DAVID COPPERFIELD

Born in 1812, **Charles Dickens** was one of the foremost authors of his time. As a youngster, he took up a number of menial jobs before he built a career as a journalist. With *Pickwick Papers* he rose to fame and success. The following years witnessed a prolific output of his works, including popular classics such as *David Copperfield*, *A Tale of Two Cities* and *Hard Times*. He died in 1870.

DAVID COPPERFIELD

CHARLES DICKENS

RUPA

Published by
Rupa Publications India Pvt. Ltd 2003
7/16, Ansari Road, Daryaganj
New Delhi 110002

Sales centres:
Bengaluru Chennai
Hyderabad Jaipur Kathmandu
Kolkata Mumbai Prayagraj

This is a work of fiction. Names, characters, places and incidents are either the product of the author's imagination or are used fictitiously and any resemblance to any actual person, living or dead, events or locales is entirely coincidental.

P-ISBN: 978-81-291-0214-0
E-ISBN: 978-81-291-4626-7

Seventh impression 2025

10 9 8 7

Printed in India

CHARLES DICKENS

CHARLES JOHN HUFFAM DICKENS WAS BORN AT PORTSEA on February 7th, 1812, the second child of John Dickens, a minor clerk in the Navy Pay Office (then at Portsmouth) and of his wife Elizabeth, née Barrow.

Owing to his father's congenital incapacity to manage his financial affairs, Charles Dickens' childhood was spent under the shadow of economic insecurity, a shadow that grew darker year by year as the family moved, first to London, then to Chatham and from there back to London, and which at one time (early in 1824) threatened to blot out for ever all prospects the boy might have had of a successful career. At that time the steadily declining family fortunes had reached their nadir with the arrest of John Dickens and his removal to the debtors' prison of the Marshalsea. Mrs. Dickens with four of her children went to join her husband in prison, and young Charles was sent to work at a blacking factory, where for six shillings a week he had to stick labels on pots of paste-blacking. Those few months were for Dickens a time of utter misery, humiliation and despair the memory of which, as he later confessed, he could never quite shake off. However, a timely legacy came to the rescue. It enabled John Dickens to leave prison and to send his son to a school at Hampstead—he had had some previous schooling at Chatham —where he remained for two or three years.

In 1827, at the age of fifteen, he entered a solicitor's office as a junior clerk. This position, though by no means well paid, enabled him to establish a certain independence for himself, to make his own friends and to indulge his taste for the theatre which he was to retain all his life.

Having taught himself shorthand, he became (in 1829) a reporter in one of the offices of "Doctors' Commons," advancing a year later to the position of a parliamentary reporter, and further still to that of a newspaper reporter on the *Morning Chronicle* at the respectable salary of five guineas a week.

In 1833 he wrote his first sketch for the *Old Monthly Magazine*; other sketches followed quickly, and a year later the name of "Boz" was attached to them. In 1836 the first series of *Sketches by Boz* appeared in volume form. Their success was immediate. The same year Dickens married Catherine Hogarth. The same year also Chapman & Hall commissioned him to write the letter-press for a projected series of Cockney sporting plates by the caricature artist Seymour. Dickens "thought of Pickwick" and this was the origin of the *Posthumous Papers of the Pickwick Club* by which Dickens established his fame for all times. They appeared first in twenty monthly instalments, beginning in April 1836 and were subsequently published in book form in 1837.

Dickens' rise from obscurity and relative poverty to a position of unique eminence and of wealth was spectacular and dramatic in its suddenness. Within a very few years of the appearance of *Pickwick* he had become the most popular novelist this country had yet known; more than that, he had become a public institution. Book followed book, and his literary activity was henceforth not to cease until the very eve of his death some thirty years later.

Oliver Twist came out in 1838; *Nicholas Nickleby* followed a year later. *Master Humphrey's Clock*, in three volumes containing *The Old Curiosity Shop* and *Barnaby Rudge* appeared in 1841.

In 1842 Dickens, accompanied by his wife, made his first tour of the United States and Canada. After his return in 1842 he published *American Notes* and in 1843 *Martin Chuzzlewit*, both works reflecting in a not very complimentary manner some of the author's impressions of America. 1843 also saw the appearance of *A Christmas Carol*, the first of Dickens' Christmas books which he continued later with *The Chimes*, *The Cricket on the Hearth*, etc.

Dickens lived with his ever growing family—in all ten children were born to him during his married life which ended in 1858 by separation from his wife—at successive residences in London, and finally at Gad's Hill near Gravesend which had been the dream place of his childhood.

He travelled a good deal abroad, staying at—among other places—Genoa (1844–45), Lausanne, Paris (1846) and Boulogne (during the summers of 1853–56).

He reached the height of his literary fame with *David Copperfield* in which he drew his father's caricatured portrait as Mr. Micawber. Shortly after its publication in 1850 Dickens re-entered journalism with the founding of the weekly magazine *Household Words* of which he was chief owner, editor and contributor. In 1859 he replaced the magazine by another almost identical one called *All the Year Round* which he continued to edit until his death.

His next main works after *David Copperfield* were *Bleak House* (1853), *Little Dorrit* (1857), *A Tale of Two Cities* (1859), *The Uncommercial Traveller* (1860) and *Great Expectations* (1861).

In later years, under the relentless pressure of work and of the many activities which his restless nature imposed on him his health began to suffer. In 1858 he had instituted public readings of his own works on a professional basis, a venture which proved an immediate and outstanding success but which perhaps more than anything else undermined his constitution. His second American tour as reader of his own works was one long triumphal —and exhausting—march. His health broke down completely in 1869, and he died from a cerebral stroke at Gad's Hill Place on June 9th, 1870, leaving behind unfinished his last work *The Mystery of Edwin Drood*. He was buried in Westminster Abbey.

H. d. R.

CONTENTS

INTRODUCTION

"OF ALL MY BOOKS," DICKENS DECLARED, "I LIKE this the best." And, even after making due allowance for the irresistible attraction which the Inimitable always felt for the most recently completed of his works, that sentence must stand as decisive.

There is, indeed, a difference in kind between Dickens' feelings towards *Copperfield* and his feelings towards his other books. He had already said, for example, of *Martin Chuzzlewit*: "I think Chuzzlewit in a hundred points immeasurably the best of my stories." But, of *Copperfield*, the all-important thing is that he did not say that it *was* the best but that he *liked* it best. And, it is precisely this same atmosphere of personal devotion and identification that invests everything that he has to say of it. This, for instance, is how he describes his feelings as he came to the last pages of the manuscript: "I seem to be sending some part of myself into the Shadowy World." And, in one of those characteristically tantalizing confessions in which he loved to indulge, he declared in his own Preface to the novel that he "did not find it easy to get sufficiently far away from it, in the first sensations of having finished it, to refer to it with . . . composure." Also, as he was at pains to make clear, he was afraid of "wearying the reader with personal confidences and private emotions."

It is that last sentence—as anyone who knows anything of Dickens will immediately have spotted—that contains the very essence of the man. For not only was he a natural actor and therefore fascinated by himself but, even more like an actor, he suffered agonies of anxiety in case other people, his audience, should fail to be fascinated, too. And it is certainly undeniable that, in *David Copperfield*, Dickens had good reason to feel a trifle self-conscious. Readers of Sir John Forster's *Life* will know what lay behind those hints and innuendoes about "personal confidences" and "private emotions." (A copy of Forster, not to mention one or two of the later biographies is, by the way, about as indispensable to the full enjoyment of the Collected Works as a copy of the Telephone Directory is indispensable to the full enjoyment of a telephone.) But for those who know Dickens only through his novels—which, after all, is not such a bad way of knowing a novelist—let me say briefly that when, at the age of thirty-six, he sat down to write *Copperfield* he had the materials for the early chapters (particularly the eleventh) already by him in his desk in the shape of notes for an unfinished autobiography. Now Dickens, remember, always saw himself as one of his own creations; and one of the most remarkable of them at that. Thus, scarcely without effort, he was able to write of the ten-year old David Copperfield's entry into Murdstone and Grinby's warehouse in almost the very words in which he had previously described the entry of the ten-year-old Charles Dickens into Warren's blacking business. Nor did he stop there. For, with somewhat more of the artistic than the filial conscience at work within him, he was able to convert his own unfortunate father, the penurious and insolvent naval pay-clerk of this life into the Mr. Micawber of immortal legend.

It would, however, be misleading to the point of downright misrepresentation of the facts to pretend that *David Copperfield* was a full-length portrait of Charles Dickens. Nothing could be further from the truth. Indeed, by chapter twelve of the novel their two ways were already diverging beyond the point of recognition. Nevertheless there is one sense in which it can be said that the most truly intimate part of the autobiography begins at the very point at which the mere record of personal incidents comes to an end. And to share in this intimacy it is necessary to bear in mind that Dickens in marrying Kate Hogarth had married the wrong woman.

It might, admittedly, be argued that, if this is so, he certainly made the most of his mistake. For, by the time he separated from Mrs. Dickens they had been married for twenty-two years and he had become the father of ten children by her—the eighth of whom was born when he had just started *Copperfield*. There he was, a veritable lion of letters and (for all the public knew to the contrary) a model family lion at that. But to himself he was something vastly different: a tragic, frustrated, infinitely pathetic sort of creature. Indeed, throughout what was nearly the quarter-of-a-century during which he was married to " silly " Kate he was desperately in love with someone else. And it was a love-affair without even the possibility of solution. For the woman whom he loved was already dead.

Indeed, even after the separation when the devoutly admiring sister-in-law, Georgina, became the mistress of his household, it was his other sister-in-law, sweet Mary Hogarth, who at the age of seventeen had died in Dickens' arms, who remained the mistress of his heart. To the end of his life he still wore on his little finger the ring that he had slipped from her hand at her death-bed and in his fifty-seventh year he could not restrain himself from saying: " She is so much in my thoughts at all times, especially when I am successful, and have greatly prospered in anything, that the recollection of her is an essential part of my being, and is inseparable from my existence as the beating of my heart is."

Now take a look at *David Copperfield* and see how, throughout, the image of young, innocent, prematurely-extinguished womanhood recurs. First there is Mrs. Copperfield, David's mother: described by the author and treated by everyone as a child, this " poor, unfortunate Baby " dies prematurely, scarcely more than an infant to the end. Then there is little Em'ly, a mere waistcoat pocket version of womankind. And again there is Dora, Copperfield's first wife who right up to *her* early death-bed actually demanded to be called by the extraordinary pet name of " Child-wife." In short, it is as though when Dickens was at work on the successor to *Dombey & Son*, he was not so much an immensely popular novelist performing in the public limelight as a secretly broken-hearted lover, wistfully dissecting his soul in the privacy of his own study; as though the ghost of poor Mary Hogarth had risen from Kensal Green Cemetery and was seated beside him in Devonshire Terrace while he wrote.

That does not mean to say, however, that the whole of *Copperfield* was conceived in gloom and uttered in despondency. On the contrary, there is a warmth and geniality about the book that is as pervasive as a good system of central-heating. The Comic Spirit is there all right; and, what is more, it is the cheerful Peggotty and company who were Dickens' own favourite characters within his own favourite novel. In fact, in 1850 when he wrote the book Dickens was at the very height of his powers, and the comic, the tragic and the frankly sentimental were all within his grasp and gathered up by the arm-full. The book abounds in characters that only Dickens could have created, described in sentences which only Dickens could have written.

It is, incidentally, only Dickens' truly astonishing proliferation of invention that has obscured his equally astonishing mastery of the craft of writing. Because of the colossal energy, vitality and exuberance which made him into a one-man Hollywood, people have failed to notice that he was also an incomparable stylist with as pretty a sense for the right word and as pretty an ear for prose rhythm (a far more subtle rhythm, by the way, than its counterparts in verse) as any English novelist has ever possessed. Consider, for example,

> " She brought with her two uncompromising black boxes, with her initials on the lids in hard brass nails. When she paid the coachman she took her money out of a hard, steel purse, and she kept the purse in a very jail of a bag which hung upon her arm by a heavy chain and shut up like a bite. I had never, at that time, seen such a metallic lady altogether as Miss Murdstone was."

or:

> " My address," said Mr. Micawber, " is Windsor Terrace, City Road. I—in short," said Mr. Micawber, with the same genteel air, and in another burst of confidence—" I live there."

or, again:

> " If Mr. Micawber's creditors *will not* give him time," said Mrs. Micawber, " they must take the consequences; and the sooner they bring it to an issue the better. Blood cannot be obtained from a stone, neither can anything on account be obtained at present (not to mention law expenses) from Mr. Micawber."

And that is to omit such phrases as " Barkis is willing " and " a lone, lorn creature " that have entered into the common coinage of the language. Try meddling with any of those passages or phrases, even to the slight extent of altering a word or lopping off a syllable, and you will soon find that it was Dickens who knew better. There was, in fact, an authentic Dickens trademark on everything he wrote; and the trademark was a hall-mark, too.

Nothing that Dickens wrote came to him more easily than *Copperfield*. Admittedly, at the outset he had flogged his brains for the right title and what ended up as *David Copperfield* (his own initials, by the way, but in reverse) had begun as *Mag's Diversions*, and had assumed six other versions of the " Copperfield " title on the way. But once it was in progress it went " wonderfully," it was " smashing," it was " splendid." The public loved it. Ruskin and Matthew Arnold cherished it above all his others; and to celebrate the book Dickens in one of his more Rajah-like moods of munificence gave a magnificent midsummer banquet at Richmond. Thackeray and Tennyson were among the guests, and Forster records that he had " rarely seen Dickens happier than he was amid the sunshine of that day."

In short, the Inimitable riding near his zenith, could afford to echo the words that he had already put between the lips of Copperfield: " I have been very fortunate, and find my name connected with some praise."

NORMAN COLLINS

CHARACTERS

RICHARD BABLEY ("MR. DICK"), a *harmless lunatic.*

MR. BARKIS, *a carrier.*

MR. CHILLIP, *a doctor; a mild little man.*

DAVID COPPERFIELD, *the hero of the story.*

MR. CREAKLE, *an ignorant and ferocious schoolmaster.*

THE REV. HORACE CREWLER, *a poor Devonshire clergyman.*

URIAH HEEP, *a clerk in the office of Mr. Wickfield.*

MR. JORAM, *the partner and son-in-law of Mr. Omer the undertaker.*

MR. JORKINS, *a proctor; partner of Mr. Spenlow.*

LITTIMER, *the confidential servant of James Steerforth.*

JACK MALDON, *an idle, bold, handsome, needy libertine.*

MR. CHARLES MELL, *an under-master at Mr. Creakle's school.*

MR. WILKINS MICAWBER, *a jaunty grandiloquent, recklessly good-natured, improvident man.*

MASTER WILKINS MICAWBER, *his eldest son.*

MR. MILLS, *the father of Julia Mills.*

MR. EDWARD MURDSTONE, *the stepfather of David Copperfield.*

MR. OMER, *a draper, tailor, undertaker, &c., at Yarmouth.*

DANIEL PEGGOTTY, *a rough but kind-hearted fisherman.*

HAM PEGGOTTY, *a boatman, boatbuilder, and fisherman; nephew to Daniel Peggotty.*

MR. QUINION, *chief manager at Murdstone and Grinby's warehouse.*

MR. FRANCIS SPENLOW, *one of the firm of Spenlow and Jorkins; the father of Dora Spenlow.*

JAMES STEERFORTH, *a young man of great personal attractions and engaging manners; formerly a school friend of David Copperfield's.*

DR. STRONG, *an amiable old gentleman, master of a school at Canterbury.*

MR. TIFFEY, *an old clerk in the office of Spenlow and Jorkins.*

THOMAS TRADDLES, *a schoolmate and friend of David Copperfield's.*

MR. WICKFIELD, *a lawyer at Canterbury.*

MRS. CLARA COPPERFIELD, *the mother of David Copperfield.*

MRS. CREAKLE, *a quiet woman, ill-treated by her husband.*

MISS CREAKLE, *daughter of the preceding.*

MRS. CREWLER, *wife of the Rev. Horace Crewler.*

THE MISSES CAROLINE, LOUISA, LUCY, MARGARET, SARAH, and SOPHY CREWLER, *daughters of the preceding.*

MRS. CRUPP, *a stout woman, who lets furnished chambers.*

ROSA DARTLE, *a lady living with Mrs. Steerforth as a companion.*

LITTLE EMILY, *the niece and adopted daughter of Mr. Peggotty.*

MARTHA ENDELL, *a young woman of evil reputation.*

MRS. GUMMIDGE, *the widow of Mr. Peggotty's partner.*

MRS. HEEP, *a widow; the mother of Uriah Heep.*

MRS. MARKLEHAM, *the mother of Mrs. Annie Strong.*

MRS. EMMA MICAWBER, *the wife of Wilkins Micawber.*

MISS EMMA MICAWBER, *her daughter.*

MISS JULIA MILLS, *the bosom-friend of Dora Spenlow.*

MISS MOWCHER, *a fashionable hairdresser.*

MISS JANE MURDSTONE, *sister to Edward Murdstone.*

MINNIE OMER, *daughter of Mr. Omer; a pretty, good-natured girl.*

CLARA PEGGOTTY, *servant to Mrs. Copperfield, and nurse and friend to David.*

MISS CLARISSA SPENLOW, *the elder of two maiden sisters of Mr. Spenlow.*

MISS DORA SPENLOW, *the only daughter of Mr. Spenlow; a timid, sensitive, artless little beauty, afterwards the "child-wife" of David Copperfield.*

MISS LAVINIA SPENLOW, *the sister of Miss Clarissa Spenlow.*

MRS. STEERFORTH, *mother of James Steerforth.*

MRS. ANNIE STRONG, *the wife of Dr. Strong.*

MISS BETSEY TROTWOOD, *an austere but kind-hearted lady; the great-aunt of David Copperfield.*

AGNES WICKFIELD, *daughter and housekeeper of Mr. Wickfield.*

PREFACE

I REMARKED IN THE ORIGINAL PREFACE TO THIS BOOK, that I did not find it easy to get sufficiently far away from it, in the first sensations of having finished it, to refer to it with the composure which this formal heading would seem to require. My interest in it was so recent and strong, and my mind was so divided between pleasure and regret—pleasure in the achievement of a long design, regret in the separation from many companions—that I was in danger of wearying the reader with personal confidences and private emotions.

Besides which, all that I could have said of the Story to any purpose, I had endeavoured to say in it.

It would concern the reader little, perhaps, to know how sorrowfully the pen is laid down at the close of a two-years' imaginative task; or how an Author feels as if he were dismissing some portion of himself into the shadow world, when a crowd of the creatures of his brain are going from him for ever. Yet, I had nothing else to tell; unless, indeed, I were to confess (which might be of less moment still), that no one can ever believe this Narrative in the reading more than I believed it in the writing.

So true are these avowals at the present day, that I can now only take the reader into one confidence more. Of all my books, I like this the best. It will be easily believed that I am a fond parent to every child of my fancy, and that no one can ever love that family as dearly as I love them. But, like many fond parents, I have in my heart of hearts a favourite child. And his name is DAVID COPPERFIELD.

1

I AM BORN

WHETHER I SHALL TURN OUT TO BE THE HERO OF MY own life, or whether that station will be held by anybody else, these pages must show. To begin my life with the beginning of my life, I record that I was born (as I have been informed and believe) on a Friday, at twelve o'clock at night. It was remarked that the clock began to strike, and I began to cry, simultaneously.

In consideration of the day and hour of my birth, it was declared by the nurse, and by some sage women in the neighbourhood who had taken a lively interest in me several months before there was any possibility of our becoming personally acquainted, first, that I was destined to be unlucky in life; and secondly, that I was privileged to see ghosts and spirits; both these gifts inevitably attaching, as they believed, to all unlucky infants of either gender, born towards the small hours on a Friday night.

I need say nothing here on the first head, because nothing can show better than my history whether that prediction was verified or falsified by the result. On the second branch of the question, I will only remark, that unless I ran through that part of my inheritance while I was still a baby, I have not come into it yet. But I do not at all complain of having been kept out of this property; and if anybody else should be in the present enjoyment of it, he is heartily welcome to keep it.

I was born with a caul, which was advertised for sale, in the newspapers, at the low price of fifteen guineas. Whether seagoing people were short of money about that time, or were short of faith and preferred cork jackets, I don't know; all I know is, that there was but one solitary bidding, and that was from an attorney connected with the bill-broking business, who offered two pounds in cash, and the balance in sherry, but declined to be guaranteed from drowning on any higher bargain. Consequently the advertisement was withdrawn at a dead loss—for as to sherry, my poor dear mother's own sherry was in the market then—and ten years afterwards the caul was put up in a raffle down in our part of the country, to fifty members at half-a-crown a head, the winner to spend five shillings. I was present myself, and I remember to have felt quite uncomfortable and confused, at a part of myself being disposed of in that way. The caul was won, I recollect, by an old lady with a hand-basket, who, very reluctantly, produced from it the stipulated five shillings, all in halfpence, and twopence halfpenny short—as it took an immense time and a great waste of arithmetic, to endeavour without any effect to prove to her. It is a fact which will be long remembered as remarkable down there, that she was never drowned, but died triumphantly in bed, at ninety-two. I have understood that it was, to the last, her proudest boast, that she never had been on the water in her life, except upon a bridge; and that over her tea (to which she was extremely partial) she, to the last, expressed her indignation at the impiety of mariners and others, who had the presumption to go " meandering " about the world. It was in vain to represent to her that some conveniences, tea perhaps included, resulted from this objectionable practice. She always returned, with greater emphasis and with an instinctive knowledge of the strength of her objection, " Let us have no meandering."

Not to meander myself, at present, I will go back to my birth.

I was born at Blunderstone, in Suffolk, or " thereby," as they say in Scotland. I was a posthumous child. My father's eyes had closed upon the light of this world six months when mine opened on it. There is something strange to me, even now, in the reflection that he never saw me; and something stranger yet in the shadowy remembrance that I have of my first childish associations with his white gravestone in the churchyard, and of the indefinable compassion I used to feel for it lying out alone there in the dark night, when our little parlour was warm and bright with fire and candle, and the doors of our house were —almost cruelly, it seemed to me sometimes—bolted and locked against it.

An aunt of my father's, and consequently a great-aunt of mine, of whom I shall have more to relate by and by, was the principal magnate of our family. Miss Trotwood, or Miss Betsey, as my poor mother always called her, when she sufficiently overcame her dread of this formidable personage to mention her at all (which was seldom), had been married to a husband younger than herself, who was very handsome, except in the sense of the homely adage, " handsome is, that handsome does "—for he was strongly suspected of having beaten Miss Betsey, and even of having once, on a disputed question of supplies, made some hasty but determined arrangements to throw her out of a two pair of stairs' window. These evidences of an incompatibility of temper induced Miss Betsey to pay him off, and effect a separation by mutual consent. He went to India with his capital, and there, according to a wild legend in our family, he was once seen riding on an elephant, in company with a Baboon; but I think it must have been a Baboo—or a Begum. Anyhow, from India tidings of his death reached home, within ten years. How they affected my aunt, nobody knew; for immediately upon the separation she took her maiden name again, bought a cottage in a hamlet on the sea-coast a long way off, established herself there as a single woman with one servant, and was understood to live secluded, ever afterwards, in an inflexible retirement.

My father had once been a favourite of hers, I believe; but she was mortally affronted by his marriage, on the ground that my mother was "a wax doll." She had never seen my mother, but she knew her to be not yet twenty. My father and Miss Betsey never met again. He was double my mother's age when he married, and of but a delicate constitution. He died a year afterwards, and, as I have said, six months before I came into the world.

This was the state of matters on the afternoon of, what *I* may be excused for calling, that eventful and important Friday. I can make no claim, therefore, to have known, at that time, how matters stood; or to have any remembrance, founded on the evidence of my own senses, of what follows.

My mother was sitting by the fire, but poorly in health, and very low in spirits, looking at it through her tears, and desponding heavily about herself and the fatherless little stranger, who was already welcomed by some grosses of prophetic pins in a drawer up-stairs, to a world not at all excited on the subject of his arrival; my mother, I saw, was sitting by the fire, that bright, windy March afternoon, very timid and sad, and very doubtful of ever coming alive out of the trial that was before her, when, lifting her eyes as she dried them, to the window opposite, she saw a strange lady coming up the garden.

My mother had a sure foreboding at the second glance, that it was Miss Betsey. The setting sun was glowing on the strange lady, over the garden-fence, and she came walking up to the door with a fell rigidity of figure and composure of countenance that could have belonged to nobody else.

When she reached the house she gave another proof of her identity. My father had often hinted that she seldom conducted herself like any ordinary Christian; and now, instead of ringing the bell, she came and looked in at that identical window, pressing the end of her nose against the glass to that extent that my poor dear mother used to say it became perfectly flat and white in a moment.

She gave my mother such a turn, that I have always been convinced I am indebted to Miss Betsey for having been born on a Friday.

My mother had left her chair in her agitation, and gone behind it in the corner. Miss Betsey, looking round the room, slowly and inquiringly, began on the other side, and carried her eyes on, like a Saracen's Head in a Dutch clock, until they reached my mother. Then she made a frown and a gesture to my mother, like one who was accustomed to be obeyed, to come and open the door. My mother went.

"Mrs. David Copperfield, I *think*," said Miss Betsey; the emphasis referring, perhaps, to my mother's mourning weeds, and her condition.

"Yes," said my mother, faintly.

"Miss Trotwood," said the visitor. "You have heard of her, I dare say?"

My mother answered she had had that pleasure. And she had a disagreeable consciousness of not appearing to imply that it had been an overpowering pleasure.

"Now you see her," said Miss Betsey. My mother bent her head, and begged her to walk in.

They went into the parlour my mother had come from, the fire in the best room on the other side of the passage not being lighted—not having been lighted, indeed, since my father's funeral; and when they were both seated, and Miss Betsey said nothing, my mother, after vainly trying to restrain herself, began to cry.

"Oh, tut tut, tut!" said Miss Betsey, in a hurry. "Don't do that! Come, come!"

My mother couldn't help it notwithstanding, so she cried until she had had her cry out.

"Take off your cap, child," said Miss Betsey, "and let me see you."

My mother was too much afraid of her to refuse compliance with this odd request, if she had any disposition to do so. Therefore she did as she was told, and did it with such nervous hands that her hair (which was luxuriant and beautiful) fell all about her face.

"Why, bless my heart!" exclaimed Miss Betsey. "You are a very Baby!"

My mother was, no doubt, unusually youthful in appearance even for her years; she hung her head, as if it were her fault, poor thing, and said, sobbing, that indeed she was afraid she was but a childish widow, and would be but a childish mother if she lived. In a short pause which ensued, she had a fancy that she felt Miss Betsey touch her hair, and that with no ungentle hand; but, looking at her, in her timid hope, she found that lady sitting with the skirt of her dress tucked up, her hands folded on one knee, and her feet upon the fender, frowning at the fire.

" In the name of Heaven," said Miss Betsey, suddenly, " why Rookery? "

" Do you mean the house, ma'am? " asked my mother.

" Why Rookery? " said Miss Betsey. " Cookery would have been more to the purpose, if you had had any practical ideas of life, either of you."

" The name was Mr. Copperfield's choice," returned my mother. " When he bought the house, he liked to think that there were rooks about it."

The evening wind made such a disturbance just now, among some tall old elm-trees at the bottom of the garden, that neither my mother nor Miss Betsey could forbear glancing that way. As the elms bent to one another, like giants who were whispering secrets, and after a few seconds of such repose, fell into a violent flurry, tossing their wild arms about, as if their late confidences were really too wicked for their peace of mind, some weather-beaten ragged old rooks'-nests burdening their higher branches, swung like wrecks upon a stormy sea.

" Where are the birds? " asked Miss Betsey.

" The——? " My mother had been thinking of something else.

" The rooks—what has become of them? " asked Miss Betsey.

" There have not been any since we have lived here," said my mother. " We thought—Mr. Copperfield thought—it was quite a large rookery; but the nests were very old ones, and the birds have deserted them a long while."

" David Copperfield all over! " cried Miss Betsey. " David Copperfield from head to foot! Calls a house a rookery when there's not a rook near it, and takes the birds on trust, because he sees the nests! "

" Mr. Copperfield," returned my mother, " is dead, and if you dare to speak unkindly of him to me——"

My poor dear mother, I suppose, had some momentary intention of committing an assault and battery upon my aunt, who could easily have settled her with one hand, even if my mother had been in far better training for such an encounter than she was that evening. But it passed with the action of rising from her chair; and she sat down again very meekly, and fainted.

When she came to herself, or when Miss Betsey had restored her, whichever it was, she found the latter standing at the window. The twilight was by this time shading down into darkness; and dimly as they saw each other, they could not have done that without the aid of the fire.

"Well?" said Miss Betsey, coming back to her chair, as if she had only been taking a casual look at the prospect; "and when do you expect——"

"I am all in a tremble," faltered my mother. "I don't know what's the matter. I shall die, I am sure!"

"No, no, no," said Miss Betsey. "Have some tea."

"Oh dear me, dear me, do you think it will do me any good?" cried my mother in a helpless manner.

"Of course it will," said Miss Betsey. "It's nothing but fancy. What do you call your girl?"

"I don't know that it will be a girl, yet, ma'am," said my mother innocently.

"Bless the Baby!" exclaimed Miss Betsey, unconsciously quoting the second sentiment of the pincushion in the drawer up-stairs, but applying it to my mother instead of me, "I don't mean that. I mean your servant."

"Peggotty," said my mother.

"Peggotty!" repeated Miss Betsey, with some indignation. "Do you mean to say, child, that any human being has gone into a Christian church, and got herself named Peggotty?"

"It's her surname," said my mother, faintly. "Mr. Copperfield called her by it, because her Christian name was the same as mine."

"Here! Peggotty!" cried Miss Betsey, opening the parlour-door. "Tea. Your mistress is a little unwell. Don't dawdle."

Having issued this mandate with as much potentiality as if she had been a recognised authority in the house ever since it had been a house, and having looked out to confront the amazed Peggotty coming along the passage with a candle at the sound of a strange voice, Miss Betsey shut the door again, and sat down as before; with her feet on the fender, the skirt of her dress tucked up, and her hands folded on one knee.

"You were speaking about its being a girl," said Miss Betsey. "I have no doubt it will be a girl. I have a presentiment that it must be a girl. Now, child, from the moment of the birth of this girl——"

"Perhaps boy," my mother took the liberty of putting in.

"I tell you I have a presentiment that it must be a girl," returned Miss Betsey. " Don't contradict. From the moment of this girl's birth, child, I intend to be her friend. I intend to be her godmother, and I beg you'll call her Betsey Trotwood Copperfield. There must be no mistakes in life with *this* Betsey Trotwood. There must be no trifling with *her* affections, poor dear. She must be well brought up, and well guarded from reposing any foolish confidences where they are not deserved. I must make that *my* care."

There was a twitch of Miss Betsey's head, after each of these sentences, as if her own old wrongs were working within her, and she repressed any plainer reference to them by strong constraint. So my mother suspected, at least, as she observed her by the low glimmer of the fire; too much scared by Miss Betsey, too uneasy in herself, and too subdued and bewildered altogether, to observe anything very clearly, or to know what to say.

" And was David good to you, child? " asked Miss Betsey, when she had been silent for a little while, and these motions of her head had gradually ceased. " Were you comfortable together? "

" We were very happy," said my mother. " Mr. Copperfield was only too good to me.'

" What, he spoilt you, I suppose? " returned Miss Betsey.

" For being quite alone and dependent on myself in this tough world again, yes, I fear he did indeed," sobbed my mother.

" Well! Don't cry! " said Miss Betsey. " You were not equally matched, child—if any two people *can* be equally matched—and so I asked the question. You were an orphan, weren't you? "

" Yes."

" And a governess? "

" I was a nursery-governess in a family where Mr. Copperfield came to visit. Mr. Copperfield was very kind to me, and took a great deal of notice of me, and paid me a good deal of attention, and at last proposed to me. And I accepted him. And so we were married," said my mother simply.

" Ha! Poor Baby! " mused Miss Betsey, with her frown still bent upon the fire. " Do you know anything? "

" I beg your pardon, ma'am," faltered my mother.

" About keeping house, for instance," said Miss Betsey.

" Not much, I fear," returned my mother. " Not so much as I could wish. But Mr. Copperfield was teaching me—"

(" Much he knew about it himself! ") said Miss Betsey in a parenthesis.

—" And I hope I should have improved, being very anxious

to learn, and he very patient to teach, if the great misfortune of his death "—my mother broke down again here, and could get no farther.

" Well, well! " said Miss Betsey.

—" I kept my housekeeping-book regularly, and balanced it with Mr. Copperfield every night," cried my mother in another burst of distress, and breaking down again.

" Well, well! " said Miss Betsey. " Don't cry any more."

—" And I am sure we never had a word of difference respecting it, except when Mr. Copperfield objected to my threes and fives being too much like each other, or to my putting curly tails to my sevens and nines," resumed my mother in another burst, and breaking down again.

" You'll make yourself ill," said Miss Betsey, " and you know that will not be good either for you or for my god-daughter. Come! You mustn't do it! "

This argument had some share in quieting my mother, though her increasing indisposition had a larger one. There was an interval of silence, only broken by Miss Betsey's occasionally ejaculating " Ha! " as she sat with her feet upon the fender.

" David had bought an annuity for himself with his money, I know," said she, by and by. " What did he do for you? "

" Mr. Copperfield," said my mother, answering with some difficulty, " was so considerate and good as to secure the reversion of a part of it to me."

" How much? " asked Miss Betsey.

" A hundred and five pounds a year," said my mother.

" He might have done worse," said my aunt.

The word was appropriate to the moment. My mother was so much worse that Peggotty, coming in with the teaboard and candles, and seeing at a glance how ill she was,—as Miss Betsey might have done sooner, if there had been light enough,—conveyed her up-stairs to her own room with all speed; and immediately despatched Ham Peggotty, her nephew, who had been for some days past secreted in the house, unknown to my mother, as a special messenger in case of emergency, to fetch the nurse and doctor.

Those allied powers were considerably astonished, when they arrived within a few minutes of each other, to find an unknown lady of portentous appearance sitting before the fire, with her bonnet tied over her left arm, stopping her ears with jewellers' cotton. Peggotty knowing nothing about her, and my mother saying nothing about her, she was quite a mystery in the parlour; and the fact of her having a magazine of jewellers' cotton in her pocket, and sticking the article in her ears in that way, did not detract from the solemnity of her presence.

The doctor having been up-stairs and come down again, and having satisfied himself, I suppose, that there was a probability of this unknown lady and himself having to sit there, face to face, for some hours, laid himself out to be polite and social. He was the meekest of his sex, the mildest of little men. He sidled in and out of a room, to take up the less space. He walked as softly as the Ghost in Hamlet, and more slowly. He carried his head on one side, partly in modest depreciation of himself, partly in modest propitiation of everybody else. It is nothing to say that he hadn't a word to throw at a dog. He couldn't have *thrown* a word at a mad dog. He might have offered him one gently, or half a one, or a fragment of one; for he spoke as slowly as he walked; but he wouldn't have been rude to him, and he couldn't have been quick with him, for any earthly consideration.

Mr. Chillip, looking mildly at my aunt with his head on one side, and making her a little bow, said, in allusion to the jewellers' cotton, as he softly touched his left ear:

" Some local irritation, ma'am? "

" What! " replied my aunt, pulling the cotton out of one ear like a cork.

Mr. Chillip was so alarmed by her abruptness—as he told my mother afterwards—that it was a mercy he didn't lose his presence of mind. But he repeated sweetly:

" Some local irritation, ma'am? "

" Nonsense! " replied my aunt, and corked herself again, at one blow.

Mr. Chillip could do nothing after this, but sit and look at her feebly, as she sat and looked at the fire, until he was called upstairs again. After some quarter of an hour's absence, he returned.

" Well? " said my aunt, taking the cotton out of the ear nearest to him.

" Well, ma'am," returned Mr. Chillip, " we are—we are progressing slowly, ma'am."

" Ba—a—ah! " said my aunt, with a perfect shake on the contemptuous interjection. And corked herself as before.

Really—really—as Mr. Chillip told my mother, he was almost shocked; speaking in a professional point of view alone he was almost shocked. But he sat and looked at her, notwithstanding, for nearly two hours, as she sat looking at the fire, until he was again called out. After another absence, he again returned.

"Well?" said my aunt, taking out the cotton on that side again.

"Well, ma'am," returned Mr. Chillip, "we are—we are progressing slowly, ma'am."

"Ya—a—ah!" said my aunt. With such a snarl at him, that Mr. Chillip absolutely could not bear it. It was really calculated to break his spirit, he said afterwards. He preferred to go and sit upon the stairs, in the dark and a strong draught, until he was again sent for.

Ham Peggotty, who went to the national school, and was a very dragon at his catechism, and who may therefore be regarded as a credible witness, reported next day, that happening to peep in at the parlour-door an hour after this, he was instantly descried by Miss Betsey, then walking to and fro in a state of agitation, and pounced upon before he could make his escape. That there were now occasional sounds of feet and voices overhead which he inferred the cotton did not exclude, from the circumstances of his evidently being clutched by the lady as a victim on whom to expend her superabundant agitation when the sounds were loudest. That, marching him constantly up and down by the collar (as if he had been taking too much laudanum), she, at those times, shook him, rumpled his hair, made light of his linen, stopped *his* ears as if she confounded them with her own, and otherwise touzled and maltreated him. This was in part confirmed by his aunt, who saw him at half-past twelve o'clock, soon after his release, and affirmed that he was then as red as I was.

The mild Mr. Chillip could not possibly bear malice at such a time, if at any time. He sidled into the parlour as soon as he was at liberty, and said to my aunt in his meekest manner:

"Well, ma'am, I am happy to congratulate you."

"What upon?" said my aunt, sharply.

Mr. Chillip was fluttered again, by the extreme severity of my aunt's manner; so he made her a little bow, and gave her a little smile, to mollify her.

"Mercy on the man, what's he doing!" cried my aunt, impatiently. "Can't he speak?"

"Be calm, my dear ma'am," said Mr. Chillip, in his softest accents. "There is no longer any occasion for uneasiness, ma'am. Be calm."

It has since been considered almost a miracle that my aunt didn't shake him, and shake what he had to say out of him. She only shook her own head at him, but in a way that made him quail.

"Well, ma'am," resumed Mr. Chillip, as soon, as he had

courage, "I am happy to congratulate you. All is now over, ma'am, and well over."

During the five minutes or so that Mr. Chillip devoted to the delivery of this oration, my aunt eyed him narrowly.

"How is she?" said my aunt, folding her arms with her bonnet still tied on one of them.

"Well, ma'am, she will soon be quite comfortable, I hope," returned Mr. Chillip. "Quite as comfortable as we can expect a young mother to be, under these melancholy domestic circumstances. There cannot be any objection to your seeing her presently, ma'am. It may do her good."

"And *she*. How is *she*?" said my aunt, sharply.

Mr. Chillip laid his head a little more on one side, and looked at my aunt like an amiable bird.

"The baby," said my aunt. "How is she?"

"Ma'am," returned Mr. Chillip, "I apprehended you had known. It's a boy."

My aunt said never a word, but took her bonnet by the strings, in the manner of a sling, aimed a blow at Mr. Chillip's head with it, put it on bent, walked out, and never came back. She vanished like a discontented fairy; or like one of those supernatural beings whom it was popularly supposed I was entitled to see: and never came back any more.

No. I lay in my basket, and my mother lay in her bed; but Betsey Trotwood Copperfield was for ever in the land of dreams and shadows, the tremendous region whence I had so lately travelled; and the light upon the window of our room shone out upon the earthly bourne of all such travellers, and the mound above the ashes and the dust that once was he, without whom I had never been.

2

I OBSERVE

THE FIRST OBJECTS THAT ASSUME A DISTINCT PRESENCE before me, as I look far back, into the blank of my infancy, are my mother with her pretty hair and youthful shape, and Peggotty, with no shape at all, and eyes so dark that they seemed to darken their whole neighbourhood in her face, and cheeks and arms so hard and red that I wondered the birds didn't peck her in preference to apples.

I believe I can remember these two at a little distance apart, dwarfed to my sight by stooping down or kneeling on the floor, and I going unsteadily from the one to the other. I have an impression on my mind which I cannot distinguish from actual remembrance, of the touch of Peggotty's forefinger as she used to hold it out to me, and of its being roughened by needlework, like a pocket nutmeg-grater.

This may be fancy, though I think the memory of most of us can go farther back into such times than many of us suppose; just as I believe the power of observation in numbers of very young children to be quite wonderful for its closeness and accuracy. Indeed, I think that most grown men who are remarkable in this respect, may with greater propriety be said not to have lost the faculty, than to have acquired it; the rather, as I generally observe such men to retain a certain freshness, and gentleness, and capacity of being pleased, which are also an inheritance they have preserved from their childhood.

I might have a misgiving that I am "meandering" in stopping to say this, but that it brings me to remark that I build these conclusions in part upon my own experience of myself; and if it should appear from anything I may set down in this narrative that I was a child of close observation, or that as a man I have a strong memory of my childhood, I undoubtedly lay claim to both of these characteristics.

Looking back, as I was saying, into the blank of my infancy, the first objects I can remember as standing out by themselves from a confusion of things, are my mother and Peggotty. What else do I remember? Let me see.

There comes out of the cloud, our house—not new to me, but quite familiar, in its earliest remembrance. On the ground-floor is Peggotty's kitchen, opening into a back yard; with a pigeon-house on a pole, in the centre, without any pigeons in it; a great dog-kennel in a corner, without any dog; and a quantity of fowls that look terribly tall to me, walking about in a menacing and ferocious manner. There is one cock who gets upon a post to crow, and seems to take particular notice of me as I look at him through the kitchen window, who makes me shiver, he is so fierce. Of the geese outside the side-gate who come waddling after me with their long necks stretched out when I go that way,

I dream at night; as a man environed by wild beasts might dream of lions.

Here is a long passage—what an enormous perspective I make of it!—leading from Peggotty's kitchen to the front-door. A dark store-room opens out of it, and that is a place to be run past at night; for I don't know what may be among those tubs and jars and old tea-chests, when there is nobody in there with a dimly-burning light, letting a mouldy air come out at the door, in which there is the smell of soap, pickles, pepper, candles and coffee, all at one whiff. Then there are the two parlours; the parlour in which we sit of an evening, my mother and I and Peggotty—for Peggotty is quite our companion, when her work is done and we are alone—and the best parlour where we sit on a Sunday; grandly, but not so comfortably. There is something of a doleful air about that room to me, for Peggotty has told me—I don't know when, but apparently ages ago—about my father's funeral, and the company having their black cloaks put on. One Sunday night my mother reads to Peggotty and me in there, how Lazarus was raised up from the dead. And I am so frightened that they are afterwards obliged to take me out of bed, and show me the quiet churchyard out of the bedroom window, with the dead all lying in their graves at rest, below the solemn moon.

There is nothing half so green that I know anywhere, as the grass of that churchyard; nothing half so shady as its trees; nothing half so quiet as its tombstones. The sheep are feeding there, when I kneel up, early in the morning, in my little bed in a closet within my mother's room, to look out at it; and I see the red light shining on the sun-dial, and think within myself, "Is the sun-dial glad, I wonder, that it can tell the time again?"

Here is our pew in the church. What a high-backed pew! With a window near it, out of which our house can be seen, and *is* seen many times during the morning's service, by Peggotty, who likes to make herself as sure as she can that it's not being robbed, or is not in flames. But though Peggotty's eye wanders, she is much offended if mine does, and frowns to me, as I stand upon the seat, that I am to look at the clergyman. But I can't always look at him—I know him without that white thing on, and I am afraid of his wondering why I stare so, and perhaps stopping the service to inquire—and what am I to do? It's a dreadful thing to gape, but I must do something. I look at my mother, but *she* pretends not to see me. I look at a boy in the aisle, and *he* makes faces at me. I look at the sunlight coming in at the open door through the porch, and there I see a stray sheep —I don't mean a sinner, but mutton—half making up his mind to come into the church. I feel that if I looked at him any longer, I might be tempted to say something out loud; and what would become of me then! I look up at the monumental tablets on the wall, and try to think of Mr. Bodgers late of this parish, and what the feelings of Mrs. Bodgers must have been, when affliction sore, long time Mr. Bodgers bore, and physicians were in vain. I wonder whether they called in Mr. Chillip, and he was in vain; and if so, how he likes to be reminded of it once a week. I look from Mr. Chillip, in his Sunday neckcloth, to the pulpit; and think what a good place it would be to play in, and what a castle it would make, with another boy coming up the stairs to attack it, and having the velvet cushion with the tassels thrown down on his head. In time my eyes gradually shut up; and, from seeming to hear the clergyman singing a drowsy song in the heat, I hear nothing, until I fall off the seat with a crash, and am taken out; more dead than alive, by Peggotty.

And now I see the outside of our house, with the latticed bedroom windows standing open to let in the sweet-smelling air, and the ragged old rooks'-nests still dangling in the elm-trees at the bottom of the front garden. Now I am in the garden at the back, beyond the yard where the empty pigeon-house and dog-kennel are—a very preserve of butterflies, as I remember it, with a high fence, and a gate and padlock; where the fruit clusters on the trees, riper and richer than fruit has ever been since, in any other garden, and where my mother gathers some in a basket, while I stand by, bolting furtive gooseberries, and trying to look unmoved. A great wind rises, and the summer is gone in a moment. We are playing in the winter twilight, dancing about the parlour. When my mother is out of breath and rests herself in an elbow-chair, I watch her winding her bright curls round her fingers, and straightening her waist, and nobody knows better than I do that she likes to look so well, and is proud of being so pretty.

That is among my very earliest impressions. That, and a sense that we were both a little afraid of Peggotty, and submitted ourselves in most things to her direction, were among the first opinions—if they may be so called—that I ever derived from what I saw.

Peggotty and I were sitting one night by the parlour fire, alone. I had been reading to Peggotty about crocodiles. I must have read very perspicuously, or the poor soul must have been deeply interested, for I remember she had a cloudy impression, after I had done, that they were a sort of vegetable. I was tired of reading, and dead sleepy; but having leave, as a high treat, to sit up until my mother came home from spending the evening at a neighbour's, I would rather have died upon my post (of course) than have gone to bed. I had reached that stage of sleepiness when Peggotty seemed to swell and grow immensely large. I propped my eyelides open with my two forefingers, and looked perseveringly at her as she sat at work; at the little bit of wax-candle she kept for her thread—how old it looked, being so wrinkled in all directions!—at the little house with a thatched roof, where the yard-measure lived; at her work-box with a sliding lid, with a view of St. Paul's Cathedral (with a pink dome) painted on the top; at the brass thimble on her finger; at herself, whom I thought lovely. I felt so sleepy, that I knew if I lost sight of anything, for a moment, I was gone.

"Peggotty," says I, suddenly, "were you ever married?"

"Lord, Master Davy," replied Peggotty. "What's put marriage in your head?"

She answered with such a start, that it quite awoke me. And then she stopped in her work, and looked at me, with her needle drawn out to its thread's length.

"But *were* you ever married, Peggotty?" says I. "You are a very handsome woman, an't you?"

I thought her in a different style from my mother, certainly; but of another school of beauty, I considered her a perfect example. There was a red velvet footstool in the best parlour, on which my mother had painted a nosegay. The groundwork of that stool and Peggotty's complexion appeared to me to be one and the same thing. The stool was smooth, and Peggotty was rough, but that made no difference.

"Me handsome, Davy!" said Peggotty. "Lawk, no, my dear! But what put marriage in your head?"

"I don't know!—You mustn't marry more than one person at a time, may you, Peggotty?"

"Certainly not," says Peggotty, with the promptest decision.

"But if you marry a person, and the person dies, why then you may marry another person, mayn't you, Peggotty?"

"You MAY," says Peggotty, "if you choose, my dear. That's a matter of opinion."

"But what is your opinion, Peggotty?" said I.

I asked her, and looked curiously at her, because she looked so curiously at me.

"My opinion is," said Peggotty, taking her eyes from me, after a little indecision and going on with her work, "that I never was married myself, Master Davy, and that I don't expect to be. That's all I know about the subject."

"You an't cross, I suppose, Peggotty, are you?" said I, after sitting quiet for a minute.

I really thought she was, she had been so short with me; but I was quite mistaken: for she laid aside her work (which was a stocking of her own), and opening her arms wide, took my curly head within them, and gave it a good squeeze. I know it was a good squeeze, because, being very plump, whenever she made any little exertion after she was dressed, some of the buttons on the back of her gown flew off. And I recollect two bursting to the opposite side of the parlour, while she was hugging me.

"Now let me hear some more about the Crorkindills," said Peggotty, who was not quite right in the name yet, "for I an't heard half enough."

I couldn't quite understand why Peggotty looked so queer, or why she was so ready to go back to the crocodiles. However, we returned to those monsters, with fresh wakefulness on my part, and we left their eggs in the sand for the sun to hatch; and we ran away from them, and baffled them by constantly turning, which they were unable to do quickly, on account of their unwieldy make; and we went into the water after them, as natives, and put sharp pieces of timber down their throats; and in short we ran the whole crocodile gauntlet. *I* did, at least; but I had my doubts of Peggotty, who was thoughtfully sticking her needle into various parts of her face and arms all the time.

We had exhausted the crocodiles, and begun with the alligators, when the garden-bell rang. We went out to the door; and there was my mother, looking unusually pretty, I thought, and with her a gentleman with beautiful black hair and whiskers, who had walked home with us from church last Sunday.

As my mother stooped down on the threshold to take me in her arms and kiss me, the gentleman said I was a more highly privileged little fellow than a monarch—or something like that; for my later understanding comes, I am sensible, to my aid here.

"What does that mean?" I asked him, over her shoulder.

He patted me on the head; but somehow, I didn't like him or his deep voice, and I was jealous that his hand should touch my mother's in touching me—which it did. I put it away as well as I could.

"Oh, Davy!" remonstrated my mother.

"Dear boy!" said the gentleman. "I cannot wonder at his devotion!"

I never saw such a beautiful colour on my mother's face before. She gently chid me for being rude; and, keeping me close to her shawl, turned to thank the gentleman for taking so much trouble as to bring her home. She put out her hand to him as she spoke, and, as he met it with his own, she glanced, I thought, at me.

" Let us say ' good night,' my fine boy," said the gentleman, when he had bent his head—*I* saw him!—over my mother's little glove.

" Good night! " said I.

" Come! Let us be the best of friends in the world! " said the gentleman, laughing. " Shake hands! "

My right hand was in my mother's left, so I gave him the other.

" Why, that's the wrong hand, Davy," laughed the gentleman.

My mother drew my right hand forward, but I was resolved, for my former reason, not to give it him, and I did not. I gave him the other, and he shook it heartily, and said I was a brave fellow, and went away.

At this minute I see him turn round in the garden, and give us a last look with his ill-omened black eyes, before the door was shut.

Peggotty, who had not said a word or moved a finger, secured the fastenings instantly, and we all went into the parlour. My mother, contrary to her usual habit, instead of coming to the elbow-chair by the fire, remained at the other end of the room, and sat singing to herself.

—" Hope you have had a pleasant evening, ma'am," said Peggotty, standing as stiff as a barrel in the centre of the room, with a candlestick in her hand.

" Much obliged to you, Peggotty," returned my mother in a cheerful voice, " I have had a *very* pleasant evening."

" A stranger or so makes an agreeable change," suggested Peggotty.

" A very agreeable change, indeed," returned my mother.

Peggotty continuing to stand motionless in the middle of the room, and my mother resuming her singing, I fell asleep, though I was not so sound asleep but that I could hear voices, without hearing what they said. When I half awoke from this uncomfortable doze, I found Peggotty and my mother both in tears, and both talking.

" Not such a one as this, Mr. Copperfield wouldn't have liked," said Peggotty. " That I say, and that I swear! "

" Good Heavens! " cried my mother, " you'll drive me mad! Was ever any poor girl so ill-used by her servants as I am! Why do I do myself the injustice of calling myself a girl? Have I never been married, Peggotty?"

"God knows you have, ma'am," returned Peggotty.

"Then, how can you dare," said my mother—"you know I don't mean how can you dare, Peggotty, but how can you have the heart—to make me so uncomfortable and say such bitter things to me, when you are well aware that I haven't, out of this place, a single friend to turn to?"

"The more's the reason," returned Peggotty, "for saying that it won't do. No! That it won't do. No! No price could make it do. No!"—I thought Peggotty would have thrown the candlestick away, she was so emphatic with it.

"How can you be so aggravating," said my mother, shedding more tears than before, "as to talk in such an unjust manner! How can you go on as if it was all settled and arranged, Peggotty, when I tell you over and over again, you cruel thing, that beyond the commonest civilities nothing has passed! You talk of admiration. What am I to do? If people are so silly as to indulge the sentiment, is it my fault? What am I to do, I ask you? Would you wish me to shave my head and black my face, or disfigure myself with a burn, or a scald, or something of that sort? I dare say you would, Peggotty. I dare say you'd quite enjoy it."

Peggotty seemed to take this aspersion very much to heart, I thought.

"And my dear boy," cried my mother, coming to the elbow-chair in which I was, and caressing me, "my own little Davy! Is it to be hinted to me that I am wanting in my affection for my precious treasure, the dearest little fellow that ever was!"

"Nobody never went and hinted no such a thing," said Peggotty.

"You did, Peggotty!" returned my mother. "You know you did. What else was it possible to infer from what you said, you unkind creature, when you know as well as I do, that on his account only last quarter I wouldn't buy myself a new parasol, though the old green one is frayed the whole way up, and the fringe is perfectly mangy? You know it is, Peggotty; you can't deny it." Then, turning affectionately to me, with her cheek against mine, "Am I a naughty mama to you, Davy? Am I a nasty, cruel, selfish, bad mama? Say I am, my child; say 'yes,' dear boy, and Peggotty will love you; and Peggotty's love is a great deal better than mine, Davy. *I* don't love you at all, do I?"

At this, we all fell a-crying together. I think I was the loudest of the party, but I am sure we were all sincere about it. I was quite heart-broken myself, and am afraid that in the first transports of wounded tenderness I called Peggotty a "Beast." That honest creature was in deep affliction, I remember, and must have become quite buttonless on the occasion; for a little volley of those explosives went off, when, after having made it up with my mother, she kneeled down by the elbow-chair, and made it up with me.

We went to bed greatly dejected. My sobs kept waking me, for a long time; and when one very strong sob quite hoisted me up in bed, I found my mother sitting on the coverlet, and leaning over me. I fell asleep in her arms, after that, and slept soundly.

Whether it was the following Sunday when I saw the gentleman again, or whether there was any greater lapse of time before he re-appeared, I cannot recall. I don't profess to be clear about dates. But there he was, in church, and he walked home with us afterwards. He came in, too, to look at a famous geranium we had, in the parlour-window. It did not appear to me that he took much notice of it, but before he went he asked my mother to give him a bit of the blossom. She begged him to choose it for himself, but he refused to do that—I could not understand why—so she plucked it for him, and gave it into his hand. He said he would never, never part with it any more; and I thought he must be quite a fool not to know that it would fall to pieces in a day or two.

Peggotty began to be less with us, of an evening, than she had always been. My mother deferred to her very much—more than usual, it occurred to me—and we were all three excellent friends; still we were different from what we used to be, and were not so comfortable among ourselves. Sometimes I fancied that Peggotty perhaps objected to my mother's wearing all the pretty dresses she had in her drawers, or to her going so often to visit at that neighbour's; but I couldn't, to my satisfaction, make out how it was.

Gradually, I became used to seeing the gentleman with the black whiskers. I liked him no better than at first, and had the same uneasy jealousy of him; but if I had any reason for it beyond a child's instinctive dislike, and a general idea that Peggotty and I could make much of my mother without any help, it certainly was not *the* reason that I might have found if I had been older. No such thing came into my mind, or near it. I could observe, in little pieces, as it were; but as to making a net of a number of these pieces, and catching anybody in it, that was, as yet, beyond me.

One autumn morning I was with my mother in the front garden, when Mr. Murdstone—I knew him by that name now—came by, on horseback. He reined up his horse to salute my mother, and said he was going to Lowestoft to see some friends who were there with a yacht, and merrily proposed to take me on the saddle before him if I would like the ride.

The air was so clear and pleasant, and the horse seemed to like the idea of the ride so much himself, as he stood snorting and pawing at the garden-gate, that I had a great desire to go. So I was sent up-stairs to Peggotty to be made spruce; and, in the meantime, Mr. Murdstone dismounted, and, with his horse's bridle drawn over his arm, walked slowly up and down on the outer side of the sweetbriar fence, while my mother walked slowly up and down on the inner, to keep him company. I recollect Peggotty and I peeping out at them from my little window; I recollect how closely they seemed to be examining the sweetbriar between them, as they strolled along; and how, from being in a perfectly angelic temper, Peggotty turned cross in a moment, and brushed my hair the wrong way, excessively hard.

Mr. Murdstone and I were soon off, and trotting along on the green turf by the side of the road. He held me quite easily with one arm, and I don't think I was restless usually; but I could not make up my mind to sit in front of him without turning my head sometimes, and looking up in his face. He had that kind of shallow black eye—I want a better word to express an eye that has no depth in it to be looked into—which, when it is abstracted, seems, from some peculiarity of light, to be disfigured, for a moment at a time, by a cast. Several times when I glanced at him, I observed that appearance with a sort of awe, and wondered what he was thinking about so closely. His hair and whiskers were blacker and thicker, looked at so near, than even I had given them credit for being. A squareness about the lower part of his face, and the dotted indication of the strong black beard he shaved close every day, reminded me of the waxwork that had travelled into our neighbourhood some half-a-year before. This, his regular eyebrows, and the rich white, and black, and brown, of his complexion—confound his complexion, and his memory!—made me think him, in spite of my misgivings, a very handsome man. I have no doubt that my poor dear mother thought him so too.

We went to an hotel by the sea, where two gentlemen were smoking cigars in a room by themselves. Each of them was lying on at least four chairs, and had a large rough jacket on. In a corner was a heap of coats and boat-cloaks, and a flag, all bundled up together.

They both rolled on to their feet, in an untidy sort of manner, when we came in, and said, "Hallo, Murdstone! We thought you were dead!"

"Not yet," said Mr. Murdstone.

"And who's this shaver?" said one of the gentlemen, taking hold of me.

"That's Davy," returned Mr. Murdstone.

"Davy who?" said the gentlemen. "Jones?"

"Copperfield," said Mr. Murdstone.

"What! Bewitching Mrs. Copperfield's incumbrance?" cried the gentleman. "The pretty little widow?"

"Quinion," said Mr. Murdstone, "take care, if you please. Somebody's sharp."

"Who is?" asked the gentleman, laughing.

I looked up, quickly; being curious to know.

"Only Brooks of Sheffield," said Mr. Murdstone.

I was quite relieved to find that it was only Brooks of Sheffield; for, at first, I really thought it was I.

There seemed to be something very comical in the reputation of Mr. Brooks of Sheffield, for both the gentlemen laughed heartily when he was mentioned, and Mr. Murdstone was a good deal amused also. After some laughing, the gentleman whom he had called Quinion said:

"And what is the opinion of Brooks of Sheffield, in reference to the projected business?"

"Why, I don't know that Brooks understands much about it at present," replied Mr. Murdstone; "but he is not generally favourable, I believe."

There was more laughter at this, and Mr. Quinion said he would ring the bell for some sherry in which to drink to Brooks. This he did; and when the wine came, he made me have a little, with a biscuit, and, before I drank it, stand up and say, "Confusion to Brooks of Sheffield!" The toast was received with great applause, and such hearty laughter that it made me laugh too; at which they laughed the more. In short, we quite enjoyed ourselves.

We walked about on the cliff after that, and sat on the grass, and looked at things through a telescope—I could make out nothing myself when it was put to my eye, but I pretended I could—and then we came back to the hotel to an early dinner. All the time we were out, the two gentlemen smoked incessantly—which, I thought, if I might judge from the smell of their rough coats, they must have been doing, ever since the coats had first come home from the tailor's. I must not forget that we went on board the yacht, where they all three descended into the cabin, and were busy with some papers. I saw them quite hard at work, when I looked down through the open skylight. They left me, during this time, with a very nice man, with a very large head of red hair and a very small shiny hat upon it, who had got a cross-barred shirt or waistcoat on, with " Skylark " in capital letters across the chest. I thought it was his name; and that as he lived on board ship and hadn't a street-door to put his name on, he put it there instead; but when I called him Mr. Skylark, he said it meant the vessel.

I observed all day that Mr. Murdstone was graver and steadier than the two gentlemen. They were very gay and careless. They joked freely with one another, but seldom with him. It appeared to me that he was more clever and cold than they were, and that they regarded him with something of my own feeling. I remarked that, once or twice, when Mr. Quinion was talking, he looked at Mr. Murdstone sideways, as if to make sure of his not being displeased; and that once when Mr. Passnidge (the other gentleman) was in high spirits, he trod upon his foot, and gave him a secret caution with his eyes, to observe Mr. Murdstone, who was sitting stern and silent. Nor do I recollect that Mr. Murdstone laughed at all that day, except at the Sheffield joke—and that, by the bye, was his own.

We went home early in the evening. It was a very fine evening, and my mother and he had another stroll by the sweetbriar, while I was sent in to get my tea. When he was gone, my mother asked me all about the day I had had, and what they had said and done. I mentioned what they had said about her, and she laughed, and told me they were impudent fellows who talked nonsense—but I knew it pleased her. I knew it quite as well as I know it now. I took the opportunity of asking if she was at all acquainted with Mr. Brooks of Sheffield, but she answered No, only she supposed he must be a manufacturer in the knife and fork way.

Can I say of her face—altered as I have reason to remember it, perished as I know it is—that it is gone, when here it comes before me at this instant, as distinct as any face that I may choose to look on in a crowded street? Can I say of her innocent and girlish beauty, that it faded, and was no more, when its breath falls on my cheek now, as it fell that night? Can I say she ever changed, when my remembrance brings her back to life, thus only; and, truer to its loving youth than I have been, or man ever is, still holds fast what it cherished then?

I write of her just as she was when I had gone to bed after this talk, and she came, to bid me good night. She kneeled down playfully by the side of the bed, and laying her chin upon her hands, and laughing, said:

" What was it they said, Davy? Tell me again. I can't believe it."

" ' Bewitching——' " I began.

My mother put her hands upon my lips to stop me.

" It was never bewitching," she said, laughing. " It never could have been bewitching, Davy. Now I know it wasn't! "

" Yes, it was. ' Bewitching Mrs. Copperfield,' " I repeated stoutly. " And, ' pretty.' "

" No, no, it was never pretty. Not pretty," interposed my mother, laying her fingers on my lips again.

" Yes, it was. ' Pretty little widow.' "

" What foolish, impudent creatures! " cried my mother, laughing and covering her face. " What ridiculous men! An't they? Davy dear——"

" Well, Ma."

" Don't tell Peggotty; she might be angry with them. I am dreadfully angry with them myself; but I would rather Peggotty didn't know."

I promised, of course; and we kissed one another over and over again, and I soon fell fast asleep.

It seems to me, at this distance of time, as if it were the next day when Peggotty broached the striking and adventurous proposition I am about to mention; but it was probably about two months afterwards.

We were sitting as before, one evening (when my mother was out as before), in company with the stocking and the yard measure, and the bit of wax, and the box with Saint Paul's on the lid, and the crocodile book, when Peggotty, after looking at me several times, and opening her mouth as if she were going to speak, without doing it—which I thought was merely gaping, or I should have been rather alarmed—said coaxingly:

" Master Davy, how should you like to go along with me and spend a fortnight at my brother's at Yarmouth? Wouldn't *that* be a treat? "

" Is your brother an agreeable man, Peggotty? " I inquired provisionally.

" Oh, what an agreeable man he is! " cried Peggotty, holding up her hands. " Then there's the sea; and the boats and ships; and the fishermen; and the beach; and Am to play with——"

Peggotty meant her nephew Ham, mentioned in my first chapter; but she spoke of him as a morsel of English Grammar.

I was flushed by her summary of delights, and replied that it would indeed be a treat, but what would my mother say?

" Why then I'll as good as bet a guinea," said Peggotty, intent upon my face, " that she'll let us go. I'll ask her, if you like, as soon as ever she comes home. There now! "

" But what's she to do while we are away? " said I, putting my small elbows on the table to argue the point. " She can't live by herself."

If Peggotty were looking for a hole, all of a sudden, in the heel of that stocking, it must have been a very little one indeed, and not worth darning.

" I say! Peggotty! She can't live by herself, you know."

" Oh, bless you! " said Peggotty, looking at me again at last. " Don't you know? She's going to stay for a fortnight with Mrs. Grayper. Mrs. Grayper's going to have a lot of company."

Oh! If that was it, I was quite ready to go. I waited, in the utmost impatience, until my mother came home from Mrs. Grayper's (for it was that identical neighbour), to ascertain if we could get leave to carry out this great idea. Without being nearly so much surprised as I expected, my mother entered into it readily; and it was all arranged that night, and my board and lodging during the visit were to be paid for.

The day soon came for our going. It was such an early day that it came soon, even to me, who was in a fever of expectation, and half afraid that an earthquake or a fiery mountain, or some other great convulsion of nature, might interpose to stop the expedition. We were to go in a carrier's cart, which departed in the morning after breakfast. I would have given any money to have been allowed to wrap myself up over-night, and sleep in my hat and boots.

It touches me nearly now, although I tell it lightly, to recollect how eager I was to leave my happy home; to think how little I suspected what I did leave for ever.

I am glad to recollect that when the carrier's cart was at the gate, and my mother stood there kissing me, a grateful fondness for her and for the old place I had never turned my back upon before, made me cry. I am glad to know that my mother cried too, and that I felt her heart beat against mine.

I am glad to recollect that when the carrier began to move, my mother ran out at the gate, and called to him to stop, that she might kiss me once more. I am glad to dwell upon the earnestness and love with which she lifted up her face to mine, and did so.

As we left her standing in the road, Mr. Murdstone came up to where she was, and seemed to expostulate with her for being so moved. I was looking back round the awning of the cart, and wondered what business it was of his. Peggotty, who was also looking back on the other side, seemed anything but satisfied; as the face she brought back in the cart denoted.

I sat looking at Peggotty for some time, in a reverie on this supposititious case; whether, if she were employed to lose me like the boy in the fairy tale, I should be able to track my way home again by the buttons she would shed.

3

I HAVE A CHANGE

THE CARRIER'S HORSE WAS THE LAZIEST HORSE IN THE world, I should hope, and shuffled along, with his head down, as if he liked to keep people waiting to whom the packages were directed. I fancied, indeed, that he sometimes chuckled audibly over this reflection, but the carrier said he was only troubled with a cough.

The carrier had a way of keeping his head down, like his horse, and of drooping sleepily forward as he drove, with one of his arms on each of his knees. I say " drove," but it struck me that the cart would have gone to Yarmouth quite as well without him, for the horse did all that; and as to conversation, he had no idea of it but whistling.

Peggotty had a basket of refreshments on her knee, which would have lasted us out handsomely, if we had been going to London by the same conveyance. We ate a good deal, and slept a good deal. Peggotty always went to sleep with her chin upon the handle of the basket, her hold of which never relaxed; and I could not have believed unless I had heard her do it, that one defenceless woman could have snored so much.

We made so many deviations up and down lanes, and were such a long time delivering a bedstead at a public-house, and calling at other places, that I was quite tired, and very glad, when we saw Yarmouth. It looked rather spongy and soppy, I thought, as I carried my eye over the great dull waste that lay across the river; and I could not help wondering, if the world were really as round as my geography-book said, how any part of it came to be so flat. But I reflected that Yarmouth might be situated at one of the poles; which would account for it.

As we drew a little nearer, and saw the whole adjacent prospect lying a straight low line under the sky, I hinted to Peggotty that a mound or so might have improved it; and also that if the land had been a little more separated from the sea, and the town and the tide had not been quite so much mixed up, like toast and water, it would have been nicer. But Peggotty said, with greater emphasis than usual, that we must take things as we found them, and that, for her part, she was proud to call herself a Yarmouth Bloater.

When we got into the street (which was strange enough to me), and smelt the fish, and pitch, and oakum, and tar, and saw the sailors walking about, and the carts jingling up and down over the stones, I felt that I had done so busy a place an injustice; and said as much to Peggotty, who heard my expressions of delight with great complacency, and told me it was well known (I suppose to those who had the good fortune to be born Bloaters) that Yarmouth was, upon the whole, the finest place in the universe.

" Here's my Am! " screamed Peggotty, " growed out of knowledge! "

He was waiting for us, in fact, at the public-house; and asked me how I found myself, like an old acquaintance. I did not feel, at first, that I knew him as well as he knew me, because he had never come to our house since the night I was born, and naturally he had the advantage of me. But our intimacy was much advanced by his taking me on his back to carry me home. He was, now, a huge, strong fellow of six feet high, broad in proportion, and round-shouldered; but with a simpering boy's face and curly light hair that gave him quite a sheepish look. He was dressed in a canvas jacket, and a pair of such very stiff trousers that they would have stood quite as well alone, without any legs in them. And you couldn't so properly have said he wore a hat, as that he was covered in a-top, like an old building, with something pitchy.

Ham carrying me on his back and a small box of ours under his arm, and Peggotty carrying another small box of ours, we turned down lanes bestrewn with bits of chips and little hillocks of sand, and went past gas-works, rope-walks, boat-builders' yards, ship-wrights' yards, ship-breakers' yards, caulkers' yards, riggers' lofts, smiths' forges, and a great litter of such places, until we came out upon the dull waste I had already seen at a distance; when Ham said,

"Yon 's our house, Mas'r Davy!"

I looked in all directions, as far as I could stare over the wilderness, and away at the sea, and away at the river, but no house could *I* make out. There was a black barge, or some other kind of superannuated boat, not far off, high and dry on the ground, with an iron funnel sticking out of it for a chimney and smoking very cosily; but nothing else in the way of a habitation that was visible to *me*.

"That's not it?" said I. "That ship-looking thing?"

"That's it, Mas'r Davy," returned Ham.

If it had been Aladdin's palace, roc's egg and all, I suppose I could not have been more charmed with the romantic idea of living in it. There was a delightful door cut in the side, and it was roofed in, and there were little windows in it; but the wonderful charm of it was, that it was a real boat which had no doubt been upon the water hundreds of times, and which had never been intended to be lived in, on dry land. That was the captivation of it to me. If it had ever been meant to be lived in, I might have thought it small, or inconvenient, or lonely; but never having been designed for any such use, it became a perfect abode.

It was beautifully clean inside, and as tidy as possible. There was a table, and a Dutch clock, and a chest of drawers, and on the chest of drawers there was a tea-tray with a painting on it of a lady with a parasol, taking a walk with a military-looking child who was trundling a hoop. The tray was kept from tumbling down, by a bible; and the tray, if it had tumbled down, would have smashed a quantity of cups and saucers and a teapot that were grouped around the book. On the walls there were some common coloured pictures, framed and glazed, of scripture subjects; such as I have never seen since in the hands of pedlars, without seeing the whole interior of Peggotty's brother's house again, at one view. Abraham in red going to sacrifice Isaac in blue, and Daniel in yellow cast into a den of green lions, were the most prominent of these. Over the little mantel-shelf, was a picture of the Sarah Jane lugger, built at Sunderland, with a real little wooden stern stuck on to it; a work of art, combining composition with carpentry, which I considered to be one of the most enviable possessions that the world could afford. There were some hooks in the beams of the ceiling, the use of which I did not divine then; and some lockers and boxes and conveniences of that sort, which served for seats and eked out the chairs.

All this I saw in the first glance after I crossed the threshold

—child-like, according to my theory—and then Peggotty opened a little door and showed me my bedroom. It was the completest and most desirable bedroom ever seen—in the stern of the vessel; with a little window, where the rudder used to go through; a little looking-glass, just the right height for me, nailed against the wall, and framed with oyster-shells; a little bed, which there was just room enough to get into; and a nosegay of seaweed in a blue mug on the table. The walls were whitewashed as white as milk, and the patchwork counterpane made my eyes quite ache with its brightness. One thing I particularly noticed in this delightful house, was the smell of fish; which was so searching, that when I took out my pocket-handkerchief to wipe my nose, I found it smelt exactly as if it had wrapped up a lobster. On my imparting this discovery in confidence to Peggotty, she informed me that her brother dealt in lobsters, crabs, and crawfish; and I afterwards found that a heap of these creatures, in a state of wonderful conglomeration with one another, and never leaving off pinching whatever they laid hold of, were usually to be found in a little wooden outhouse where the pots and kettles were kept.

We were welcomed by a very civil woman in a white apron, whom I had seen curtseying at the door when I was on Ham's back, about a quarter of a mile off. Likewise by a most beautiful little girl (or I thought her so), with a necklace of blue beads on, who wouldn't let me kiss her when I offered to, but ran away and hid herself. By and by, when we had dined in a sumptuous manner off boiled dabs, melted butter, and potatoes, with a chop for me, a hairy man with a very good-natured face came home. As he called Peggotty " Lass," and gave her a hearty smack on the cheek, I had no doubt, from the general propriety of her conduct, that he was her brother; and so he turned out—being presently introduced to me as Mr. Peggotty, the master of the house.

" Glad to see you, sir," said Mr. Peggotty. " You'll find us rough, sir, but you'll find us ready."

I thanked him, and replied that I was sure I should be happy in such a delightful place.

" How's your Ma, sir? " said Mr. Peggotty. " Did you leave her pretty jolly? "

I gave Mr. Peggotty to understand that she was as jolly as I could wish—and that she desired her compliments—which was a polite fiction on my part.

" I'm much obleeged to her, I'm sure," said Mr. Peggotty. " Well, sir, if you can make out here, for a fortnut, 'long wit' her," nodding at his sister, " and Ham, and little Em'ly, we shall be proud of your company."

Having done the honours of his house in this hospitable manner, Mr. Peggotty went out to wash himself in a kettleful of hot water, remarking that " cold would never get *his* muck off." He soon returned, greatly improved in appearance; but so rubicund, that I couldn't help thinking his face had this in common with the lobsters, crabs, and crawfish—that it went into the hot water very black and came out very red.

After tea, when the door was shut and all was made snug (the nights being cold and misty now), it seemed to me the most delicious retreat that the imagination of man could conceive. To hear the wind getting up out at sea, to know that the fog was creeping over the desolate flat outside, and to look at the fire and think that there was no house near but this one, and this one a boat, was like enchantment. Little Em'ly had overcome her shyness, and was sitting by my side upon the lowest and least of the lockers, which was just large enough for us two, and just fitted into the chimney corner. Mrs. Peggotty, with the white apron, was knitting on the opposite side of the fire. Peggotty at her needlework was as much at home with Saint Paul's and the bit of wax-candle, as if they had never known any other roof. Ham, who had been giving me my first lesson in all-fours, was trying to recollect a scheme of telling fortunes with the dirty cards, and was printing off fishy impressions of his thumb on all the cards he turned. Mr. Peggotty was smoking his pipe. I felt it was a time for conversation and confidence.

" Mr. Peggotty! " said I.

" Sir," says he.

" Did you give your son the name of Ham, because you lived in a sort of ark? "

Mr. Peggotty seemed to think it a deep idea, but answered:

" No, sir. I never giv him no name."

" Who gave him that name, then? " said I, putting question number two of the catechism to Mr. Peggotty.

" Why, sir, his father giv it him," said Mr. Peggotty.

" I thought you were his father! "

" My brother Joe was *his* father," said Mr. Peggotty.

" Dead, Mr. Peggotty? " I hinted, after a respectful pause.

" Drowndead," said Mr. Peggotty.

I was very much surprised that Mr. Peggotty was not Ham's father, and began to wonder whether I was mistaken about his relationship to anybody else there. I was so curious to know, that I made up my mind to have it out with Mr. Peggotty.

"Little Em'ly," I said, glancing at her. "She is your daughter, isn't she, Mr. Peggotty?"

"No, sir. My brother-in-law, Tom, was *her* father."

I couldn't help it. "—Dead, Mr. Peggotty?" I hinted, after another respectful silence.

"Drowndead," said Mr. Peggotty.

I felt the difficulty of resuming the subject, but had not got to the bottom of it yet, and must get to the bottom somehow. so I said:

"Haven't you *any* children, Mr. Peggotty?"

"No, master," he answered, with a short laugh. "I'm a bacheldore."

"A bachelor!" I said, astonished. "Why, who's that, Mr. Peggotty?" pointing to the person in the apron who was knitting.

"That's Missis Gummidge," said Mr. Peggotty.

"Gummidge, Mr. Peggotty?"

But at this point Peggotty—I mean my own peculiar Peggotty—made such impressive motions to me not to ask any more questions, that I could only sit and look at all the silent company, until it was time to go to bed. Then, in the privacy of my own little cabin, she informed me that Ham and Em'ly were an orphan nephew and niece, whom my host had at different times adopted in their childhood, when they were left destitute; and that Mrs. Gummidge was the widow of his partner in a boat; who had died very poor. He was but a poor man himself, said Peggotty, but as good as gold and as true as steel—those were her similes. The only subject, she informed me, on which he ever showed a violent temper or swore an oath, was this generosity of his; and if it were ever referred to, by any of them, he struck the table a heavy blow with his right hand (had split it on one such occasion), and swore a dreadful oath that he would be "Gormed" if he didn't cut and run for good, if it was ever mentioned again. It appeared, in answer to my inquiries, that nobody had the least idea of the etymology of this terrible verb passive to be gormed; but that they all regarded it as constituting a most solemn imprecation.

I was very sensible of my entertainer's goodness, and listened to the women's going to bed in another little crib like mine at the opposite end of the boat, and to him and Ham hanging up two hammocks for themselves on the hooks I had noticed in the roof, in a very luxurious state of mind, enhanced by my being sleepy. As slumber gradually stole upon me, I heard the wind howling out at sea and coming on across the flat so fiercely, that I had a lazy apprehension of the great deep rising in the night. But I bethought myself that I was in a boat, after all; and that a man like Mr. Peggotty was not a bad person to have on board if anything did happen.

Nothing happened, however, worse than morning. Almost as soon as it shone upon the oyster-shell frame of my mirror I was out of bed, and out with little Em'ly, picking up stones upon the beach.

"You're quite a sailor, I suppose?" I said to Em'ly. I don't know that I supposed anything of the kind, but I felt it an act of gallantry to say something; and a shining sail close to us made such a pretty little image of itself, at the moment, in her bright eye, that it came into my head to say this.

"No," replied Em'ly, shaking her head, "I'm afraid of the sea,"

"Afraid!" I said, with a becoming air of boldness, and looking very big at the mighty ocean. "*I* an't!"

"Ah! but it's cruel," said Em'ly. "I have seen it very cruel to some of our men. I have seen it tear a boat as big as our house all to pieces."

"I hope it wasn't the boat that——"

"That father was drownded in?" said Em'ly. "No. Not that one, I never see that boat."

"Nor him?" I asked her.

Little Em'ly shook her head. "Not to remember!"

Here was a coincidence! I immediately went into an explanation how I had never seen my own father; and how my mother and I had always lived by ourselves in the happiest state imaginable, and lived so then, and always meant to live so; and how my father's grave was in the churchyard near our house, and shaded by a tree, beneath the boughs of which I had walked and heard the birds sing many a pleasant morning. But there were some differences between Em'ly's orphanhood and mine, it appeared. She had lost her mother before her father; and where her father's grave was no one knew, except that it was somewhere in the depths of the sea.

"Besides," said Em'ly, as she looked about for shells and pebbles, "your father was a gentleman and your mother is a lady; and my father was a fisherman and my mother was a fisherman's daughter, and my uncle Dan is a fisherman."

"Dan is Mr. Peggotty, is he?" said I.

"Uncle Dan—yonder," answered Em'ly, nodding at the boat-house.

"Yes, I mean him. He must be very good, I should think?"

"Good?" said Em'ly. "If I was ever to be a lady, I'd give him a sky-blue coat with diamond buttons, nankeen trousers, a red velvet waistcoat, a cocked hat, a large gold watch, a silver pipe, and a box of money."

I said I had no doubt that Mr. Peggotty well deserved these treasures. I must acknowledge that I felt it difficult to picture him quite at his ease in the raiment proposed for him by his grateful little niece, and that I was particularly doubtful of the policy of the cocked hat; but I kept these sentiments to myself.

Little Em'ly had stopped and looked up at the sky in her enumeration of these articles, as if they were a glorious vision. We went on again, picking up shells and pebbles.

" You would like to be a lady?" I said.

Emily looked at me, and laughed and nodded " yes."

" I should like it very much. We would all be gentlefolks together, then. Me, and uncle, and Ham, and Mrs. Gummidge. We wouldn't mind then, when there comes stormy weather.—Not for our own sakes, I mean. We would for the poor fishermen's, to be sure, and we'd help 'em with money when they come to any hurt."

This seemed to me to be a very satisfactory, and therefore not at all improbable, picture. I expressed my pleasure in the contemplation of it, and little Em'ly was emboldened to say, shyly,

" Don't you think you are afraid of the sea, now?"

It was quiet enough to reassure me, but I have no doubt if I had seen a moderately large wave come tumbling in, I should have taken to my heels, with an awful recollection of her drowned relations. However, I said " No," and I added, " You don't seem to be, either, though you say you are;"—for she was walking much too near the brink of a sort of old jetty or wooden causeway we had strolled upon, and I was afraid of her falling over.

" I'm not afraid in this way," said little Em'ly. " But I wake when it blows, and tremble to think of Uncle Dan and Ham, and believe I hear 'em crying out for help. That's why I should like so much to be a lady. But I'm not afraid in this way. Not a bit. Look here!"

She started from my side, and ran along a jagged timber which protruded from the place we stood upon, and overhung the deep water at some height, without the least defence. The incident is so impressed on my remembrance, that if I were a draughtsman I could draw its form here, I dare say, accurately as it was that day, and little Em'ly springing forward to her destruction (as it appeared to me), with a look that I have never forgotten, directed far out to sea.

The light, bold, fluttering little figure turned and came back safe to me, and I soon laughed at my fears, and at the cry I had uttered; fruitlessly in any case, for there was no one near. But there have been times since, in my manhood, many times there have been, when I have thought, Is it possible, among the possibilities of hidden things, that in the sudden rashness of the child and her wild look so far off, there was any merciful attraction of her into danger, any tempting her towards him permitted on the part of her dead father, that her life might have a chance of ending that day? There has been a time since when I have wondered whether, if the life before her could have been revealed to me at a glance, and so revealed as that a child could fully comprehend it, and if her preservation could have depended on a motion of my hand, I ought to have held it up to save her. There has been a time since—I do not say it lasted long, but it has been—when I have asked myself the question, would it have been better for little Em'ly to have had the waters close above her head that morning in my sight; and when I have answered Yes, it would have been.

This may be premature. I have set it down too soon, perhaps. But let it stand.

We strolled a long way, and loaded ourselves with things that we thought curious, and put some stranded starfish carefully back into the water. I hardly know enough of the race at this moment to be quite certain whether they had reason to feel obliged to us for doing so, or the reverse—and then made our way home to Mr. Peggotty's dwelling. We stopped under the lee of the lobster-outhouse to exchange an innocent kiss, and went into breakfast glowing with health and pleasure.

"Like two young mavishes," Mr. Peggotty said. I knew this meant, in our local dialect, like two young thrushes, and received it as a compliment.

Of course I was in love with little Em'ly. I am sure I loved that baby quite as truly, quite as tenderly, with greater purity and more disinterestedness, than can enter into the best love of a later time of life, high and ennobling as it is. I am sure my fancy raised up something round that blue-eyed mite of a child, which etherealised, and made a very angel of her. If, any sunny forenoon, she had spread a little pair of wings, and flown away before my eyes, I don't think I should have regarded it as much more than I had reason to expect.

We used to walk about that dim old flat at Yarmouth in a loving manner, hours and hours. The days sported by us, as if Time had not grown up himself yet, but were a child too, and always at play. I told Em'ly I adored her, and that unless she confessed she adored me I should be reduced to the necessity of killing myself with a sword. She said she did, and I have no doubt she did.

As to any sense of inequality, or youthfulness, or other difficulty in our way, little Em'ly and I had no such trouble, because we had no future. We made no more provision for growing older, than we did for growing younger. We were the admiration of Mrs. Gummidge and Peggotty, who used to whisper of an evening when we sat lovingly, on our little locker side by side, "Lor! wasn't it beautiful!" Mr. Peggotty smiled at us from behind his pipe, and Ham grinned all the evening and did nothing else. They had something of the sort of pleasure in us, I suppose, that they might have had in a pretty toy, or a pocket model of the Colosseum.

I soon found out that Mrs. Gummidge did not always make herself so agreeable as she might have been expected to do, under the circumstances of her residence with Mr. Peggotty. Mrs. Gummidge's was rather a fretful disposition, and she whimpered more sometimes than was comfortable for other parties in so small an establishment. I was very sorry for her; but there were moments when it would have been more agreeable, I thought, if Mrs. Gummidge had had a convenient apartment of her own to retire to, and had stopped there until her spirits revived.

Mr. Peggotty went occasionally to a public-house called The Willing Mind. I discovered this, by his being out on the second or third evening of our visit, and by Mrs. Gummidge's looking up at the Dutch clock, between eight and nine, and saying he was there, and that, what was more, she had known in the morning he would go there.

Mrs. Gummidge had been in a low state all day, and had burst into tears in the forenoon, when the fire smoked. "I am a lone lorn creetur'," were Mrs. Gummidge's words, when that unpleasant occurrence took place, "and everythink goes contrairy with me."

"Oh, it'll soon leave off," said Peggotty—I again mean our Peggotty—"and besides, you know, it's not more disagreeable to you than to us."

"I feel it more," said Mrs. Gummidge.

It was a very cold day, with cutting blasts of wind. Mrs. Gummidge's peculiar corner of the fireside seemed to me to be the warmest and snuggest in the place, as her chair was certainly the easiest, but it didn't suit her that day at all. She was constantly complaining of the cold, and of its occasioning a visitation in her back which she called 'the creeps.' At last she shed tears on that subject, and said again that she was "a lone lorn creetur' and everythink went contrairy with her."

"It is certainly very cold," said Peggotty. "Everybody must feel it so."

"I feel it more than other people," said Mrs. Gummidge.

So at dinner; when Mrs. Gummidge was always helped immediately after me, to whom the preference was given as a visitor of distinction. The fish were small and bony, and the potatoes were a little burnt. We all acknowledged that we felt this something of a disappointment; but Mrs. Gummidge said she felt it more than we did, and shed tears again, and made that former declaration with great bitterness.

Accordingly, when Mr. Peggotty came home about nine o'clock, this unfortunate Mrs. Gummidge was knitting in her corner, in a very wretched and miserable condition. Peggotty had been working cheerfully. Ham had been patching up a great pair of waterboots; and I, with little Em'ly by my side, had been reading to them. Mrs. Gummidge had never made any other remark than a forlorn sigh, and had never raised her eyes since tea.

"Well, mates," said Mr. Peggotty, taking his seat, "and how are you?"

We all said something or looked something, to welcome him, except Mrs. Gummidge, who only shook her head over her knitting.

"What's amiss?" said Mr. Peggotty, with a clap of his hands. "Cheer up, old mawther!" (Mr. Peggotty meant old girl.)

Mrs. Gummidge did not appear to be able to cheer up. She took out an old black silk handkerchief and wiped her eyes; but instead of putting it in her pocket, kept it out, and wiped them again, and still kept it out, ready for use.

"What's amiss, dame?" said Mr. Peggotty.

"Nothing," returned Mrs. Gummidge. "You've come from The Willing Mind, Dan'l?"

"Why yes, I've took a short spell at The Willing Mind tonight," said Mr. Peggotty.

"I'm sorry I should drive you there," said Mrs. Gummidge.

"Drive! I don't want no driving," returned Mr. Peggotty with an honest laugh. "I only go too ready."

"Very ready," said Mrs. Gummidge, shaking her head, and wiping her eyes. "Yes, yes, very ready. I am sorry it should be along of me that you're so ready."

"Along o' you! It an't along o' you!" said Mr. Peggotty. "Don't ye believe a bit on it."

"Yes, yes, it is," cried Mrs. Gummidge, "I know what I am. I know that I am a lone lorn creetur', and not only that every-think goes contrairy with me, but that I go contrairy with every-body. Yes, yes, I feel more than other people do, and I show it more. It's my misfortun'."

I really couldn't help thinking, as I sat taking in all this, that the misfortune extended to some other members of that family besides Mrs. Gummidge. But Mr. Peggotty made no such retort, only answering with another entreaty to Mrs. Gummidge to cheer up.

"I an't what I could wish myself to be," said Mrs. Gummidge. "I am far from it. I know what I am. My troubles has made me contrairy. I feel my troubles, and they make me contrairy. I wish I didn't feel 'em, but I do. I wish I could be hardened to 'em, but I an't. I make the house uncomfortable. I don't wonder at it. I've made your sister so all day, and Master Davy."

Here I was suddenly melted, and roared out. "No, you haven't, Mrs. Gummidge," in great mental distress.

"It's far from right that I should do it," said Mrs. Gummidge. "It an't a fit return. I had better go into the house and die. I am a lone lorn creetur', and had much better not make myself con-trairy here. If thinks must go contrairy with me, and I must go contrairy myself, let me go contrairy in my parish. Dan'l, I'd better go into the house, and die and be a riddance!"

Mrs. Gummidge retired with these words, and betook herself to bed. When she was gone, Mr. Peggotty, who had not exhibited a trace of any feeling but the profoundest sympathy, looked round upon us, and nodding his head with a lively expression of that sentiment still animating his face, said in a whisper:

"She's been thinking of the old 'un!"

I did not quite understand what old one Mrs. Gummidge was supposed to have fixed her mind upon, until Peggotty, on seeing me to bed, explained that it was the late Mr. Gum-midge; and that her brother always took that for a received truth on such occasions, and that it always had a moving effect upon him. Some time after he was in his hammock that night, I heard him myself repeat to Ham, "Poor thing! She's been thinking of the old 'un!" And whenever Mrs. Gummidge was overcome in a similar manner during the remainder of our stay (which happened some few times), he always said the same thing in extenuation of the circumstance, and always with the tenderest commiseration.

So the fortnight slipped away, varied by nothing but the variation of the tide, which altered Mr. Peggotty's times of going out and coming in, and altered Ham's engagements also. When the latter was unemployed, he sometimes walked with us to show us the boats and ships, and once or twice he took us for a row. I don't know why one slight set of impressions should be more particularly associated with a place than another, though I believe this obtains with most people, in reference especially to the associations of their childhood. I never hear the name, or read the name, of Yarmouth, but I am reminded of a certain Sunday morning on the beach, the bells ringing for church, little Em'ly leaning on my shoulder, Ham lazily dropping stones into the water, and the sun, away at sea, just breaking through the heavy mist, and showing us the ships, like their own shadows.

At last the day came for going home. I bore up against the separation from Mr. Peggotty and Mrs. Gummidge, but my agony of mind at leaving little Em'ly was piercing. We went arm-in-arm to the public-house where the carrier put up, and I promised, on the road, to write to her. (I redeemed that promise afterwards, in characters larger than those in which apartments are usually announced in manuscript, as being to let.) We were greatly overcome at parting; and if ever, in my life, I have had a void made in my heart, I had one made that day.

Now, all the time I had been on my visit, I had been ungrateful to my home again, and had thought little or nothing about it. But I was no sooner turned towards it, than my reproachful young conscience seemed to point that way with a steady finger; and I felt, all the more for the sinking of my spirits, that it was my nest, and that my mother was my comforter and friend.

This gained upon me as we went along; so that the nearer we drew, and the more familiar the objects became that we passed, the more excited I was to get there, and to run into her arms. But Peggotty, instead of sharing in these transports, tried to check them (though very kindly), and looked confused and out of sorts.

Blunderstone Rookery would come, however, in spite of her, when the carrier's horse pleased—and did. How well I recollect it, on a cold grey afternoon, with a dull sky, threatening rain!

The door opened, and I looked, half laughing and half crying in my pleasant agitation, for my mother. It was not she, but a strange servant.

"Why, Peggotty!" I said, ruefully, "isn't she come home?"

"Yes, yes, Master Davy," said Peggotty. "She's come home. Wait a bit, Master Davy, and I'll—I'll tell you something."

Between her agitation, and her natural awkwardness in getting out of the cart, Peggotty was making a most extraordinary festoon of herself, but I felt too blank and strange to tell her so. When she had got down, she took me by the hand; led me, wondering into, the kitchen; and shut the door.

"Peggotty!" said I, quite frightened. "What's the matter?"

"Nothing's the matter, bless you, Master Davy dear!" she answered, assuming an air of sprightliness.

"Something's the matter, I'm sure. Where's mama?"

"Where's mama, Master Davy?" repeated Peggotty.

"Yes. Why hasn't she come out to the gate, and what have we come in here for? Oh, Peggotty!" My eyes were full, and I felt as if I were going to tumble down.

"Bless the precious boy!" cried Peggotty, taking hold of me. "What is it? Speak, my pet!"

"Not dead, too! Oh, she's not dead, Peggotty?"

Peggotty cried out No! with an astonishing volume of voice; and then sat down, and began to pant, and said I had given her a turn.

I gave her a hug to take away the turn, or to give her another turn in the right direction, and then stood before her, looking at her in anxious inquiry.

"You see, dear, I should have told you before now," said Peggotty, "but I hadn't an opportunity. I ought to have made it, perhaps, but I couldn't azackly"—that was always the substitute for exactly, in Peggotty's militia of words—"bring my mind to it."

"Go on, Peggotty," said I, more frightened than before.

"Master Davy," said Peggotty, untying her bonnet with a shaking hand, and speaking in a breathless sort of way. "What do you think? You have got a Pa!"

I trembled, and turned white. Something—I don't know what, or how—connected with the grave in the churchyard and the raising of the dead, seemed to strike me like an unwholesome wind.

"A new one," said Peggotty.

"A new one?" I repeated.

Peggotty gave a gasp, as if she were swallowing something that was very hard, and, putting out her hand, said:

"Come and see him."

"I don't want to see him."

—"And your mama," said Peggotty.

I ceased to draw back, and we went straight to the best parlour, where she left me. On one side of the fire, sat my mother;

on the other, Mr. Murdstone. My mother dropped her work, and arose hurriedly, but timidly I thought.

"Now, Clara, my dear," said Mr. Murdstone. "Recollect! control yourself, always control yourself! Davy boy, how do you do?"

I gave him my hand. After a moment of suspense, I went and kissed my mother: she kissed me, patted me gently on the shoulder, and sat down again to her work. I could not look at her, I could not look at him, I knew quite well that he was looking at us both: and I turned to the window and looked out there at some shrubs that were drooping their heads in the cold.

As soon as I could creep away, I crept up-stairs. My old dear bedroom was changed, and I was to lie a long way off. I rambled down-stairs to find anything that was like itself, so altered it all seemed; and roamed into the yard. I very soon started back from there, for the empty dog-kennel was filled up with a great dog—deep-mouthed and black-haired like Him—and he was very angry at the sight of me, and sprang out to get at me.

4

I FALL INTO DISGRACE

IF THE ROOM TO WHICH MY BED WAS REMOVED WERE A sentient thing that could give evidence, I might appeal to it at this day—who sleeps there now, I wonder!—to bear witness for me what a heavy heart I carried to it. I went up there, hearing the dog in the yard bark after me all the way while I climbed the stairs; and, looking as blank and strange upon the room as the room looked upon me, sat down with my small hands crossed, and thought.

I thought of the oddest things. Of the shape of the room, of the cracks in the ceiling, of the paper on the wall, of the flaws in the window-glass making ripples and dimples on the prospect, of the washing-stand being ricketty on its three legs, and having a discontented something about it, which reminded me of Mrs. Gummidge under the influence of the old one. I was crying all the time, but, except that I was conscious of being cold and dejected, I am sure I never thought why I cried. At last in my desolation I began to consider that I was dreadfully in love with little Em'ly, and had been torn away from her to come here where no one seemed to want me, or to care about me, half as much as she did. This made such a very miserable piece of business of it, that I rolled myself up in a corner of the counterpane, and cried myself to sleep.

I was awakened by somebody saying "Here he is!" and uncovering my hot head. My mother and Peggotty had come to look for me, and it was one of them who had done it.

"Davy," said my mother. "What's the matter?"

I thought it was very strange that she should ask me, and answered, "Nothing." I turned over on my face, I recollect, to hide my trembling lip, which answered her with greater truth.

"Davy," said my mother. "Davy, my child!"

I dare say no words she could have uttered would have affected me so much, then, as her calling me her child. I hid my tears in the bedclothes, and pressed her from me with my hand, when she would have raised me up.

"This is your doing, Peggotty, you cruel thing!" said my mother. "I have no doubt at all about it. How can you reconcile it to your conscience, I wonder, to prejudice my own boy against me, or against anybody who is dear to me? What do you mean by it, Peggotty?"

Poor Peggotty lifted up her hands and eyes, and only answered, in a sort of paraphrase of the grace I usually repeated after dinner, "Lord forgive you, Mrs. Copperfield, and for what you have said this minute, may you never be truly sorry!"

"It's enough to distract me," cried my mother. "In my honeymoon, too, when my most inveterate enemy might relent, one would think, and not envy me a little peace of mind and happiness. Davy, you naughty boy! Peggotty, you savage creature! Oh, dear me!" cried my mother, turning from one of us to the other, in her pettish, wilful manner. "What a troublesome world this is, when one has the most right to expect it to be as agreeable as possible!"

I felt the touch of a hand that I knew was neither hers nor Peggotty's, and slipped to my feet at the bed-side. It was Mr. Murdstone's hand, and he kept it on my arm as he said:

"What's this? Clara, my love, have you forgotten?—Firmness, my dear!"

"I am very sorry, Edward," said my mother. "I meant to be very good, but I am so uncomfortable."

"Indeed!" he answered. "That's a bad hearing, so soon, Clara."

"I say it's very hard I should be made so now," returned my mother, pouting; "and it is —very hard—isn't it?"

He drew her to him, whispered in her ear, and kissed her. I knew as well, when I saw my mother's head lean down upon his shoulder, and her arm touch his neck—I knew as well that he could mould her pliant nature into any form he chose, as I know, now, that he did it.

"Go you below, my love," said Mr. Murdstone. "David and I will come down, together. My friend," turning a darkening face on Peggotty, when he had watched my mother out, and dismissed her with a nod and a smile; "do you know your mistress's name?"

"She has been my mistress a long time, sir," answered Peggotty, "I ought to know it."

"That's true," he answered. "But I thought I heard you, as I came up-stairs, address her by a name that is not hers. She has taken mine, you know. Will you remember that?"

Peggotty, with some uneasy glances at me, curtseyed herself out of the room without replying; seeing, I suppose, that she was expected to go, and had no excuse for remaining. When we two were left alone, he shut the door, and sitting on a chair, and holding me standing before him, looked steadily into my eyes. I felt my own attracted, no less steadily, to his. As I recall our being opposed thus, face to face, I seem again to hear my heart beat fast and high.

"David," he said, making his lips thin, by pressing them together, "if I have an obstinate horse or dog to deal with, what do you think I do?"

"I don't know."

"I beat him."

I had answered in a kind of breathless whisper, but I felt, in my silence, that my breath was shorter now.

"I make him wince, and smart. I say to myself, 'I'll conquer that fellow;' and if it were to cost him all the blood he had, I should do it. What is that upon your face?"

"Dirt," I said.

He knew it was the mark of tears as well as I. But if he had asked the question twenty times, each time with twenty blows, I believe my baby heart would have burst before I would have told him so.

"You have a good deal of intelligence for a little fellow," he said, with a grave smile that belonged to him, "and you understood me very well, I see. Wash that face, sir, and come down with me."

He pointed to the washing-stand, which I had made out to be like Mrs. Gummidge, and motioned me with his head to obey him directly. I had little doubt then, and I have less doubt now, that he would have knocked me down without the least compunction, if I had hesitated.

" Clara, my dear," he said, when I had done his bidding, and he walked me into the parlour, with his hand still on my arm; " you will not be made uncomfortable any more, I hope. We shall soon improve our youthful humours."

God help me, I might have been improved for my whole life, I might have been made another creature perhaps, for life, by a kind word at that season. A word of encouragement and explanation, of pity for my childish ignorance, of welcome home, of reassurance to me that it *was* home, might have made me dutiful to him in my heart henceforth, instead of in my hypocritical outside, and might have made me respect instead of hate him. I thought my mother was sorry to see me standing in the room so sacred and strange, and that, presently, when I stole to a chair, she followed me with her eyes more sorrowfully still—missing, perhaps, some freedom in my childish tread—but the word was not spoken, and the time for it was gone.

We dined alone, we three together. He seemed to be very fond of my mother—I am afraid I liked him none the better for that—and she was very fond of him. I gathered from what they said, that an elder sister of his was coming to stay with them, and that she was expected that evening. I am not certain whether I found out then or afterwards, that, without being actively concerned in any business, he had some share in, or some annual charge upon the profits of, a wine-merchant's house in London, with which his family had been connected from his great-grandfather's time, and in which his sister had a similar interest; but I may mention it in this place, whether or no.

After dinner, when we were sitting by the fire, and I was meditating an escape to Peggotty without having the hardihood to slip away, lest it should offend the master of the house, a coach drove up to the garden-gate, and he went out to receive the visitor. My mother followed him. I was timidly following her, when she turned round at the parlour-door, in the dusk, and taking me in her embrace as she had been used to do, whispered me to love my new father and be obedient to him. She did this hurriedly and secretly, as if it were wrong, but tenderly; and, putting out her hand behind her, held mine in it, until we came near to where he was standing in the garden, where she let mine go, and drew hers through his arm.

It was Miss Murdstone who was arrived, and a gloomy-looking lady she was; dark, like her brother, whom she greatly resembled in face and voice; and with very heavy eyebrows, nearly meeting over her large nose, as if, being disabled by the wrongs of her sex from wearing whiskers, she had carried them to that account. She brought with her two uncompromising hard black boxes, with her initials on the lids in hard brass nails. When she paid the coachman she took her money out of a hard steel purse, and she kept the purse in a very jail of a bag which hung upon her arm by a heavy chain, and shut up like a bite. I had never, at that time, seen such a metallic lady altogether as Miss Murdstone was.

She was brought into the parlour with many tokens of welcome, and there formally recognized my mother as a new and near relation. Then she looked at me, and said:

" Is that your boy, sister-in-law? "

My mother acknowledged me.

" Generally speaking," said Miss Murdstone, " I don't like boys. How d'ye do, boy? "

Under these encouraging circumstances, I replied that I was very well, and that I hoped she was the same; with such an indifferent grace, that Miss Murdstone disposed of me in two words:

" Wants manner! "

Having uttered which with great distinctness, she begged the favour of being shown to her room, which became to me from that time forth a place of awe and dread, wherein the two black boxes were never seen open or known to be left unlocked, and where (for I peeped in once or twice when she was out) numerous little steel fetters and rivets, with which Miss Murdstone embellished herself when she was dressed, generally hung upon the looking-glass in formidable array.

As well as I could make out, she had come for good, and had no intention of ever going again. She began to " help " my mother next morning, and was in and out of the store-closet all day, putting things to rights, and making havoc in the old arrangements. Almost the first remarkable thing I observed in Miss Murdstone was, her being constantly haunted by a suspicion that the servants had a man secreted somewhere on the premises. Under the influence of this delusion, she dived into the coal-cellar at the most untimely hours, and scarcely ever opened the door of a dark cupboard without clapping it to again, in the belief that she had got him.

Though there was nothing very airy about Miss Murdstone, she was a perfect lark in point of getting up. She was up (and, as I believe to this hour, looking for that man) before anybody in the house was stirring. Peggotty gave it as her opinion that she even slept with one eye open; but I could not concur in this idea; for I tried it myself after hearing the suggestion thrown out, and found it couldn't be done.

On the very first morning after her arrival she was up and ringing her bell at cock-crow. When my mother came down to breakfast and was going to make the tea, Miss Murdstone gave her a kind of peck on the cheek, which was her nearest approach to a kiss, and said:

" Now, Clara, my dear, I am come here, you know, to relieve you of all the trouble I can. You're much too pretty and thoughtless "—my mother blushed but laughed, and seemed not to dislike this character—" to have any duties imposed upon you that can be undertaken by me. If you'll be so good as give me your keys, my dear, I'll attend to all this sort of thing in future."

From that time, Miss Murdstone kept the keys in her own little jail all day, and under her pillow all night, and my mother had no more to do with them than I had.

My mother did not suffer her authority to pass from her without a shadow of protest. One night when Miss Murdstone had been developing certain household plans to her brother, of which he signified his approbation, my mother suddenly began to cry, and said she thought she might have been consulted.

" Clara! " said Mr. Murdstone sternly. " Clara! I wonder at you."

" Oh, it's very well to say you wonder, Edward! " cried my mother, " and it's very well for you to talk about firmness, but you wouldn't like it yourself."

Firmness, I may observe, was the grand quality on which both Mr. and Miss Murdstone took their stand. However I might have expressed my comprehension of it at that time, if I had been called upon, I nevertheless did clearly comprehend in my own way, that it was another name for tyranny; and for a certain gloomy, arrogant, devil's humour, that was in them both. The creed, as I should state it now, was this. Mr. Murdstone was firm; nobody in his world was to be so firm as Mr. Murdstone; nobody else in his world was to be firm at all, for everybody was to be bent to his firmness. Miss Murdstone was an exception. She might be firm, but only by relationship, and in an inferior and tributary degree. My mother was another exception. She might be firm, and must be; but only in bearing their firmness, and firmly believing there was no other firmness upon earth.

"It's very hard," said my mother, "that in my own house——"

"*My* own house?" repeated Mr. Murdstone. "Clara!"

"*Our* own house, I mean," faltered my mother, evidently frightened—"I hope you must know what I mean, Edward—it's very hard that in *your* own house I may not have a word to say about domestic matters. I am sure I managed very well before we were married. There's evidence," said my mother sobbing; "ask Peggotty if I didn't do very well when I wasn't interfered with!"

"Edward," said Miss Murdstone, "let there be an end of this. I go to-morrow."

"Jane Murdstone," said her brother, "be silent! How dare you to insinuate that you don't know my character better than your words imply?"

"I am sure," my poor mother went on at a grievous disadvantage, and with many tears, "I don't want anybody to go. I should be very miserable and unhappy if anybody was to go. I don't ask much. I am not unreasonable. I only want to be consulted sometimes. I am very much obliged to anybody who assists me, and I only want to be consulted as a mere form, sometimes. I thought you were pleased, once with my being a little, inexperienced and girlish, Edward—I am sure you said so—but you seem to hate me for it now, you are so severe."

"Edward," said Miss Murdstone, again, "let there be an end of this. I go to-morrow."

"Jane Murdstone," thundered Mr. Murdstone. "Will you be silent? How dare you?"

Miss Murdstone made a jail-delivery of her pocket-handkerchief, and held it before her eyes.

"Clara," he continued, looking at my mother, "you surprise me! You astound me! Yes, I had a satisfaction in the thought of marrying an inexperienced and artless person, and forming her character, and infusing into it some amount of that firmness and decision of which it stood in need. But when Jane Murdstone is kind enough to come to my assistance in this endeavour, and to assume, for my sake, a condition something like a housekeeper's, and when she meets with a base return——"

"Oh, pray, pray, Edward," cried my mother, "don't accuse me of being ungrateful. I am sure I am not ungrateful. No one ever said I was before. I have many faults, but not that. Oh, don't, my dear!"

"When Jane Murdstone meets, I say," he went on, after

waiting until my mother was silent, " with a base return, that feeling of mine is chilled and altered."

" Don't, my love, say that! " implored my mother very piteously. " Oh, don't, Edward! I can't bear to hear it. Whatever I am, I am affectionate. I know I am affectionate. I wouldn't say it, if I wasn't sure that I am. Ask Peggotty. I am sure she'll tell you I'm affectionate."

" There is no extent of mere weakness, Clara," said Mr. Murdstone in reply, " that can have the least weight with me. You lose breath."

" Pray let us be friends," said my mother, " I couldn't live under coldness or unkindness. I am so sorry. I have a great many defects, I know, and it's very good of you, Edward, with your strength of mind, to endeavour to correct them for me. Jane, I don't object to anything. I should be quite broken-hearted if you thought of leaving——" My mother was too much overcome to go on.

" Jane Murdstone," said Mr. Murdstone to his sister, " any harsh words between us are, I hope, uncommon. It is not my fault that so unusual an occurrence has taken place to-night. I was betrayed into it by another. Nor is it your fault. You were betrayed into it by another. Let us both try to forget it. And as this," he added, after these magnanimous words, " is not a fit scene for the boy—David, go to bed! "

I could hardly find the door, through the tears that stood in my eyes. I was so sorry for my mother's distress; but I groped my way out, and groped my way up to my room in the dark, without even having the heart to say good night to Peggotty, or to get a candle from her. When her coming up to look for me, an hour or so afterwards, awoke me, she said that my mother had gone to bed poorly, and that Mr. and Miss Murdstone were sitting alone.

Going down next morning rather earlier than usual, I paused outside the parlour-door, on hearing my mother's voice. She was very earnestly and humbly entreating Miss Murdstone's pardon, which that lady granted, and a perfect reconciliation took place. I never knew my mother afterwards to give an opinion on any matter, without first appealing to Miss Murdstone, or without having first ascertained by some sure means, what Miss Murdstone's opinion was; and I never saw Miss Murdstone, when out of temper (she was infirm that way), move her hand towards her bag as if she were going to take out the keys and offer to resign them to my mother, without seeing that my mother was in a terrible fright.

The gloomy taint that was in the Murdstone blood, darkened the Murdstone religion, which was austere and wrathful. I have thought, since, that its assuming that character was a necessary consequence of Mr. Murdstone's firmness, which wouldn't allow him to let anybody off from the utmost weight of the severest penalties he could find any excuse for. Be this as it may, I well remember the tremendous visages with which we used to go to church, and the changed air of the place. Again the dreaded Sunday comes round, and I file into the old pew first, like a guarded captive brought to a condemned service. Again, Miss Murdstone, in a black velvet gown, that looks as if it had been made out of a pall, follows close upon me; then my mother; then her husband. There is no Peggotty now, as in the old time. Again, I listen to Miss Murdstone mumbling the responses, and emphasising all the dread words with cruel relish. Again, I see her dark eyes roll round the church when she says " miserable sinners," as if she were calling all the congregation names. Again, I catch rare glimpses of my mother, moving her lips timidly between the two, with one of them muttering at each ear like low thunder. Again, I wonder with a sudden fear whether it is likely that our good old clergyman can be wrong, and Mr. and Miss Murdstone right, and that all the angels in Heaven can be destroying angels. Again, if I move a finger or relax a muscle of my face, Miss Murdstone pokes me with her prayer-book, and makes my side ache.

Yes, and again, as we walk home, I note some neighbours looking at my mother and at me, and whispering. Again, as the three go on arm-in-arm, and I linger behind alone, I follow some of those looks, and wonder if my mother's step be really not so light as I have seen it, and if the gaiety of her beauty be really almost worried away. Again, I wonder whether any of the neighbours call to mind, as I do, how we used to walk home together, she and I; and I wonder stupidly about that, all the dreary, dismal day.

There had been some talk on occasions of my going to boarding-school. Mr. and Miss Murdstone had originated it, and my mother had of course agreed with them. Nothing, however, was concluded on the subject yet. In the meantime I learnt lessons at home.

Shall I ever forget those lessons! They were presided over nominally by my mother, but really by Mr. Murdstone and his sister, who were always present, and found them a favourable occasion for giving my mother lessons in that miscalled firmness, which was the bane of both our lives. I believe I was kept at home for that purpose. I had been apt enough to learn, and willing enough, when my mother and I had lived alone together. I can faintly remember learning the alphabet at her knee. To this day, when I look upon the fat black letters in the primer, the puzzling novelty of their shapes, and the easy good-nature of O and Q and S, seem to present themselves again before me as they used to do. But they recall no feeling of disgust or reluctance. On the contrary, I seem to have walked along a path of flowers as far as the crocodile book, and to have been cheered by the gentleness of my mother's voice and manner all the way. But these solemn lessons which succeeded those, I remember as the death-blow at my peace, and a grievous daily drudgery and misery. They were very long, very numerous, very hard—perfectly unintelligible, some of them, to me—and I was generally as much bewildered by them as I believe my poor mother was herself.

Let me remember how it used to be, and bring one morning back again.

I come into the second-best parlour after breakfast, with my books, and an exercise-book, and a slate. My mother is ready for me at her writing desk, but not half so ready as Mr. Murdstone in his easy-chair by the window (though he pretends to be reading a book), or as Miss Murdstone, sitting near my mother stringing steel beads. The very sight of these two has such an influence over me, that I begin to feel the words I have been at infinite pains to get into my head, all sliding away, and going I don't know where. I wonder where they *do* go, by-the-bye?

I hand the first book to my mother. Perhaps it is a grammar, perhaps a history or geography. I take a last drowning look at the page as I give it into her hand, and start off aloud at a racing pace while I have got it fresh. I trip over a word. Mr. Murdstone looks up. I trip over another word. Miss Murdstone looks up. I redden, tumble over half-a-dozen words, and stop. I think my mother would show me the book if she dared, but she does not dare, and she says softly:

"Oh, Davy, Davy!"

"Now, Clara," says Mr. Murdstone, "be firm with the boy. Don't say, 'Oh, Davy, Davy!' That's childish. He knows his lesson, or he does not know it."

"He does *not* know it," Miss Murdstone interposes awfully.

"I am really afraid he does not," says my mother.

"Then you see, Clara," returns Miss Murdstone, "you should just give him the book back, and make him know it."

"Yes, certainly," says my mother; "that is what I intend to do, my dear Jane. Now, Davy, try once more, and don't be stupid."

I obey the first clause of the injunction by trying once more, but am not so successful with the second, for I am very stupid. I tumble down before I get to the old place, at a point where I was all right before, and stop to think. But I can't think about the lesson. I think of the number of yards of net in Miss Murdstone's cap, or of the price of Mr. Murdstone's dressing-gown, or any such ridiculous problem that I have no business with, and don't want to have anything at all to do with. Mr. Murdstone makes a movement of impatience which I have been expecting for a long time. Miss Murdstone does the same. My mother glances submissively at them, shuts the book, and lays it by as an arrear to be worked out when my other tasks are done.

There is a pile of these arrears very soon, and it swells like a rolling snowball. The bigger it gets, the more stupid *I* get. The case is so hopeless, and I feel that I am wallowing in such a bog of nonsense, that I give up all idea of getting out, and abandon myself to my fate. The despairing way in which my mother and I look at each other, as I blunder on, is truly melancholy. But the greatest effect in these miserable lessons is when my mother (thinking nobody is observing her) tries to give me the cue by the motion of her lips. At that instant, Miss Murdstone, who has been lying in wait for nothing else all along, says in a deep warning voice:

"Clara!"

My mother starts, colours, and smiles faintly. Mr. Murdstone comes out of his chair, takes the book, throws it at me or boxes my ears with it, and turns me out of the room by the shoulders.

Even when the lessons are done, the worst is yet to happen, in the shape of an appalling sum. This is invented for me, and delivered to me orally by Mr. Murdstone, and begins, "If I go into a cheesemonger's shop, and buy five thousand double-Gloucester cheeses at fourpence-halfpenny each, present payment"—at which I see Miss Murdstone secretly overjoyed. I pore over these cheeses without any result or enlightenment until dinner-time, when, having made a Mulatto of myself by getting the dirt of the slate into the pores of my skin, I have a slice of bread to help me out with the cheeses, and am considered in disgrace for the rest of the evening.

It seems to me, at this distance of time, as if my unfortunate studies generally took this course. I could have done very well if I had been without the Murdstones; but the influence of the Murdstones upon me was like the fascination of two snakes on a wretched young bird. Even when I did get through the morning with tolerable credit, there was not much gained but dinner; for Miss Murdstone never could endure to see me untasked, and if I rashly made any show of being unemployed, called her brother's attention to me by saying, " Clara, my dear, there's nothing like work—give your boy an exercise;" which caused me to be clapped down to some new labour there and then. As to any recreation with other children of my age, I had very little of that; for the gloomy theology of the Murdstones made all children out to be a swarm of little vipers (though there *was* a child once set in the midst of the Disciples), and held that they contaminated one another.

The natural result of this treatment, continued, I suppose, for some six months or more, was to make me sullen, dull, and dogged. I was not made the less so by my sense of being daily more and more shut out and alienated from my mother. I believe I should have been almost stupefied but for one circumstance.

It was this. My father had left a small collection of books in a little room up-stairs, to which I had access (for it adjoined my own) and which nobody else in our house ever troubled. From that blessed little room, Roderick Random, Peregrine Pickle, Humphry Clinker, Tom Jones, The Vicar of Wakefield, Don Quixote, Gil Blas, and Robinson Crusoe, came out, a glorious host, to keep me company. They kept alive my fancy, and my hope of something beyond that place and time,—they, and the Arabian Nights, and the Tales of the Genii,—and did me no harm; for whatever harm was in some of them was not there for me; *I* knew nothing of it. It is astonishing to me now, how I found time, in the midst of my porings and blunderings over heavier themes, to read those books as I did. It is curious to me how I could ever have consoled myself under my small troubles (which were great troubles to me), by impersonating my favourite characters in them—as I did—and by putting Mr. and Miss Murdstone into all the bad ones—which I did too. I have been Tom Jones (a child's Tom Jones, a harmless creature) for a week together. I have sustained my own idea of Roderick Random for a month at a stretch, I verily believe. I had a greedy relish for a few volumes of Voyages and Travels—I forget what, now—that were on those shelves; and for days and days I can remember to have gone about my region of our house, armed with the centre-piece out of an old set of boot-trees—the perfect realisation of Captain Somebody, of the Royal British Navy, in danger of being beset by savages, and resolved to sell his life at a great price. The Captain never lost dignity, from having his ears boxed with the Latin Grammar. I did; but the Captain was a Captain and a hero, in despite of all the grammars of all the languages in the world, dead or alive.

This was my only and my constant comfort. When I think of it, the picture always rises in my mind, of a summer evening, the boys at play in the churchyard, and I sitting on my bed, reading as if for life. Every barn in the neighbourhood, every stone in the church, and every foot of the churchyard, had some association of its own, in my mind, connected with these books, and stood for some locality made famous in them. I have seen Tom Pipes go climbing up the church-steeple; I have watched Strap, with the knapsack on his back, stopping to rest himself upon the wicket-gate; and I *know* that Commodore Trunnion held that club with Mr. Pickle, in the parlour of our little village alehouse.

The reader now understands, as well as I do, what I was when I came to that point of my youthful history to which I am now coming again.

One morning when I went into the parlour with my books, I found my mother looking anxious, Miss Murdstone looking firm, and Mr. Murdstone binding something round the bottom of a cane—a lithe and limber cane, which he left off binding when I came in, and poised and switched in the air.

" I tell you, Clara," said Mr. Murdstone, " I have been often flogged myself."

" To be sure; of course," said Miss Murdstone.

" Certainly, my dear Jane," faltered my mother, meekly. " But —but do you think it did Edward good?"

" Do you think it did Edward harm, Clara?" asked Mr. Murdstone, gravely.

" That's the point," said his sister.

To this my mother returned, " Certainly, my dear Jane," and said no more.

I felt apprehensive that I was personally interested in this dialogue, and sought Mr. Murdstone's eye as it lighted on mine.

" Now, David," he said—and I saw that cast again as he said it—" you must be far more careful to-day than usual." He gave the cane another poise, and another switch; and having finished his preparation of it, laid it down beside him, with an impressive look, and took up his book.

This was a good freshener to my presence of mind, as a beginning. I felt the words of my lessons slipping off, not one by one, or line by line, but by the entire page; I tried to lay hold of them; but they seemed, if I may so express it, to have put skates on, and to skim away from me with a smoothness there was no checking.

We began badly, and went on worse. I had come in with an idea of distinguishing myself rather, conceiving that I was very well prepared; but it turned out to be quite a mistake. Book after book was added to the heap of failures, Miss Murdstone being firmly watchful of us all the time. And when we came at last to the five thousand cheeses (canes he made it that day, I remember), my mother burst out crying.

"Clara!" said Miss Murdstone, in her warning voice.

"I am not quite well, my dear Jane, I think," said my mother.

I saw him wink, solemnly at his sister, as he rose and said, taking up the cane:

"Why, Jane, we can hardly expect Clara to bear, with perfect firmness, the worry and torment that David has occasioned her to-day. That would be stoical. Clara is greatly strengthened and improved, but we can hardly expect so much from her. David, you and I will go up-stairs, boy."

As he took me out at the door, my mother ran towards us. Miss Murdstone said, "Clara! are you a perfect fool?" and interfered. I saw my mother stop her ears then, and I heard her crying.

He walked me up to my room slowly and gravely—I am certain he had a delight in that formal parade of executing justice—and when we got there, suddenly twisted my head under his arm.

"Mr. Murdstone! Sir!" I cried to him. "Don't! Pray don't beat me! I have tried to learn, sir, but I can't learn while you and Miss Murdstone are by. I can't indeed!"

"Can't you, indeed, David?" he said. "We'll try that."

He had my head as in a vice, but I twined round him somehow, and stopped him for a moment, entreating him not to beat me. It was only for a moment that I stopped him, for he cut me heavily an instant afterwards, and in the same instant I caught the hand with which he held me in my mouth, between my teeth, and bit it through. It sets my teeth on edge to think of it.

He beat me then as if he would have beaten me to death. Above all the noise we made, I heard them running up the stairs and crying out—I heard my mother crying out—and Peggotty. Then he was gone; and the door was locked outside; and I was lying, fevered and hot, and torn, and sore, and raging in my puny way, upon the floor.

How well I recollect, when I became quiet, what an unnatural stillness seemed to reign through the whole house! How well I remember, when my smart and passion began to cool, how wicked I began to feel!

I sat listening for a long while, but there was not a sound.

I crawled up from the floor, and saw my face in the glass, so swollen, red, and ugly that it almost frightened me. My stripes were sore and stiff, and made me cry afresh, when I moved; but they were nothing to the gulit I felt. It lay heavier on my breast than if I had been a most atrocious criminal, I dare say.

It had begun to grow dark, and I had shut the window (I had been lying, for the most part, with my head upon the sill, by turns crying, dozing, and looking listlessly out), when the key was turned, and Miss Murdstone came in with some bread and meat, and milk. These she put down upon the table without a word, glaring at me the while with exemplary firmness, and then retired, locking the door after her.

Long after it was dark I sat there, wondering whether anybody else would come. When this appeared improbable for that night, I undressed, and went to bed; and there, I began to wonder fearfully what would be done to me. Whether it was a criminal act that I had committed? Whether I should be taken into custody, and sent to prison? Whether I was at all in danger of being hanged?

I never shall forget the waking next morning; the being cheerful and fresh for the first moment, and then the being weighed down by the stale and dismal oppression of remembrance. Miss Murdstone reappeared before I was out of bed; told me, in so many words, that I was free to walk in the garden for half an hour and no longer; and retired, leaving the door open, that I might avail myself of that permission.

I did so, and did so every morning of my imprisonment, which lasted five days. If I could have seen my mother alone, I should have gone down on my knees to her and besought her forgiveness; but I saw no one, Miss Murdstone excepted, during the whole time—except at evening prayers in the parlour; to which I was escorted by Miss Murdstone after everybody else was placed; where I was stationed, a young outlaw, all alone by myself near the door; and whence I was solemnly conducted by my jailer, before any one arose from the devotional posture. I only observed that my mother was as far off from me as she could be, and kept her face another way, so that I never saw it; and that Mr. Murdstone's hand was bound up in a large linen wrapper.

The length of those five days I can convey no idea of to any one. They occupy the place of years in my remembrance. The way in which I listened to all the incidents of the house that made themselves audible to me; the ringing of bells, the opening and shutting of doors, the murmuring of voices, the footsteps on the stairs; to any laughing, whistling, or singing, outside, which seemed more dismal than anything else to me in my solitude and disgrace—the uncertain pace of the hours, especially at night, when I would wake thinking it was morning, and find that the family were not yet gone to bed, and that all the length of night had yet to come—the depressed dreams and nightmares I had—the return of day, noon, afternoon, evening, when the boys played in the churchyard, and I watched them from a distance within the room, being ashamed to show myself at the window lest they should know I was a prisoner—the strange sensation of never hearing myself speak—the fleeting intervals of something like cheerfulness, which came with eating and drinking, and went away with it—the setting in of rain one evening, with a fresh smell, and its coming down faster and faster between me and the church, until it and gathering night seemed to quench me in gloom, and fear, and remorse—all this appears to have gone round and round for years instead of days, it is so vividly and strongly stamped on my remembrance.

On the last night of my restraint, I was awakened by hearing my own name spoken in a whisper. I started up in bed, and putting out my arms in the dark, said:

" Is that you, Peggotty? "

There was no immediate answer, but presently I heard my name again, in a tone so very mysterious and awful that I think I should have gone into a fit, if it had not occurred to me that it must have come through the keyhole.

I groped my way to the door and putting my own lips to the keyhole whispered:

" Is that you Peggotty dear? "

" Yes, my own precious Davy " she replied. " Be as soft as a mouse, or the Cat'll hear us."

I understand this to mean Miss Murdstone, and was sensible of the urgency of the case; her room being close by.

" How's mama, dear Peggotty? Is she very angry with me? "

I could hear Peggotty crying softly on her side of the keyhole as I was doing on mine, before she answered. " No. Not very."

" What is going to be done with me, Peggotty dear? Do you know? "

" School. Near London," was Peggotty's answer. I was obliged to get her to repeat it, for she spoke it the first time quite down my throat, in consequence of my having forgotten to take my mouth away from the keyhole and put my ear there; and though her words tickled me a good deal, I didn't hear them.

" When, Peggotty? "

"To-morrow."

"Is that the reason why Miss Murdstone took the clothes out of my drawers?" which she had done, though I have forgotten to mention it.

"Yes" said Peggotty. "Box."

"Shan't I see mama?"

"Yes" said Peggotty. "Morning."

Then Peggotty fitted her mouth close to the keyhole, and delivered these words through it with as much feeling and earnestness as a keyhole has ever been the medium of communicating, I will venture to assert: shooting in each broken little sentence in a convulsive little burst of its own.

"Davy, dear. If I ain't been azackly as intimate with you. Lately, as I used to be. It ain't because I don't love you. Just as well and more, my pretty poppet. It's because I thought it better for you. And for some one else besides. Davy, my darling, are you listening? Can you hear?"

"Ye—ye—ye—yes, Peggotty!" I sobbed.

"My own!" said Peggotty, with infinite compassion. "What I want to say, is. That you must never forget me. For I'll never forget you. And I'll take as much care of your mama, Davy. As ever I took of you. And I won't leave her. The day may come when she'll be glad to lay her poor head. On her stupid, cross, old Peggotty's arm again. And I'll write to you, my dear. Though I ain't no scholar. And I'll—I'll——" Peggotty fell to kissing the keyhole, as she couldn't kiss me.

"Thank you, dear Peggotty!" said I. "Oh, thank you! Thank you! Will you promise me one thing, Peggotty? Will you write and tell Mr. Peggotty and little Em'ly, and Mrs. Gummidge and Ham, that I am not so bad as they might suppose, and that I sent 'em all my love—especially to little Em'ly? Will you, if you please, Peggotty?"

The kind soul promised, and we both of us kissed the keyhole with the greatest affection—I patted it with my hand, I recollect, as if it had been her honest face—and parted. From that night there grew up in my breast a feeling for Peggotty which I cannot very well define. She did not replace my mother; no one could do that; but she came into a vacancy in my heart, which closed upon her, and I felt towards her something I have never felt for any other human being. It was a sort of comical affection too; and yet if she had died, I cannot think what I should have done, or how I should have acted out the tragedy it would have been to me.

In the morning Miss Murdstone appeared as usual, and told

me I was going to school; which was not altogether such news to me as she supposed. She also informed me that when I was dressed, I was to come down-stairs into the parlour, and have my breakfast. There I found my mother, very pale and with red eyes: into whose arms I ran, and begged her pardon from my suffering soul.

" Oh, Davy! " she said. " That you could hurt any one I love! Try to be better, pray to be better! I forgive you; but I am so grieved, Davy, that you should have such bad passions in your heart."

They had persuaded her that I was a wicked fellow, and she was more sorry for that than for my going away. I felt it sorely. I tried to eat my parting breakfast, but my tears dropped upon my bread-and-butter, and trickled into my tea. I saw my mother look at me sometimes, and then glance at the watchful Miss Murdstone, and then look down, or look away.

" Master Copperfield's box there! " said Miss Murdstone, when wheels were heard at the gate.

I looked for Peggotty, but it was not she; neither she nor Mr. Murdstone appeared. My former acquaintance, the carrier, was at the door; the box was taken out to his cart, and lifted in.

" Clara! " said Miss Murdstone, in her warning note.

" Ready, my dear Jane," returned my mother. " Good-bye, Davy. You are going for your own good. Good-bye, my child. You will come home in the holidays, and be a better boy."

" Clara! " Miss Murdstone repeated.

" Certainly, my dear Jane," replied my mother, who was holding me. " I forgive you my dear boy. God bless you! "

" Clara! " Miss Murdstone repeated.

Miss Murdstone was good enough to take me out to the cart, and to say on the way that she hoped I would repent, before I came to a bad end; and then I got into the cart, and the lazy horse walked off with it.

5

I AM SENT AWAY FROM HOME

WE MIGHT HAVE GONE ABOUT HALF A MILE, AND MY pocket-handkerchief was quite wet through, when the carrier stopped short.

Looking out to ascertain for what, I saw, to my amazement, Peggotty burst from a hedge and climb into the cart. She took me in both her arms, and squeezed me to her stays until the pressure on my nose was extremely painful, though I never thought of that till afterwards when I found it very tender. Not a single word did Peggotty speak. Releasing one of her arms, she put it down in her pocket to the elbow, and brought out some paper bags of cakes which she crammed into my pockets, and a purse which she put into my hand, but not one word did she say. After another and a final squeeze with both arms, she got down from the cart and ran away; and my belief is, and has always been, without a solitary button on her gown. I picked up one, of several that were rolling about, and treasured it as a keepsake for a long time.

The carrier looked at me, as if to inquire if she were coming back. I shook my head, and said I thought not. " Then, come up," said the carrier to the lazy horse; who came up accordingly.

Having by this time cried as much as I possibly could, I began to think it was of no use crying any more, especially as neither Roderick Random, nor that Captain in the Royal British Navy had ever cried, that I could remember, in trying situations. The carrier seeing me in this resolution, proposed that my pocket-handkerchief should be spread upon the horse's back to dry. I thanked him, and assented; and particularly small it looked, under those circumstances.

I had now leisure to examine the purse. It was a stiff leather purse, with a snap, and had three bright shillings in it, which Peggotty had evidently polished up with whitening, for my greater delight. But its most precious contents were two half-crowns folded together in a bit of paper, on which was written, in my mother's hand, " For Davy. With my love." I was so overcome by this, that I asked the carrier to be so good as to reach me my pocket-handkerchief again; but he said he thought I had better do without it, and I thought I really had, so I wiped my eyes on my sleeve and stopped myself.

For good, too; though in consequence of my previous emotions I was still occasionally seized with a stormy sob. After we had jogged on for some little time, I asked the carrier if he was going all the way?

" All the way where?" inquired the carrier.

" There," I said.

" Where's there?" inquired the carrier.

" Near London," I said.

" Why, that horse," said the carrier, jerking the rein to point him out, " would be deader than pork afore he got over half the ground."

" Are you only going to Yarmouth, then?" I asked.

" That's about it," said the carrier. " And there I shall take you to the stage-cutch, and the stage-cutch that'll take you to—wherever it is."

As this was a great deal for the carrier (whose name was Mr. Barkis) to say—he being, as I observed in a former chapter, of a phlegmatic temperament, and not at all conversational—I offered him a cake as a mark of attention, which he ate at one gulp, exactly like an elephant, and which made no more impression on his big face than it would have done on an elephant's.

" Did *she* make 'em now?" said Mr. Barkis, always leaning forward, in his slouching way, on the footboard of the cart with an arm on each knee.

" Peggotty, do you mean, sir?"

" Ah!" said Mr. Barkis. " Her."

" Yes. She makes all our pastry and does all our cooking."

" Do she though?" said Mr. Barkis.

He made up his mouth as if to whistle, but he didn't whistle. He sat looking at the horse's ears, as if he saw something new there; and sat so for a considerable time. By-and-by, he said:

" No sweethearts, I b'lieve?"

" Sweetmeats did you say, Mr. Barkis?" For I thought he wanted something else to eat, and had pointedly alluded to that description of refreshment.

" Hearts," said Mr. Barkis. " Sweethearts; no person walks with her?"

" With Peggotty?"

" Ah!" he said. " Her."

" Oh, no. She never had a sweetheart."

"Didn't she, though?" said Mr. Barkis.

Again he made up his mouth to whistle, and again he didn't whistle, but sat looking at the horse's ears.

"So she makes," said Mr. Barkis, after a long interval of reflection, "all the apple pasties, and does all the cooking, do she?"

I replied that such was the fact.

"Well, I'll tell you what," said Mr. Barkis. "P'raps you might be writin' to her?"

"I shall certainly write to her," I rejoined.

"Ah!" he said, slowly turning his eyes towards me. "Well! If you was writin' to her, p'raps you'd recollect to say that Barkis was willin'; would you?"

"That Barkis was willing," I repeated, innocently. "Is that all the message?"

"Ye—es," he said, considering. "Ye—es. Barkis is willin'."

"But you will be at Blunderstone again to-morrow, Mr. Barkis," I said, faltering a little at the idea of my being far away from it then, "and could give your own message so much better."

As he repudiated this suggestion, however, with a jerk of his head, and once more confirmed his previous request by saying, with profound gravity, "Barkis is willin'. That's the message," I readily undertook its transmission. While I was waiting for the coach in the hotel at Yarmouth that very afternoon, I procured a sheet of paper and an inkstand and wrote a note to Peggotty, which ran thus: "My dear Peggotty. I have come here safe. Barkis is willing. My love to mama. Yours affectionately. P.S. He says he particularly wants you to know—*Barkis is willing*."

When I had taken this commission on myself prospectively, Mr. Barkis relapsed into perfect silence; and I, feeling quite worn out by all that had happened lately, lay down on a sack in the cart and fell asleep. I slept soundly until we got to Yarmouth: which was so entirely new and strange to me in the inn-yard to which we drove, that I at once abandoned a latent hope I had had of meeting with some of Mr. Peggotty's family there, perhaps even with little Em'ly herself.

The coach was in the yard, shining very much all over, but without any horses to it as yet; and it looked in that state as if nothing was more unlikely than its ever going to London. I was thinking this, and wondering what would ultimately become of my box, which Mr. Barkis had put down on the yard-pavement by the pole (he having driven up the yard to turn his cart), and also what would ultimately become of me, when a lady looked out of a bow-window where some fowls and joints of meat were hanging up, and said:

" Is that the little gentleman from Blunderstone? "

" Yes, ma'am," I said.

" What name? " inquired the lady.

" Copperfield, ma'am," I said.

" That won't do," returned the lady. "Nobody's dinner is paid for here, in that name."

" Is it Murdstone, ma'am? " I said.

" If you're Master Murdstone," said the lady, " why do you go and give me another name, first? "

I explained to the lady how it was, who then rang a bell, and called out, " William! show the coffee-room! " upon which a waiter came running out of a kitchen on the opposite side of the yard to show it, and seemed a good deal surprised when he was only to show it to me.

It was a large long room with some large maps in it. I doubt if I could have felt much stranger if the maps had been real foreign countries, and I cast away in the middle of them. I felt it was taking a liberty to sit down, with my cap in my hand, on the corner of the chair nearest the door; and when the waiter laid a cloth on purpose for me, and put a set of casters on it, I think I must have turned red all over with modesty.

He brought me some chops, and vegetables, and took the covers off in such a bouncing manner that I was afraid I must have given him some offence. But he greatly relieved my mind by putting a chair for me at the table, and saying very affably, " Now, six-foot! come on! "

I thanked him, and took my seat at the board; but found it extremely difficult to handle my knife and fork with anything like dexterity, or to avoid splashing myself with the gravy, while he was standing opposite, staring so hard, and making me blush in the most dreadful manner every time I caught his eye. After watching me into the second chop, he said:

" There's half a pint of ale for you. Will you have it now? "

I thanked him and said " Yes." Upon which he poured it out of a jug into a large tumbler, and held it up against the light, and made it look beautiful.

" My eye! " he said. " It seems a good deal, don't it? "

" It does seem a good deal," I answered with a smile. For it was quite delightful to me to find him so pleasant. He was a twinkling-eyed, pimple-faced man, with his hair standing upright all over his head; and as he stood with one arm akimbo, holding up the glass to the light with the other hand, he looked quite friendly.

"There was a gentleman here yesterday," he said—"a stout gentleman, by the name of Topsawyer—perhaps you know him?"

"No," I said, "I don't think——"

"In breeches and gaiters, broad-brimmed hat, grey coat, speckled choker," said the waiter.

"No," I said bashfully, "I haven't the pleasure——"

"He came in here," said the waiter, looking at the light through the tumbler, "ordered a glass of this ale—*would* order it—I told him not—drank it, and fell dead. It was too old for him. It oughn't to be drawn; that's the fact."

I was very much shocked to hear of this melancholy accident, and said I thought I had better have some water.

"Why, you see," said the waiter, still looking at the light through the tumbler, with one of his eyes shut up, "our people don't like things being ordered and left. It offends 'em. But *I*'ll drink it, if you like. I'm used to it, and use is everything. I don't think it'll hurt me, if I throw my head back, and take it off quick. Shall I?"

I replied that he would much oblige me by drinking it, if he thought he could do it safely, but by no means otherwise. When he did throw his head back, and take it off quick, I had a horrible fear, I confess, of seeing him meet the fate of the lamented Mr. Topsawyer, and fall lifeless on the carpet. But it didn't hurt him. On the contrary, I thought he seemed the fresher for it.

"What have we got here?" he said, putting a fork into my dish. "Not chops?"

"Chops," I said.

"Lord bless my soul!" he exclaimed, "I didn't know they were chops. Why a chop's the very thing to take off the bad effects of that beer! Ain't it lucky?"

So he took a chop by the bone in one hand, and a potato in the other, and ate away with a very good appetite, to my extreme satisfaction. He afterwards took another chop, and another potato; and after that another chop and another potato. When he had done, he brought me a pudding, and having set it before me, seemed to ruminate, and to become absent in his mind for some moments.

"How's the pie?" he said, rousing himself.

"It's a pudding," I made answer.

"Pudding!" he exclaimed. "Why, bless me, so it is! What!" looking at it nearer. "You don't mean to say it's a batter-pudding?"

" Yes, it is indeed."

" Why, a batter-pudding," he said, taking up a table-spoon, " is my favourite pudding! Ain't that lucky? Come on, little 'un, and let's see who'll get most."

The waiter certainly got most. He entreated me more than once to come in and win, but what with his table-spoon to my tea-spoon, his dispatch to my dispatch, and his appetite to my appetite, I was left far behind at the first mouthful, and had no chance with him. I never saw any one enjoy a pudding so much, I think; and he laughed, when it was all gone, as if his enjoyment of it lasted still.

Finding him so very friendly and companionable, it was then that I asked for the pen and ink and paper, to write to Peggotty. He not only brought it immediately, but was good enough to look over me while I wrote the letter. When I had finished it, he asked me where I was going to school.

I said, " Near London," which was all I knew.

" Oh! my eye! " he said, looking very low-spirited, " I am sorry for that."

" Why? " I asked him.

" Oh, Lord! " he said, shaking his head, " that's the school where they broke the boy's ribs—two ribs—a little boy he was, I should say he was—let me see—how old are you, about? "

I told him between eight and nine.

" That's just his age," he said. " He was eight years and six months old when they broke his first rib; eight years and eight months old when they broke his second, and did for him."

I could not disguise from myself, or from the waiter, that this was an uncomfortable coincidence, and inquired how it was done. His answer was not cheering to my spirits, for it consisted of two dismal words, " With whopping."

The blowing of the coach-horn in the yard was a seasonable diversion, which made me get up and hesitatingly inquire, in the mingled pride and diffidence of having a purse (which I took out of my pocket), if there were anything to pay.

"There's a sheet of letter-paper," he returned. "Did you ever buy a sheet of letter-paper? "

I could not remember that I ever had.

" It's dear," he said, " on account of the duty. Threepence. That's the way we're taxed in this country. There's nothing else, except the waiter. Never mind the ink. *I* lose by that."

" What should you—what should I—how much ought I to—what would it be right to pay the waiter, if you please? " I stammered, blushing.

" If I hadn't a family, and that family hadn't the cow-pock," said the waiter, " I wouldn't take a sixpence. If I didn't support a aged pairint, and a lovely sister,"—here the waiter was greatly agitated—"I wouldn't take a farthing. If I had a good place, and was treated well here, I should beg acceptance of a trifle, instead of taking of it. But I live on broken wittles—and I sleep on the coals "—here the waiter burst into tears.

I was very much concerned for his misfortunes, and felt that any recognition short of ninepence would be mere brutality and hardness of heart. Therefore I gave him one of my three bright shillings, which he received with much humility and veneration, and spun up with his thumb, directly afterwards, to try the goodness of.

It was a little disconcerting to me, to find, when I was being helped up behind the coach, that I was supposed to have eaten all the dinner without any assistance. I discovered this, from overhearing the lady in the bow-window say to the guard, " Take care of that child, George, or he'll burst! " and from observing that the women-servants who were about the place came out to look and giggle at me as a young phenomenon. My unfortunate friend the waiter, who had quite recovered his spirits, did not appear to be disturbed by this, but joined in the general admiration without being at all confused. If I had any doubt of him, I suppose this half awakened it; but I am inclined to believe that with the simple confidence of a child, and the natural reliance of a child upon superior years (qualities I am very sorry any children should prematurely change for worldly wisdom), I had no serious mistrust of him on the whole, even then.

I felt it rather hard, I must own, to be made, without deserving it, the subject of jokes between the coachman and guard as to the coach drawing heavy behind, on account of my sitting there, and as to the greater expediency of my travelling by wagon. The story of my supposed appetite getting wind among the outside passengers, they were merry upon it likewise; and asked me whether I was going to be paid for, at school, as two brothers or three, and whether I was contracted for, or went upon the regular terms; with other pleasant questions. But the worst of it was, that I knew I should be ashamed to eat anything, when an opportunity offered, and that, after a rather light dinner, I should remain hungry all night—for I had left my cakes behind, at the hotel, in my hurry. My apprehensions were realised. When we stopped for supper I couldn't muster courage to take any, though I should have liked it very much, but sat by the fire and said I didn't want anything. This did not save me from more jokes, either; for a husky-voiced gentleman with a rough face, who had been eating out of a sandwich-box nearly all the way, except when he had been drinking out of a bottle, said I was like a boa-constrictor, who took enough at one meal to last him a long time; after which he actually brought a rash out upon himself with boiled beef.

We had started from Yarmouth at three o'clock in the afternoon, and were due in London about eight next morning. It was Midsummer weather, and the evening was very pleasant. When we passed through a village, I pictured to myself what the insides of the houses were like, and what the inhabitants were about; and when boys came running after us, and got up behind and swung there for a little way, I wondered whether their fathers were alive, and whether they were happy at home. I had plenty to think of, therefore, besides my mind running continually on the kind of place I was going to—which was an awful speculation. Sometimes, I remember, I resigned myself to thoughts of home and Peggotty; and to endeavouring, in a confused blind way, to recall how I had felt, and what sort of boy I used to be, before I bit Mr. Murdstone: which I couldn't satisfy myself about by any means, I seemed to have bitten him in such a remote antiquity.

The night was not so pleasant as the evening, for it got chilly; and being put between two gentlemen (the rough-faced one and another) to prevent my tumbling off the coach, I was nearly smothered by their falling asleep, and completely blocking me up. They squeezed me so hard sometimes, that I could not help crying out, " Oh, if you please! "—which they didn't like at all, because it woke them. Opposite me was an elderly lady in a great fur cloak, who looked in the dark more like a haystack than a lady, she was wrapped up to such a degree. This lady had a basket with her, and she hadn't known what to do with it, for a long time, until she found that, on account of my legs being short, it could go underneath me. It cramped and hurt me so, that it made me perfectly miserable; but if I moved in the least, and made a glass that was in the basket rattle against something else (as it was sure to do), she gave me the cruellest poke with her foot, and said, " Come, don't *you* fidget. *Your* bones are young enough, *I*'m sure! "

At last the sun rose, and then my companions seemed to sleep easier. The difficulties under which they had laboured all night, and which had found utterance in the most terrific gasps and snorts, are not to be conceived. As the sun got higher, their sleep became lighter, and so they gradually one by one awoke. I recollect being very much surprised by the feint everybody made, then, of not having been to sleep at all, and by the uncommon indignation with which every one repelled the charge. I labour under the same kind of astonishment to this day, having invariably observed that of all human weaknesses, the one to which our common nature is the least disposed to confess (I cannot imagine why) is the weakness of having gone to sleep in a coach.

What an amazing place London was to me when I saw it in the distance, and how I believed all the adventures of all my favourite heroes to be constantly enacting and re-enacting there, and how I vaguely made it out in my own mind to be fuller of wonders and wickedness than all the cities of the earth, I need not stop here to relate. We approached it by degrees, and got, in due time, to the inn in the Whitechapel district, for which we were bound. I forget whether it was the Blue Bull, or the Blue Boar; but I know it was the Blue Something, and that its likeness was painted up on the back of the coach.

The guard's eye lighted on me as he was getting down, and he said at the booking-office door:

" Is there anybody here for a yoongster booked in the name of Murdstone, from Bloonderstone, Sooffolk, to be left till called for? "

Nobody answered.

" Try Copperfield, if you please, sir," said I, looking helplessly down.

" Is there anybody here for a yoongster, booked in the name of Murdstone, from Bloonderstone, Sooffolk, but owning to the name of Copperfield, to be left till called for? " said the guard. " Come! *Is* there anybody? "

No. There was nobody. I looked anxiously around; but the inquiry made no impression on any of the bystanders, if I except a man in gaiters, with one eye, who suggested that they had better put a brass collar round my neck, and tie me up in the stable.

A ladder was brought, and I got down after the lady, who was like a haystack: not daring to stir until her basket was removed. The coach was clear of passengers by that time, the luggage was very soon cleared out, the horses had been taken out before the luggage, and now the coach itself was wheeled and backed off by some hostlers, out of the way. Still nobody appeared to claim the dusty youngster from Blunderstone, Suffolk.

More solitary than Robinson Crusoe, who had nobody to look at him, and see that he was solitary, I went into the booking-office, and by invitation of the clerk on duty, passed behind the counter, and sat down on the scale at which they weighed the luggage. Here, as I sat looking at the parcels, packages, and books, and inhaling the smell of stables (ever since associated with that morning), a procession of most tremendous considerations began to march through my mind. Supposing nobody should ever fetch me, how long would they consent to keep me there? Would they keep me long enough to spend seven shillings? Should I sleep at night in one of those wooden bins, with the other luggage, and wash myself at the pump in the yard in the morning; or should I be turned out every night, and expected to come again to be left till called for, when the office opened next day? Supposing there was no mistake in the case, and Mr. Murdstone had devised this plan to get rid of me, what should I do? If they allowed me to remain there until my seven shillings were spent, I couldn't hope to remain there when I began to starve. That would obviously be inconvenient and unpleasant to the customers, besides entailing on the Blue Whatever-it-was, the risk of funeral expenses. If I started off at once, and tried to walk back home, how could I ever find my way, how could I ever hope to walk so far, how could I make sure of any one but Peggotty, even if I got back? If I found out the nearest proper authorities, and offered myself to go for a soldier, or a sailor, I was such a little fellow that it was most likely they wouldn't take me in. These thoughts, and a hundred other such thoughts, turned me burning hot, and made me giddy with apprehension and dismay. I was in the height of my fever when a man entered and whispered to the clerk, who presently slanted me off the scale, and pushed me over to him, as if I were weighed, bought, delivered, and paid for.

As I went out of the office, hand in hand with this new acquaintance, I stole a look at him. He was a gaunt, sallow young man, with hollow cheeks, and a chin almost as black as Mr. Murdstone's; but there the likeness ended, for his whiskers were shaved off, and his hair, instead of being glossy, was rusty and dry. He was dressed in a suit of black clothes which were rather rusty and dry too, and rather short in the sleeves and legs; and he had a white neckerchief on, that was not over-clean. I did not, and do not, suppose that this neckerchief was all the linen he wore, but it was all he showed or gave any hint of.

"You're the new boy?" he said.

"Yes, sir," I said.

I supposed I was. I didn't know.

"I'm one of the masters at Salem House," *he* said.

I made him a bow and felt very much overawed. I was so ashamed to allude to a commonplace thing like my box, to a scholar and a master at Salem House, that we had gone some little distance from the yard before I had the hardihood to mention it. We turned back, on my humbly insinuating that it might be useful to me hereafter; and he told the clerk that the carrier had instructions to call for it at noon.

" If you please, sir," I said, when we had accomplished about the same distance as before, " is it far? "

" It's down by Blackheath," he said.

" Is *that* far, sir? " I diffidently asked.

" It's a good step," he said, " We shall go by the stage-coach. It's about six miles."

I was so faint and tired, that the idea of holding out for six miles more was too much for me. I took heart to tell him that I had had nothing all night, and that if he would allow me to buy something to eat, I should be very much obliged to him. He appeared surprised at this—I see him stop and look at me now —and after considering for a few moments, said he wanted to call on an old person who lived not far off, and that the best way would be for me to buy some bread, or whatever I liked best that was wholesome, and make my breakfast at her house, where we could get some milk.

Accordingly we looked in at a baker's window, and after I had made a series of proposals to buy everything that was bilious in the shop, and he had rejected them one by one, we decided in favour of a nice little loaf of brown bread, which cost me threepence. Then, at a grocer's shop, we bought an egg and a slice of streaky bacon; which still left what I thought a good deal of change, out of the second of the bright shillings, and made me consider London a very cheap place. These provisions laid in, we went on through a great noise and uproar that confused my weary head beyond description, and over a bridge which, no doubt, was London Bridge (indeed I think he told me so, but I was half asleep), until we came to the poor person's house, which was a part of some alms-houses, as I knew by their look, and by an inscription on a stone over the gate, which said they were established for twenty-five poor women.

The Master at Salem House lifted the latch of one of a number of little black doors that were all alike, and had each a little diamond-paned window on one side, and another little diamond-paned window above; and we went into the little house of one of these poor old women, who was blowing a fire to make a little saucepan boil. On seeing the Master enter, the old woman stopped with the bellows on her knee, and said something that I thought sounded like " My Charley! " but on seeing me come in too, she got up, and rubbing her hands made a confused sort of half curtsey.

"Can you cook this young gentleman's breakfast for him, if you please?" said the Master at Salem House.

"Can I?" said the old woman. "Yes can I, sure!"

"How's Mrs. Fibbitson to-day?" said the Master, looking at another old woman in a large chair by the fire, who was such a bundle of clothes that I feel grateful to this hour for not having sat upon her by mistake.

"Ah, she's poorly," said the first old woman. "It's one of her bad days. If the fire was to go out, through any accident, I verily believe she'd go out too, and never come to life again."

As they looked at her, I looked at her also. Although it was a warm day, she seemed to think of nothing but the fire. I fancied she was jealous even of the saucepan on it; and I have reason to know that she took its impressment into the service of boiling my egg and broiling my bacon, in dudgeon; for I saw her, with my own discomfited eyes, shake her fist at me once, when those culinary operations were going on, and no one else was looking. The sun streamed in at the little window, but she sat with her own back and the back of the large chair towards it, screening the fire as if she were sedulously keeping *it* warm, instead of it keeping her warm, and watching it in a most distrustful manner. The completion of the preparations for my breakfast, by relieving the fire, gave her such extreme joy that she laughed aloud—and a very unmelodious laugh she had, I must say.

I sat down to my brown loaf, my egg, and my rasher of bacon, with a basin of milk besides, and made a most delicious meal. While I was yet in the full enjoyment of it, the old woman of the house said to the Master:

"Have you got your flute with you?"

"Yes," he returned.

"Have a blow at it," said the old woman, coaxingly. "Do!"

The Master, upon this, put his hand underneath the skirts of his coat, and brought out his flute in three pieces, which he screwed together, and began immediately to play. My impression is, after many years of consideration, that there never can have been anybody in the world who played worse. He made the most dismal sounds I have ever heard produced by any means, natural or artificial. I don't know what the tunes were—if there were such things in the performance at all, which I doubt—but the influence of the strain upon me was, first, to make me think of all my sorrows until I could hardly keep my tears back; then to take away my appetite; and lastly, to make me so sleepy that I couldn't keep my eyes open. They begin to close again, and I begin to nod, as the recollection rises fresh upon me. Once more the little room, with its open corner cupboard, and its square-backed chairs, and its angular little staircase leading to the room above, and its three peacock's feathers displayed over the mantelpiece—I remember wondering when I first went in, what that peacock would have thought if he had known what his finery was doomed to come to—fades from before me, and I nod, and sleep. The flute becomes inaudible, the wheels of the coach are heard instead, and I am on my journey. The coach jolts, I wake up with a start, and the flute has come back again, and the Master at Salem House is sitting with his legs crossed, playing it dolefully, while the old woman of the house looks on delighted. She fades in her turn, and he fades, and all fades, and there is no flute, no Master, no Salem House, no David Copperfield, no anything but heavy sleep.

I dreamed, I thought, that once while he was blowing into this dismal flute, the old woman of the house, who had gone nearer and nearer to him in her ecstatic admiration, leaned over the back of his chair and gave him an affectionate squeeze round the neck, which stopped his playing for a moment. I was in the middle state between sleeping and waking, either then or immediately afterwards; for, as he resumed—it was a real fact that he had stopped playing—I saw and heard the same old woman ask Mrs. Fibbitson if it wasn't delicious (meaning the flute), to which Mrs. Fibbitson replied, "Ay, ay! yes!" and nodded at the fire; to which, I am persuaded, she gave the credit of the whole performance.

When I seemed to have been dozing a long while, the Master at Salem House unscrewed his flute into the three pieces, put them up as before, and took me away. We found the coach very near at hand, and got upon the roof; but I was so dead sleepy, that when we stopped on the road to take up somebody else, they put me inside where there were no passengers, and where I slept profoundly, until I found the coach going at a footpace up a steep hill among green leaves. Presently, it stopped, and had come to its destination.

A short walk brought us—I mean the Master and me—to Salem House, which was enclosed with a high brick wall, and looked very dull. Over a door in this wall was a board with SALEM HOUSE upon it; and through a grating in this door we were surveyed, when we rang the bell, by a surly face, which I found, on the door being opened, belonged to a stout man with a bull-neck, a wooden leg, overhanging temples, and his hair cut close all round his head.

"The new boy," said the Master.

The man with the wooden leg eyed me all over—it didn't take long, for there was not much of me—and locked the gate behind us, and took out the key. We were going up to the house, among some dark heavy trees, when he called after my conductor.

"Hallo!"

We looked back, and he was standing at the door of a little lodge, where he lived, with a pair of boots in his hand.

"Here! The cobbler's been," he said, "since you've been out, Mr. Mell, and he says he can't mend 'em any more. He says there ain't a bit of the original boot left, and he wonders you expect it."

With these words he threw the boots towards Mr. Mell, who went back a few paces to pick them up, and looked at them (very disconsolately, I was afraid) as we went on together. I observed then, for the first time, that the boots he had on were a good deal the worse for wear, and that his stocking was just breaking out in one place, like a bud.

Salem House was a square brick building with wings, of a bare and unfurnished appearance. All about it was so very quiet, that I said to Mr. Mell I supposed the boys were out; but he seemed surprised at my not knowing that it was holiday-time. That all the boys were at their several homes. That Mr. Creakle, the proprietor, was down by the sea-side with Mrs. and Miss Creakle. And that I was sent in holiday-time as a punishment for my misdoing. All of which he explained to me as we went along.

I gazed upon the schoolroom into which he took me, as the most forlorn and desolate place I had ever seen. I see it now. A long room, with three long rows of desks, and six of forms, and bristling all round with pegs for hats and slates. Scraps of old copy-books and exercises litter the dirty floor. Some silk-worms' houses, made of the same materials, are scattered over the desks. Two miserable little white mice, left behind by their owner, are running up and down in a fusty castle made of paste-board and wire, looking in all the corners with their red eyes for anything to eat. A bird, in a cage very little bigger than himself, makes a mournful rattle now and then in hopping on his perch, two inches high, or dropping from it; but neither sings nor chirps. There is a strange unwholesome smell upon the room, like mildewed corduroys, sweet apples wanting air, and rotten books. There could not well be more ink splashed about it, if it had been roofless from its first construction, and the skies had rained, snowed, hailed, and blown ink through the varying seasons of the year.

Mr. Mell having left me while he took his irreparable boots up-stairs, I went softly to the upper end of the room, observing all this as I crept along. Suddenly I came upon a pasteboard placard, beautifully written, which was lying on the desk, and bore these words: " *Take care of him. He bites.*"

I got upon the desk immediately, apprehensive of at least a great dog underneath. But, though I looked all round with anxious eyes, I could see nothing of him. I was still engaged in peering about, when Mr. Mell came back, and asked me what I did up there?

" I beg your pardon, sir," says I, " if you please, I'm looking for the dog."

" Dog? " says he. " What dog? "

" Isn't it a dog, sir? "

" Isn't what a dog? "

" That's to be taken care of, sir; that bites? "

" No, Copperfield," says he, gravely, " that's not a dog. That's a boy. My instructions are, Copperfield, to put this placard on your back. I am sorry to make such a beginning with you, but I must do it."

With that he took me down, and tied the placard, which was neatly constructed for the purpose, on my shoulders like a knapsack; and wherever I went, afterwards, I had the consolation of carrying it.

What I suffered from that placard nobody can imagine. Whether it was possible for people to see me or not, I always fancied that somebody was reading it. It was no relief to turn round and find nobody; for wherever my back was, there I imagined somebody always to be. That cruel man with the wooden leg aggravated my sufferings. He was in authority, and if he ever saw me leaning against a tree, or a wall, or the house, he roared out from his lodge-door in a stupendous voice, " Hallo, you sir! You Copperfield! Show that badge conspicuous, or I'll report you! " The playground was a bare gravelled yard, open to all the back of the house and the offices; and I knew that the servants read it, and the butcher read it, and the baker read it; that everybody, in a word, who came backwards and forwards to the house, of a morning when I was ordered to walk there, read that I was to be taken care of, for I bit. I recollect that I positively began to have a dread of myself, as a kind of wild boy who did bite.

There was an old door in this playground, on which the boys had a custom of carving their names. It was completely covered with such inscriptions. In my dread of the end of the vacation and their coming back, I could not read a boy's name, without inquiring in what tone and with what emphasis *he* would read,

"Take care of him. He bites." There was one boy—a certain J. Steerforth—who cut his name very deep and very often, who, I conceived, would read it in a rather strong voice, and afterwards pull my hair. There was another boy, one Tommy Traddles, who I dreaded would make game of it, and pretend to be dreadfully frightened of me. There was a third, George Demple, who I fancied would sing it. I have looked, a little shrinking creature, at that door, until the owners of all the names—there were five-and-forty of them in the school then, Mr. Mell said—seemed to send me to Coventry by general acclamation, and to cry out, each in his own way, "Take care of him. He bites!"

It was the same with the places at the desks and forms. It was the same with the groves of deserted bedsteads I peeped at, on my way to, and when I was in, my own bed. I remember dreaming night after night, of being with my mother as she used to be, or of going to a party at Mr. Peggotty's, or of travelling outside the stage-coach, or of dining again with my unfortunate friend the waiter, and in all these circumstances making people scream and stare, by the unhappy disclosure that I had nothing on but my little night-shirt, and that placard.

In the monotony of my life, and in my constant apprehension of the re-opening of the school, it was such an insupportable affliction! I had long tasks every day to do with Mr. Mell; but I did them, there being no Mr. and Miss Murdstone here, and got through them without disgrace. Before, and after them, I walked about—supervised, as I have mentioned, by the man with the wooden leg. How vividly I call to mind the damp about the house, the green cracked flagstones in the court, an old leaky water-butt, and the discoloured trunks of some of the grim trees, which seemed to have dripped more in the rain than other trees, and to have blown less in the sun! At one we dined, Mr. Mell and I, at the upper end of a long bare dining-room, full of deal tables, and smelling of fat. Then, we had more tasks until tea, which Mr. Mell drank out of a blue tea-cup, and I out of a tin pot. All day long, and until seven or eight in the evening, Mr. Mell, at his own detached desk in the school-room, worked hard with pen, ink, ruler, books, and writing-paper, making out the bills (as I found) for last half-year. When he had put up his things for the night, he took out his flute, and blew at it, until I almost thought he would gradually blow his whole being into the large hole at the top, and ooze away at the keys.

I picture my small self in the dimly-lighted rooms, sitting with my head upon my hand, listening to the doleful performance of Mr. Mell, and conning to-morrow's lessons. I picture myself with my books shut up, still listening to the doleful performance of Mr. Mell, and listening through it to what used to be at home, and to the blowing of the wind on Yarmouth flats, and feeling very sad and solitary. I picture myself going up to bed, among the unused rooms, and sitting on my bedside crying for a comfortable word from Peggotty. I picture myself coming down-stairs in the morning, and looking through a long ghastly gash of a staircase window at the school-bell hanging on the top of an outhouse with a weathercock above it; and dreading the time when it shall ring J. Steerforth and the rest to work. Such time is only second, in my foreboding apprehensions, to the time when the man with the wooden leg shall unlock the rusty gate to give admission to the awful Mr. Creakle. I cannot think I was a very dangerous character in any of these aspects, but in all of them I carried the same warning on my back.

Mr. Mell never said much to me, but he was never harsh to me. I suppose we were company to each other, without talking. I forgot to mention that he would talk to himself sometimes, and grin, and clench his fist, and grind his teeth, and pull his hair in an unaccountable manner. But he had these peculiarities. At first they frightened me, though I soon got used to them.

6

I ENLARGE MY CIRCLE OF ACQUAINTANCE

I HAD LED THIS LIFE ABOUT A MONTH, WHEN THE MAN with the wooden leg began to stump about with a mop and a bucket of water, from which I inferred that preparations were making to receive Mr. Creakle and the boys. I was not mistaken; for the mop came into the schoolroom before long, and turned out Mr. Mell and me, who lived where we could, and got on how we could, for some days, during which we were always in the way of two or three young women, who had rarely shown themselves before, and were so continually in the midst of dust that I sneezed almost as much as if Salem House had been a great snuff-box.

One day I was informed by Mr. Mell that Mr. Creakle would be home that evening. In the evening, after tea, I heard that he was come. Before bed-time, I was fetched by the man with the wooden leg to appear before him.

Mr. Creakle's part of the house was a good deal more comfortable than ours, and he had a snug bit of garden that looked pleasant after the dusty playground, which was such a desert in miniature that I thought no one but a camel, or a dromedary, could have felt at home in it. It seemed to me a bold thing even to take notice that the passage looked comfortable, as I went on my way, trembling, to Mr. Creakle's presence: which so abashed me, when I was ushered into it, that I hardly saw Mrs. Creakle or Miss Creakle (who were both there, in the parlour), or anything but Mr. Creakle, a stout gentleman with a bunch of watch-chain and seals, in an arm-chair, with a tumbler and bottle beside him.

" So! " said Mr. Creakle. " This is the young gentleman whose teeth are to be filed! Turn him round."

The wooden-legged man turned me about so as to exhibit the placard; and having afforded time for a full survey of it, turned me about again, with my face to Mr. Creakle, and posted himself at Mr. Creakle's side. Mr. Creakle's face was fiery, and his eyes were small, and deep in his head; he had thick veins in his forehead, a little nose, and a large chin. He was bald on the top of his head: and had some thin wet-looking hair that was just turning grey, brushed across each temple, so that the two sides interlaced on his forehead. But the circumstance about him which impressed me most, was, that he had no voice, but spoke in a whisper. The exertion this cost him, or the consciousness of talking in that feeble way, made his angry face so much more angry, and his thick veins so much thicker, when he spoke, that I am not surprised, on looking back, at this peculiarity striking me as his chief one.

" Now," said Mr. Creakle. " What's the report of this boy? "

" There's nothing against him yet," returned the man with the wooden leg. " There has been no opportunity."

I thought Mr. Creakle was disappointed. I thought Mrs. and Miss Creakle (at whom I now glanced for the first time, and who were, both, thin and quiet) were not disappointed.

" Come here, sir! " said Mr. Creakle, beckoning to me.

" Come here! " said the man with the wooden leg, repeating the gesture.

" I have the happiness of knowing your father-in-law," whispered Mr. Creakle, taking me by the ear; " and a worthy man he is, and a man of a strong character. He knows me, and I know him. Do *you* know me? Hey?" said Mr. Creakle, pinching my ear with ferocious playfulness.

"Not yet, sir," I said, flinching with the pain.

"Not yet? Hey?" repeated Mr. Creakle. "But you will soon. Hey?"

"You will soon. Hey?" repeated the man with the wooden leg. I afterwards found that he generally acted, with his strong voice, as Mr. Creakle's interpreter to the boys.

I was very much frightened, and said I hoped so, if he pleased. I felt, all this while, as if my ear were blazing; he pinched it so hard.

"I'll tell you what I am," whispered Mr. Creakle, letting it go at last, with a screw at parting that brought the water into my eyes. "I'm a Tartar."

"A Tartar," said the man with the wooden leg.

"When I say I'll do a thing, I do it," said Mr. Creakle; "and when I say I will have a thing done, I will have it done."

"—Will have a thing done, I will have it done," repeated the man with the wooden leg.

"I am a determined character," said Mr. Creakle. "That's what I am. I do my duty. That's what *I* do. My flesh and blood," he looked at Mrs. Creakle as he said this, "when it rises against me, is not my flesh and blood. I discard it. Has that fellow," to the man with the wooden leg, "been here again?"

"No," was the answer.

"No," said Mr. Creakle. "He knows better. He knows me. Let him keep away. I say let him keep away," said Mr. Creakle, striking his hand upon the table, and looking at Mrs. Creakle, "for he knows me. Now you have begun to know me too, my young friend, and you may go. Take him away."

I was very glad to be ordered away, for Mrs. and Miss Creakle were both wiping their eyes, and I felt as uncomfortable for them as I did for myself. But I had a petition on my mind which concerned me so nearly, that I couldn't help saying, though I wondered at my own courage:

"If you please, sir——"

Mr. Creakle whispered, "Hah! What's this?" and bent his eyes upon me, as if he would have burnt me up with them.

"If you please, sir," I faltered, "if I might be allowed (I am very sorry indeed, sir, for what I did) to take this writing off, before the boys come back——"

Whether Mr. Creakle was in earnest, or whether he only did it to frighten me, I don't know, but he made a burst out of his chair, before which I precipitately retreated, without waiting for the escort of the man with the wooden leg, and never once stopped until I reached my own bedroom, where, finding I was not pursued, I went to bed, as it was time, and lay quaking, for a couple of hours.

Next morning Mr. Sharp came back. Mr. Sharp was the first master, and superior to Mr. Mell. Mr. Mell took his meals with the boys, but Mr. Sharp dined and supped at Mr. Creakle's table. He was a limp, delicate-looking gentleman, I thought, with a good deal of nose, and a way of carrying his head on one side, as if it were a little too heavy for him. His hair was very smooth and wavy; but I was informed by the very first boy who came back that it was a wig (a second-hand one *he* said), and that Mr. Sharp went out every Saturday afternoon to get it curled.

It was no other than Tommy Traddles who gave me this piece of intelligence. He was the first boy who returned. He introduced himself by informing me that I should find his name on the right-hand corner of the gate, over the top-bolt; upon that I said, "Traddles?" to which he replied, "The same," and then he asked me for a full account of myself and family.

It was a happy circumstance for me that Traddles came back first. He enjoyed my placard so much, that he saved me from the embarrassment of either disclosure or concealment, by presenting me to every other boy who came back, great or small, immediately on his arrival, in this form of introduction, "Look here! Here's a game!" Happily, too, the greater part of the boys came back low-spirited, and were not so boisterous at my expense as I had expected. Some of them certainly did dance about me like wild Indians, and the greater part could not resist the temptation of pretending that I was a dog, and patting and smoothing me, lest I should bite, and saying, "Lie down, sir!" and calling me Towzer. This was naturally confusing, among so many strangers, and cost me some tears, but on the whole it was much better than I had anticipated.

I was not considered as being formally received into the school, however, until J. Steerforth arrived. Before this boy, who was reputed to be a great scholar, and was very good-looking, and at least half-a-dozen years my senior, I was carried as before a magistrate. He inquired, under a shed in the playground, into the particulars of my punishment, and was pleased to express his opinion that it was "a jolly shame"; for which I became bound to him ever afterwards.

"What money have you got, Copperfield?" he said, walking

aside with me when he had disposed of my affair in these terms.

I told him seven shillings.

"You had better give it to me to take care of," he said. "At least, you can if you like. You needn't if you don't like."

I hastened to comply with his friendly suggestion, and opening Peggotty's purse, turned it upside down into his hand.

"Do you want to spend anything now?" he asked me.

"No, thank you," I replied.

"You can, if you like, you know," said Steerforth. "Say the word."

"No, thank you, sir," I repeated.

"Perhaps you'd like to spend a couple of shillings or so, in a bottle of currant wine by-and-by, up in the bedroom?" said Steerforth. "You belong to my bedroom, I find."

It certainly had not occurred to me before, but I said, Yes, I should like that.

"Very good," said Steerforth. "You'll be glad to spend another shilling or so, in almond cakes, I dare say?"

I said, Yes, I should like that, too.

"And another shilling or so in biscuits, and another in fruit, eh?" said Steerforth. "I say, young Copperfield, you're going it!"

I smiled because he smiled, but I was a little troubled in my mind, too.

"Well!" said Steerforth. "We must make it stretch as far as we can; that's all. I'll do the best in my power for you. I can go out when I like, and I'll smuggle the prog in." With these words he put the money in his pocket, and kindly told me not to make myself uneasy; he would take care it should be all right.

He was as good as his word, if that were all right which I had a secret misgiving were nearly all wrong—for I feared it was a waste of my mother's two half-crowns—though I had preserved the piece of paper they were wrapped in: which was a precious saving. When we went up-stairs to bed, he produced the whole seven shillings' worth, and laid it out on my bed in the moonlight, saying:

"There you are, young Copperfield, and a royal spread you've got."

I couldn't think of doing the honours of the feast, at my time of life, while he was by: my hand shook at the very thought of it. I begged him to do me the favour of presiding; and my request being seconded by the other boys who were in that room, he acceded to it, and sat upon my pillow, handing round the viands—with perfect fairness, I must say—and dispensing the currant wine in a little glass without a foot, which was his own property. As to me, I sat on his left hand, and the rest were grouped about us, on the nearest beds and on the floor.

How well I recollect our sitting there, talking in whispers: or their talking, and my respectfully listening, I ought rather to say; the moonlight falling a little way into the room, through the window, painting a pale window on the floor, and the greater part of us in shadow, except when Steerforth dipped a match into a phosphorus-box, when he wanted to look for anything on the board, and shed a blue glare over us that was gone directly! A certain mysterious feeling, consequent on the darkness, the secrecy of the revel, and the whisper in which everything was said, steals over me again, and I listen to all they tell me with a vague feeling of solemnity and awe, which makes me glad that they are all so near, and frightens me (though I feign to laugh) when Traddles pretends to see a ghost in the corner.

I heard all kinds of things about the school and all belonging to it. I heard that Mr. Creakle had not preferred his claim to being a Tartar without reason; but he was the sternest and most severe of masters; that he laid about him, right and left, every day of his life, charging in among the boys like a trooper, and slashing away, unmercifully. That he knew nothing himself, but the art of slashing, being more ignorant (J. Steerforth said) than the lowest boy in the school; that he had been, a good many years ago, a small hop-dealer in the Borough, and had taken to the schooling business after being bankrupt in hops, and making away with Mrs. Creakle's money. With a good deal more of that sort, which I wondered how they knew.

I heard that the man with the wooden leg, whose name was Tungay, was an obstinate barbarian who had formerly assisted in the hop business, but had come into the scholastic line with Mr. Creakle, in consequence, as was supposed among the boys, of his having broken his leg in Mr. Creakle's service, and having done a deal of dishonest work for him, and knowing his secrets. I heard that with the single exception of Mr. Creakle, Tungay considered the whole establishment, masters and boys, as his natural enemies, and that the only delight of his life was to be sour and malicious. I heard that Mr. Creakle had a son, who had not been Tungay's friend, and who, assisting in the school, had once held some remonstrance with his father on an occasion when its discipline was very cruelly exercised, and was supposed, besides, to have protested against his father's usage of his mother. I heard that Mr. Creakle had turned him out of doors, in consequence, and that Mrs. and Miss Creakle had been in a sad way, ever since.

But the greatest wonder that I heard of Mr. Creakle was, there being one boy in the school on whom he never ventured to lay a hand, and that boy being J. Steerforth. Steerforth himself confirmed this when it was stated, and said that he should like to begin to see him do it. On being asked by a mild boy (not me) how he would proceed if he did begin to see him do it, he dipped a match into his phosphorus-box on purpose to shed a glare over his reply, and said he would commence by knocking him down with a blow on the forehead from the seven-and-sixpenny ink-bottle that was always on the mantelpiece. We sat in the dark for some time, breathless.

I heard that Mr. Sharp and Mr. Mell were both supposed to be wretchedly paid; and that when there was hot and cold meat for dinner at Mr. Creakle's table, Mr. Sharp was always expected to say he preferred cold; which was again corroborated by J. Steerforth, the only parlour-boarder. I heard that Mr. Sharp's wig didn't fit him; and that he needn't be so " bounceable "—somebody else said " bumptious "—about it, because his own red hair was very plainly to be seen behind.

I heard that one boy, who was a coal-merchant's son, came as a set-off against the coal-bill, and was called, on that account, " Exchange or Barter "—a name selected from the arithmetic-book as expressing this arrangement. I heard that the table-beer was a robbery of parents, and the pudding an imposition. I heard that Miss Creakle was regarded by the school in general as being in love with Steerforth; and I am sure, as I sat in the dark, thinking of his nice voice, and his fine face, and his easy manner, and his curling hair, I thought it very likely. I heard that Mr. Mell was not a bad sort of fellow, but hadn't a sixpence to bless himself with; and that there was no doubt that old Mrs. Mell, his mother, was as poor as Job. I thought of my breakfast then, and what had sounded like " My Charley! " but I was, I am glad to remember, as mute as a mouse about it.

The hearing of all this, and a good deal more, outlasted the banquet some time. The greater part of the guests had gone to bed as soon as the eating and drinking were over; and we, who had remained whispering and listening half undressed, at last betook ourselves to bed, too.

" Good night, young Copperfield," said Steerforth. " I'll take care of you."

" You're very kind," I gratefully returned. " I am very much obliged to you."

" You haven't got a sister, have you? " said Steerforth, yawning.

" No," I answered.

" That's a pity," said Steerforth. " If you had had one, I should think she would have been a pretty, little, bright-eyed sort of girl. I should have liked to know her. Good night, young Copperfield."

" Good night, sir," I replied.

I thought of him very much after I went to bed, and raised myself, I recollect, to look at him where he lay in the moonlight, with his handsome face turned up, and his head reclining easily on his arm. He was a person of great power in my eyes; that was, of course, the reason of my mind running on him. No veiled future dimly glanced upon him in the moonbeams. There was no shadowy picture of his footsteps, in the garden that I dreamed of walking in all night.

7

MY " FIRST HALF " AT SALEM HOUSE

SCHOOL BEGAN IN EARNEST NEXT DAY. A PROFOUND impression was made upon me, I remember, by the roar of voices in the schoolroom suddenly becoming hushed as death when Mr. Creakle entered after breakfast, and stood in the doorway looking round upon us like a giant in a story-book surveying his captives.

Tungay stood at Mr. Creakle's elbow. He had no occasion, I thought, to cry out " Silence! " so ferociously, for the boys were all struck speechless and motionless.

Mr. Creakle was seen to speak, and Tungay was heard, to this effect.

" Now, boys, this is a new half. Take care what you're about, in this new half. Come fresh up to the lessons, I advise you, for I come fresh up to the punishment. I won't flinch. It will be of no use your rubbing yourselves; you won't rub the marks out that I shall give you. Now get to work, every boy! "

When this dreadful exordium was over, and Tungay had stumped out again, Mr. Creakle came to where I sat, and told me that if I were famous for biting, he was famous for biting, too. He then showed me the cane, and asked me what I thought of *that*, for a tooth? Was it a sharp tooth, hey? Was it a double tooth, hey? Had it a deep prong, hey? Did it bite, hey? Did it bite? At every question he gave me a fleshy cut with it that made me writhe; so I very soon made free of Salem House (as Steerforth said), and was very soon in tears also.

Not that I mean to say these were special marks of distinction, which only I received. On the contrary, a large majority of the boys (especially the smaller ones) were visited with similar instances of notice, as Mr. Creakle made the round of the schoolroom. Half the establishment was writhing and crying, before the day's work began; and how much of it had writhed and cried before the day's work was over I am really afraid to recollect, lest I should seem to exaggerate.

I should think there never can have been a man who enjoyed his profession more than Mr. Creakle did. He had a delight in cutting at the boys, which was like the satisfaction of a craving appetite. I am confident that he couldn't resist a chubby boy, especially; that there was a fascination in such a subject, which made him restless in his mind, until he had scored and marked him for the day. I was chubby myself, and ought to know. I am sure when I think of the fellow now, my blood rises against him with the disinterested indignation I should feel if I could have known all about him without having ever been in his power; but it rises hotly, because I know him to have been an incapable brute, who had no more right to be possessed of the great trust he held, than to be Lord High Admiral, or Commander-in-Chief—in either of which capacities it is probable that he would have done infinitely less mischief.

Miserable little propitiators of a remorseless Idol, how abject we were to him! What a launch in life I think it now, on looking back, to be so mean and servile to a man of such parts and pretensions!

Here I sit at the desk again, watching his eye—humbly watching his eye, as he rules a ciphering book for another victim whose hands have just been flattened by that identical ruler, and who is trying to wipe the sting out with a pocket-handkerchief. I have plenty to do. I don't watch his eye in idleness, but because I am morbidly attracted to it, in a dread desire to know what he will do next, and whether it will be my turn to suffer, or somebody else's. A lane of small boys beyond me, with the same interest in his eye, watch it too. I think he knows it, though he pretends he don't. He makes dreadful mouths as he rules the ciphering book; and now he throws his eye sideways down our lane, and we all droop over our books and tremble. A moment afterwards we are again eyeing him. An unhappy culprit, found guilty of imperfect exercise, approaches at his command. The culprit falters excuses, and professes a determination to do better to-morrow. Mr. Creakle cuts a joke before he beats him, and we laugh at it—miserable little dogs, we laugh, with our visages as white as ashes, and our hearts sinking into our boots.

Here I sit at the desk again, on a drowsy summer afternoon. A buzz and hum go up around me, as if the boys were so many blue-bottles. A cloggy sensation of the lukewarm fat of meat is upon me (we dined an hour or two ago), and my head is as heavy as so much lead. I would give the world to go to sleep. I sit with my eye on Mr. Creakle blinking at him like a young owl; when sleep overpowers me for a minute, he still looms through my slumber, ruling those ciphering books, until he softly comes behind me and wakes me to plainer perception of him, with a red ridge across my back.

Here I am in the playground, with my eye still fascinated by him, though I can't see him. The window at a little distance from which I know he is having his dinner, stands for him, and I eye that instead. If he shows his face near it, mine assumes an imploring and submissive expression. If he looks out through the glass, the boldest boy (Steerforth excepted) stops in the middle of a shout or yell, and becomes contemplative. One day, Traddles (the most unfortunate boy in the world) breaks that window accidentally with a ball. I shudder at this moment with the tremendous sensation of seeing it done, and feeling that the ball has bounded on to Mr. Creakle's sacred head.

Poor Traddles! In a tight sky-blue suit that made his arms and legs like German sausages, or roly-poly puddings, he was the merriest and most miserable of all the boys. He was always being caned—I think he was caned every day that half-year, except one holiday Monday when he was only ruler'd on both hands—and was always going to write to his uncle about it, and never did. After laying his head on the desk for a little while, he would cheer up somehow, begin to laugh again, and draw skeletons all over his slate, before his eyes were dry. I used at first to wonder what comfort Traddles found in drawing skeletons; and for some time looked upon him as a sort of hermit, who reminded himself by those symbols of mortality that caning couldn't last for ever. But I believe he only did it because they were easy, and didn't want any features.

He was very honourable, Traddles was, and held it as a solemn duty in the boys to stand by one another. He suffered for this on several occasions; and particularly once, when Steerforth laughed in church, and the Beadle thought it was Traddles, and took him out. I see him now, going away in custody, despised by the congregation. He never said who was the real offender, though he smarted for it next day, and was imprisoned so many hours that he came forth with a whole churchyardful of skeletons swarming all over his Latin Dictionary. But he had his reward. Steerforth said there was nothing of the sneak in Traddles, and we all felt that to be the highest praise. For my part, I could have gone through a good deal (though I was much less brave than Traddles, and nothing like so old) to have won such a recompense.

To see Steerforth walk to church before us, arm-in-arm with Miss Creakle, was one of the great sights of my life. I didn't think Miss Creakle equal to little Em'ly in point of beauty, and I didn't love her (I didn't dare); but I thought her a young lady of extraordinary attractions, and in point of gentility not to be surpassed. When Steerforth, in white trousers, carried her parasol for her, I felt proud to know him; and believed that she could not choose but adore him with all her heart. Mr. Sharp and Mr. Mell were both notable personages in my eyes; but Steerforth was to them what the sun was to two stars.

Steerforth continued his protection of me, and proved a very useful friend, since nobody dared to annoy one whom he honoured with his countenance. He couldn't—or at all events he didn't—defend me from Mr. Creakle, who was very severe with me; but whenever I had been treated worse than usual, he always told me that I wanted a little of his pluck, and that he wouldn't have stood it himself; which I felt he intended for encouragement, and considered to be very kind of him. There was one advantage, and only one that I know of, in Mr. Creakle's severity. He found my placard in his way when he came up or down behind the form on which I sat, and wanted to make a cut at me in passing; for this reason it was soon taken off, and I saw it no more.

An accidental circumstance cemented the intimacy between Steerforth and me, in a manner that inspired me with great pride and satisfaction, though it sometimes led to inconvenience. It happened on one occasion, when he was doing me the honour of talking to me in the playground, that I hazarded the observation that something or somebody—I forget what now—was like something or somebody in Peregrine Pickle. He said nothing at the time; but when I was going to bed at night, asked me if I had got that book?

I told him no, and explained how it was that I had read it, and all those other books of which I have made mention.

"And do you recollect them?" Steerforth said.

"Oh, yes," I replied; I had a good memory, and I believed I recollected them very well.

"Then I tell you what, young Copperfield," said Steerforth, "you shall tell 'em to me. I can't get to sleep very early at night, and I generally wake rather early in the morning. We'll go over 'em one after another. We'll make some regular Arabian Nights of it."

I felt extremely flattered by this arrangement, and we commenced carrying it into execution that very evening. What ravages I committed on my favourite authors in the course of my interpretation of them, I am not in a condition to say, and should be very unwilling to know; but I had a profound faith in them, and I had, to the best of my belief, a simple earnest manner of narrating what I did narrate; and these qualities went a long way.

The drawback was, that I was often sleepy at night, or out of spirits and indisposed to resume the story, and then it was rather hard work, and it must be done; for to disappoint or to displease Steerforth was of course out of the question. In the morning too, when I felt weary, and should have enjoyed another hour's repose very much, it was a tiresome thing to be roused, like the Sultana Scheherazade, and forced into a long story before the getting-up bell rang; but Steerforth was resolute; and as he explained to me, in return, my sums and exercises, and anything in my tasks that was too hard for me, I was no loser by the transaction. Let me do myself justice, however. I was moved by no interested or selfish motive, nor was I moved by fear of him. I admired and loved him, and his approval was return enough. It was so precious to me, that I look back on these trifles, now, with an aching heart.

Steerforth was considerate too, and showed his consideration, in one particular instance, in an unflinching manner that was a little tantalising, I suspect, to poor Traddles and the rest. Peggotty's promised letter—what a comfortable letter it was!—arrived before "the half" was many weeks old, and with it a cake in a perfect nest of oranges, and two bottles of cowslip wine. This treasure, as in duty bound, I laid at the feet of Steerforth, and begged him to dispense.

"Now, I'll tell you what, young Copperfield," said he: "the wine shall be kept to wet your whistle when you are story-telling."

I blushed at the idea, and begged him, in my modesty, not to think of it. But he said he had observed I was sometimes hoarse—a little roopy was his exact expression—and it should be, every drop, devoted to the purpose he had mentioned. Accordingly, it was locked up in his box, and drawn off by himself in a phial, and administered to me through a piece of quill in the cork, when I was supposed to be in want of a restorative. Sometimes, to make it a more sovereign specific, he was so kind as to squeeze orange juice into it, or to stir it up with ginger, or dissolve a peppermint drop in it; and although I cannot assert that the flavour was improved by these experiments, or that it was exactly the compound one would have chosen for a stomachic, the last thing at night and the first thing in the morning, I drank it gratefully, and was very sensible of his attention.

We seem, to me, to have been months over Peregrine, and months more over the other stories. The institution never flagged for want of a story, I am certain, and the wine lasted out almost as well as the matter. Poor Traddles—I never think of that boy but with a strange disposition to laugh, and with tears in my eyes—was a sort of chorus, in general, and affected to be convulsed with mirth at the comic parts, and to be overcome with fear when there was any passage of an alarming character in the narrative. This rather put me out, very often. It was a great jest of his, I recollect, to pretend that he couldn't keep his teeth from chattering, whenever mention was made of an alguazil in connection with the adventures of Gil Blas; and I remember that when Gil Blas met the captain of the robbers in Madrid, this unlucky joker counterfeited such an ague of terror, that he was overheard by Mr. Creakle, who was prowling about the passage, and handsomely flogged for disorderly conduct in the bedroom.

Whatever I had within me that was romantic and dreamy, was encouraged by so much story-telling in the dark; and in that respect the pursuit may not have been very profitable to me. But the being cherished as a kind of plaything in my room, and the consciousness that this accomplishment of mine was bruited about among the boys, and attracted a good deal of notice to me though I was the youngest there, stimulated me to exertion. In a school carried on by sheer cruelty, whether it is presided over by a dunce or not, there is not likely to be much learnt. I believe our boys were, generally, as ignorant a set as any schoolboys in existence; they were too much troubled and knocked about to learn; they could no more do that to advantage, than any one can do anything to advantage in a life of constant misfortune, torment, and worry. But my little vanity, and Steerforth's help, urged me on somehow; and without saving me from much, if anything, in the way of punishment, made me, for the time I was there, an exception to the general body, inasmuch that I did steadily pick up some crumbs of knowledge.

In this I was much assisted by Mr. Mell, who had a liking for me that I am grateful to remember. It always gave me pain to observe that Steerforth treated him with systematic disparagement, and seldom lost an occasion of wounding his feelings, or inducing others to do so. This troubled me the more for a long time, because I had soon told Steerforth, from whom I could no more keep such a secret than I could keep a cake or any other tangible possession, about the two old women Mr. Mell had taken me to see; and I was always afraid that Steerforth would let it out, and twit him with it.

We little thought, any one of us, I dare say, when I ate my breakfast that first morning, and went to sleep under the shadow of the peacock's feathers to the sound of the flute, what consequences would come of the introduction into those alms-houses of my insignificant person. But the visit had its unforeseen consequences; and of a serious sort, too, in their way.

One day when Mr. Creakle kept the house from indisposition, which naturally diffused a lively joy through the school, there was a good deal of noise in the course of the morning's work. The great relief and satisfaction experienced by the boys made them difficult to manage; and though the dreaded Tungay brought his wooden leg in twice or thrice, and took notes of the principal offenders' names, no great impression was made by it, as they were pretty sure of getting into trouble to-morrow, do what they would, and thought it wise, no doubt, to enjoy themselves to-day.

It was, properly, a half-holiday; being Saturday. But as the noise in the playground would have disturbed Mr. Creakle, and the weather was not favourable for going out walking, we were ordered into school in the afternoon, and set some lighter tasks than usual, which were made for the occasion. It was the day of the week on which Mr. Sharp went out to get his wig curled; so Mr. Mell, who always did the drudgery, whatever it was, kept school by himself.

If I could associate the idea of a bull or a bear with any one so mild as Mr. Mell, I should think of him, in connection with that afternoon when the uproar was at its height, as of one of those animals, baited by a thousand dogs. I recall him bending his aching head, supported on his bony hand, over the book on his desk, and wretchedly endeavouring to get on with his tiresome work, amidst an uproar that might have made the Speaker of the House of Commons giddy. Boys started in and out of their places, playing at puss-in-the-corner with other boys; there were laughing boys, singing boys, talking boys, dancing boys, howling boys; boys shuffled with their feet, boys whirled about him, grinning, making faces, mimicking him behind his back and before his eyes; mimicking his poverty, his boots, his coat, his mother, everything belonging to him that they should have had consideration for.

" Silence! " cried Mr. Mell, suddenly rising up, and striking his desk with the book. " What does this mean? It's impossible to bear it. It's maddening. How can you do it to me, boys? "

It was my book that he struck his desk with; and as I stood beside him, following his eye as it glanced round the room, I saw the boys all stop, some suddenly surprised, some half afraid, and some sorry perhaps.

Steerforth's place was at the bottom of the school, at the opposite end of the long room. He was lounging with his back against the wall, and his hands in his pockets, and looked at Mr. Mell with his mouth shut up as if he were whistling, when Mr. Mell looked at him.

" Silence, Mr. Steerforth! " said Mr. Mell.

" Silence yourself," said Steerforth, turning red. " Whom are you talking to? "

" Sit down," said Mr. Mell.

" Sit down yourself," said Steerforth, " and mind your business."

There was a titter, and some applause; but Mr. Mell was so white, that silence immediately succeeded; and one boy, who had darted out behind him to imitate his mother again, changed his mind, and pretended to want a pen mended.

" If you think, Steerforth," said Mr. Mell, " that I am not acquainted with the power you can establish over any mind here "—he laid his hand, without considering what he did (as I supposed), upon my head—" or that I have not observed you, within a few minutes, urging your juniors on to every sort of outrage against me, you are mistaken."

" I don't give myself the trouble of thinking at all about you," said Steerforth, coolly; " so I'm not mistaken, as it happens."

" And when you make use of your position of favouritism here, sir," pursued Mr. Mell, with his lip trembling very much, " to insult a gentleman—"

" A what?—where is he? " said Steerforth.

Here somebody cried out, " Shame, J. Steerforth! Too bad! " It was Traddles; whom Mr. Mell instantly discomfited by bidding him hold his tongue.

—" To insult one who is not fortunate in life, sir, and who never gave you the least offence, and the many reasons for not insulting whom you are old enough and wise enough to understand," said Mr. Mell, with his lip trembling more and more, " you commit a mean and base action. You can sit down or stand up as you please, sir. Copperfield, go on."

" Young Copperfield," said Steerforth, coming forward up the room, " stop a bit. I tell you what, Mr. Mell, once for all. When you take the liberty of calling me mean or base, or anything of that sort, you are an impudent beggar. You are always a beggar, you know; but when you do that, you are an impudent beggar."

I am not clear whether he was going to strike Mr. Mell, or Mr. Mell was going to strike him, or there was any such intention on either side. I saw a rigidity come upon the whole school as if they had been turned into stone, and found Mr. Creakle in the midst of us, with Tungay at his side, and Mrs. and Miss Creakle looking in at the door as if they were frightened. Mr. Mell, with his elbows on his desk and his face in his hands, sat, for some moments, quite still.

" Mr. Mell," said Mr. Creakle, shaking him by the arm; and his whisper was so audible now, that Tungay felt it unnecessary to repeat his words; " you have not forgotten yourself, I hope? "

" No, sir, no," returned the Master, showing his face, and shaking his head, and rubbing his hands in great agitation. " No, sir, no. I have remembered myself, I—no, Mr. Creakle, I have not forgotten myself, I—I have remembered myself, sir. I—I—could wish you had remembered me a little sooner, Mr. Creakle. It—it—would have been more kind, sir, more just, sir. It would have saved me something, sir."

Mr. Creakle, looking hard at Mr. Mell, put his hand on Tungay's shoulder, and got his feet upon the form close by, and sat upon the desk. After still looking hard at Mr. Mell from his throne, as he shook his head, and rubbed his hands, and remained in the same state of agitation, Mr. Creakle turned to Steerforth, and said:

" Now, sir, as he don't condescend to tell me, what *is* this? "

Steerforth evaded the question for a little while; looking in scorn and anger on his opponent, and remaining silent. I could not help thinking even in that interval, I remember, what a noble fellow he was in appearance, and how homely and plain Mr. Mell looked opposed to him.

"What did he mean by talking about favourites, then?" said Steerforth, at length.

"Favourites?" repeated Mr. Creakle, with the veins in his forehead swelling quickly. "Who talked about favourites?"

"He did," said Steerforth.

"And pray, what did you mean by that, sir?" demanded Mr. Creakle, turning angrily on his assistant.

"I meant, Mr. Creakle," he returned in a low voice, "as I said; that no pupil had a right to avail himself of his position of favouritism to degrade me."

"To degrade *you*?" said Mr. Creakle. "But give me leave to ask you, Mr. What's-your-name;" and here Mr. Creakle folded his arms, cane and all, upon his chest, and made such a knot of his brows that his little eyes were hardly visible below them; "whether, when you talk about favourites, you showed proper respect to me? To me, sir," said Mr. Creakle, darting his head at him suddenly, and drawing it back again, "the principal of this establishment, and your employer."

"It was not judicious, sir, I am willing to admit," said Mr. Mell. "I should not have done so, if I had been cool."

Here Steerforth struck in.

"Then he said I was mean, and then he said I was base, and then I called him a beggar. If I had been cool, perhaps I shouldn't have called him a beggar. But I did, and I am ready to take the consequences of it."

Without considering, perhaps, whether there were any consequences to be taken, I felt quite in a glow at this gallant speech. It made an impression on the boys, too, for there was a low stir among them, though no one spoke a word.

"I am surprised, Steerforth—although your candour does you honour," said Mr. Creakle, "does you honour, certainly—I am surprised, Steerforth, I must say, that you should attach such an epithet to any person employed and paid in Salem House, sir."

Steerforth gave a short laugh.

"That's not an answer, sir," said Mr. Creakle, "to my remark. I expect more than that from you, Steerforth."

If Mr. Mell looked homely, in my eyes, before the handsome boy, it would be quite impossible to say how homely Mr. Creakle looked.

"Let him deny it," said Steerforth.

"Deny that he is a beggar, Steerforth?" cried Mr. Creakle. "Why, where does he go a-begging?"

"If he is not a beggar himself, his near relation's one," said Steerforth. "It's all the same."

He glanced at me, and Mr. Mell's hand gently patted me upon the shoulder. I looked up with a flush upon my face and remorse in my heart, but Mr. Mell's eyes were fixed on Steerforth. He continued to pat me kindly on the shoulder, but he looked at him.

"Since you expect me, Mr. Creakle, to justify myself," said Steerforth, "and to say what I mean,—what I have to say is, that his mother lives on charity in an alms-house."

Mr. Mell still looked at him, and still patted me kindly on the shoulder, and said to himself in a whisper, if I heard right: "Yes, I thought so."

Mr. Creakle turned to his assistant, with a severe frown and laboured politeness:

"Now you hear what this gentleman says, Mr. Mell. Have the goodness, if you please, to set him right before the assembled school."

"He is right, sir, without correction," returned Mr. Mell, in the midst of a dead silence; "what he has said is true."

"Be so good then as declare publicly, will you," said Mr. Creakle, putting his head on one side, and rolling his eyes round the school, "whether it ever came to my knowledge until this moment?"

"I believe not directly," he returned.

"Why, you know not," said Mr. Creakle. "Don't you, man?"

"I apprehend you never supposed my worldly circumstances to be very good," replied the assistant. "You know what my position is, and always has been here."

"I apprehend, if you come to that," said Mr. Creakle, with his veins swelling again bigger than ever, "that you've been in a wrong position altogether, and mistook this for a charity school. Mr. Mell, we'll part, if you please. The sooner the better."

"There is no time," answered Mr. Mell, rising, "like the present."

"Sir, to you!" said Mr. Creakle.

"I take my leave of you, Mr. Creakle, and all of you," said Mr. Mell, glancing round the room, and again patting me gently on the shoulder. "James Steerforth, the best wish I can leave you is that you may come to be ashamed of what you have done to-day. At present I would prefer to see you anything rather than a friend to me, or to any one in whom I feel an interest."

Once more he laid his hand upon my shoulder; and then taking his flute and a few books from his desk, and leaving the key in it for his successor, he went out of the school, with his property under his arm. Mr. Creakle then made a speech, through Tungay, in which he thanked Steerforth for asserting (though perhaps too warmly) the independence and respectability of Salem House; and which he wound up by shaking hands with Steerforth, while we gave three cheers—I did not quite know what for, but I supposed for Steerforth, and so joined in them ardently, though I felt miserable. Mr. Creakle then caned Tommy Traddles for being discovered in tears, instead of cheers, on account of Mr. Mell's departure; and went back to his sofa, or his bed, or wherever he had come from.

We were left to ourselves now, and looked very blank, I recollect, on one another. For myself, I felt so much self-reproach and contrition for my part in what had happened, that nothing would have enabled me to keep back my tears but the fear that Steerforth, who often looked at me, I saw, might think it unfriendly—or, I should rather say, considering our relative ages, and the feeling with which I regarded him, undutiful—if I showed the emotion which distressed me. He was very angry with Traddles, and said he was glad he had caught it.

Poor Traddles, who had passed the stage of lying with his head upon the desk, and was relieving himself as usual with a burst of skeletons, said he didn't care. Mr. Mell was ill-used.

" Who has ill-used him, you girl? " said Steerforth.

" Why, you have," returned Traddles.

" What have I done? " said Steerforth.

" What have you done? " retorted Traddles. " Hurt his feelings and lost him his situation."

" His feelings? " repeated Steerforth disdainfully. " His feelings will soon get the better of it, I'll be bound. His feelings are not like yours, Miss Traddles. As to his situation—which was a precious one, wasn't it?—do you suppose I am not going to write home, and take care that he gets some money, Polly? "

We thought this intention very noble in Steerforth, whose mother was a widow and rich, and would do almost anything, it was said, that he asked her. We were all extremely glad to see Traddles so put down, and exalted Steerforth to the skies: especially when he told us, as he condescended to do, that what he had done had been done expressly for us, and for our cause, and that he had conferred a great boon upon us by unselfishly doing it.

But I must say that when I was going on with a story in the dark that night, Mr. Mell's old flute seemed more than once to sound mournfully in my ears; and that when at last Steerforth was tired, and I lay down in my bed, I fancied it playing so sorrowfully somewhere, that I was quite wretched..

I soon forgot him in the contemplation of Steerforth, who, in an easy amateur way, and without any book (he seemed to me to know everything by heart), took some of his classes until a new master was found. The new master came from a grammar-school, and before he entered on his duties, dined in the parlour one day, to be introduced to Steerforth. Steerforth approved of him highly, and told us he was a Brick. Without exactly understanding what learned distinction was meant by this, I respected him greatly for it, and had no doubt whatever of his superior knowledge: though he never took the pains with me—not that *I* was anybody—that Mr. Mell had taken.

There was only one other event in this half-year, out of the daily school-life, that made an impression upon me which still survives. It survives for many reasons.

One afternoon, when we were all harassed into a state of dire confusion, and Mr. Creakle was laying about him dreadfully, Tungay came in and called out in his usual strong way: " Visitors for Copperfield! "

A few words were interchanged between him and Mr. Creakle, as, who the visitors were, and what room they were to be shown into; and then I, who had, according to custom, stood up on the announcement being made, and felt quite faint with astonishment, was told to go by the back stairs and get a clean frill on, before I repaired to the dining-room. These orders I obeyed, in such a flutter and hurry of my young spirits as I had never known before; and when I got to the parlour-door, and the thought came into my head that it might be my mother—I had only thought of Mr. or Miss Murdstone until then—I drew back my hand from the lock, and stopped to have a sob before I went in.

At first I saw nobody; but feeling a pressure against the door, I looked round it, and there, to my amazement, were Mr. Peggotty and Ham, ducking at me with their hats, and squeezing one another against the wall. I could not help laughing; but it was much more in the pleasure of seeing them, than at the appearance they made. We shook hands in a very cordial way, and I laughed and laughed, until I pulled out my pocket-handkerchief and wiped my eyes.

Mr. Peggotty (who never shut his mouth once, I remember, during the visit) showed great concern when he saw me do this, and nudged Ham to say something.

" Cheer up, Mas'r Davy bor'! " said Ham, in his simpering way. " Why, how you have growed! "

" Am I grown?" I said, drying my eyes. I was not crying at anything in particular that I know of; but somehow it made me cry, to see old friends.

" Growed, Mas'r Davy bor'? Ain't he growed!" said Ham.

" Ain't he growed!" said Mr. Peggotty.

They made me laugh again by laughing at each other, and then we all three laughed until I was in danger of crying again.

" Do you know how mama is, Mr. Peggotty?" I said. " And how my dear, dear old Peggotty is?"

" Oncommon," said Mr. Peggotty.

" And little Em'ly, and Mrs. Gummidge?"

" On—common," said Mr. Peggotty.

There was a silence. Mr. Peggotty, to relieve it, took two prodigious lobsters, and an enormous crab, and a large canvas bag of shrimps, out of his pockets, and piled them up in Ham's arms.

" You see," said Mr. Peggotty, " knowing as you was partial to a little relish with your wittles when you was along with us, we took the liberty. The old Mawther biled 'em, she did. Mrs. Gummidge biled 'em. Yes," said Mr. Peggotty, slowly, who I thought appeared to stick to the subject on account of having no other subject ready, " Mrs. Gummidge, I do assure you, she biled 'em."

I expressed my thanks. Mr. Peggotty, after looking at Ham, who stood smiling sheepishly over the shell-fish, without making any attempt to help him, said:

" We come, you see, the wind and tide making in our favour, in one of our Yarmouth lugs to Gravesen'. My sister she wrote to me the name of this here place, and wrote to me as if ever I chanced to come to Gravesen', I was to come over and inquire for Mas'r Davy, and give her dooty, humbly wishing him well, and reporting of the fam'ly as they was oncommon toe-be-sure. Little Em'ly, you see, she'll write to my sister when I go back as I see you, and as you was similarly oncommon, and so we make it quite a merry-go-rounder."

I was obliged to consider a little before I understood what Mr. Peggotty meant by this figure, expressive of a complete circle of intelligence. I then thanked him heartily; and said, with a consciousness of reddening, that I supposed little Em'ly was altered too, since we used to pick up shells and pebbles on the beach.

" She's getting to be a woman, that's wot she's getting to be," said Mr. Peggotty, " Ask *him*."

He meant Ham, who beamed with delight and assent over the bag of shrimps.

" Her pretty face! " said Mr. Peggotty, with his own shining like a light.

" Her learning! " said Ham.

" Her writing! " said Mr. Peggotty. " Why it's as black as jet! And so large it is, you might see it anywheres."

It was perfectly delightful to behold with what enthusiasm Mr. Peggotty became inspired when he thought of his little favourite. He stands before me again, his bluff hairy face irradiating with a joyful love and pride for which I can find no description. His honest eyes fire up, and sparkle, as if their depths were stirred by something bright. His broad chest heaves with pleasure. His strong loose hands clench themselves, in his earnestness; and he emphasises what he says with a right arm that shows, in my pigmy view, like a sledge-hammer.

Ham was quite as earnest as he. I dare say they would have said much more about her, if they had not been abashed by the unexpected coming in of Steerforth, who, seeing me in a corner speaking with two strangers, stopped in a song he was singing, and said: " I didn't know you were here, young Copperfield! " (for it was not the usual visiting room) and crossed by us on his way out.

I am not sure whether it was in the pride of having such a friend as Steerforth, or in the desire to explain to him how I came to have such a friend as Mr. Peggotty, that I called to him as he was going away. But I said, modestly—Good Heaven, how it all comes back to me this long time afterwards!—

" Don't go, Steerforth, if you please. These are two Yarmouth boatmen—very kind, good people—who are relations of my nurse, and have come from Gravesend to see me."

" Aye, aye! " said Steerforth, returning. " I am glad to see them. How are you both? "

There was an ease in his manner—a gay and light manner it was, but not swaggering—which I still believe to have borne a kind of enchantment with it. I still believe him, in virtue of this carriage, his animal spirits, his delightful voice, his handsome face and figure, and, for aught I know, of some inborn power of attraction besides (which I think a few people possess), to have carried a spell with him to which it was a natural weakness to yield, and which not many persons could withstand. I could not but see how pleased they were with him, and how they seemed to open their hearts to him in a moment.

" You must let them know at home, if you please Mr. Peggotty," I said, "when that letter is sent, that Mr. Steerforth is very kind to me, and that I don't know what I should ever do here without him."

"Nonsense!" said Steerforth, laughing. "You mustn't tell them anything of the kind."

"And if Mr. Steerforth ever comes into Norfolk or Suffolk, Mr. Peggotty," I said, "while I am there, you may depend upon it I shall bring him to Yarmouth, if he will let me, to see your house. You never saw such a good house, Steerforth. It's made out of a boat!"

"Made out of a boat, is it?" said Steerforth. "It's the right sort of a house for such a thorough-built boatman."

"So 'tis, sir, so 'tis, sir," said Ham, grinning. "You're right, young gen'l'm'n! Mas'r Davy bor', gen'l'm'n's right. A thorough-built boatman! Hor, hor! That's what he is, too!"

Mr. Peggotty was no less pleased than his nephew, though his modesty forbade him to claim a personal compliment so vociferously.

"Well, sir," he said, bowing and chuckling, and tucking in the ends of his neckerchief at his breast: "I thankee, sir, I thankee! I do my endeavours in my line of life, sir."

"The best of men can do no more, Mr. Peggotty," said Steerforth. He had got his name already.

"I'll pound it it's wot you do yourself, sir," said Mr. Peggotty, shaking his head, "and wot you do well—right well! I thankee, sir. I'm obleeged to you, sir, for your welcoming manner of me. I'm rough, sir, but I'm ready—least ways, I *hope* I'm ready, you understand. My house ain't much for to see, sir, but it's hearty at your service if ever you should come along with Mas'r Davy to see it. I'm a reg'lar Dodman, I am," said Mr. Peggotty, by which he meant snail, and this was in allusion to his being slow to go, for he had attempted to go after every sentence, and had somehow or other come back again; "but I wish you both well, and I wish you happy!"

Ham echoed this sentiment, and we parted with them in the heartiest manner. I was almost tempted that evening to tell Steerforth about pretty little Em'ly, but I was too timid of mentioning her name, and too much afraid of his laughing at me. I remember that I thought a good deal, and in an uneasy sort of way, about Mr. Peggotty having said that she was getting on to be a woman; but I decided that was nonsense.

We transported the shell-fish, or the "relish" as Mr. Peggotty had modestly called it, up into our room unobserved, and made a great supper that evening. But Traddles couldn't get happily out of it. He was too unfortunate even to come through a supper like anybody else. He was taken ill in the night—quite prostrate he was—in consequence of Crab; and after being drugged with black draughts and blue pills, to an extent which Demple (whose father was a doctor) said was enough to undermine a horse's constitution, received a caning and six chapters of Greek Testament for refusing to confess.

The rest of the half-year is a jumble in my recollection of the daily strife and struggle of our lives; of the waning summer and the changing season; of the frosty mornings when we were rung out of bed, and the cold, cold smell of the dark nights when we were rung into bed; of the evening schoolroom dimly lighted and indifferently warmed, and the morning schoolroom which was nothing but a great shivering-machine; of the alternation of boiled beef with roast beef, and boiled mutton with roast mutton; of clods of bread-and-butter, dog's-eared lesson-books, cracked slates, tear-blotted copy-books, canings, rulerings, hair-cuttings, rainy Sundays, suet-puddings, and a dirty atmosphere of ink surrounding all.

I well remember though, how the distant idea of the holidays, after seeming for an immense time to be a stationary speck, began to come towards us, and to grow and grow. How from counting months, we came to weeks, and then to days; and how I then began to be afraid that I should not be sent for and when I learnt from Steerforth that I *had* been sent for, and was certainly to go home, had dim forebodings that I might break my leg first. How the breaking-up day changed its place fast, at last, from the week after next to next week, this week, the day after to-morrow, to-morrow, to-day, to-night—when I was inside the Yarmouth mail, and going home.

I had many a broken sleep inside the Yarmouth mail, and many an incoherent dream of all these things. But when I awoke at intervals, the ground outside the window was not the playground of Salem House, and the sound in my ears was not the sound of Mr. Creakle giving it to Traddles, but was the sound of the coachman touching up the horses.

8

MY HOLIDAYS. ESPECIALLY ONE HAPPY AFTERNOON

WHEN WE ARRIVED BEFORE DAY AT THE INN WHERE THE mail stopped, which was not the inn where my friend the waiter lived, I was shown up to a nice little bedroom, with DOLPHIN painted on the door. Very cold I was, I know, notwithstanding the hot tea they had given me before a large fire down-stairs; and very glad I was to turn into the Dolphin's bed, pull the Dolphin's blankets round my head, and go to sleep.

Mr. Barkis the carrier was to call for me in the morning at nine o'clock. I got up at eight, a little giddy from the shortness of my night's rest, and was ready for him before the appointed time. He received me exactly as if not five minutes had elapsed since we were last together, and I had only been into the hotel to get change for sixpence, or something of that sort.

As soon as I and my box were in the cart, and the carrier was seated, the lazy horse walked away with us all at his accustomed pace.

"You look very well, Mr. Barkis," I said, thinking he would like to know it.

Mr. Barkis rubbed his cheek with his cuff, and then looked at his cuff as if he expected to find some of the bloom upon it; but made no other acknowledgement of the compliment.

"I gave your message, Mr. Barkis," I said: "I wrote to Peggotty."

"Ah!" said Mr. Barkis.

Mr. Barkis seemed gruff, and answered drily.

"Wasn't it right, Mr. Barkis?" I asked, after a little hesitation.

"Why, no," said Mr. Barkis.

"Not the message?"

"The message was right enough, perhaps," said Mr. Barkis; "but it come to an end there."

Not understanding what he meant, I repeated inquisitively: "Came to an end, Mr. Barkis?"

"Nothing come of it," he explained, looking at me sideways. "No answer."

"There was an answer expected, was there, Mr. Barkis?" said I, opening my eyes. For this was a new light to me.

"When a man says he's willin'," said Mr. Barkis, turning his glance slowly on me again, "it's as much as to say, that man's a-waitin' for a answer."

"Well, Mr. Barkis?"

"Well," said Mr. Barkis, carrying his eyes back to his horse's ears; "that man's been a-waitin' for a answer ever since."

"Have you told her so, Mr. Barkis?"

"N—no," growled Mr. Barkis, reflecting about it. "I ain't got no call to go and tell her so. I never said six words to her myself. *I* ain't a-goin' to tell her so."

"Would you like me to do it, Mr. Barkis?" said I, doubtfully.

"You might tell her, if you would," said Mr. Barkis, with another slow look at me, "that Barkis was a-waitin' for a answer. Says you—what name is it?"

"Her name?"

"Ah!" said Mr. Barkis, with a nod of his head.

"Peggotty."

"Chrisen name? Or nat'ral name?" said Mr. Barkis.

"Oh, it's not her Christian name. Her Christian name is Clara."

"Is it though?" said Mr. Barkis.

He seemed to find an immense fund of reflection in this circumstance, and sat pondering and inwardly whistling for some time.

"Well!" he resumed at length. "Says you, 'Peggotty! Barkis is waitin' for a answer.' Says she, perhaps, 'Answer to what?' Says you, 'To what I told you.' 'What is that?' says she. 'Barkis is willin',' says you."

This extremely artful suggestion Mr. Barkis accompanied with a nudge of his elbow that gave me quite a stitch in my side, After that, he slouched over his horse in his usual manner; and made no other reference to the subject except, half an hour afterwards, taking a piece of chalk from his pocket, and writing up, inside the tilt of the cart, "Clara Peggotty"—apparently as a private memorandum.

Ah, what a strange feeling it was to be going home when it was not home, and to find that every object I looked at, reminded me of the happy old home, which was like a dream I could never dream again! The days when my mother and I and Peggotty were all in all to one another, and there was no one to come between us, rose up before me so sorrowfully on the road, that I am not sure I was glad to be there—not sure but that I would rather have remained away, and forgotten it in Steerforth's company. But there I was; and soon I was at our house, where the bare old elm trees wrung their many hands in the bleak wintry air, and shreds of the old rooks' nests drifted away upon the wind.

The carrier put my box down at the garden-gate, and left me. I walked along the path towards the house, glancing at the windows, and fearing at every step to see Mr. Murdstone or Miss Murdstone lowering out of one of them. No face appeared, however; and being come to the house, and knowing how to open the door, before dark, without knocking, I went in with a quiet, timid step.

God knows how infantine the memory may have been, that was awakened within me by the sound of my mother's voice in the old parlour, when I set foot in the hall. She was singing in a low tone. I think I must have lain in her arms, and heard her singing so to me when I was but a baby. The strain was new to me, and yet it was so old that it filled my heart brimful; like a friend come back from a long absence.

I believed, from the solitary and thoughtful way in which my mother murmured her song, that she was alone. And I went softly into the room. She was sitting by the fire, suckling an infant, whose tiny hand she held against her neck. Her eyes were looking down upon its face, and she sat singing to it. I was so far right, that she had no other companion.

I spoke to her, and she started, and cried out. But seeing me, she called me her dear Davy, her own boy! and coming half across the room to meet me, kneeled down upon the ground and kissed me, and laid my head down on her bosom near the little creature that was nestling there, and put its hand to my lips.

I wish I had died. I wish I had died then, with that feeling in my heart! I should have been more fit for Heaven than I ever have been since.

" He is your brother," said my mother, fondling me. " Davy, my pretty boy! My poor child! " Then she kissed me more and more, and clasped me round the neck. This she was doing when Peggotty came running in, and bounced down on the ground beside us, and went mad about us both for a quarter of an hour.

It seemed that I had not been expected so soon, the carrier being much before his usual time. It seemed, too, that Mr. and Miss Murdstone had gone out upon a visit in the neighbourhood, and would not return before night. I had never hoped for this. I had never thought it possible that we three could be together undisturbed, once more; and I felt, for the time, as if the old days were come back.

We dined together by the fireside. Peggotty was in attendance to wait upon us but my mother wouldn't let her do it and made her dine with us. I had my own old plate, with a brown view of a man-of-war in full sail upon it, which Peggotty had hoarded somewhere all the time I had been away, and would not have had broken, she said, for a hundred pounds. I had my own old mug with David on it, and my own old little knife and fork that wouldn't cut.

While we were at table, I thought it a favourable occasion to tell Peggotty about Mr. Barkis, who, before I had finished what I had to tell her, began to laugh, and throw her apron over her face.

" Peggotty," said my mother. " What's the matter? "

Peggotty only laughed the more, and held her apron tight over her face when my mother tried to pull it away, and sat as if her head were in a bag.

" What are you doing, you stupid creature? " said my mother, laughing.

" Oh, drat the man! " cried Peggotty. " He wants to marry me."

" It would be a very good match for you; wouldn't it? " said my mother.

" Oh! I don't know," said Peggotty. " Don't ask me. I wouldn't have him if he was made of gold. Nor I wouldn't have anybody."

" Then, why don't you tell him so, you ridiculous thing? " said my mother.

" Tell him so," retorted Peggotty, looking out of her apron. " He has never said a word to me about it. He knows better. If he was to make so bold as say a word to me, I should slap his face."

Her own was as red as ever I saw it, or any other face, I think; but she only covered it again, for a few moments at a time, when she was taken with a violent fit of laughter; and after two or three of those attacks, went on with her dinner.

I remarked that my mother, though she smiled when Peggotty looked at her, became more serious and thoughtful. I had seen at first that she was changed. Her face was very pretty still, but it looked careworn, and too delicate; and her hand was so thin and white that it seemed to me to be almost transparent. But the change to which I now refer was superadded to this: it was in her manner, which became anxious and fluttered. At last she said, putting out her hand, and laying it affectionately on the hand of her old servant:

" Peggotty dear, you are not going to be married? "

" Me, ma'am? " returned Peggotty, staring: " Lord bless you, no! "

" Not just yet? " said my mother, tenderly.

" Never! " cried Peggotty.

My mother took her hand, and said:

" Don't leave me, Peggotty. Stay with me. It will not be for long, perhaps. What should I ever do without you! "

" Me leave you, my precious! " cried Peggotty. " Not for all the world and his wife. Why what's put that in your silly little head? " for Peggotty had been used of old to talk to my mother sometimes, like a child.

But my mother made no answer, except to thank her, and Peggotty went running on in her own fashion.

" Me leave you? I think I see myself. Peggotty go away from you? I should like to catch her at it! No, no, no," said Peggotty, shaking her head, and folding her arms; " not she, my dear. It isn't that there ain't some Cats that would be well enough pleased if she did, but they sha'n't be pleased. They shall be aggravated. I'll stay with you till I am a cross cranky old woman. And when I'm too deaf, and too lame, and too blind, and too mumbly for want of teeth, to be of any use at all, even to be found fault with, then I shall go to my Davy, and ask him to take me in."

" And Peggotty," says I, " I shall be glad to see you, and I'll make you as welcome as a queen."

" Bless your dear heart! " cried Peggotty. " I know you will! " And she kissed me beforehand, in grateful acknowledgement of my hospitality. After that, she covered her head up with her apron again, and had another laugh about Mr. Barkis. After that, she took the baby out of its little cradle, and nursed it. After that, she cleared the dinner-table; after that, came in with another cap on, and her work-box, and the yard-measure, and the bit of wax-candle, all just the same as ever.

We sat round the fire, and talked delightfully. I told them what a hard master Mr. Creakle was, and they pitied me very much. I told them what a fine fellow Steerforth was, and what a patron of mine, and Peggotty said she would walk a score of miles to see him. I took the little baby in my arms when it was awake, and nursed it lovingly. When it was asleep again, I crept close to my mother's side, according to my old custom, broken now a long time, and sat with my arms embracing her waist, and my little red cheek on her shoulder, and once more felt her beautiful hair drooping over me—like an angel's wing as I used to think, I recollect—and was very happy indeed.

While I sat thus, looking at the fire, and seeing pictures in the red-hot coals, I almost believed that I had never been away; that Mr. and Miss Murdstone were such pictures, and would vanish when the fire got low; and that there was nothing real in all that I remembered, save my mother, Peggotty, and I.

Peggotty darned away at a stocking as long as she could see, and then sat with it drawn on her left hand like a glove, and her needle in her right, ready to take another stitch whenever there was a blaze. I cannot conceive whose stockings they can have been that Peggotty was always darning, or where such an unfailing supply of stockings in want of darning can have come from. From my earliest infancy she seems to have been always employed in that class of needlework, and never by any chance in any other.

"I wonder," said Peggotty, who was sometimes seized with a fit of wondering on some most unexpected topic, "what's become of Davy's great-aunt?"

"Lor, Peggotty!" observed my mother, rousing herself from a reverie, "what nonsense you talk!"

"Well, but I really do wonder, ma'am," said Peggotty.

"What can have put such a person in your head?" inquired my mother. "Is there nobody else in the world to come there?"

"I don't know how it is," said Peggotty, "unless it's on account of being stupid, but my head never can pick and choose its people. They come and they go, and they don't come and they don't go, just as they like. I wonder what's become of her?"

"How absurd you are, Peggotty!" returned my mother. "One would suppose you wanted a second visit from her."

"Lord forbid!" cried Peggotty.

"Well, then, don't talk about such uncomfortable things, there's a good soul," said my mother. "Miss Betsey is shut up in her cottage by the sea, no doubt, and will remain there. At all events, she is not likely ever to trouble us again."

"No!" mused Peggotty. "No, that ain't likely at all—I wonder, if she was to die, whether she'd leave Davy anything?"

"Good gracious me, Peggotty," returned my mother, "what a nonsensical woman you are! when you know that she took offence at the poor dear boy's ever being born at all."

"I suppose she wouldn't be inclined to forgive him now," hinted Peggotty.

"Why should she be inclined to forgive him now?" said my mother, rather sharply.

"Now that he's got a brother, I mean," said Peggotty.

My mother immediately began to cry, and wondered how Peggotty dared to say such a thing.

"As if this poor little innocent in its cradle had ever done any harm to you or anybody else, you jealous thing!" said she. "You had much better go and marry Mr. Barkis, the carrier. Why don't you?"

"I should make Miss Murdstone happy, if I was to," said Peggotty.

"What a bad disposition you have, Peggotty!" returned my mother. "You are as jealous of Miss Murdstone as it is possible for a ridiculous creature to be. You want to keep the keys yourself, and give out all the things, I suppose? I shouldn't be surprised if you did. When you know that she only does it out of kindness and the best intentions! You know she does, Peggotty—you know it well."

Peggotty muttered something to the effect of "Bother the best intentions!" and something else to the effect that there was a little too much of the best intentions going on.

"I know what you mean, you cross thing," said my mother. "I understand you, Peggotty, perfectly. You know I do, and I wonder you don't colour up like fire. But one point at a time. Miss Murdstone is the point now, Peggotty, and you sha'n't escape from it. Haven't you heard her say, over and over again, that she thinks I am too thoughtless and too—a—a——"

"Pretty," suggested Peggotty.

"Well," returned my mother, half laughing, "and if she is so silly as to say so, can I be blamed for it?"

"No one says you can," said Peggotty.

"No, I should hope not, indeed!" returned my mother. "Haven't you heard her say, over and over again, that on this account she wished to spare me a great deal of trouble, which she thinks I am not suited for, and which I really don't know myself that I *am* suited for; and isn't she up early and late, and going to and fro continually—and doesn't she do all sorts of things, and grope into all sorts of places, coal-holes and pantries and I don't know where, that can't be very agreeable—and do you mean to insinuate that there is not a sort of devotion in that?"

"I don't insinuate at all," said Peggotty.

"You do, Peggotty," returned my mother. "You never do anything else, except your work. You are always insinuating. You revel in it. And when you talk of Mr. Murdstone's good intentions——"

"I never talked of 'em," said Peggotty.

"No, Peggotty," returned my mother, "but you insinuated. That's what I told you just now. That's the worst of you. You *will* insinuate. I said, at the moment, that I understood you, and you see I did. When you talk of Mr. Murdstone's good intentions, and pretend to slight them (for I don't believe you really do, in your heart, Peggotty), you must be as well convinced as I am how good they are, and how they actuate him in everything. If he seems to have been at all stern with a certain person, Peggotty—you understand, and so I am sure does Davy, that I am not alluding to anybody present—it is solely because he is satisfied that it is for a certain person's benefit. He naturally loves a certain person, on my account; and acts solely for a certain person's good. He is better able to judge of it than I am; for I very well know that I am a weak, light, girlish creature, and that he is a firm, grave, serious man. And he takes," said my mother, with the tears which were engendered in her affectionate nature, stealing down her face, "he takes great pains with me; and I ought to be very thankful to him, and very submissive to him even in my thoughts; and when I am not, Peggotty, I worry and condemn myself, and feel doubtful of my own heart, and don't know what to do."

Peggotty sat with her chin on the foot of the stocking, looking silently at the fire.

"There, Peggotty," said my mother, changing her tone, "don't let us fall out with one another, for I couldn't bear it. You are my true friend, I know, if I have any in the world. When I call you a ridiculous creature, or a vexatious thing, or anything of that sort, Peggotty, I only mean that you are my true friend, and always have been, ever since the night when Mr. Copperfield first brought me home here, and you came out to the gate to meet me."

Peggotty was not slow to respond, and ratify the treaty of friendship by giving me one of her best hugs. I think I had some glimpses of the real character of this conversation at the time; but I am sure, now, that the good creature originated it, and took her part in it, merely that my mother might comfort herself with the little contradictory summary in which she had indulged. The design was efficacious; for I remember that my mother seemed more at ease during the rest of the evening, and that Peggotty observed her less.

When we had had our tea, and the ashes were thrown up, and the candles snuffed, I read Peggotty a chapter out of the Crocodile Book, in remembrance of old times—she took it out of her pocket: I don't know whether she had kept it there ever since—and then we talked about Salem House, which brought me round again to Steerforth, who was my great subject. We were very happy; and that evening, as the last of its race, and destined evermore to close that volume of my life, will never pass out of my memory.

It was almost ten o'clock before we heard the sound of wheels. We all got up then; and my mother said hurriedly that, as it was so late, and Mr. and Miss Murdstone approved of early hours for young people, perhaps I had better go to bed. I kissed her, and went up-stairs with my candle directly, before they came in. It appeared to my childish fancy, as I ascended to the bedroom where I had been imprisoned, that they brought a cold blast of air into the house which blew away the old familiar feeling like a feather.

I felt uncomfortable about going down to breakfast in the morning, as I had never set eyes on Mr. Murdstone since the day when I committed my memorable offence. However, as it must be done, I went down, after two or three false starts halfway, and as many runs back on tiptoe to my own room, and presented myself in the parlour.

He was standing before the fire with his back to it, while Miss Murdstone made the tea. He looked at me steadily as I entered, but made no sign of recognition whatever.

I went up to him, after a moment of confusion, and said:

"I beg your pardon, sir. I am very sorry for what I did, and I hope you will forgive me."

"I am glad to hear you are sorry, David," he replied.

The hand he gave me was the hand I had bitten. I could not restrain my eye from resting for an instant on a red spot upon it; but it was not so red as I turned, when I met that sinister expression in his face.

"How do you do, ma'am?" I said to Miss Murdstone.

"Ah, dear me!" sighed Miss Murdstone, giving me the tea-caddy scoop instead of her fingers. "How long are the holidays?"

"A month, ma'am."

"Counting from when?"

"From to-day, ma'am."

"Oh!" said Miss Murdstone. "Then here's *one* day off."

She kept a calendar of the holidays in this way, and every morning checked a day off in exactly the same manner. She did it gloomily until she came to ten, but when she got into two figures she became more hopeful, and, as the time advanced, even jocular.

It was on this very first day that I had the misfortune to throw her, though she was not subject to such weakness in general, into a state of violent consternation. I came into the room where she and my mother were sitting; and the baby (who was only a few weeks old) being on my mother's lap, I took it very carefully in my arms. Suddenly Miss Murdstone gave such a scream that I all but dropped it.

"My dear Jane!" cried my mother.

"Good heavens, Clara, do you see?" exclaimed Miss Murdstone.

"See what, my dear Jane?" said my mother; "where?"

"He's got it!" cried Miss Murdstone. "The boy has got the baby!"

She was limp with horror; but stiffened herself to make a dart at me, and take it out of my arms. Then she turned faint, and was so very ill that they were obliged to give her cherry-brandy. I was solemnly interdicted by her, on her recovery, from touching my brother any more on any pretence whatever; and my poor mother, who, I could see, wished otherwise, meekly confirmed the interdict, by saying, "No doubt you are right, my dear Jane."

On another occasion, when we three were together, this same dear baby—it was truly dear to me, for our mother's sake—was the innocent occasion of Miss Murdstone's going into a passion. My mother, who had been looking at its eyes as it lay upon her lap, said:

"Davy! come here!" and looked at mine.

I saw Miss Murdstone lay her beads down.

"I declare," said my mother, gently, "they are exactly alike. I suppose they are mine. I think they are the colour of mine. But they are wonderfully alike."

"What are you talking about, Clara?" said Miss Murdstone.

"My dear Jane," faltered my mother, a little abashed by the harsh tone of this inquiry, "I find that the baby's eyes and Davy's are exactly alike."

"Clara!" said Miss Murdstone, rising angrily, "you are a positive fool sometimes."

"My dear Jane," remonstrated my mother.

"A positive fool," said Miss Murdstone. "Who else could compare my brother's baby with your boy? They are not at all alike. They are exactly unlike. They are utterly dissimilar in all respects. I hope they will ever remain so. I will not sit here, and hear such comparisons made." With that she stalked out, and made the door bang after her.

In short, I was not a favourite with Miss Murdstone. In short,

I was not a favourite there with anybody, not even with myself; for those who did like me could not show it, and those who did not showed it so plainly that I had a sensitive consciousness of always appearing constrained, boorish, and dull.

I felt that I made them as uncomfortable as they made me. If I came into the room where they were, and they were talking together and my mother seemed cheerful, an anxious cloud would steal over her face from the moment of my entrance. If Mr. Murdstone were in his best humour, I checked him. If Miss Murdstone were in her worst, I intensified it. I had perception enough to know that my mother was the victim always; that she was afraid to speak to me, or to be kind to me, lest she should give them some offence by her manner of doing so, and receive a lecture afterwards; that she was not only ceaselessly afraid of her own offending, but of my offending, and uneasily watched their looks if I only moved. Therefore I resolved to keep myself as much out of their way as I could; and many a wintry hour did I hear the church-clock strike, when I was sitting in my cheerless bed-room, wrapped in my little greatcoat, poring over a book.

In the evening, sometimes, I went and sat with Peggotty in the kitchen. There I was comfortable, and not afraid of being myself. But neither of these resources was approved of in the parlour. The tormenting humour which was dominant there stopped them both. I was still held to be necessary to my poor mother's training, and, as one of her trials, could not be suffered to absent myself.

" David," said Mr. Murdstone, one day after dinner when I was going to leave the room as usual; " I am sorry to observe that you are of a sullen disposition."

" As sulky as a bear! " said Miss Murdstone.

I stood still, and hung my head.

" Now, David," said Mr. Murdstone, " a sullen obdurate disposition is, of all tempers, the worst."

" And the boy's is, of all such dispositions that ever I have seen," remarked his sister, " the most confirmed and stubborn. I think, my dear Clara, even you must observe it? "

" I beg your pardon, my dear Jane," said my mother, " but are you quite sure—I am certain you'll excuse me, my dear Jane —that you understand Davy? "

" I should be somewhat ashamed of myself, Clara," returned Miss Murdstone, " if I could not understand the boy, or any boy. I don't profess to be profound; but I do lay claim to common sense."

"No doubt, my dear Jane," returned my mother, "your understanding is very vigorous."

"Oh dear, no! Pray don't say that, Clara," interposed Miss Murdstone, angrily.

"But I am sure it is," resumed my mother; "and everybody knows it is. I profit so much by it myself, in many ways—at least I ought to—that no one can be more convinced of it than myself; and therefore I speak with great diffidence, my dear Jane, I assure you."

"We'll say I don't understand the boy, Clara," returned Miss Murdstone, arranging the little fetters on her wrists. "We'll agree, if you please, that I don't understand him at all. He is much too deep for me. But perhaps my brother's penetration may enable him to have some insight into his character. And I believe my brother was speaking on the subject when we—not very decently—interrupted him."

"I think, Clara," said Mr. Murdstone, in a low grave voice, "that there may be better and more dispassionate judges of such a question than you."

"Edward," replied my mother, timidly, "you are a far better judge of all questions than I pretend to be. Both you and Jane are. I only said——"

"You only said something weak and inconsiderate," he replied. "Try not to do it again, my dear Clara, and keep a watch upon yourself."

My mother's lips moved, as if she answered "Yes, my dear Edward," but she said nothing aloud.

"I was sorry, David, I remarked," said Mr. Murdstone, turning his head and his eyes stiffly towards me, "to observe that you are of a sullen disposition. This is not a character that I can suffer to develop itself beneath my eyes without an effort at improvement. You must endeavour, sir, to change it. We must endeavour to change it for you."

"I beg your pardon, sir," I faltered. "I have never meant to be sullen since I came back."

"Don't take refuge in a lie, sir!" he returned so fiercely, that I saw my mother involuntarily put out her trembling hand as if to interpose between us. "You have withdrawn yourself in your sullenness to your own room. You have kept your own room when you ought to have been here. You know now, once for all, that I require you to be here, and not there. Further, that I require you to bring obedience here. You know me, David. I will have it done."

Miss Murdstone gave a hoarse chuckle.

" I will have a respectful, prompt, and ready bearing towards myself," he continued, " and towards Jane Murdstone, and towards your mother. I will not have this room shunned as if it were infected, at the pleasure of a child. Sit down."

He ordered me like a dog, and I obeyed like a dog.

" One thing more," he said. " I observe that you have an attachment to low and common company. You are not to associate with servants. The kitchen will not improve you, in the many respects in which you need improvement. Of the woman who abets you, I say nothing—since you, Clara," addressing my mother in a lower voice, " from old associations and long-established fancies, have a weakness respecting her which is not yet overcome."

" A most unaccountable delusion it is! " cried Miss Murdstone.

" I only say," he resumed, addressing me, " that I disapprove of your preferring such company as Mistress Peggotty, and that it is to be abandoned. Now, David, you understand me, and you know what will be the consequence if you fail to obey me to the letter."

I knew well—better perhaps than he thought, as far as my poor mother was concerned—and I obeyed him to the letter. I retreated to my own room no more; I took refuge with Peggotty no more; but sat wearily in the parlour day after day looking forward to night, and bedtime.

What irksome constraint I underwent, sitting in the same attitude hours upon hours, afraid to move an arm or a leg lest Miss Murdstone should complain (as she did on the least pretence) of my restlessness, and afraid to move an eye lest she should light on some look of dislike or scrutiny that would find new cause for complaint in mine! What intolerable dullness to sit listening to the ticking of the clock; and watching Miss Murdstone's little shiny steel beads as she strung them; and wondering whether she would ever be married, and if so, to what sort of unhappy man; and counting the divisions in the moulding on the chimney-piece; and wandering away, with my eyes, to the ceiling, among the curls and corkscrews in the paper on the wall!

What walks I took alone, down muddy lanes, in the bad winter weather, carrying that parlour, and Mr. and Miss Murdstone in it, everywhere: a monstrous load that I was obliged to bear, a daymare that there was no possibility of breaking in, a weight that brooded on my wits, and blunted them!

What meals I had in silence and embarrassment, always feeling that there were a knife and fork too many, and those mine; an appetite too many, and that mine; a plate and chair too many, and those mine; a somebody too many, and that I!

What evenings, when the candles came, and I was expected to employ myself, but not daring to read an entertaining book, pored over some hard-headed harder-hearted treatise on arithmetic; when the tables of weights and measures set themselves to tunes, as Rule Britannia, or Away with Melancholy; when they wouldn't stand still to be learnt, but would go threading my grandmother's needle through my unfortunate head, in at one ear and out at the other!

What yawns and dozes I lapsed into, in spite of all my care; what starts I came out of concealed sleeps with; what answers I never got, to little observations that I rarely made; what a blank space I seemed, which everybody overlooked, and yet was in everybody's way; what a heavy relief it was to hear Miss Murdstone hail the first stroke of nine at night, and order me to bed!

Thus the holidays lagged away, until the morning came when Miss Murdstone said: " Here's the last day off! " and gave me the closing cup of tea of the vacation.

I was not sorry to go. I had lapsed into a stupid state; but I was recovering a little and looking forward to Steerforth, albeit Mr. Creakle loomed behind him. Again Mr. Barkis appeared at the gate, and again Miss Murdstone in her warning voice, said: " Clara! " when my mother bent over me, to bid me farewell.

I kissed her, and my baby brother, and was very sorry then; but not sorry to go away, for the gulf between us was there, and the parting was there, every day. And it is not so much the embrace she gave me, that lives in my mind, though it was as fervent as could be, as what followed the embrace.

I was in the carrier's cart when I heard her calling to me. I looked out, and she stood at the garden-gate alone, holding her baby up in her arms for me to see. It was cold still weather; and not a hair of her head, nor a fold of her dress, was stirred, as she looked intently at me, holding up her child.

So I lost her. So I saw her afterwards, in my sleep at school—a silent presence near my bed—looking at me with the same intent face—holding up her baby in her arms.

9

I HAVE A MEMORABLE BIRTHDAY

I PASS OVER ALL THAT HAPPENED AT SCHOOL, UNTIL the anniversary of my birthday came round in March. Except that Steerforth was more to be admired than ever, I remember nothing. He was going away at the end of the half-year, if not sooner, and was more spirited and independent than before in my eyes, and therefore more engaging than before; but beyond this I remember nothing. The great remembrance by which the time is marked in my mind, seems to have swallowed up all lesser recollections, and to exist alone.

It is even difficult for me to believe that there was a gap of full two months between my return to Salem House and the arrival of that birthday. I can only understand that the fact was so, because I know it must have been so; otherwise I should feel convinced that there was no interval, and that the one occasion trod upon the other's heels.

How well I recollect the kind of day it was! I smell the fog that hung about the place; I see the hoar frost, gnostly, through it; I feel my rimy hair fall clammy on my cheek; I look along the dim perspective of the schoolroom, with a sputtering candle here and there to light up the foggy morning, and the breath of the boys wreathing and smoking in the raw cold as they blow upon their fingers, and tap their feet upon the floor.

It was after breakfast, and we had been summoned in from the playground, when Mr. Sharp entered and said:

" David Copperfield is to go into the parlour."

I expected a hamper from Peggotty, and brightened at the order. Some of the boys about me put in their claim not to be forgotten in the distribution of the good things, as I got out of my seat with great alacrity.

" Don't hurry, David," said Mr. Sharp. " There's time enough, my boy, don't hurry."

I might have been surprised by the feeling tone in which he spoke, if I had given it a thought; but I gave it none until afterwards. I hurried away to the parlour; and there I found Mr.

Creakle, sitting at his breakfast with the cane and a newspaper before him, and Mrs. Creakle with an opened letter in her hand. But no hamper.

" David Copperfield," said Mrs. Creakle, leading me to a sofa, and sitting down beside me. " I want to speak to you very particularly. I have something to tell you, my child."

Mr. Creakle, at whom of course I looked, shook his head without looking at me, and stopped up a sigh with a very large piece of buttered toast.

" You are too young to know how the world changes every day," said Mrs. Creakle, " and how the people in it pass away. But we all have to learn it, David; some of us when we are young, some of us when we are old, some of us at all times of our lives."

I looked at her earnestly.

" When you came away from home at the end of the vacation," said Mrs. Creakle, after a pause, " were they all well? " After another pause, " Was your mama well? "

I trembled without distinctly knowing why, and still looked at her earnestly, making no attempt to answer.

" Because," said she, " I grieve to tell you that I hear this morning your mama is very ill."

A mist rose between Mrs. Creakle and me, and her figure seemed to move in it for an instant. Then I felt the burning tears run down my face, and it was steady again.

" She is very dangerously ill," she added.

I knew all now.

" She is dead."

There was no need to tell me so. I had already broken out into a desolate cry, and felt an orphan in the wide world.

She was very kind to me. She kept me there all day, and left me alone sometimes; and I cried, and wore myself to sleep, and awoke and cried again. When I could cry no more, I began to think; and then the oppression on my breast was heaviest, and my grief a dull pain that there was no ease for.

And yet my thoughts were idle; not intent on the calamity that weighed upon my heart, but idly loitering near it. I thought of our house shut up and hushed. I thought of the little baby, who, Mrs. Creakle said, had been pining away for some time, and who, they believed would die too. I thought of my father's grave in the churchyard by our house, and of my mother lying there beneath the tree I knew so well. I stood upon a chair when I was left alone, and looked into the glass to see how red my eyes were, and how sorrowful my face. I considered, after some hours were gone, if my tears were really hard to flow now, as they seemed to be, what, in connection with my loss, it would affect me most to think of when I drew near home—for I was going home to the funeral. I am sensible of having felt that a dignity attached to me among the rest of the boys, and that I was important in my affliction.

If ever child were stricken with sincere grief, I was. But I remember that this importance was a kind of satisfaction to me, when I walked in the playground that afternoon while the boys were in school. When I saw them glancing at me out of the windows, as they went up to their classes, I felt distinguished, and looked more melancholy, and walked slower. When school was over, and they came out and spoke to me, I felt it rather good in myself not to be proud to any of them, and to take exactly the same notice of them all, as before.

I was to go home next night; not by the mail, but by the heavy night-coach, which was called the Farmer, and was principally used by country-people travelling short intermediate distances upon the road. We had no story-telling that evening, and Traddles insisted on lending me his pillow. I don't know what good he thought it would do me, for I had one of my own; but it was all he had to lend, poor fellow, except a sheet of letterpaper full of skeletons; and that he gave me at parting, as a soother of my sorrows and a contribution to my peace of mind.

I left Salem House upon the morrow afternoon. I little thought then that I left it, never to return. We travelled very slowly all night, and did not get into Yarmouth before nine or ten o'clock in the morning. I looked out for Mr. Barkis, but he was not there; and instead of him a fat, short-winded, merry-looking little old man in black, with rusty little bunches of ribbons at the knees of his breeches, black stockings, and a broad-brimmed hat, came puffing up to the coach-window, and said:

" Master Copperfield? "

" Yes, sir."

" Will you come with me young sir, if you please," he said, opening the door, " and I shall have the pleasure of taking you home? "

I put my hand in his, wondering who he was, and we walked away to a shop in a narrow street, on which was written OMER, DRAPER, TAILOR, HABERDASHER, FUNERAL FURNISHER, &c. It was a close and stifling little shop; full of all sorts of clothing, made and unmade, including one window full of beaver-hats and bonnets. We went into a little back-parlour behind the shop, where we found three young women at work on a quantity of black materials, which were heaped upon the table, and little bits and cuttings of which were littered all over the floor. There was a good fire in the room, and a breathless smell of warm black crape. I did not know what the smell was then, but I know now.

The three young women, who appeared to be very industrious and comfortable, raised their heads to look at me, and then went on with their work. Stitch, stitch, stitch. At the same time there came from a workshop across a little yard outside the window, a regular sound of hammering that kept a kind of tune: RAT—tat-tat, RAT—tat-tat, RAT—tat-tat, without any variation.

"Well," said my conductor to one of the three young women, "How do you get on, Minnie?"

"We shall be ready by the trying-on time," she replied gaily, without looking up. "Don't you be afraid, father."

Mr. Omer took off his broad-brimmed hat, and sat down and panted. He was so fat that he was obliged to pant some time before he could say:

"That's right."

"Father!" said Minnie, playfully. "What a porpoise you do grow!"

"Well, I don't know how it is, my dear," he replied, considering about it. "I *am* rather so."

"You are such a comfortable man, you see," said Minnie. "You take things so easy."

"No use taking 'em otherwise, my dear," said Mr. Omer.

"No, indeed," returned his daughter. "We are all pretty gay here, thank Heaven! Ain't we, father?"

"I hope so, my dear," said Mr. Omer. "As I have got my breath now, I think I'll measure this young scholar. Would you walk into the shop, Master Copperfield?"

I preceded Mr. Omer, in compliance with his request; and after showing me a roll of cloth which he said was extra super, and too good mourning for anything short of parents, he took my various dimensions, and put them down in a book. While he was recording them he called my attention to his stock in trade, and to certain fashions which he said had "just come up, and to certain other fashions which he said had "just gone out."

"And by that sort of thing we very often lose a little mint of money," said Mr. Omer. "But fashions are like human beings. They come in, nobody knows when, why, or how; and they go out, nobody knows when, why, or how. Everything is like life, in my opinion, if you look at it in that point of view."

I was too sorrowful to discuss the question, which would possibly have been beyond me under any circumstances; and Mr. Omer took me back into the parlour, breathing with some difficulty on the way.

He then called down a little break-neck range of steps behind a door: " Bring up that tea and bread-and-butter! " which, after some time, during which I sat looking about me and thinking, and listening to the stitching in the room and the tune that was being hammered across the yard, appeared on a tray, and turned out to be for me.

" I have been acquainted with you," said Mr. Omer, after watching me for some minutes, during which I had not made much impression on the breakfast, for the black things destroyed my appetite, " I have been acquainted with you a long time, my young friend."

" Have you, sir? "

" All your life," said Mr. Omer. " I may say before it. I knew your father before you. He was five foot nine and a half, and he lays in five and twen-ty foot of ground."

" RAT—tat-tat, RAT—tat-tat, RAT—tat-tat," across the yard.

" He lays in five and twen-ty foot of ground, if he lays in a fraction," said Mr. Omer, pleasantly. " It was either his request or her direction, I forget which."

" Do you know how my little brother is, sir? " I inquired.

Mr. Omer shook his head.

" RAT—tat-tat, RAT—tat-tat, RAT—tat-tat."

" He is in his mother's arms," said he.

" Oh, poor little fellow! Is he dead? "

" Don't mind it more than you can help," said Mr. Omer. " Yes. The baby's dead."

My wounds broke out afresh at this intelligence. I left the scarcely tasted breakfast, and went and rested my head on another table, in a corner of the little room, which Minnie hastily cleared, lest I should spot the mourning that was lying there with my tears. She was a pretty good-natured girl, and put my hair away from my eyes with a soft kind touch; but she was very cheerful at having nearly finished her work and being in good time, and was so different from me!

Presently the tune left off, and a good-looking young fellow came across the yard into the room. He had a hammer in his hand, and his mouth was full of little nails, which he was obliged to take out before he could speak.

" Well, Joram! " said Mr. Omer. " How do *you* get on? "

" All right," said Joram. " Done, sir."

Minnie coloured a little, and the other two girls smiled at one another.

" What! you were at it by candle-light last night, when I was at the club, then? Were you? " said Mr. Omer, shutting up one eye.

" Yes," said Joram. "As you said we could make a little trip of it, and go over together, if it was done, Minnie and me—and you."

" Oh! I thought you were going to leave me out altogether," said Mr. Omer, laughing till he coughed.

"—As you was so good as to say that," resumed the young man, " why I turned to with a will, you see. Will you give me your opinion of it? "

" I will," said Mr. Omer, rising. " My dear; " and he stopped and turned to me: " would you like to see your——"

" No, father," Minnie interposed.

" I thought it might be agreeable, my dear," said Mr. Omer. " But perhaps you're right."

I can't say how I knew it was my dear, dear mother's coffin that they went to look at. I had never heard one making; I had never seen one that I know of: but it came into my mind what the noise was, while it was going on; and when the young man entered, I am sure I knew what he had been doing.

The work being now finished, the two girls, whose names I had not heard, brushed the shreds and threads from their dresses, and went into the shop to put that to rights, and wait for customers. Minnie stayed behind to fold up what they had made, and pack it in two baskets. This she did upon her knees, humming a lively little tune the while. Joram, who I had no doubt was her lover, came in and stole a kiss from her while she was busy (he didn't appear to mind me, at all), and said her father was gone for the chaise, and he must make haste and get himself ready. Then he went out again; and then she put her thimble and scissors in her pocket, and stuck a needle threaded with black thread neatly in the bosom of her gown, and put on her outer clothing smartly, at a little glass behind the door, in which I saw the reflection of her pleased face.

All this I observed, sitting at the table in the corner with my head leaning on my hand, and my thoughts running on very different things. The chaise soon came round to the front of the shop, and the baskets being put in first, I was put in next, and those three followed. I remember it as a kind of half chaise-cart, half pianoforte-van, painted of a sombre colour, and drawn by a black horse with a long tail. There was plenty of room for us all.

I do not think I have ever experienced so strange a feeling in my life (I am wiser now, perhaps) as that of being with them, remembering how they had been employed, and seeing them enjoy the ride. I was not angry with them; I was more afraid of them, as if I were cast away among creatures with whom I had no community of nature. They were very cheerful. The old man sat in front to drive, and the two young people sat behind him, and whenever he spoke to them leaned forward, the one on one side of his chubby face and the other on the other, and made a great deal of him. They would have talked to me too, but I held back, and moped in my corner; scared by their love-making and hilarity, though it was far from boisterous, and almost wondering that no judgment came upon them for their hardness of heart.

So, when they stopped to bait the horse, and ate and drank and enjoyed themselves, I could touch nothing that they touched, but kept my fast unbroken. So, when we reached home, I dropped out of the chaise behind, as quickly as possible, that I might not be in their company before those solemn windows, looking blindly on me like closed eyes once bright. And oh, how little need I had had to think what would move me to tears when I came back—seeing the window of my mother's room, and next it that which, in the better time, was mine!

I was in Peggotty's arms before I got to the door, and she took me into the house. Her grief burst out when she first saw me; but she controlled it soon, and spoke in whispers, and walked softly, as if the dead could be disturbed. She had not been in bed, I found, for a long time. She sat up at night still, and watched. As long as her poor dear pretty was above the ground, she said, she would never desert her.

Mr. Murdstone took no heed of me when I went into the parlour, where he was, but sat by the fireside, weeping silently, and pondering in his elbow-chair. Miss Murdstone, who was busy at her writing-desk, which was covered with letters and papers, gave me her cold finger-nails, and asked me, in an iron whisper, if I had been measured for my mourning.

I said: " Yes."

" And your shirts," said Miss Murdstone; " have you brought 'em home? "

" Yes, ma'am. I have brought home all my clothes."

This was all the consolation that her firmness administered to me. I do not doubt that she had a choice pleasure in exhibiting what she called her self-command, and her firmness, and her strength of mind, and her common sense, and the whole diabolical catalogue of her unamiable qualities, on such an occasion. She was particularly proud of her turn for business; and she showed it now in reducing everything to pen and ink, and being moved by nothing. All the rest of that day, and from morning to night afterwards, she sat at that desk; scratching composedly with a hard pen, speaking in the same imperturbable whisper to everybody; never relaxing a muscle of her face, or softening a tone of her voice, or appearing with an atom of her dress astray.

Her brother took a book sometimes, but never read it that I saw. He would open it and look at it as if he were reading, but would remain for a whole hour without turning the leaf, and then put it down and walk to and fro in the room. I used to sit with folded hands watching him, and counting his foot-steps, hour after hour. He very seldom spoke to her, and never to me. He seemed to be the only restless thing, except the clocks, in the whole motionless house.

In these days before the funeral, I saw but little of Peggotty, except that, in passing up or down stairs, I always found her close to the room where my mother and her baby lay, and except that she came to me every night, and sat by my bed's head while I went to sleep. A day or two before the burial—I think it was a day or two before, but I am conscious of confusion in my mind about that heavy time, with nothing to mark its progress—she took me into the room. I only recollect that underneath some white covering on the bed, with a beautiful cleanliness and freshness all around it, there seemed to me to lie embodied the solemn stillness that was in the house; and that when she would have turned the cover gently back, I cried: "Oh no! oh no!" and held her hand.

If the funeral had been yesterday, I could not recollect it better. The very air of the best parlour, when I went in at the door, the bright condition of the fire, the shining of the wine in the decanters, the patterns of the glasses and plates, the faint sweet smell of cake, the odour of Miss Murdstone's dress, and our black clothes. Mr. Chillip is in the room, and comes to speak to me.

"And how is Master David?" he says, kindly.

I cannot tell him very well. I give him my hand, which he holds in his.

"Dear me!" says Mr. Chillip, meekly smiling, with something shining in his eye. "Our little friends grow up around us. They grow out of our knowledge, ma'am?"

This is to Miss Murdstone, who makes no reply.

"There is a great improvement here, ma'am?" says Mr. Chillip.

Miss Murdstone merely answers with a frown and a formal bend: Mr. Chillip, discomfited, goes into a corner, keeping me with him, and opens his mouth no more.

I remark this, because I remark everything that happens, not because I care about myself, or have done since I came home. And now the bell begins to sound, and Mr. Omer and another come to make us ready. As Peggotty was wont to tell me, long ago, the followers of my father to the same grave were made ready in the same room.

There are Mr. Murdstone, our neighbour Mr. Grayper, Mr. Chillip, and I. When we go out to the door, the Bearers and their load are in the garden; and they move before us down the path, and past the elms, and through the gate, and into the churchyard, where I have so often heard the birds sing on a summer morning.

We stand around the grave. The day seems different to me from every other day, and the light not of the same colour—of a sadder colour. Now there is a solemn hush, which we have brought from home with what is resting in the mould; and while we stand bare-headed, I hear the voice of the clergyman, sounding remote in the open air, and yet distinct and plain, saying: "I am the Resurrection and the Life, saith the Lord!" Then I hear sobs; and, standing apart among the lookers-on, I see that good and faithful servant, whom of all the people upon earth I love the best, and unto whom my childish heart is certain that the Lord will one day say: "Well done."

There are many faces that I know, among the little crowd; faces that I knew in church, when mine was always wondering there; faces that first saw my mother, when she came to the village in her youthful bloom. I do not mind them—I mind nothing but my grief—and yet I see and know them all; and even in the background, far away, see Minnie looking on, and her eye glancing on her sweetheart, who is near me.

It is over, and the earth is filled in, and we turn to come away. Before us stands our house, so pretty and unchanged, so linked in my mind with the young idea of what is gone, that all my sorrow has been nothing to the sorrow it calls forth. But they take me on; and Mr. Chillip, talks to me; and when we get home, puts some water to my lips; and when I ask his leave to go up to my room, dismisses me with the gentleness of a woman.

All this, I say, is yesterday's event. Events of later date have floated from me to the shore where all forgotten things will reappear, but this stands like a high rock in the ocean.

I knew that Peggotty would come to me in my room. The Sabbath stillness of the time (the day was so like Sunday! I have forgotten that) was suited to us both. She sat down by my side upon my little bed; and holding my hand, and sometimes putting it to her lips, and sometimes smoothing it with hers, as she might have comforted my little brother, told me, in her way, all that she had to tell concerning what had happened.

" She was never well," said Peggotty, " for a long time. She was uncertain in her mind, and not happy. When her baby was born, I thought at first she would get better, but she was more delicate, and sunk a little every day. She used to like to sit alone before her baby came, and then she cried; but afterwards she used to sing to it—so soft, that I once thought, when I heard her, it was like a voice up in the air, that was rising away.

" I think she got to be more timid, and more frightened-like, of late; and that a hard word was like a blow to her. But she was always the same to me. She never changed to her foolish Peggotty, didn't my sweet girl."

Here Peggotty stopped, and softly beat upon my hand a little while.

" The last time that I saw her like her own old self, was the night when you came home, my dear. The day you went away, she said to me, ' I never shall see my pretty darling again. Something tells me so, that tells the truth, I know.'

" She tried to hold up after that; and many a time, when they told her she was thoughtless and light-hearted, made believe to be so; but it was all a bygone then. She never told her husband what she had told me—she was afraid of saying it to anybody else—till one night, a little more than a week before it happened, when she said to him: ' My dear, I think I am dying.'

" ' It's off my mind now, Peggotty,' she told me, when I laid her in her bed that night. ' He will believe it more and more, poor fellow, every day for a few days to come; and then it will be past. I am very tired. If this is sleep, sit by me while I sleep; don't leave me. God bless both my children! God protect and keep my fatherless boy! "

" I never left her afterwards," said Peggotty. " She often talked to them two down-stairs—for she loved them; she couldn't bear not to love any one who was about her—but when they went away from her bedside, she always turned to me, as if there was rest where Peggotty was, and never fell asleep in any other way.

" On the last night, in the evening, she kissed me, and said:

" If my baby should die too, Peggotty, please let them lay him in my arms, and bury us together.' (It was done; for the poor lamb lived but a day beyond her.) ' Let my dearest boy go with us to our resting-place,' she said, ' and tell him that his mother, when she lay here, blessed him not once, but a thousand times.' "

Another silence followed this, and another gentle beating on my hand.

" It was pretty far in the night," said Peggotty, " when she asked me for some drink; and when she had taken it, gave me such a patient smile, the dear!—so beautiful!

" Daybreak had come, and the sun was rising, when she said to me, how kind and considerate Mr. Copperfield had always been to her, and how he had borne with her, and told her, when she doubted herself, that a loving heart was better and stronger than wisdom, and that he was a happy man in hers.

" ' Peggotty, my dear,' she said then, ' put me nearer to you,' for she was very weak. ' Lay your good arm underneath my neck,' she said, ' and turn me to you, for your face is going far off, and I want it to be near.' I put it as she asked; and oh Davy! the time had come when my first parting words to you were true—when she was glad to lay her poor head on her stupid cross old Peggotty's arm—and she died like a child that had gone to sleep! "

Thus ended Peggotty's narration. From the moment of my knowing of the death of my mother, the idea of her as she had been of late had vanished from me. I remembered her, from that instant, only as the young mother of my earliest impressions, who had been used to wind her bright curls round and round her finger, and to dance with me at twilight in the parlour. What Peggotty had told me now, was so far from bringing me back to the later period, that it rooted the earlier image in my mind. It may be curious, but it is true. In her death she winged her way back to her calm untroubled youth, and cancelled all the rest.

The mother who lay in the grave was the mother of my infancy; the little creature in her arms was myself, as I had once been, hushed for ever on her bosom.

10

I BECOME NEGLECTED, AND AM PROVIDED FOR

THE FIRST ACT OF BUSINESS MISS MURDSTONE performed when the day of the solemnity was over, and light was freely admitted into the house, was to give Peggotty a month's warning. Much as Peggotty would have disliked such a service, I believe she would have retained it, for my sake, in preference to the best upon earth. She told me we must part, and told me why; and we condoled with one another in all sincerity.

As to me or my future, not a word was said, or a step taken. Happy they would have been, I dare say, if they could have dismissed me at a month's warning too. I mustered courage once, to ask Miss Murdstone when I was going back to school; and she answered drily, she believed I was not going back at all. I was told nothing more. I was very anxious to know what was going to be done with me, and so was Peggotty; but neither she nor I could pick up any information on the subject.

There was one change in my condition, which, while it relieved me of a great deal of present uneasiness, might have made me, if I had been capable of considering it closely, yet more uncomfortable about the future. It was this. The constraint that had been put upon me was quite abandoned. I was so far from being required to keep my dull post in the parlour, that on several occasions, when I took my seat there, Miss Murdstone frowned to me to go away. I was so far from being warned off from Peggotty's society, that, provided I was not in Mr. Murdstone's, I was never sought out or inquired for. At first I was in daily dread of his taking my education in hand again, or of Miss Murdstone's devoting herself to it; but I soon began to think that such fears were groundless, and that all I had to anticipate was neglect.

I do not conceive that this discovery gave me much pain then. I was still giddy with the shock of my mother's death, and in a kind of stunned state as to all tributary things. I can recollect, indeed, to have speculated, at odd times, on the possibility of my not being taught any more, or cared for any more; and growing up to be a shabby moody man, lounging an idle life away, about the village; as well as on the feasibility of my getting rid of this picture by going away somewhere, like the hero in a story, to seek my fortune: but these were transient visions, day-dreams I sat looking at sometimes, as if they were faintly painted or written on the wall of my room, and which, as they melted away, left the wall blank again.

"Peggotty," I said in a thoughtful whisper, one evening, when I was warming my hands at the kitchen fire, "Mr. Murdstone likes me less than he used to. He never liked me much, Peggotty; but he would rather not even see me now, if he can help it."

"Perhaps it's his sorrow," said Peggotty, stroking my hair.

"I am sure, Peggotty, I am sorry too. If I believed it was his sorrow, I should not think of it at all. But it's not that; oh, no, it's not that."

"How do you know it's not that?" said Peggotty, after a silence.

"Oh, his sorrow is another and quite a different thing. He is sorry at this moment, sitting by the fireside with Miss Murdstone; but if I was to go in, Peggotty, he would be something besides."

"What would he be?" said Peggotty.

"Angry," I answered, with an involuntary imitation of his dark frown. "If he was only sorry, he wouldn't look at me as he does. *I* am only sorry, and it makes me feel kinder."

Peggotty said nothing for a little while; and I warmed my hands, as silent as she.

"Davy," she said at length.

"Yes, Peggotty?"

"I have tried, my dear, all ways I could think of—all the ways there are, and all the ways there ain't, in short—to get a suitable service here, in Blunderstone; but there's no such a thing, my love."

"And what do you mean to do, Peggotty?" says I, wistfully. "Do you mean to go and seek your fortune?"

"I expect I shall be forced to go to Yarmouth," replied Peggotty, "and live there."

"You might have gone farther off," I said brightening a little, "and been as bad as lost. I shall see you sometimes, my dear old Peggotty, there. You won't be quite at the other end of the world, will you?"

"Contrary ways, please God!" cried Peggotty, with great animation. "As long as you are here, my pet, I shall come over every week of my life to see you. One day every week of my life!"

I felt a great weight taken off my mind by this promise: but even this was not all for Peggotty went on to say:

" I'm a-going, Davy, you see, to my brother's, first, for another fortnight's visit—just till I have had time to look about me, and get to be something like myself again. Now, I have been thinking that perhaps, as they don't want you here at present, you might be let to go along with me."

If anything, short of being in a different relation to every one about me, Peggotty excepted, could have given me a sense of pleasure at that time, it would have been this project of all others. The idea of being again surrounded by those honest faces, shining welcome on me; of renewing the peacefulness of the sweet Sunday morning, when the bells were ringing, the stones dropping in the water, and the shadowy ships breaking through the mist; of roaming up and down with little Em'ly, telling her my troubles, and finding charms against them in the shells and pebbles on the beach; made a calm in my heart. It was ruffled next moment, to be sure, by a doubt of Miss Murdstone giving her consent; but even that was set at rest soon, for she came out to take an evening grope in the store-closet while we were yet in conversation, and Peggotty, with a boldness that amazed me, broached the topic on the spot.

" The boy will be idle there," said Miss Murdstone, looking into a pickle-jar, " and idleness is the root of all evil. But, to be sure, he would be idle here—or anywhere, in my opinion."

Peggotty had an angry answer ready, I could see; but she swallowed it for my sake, and remained silent.

" Humph! " said Miss Murdstone, still keeping her eye on the pickles; " it is of more importance than anything else—it is of paramount importance—that my brother should not be disturbed or made uncomfortable. I suppose I had better say yes."

I thanked her, without making any demonstration of joy, lest it should induce her to withdraw her assent. Nor could I help thinking this a prudent course, since she looked at me out of the pickle-jar, with as great an access of sourness as if her black eyes had absorbed its contents. However, the permission was given, and was never retracted; for when the month was out, Peggotty and I were ready to depart.

Mr. Barkis came into the house for Peggotty's boxes. I had never known him to pass the garden-gate before, but on this occasion he came into the house. And he gave me a look as he shouldered the largest box and went out, which I thought had meaning in it, if meaning could ever be said to find its way into Mr. Barkis's visage.

Peggotty was naturally in low spirits at leaving what had been her home so many years, and where the two strong attachments of her life—for my mother and myself—had been formed. She had been walking in the churchyard, too, very early; and she got into the cart, and sat in it with her handkerchief at her eyes.

So long as she remained in this condition, Mr. Barkis gave no sign of life whatever. He sat in his usual place and attitude, like a great stuffed figure. But when she began to look about her, and to speak to me, he nodded his head and grinned several times. I have not the least notion at whom, or what he meant by it.

"It's a beautiful day, Mr. Barkis!" I said, as an act of politeness.

"It ain't bad," said Mr. Barkis, who generally qualified his speech, and rarely committed himself.

"Peggotty is quite comfortable now, Mr. Barkis," I remarked, for his satisfaction.

"Is she, though?" said Mr. Barkis.

After reflecting about it, with a sagacious air, Mr. Barkis eyed her, and said:

"*Are* you pretty comfortable?"

Peggotty laughed, and answered in the affirmative.

"But really and truly, you know. Are you?" growled Mr. Barkis, sliding nearer to her on the seat, and nudging her with his elbow. "Are you? Really and truly, pretty comfortable? Are you? Eh?" At each of these inquiries Mr. Barkis shuffled nearer to her, and gave her another nudge; so that at last we were all crowded together in the left-hand corner of the cart, and I was so squeezed that I could hardly bear it.

Peggotty calling his attention to my sufferings, Mr. Barkis gave me a little more room at once, and got away by degrees. But I could not help observing that he seemed to think he had hit upon a wonderful expedient for expressing himself in a neat, agreeable, and pointed manner, without the inconvenience of inventing conversation. He manifestly chuckled over it for some time. By-and-by he turned to Peggotty again, and repeating, "Are you pretty comfortable, though?" bore down upon us as before, until the breath was nearly wedged out of my body. By-and-by he made another descent upon us with the same inquiry and the same result. At length, I got up whenever I saw him coming, and standing on the foot-board, pretended to look at the prospect; after which I did very well.

He was so polite as to stop at a public-house, expressly on

our account, and entertain us with broiled mutton and beer. Even when Peggotty was in the act of drinking, he was seized with one of those approaches, and almost choked her. But as we drew nearer to the end of our journey, he had more to do and less time for gallantry; and when we got on Yarmouth pavement, we were all too much shaken and jolted, I apprehend, to have any leisure for anything else.

Mr. Peggotty and Ham waited for us at the old place. They received me and Peggotty in an affectionate manner, and shook hands with Mr. Barkis, who, with his hat on the very back of his head, and a shamefaced leer upon his countenance, and pervading his very legs, presented but a vacant appearance, I thought. They each took one of Peggotty's trunks, and were going away, when Mr. Barkis solemnly made a sign to me with his forefinger to come under an archway.

" I say," growled Mr. Barkis, " it was all right."

I looked up into his face, and answered, with an attempt to be very profound; " Oh! "

" It didn't come to a end there," said Mr. Barkis, nodding confidentially. " It was all right."

Again I answered, " Oh! "

" You know who was willin'," said my friend. " It was Barkis, and Barkis only."

I nodded assent.

" It's all right," said Mr. Barkis, shaking hands: " I'm a friend of your'n. You made it all right, first. It's all right."

In his attempts to be particularly lucid, Mr. Barkis was so extremely mysterious that I might have stood looking in his face for an hour, and most assuredly should have got as much information out of it as out of the face of a clock that had stopped, but for Peggotty's calling me away. As we were going along, she asked me what he had said; and I told her he had said it was all right.

" Like his impudence," said Peggotty, " but I don't mind that! Davy dear, what should you think if I was to think of being married? "

" Why—I suppose you would like me as much then, Peggotty, as you do now? " I returned, after a little consideration.

Greatly to the astonishment of the passengers in the street, as well as of her relations going on before, the good soul was obliged to stop and embrace me on the spot, with many protestations of her unalterable love.

" Tell me what should you say, darling? " she asked again, when this was over, and we were walking on.

" If you were thinking of being married—to Mr. Barkis, Peggotty? "

" Yes," said Peggotty.

" I should think it would be a very good thing. For then you know, Peggotty, you would always have the horse and cart to bring you over to see me, and could come for nothing, and be sure of coming."

" The sense of the dear! " cried Peggotty. " What I have been thinking of, this month back! Yes, my precious; and I think I should be more independent altogether, you see; let alone my working with a better heart in my own house, than I could in anybody else's now. I don't know what I might be fit for, now, as a servant to a stranger. And I shall be always near my pretty's resting-place," said Peggotty, musing, " and be able to see it when I like; and when *I* lie down to rest, I may be laid not far from my darling girl! "

We neither of us said anything for a little while.

" But I wouldn't so much as give it another thought," said Peggotty, cheerily, " if my Davy was anyways against it—not if I had been asked in church thirty times three times over, and was wearing out the ring in my pocket."

" Look at me, Peggotty," I replied; " and see if I am not really glad, and don't truly wish it! " As indeed I did, with all my heart.

" Well, my life," said Peggotty, giving me a squeeze, " I have thought of it night and day, every way I can, and I hope the right way; but I'll think of it again, and speak to my brother about it, and in the meantime we'll keep it to ourselves, Davy, you and me. Barkis is a good plain creatur'," said Peggotty, " and if I tried to do my duty by him, I think it would be my fault if I wasn't—if I wasn't pretty comfortable," said Peggotty, laughing heartily.

This quotation from Mr. Barkis was so appropriate, and tickled us both so much, that we laughed again and again, and were quite in a pleasant humour when we came within view of Mr. Peggotty's cottage.

It looked just the same, except that it may, perhaps, have shrunk a little in my eyes; and Mrs. Gummidge was waiting at the door as if she had stood there ever since. All within was the same, down to the seaweed in the blue mug in my bedroom. I went into the outhouse to look about me; and the very same lobsters, crabs, and crawfish possessed by the same desire to pinch the world in general, appeared to be in the same state of conglomeration in the same old corner.

But there was no little Em'ly to be seen, so I asked Mr. Peggotty where she was.

"She's at school, sir," said Mr. Peggotty, wiping the heat consequent on the porterage of Peggotty's box from his forehead; "she'll be home," looking at the Dutch clock, "in from twenty minutes to half-an-hour's time. We all on us feel the loss of her, bless ye!"

Mrs. Gummidge moaned.

"Cheer up, mawther!" cried Mr. Peggotty.

"I feel it more than anybody else," said Mrs. Gummidge: "I'm a lone lorn creetur', and she used to be a'most the only thing that didn't go contrairy with me."

Mrs. Gummidge, whimpering and shaking her head, applied herself to blowing the fire. Mr. Peggotty, looking round upon us while she was so engaged, said in a low voice, which he shaded with his hand: "The old 'un!" From this I rightly conjectured that no improvement had taken place since my last visit in the state of Mrs. Gummidge's spirits.

Now, the whole place was, or it should have been, quite as delightful a place as ever; and yet it did not impress me in the same way. I felt rather disappointed with it. Perhaps it was because little Em'ly was not at home. I knew the way by which she would come, and presently found myself strolling along the path to meet her.

A figure appeared in the distance before long, and I soon knew it to be Em'ly, who was a little creature still in stature, though she was grown. But when she drew nearer, and I saw her blue eyes looking bluer, and her dimpled face looking brighter, and her whole self prettier and gayer, a curious feeling came over me that made me pretend not to know her, and pass by as if I were looking at something a long way off. I have done such a thing since in later life, or I am mistaken.

Little Em'ly didn't care a bit. She saw me well enough; but instead of turning round and calling after me, ran away laughing. This obliged me to run after her, and she ran so fast that we were very near the cottage before I caught her.

"Oh, it's you, is it?" said little Em'ly.

"Why, you knew who it was, Em'ly," said I.

"And didn't *you* know who it was?" said Em'ly. I was going to kiss her, but she covered her cherry lips with her hands, and said she wasn't a baby now, and ran away, laughing more than ever, into the house.

She seemed to delight in teasing me, which was a change in her I wondered at very much. The tea-table was ready, and our little locker was put out in its old place, but instead of coming to sit by me, she went and bestowed her company upon that grumbling Mrs. Gummidge: and on Mr. Peggotty's inquiring why, rumpled her hair all over her face to hide it, and would do nothing but laugh.

" A little puss it is! " said Mr. Peggotty, patting her with his great hand.

" So sh'is! so sh'is! " cried Ham. " Mas'r Davy bor', so sh'is! " and he sat and chuckled at her for some time, in a state of mingled admiration and delight, that made his face a burning red.

Little Em'ly was spoiled by them all, in fact; and by no one more than Mr. Peggotty himself, whom she could have coaxed into anything by only going and laying her cheek against his rough whisker. That was my opinion, at least, when I saw her do it; and I held Mr. Peggotty to be thoroughly in the right. But she was so affectionate and sweet-natured, and had such a pleasant manner of being both sly and shy at once, that she captivated me more than ever.

She was tender-hearted, too; for when, as we sat round the fire after tea, an allusion was made by Mr. Peggotty over his pipe to the loss I had sustained, the tears stood in her eyes, and she looked at me so kindly across the table, that I felt quite thankful to her.

" Ah! " said Mr. Peggotty, taking up her curls, and running them over his hand like water, " here's another orphan, you see, sir. And here," said Mr. Peggotty, giving Ham a back-handed knock in the chest, " is another of 'm, though he don't look much like it."

" If I had you for my guardian, Mr. Peggotty," said I, shaking my head, " I don't think I should *feel* much like it."

" Well said, Mas'r Davy bor'! " cried Ham in an ecstasy. " Hoorah! Well said! Nor more you wouldn't! Hor! Hor! "—Here he returned Mr. Peggotty's back-hander, and little Em'ly got up and kissed Mr. Peggotty.

" And how's your friend, sir? " said Mr. Peggotty to me.

" Steerforth? " said I.

" That's the name! " cried Mr. Peggotty, turning to Ham. " I knowed it was something in our way."

" You said it was Rudderford," observed Ham, laughing.

" Well! " retorted Mr. Peggotty. " And ye steer with a rudder, don't ye? It ain't fur off. How is he, sir? "

" He was very well indeed when I came away, Mr. Peggotty."

" There's a friend! " said Mr. Peggotty, stretching out his

pipe. " There's a friend, if you talk of friends! Why, Lord love my heart alive, if it ain't a treat to look at him! "

" He is very handsome, is he not? " said I, my heart warming with his praise.

" Handsome! " cried Mr. Peggotty. " He stands up to you like —like a—why I don't know what he *don't* stand up to you like. He's so bold! "

" Yes! That's just his character," said I. " He's as brave as a lion, and you can't think how frank he is, Mr. Peggotty."

" And I do suppose, now," said Mr. Peggotty, looking at me through the smoke of his pipe, " that in the way of book-larning he'd take the wind out of a'most anything."

" Yes," said I, delighted; " he knows everything. He is astonishingly clever."

" There's a friend! " murmured Mr. Peggotty, with a grave toss of his head.

" Nothing seems to cost him any trouble," said I. " He knows a task if he only looks at it. He is the best cricketer you ever saw. He will give you almost as many men as you like at draughts, and beat you easily."

Mr. Peggotty gave his head another toss, as much as to say: " Of course he will."

" He is such a speaker," I pursued, " that he can win anybody over; and I don't know what you'd say if you were to hear him sing, Mr. Peggotty."

Mr. Peggotty gave his head another toss, as much as to say: " I have no doubt of it."

" Then, he's such a generous, fine, noble fellow," said I, quite carried away by my favourite theme, " that it's hardly possible to give him as much praise as he deserves. I am sure I can never feel thankful enough for the generosity with which he has protected me, so much younger and lower in the school than himself."

I was running on, very fast indeed, when my eyes rested on little Em'ly's face, which was bent forward over the table, listening with the deepest attention, her breath held, her blue eyes sparkling like jewels, and the colour mantling her cheeks. She looked so extraordinarily earnest and pretty, that I stopped in a sort of wonder; and they all observed her at the same time, for as I stopped, they laughed and looked at her.

" Em'ly is like me," said Peggotty, " and would like to see him."

Em'ly was confused by our all observing her, and hung down her head, and her face was covered with blushes. Glancing up presently through her stray curls, and seeing that we were all looking at her still (I am sure I, for one, could have looked at her for hours), she ran away, and kept away till it was nearly bedtime.

I lay down in the old little bed in the stern of the boat, and the wind came moaning on across the flat as it had done before. But I could not help fancying, now, that it moaned of those who were gone; and instead of thinking that the sea might rise in the night and float the boat away, I thought of the sea that had risen, since I last heard those sounds, and drowned my happy home. I recollect, as the wind and water began to sound fainter in my ears, putting a short clause into my prayers, petitioning that I might grow up to marry little Em'ly, and so dropping lovingly asleep.

The days passed pretty much as they had passed before, except—it was a great exception—that little Em'ly and I seldom wandered on the beach now. She had tasks to learn, and needle-work to do; and was absent during a great part of each day. But I felt that we should not have had these old wanderings, even if it had been otherwise. Wild and full of childish whims as Em'ly was, she was more of a little woman than I had supposed. She seemed to have got a great distance away from me, in little more than a year. She liked me, but she laughed at me, and tormented me; and when I went to meet her, stole home another way, and was laughing at the door when I came back, disappointed. The best times were when she sat quietly at work in the doorway, and I sat on the wooden steps at her feet, reading to her. It seems to me at this hour, that I have never seen such sunlight as on those bright April afternoons; but I have never seen such a sunny little figure as I used to see, sitting in the doorway of the old boat; that I have never beheld such sky, such water, such glorified ships sailing away into golden air.

On the very first evening after our arrival, Mr. Barkis appeared in an exceedingly vacant and awkward condition, and with a bundle of oranges tied up in a handkerchief. As he made no allusion of any kind to this property, he was supposed to have left it behind him by accident when he went away; until Ham, running after him to restore it, came back with the information that it was intended for Peggotty. After that occasion he appeared every evening at exactly the same hour, and always with a little bundle, to which he never alluded, and which he regularly put behind the door, and left there. These offerings of affection were of a most various and eccentric description. Among them I remember a double set of pigs' trotters, a huge pin-cushion, half a bushel or so of apples, a pair of jet earrings, some Spanish onions, a box of dominoes, a canary bird and cage, and a leg of pickled pork.

Mr. Barkis's wooing, as I remember it, was altogether of a peculiar kind. He very seldom said anything; but would sit by the fire in much the same attitude as he sat in his cart, and stare heavily at Peggotty, who was opposite. One night, being, as I suppose, inspired by love, he made a dart at the bit of wax-candle she kept for her thread, and put it in his waistcoat-pocket and carried it off. After that, his great delight was to produce it when it was wanted, sticking to the lining of his pocket, in a partially melted state, and pocket it again when it was done with. He seemed to enjoy himself very much, and not to feel at all called upon to talk. Even when he took Peggotty out for a walk on the flats, he had no uneasiness on that head, I believe; contenting himself with now and then asking her if she was pretty comfortable; and I remember that sometimes, after he was gone, Peggotty would throw her apron over her face, and laugh for half-an-hour. Indeed, we were all more or less amused, except that miserable Mrs. Gummidge, whose courtship would appear to have been of an exactly parallel nature, she was so continually reminded by these transactions of the old one.

At length, when the term of my visit was nearly expired, it was given out that Peggotty and Mr. Barkis were going to make a day's holiday together, and that little Em'ly and I were to accompany them. I had but a broken sleep the night before, in anticipation of the pleasure of a whole day with Em'ly. We were all astir betimes in the morning; and while we were yet at breakfast, Mr. Barkis appeared in the distance, driving a chaise-cart towards the object of his affections.

Peggotty was dressed as usual, in her neat and quiet mourning; but Mr. Barkis bloomed in a new blue coat, of which the tailor had given him such good measure, that the cuffs would have rendered gloves unnecessary in the coldest weather, while the collar was so high that it pushed his hair up on end on the top of his head. His bright buttons, too, were of the largest size. Rendered complete by drab pantaloons and a buff waistcoat, I thought Mr. Barkis a phenomenon of respectability.

When we were all in a bustle outside the door, I found that Mr. Peggotty was prepared with an old shoe, which was to be thrown after us for luck, and which he offered to Mrs. Gummidge for that purpose.

"No. It had better be done by somebody else, Dan'l," said Mrs. Gummidge. "I'm a lone lorn creetur' myself, and everythink that reminds me of creeturs that ain't lone and lorn, goes contrairy with me."

"Come, old gal!" cried Mr. Peggotty. "Take and heave it."

"No, Dan'l," returned Mrs. Gummidge, whimpering and shaking her head. "If I felt less, I could do more. You don't feel like me, Dan'l; thinks don't go contrairy with you, nor you with them; you had better do it yourself."

But here Peggotty, who had been going about from one to another in a hurried way, kissing everybody, called out from the cart, in which we all were by this time (Em'ly and I on two little chairs, side by side), that Mrs. Gummidge must do it. So Mrs. Gummidge did it; and, I am sorry to relate, cast a damp upon the festive character of our departure, by immediately bursting into tears, and sinking subdued into the arms of Ham, with the declaration that she knowed she was a burden, and had better be carried to the House at once. Which I really thought was a sensible idea, that Ham might have acted on.

Away we went, however, on our holiday excursion; and the first thing we did was to stop at a church, where Mr. Barkis tied the horse to some rails, and went in with Peggotty, leaving little Em'ly and me alone in the chaise. I took that occasion to put my arm round Em'ly's waist, and propose that as I was going away so very soon now, we should determine to be very affectionate to one another, and very happy, all day. Little Em'ly consenting, and allowing me to kiss her, I became desperate; informing her, I recollect, that I never could love another, and that I was prepared to shed the blood of anybody who should aspire to her affections.

How merry little Em'ly made herself about it! With what a demure assumption of being immensely older and wiser than I, the fairy little woman said I was "a silly boy"; and then laughed so charmingly that I forgot the pain of being called by that disparaging name, in the pleasure of looking at her.

Mr. Barkis and Peggotty were a good while in the church, but came out at last, and then we drove away into the country. As we were going along, Mr. Barkis turned to me, and said, with a wink,—by-the-bye, I should hardly have thought, before, that he *could* wink:

"What name was it as I wrote up in the cart?"

"Clara Peggotty," I answered.

"What name would it be as I should write up now, if there was a tilt here?"

"Clara Peggotty, again?" I suggested.

"Clara Peggotty BARKIS!" he returned, and burst into a roar of laughter that shook the chaise.

In a word, they were married, and had gone into the church for no other purpose. Peggotty was resolved that it should be quietly done; and the clerk had given her away, and there had been no witnesses of the ceremony. She was a little confused when Mr. Barkis made this abrupt announcement of their union, and could not hug me enough in token of her unimpaired affection; but she soon became herself again, and said she was very glad it was over.

We drove to a little inn in a by-road, where we were expected, and where we had a very comfortable dinner, and passed the day with great satisfaction. If Peggotty had been married every day for the last ten years, she could hardly have been more at her ease about it; it made no sort of difference in her: she was just the same as ever, and went out for a stroll with little Em'ly and me before tea, while Mr. Barkis philosophically smoked his pipe, and enjoyed himself, I suppose, with the contemplation of his happiness. If so, it sharpened his appetite, for I distinctly called to mind that, although he had eaten a good deal of pork and greens at dinner, and had finished off with a fowl or two, he was obliged to have cold boiled bacon for tea, and disposed of a large quantity without any emotion.

I have often thought, since, what an odd, innocent, out-of-the-way kind of wedding it must have been! We got into the chaise again soon after dark, and drove cosily back, looking up at the stars, and talking about them. I was their chief exponent, and opened Mr. Barkis's mind to an amazing extent. I told him all I knew, but he would have believed anything I might have taken it into my head to impart to him; for he had a profound veneration for my abilities, and informed his wife in my hearing, on that very occasion, that I was "a young Roeshus"—by which I think he meant prodigy.

When we had exhausted the subject of the stars, or rather when I had exhausted the mental faculties of Mr. Barkis, little Em'ly and I made a cloak of an old wrapper, and sat under it for the rest of the journey. Ah, how I loved her! What happiness (I thought) if we were married, and were going away anywhere to live among the trees and in the fields, never growing older, never growing wiser, children ever, rambling hand in hand through sunshine and among flowery meadows, laying down our heads on moss at night, in a sweet sleep of purity and peace, and buried by the birds when we were dead! Some such picture, with no real world in it, bright with the light of our innocence, and vague as the stars afar off, was in my mind all the way. I am glad to think there were two such guileless hearts at Peggotty's marriage as little Em'ly's and mine. I am glad to think the Loves and Graces took such airy forms in its homely procession.

Well, we came to the old boat again in good time at night; and there Mr. and Mrs. Barkis bade us good-bye, and drove away snugly to their own home. I felt then, for the first time, that I had lost Peggotty. I should have gone to bed with a sore heart indeed under any other roof but that which sheltered little Em'ly's head.

Mr. Peggotty and Ham knew what was in my thoughts as well as I did, and were ready with some supper and their hospitable faces to drive it away. Little Em'ly came and sat beside me on the locker for the only time in all that visit; and it was altogether a wonderful close to a wonderful day.

It was a night tide: and soon after we went to bed, Mr. Peggotty and Ham went out to fish. I felt very brave at being left alone in the solitary house, the protector of Em'ly and Mrs. Gummidge, and only wished that a lion or a serpent, or any ill-disposed monster, would make an attack upon us, that I might destroy him, and cover myself with glory. But as nothing of the sort happened to be walking about on Yarmouth flats that night, I provided the best substitute I could by dreaming of dragons until morning.

With morning came Peggotty; who called to me, as usual, under my window, as if Mr. Barkis the carrier had been from first to last a dream too. After breakfast she took me to her own home, and a beautiful little home it was. Of all the moveables in it, I must have been most impressed by a certain old bureau of some dark wood in the parlour (the tile-floored kitchen was the general sitting-room), with a retreating top which opened, let down, and became a desk, within which was a large quarto edition of Foxe's *Book of Martyrs*. This precious volume, of which I do not recollect one word, I immediately discovered and immediately applied myself to; and I never visited the house afterwards, but I kneeled on a chair, opened the casket where this gem was enshrined, spread my arms over the desk, and fell to devouring the book afresh. I was chiefly edified, I am afraid, by the pictures, which were numerous, and represented all kinds of dismal horrors; but the Martyrs and Peggotty's house have been inseparable in my mind ever since, and are now.

I took leave of Mr. Peggotty, and Ham, and Mrs. Gummidge, and little Em'ly, that day; and passed the night at Peggotty's in a little room in the roof (with the crocodile-book on a shelf by the bed's head), which was to be always mine, Peggotty said, and should always be kept for me in exactly the same state.

"Young or old, Davy dear, as long as I am alive and have this house over my head," said Peggotty, "you shall find it as if I expected you here directly minute. I shall keep it every day, as I used to keep your old little room, my darling; and if you was to go to China, you might think of it as being kept just the same, all the time you were away."

I felt the truth and constancy of my dear old nurse, with all my heart, and thanked her as well as I could. That was not very well, for she spoke to me thus, with her arms round my neck, in the morning, and I was going home in the morning, and I went home in the morning, with herself and Mr. Barkis in the cart. They left me at the gate, not easily or lightly; and it was a strange sight to me to see the cart go on, taking Peggotty away, and leaving me under the old elm-trees looking at the house in which there was no face to look on mine with love or liking any more.

And now I fell into a state of neglect, which I cannot look back upon without compassion. I fell at once into a solitary condition,—apart from all friendly notice, apart from the society of all other boys of my own age, apart from all companionship but my own spiritless thoughts,—which seems to cast its gloom upon this paper as I write.

What would I have given, to have been sent to the hardest school that ever was kept!—to have been taught something, anyhow, anywhere! No such hope dawned upon me. They disliked me; and they sullenly, sternly, steadily, overlooked me. I think Mr. Murdstone's means were straitened at about this time; but it is little to the purpose. He could not bear me; and in putting me from him, he tried, as I believe, to put away the notion that I had any claim upon him—and succeeded.

I was not actively ill-used. I was not beaten, or starved; but the wrong that was done to me had no intervals of relenting, and was done in a systematic, passionless manner. Day after day, week after week, month after month, I was coldly neglected. I wonder sometimes, when I think of it, what they would have done if I had been taken with an illness; whether I should have lain down in my lonely room, and languished through it in my usual solitary way, or whether anybody would have helped me out.

When Mr. and Miss Murdstone were at home, I took my meals with them; in their absence, I ate and drank by myself. At all times I lounged about the house and neighbourhood quite disregarded, except that they were jealous of my making any friends: thinking, perhaps, that if I did, I might complain to some one. For this reason, though Mr. Chillip often asked me to go and see him (he was a widower, having, some years before that, lost a little small light-haired wife, whom I can just remember connecting in my own thoughts with a pale tortoise-shell cat), it was but seldom that I enjoyed the happiness of passing an afternoon in his closet of a surgery; reading some book that was new to me, with the smell of the whole pharmacopœia coming up my nose, or pounding something in a mortar under his mild directions.

For the same reason, added no doubt to the old dislike of her, I was seldom allowed to visit Peggotty. Faithful to her promise, she either came to see me, or met me somewhere near, once every week, and never empty-handed; but many and bitter were the disappointments I had, in being refused permission to pay a visit to her at her house. Some few times, however, at long intervals, I was allowed to go there, and then I found out that Mr. Barkis was something of a miser, or, as Peggotty dutifully expressed it, was "a little near," and kept a heap of money in a box under his bed, which he pretended was only full of coats and trousers. In this coffer, his riches hid themselves with such a tenacious modesty, that the smallest instalments could only be tempted out by artifice; so that Peggotty had to prepare a long and elaborate scheme, a very Gunpowder Plot, for every Saturday's expenses.

All this time I was so conscious of the waste of any promise I had given, and of my being utterly neglected, that I should have been perfectly miserable, I have no doubt, but for the old books. They were my only comfort; and I was as true to them as they were to me, and read them over and over I don't know how many times more.

I now approach a period of my life, which I can never lose the remembrance of, while I remember anything; and the recollection of which has often, without my invocation, come before me like a ghost, and haunted my happier times.

I had been out, one day, loitering somewhere, in the listless meditative manner that my way of life engendered, when, turning the corner of a lane near our house, I came upon Mr. Murdstone walking with a gentleman. I was confused, and was going by them, when the gentleman cried:

"What! Brooks!"

"No, sir, David Copperfield," I said.

"Don't tell me. You are Brooks," said the gentleman. "You are Brooks of Sheffield. That's your name."

At these words, I observed the gentleman more attentively.

His laugh coming to my remembrance too, I knew him to be Mr. Quinion, whom I had gone over to Lowestoft with Mr. Murdstone to see, before—it is no matter—I need not recall when.

"And how do you get on, and where are you being educated, Brooks?" said Mr. Quinion.

He had put his hand upon my shoulder, and turned me about, to walk with them. I did not know what to reply, and glanced dubiously at Mr. Murdstone.

"He is at home at present," said the latter. "He is not being educated anywhere. I don't know what to do with him. He is a difficult subject.

That old, double look was on me for a moment; and then his eyes darkened with a frown, as it turned, in its aversion, elsewhere.

"Humph!" said Mr. Quinion, looking at us both, I thought. "Fine weather."

Silence ensued, and I was considering how I could best disengage my shoulder from his hand, and go away, when he said:

"I suppose you are a pretty sharp fellow still? Eh, Brooks?"

"Ay! He is sharp enough," said Mr. Murdstone, impatiently. "You had better let him go. He will not thank you for troubling him."

On this hint, Mr. Quinion released me, and I made the best of my way home. Looking back as I turned into the front garden, I saw Mr. Murdstone leaning against the wicket of the churchyard, and Mr. Quinion talking to him. They were both looking after me, and I felt that they were speaking of me.

Mr. Quinion lay at our house that night. After breakfast, the next morning, I had put my chair away, and was going out of the room, when Mr. Murdstone called me back. He then gravely repaired to another table, where his sister sat herself at her desk. Mr. Quinion, with his hands in his pockets, stood looking out of window; and I stood looking at them all.

"David," said Mr. Murdstone, "to the young this is a world for action; not for moping and droning in."

—"As you do," added his sister.

"Jane Murdstone, leave it to me, if you please. I say, David, to the young this is a world for action, and not for moping and droning in. It is especially so for a young boy of your disposition, which requires a great deal of correcting; and to which no greater service can be done than to force it to conform to the ways of the working world, and to bend it and break it."

"For stubbornness won't do here," said his sister. "What it wants is, to be crushed. And crushed it must be. Shall be, too!"

He gave her a look, half in remonstrance, half in approval, and went on:

" I suppose you know, David, that I am not rich. At any rate, you know it now. You have received some considerable education already. Education is costly; and even if it were not, and I could afford it, I am of opinion that it would not be at all advantageous to you to be kept at school. What is before you is a fight with the world; and the sooner you begin it, the better."

I think it occurred to me that I had already begun it, in my poor way: but it occurs to me now, whether or no.

" You have heard the 'counting-house' mentioned sometimes," said Mr. Murdstone.

" The counting-house, sir?" I repeated.

" Of Murdstone and Grinby, in the wine trade," he replied.

I suppose I looked uncertain, for he went on hastily:

" You have heard the 'counting-house' mentioned, or the business, or the cellars, or the wharf, or something about it."

" I think I have heard the business mentioned, sir," I said, remembering what I vaguely knew of his and his sister's resources. " But I don't know when."

" It does not matter when," he returned. " Mr. Quinion manages that business."

I glanced at the latter deferentially as he stood looking out of window.

" Mr. Quinion suggests that it gives employment to some other boys, and that he sees no reason why it shouldn't, on the same terms, give employment to you."

" He having," Mr. Quinion observed in a low voice, and half turning round, " no other prospect, Murdstone."

Mr. Murdstone, with an impatient, even an angry gesture, resumed, without noticing what he had said:

" Those terms are, that you will earn enough for yourself to provide for your eating and drinking, and pocket-money. Your lodging (which I have arranged for) will be paid by me. So will your washing."

" Which will be kept down to my estimate," said his sister.

" Your clothes will be looked after for you, too," said Mr. Murdstone; " as you will not be able, yet awhile, to get them for yourself. So you are now going to London, David, with Mr. Quinion, to begin the world on your own account."

" In short, you are provided for," observed his sister; " and will please to do your duty."

Though I quite understood that the purpose of this announcement was to get rid of me, I have no distinct remembrance whether it pleased or frightened me. My impression is, that I was in a state of confusion about it, and, oscillating between the two points, touched neither. Nor had I much time for the clearing of my thoughts, as Mr. Quinion was to go upon the morrow.

Behold me, on the morrow, in a much-worn little white hat, with a black crape round it for my mother, a black jacket, and a pair of hard stiff corduroy trousers—which Miss Murdstone considered the best armour for the legs in that fight with the world which was now to come off—behold me so attired, and with my little worldly all before me in a small trunk, sitting, a lone lorn child (as Mrs. Gummidge might have said), in the post-chaise that was carrying Mr. Quinion to the London coach at Yarmouth! See, how our house and church are lessening in the distance; how the grave beneath the tree is blotted out by intervening objects: how the spire points upwards from my old playground no more, and the sky is empty!

11

I BEGIN LIFE ON MY OWN ACCOUNT, AND DON'T LIKE IT

I KNOW ENOUGH OF THE WORLD NOW, TO HAVE almost lost the capacity of being surprised by anything; but it is matter of some surprise to me, even now, that I can have been so easily thrown away at such an age. A child of excellent abilities and with strong powers of observation, quick, eager, delicate, and soon hurt bodily or mentally, it seems wonderful to me that nobody should have made any sign in my behalf. But none was made; and I became, at ten years old, a little labouring hind in the service of Murdstone and Grinby.

Murdstone and Grinby's warehouse was at the water-side. It was down in Blackfriars. Modern improvements have altered the place; but it was the last house at the bottom of a narrow street, curving down hill to the river, with some stairs at the end, where people took boat. It was a crazy old house with a wharf of its own, abutting on the water when the tide was in, and on the mud when the tide was out, and literally overrun with rats. Its panelled rooms, discoloured with the dirt and smoke of a hundred years, I dare say; its decaying floors and staircase; the squeaking and scuffling of the old grey rats down in the cellars; and the dirt and rottenness of the place; are things, not of many years ago, in my mind, but of the present instant. They are all before me, just as they were in the evil hour when I went among them for the first time, with my trembling hand in Mr. Quinion's.

Murdstone and Grinby's trade was among a good many kinds of people, but an important branch of it was the supply of wines and spirits to certain packet ships. I forget now where they chiefly went, but I think there were some among them that made voyages both to the East and West Indies. I know that a great many empty bottles were one of the consequences of this traffic, and that certain men and boys were employed to examine them against the light, and reject those that were flawed, and to rinse and wash them. When the empty bottles ran short, there were labels to be pasted on full ones, or corks to be fitted to them, or seals to be put upon the corks, or finished bottles to be packed in casks. All this work was my work, and of the boys employed upon it I was one.

There were three or four of us, counting me. My working place was established in a corner of the warehouse, where Mr. Quinion could see me, when he chose to stand up on the bottom rail of his stool in the counting-house, and look at me through a window above the desk. Hither, on the first morning of my so auspiciously beginning life on my own account, the oldest of the regular boys was summoned to show me my business. His name was Mick Walker, and he wore a ragged apron and a paper cap. He informed me that his father was a bargeman, and walked, in a black velvet head-dress, in the Lord Mayor's Show. He also informed me that our principal associate would be another boy whom he introduced by the—to me—extraordinary name of Mealy Potatoes. I discovered, however, that this youth had not been christened by that name, but that it had been bestowed upon him in the warehouse, on account of his complexion, which was pale or mealy. Mealy's father was a waterman, who had the additional distinction of being a fireman, and was engaged as such at one of the large theatres; where some young relation of Mealy's—I think his little sister—did Imps in the Pantomimes.

No words can express the secret agony of my soul as I sunk into this companionship; compared these henceforth every-day associates with those of my happier childhood—not to say with Steerforth, Traddles, and the rest of those boys; and felt my hopes of growing up to be a learned and distinguished man crushed in my bosom. The deep remembrance of the sense I had, of being utterly without hope now; of the shame I felt in my position; of the misery it was to my young heart to believe that day by day what I had learned, and thought, and delighted in, and raised my fancy and my emulation up by, would pass away from me, little by little, never to be brought back any more; cannot be written. As often as Mick Walker went away in the course of that forenoon, I mingled my tears with the water in which I was washing the bottles; and sobbed as if there were a flaw in my own breast, and it were in danger of bursting.

The counting-house clock was at half-past twelve, and there was general preparation for going to dinner, when Mr. Quinion tapped at the counting-house window, and beckoned to me to go in. I went in, and found there a stoutish, middle-aged person, in a brown surtout and black tights and shoes, with no more hair upon his head (which was a large one, and very shining) than there is upon an egg, and with a very extensive face, which he turned full upon me. His clothes were shabby, but he had an imposing shirt-collar on. He carried a jaunty sort of a stick, with a large pair of rusty tassels to it; and a quizzing-glass hung outside his coat,—for ornament, I afterwards found, as he very seldom looked through it, and couldn't see anything when he did.

"This," said Mr. Quinion, in allusion to myself, "is he."

"This," said the stranger, with a certain condescending roll in his voice, and a certain indescribable air of doing something genteel, which impressed me very much, "is Master Copperfield. I hope I see you well, sir?"

I said I was very well, and hoped he was. I was sufficiently ill at ease, Heaven knows; but it was not in my nature to complain much at that time of life, so I said I was very well, and hoped he was.

"I am," said the stranger, "thank Heaven, quite well. I have received a letter from Mr. Murdstone, in which he mentions that he would desire me to receive into an apartment in the rear of my house, which is at present unoccupied—and is, in short, to be let as a—in short," said the stranger, with a smile and in a burst of confidence, "as a bedroom—the young beginner whom I have now the pleasure to—" and the stranger waved his hand, and settled his chin in his shirt-collar.

"This is Mr. Micawber," said Mr. Quinion to me.

"Ahem!" said the stranger, "that is my name."

"Mr. Micawber," said Mr. Quinion, "is known to Mr. Murdstone. He takes orders for us on commission, when he can get any. He has been written to by Mr. Murdstone, on the subject of your lodgings, and he will receive you as a lodger."

"My address," said Mr. Micawber, "is Windsor Terrace, City Road. I—in short," said Mr. Micawber, with the same genteel air, and in another burst of confidence—"I live there."

I made him a bow.

"Under the impression," said Mr. Micawber, "that your peregrinations in this metropolis have not as yet been extensive, and that you might have some difficulty in penetrating the arcana of the Modern Babylon in the direction of the City Road,—in short," said Mr. Micawber, in another burst of confidence, "that you might lose yourself—I shall be happy to call this evening, and install you in the knowledge of the nearest way."

I thanked him with all my heart, for it was friendly in him to offer to take that trouble.

"At what hour," said Mr. Micawber, "shall I——"

"At about eight," said Mr. Quinion.

"At about eight," said Mr. Micawber. "I beg to wish you good day, Mr. Quinion. I will intrude no longer."

So he put on his hat, and went out with his cane under his arm: very upright, and humming a tune when he was clear of the counting-house.

Mr. Quinion then formally engaged me to be as useful as I could in the warehouse of Murdstone and Grinby, at a salary, I think, of six shillings a week. I am not clear whether it was six or seven. I am inclined to believe, from my uncertainty on this head, that it was six at first and seven afterwards. He paid me a week down (from his own pocket, I believe), and I gave Mealy sixpence out of it to get my trunk carried to Windsor Terrace that night: it being too heavy for my strength, small as it was. I paid sixpence more for my dinner, which was a meat pie and a turn at a neighbouring pump; and passed the hour which was allowed for that meal, in walking about the streets.

At the appointed time in the evening, Mr. Micawber reappeared. I washed my hands and face, to do the greater honour to his gentility, and we walked to our house, as I suppose I must now call it, together; Mr. Micawber impressing the names of streets, and the shapes of corner houses upon me, as we went along, that I might find my way back, easily, in the morning.

Arrived at this house in Windsor Terrace (which I noticed was shabby like himself, but also, like himself, made all the show it could), he presented me to Mrs. Micawber, a thin and faded lady, not at all young, who was sitting in the parlour (the first floor was altogether unfurnished, and the blinds were kept down to delude the neighbours), with a baby at her breast. This baby was one of twins; and I may remark here that I hardly ever, in all my experience of the family, saw both the twins detached from Mrs. Micawber at the same time. One of them was always taking refreshment.

There were two other children; Master Micawber, aged about four, and Miss Micawber, aged about three. These, and a dark-complexioned young woman, with a habit of snorting, who was servant to the family, and informed me, before half-an-hour had expired, that she was "a Orfling", and came from St. Luke's workhouse, in the neighbourhood, completed the establishment. My room was at the top of the house, at the back: a close chamber; stencilled all over with an ornament which my young imagination represented as a blue muffin; and very scantily furnished.

"I never thought," said Mrs. Micawber, when she came up, twin and all, to show me the apartment, and sat down to take breath, "before I was married, when I lived with papa and mama, that I should ever find it necessary to take a lodger. But Mr. Micawber being in difficulties, all considerations of private feeling must give way."

I said: "Yes, ma'am."

"Mr. Micawber's difficulties are almost overwhelming just at present," said Mrs. Micawber; "and whether it is possible to bring him through them, I don't know. When I lived at home with papa and mama, I really should have hardly understood what the word meant, in the sense in which I now employ it, but experientia does it—as papa used to say."

I cannot satisfy myself whether she told me that Mr. Micawber had been an officer in the Marines, or whether I have imagined it. I only know that I believe to this hour that he *was* in the Marines once upon a time, without knowing why. He was a sort of town traveller for a number of miscellaneous houses, now; but made little or nothing of it, I am afraid.

"If Mr. Micawber's creditors *will not* give him time," said Mrs. Micawber, "they must take the consequences; and the sooner they bring it to an issue the better. Blood cannot be obtained from a stone, neither can anything on account be obtained at present (not to mention law expenses) from Mr. Micawber."

I never can quite understand whether my precocious self-dependence confused Mrs. Micawber in reference to my age, or whether she was so full of the subject that she would have talked about it to the very twins if there had been nobody else to communicate with, but this was the strain in which she began, and she went on accordingly all the time I knew her.

Poor Mrs. Micawber! She said she had tried to exert herself; and so, I have no doubt, she had. The centre of the street-door was perfectly covered with a great brass-plate, on which was engraved " Mrs. Micawber's Boarding Establishment for Young Ladies:" but I never found that any young lady had ever been to school there; or that any young lady ever came, or proposed to come; or that the least preparation was ever made to receive any young lady. The only visitors I ever saw, or heard of, were creditors. *They* used to come at all hours, and some of them were quite ferocious. One dirty-faced man, I think he was a boot-maker, used to edge himself into the passage as early as seven o'clock in the morning, and call up the stairs to Mr. Micawber—" Come! You ain't out yet, you know. Pay us, will you? Don't hide, you know; that's mean. I wouldn't be mean if I was you. Pay us, will you? You just pay us, d'ye hear? Come!" Receiving no answer to these taunts, he would mount in his wrath to the words " swindlers " and " robbers "; and these being ineffectual too, would sometimes go to the extremity of crossing the street, and roaring up at the windows of the second floor, where he knew Mr. Micawber was. At these times, Mr. Micawber would be transported with grief and mortification, even to the length (as I was once made aware by a scream from his wife) of making motions at himself with a razor; but within half-an-hour afterwards, he would polish up his shoes with extraordinary pains, and go out, humming a tune with a greater air of gentility than ever. Mrs. Micawber was quite as elastic. I have known her to be thrown into fainting fits by the king's taxes at three o'clock, and to eat lamb-chops breaded, and drink warm ale (paid for with two tea-spoons that had gone to the pawnbroker's) at four. On one occasion, when an execution had just been put in, coming home through some chance as early as six o'clock, I saw her lying (of course with a twin) under the grate in a swoon, with her hair all torn about her face; but I never knew her more cheerful than she was, that very same night, over a veal cutlet before the kitchen fire, telling me stories about her papa and mama, and the company they used to keep.

In this house, and with this family, I passed my leisure time. My own exclusive breakfast of a penny loaf and a pennyworth of milk, I provided myself; I kept another small loaf, and a modicum of cheese, on a particular shelf of a particular cupboard, to make my supper on when I came back at night. This made a hole in the six or seven shillings, I know well; and I was out at the warehouse all day, and had to support myself on that money all the week. From Monday morning until Saturday night, I had no advice, no counsel, no encouragement, no consolation, no assistance, no support, of any kind, from any one, that I can call to mind, as I hope to go to heaven!

I was so young and childish, and so little qualified—how could I be otherwise?—to undertake the whole charge of my own existence, that often, in going to Murdstone and Grinby's, of a morning, I could not resist the stale pastry put out for sale at half-price at the pastrycooks' doors, and spent in that the money I should have kept for my dinner. Then, I went without my dinner, or bought a roll or a slice of pudding. I remember two pudding-shops, between which I was divided, according to my finances. One was in a court close to St. Martin's Church—at the back of the church,—which is now removed altogether. The pudding at that shop was made of currants, and was rather a special pudding, but was dear, twopennyworth not being larger than a pennyworth of more ordinary pudding. A good shop for the latter was in the Strand—somewhere in that part which has been rebuilt since. It was a stout pale pudding, heavy and flabby, and with great flat raisins in it, stuck in whole at wide distances apart. It came up hot at about my time every day, and many a day did I dine off it. When I dined regularly and handsomely, I had a saveloy and a penny loaf, or a fourpenny plate of red beef from a cook's shop; or a plate of bread and cheese and a glass of beer, from a miserable old public-house opposite our place of business, called the Lion, or the Lion and something else that I have forgotten. Once, I remember carrying my own bread (which I had brought from home in the morning) under my arm, wrapped in a piece of paper, like a book, and going to a famous alamode beef-house near Drury Lane, and ordering a "small plate" of that delicacy to eat with it. What the waiter thought of such a strange little apparition coming in all alone, I don't know; but I can see him now, staring at me as I ate my dinner, and bringing up the other waiter to look. I gave him a halfpenny for himself and I wish he hadn't taken it.

We had half-an-hour, I think, for tea. When I had money enough, I used to get half-a-pint of ready-made coffee and a slice of bread and butter. When I had none, I used to look at a venison-shop in Fleet Street; or I have strolled, at such a time, as far as Covent Garden Market, and stared at the pineapples. I was fond of wandering about the Adelphi, because it was a mysterious place, with those dark arches. I see myself emerging one evening from some of these arches, on a little public-house close to the river, with an open space before it, where some coal-heavers were dancing; to look at whom I sat down upon a bench. I wonder what they thought of me!

I was such a child, and so little, that frequently when I went into the bar of a strange public-house for a glass of ale or porter, to moisten what I had had for dinner, they were afraid to give it me. I remember one hot evening I went into the bar of a public-house, and said to the landlord:

" What is your best—your *very best*—ale a glass ? " For it was a special occasion. I don't know what. It may have been my birthday.

" Twopence-halfpenny," says the landlord, " is the price of the Genuine Stunning ale."

" Then," says I, producing the money, " just draw me a glass of the Genuine Stunning, if you please, with a good head to it."

The landlord looked at me in return over the bar, from head to foot, with a strange smile on his face; and instead of drawing the beer, looked round the screen and said something to his wife. She came out from behind it, with her work in her hand, and joined him in surveying me. Here we stand, all three, before me now. The landlord in his shirt-sleeves, leaning against the bar window-frame; his wife looking over the little half-door and I, in some confusion, looking up at them from outside the partition. They asked me a good many questions; as, what my name was, how old I was, where I lived, how I was employed, and how I came there. To all of which, that I might commit nobody, I invented, I am afraid, appropriate answers. They served me with the ale, though I suspect it was not the Genuine Stunning: and the landlord's wife, opening the little half-door of the bar, and bending down, gave me my money back, and gave me a kiss that was half admiring, and half compassionate, but all womanly and good, I am sure.

I know I do not exaggerate, unconsciously and unintentionally, the scantiness of my resources or the difficulties of my life. I know that if a shilling were given me by Mr. Quinion at any time, I spent it in a dinner or a tea. I know that I worked from morning until night, with common men and boys, a shabby child. I know that I lounged about the streets, insufficiently and unsatisfactorily fed. I know that, but for the mercy of God, I might easily have been, for any care that was taken of me, a little robber or a little vagabond.

Yet I had some station at Murdstone and Grinby's too. Besides that Mr. Quinion did what a careless man so occupied, and dealing with a thing so anomalous, could, to treat me as one upon a different footing from the rest, I never said, to man or boy, how it was that I came to be there, or gave the least indication of being sorry that I was there. That I suffered in secret, and that I suffered exquisitely, no one ever knew but I. How much I suffered, it is, as I have said already, utterly beyond my power to tell. But I kept my own counsel, and I did my work. I knew from the first, that, if I could not do my work as well as any of the rest, I could not hold myself above slight and contempt. I soon became at least as expeditious and as skilful as either of the other boys. Though perfectly familiar with them, my conduct and manner were different enough from theirs to place a space between us. They and the men generally spoke of me as " the little gent," or " the young Suffolker." A certain man named Gregory, who was foreman of the packers, and another named Tipp, who was the carman, and wore a red jacket, used to address me sometimes as " David": but I think it was mostly when we were very confidential, and when I had made some efforts to entertain them, over our work, with some results of the old readings; which were fast perishing out of my remembrance. Mealy Potatoes uprose once, and rebelled against my being so distinguished; but Mick Walker settled him in no time.

My rescue from this kind of existence I considered quite hopeless, and abandoned, as such, altogether. I am solemnly convinced that I never for one hour was reconciled to it, or was otherwise than miserably unhappy; but I bore it; and even to Peggotty, partly for the love of her and partly for shame, never in any letter (though many passed between us) revealed the truth.

Mr. Micawber's difficulties were an addition to the distressed state of my mind. In my forlorn state I became quite attached to the family, and used to walk about, busy with Mrs. Micawber's calculations of ways and means, and heavy with the weight of Mr. Micawber's debts. On a Saturday night, which was my grand treat,—partly because it was a great thing to walk home with six or seven shillings in my pocket, looking into the shops and thinking what such a sum would buy, and partly because I went home early,—Mrs. Micawber would make the most heart-rending confidences to me; also on a Sunday morning, when I mixed the portion of tea or coffee I had bought over-night, in a little shaving-pot, and sat late at my breakfast. It was nothing at all unusual for Mr. Micawber to sob violently at the beginning of one of these Saturday night conversations, and sing about Jack's delight being his lovely Nan, towards the end of it. I have known him come home to supper with a flood of tears, and a declaration that nothing was now left but a jail; and go to bed making a calculation of the expense of putting bow-windows to the house, " in case anything turned up," which was his favourite expression. And Mrs. Micawber was just the same.

A curious equality of friendship, originating, I suppose, in our respective circumstances, sprung up between me and these people, notwithstanding the ludicrous disparity in our years. But I never allowed myself to be prevailed upon to accept any invitation to eat and drink with them out of their stock (knowing that they got on badly with the butcher and baker, and had often not too much for themselves), until Mrs. Micawber took me into her entire confidence. This she did one evening as follows:

" Master Copperfield," said Mrs. Micawber, " I make no stranger of you, and therefore do not hesitate to say that Mr. Micawber's difficulties are coming to a crisis."

It made me very miserable to hear it, and I looked at Mrs. Micawber's red eyes with the utmost sympathy.

" With the exception of the heel of a Dutch cheese—which is not adapted to the wants of a young family "—said Mrs. Micawber, " there is really not a scrap of anything in the larder. I was accustomed to speak of the larder when I lived with papa and mama, and I use the word almost unconsciously. What I mean to express is, that there is nothing to eat in the house."

" Dear me! " I said, in great concern.

I had two or three shillings of my week's money in my pocket —from which I presume that it must have been on a Wednesday night when we held this conversation—and I hastily produced them, and with heartfelt emotion begged Mrs. Micawber to accept of them as a loan. But that lady, kissing me, and making me put them back in my pocket, replied that she couldn't think of it.

" No, my dear Master Copperfield," said she, " far be it from my thoughts! But you have a discretion beyond your years, and can render me another kind of service, if you will; and a service I will thankfully accept of."

I begged Mrs. Micawber to name it.

" I have parted with the plate myself," said Mrs. Micawber. " Six tea, two salt, and a pair of sugars, I have at different times borrowed money on, in secret, with my own hands. But the twins are a great tie; and to me, with my recollections of papa and mama, these transactions are very painful. There are still a few trifles that we could part with. Mr. Micawber's feelings would never allow *him* to dispose of them; and Clickett "—this was the girl from the workhouse—" being of a vulgar mind, would take painful liberties if so much confidence was reposed in her. Master Copperfield, if I might ask you——"

I understood Mrs. Micawber now, and begged her to make use of me to any extent. I began to dispose of the more portable articles of property that very evening; and went out on a similar expedition almost every morning, before I went to Murdstone and Grinby's.

Mr. Micawber had a few books on a little chiffonier, which he called the library; and those went first. I carried them, one after another, to a bookstall in the City Road—one part of which, near our house, was almost all bookstalls and bird-shops then—and sold them for whatever they would bring. The keeper of this bookstall, who lived in a little house behind it, used to get tipsy every night, and to be violently scolded by his wife every morning. More than once, when I went there early, I had audience of him in a turn-up bedstead, with a cut in his forehead or a black eye, bearing witness to his excesses over-night (I am afraid he was quarrelsome in his drink), and he with a shaking hand, endeavouring to find the needful shillings in one or other of the pockets of his clothes, which lay upon the floor, while his wife, with a baby in her arms and her shoes down at heel, never left off rating him. Sometimes he had lost his money, and then he would ask me to call again; but his wife had always got some—had taken his, I dare say, while he was drunk—and secretly completed the bargain on the stairs, as we went down together.

At the pawnbroker's shop, too, I began to be very well known. The principal gentleman who officiated behind the counter, took a good deal of notice of me; and often got me, I recollect, to decline a Latin noun or adjective, or to conjugate a Latin verb, in his ear, while he transacted my business. After all these occasions Mrs. Micawber made a little treat, which was generally a supper; and there was a peculiar relish in these meals which I well remember.

At last Mr. Micawber's difficulties came to a crisis, and he was arrested early one morning, and carried over to the King's Bench Prison in the Borough. He told me, as he went out of the house, that the God of day had now gone down upon him—and I really thought his heart was broken and mine too. But I heard, afterwards, that he was seen to play a lively game at skittles, before noon.

On the first Sunday after he was taken there, I was to go and see him, and have dinner with him. I was to ask my way to such a place, and just short of that place I should see such another place, and just short of that I should see a yard, which

I was to cross, and keep straight on until a saw a turnkey. All this I did; and when at last I did see a turnkey (poor little fellow that I was!), and thought how, when Roderick Random was in a debtors' prison, there was a man there with nothing on him but an old rug, the turnkey swam before my dimmed eyes and my beating heart.

Mr. Micawber was waiting for me within the gate, and we went up to his room top story but one), and cried very much. He solemnly conjured me, I remember, to take warning by his fate; and to observe that if a man had twenty pounds a year for his income, and spent nineteen pounds nineteen shillings and sixpence, he would be happy, but that if he spent twenty pounds one he would be miserable. After which he borrowed a shilling of me for porter, gave me a written order on Mrs. Micawber for the amount, and put away his pocket-handkerchief, and cheered up.

We sat before a little fire, with two bricks put within the rusted grate, one on each side, to prevent its burning too many coals; until another debtor, who shared the room with Mr. Micawber, came in from the bakehouse with the loin of mutton which was our joint-stock repast. Then I was sent up to "Captain Hopkins" in the room overhead, with Mr. Micawber's compliments, and I was his young friend, and would Captain Hopkins lend me a knife and fork.

Captain Hopkins lent me the knife and fork, with his compliments to Mr. Micawber. There was a very dirty lady in his little room, and two wan girls, his daughters, with shock heads of hair. I thought it was better to borrow Captain Hopkins's knife and fork, than Captain Hopkins's comb. The Captain himself was in the last extremity of shabbiness, with large whiskers, and an old, old brown greatcoat, with no other coat below it. I saw his bed rolled up in a corner; and what plates and dishes and pots he had, on a shelf; and I divined (God knows how) that though the two girls with the shock heads of hair were Captain Hopkins's children, the dirty lady was not married to Captain Hopkins. My timid station on his threshold was not occupied more than a couple of minutes at most; but I came down again with all this in my knowledge, as surely as the knife and fork were in my hand.

There was something gipsy-like and agreeable in the dinner, after all. I took back Captain Hopkins's knife and fork early in the afternoon, and went home to comfort Mrs. Micawber with an account of my visit. She fainted when she saw me return, and made a little jug of egg-hot afterwards to console us while we talked it over.

I don't know how the household furniture came to be sold for the family benefit, or who sold it, except that *I* did not. Sold it was, however, and carried away in a van; except the bed, a few chairs, and the kitchen-table. With these possessions we encamped, as it were, in the two parlours of the emptied house in Windsor Terrace; Mrs. Micawber, the children, the Orfling, and myself; and lived in those rooms night and day. I have no idea for how long, though it seems to me for a long time. At last Mrs. Micawber resolved to move into the prison, where Mr. Micawber had now secured a room to himself. So I took the key of the house to the landlord, who was very glad to get it; and the beds were sent over to the King's Bench, except mine, for which a little room was hired outside the walls in the neighbourhood of that Institution, very much to my satisfaction since the Micawbers and I had become too used to one another, in our troubles, to part. The Orfling was likewise accommodated with an inexpensive lodging in the same neighbourhood. Mine was a quiet back-garret with a sloping roof, commanding a pleasant prospect of a timberyard, and when I took possession of it, with the reflection that Mr. Micawber's troubles had come to a crisis at last, I thought it quite a paradise.

All this time I was working at Murdstone and Grinby's in the same common way, and with the same common companions, and with the same sense of unmerited degradation as at first. But I never, happily for me no doubt, made a single acquaintance, or spoke to any of the many boys whom I saw daily in going to the warehouse, in coming from it, and in prowling about the streets at meal-times. I led the same secretly unhappy life; but I led it in the same lonely, self-reliant manner. The only changes I am conscious of are, firstly, that I had grown more shabby, and secondly, that I was now relieved of much of the weight of Mr. and Mrs. Micawber's cares; for some relatives or friends had engaged to help them at their present pass, and they lived more comfortably in the prison than they had lived for a long while out of it. I used to breakfast with them now, in virtue of some arrangement, of which I have forgotten the details. I forget, too, at what hour the gates were opened in the morning, admitting of my going in; but I know that I was often up at six o'clock, and that my favourite lounging-place in the interval was old London Bridge, where I was wont to sit in one of the stone recesses, watching the people going by, or to look over the balustrades at the sun shining in the water, and lighting up the golden flame on the top of the Monument. The Orfling met me here sometimes, to be told some astonishing fictions respecting the wharves and the Tower; of which I can say no more than that I hope I believed them myself. In the evening I used to go back to the prison, and walk up and down the parade with Mr. Micawber; or play casino with Mrs. Micawber, and hear reminiscences of her papa and mama. Whether Mr. Murdstone knew where I was, I am unable to say. I never told them at Murdstone and Grinby's.

Mr. Micawber's affairs, although past their crisis, were very much involved by reason of a certain "Deed," of which I used to hear a great deal, and which I suppose, now, to have been some former composition with his creditors, though I was so far from being clear about it then, that I am conscious of having confounded it with those demoniacal parchments which are held to have, once upon a time, obtained to a great extent in Germany. At last this document appeared to be got out of the way, somehow; at all events it ceased to be the rock ahead it had been; and Mrs. Micawber informed me that "her family" had decided that Mr. Micawber should apply for his release under the Insolvent Debtors' Act, which would set him free, she expected, in about six weeks.

"And then," said Mr. Micawber, who was present, "I have no doubt I shall, please Heaven, begin to be beforehand with the world, and to live in a perfectly new manner, if—in short, if anything turns up."

By way of going in for anything that might be on the cards, I call to mind that Mr. Micawber, about this time, composed a petition to the House of Commons, praying for an alteration in the law of imprisonment for debt. I set down this remembrance here, because it is an instance to myself of the manner in which I fitted my old books to my altered life, and made stories for myself, out of the streets, and out of men and women; and how some main points in the character I shall unconsciously develop, I suppose, in writing my life, were gradually forming all this while.

There was a club in the prison, in which Mr. Micawber, as a gentleman, was a great authority. Mr. Micawber had stated his idea of this petition to the club, and the club had strongly approved of the same. Wherefore Mr. Micawber (who was a thoroughly good-natured man, and as active a creature about everything but his own affairs as ever existed, and never so happy as when he was busy about something that could never be of any profit to him) set to work at the petition, invented it, engrossed it on an immense sheet of paper, spread it out on a table, and appointed a time for all the club, and all within the walls if they chose, to come up to his room and sign it.

When I heard of this approaching ceremony, I was so anxious to see them all come in, one after another, though I knew the greater part of them already, and they me, that I got an hour's leave of absence from Murdstone and Grinby's, and established myself in a corner for that purpose. As many of the principal members of the club as could be got into the small room without filling it, supported Mr. Micawber in front of the petition, while my old friend Captain Hopkins (who had washed himself, to do honour to so solemn an occasion) stationed himself close to it, to read it to all who were unacquainted with its contents. The door was then thrown open, and the general population began to come in, in a long file: several waiting outside, while one entered, affixed his signature, and went out. To everybody in succession, Captain Hopkins said: "Have you read it?"—"No." "Would you like to hear it read?" If he weakly showed the least disposition to hear it, Captain Hopkins, in a loud sonorous voice, gave him every word of it. The Captain would have read it twenty thousand times, if twenty thousand people would have heard him, one by one. I remember a certain luscious roll he gave to such phrases as "The people's representatives in Parliament assembled," "Your petitioners therefore humbly approach your honourable house," "His gracious Majesty's unfortunate subjects," as if the words were something real in his mouth, and delicious to taste; Mr. Micawber, meanwhile, listening with a little of an author's vanity, and contemplating (not severely) the spikes on the opposite wall.

As I walked to and fro daily between Southwark and Blackfriars, and lounged about at meal-times in obscure streets, the stones of which may, for anything I know, be worn at this moment by my childish feet, I wonder how many of these people were wanting in the crowd that used to come filing before me in review again, to the echo of Captain Hopkins's voice! When my thoughts go back now, to that slow agony of my youth, I wonder how much of the histories I invented for such people hangs like a mist of fancy over well-remembered facts! When I tread the old ground, I do not wonder that I seem to see and pity, going on before me, an innocent romantic boy, making his imaginative world out of such strange experiences and sordid things.

12

LIKING LIFE ON MY OWN ACCOUNT NO BETTER, I FORM A GREAT RESOLUTION

IN DUE TIME, MR. MICAWBER'S PETITION WAS RIPE for hearing; and that gentleman was ordered to be discharged under the Act, to my great joy. His creditors were not implacable; and Mrs. Micawber informed me that even the revengeful bootmaker had declared in open court that he bore him no malice, but that when money was owing to him he liked to be paid. He said he thought it was human nature.

Mr. Micawber returned to the King's Bench when his case was over, as some fees were to be settled, and some formalities observed, before he could be actually released. The club received him with transport, and held an harmonic meeting that evening in his honour; while Mrs. Micawber and I had a lamb's fry in private, surrounded by the sleeping family.

" On such an occasion I will give you, Master Copperfield," said Mrs. Micawber, " in a little more flip," for we had been having some already, " the memory of my papa and mama."

" Are they dead, ma'am ? " I inquired, after drinking the toast in a wine-glass.

" My mama departed this life," said Mrs. Micawber, " before Mr. Micawber's difficulties commenced, or at least before they became pressing. My papa lived to bail Mr. Micawber several times, and then expired, regretted by a numerous circle."

Mrs. Micawber shook her head, and dropped a pious tear upon the twin who happened to be in hand.

As I could hardly hope for a more favourable opportunity of putting a question in which I had a near interest, I said to Mrs. Micawber:

" May I ask, ma'am, what you and Mr. Micawber intend to do, now that Mr. Micawber is out of his difficulties, and at liberty? Have you settled yet? "

" My family " said Mrs. Micawber, who always said those two words with an air, though I never could discover who came under the denomination, " my family are of opinion that Mr.

Micawber should quit London, and exert his talents in the country. Mr. Micawber is a man of great talent, Master Copperfield."

I said I was sure of that.

"Of great talent," repeated Mrs. Micawber. "My family are of opinion, that, with a little interest, something might be done for a man of his ability in the Custom House. The influence of my family being local, it is their wish that Mr. Micawber should go down to Plymouth. They think it indispensable that he should be upon the spot."

"That he may be ready?" I suggested.

"Exactly," returned Mrs. Micawber. "That he may be ready, in case of anything turning up."

"And do you go too, ma'am?"

The events of the day, in combination with the twins, if not with the flip, had made Mrs. Micawber hysterical, and she shed tears as she replied:

"I never will desert Mr. Micawber. Mr. Micawber may have concealed his difficulties from me in the first instance, but his sanguine temper may have led him to expect that he would overcome them. The pearl necklace and bracelets which I inherited from mama, have been disposed of for less than half their value; and the set of coral, which was the wedding gift of my papa, has been actually thrown away for nothing. But I never will desert Mr. Micawber. No!" cried Mrs. Micawber, more affected than before, "I never will do it! It's of no use asking me!"

I felt quite uncomfortable—as if Mrs. Micawber supposed I had asked her to do anything of the sort!—and sat looking at her in alarm.

"Mr. Micawber has his faults. I do not deny that he is improvident. I do not deny that he has kept me in the dark as to his resources and his liabilities both," she went on, looking at the wall; "but I never will desert Mr. Micawber!"

Mrs. Micawber having now raised her voice into a perfect scream, I was so frightened that I ran off to the club-room, and disturbed Mr. Micawber in the act of presiding at a long table, and leading the chorus of

Gee up, Dobbin,
Gee ho, Dobbin,
Gee up, Dobbin,
Gee up, and gee ho—o—o—!

—with the tidings that Mrs. Micawber was in an alarming state, upon which he immediately burst into tears, and came away with me with his waistcoat full of the heads and tails of shrimps, of which he had been partaking.

" Emma, my angel! " cried Mr. Micawber, running into the room; " what is the matter? "

" I never will desert you, Micawber! " she exclaimed.

" My life! " said Mr. Micawber, taking her in his arms. " I am perfectly aware of it."

" He is the parent of my children! He is the father of my twins! He is the husband of my affections," cried Mrs. Micawber, struggling; " and I ne—ver—will—desert Mr. Micawber! "

Mr. Micawber was so deeply affected by this proof of her devotion (as to me, I was dissolved in tears), that he hung over her in a passionate manner, imploring her to look up, and to be calm. But the more he asked Mrs. Micawber to look up, the more she fixed her eyes on nothing; and the more he asked her to compose herself, the more she wouldn't. Consequently Mr. Micawber was soon so overcome, that he mingled his tears with hers and mine; until he begged me to do him the favour of taking a chair on the staircase, while he got her into bed. I would have taken my leave for the night, but he would not hear of my doing that until the strangers' bell should ring. So I sat at the staircase window, until he came out with another chair and joined me.

" How is Mrs. Micawber now, sir? " I said.

" Very low," said Mr. Micawber, shaking his head; " reaction. Ah, this has been a dreadful day! We stand alone now—everything is gone from us! "

Mr. Micawber pressed my hand, and groaned, and afterwards shed tears. I was greatly touched, and disappointed too, for I had expected that we should be quite gay on this happy and long-looked-for occasion. But Mr. and Mrs. Micawber were so used to their old difficulties, I think, that they felt quite ship-wrecked when they came to consider that they were released from them. All their elasticity was departed, and I never saw them half so wretched as on this night; insomuch that when the bell rang, and Mr. Micawber walked with me to the lodge, and parted from me there with a blessing, I felt quite afraid to leave him by himself, he was so profoundly miserable.

But through all the confusion and lowness of spirits in which we had been, so unexpectedly to me, involved, I plainly discerned that Mr. and Mrs. Micawber and their family were going away from London, and that a parting between us was near at hand. It was in my walk home that night, and in the sleepless hours which followed when I lay in bed, that the thought first occurred to me—though I don't know how it came into my head—which afterwards shaped itself into a settled resolution.

I had grown to be so accustomed to the Micawbers, and had been so intimate with them in their distresses, and was so utterly friendless without them, that the prospect of being thrown upon some new shift for a lodging, and going once more among unknown people, was like being that moment turned adrift into my present life, with such a knowledge of it ready made as experience had given me. All the sensitive feelings it wounded so cruelly, all the shame and misery it kept alive within my breast, became more poignant as I thought of this; and I determined that the life was unendurable.

That there was no hope of escape from it, unless the escape was my own act, I knew quite well. I rarely heard from Miss Murdstone, and never from Mr. Murdstone; but two or three parcels of made or mended clothes had come up for me, consigned to Mr. Quinion, and in each there was a scrap of paper to the effect that J. M. trusted D.C. was applying himself to business, and devoting himself wholly to his duties—not the least hint of my ever being anything else than the common drudge into which I was fast settling down.

The very next day showed me, while my mind was in the first agitation of what it had conceived, that Mrs. Micawber had not spoken of their going away without warrant. They took a lodging in the house where I lived, for a week; at the expiration of which time they were to start for Plymouth. Mr. Micawber himself came down to the counting-house, in the afternoon, to tell Mr. Quinion that he must relinquish me on the day of his departure, and to give me a high character, which I am sure I deserved. And Mr. Quinion, calling in Tipp the carman, who was a married man, and had a room to let, quartered me prospectively on him—by our mutual consent, as he had every reason to think; for I said nothing, though my resolution was now taken.

I passed my evenings with Mr. and Mrs. Micawber, during the remaining term of our residence under the same roof; and I think we became fonder of one another as the time went on. On the last Sunday, they invited me to dinner; and we had a loin of pork and apple sauce, and a pudding. I had bought a spotted wooden horse over-night as a parting gift to little Wilkins Micawber—that was the boy—and a doll for little Emma. I had also bestowed a shilling on the Orfling, who was about to be disbanded.

We had a very pleasant day, though we were all in a tender state about our approaching separation.

" I shall never, Master Copperfield," said Mrs. Micawber, " revert to the period when Mr. Micawber was in difficulties, without thinking of you. Your conduct has always been of the most delicate and obliging description. You have never been a lodger. You have been a friend."

" My dear," said Mr. Micawber; " Copperfield," for so he had been accustomed to call me of late, " has a heart to feel for the distresses of his fellow-creatures when they are behind a cloud, and a head to plan, and a hand to—in short, a general ability to dispose of such available property as could be made away with."

I expressed my sense of this commendation, and said I was very sorry we were going to lose one another.

" My dear young friend," said Mr. Micawber, " I am older than you; a man of some experience in life, and—and of some experience, in short, in difficulties, generally speaking. At present, and until something turns up (which I am, I may say, hourly expecting), I have nothing to bestow but advice. Still my advice is so far worth taking that—in short, that I have never taken it myself, and am the "—here Mr. Micawber, who had been beaming and smiling, all over his head and face, up to the present moment, checked himself and frowned—" the miserable wretch you behold."

" My dear Micawber! " urged his wife.

" I say," returned Mr. Micawber, quite forgetting himself, and smiling again, " the miserable wretch you behold. My advice is, never do to-morrow what you can do to-day. Procrastination is the thief of time. Collar him! "

" My poor papa's maxim," Mrs. Micawber observed.

" My dear," said Mr. Micawber, " your papa was very well in his way, and Heaven forbid that I should disparage him. Take him for all in all, we ne'er shall—in short, make the acquaintance, probably, of anybody else possessing, at his time of life, the same legs for gaiters; and able to read the same description of print, without spectacles. But he applied that maxim to our marriage, my dear; and that was so far prematurely entered into, in consequence, that I never recovered the expense."

Mr. Micawber looked aside at Mrs. Micawber, and added: " Not that I am sorry for it. Quite the contrary, my love." After which he was grave for a minute or so.

" My other piece of advice, Copperfield," said Mr. Micawber, " you know. Annual income twenty pounds, annual expenditure nineteen and six, result happiness. Annual income twenty pounds, annual expenditure twenty pounds ought and six, result misery. The blossom is blighted, the leaf is withered, the God of day goes down upon the dreary scene, and—and in short you are for ever floored. As I am! "

To make his example the more impressive, Mr. Micawber drank a glass of punch with an air of great enjoyment and satisfaction, and whistled the College Hornpipe.

I did not fail to assure him that I would store these precepts in my mind, though indeed I had no need to do so, for, at the time, they affected me visibly. Next morning I met the whole family at the coach-office, and saw them, with a desolate heart, take their places outside, at the back.

" Master Copperfield," said Mrs. Micawber, " God bless you! I never can forget all that, you know, and I never would if I could."

" Copperfield," said Mr. Micawber, " farewell! Every happiness and prosperity! If, in the progress of revolving years, I could persuade myself that my blighted destiny had been a warning to you, I should feel that I had not occupied another man's place in existence altogether in vain. In case of anything turning up (of which I am rather confident), I shall be extremely happy if it should be in my power to improve your prospects."

I think, as Mrs. Micawber sat at the back of the coach, with the children, and I stood in the road looking wistfully at them, a mist cleared from her eyes, and she saw what a little creature I really was. I think so, because she beckoned to me to climb up, with quite a new and motherly expression in her face, and put her arm round my neck, and gave me just such a kiss as she might have given to her own boy. I had barely time to get down again before the coach started, and I could hardly see the family for the handkerchiefs they waved. It was gone in a minute. The Orfling and I stood looking vacantly at each other in the middle of the road, and then shook hands and said good-bye; she going back, I suppose, to St. Luke's work-house, as I went to begin my weary day at Murdstone and Grinby's.

But with no intention of passing many more weary days there. No. I had resolved to run away.—To go, by some means or other, down into the country, to the only relation I had in the world, and tell my story to my aunt, Miss Betsey.

I have already observed that I don't know how this desperate idea came into my brain. But, once there, it remained there; and hardened into a purpose than which I have never entertained a more determined purpose in my life. I am far from sure that I believed there was anything hopeful in it, but my mind was thoroughly made up that it must be carried into execution.

Again, and again, and a hundred times again, since the night when the thought had first occurred to me and banished sleep, I had gone over that old story of my poor mother's about my birth, which it had been one of my great delights in the old time to hear her tell, and which I knew by heart. My aunt walked into that story, and walked out of it, a dread and awful personage; but there was one little trait in her behaviour which I liked to dwell on, and which gave me some faint shadow of encouragement. I could not forget how my mother had thought that she felt her touch her pretty hair with no ungentle hand; and though it might have been altogether my mother's fancy, and might have had no foundation whatever in fact, I made a little picture, out of it, of my terrible aunt relenting towards the girlish beauty that I recollect so well and loved so much, which softened the whole narrative. It is very possible that it had been in my mind a long time, and had gradually engendered my determination.

As I did not even know where Miss Betsy lived, I wrote a long letter to Peggotty, and asked her, incidentally, if she remembered; pretending that I had heard of such a lady living at a certain place I named at random, and had a curiosity to know if it were the same. In the course of that letter, I told Peggotty that I had a particular occasion for half a guinea; and that if she could lend me that sum until I could repay it, I should be very much obliged to her, and would tell her afterwards what I had wanted it for.

Peggotty's answer soon arrived, and was, as usual, full of affectionate devotion. She enclosed the half-guinea (I was afraid she must have had a world of trouble to get it out of Mr. Barkis's box), and told me that Miss Betsey lived near Dover, but whether at Dover itself, at Hythe, Sandgate, or Folkestone, she could not say. One of our men, however, informing me on my asking him about these places, that they were all close together, I deemed this enough for my object, and resolved to set out at the end of that week.

Being a very honest little creature, and unwilling to disgrace the memory I was going to leave behind me at Murdstone and Grinby's, I considered myself bound to remain until Saturday night; and, as I had been paid a week's wages in advance when I first came there, not to present myself in the counting-house at the usual hour, to receive my stipend. For this express reason I had borrowed the half-guinea, that I might not be without a fund for my travelling expenses. Accordingly, when the Saturday night came, and we were all waiting in the warehouse to be paid, and

Tipp the carman, who always took precedence, went in first to draw his money, I shook Mick Walker by the hand; asked him, when it came to his turn to be paid, to say to Mr. Quinion that I had gone to move my box to Tipp's; and, bidding a last good-night to Mealy Potatoes, ran away.

My box was at my old lodging over the water, and I had written a direction for it on the back of one of our address cards that we nailed on the casks: " Master David, to be left till called for, at the Coach Office, Dover." This I had in my pocket ready to put on the box, after I should have got it out of the house; and as I went towards my lodging, I looked about me for some one who would help me to carry it to the booking-office.

There was a long-legged young man, with a very little empty donkey-cart, standing near the Obelisk, in the Blackfriars Road, whose eye I caught as I was going by, and who, addressing me as " Sixpenn'orth of bad ha'pence," hoped " I should know him agin to swear to "—an allusion, I have no doubt, to my staring at him. I stopped to assure him that I had not done so in bad manners, but uncertain whether he might or might not like a job.

" Wot job? " said the long-legged young man.

" To move a box," I answered.

" Wot box? " said the long-legged young man.

I told him mine, which was down that street there, and which I wanted him to take to the Dover coach-office for sixpence.

" Done with you for a tanner! " said the long-legged young man, and directly got upon his cart, which was nothing but a large wooden tray on wheels, and rattled away at such a rate, that it was as much as I could do to keep pace with the donkey.

There was a defiant manner about this young man, and particularly about the way in which he chewed straw as he spoke to me, that I did not much like; as the bargain was made, however, I took him up-stairs to the room I was leaving, and we brought the box down, and put it on his cart. Now, I was unwilling to put the direction-card on there, lest any of my landlord's family should fathom what I was doing, and detain me; so I said to the young man that I would be glad if he would stop for a minute, when he came to the dead-wall of the King's Bench prison. The words were no sooner out of my mouth, than he rattled away as if he, my box, the cart, and the donkey, were all equally mad; and I was quite out of breath with running and calling after him, when I caught him at the place appointed.

Being much flushed and excited, I tumbled my half-guinea out of my pocket in pulling the card out. I put it in my mouth for safety, and though my hands trembled a good deal, had just tied the card on very much to my satisfaction, when I felt myself violently, chucked under the chin by the long-legged young man, and saw my half-guinea fly out of my mouth into his hand.

" Wot! " said the young man, seizing me by my jacket collar, with a frightful grin. " This is a pollis case, is it? You're a-going to bolt, are you? Come to the pollis, you young warmin, come to the pollis! "

" You give me my money back, if you please," said I, very much frightened; " and leave me alone."

" Come to the pollis! " said the young man. " You shall prove it yourn to the pollis."

" Give me my box and money, will you? " I cried, bursting into tears.

The young man still replied: " Come to the pollis! " and was dragging me against the donkey in a violent manner, as if there were any affinity between that animal and a magistrate, when he changed his mind, jumped into the cart, sat upon my box, and, exclaiming that he would drive to the pollis straight, rattled away harder than ever.

I ran after him as fast as I could, but I had no breath to call out with, and should not have dared to call out, now, if I had. I narrowly escaped being run over, twenty times at least, in half a mile. Now I lost him, now I saw him, now I lost him, now I was cut at with a whip, now shouted at, now down in the mud, now up again, now running into somebody's arms, now running headlong at a post. At length, confused by fright and heat, and doubting whether half London might not by this time be turning out for my apprehension, I left the young man to go where he would with my box and money; and, panting and crying, but never stopping, faced about for Greenwich, which I had understood was on the Dover Road: taking very little more out of the world, towards the retreat of my aunt, Miss Betsey, than I had brought into it, on the night when my arrival gave her so much umbrage.

13

THE SEQUEL OF MY RESOLUTION

FOR ANYTHING I KNOW, I MAY HAVE HAD SOME wild idea of running all the way to Dover, when I gave up the pursuit of the young man with the donkey-cart, and started for Greenwich. My scattered senses were soon collected as to that point, if I had; for I came to a stop in the Kent Road, at a terrace with a piece of water before it, and a great foolish image in the middle, blowing a dry shell. Here I sat down on a doorstep, quite spent and exhausted with the efforts I had already made, and with hardly breath enough to cry for the loss of my box and half-guinea.

It was by this time dark; I heard the clocks strike ten, as I sat resting. But it was a summer night, fortunately, and fine weather. When I had recovered my breath, and had got rid of a stifling sensation in my throat, I rose up and went on. In the midst of my distress, I had no notion of going back. I doubt if I should have had any, though there had been a Swiss snow-drift in the Kent Road.

But my standing, possessed of only three-halfpence in the world (and I am sure I wonder how *they* came to be left in my pocket on a Saturday night!) troubled me none the less because I went on. I began to picture to myself, as a scrap of newspaper intelligence, my being found dead in a day or two, under some hedge; and I trudged on miserably, though as fast as I could, until I happened to pass a little shop, where it was written up that ladies' and gentlemen's wardrobes were bought, and that the best price was given for rags, bones, and kitchen-stuff. The master of this shop was sitting at the door in his shirt-sleeves, smoking; and as there were a great many coats and pairs of trousers dangling from the low ceiling, and only two feeble candles burning inside to show what they were, I fancied that he looked like a man of a revengeful disposition, who had hung all his enemies, and was enjoying himself.

My late experiences with Mr. and Mrs. Micawber suggested to me that here might be a means of keeping off the wolf for a little while. I went up the next bye-street, took off my waistcoat, rolled it neatly under my arm, and came back to the shop-door. " If you please, sir," I said, " I am to sell this for a fair price."

Mr. Dolloby—Dolloby was the name over the shop-door, at least—took the waistcoat, stood his pipe on its head against the door-post, went into the shop, followed by me, snuffed the two candles with his fingers, spread the waistcoat on the counter, and looked at it there, held it up against the light, and looked at it there, and ultimately said:

" What do you call a price, now, for this here little weskit? "

" Oh! you know best, sir," I returned, modestly.

" I can't be buyer and seller too," said Mr. Dolloby. " Put a price on this here little weskit."

" Would eighteenpence be? "—I hinted, after some hesitation.

Mr. Dolloby rolled it up again, and gave it me back. " I should rob my family," he said, " if I was to offer ninepence for it."

This was a disagreeable way of putting the business; because it imposed upon me, a perfect stranger, the unpleasantness of asking Mr. Dolloby to rob his family on my account. My circumstances being so very pressing, however, I said I would take ninepence for it, if he pleased. Mr. Dolloby, not without some grumbling, gave ninepence. I wished him good-night, and walked out of the shop, the richer by that sum, and the poorer by a waistcoat. But when I buttoned my jacket, that was not much.

Indeed, I foresaw pretty clearly that my jacket would go next and that I should have to make the best of my way to Dover in a shirt and a pair of trousers, and might deem myself lucky if I got there even in that trim. But my mind did not run so much on, this as might be supposed. Beyond a general impression of the distance before me, and of the young man with the donkey-cart having used me cruelly, I think I had no very urgent sense of my difficulties when I once again set off with my ninepence in my pocket.

A plan had occurred to me for passing the night, which I was going to carry into execution. This was, to lie behind the wall at the back of my old school, in a corner where there used to be a haystack. I imagined it would be a kind of company to have the boys, and the bedroom where I used to tell the stories, so near me: although the boys would know nothing of my being there, and the bedroom would yield me no shelter.

I had had a hard day's work, and was pretty well jaded when I came climbing out, at last, upon the level of Blackheath. It cost me some trouble to find out Salem House; but I found it, and I found a haystack in the corner, and I lay down by it; having first walked round the wall, and looked up at the windows, and seen that all was dark and silent within. Never shall I forget the lonely sensation of first lying down, without a roof above my head!

Sleep came upon me as it came on many other outcasts, against whom house-doors were locked, and house-dogs barked, that night—and I dreamed of lying on my old school-bed, talking to the boys in my room; and found myself sitting upright, with Steerforth's name upon my lips, looking wildly at the stars that were glistening and glimmering above me. When I remembered where I was at that untimely hour, a feeling stole upon me that made me get up, afraid of I don't know what, and walk about. But the fainter glimmering of the stars, and the pale light in the sky where the day was coming, reassured me: and my eyes being very heavy, I lay down again, and slept—though with a knowledge in my sleep that it was cold—until the warm beams of the sun, and the ringing of the getting-up bell at Salem House, awoke me. If I could have hoped that Steerforth was there, I would have lurked about until he came out alone; but I knew he must have left long since. Traddles still remained, perhaps, but it was very doubtful; and I had not sufficient confidence in his discretion or good luck, however strong my reliance was on his good-nature, to wish to trust him with my situation. So I crept away from the wall as Mr. Creakle's boys were getting up, and struck into the long dusty track which I had first known to be the Dover Road when I was one of them, and when I little expected that any eyes would ever see me the wayfarer I was now, upon it.

What a different Sunday morning from the old Sunday morning at Yarmouth! In due time I heard the church-bells ringing, as I plodded on; and I met people who were going to church; and I passed a church or two where the congregation were inside, and the sound of singing came out into the sunshine, while the beadle sat and cooled himself in the shade of the porch, or stood beneath the yew-tree, with his hand to his forehead, glowering at me going by. But the peace and rest of the old Sunday morning were on everything, except me. That was the difference. I felt quite wicked in my dirt and dust, with my tangled hair. But for the quiet picture I had conjured up, of my mother in her youth and beauty, weeping by the fire, and my aunt relenting to her, I hardly think I should have had the courage to go on until next day. But it always went before me, and I followed.

I got, that Sunday, through three-and-twenty miles on the straight road, though not very easily, for I was new to that kind of toil. I see myself, as evening closes in, coming over the bridge at Rochester, footsore and tired, and eating bread that I had bought for supper. One or two little houses, with the notice, "Lodgings for Travellers," hanging out, had tempted me; but I was afraid of spending the few pence I had, and was even more afraid of the vicious looks of the trampers I had met or overtaken. I sought no shelter, therefore, but the sky; and toiling into Chatham,—which, in that night's aspect, is a mere dream of chalk, and drawbridges, and mastless ships in a muddy river, roofed like Noah's arks,—crept, at last, upon a sort of grass-grown battery overhanging a lane, where a sentry was walking to and fro. Here I lay down, near a cannon; and, happy in the society of the sentry's footsteps, though he knew no more of my being above him than the boys at Salem House had known of my lying by the wall, slept soundly until morning.

Very stiff and sore of foot I was in the morning, and quite dazed by the beating of drums and marching of troops, which seemed to hem me in on every side when I went down towards the long narrow street. Feeling that I could go but a very little way that day, if I were to reserve any strength for getting to my journey's end, I resolved to make the sale of my jacket its principal business. Accordingly, I took the jacket off, that I might learn to do without it; and carrying it under my arm, began a tour of inspection of the various slop-shops.

It was a likely place to sell a jacket in; for the dealers in second-hand clothes were numerous, and were, generally speaking, on the look-out for customers at their shop-doors. But, as most of them had, hanging up among their stock, an officer's coat or two, epaulettes and all, I was rendered timid by the costly nature of their dealings, and walked about for a long time without offering my merchandise to any one.

This modesty of mine directed my attention to the marine-store shops, and such shops as Mr. Dolloby's, in preference to the regular dealers. At last I found one that I thought looked promising, at the corner of a dirty lane, ending in an inclosure full of stinging-nettles, against the palings of which some second-hand sailors' clothes, that seemed to have overflowed the shop, were fluttering among some cots, and rusty guns, and oilskin hats, and certain trays full of so many old rusty keys of so many sizes that they seemed various enough to open all the doors in the world.

Into this shop, which was low and small, and which was darkened rather than lighted by a little window, overhung with clothes, and was descended into by some steps, I went with a palpitating heart; which was not relieved when an ugly old man, with the lower part of his face all covered with a stubbly grey beard, rushed out of a dirty den behind it, and seized me by the hair of my head. He was a dreadful old man to look at, in a filthy flannel waistcoat, and smelling terribly of rum. His bedstead, covered with a tumbled and ragged piece of patchwork, was in the den he had come from, where another little window showed a prospect of more stinging-nettles, and a lame donkey.

" Oh, what do you want? " grinned this old man, in a fierce, monotonous whine. " Oh, my eyes and limbs, what do you want? Oh, my lungs and liver, what do you want? Oh, goroo, goroo! "

I was so much dismayed by these words, and particularly by the repetition of the last unknown one, which was a kind of rattle in his throat, that I could make no answer; hereupon the old man, still holding me by the hair, repeated:

" Oh, what do you want? Oh, my eyes and limbs, what do you want? Oh, my lungs and liver, what do you want? Oh, goroo! "—which he screwed out of himself, with an energy that made his eyes start in his head.

" I wanted to know," I said, trembling, " if you would buy a jacket."

" Oh, let's see the jacket! " cried the old man. " Oh, my heart on fire, show the jacket to us! Oh, my eyes and limbs, bring the jacket out! "

With that he took his trembling hands, which were like the claws of a great bird, out of my hair; and put on a pair of spectacles, not at all ornamental to his inflamed eyes.

" Oh, how much for the jacket? " cried the old man, after examining it. " Oh—goroo!—how much for the jacket? "

" Half-a-crown," I answered, recovering myself.

" Oh, my lungs and liver," cried the old man, " no! Oh, my eyes, no! Oh, my limbs, no! Eighteenpence. Goroo! "

Every time he uttered this ejaculation, his eyes seemed to be in danger of starting out; and every sentence he spoke, he delivered in a sort of tune, always exactly the same, and more like a gust of wind, which begins low, mounts up high, and falls again, than any other comparison I can find for it.

" Well," said I, glad to have closed the bargain, " I'll take eighteenpence."

" Oh, my liver! " cried the old man, throwing the jacket on a shelf. " Get out of the shop! Oh, my lungs, get out of the shop! Oh, my eyes and limbs—goroo!—don't ask for money; make it an exchange."

I never was so frightened in my life, before or since; but I told him humbly that I wanted money, and that nothing else was of any use to me, but that I would wait for it, as he desired, outside, and had no wish to hurry him. So I went outside, and sat down in the shade in a corner. And I sat there so many hours, that the shade became sunlight, and the sunlight became shade again, and still I sat there waiting for the money.

There never was such another drunken madman in that line of business, I hope. That he was well known in the neighbourhood, and enjoyed the reputation of having sold himself to the devil, I soon understood from the visit he received from the boys, who continually came skirmishing about the shop, shouting that legend, and calling to him to bring out his gold. " You ain't poor, you know, Charley, as you pretend. Bring out your gold. Bring out some of the gold you sold yourself to the devil for. Come! It's in the lining of the mattress, Charley. Rip it open and let's have some! " This, and many offers to lend him a knife for the purpose, exasperated him to such a degree, that the whole day was a succession of rushes on his part, and flights on the part of the boys. Sometimes in his rage he would take me for one of them, and come at me, mouthing as if he were going to tear me in pieces; then, remembering me, just in time, would dive into the shop, and lie upon his bed, as I thought from the sound of his voice, yelling in a frantic way, to his own windy tune, the " Death of Nelson "; with an Oh! before every line, and innumerable Goroos interspersed. As if this were not bad enough for me, the boys, connecting me with the establishment, on account of the patience and perseverence with which I sat outside, half-dressed, pelted me, and used me very ill all day.

He made many attempts to induce me to consent to an exchange; at one time coming out with a fishing-rod, at another with a fiddle, at another with a cocked hat, at another with a flute. But I resisted all these overtures, and sat there in desperation; each time asking him, with tears in my eyes, for my money or my jacket. At last he began to pay me in halfpence at a time; and was full two hours getting by easy stages to a shilling.

" Oh, my eyes and limbs! " he then cried, peeping hideously out of the shop, after a long pause, " will you go for twopence more? "

" I can't," I said; " I shall be starved."

" Oh, my lungs and liver, will you go for threepence? "

" I would go for nothing, if I could," I said, " but I want the money badly."

" Oh, go-roo! " (it is really impossible to express how he twisted this ejaculation out of himself, as he peeped round the doorpost at me, showing nothing but his crafty old head;) " will you go for fourpence? "

I was so faint and weary that I closed with this offer; and taking the money out of his claw, not without trembling, went away more hungry and thirsty than I had ever been, a little before sunset. But at an expense of threepence I soon refreshed myself completely; and, being in better spirits then, limped seven miles upon my road.

My bed at night was under another haystack, where I rested comfortably, after having washed my blistered feet in a stream, and dressed them as well as I was able, with some cool leaves. When I took the road again next morning, I found that it lay through a succession of hop-grounds and orchards. It was sufficiently late in the year for the orchards to be ruddy with ripe apples; and in a few places the hop-pickers were already at work. I thought it all extremely beautiful, and made up my mind to sleep among the hops that night: imagining some cheerful companionship in the long perspectives of poles, with the graceful leaves twining round them.

The trampers were worse than ever that day, and inspired me with a dread that is yet quite fresh in my mind. Some of them were most ferocious-looking ruffians, who stared at me as I went by; and stopped, perhaps, and called after me to come back and speak to them, and when I took to my heels, stoned me. I recollect one young fellow—a tinker, I suppose, from his wallet and brazier—who had a woman with him, and who faced about and stared at me thus; and then roared to me in such a tremendous voice to come back, that I halted and looked round.

" Come here, when you're called," said the tinker, " or I'll rip your young body open."

I thought it best to go back. As I drew nearer to them, trying to propitiate the tinker by my looks, I observed that the woman had a black eye.

" Where are you going? " said the tinker, gripping the bosom of my shirt with his blackened hand.

" I am going to Dover," I said.

" Where do you come from? " asked the tinker, giving his hand another turn in my shirt, to hold me more securely.

" I come from London," I said.

" What lay are you upon? " asked the tinker. " Are you a prig? "

" N—no," I said.

" Ain't you, by G—? If you make a brag of your honesty to me," said the tinker, " I'll knock your brains out."

With his disengaged hand he made a menace of striking me, and then looked at me from head to foot.

" Have you got the price of a pint of beer about you? " said the tinker. 'If you have, out with it, afore I take it away! "

I should certainly have produced it, but that I met the woman's look, and saw her very slightly shake her head, and form " No! " with her lips.

" I am very poor," I said, attempting to smile, " and have got no money."

" Why, what do you mean? " said the tinker, looking so sternly at me, that I almost feared he saw the money in my pocket.

" Sir! " I stammered.

" What do you mean," said the tinker, " by wearing my brother's silk handkercher! Give it over here! " And he had mine off my neck in a moment, and tossed it to the woman.

The woman burst into a fit of laughter, as if she thought this a joke, and tossed it back to me, nodded once, as slightly as before, and made the word " Go! " with her lips. Before I could obey, however, the tinker seized the handkerchief out of my hand with a roughness that threw me away like a feather, and putting it loosely round his own neck, turned upon the woman with an oath, and knocked her down. I never shall forget seeing her fall backward on the hard road, and lie there with her bonnet tumbled off, and her hair all whitened in the dust; nor, when I looked back from a distance, seeing her sitting on the pathway, which was a bank by the roadside, wiping the blood from her face with a corner of her shawl, while he went on ahead.

This adventure frightened me so, that, afterwards, when I saw any of these people coming, I turned back until I could find a hiding-place, where I remained until they had gone out of sight; which happened so often, that I was very seriously delayed. But under this difficulty, as under all the other difficulties of my journey, I seemed to be sustained and led on by my fanciful picture of my mother in her youth, before I came into the world. It always kept me company. It was there, among the hops, when I lay down to sleep; it was with me on my waking in the morning; it went before me all day. I have associated it, ever since, with the sunny street of Canterbury, dozing as it were in the hot light; and with the sight of its old houses and gateways, and the stately, grey Cathedral, with the rooks sailing round the towers. When I came, at last, upon the bare, wide downs near Dover, it relieved the solitary aspect of the scene with hope; and not until I reached that first great aim of my journey, and actually set foot in the town itself, on the sixth day of my flight, did it desert me. But then, strange to say, when I stood with my ragged shoes, and my dusty, sunburnt, half-clothed figure, in the place so long desired, it seemed to vanish like a dream, and to leave me helpless and dispirited.

I inquired about my aunt among the boatmen first, and received various answers. One said she lived in the South Foreland Light, and had singed her whiskers by doing so; another, that she was made fast to the great buoy outside the harbour, and could only be visited at half-tide; a third, that she was locked up in Maidstone Jail for child-stealing; a fourth, that she was seen to mount a broom, in the last high wind, and make direct for Calais. The fly-drivers, among whom I inquired next, were equally jocose and equally disrespectful; and the shopkeepers, not liking my appearance, generally replied, without hearing what I had to say, that they had got nothing for me. I felt more miserable and destitute than I had done at any period of my running away. My money was all gone, I had nothing left to dispose of; I was hungry, thirsty, and worn out; and seemed as distant from my end as if I had remained in London.

The morning had worn away in these inquiries, and I was sitting on the step of an empty shop at a street corner, near the market-place, deliberating upon wandering towards those other places which had been mentioned, when a fly-driver, coming by with his carriage, dropped a horsecloth. Something good-natured in the man's face, as I handed it up, encouraged me to ask him if he could tell me where Miss Trotwood lived; though I had asked the question so often, that it almost died upon my lips.

"Trotwood," said he. "Let me see. I know the name, too. Old lady?"

"Yes," I said, "rather."

"Pretty stiff in the back?" said he, making himself upright.

"Yes," I said. "I should think it very likely."

"Carries a bag?" said he: "bag with a good deal of room in it: is gruffish, and comes down upon you, sharp?"

My heart sank within me as I acknowledged the undoubted accuracy of this description.

"Why then, I tell you what," said he. "If you go up there," pointing with his whip towards the heights, "and keep right on till you come to some houses facing the sea, I think you'll hear of her. My opinion is, she won't stand anything, so here's a penny for you."

I accepted the gift thankfully, and bought a loaf with it. Dispatching this refreshment by the way, I went in the direction my friend had indicated, and walked on a good distance without coming to the houses he had mentioned. At length I saw some before me; and approaching them, went into a little shop (it was what we used to call a general shop, at home), and inquired if they could have the goodness to tell me where Miss Trotwood lived. I addressed myself to a man behind the counter, who was weighing some rice for a young woman; but the latter, taking the inquiry to herself, turned round quickly.

"My mistress?" she said. "What do you want with her, boy?"

"I want," I replied, "to speak to her, if you please."

"To beg of her, you mean," retorted the damsel.

"No," I said, "indeed." But suddenly remembering that in truth I came for no other purpose, I held my peace in confusion, and felt my face burn.

My aunt's handmaid, as I supposed she was from what she had said, put her rice in a little basket and walked out of the shop; telling me that I could follow her, if I wanted to know where Miss Trotwood lived. I needed no second permission; though I was by this time in such a state of consternation and agitation, that my legs shook under me. I followed the young woman, and we soon came to a very neat little cottage with cheerful bow-windows; in front of it, a small square gravelled court or garden full of flowers, carefully tended, and smelling deliciously.

"This is Miss Trotwood's," said the young woman. "Now you know; and that's all I have got to say." With which words she hurried into the house, as if to shake off the responsibility of my appearance; and left me standing at the garden-gate, looking disconsolately over the top of it towards the parlour-window, where a muslin curtain partly undrawn in the middle, a large round green screen or fan fastened on to the window-sill, a small table, and a great chair, suggested to me that my aunt might be at that moment seated in awful state.

My shoes were by this time in a woeful condition. The soles had shed themselves bit by bit, and the upper leathers had broken and burst until the very shape and form of shoes had departed from them. My hat (which had served me for a night-cap, too) was so crushed and bent, that no old battered handleless saucepan on a dunghill need have been ashamed to vie with it. My shirt and trousers, stained with heat, dew, grass, and the Kentish soil on which I had slept—and torn besides—might have frightened the birds from my aunt's garden, as I stood at the gate. My hair had known no comb or brush since I left London.

My face, neck, and hands, from unaccustomed exposure to the air and sun, were burnt to a berry-brown. From head to foot I was powdered almost as white with chalk and dust, as if I had come out of a lime-kiln. In this plight, and with a strong consciousness of it, I waited to introduce myself to, and make my first impression on, my formidable aunt.

The unbroken stillness of the parlour-window leading me to infer, after a while, that she was not there, I lifted up my eyes to the window above it, where I saw a florid, pleasant-looking gentleman, with a grey head, who shut up one eye in a grotesque manner, nodded his head at me several times, shook it at me as often, laughed, and went away.

I had been discomposed enough before; but I was so much the more discomposed by this unexpected behaviour, that I was on the point of slinking off, to think how I had best proceed, when there came out of the house a lady with her handkerchief tied over her cap, and a pair of gardening gloves on her hands, wearing a gardening pocket like a toll-man's apron, and carrying a great knife. I knew her immediately to be Miss Betsey, for she came stalking out of the house exactly as my poor mother had so often described her stalking up our garden at Blunderstone Rookery.

"Go away!" said Miss Betsey, shaking her head, and making a distant chop in the air with her knife. "Go along! No boys here!"

I watched her, with my heart at my lips, as she marched to a corner of her garden, and stooped to dig up some little root there. Then, without a scrap of courage, but with a great deal of desperation, I went softly in and stood beside her, touching her with my finger.

"If you please, ma'am," I began.

She started and looked up.

"If you please, aunt."

"EH?" exclaimed Miss Betsey, in a tone of amazement I have never heard approached.

"If you please, aunt, I am your nephew."

"Oh, Lord!" said my aunt. And sat flat down in the garden-path.

"I am David Copperfield, of Blunderstone, in Suffolk—where you came, on the night when I was born, and saw my dear mama. I have been very unhappy since she died. I have been slighted, and taught nothing, and thrown upon myself, and put to work not fit for me. It made me run away to you. I was robbed at first setting out, and have walked all the way, and have never slept in a bed since I began the journey." Here my self-support gave way all at once; and with a movement of my hands, intended to show her my ragged state, and call it to witness that I had suffered something, I broke into a passion of crying, which I suppose had been pent up within me all the week.

My aunt, with every sort of expression but wonder discharged from her countenance, sat on the gravel, staring at me, until I began to cry; when she got up in a great hurry, collared me, and took me into the parlour. Her first proceeding there was to unlock a tall press, bring out several bottles, and pour some of the contents of each into my mouth. I think they must have been taken out at random, for I am sure I tasted aniseed water, anchovy sauce, and salad dressingl When she had administered these restoratives, as I was still quite hysterical, and unable to control my sobs, she put me on the sofa, with a shawl under my head, and the handkerchief from her own head under my feet, lest I should sully the cover; and then, sitting herself down behind the green fan or screen I have already mentioned, so that I could not see her face, ejaculated at intervals, " Mercy on us! " letting those exclamations off like minute guns.

After a time she rang the bell. " Janet," said my aunt, when her servant came in. "Go up-stairs, give my compliments to Mr. Dick, and say I wish to speak to him."

Janet looked a little surprised to see me lying stiffly on the sofa (I was afraid to move lest it should be displeasing to my aunt), but went on her errand. My aunt, with her hands behind her, walked up and down the room, until the gentleman who had squinted at me from the upper window came in laughing.

" Mr. Dick," said my aunt, " don't be a fool, because nobody can be more discreet than you can, when you choose. We all know that. So don't be a fool, whatever you are."

The gentleman was serious immediately, and looked at me, I thought, as if he would entreat me to say nothing about thc window.

" Mr. Dick," said my aunt, " you have heard me mention David Copperfield? Now don't pretend not to have a memory, because you and I know better."

" David Copperfield? " said Mr. Dick, who did not appear to me to remember much about it. " *David* Copperfield? Oh yes, to be sure. David, certainly."

" Well," said my aunt, " this is his boy, his son. He would be as like his father as it's possible to be, if he was not so like his mother, too."

" His son? " said Mr. Dick. " David's son? Indeed! "

"Yes," pursued my aunt, "and he has done a pretty piece of business. He has run away. Ah! His sister, Betsey Trotwood, never would have run away." My aunt shook her head firmly, confident in the character and behaviour of the girl who never was born.

"Oh! you think she wouldn't have run away?" said Mr. Dick.

"Bless and save the man," exclaimed my aunt, sharply, "how he talks! Don't I know she wouldn't? She would have lived with her god-mother, and we should have been devoted to one another. Where, in the name of wonder, should his sister, Betsey Trotwood, have run from, or to?"

"Nowhere," said Mr. Dick.

"Well then," returned my aunt, softened by the reply, "how can you pretend to be wool-gathering, Dick, when you are as sharp as a surgeon's lancet? Now, here you see young David Copperfield, and the question I put to you is, what shall I do with him?"

"What shall you do with him?" said Mr. Dick, feebly, scratching his head. "Oh! do with him?"

"Yes," said my aunt, with a grave look, and her forefinger held up. "Come! I want some very sound advice,"

"Why, if I was you," said Mr. Dick, considering, and looking vacantly at me, "I should—" The contemplation of me seemed to inspire him with a sudden idea, and he added, briskly, "I should wash him!"

"Janet," said my aunt, turning round with a quiet triumph, which I did not then understand, "Mr. Dick sets us all right. Heat the bath!"

Although I was deeply interested in this dialogue, I could not help observing my aunt, Mr. Dick, and Janet, while it was in progress, and completing a survey I had already been engaged in making of the room.

My aunt was a tall, hard-featured lady, but by no means ill-looking. There was an inflexibility in her face, in her voice, in her gait and carriage, amply sufficient to account for the effect she had made upon a gentle creature like my mother; but her features were rather handsome than otherwise, though unbending and austere. I particularly noticed that she had a very quick, bright eye. Her hair, which was grey, was arranged in two plain divisions, under what I believe would be called a mob-cap; I mean a cap, much more common then than now, with side-pieces fastening under the chin. Her dress was of a lavender colour, and perfectly neat; but scantily made, as if she desired to be as little encumbered as possible. I remember that I thought it, in form, more like a riding-habit with the superfluous skirt cut off, than anything else. She wore at her side a gentleman's gold watch, if I might judge from its size and make, with an appropriate chain and seals; she had some linen at her throat not unlike a shirt-collar, and things at her wrists like little shirt-wristbands.

Mr. Dick, as I have already said, was grey-headed and florid; I should have said all about him, in saying so, had not his head been curiously bowed—not by age; it reminded me of one of Mr. Creakle's boys' heads after a beating—and his grey eyes prominent and large, with a strange kind of watery brightness in them that made me, in combination with his vacant manner, his submission to my aunt, and his childish delight when she praised him, suspect him of being a little mad; though, if he were mad, how he came to be there, puzzled me extremely. He was dressed like any other ordinary gentleman, in a loose grey morning coat and waistcoat, and white trousers; and had his watch in his fob, and his money in his pockets: which he rattled as if he were very proud of it.

Janet was a pretty blooming girl, of about nineteen or twenty, and a perfect picture of neatness. Though I made no further observation of her at the moment, I may mention here what I did not discover until afterwards, namely, that she was one of a series of protégées whom my aunt had taken into her service expressly to educate in a renouncement of mankind, and who had generally completed their abjuration by marrying the baker.

The room was as neat as Janet or my aunt. As I laid down my pen, a moment since, to think of it, the air from the sea came blowing in again, mixed with the perfume of the flowers; and I saw the old-fashioned furniture brightly rubbed and polished, my aunt's inviolable chair and table by the round green fan in the bow-window, the drugget-covered carpet, the cat, the kettle-holder, the two canaries, the old china, the punch-bowl full of dried rose-leaves, the tall press guarding all sorts of bottles and pots, and, wonderfully out of keeping with the rest, my dusty self upon the sofa, taking note of everything.

Janet had gone away to get the bath ready, when my aunt, to my great alarm, became in one moment rigid with indignation, and had hardly voice to cry out, " Janet! Donkeys! "

Upon which, Janet came running up the stairs as if the house were in flames, darted out on a little piece of green in front, and warned off two saddle-donkeys, lady-ridden, that had presumed to set hoof upon it; while my aunt, rushing out of the house, seized the bridle of a third animal laden with a bestriding child, turned him, led him forth from those sacred precincts, and boxed the ears of the unlucky urchin in attendance who had dared to profane that hallowed ground.

To this hour I don't know whether my aunt had any lawful right of way over that patch of green; but she had settled it in her own mind that she had, and it was all the same to her. The one great outrage of her life, demanding to be constantly avenged, was the passage of a donkey over that immaculate spot. In whatever occupation she was engaged, however interesting to her the conversation in which she was taking part, a donkey turned the current of her ideas in a moment, and she was upon him straight. Jugs of water, and watering-pots, were kept in secret places ready to be discharged on the offending boys; sticks were laid in ambush behind the door; sallies were made at all hours; and incessant water prevailed. Perhaps this was an agreeable excitement to the donkey-boys; or perhaps the more sagacious of the donkeys, understanding how the case stood, delighted with constitutional obstinacy in coming that way. I only know that there were three alarms before the bath was ready; and that on the occasion of the last and most desperate of all, I saw my aunt engage, single-handed, with a sandy-headed lad of fifteen, and bump his sandy head against her own gate, before he seemed to comprehend what was the matter. These interruptions were the more ridiculous to me, because she was giving me broth out of a table-spoon at the time (having firmly persuaded herself that I was actually starving, and must receive nourishment at first in very small quantities), and while my mouth was yet open to receive the spoon, she would put it back into the basin, cry " Janet! Donkeys! " and go out to the assault.

The bath was a great comfort. For I began to be sensible of acute pains in my limbs from lying out in the fields, and was now so tired and low that I could hardly keep myself awake for five minutes together. When I had bathed, they (I mean my aunt and Janet) enrobed me in a shirt and a pair of trousers belonging to Mr. Dick, and tied me up in two or three great shawls. What sort of bundle I looked like, I don't know, but I felt a very hot one. Feeling also very faint and drowsy, I soon lay down on the sofa again and fell asleep.

It might have been a dream, originating in the fancy which had occupied my mind so long, but I awoke with the impression that my aunt had come and bent over me, and had put my hair away from my face, and laid my head more comfortably, and had then stood looking at me. The words, " Pretty fellow," or " Poor fellow," seemed to be in my ears, too; but certainly there was nothing else, when I awoke, to lead me to believe that they had been uttered by my aunt, who sat in the bow-window gazing at the sea from behind the green fan, which was mounted on a kind of swivel, and turned any way.

We dined soon after I awoke, off a roast fowl and a pudding; I sitting at table, not unlike a trussed bird myself, and moving my arms with considerable difficulty. But as my aunt had swathed me up, I made no complaint of being inconvenienced. All this time I was deeply anxious to know what she was going to do with me; but she took her dinner in profound silence, except when she occasionally fixed her eyes on me sitting opposite, and said, " Mercy upon us! " which did not by any means relieve my anxiety.

The cloth being drawn, and some sherry put upon the table (of which I had a glass), my aunt sent up for Mr. Dick again, who joined us, and looked as wise as he could when she requested him to attend to my story, which she elicited from me, gradually, by a course of questions. During my recital, she kept her eyes on Mr. Dick, who I thought would have gone to sleep but for that, and who, whensoever he lapsed into a smile, was checked by a frown from my aunt.

" Whatever possessed that poor unfortunate Baby, that she must go and be married again," said my aunt, when I had finished, " *I* can't conceive."

" Perhaps she fell in love with her second husband," Mr. Dick suggested.

" Fell in love! " repeated my aunt. " What do you mean? What business had she to do it? "

" Perhaps," Mr. Dick simpered, after thinking a little, " she did it for pleasure."

" Pleasure, indeed! " replied my aunt. " A mighty pleasure for the poor Baby to fix her simple faith upon any dog of a fellow, certain to ill-use her in some way or other. What did she propose to herself, I should like to know! She had had one husband. She had seen David Copperfield out of the world, who was always running after wax dolls from his cradle. She had got a baby—oh, there were a pair of babies when she gave birth to this child sitting here, that Friday night!—and what more did she want? "

Mr. Dick secretly shook his head at me, as if he thought there was no getting over this.

" She couldn't even have a baby like anybody else," said my aunt. " Where was this child's sister, Betsey Trotwood? Not forthcoming. Don't tell me! "

Mr. Dick seemed quite frightened.

" That little man of a doctor, with his head on one side," said my aunt, " Jellips, or whatever his name was, what was *he* about? All he could do was to say to me, like a robin red-breast —as he *is*—' It's a boy.' A boy! Yah, the imbecility of the whole set of 'em! "

The heartiness of the ejaculation startled Mr. Dick exceedingly; and me, too, if I am to tell the truth.

" And then, as if this was not enough, and she had not stood sufficiently in the light of this child's sister, Betsey Trotwood," said my aunt, " she marries a second time—goes and marries a Murderer—or a man with a name like it—and stands in *this* child's light! And the natural consequence is, as anybody but a baby might have foreseen, that he prowls and wanders. He's as like Cain before he was grown up, as he can be."

Mr. Dick looked hard at me, as if to identify me in this character.

" And then there's that woman with the Pagan name," said my aunt, " that Peggotty, *she* goes and gets married next. Because she has not seen enough of the evil attending such things, *she* goes and gets married next, as the child relates. I only hope," said my aunt, shaking her head, " that her husband is one of those Poker husbands who abound in the newspapers, and will beat her well with one."

I could not bear to hear my old nurse so decried, and made the subject of such a wish. I told my aunt that indeed she was mistaken. That Peggotty was the best, the truest, the most faithful, most devoted, and most self-denying friend and servant in the world; who had ever loved me dearly, who had ever loved my mother dearly; who had held my mother's dying head upon her arm, on whose face my mother had imprinted her last grateful kiss. And my remembrance of them both, choking me, I broke down as I was trying to say that her home was my home, and that all she had was mine, and that I would have gone to her for shelter, but for her humble station, which made me fear that I might bring some trouble on her—I broke down, I say, as I was trying to say so, and laid my face in my hands upon the table.

" Well, well! " said my aunt, " the child is right to stand by those who have stood by him.—Janet! Donkeys! "

I thoroughly believe that but for those unfortunate donkeys, we should have come to a good understanding; for my aunt had laid her hand on my shoulder, and the impulse was upon me, thus emboldened, to embrace her and beseech her protection.

But the interruption, and the disorder she was thrown into by the struggle outside, put an end to all softer ideas for the present, and kept my aunt indignantly declaiming to Mr. Dick about her determination to appeal for redress to the laws of her country, and to bring actions for trespass against the whole donkey proprietorship of Dover, until tea-time.

After tea, we sat at the window, on the look-out, as I imagined, from my aunt's sharp expression of face, for more invaders—until dusk, when Janet set candles, and a back-gammon-board, on the table, and pulled down the blinds.

"Now, Mr. Dick," said my aunt, with her grave look, and her forefinger up as before, "I am going to ask you another question. Look at this child."

"David's son?" said Mr. Dick, with an attentive, puzzled face.

"Exactly so," returned my aunt, "What would you do with him, now?"

"Do with David's son?" said Mr. Dick.

"Ay," replied my aunt, "with David's son."

"Oh!" said Mr. Dick. "Yes. Do with—I should put him to bed."

"Janet!" cried my aunt, with the same complacent triumph that I had remembered before. "Mr. Dick sets us all right. If the bed is ready, we'll take him up to it."

Janet reporting it to be quite ready, I was taken up to it; kindly, but in some sort like a prisoner; my aunt going in front, and Janet bringing up the rear. The only circumstance which gave me any new hope, was my aunt's stopping on the stairs to inquire about a smell of fire that was prevalent there; and Janet's replying that she had been making tinder down in the kitchen, of my old shirt. But there were no other clothes in my room than the odd heap of things I wore; and when I was left there, with a little taper which my aunt forewarned me would burn exactly five minutes, I heard them lock my door on the outside. Turning these things over in my mind, I deemed it possible that my aunt, who could know nothing of me, might suspect I had a habit of running away, and took precautions, on that account, to have me in safe keeping.

The room was a pleasant one, at the top of the house, overlooking the sea, on which the moon was shining brilliantly. After I had said my prayers, and the candle had burnt out, I remember how I still sat looking at the moonlight on the water, as if I could hope to read my fortune in it, as in a bright book; or to see my mother with her child, coming from Heaven, along that shining path, to look upon me as she had looked when I last saw her sweet face. I remember how the solemn feeling with which at length I turned my eyes away, yielded to the sensation of gratitude and rest which the sight of the white-curtained bed—and how much more the lying softly down upon it, nestling in the show-white sheets!—inspired. I remember how I thought of all the solitary places under the night sky where I had slept, and how I prayed that I never might be houseless any more, and never might forget the houseless. I remember how I seemed to float, down the melancholy glory of that track upon the sea, away into the world of dreams.

14

MY AUNT MAKES UP HER MIND ABOUT ME

ON GOING DOWN IN THE MORNING, I FOUND MY aunt musing so profoundly over the breakfast-table, with her elbow on the tray, that the contents of the urn had overflowed the teapot and were laying the whole table-cloth under water, when my entrance put her meditations to flight. I felt sure that I had been the subject of her reflections, and was more than ever anxious to know her intentions towards me. Yet I dared not express my anxiety, lest it should give her offence.

My eyes, however, not being so much under control as my tongue, were attracted towards my aunt very often during breakfast. I never could look at her for a few moments together but I found her looking at me—in an odd thoughtful manner, as if I were an immense way off, instead of being on the other side of the small round table. When she had finished her breakfast, my aunt very deliberately leaned back in her chair, knitted her brows, folded her arms, and contemplated me at her leisure, with such a fixedness of attention that I was quite overpowered by embarrassment. Not having as yet finished my own breakfast, I attempted to hide my confusion by proceeding with it; but my knife tumbled over my fork, my fork tripped up my knife, I chipped bits of bacon a surprising height into the air instead of cutting them for my own eating, and choked myself with my tea, which persisted in going the wrong way instead of the right one, until I gave in altogether, and sat blushing under my aunt's close scrutiny.

"Hallo!" said my aunt, after a long time.

I looked up, and met her sharp bright glance respectfully.

"I have written to him," said my aunt.

"To—?"

"To your father-in-law," said my aunt. "I have sent him a letter that I'll trouble him to attend to, or he and I will fall out, I can tell him!"

"Does he know where I am, aunt?" I inquired, alarmed.

"I have told him," said my aunt, with a nod.

"Shall I—be—given up to him?" I faltered.

"I don't know," said my aunt. "We shall see."

"Oh! I can't think what I shall do," I exclaimed, "if I have to go back to Mr. Murdstone!"

"I don't know anything about it," said my aunt, shaking her head. "I can't say, I am sure. We shall see."

My spirits sank under these words, and I became very downcast and heavy of heart. My aunt, without appearing to take much heed of me, put on a coarse apron with a bib, which she took out of the press; washed up the teacups with her own hands; and, when everything was washed and set in the tray again, and the cloth folded and put on the top of the whole, rang for Janet to remove it. She next swept up the crumbs with a little broom (putting on a pair of gloves first), until there did not appear to be one microscopic speck left on the carpet; next dusted and arranged the room, which was dusted and arranged to a hair's-breadth already. When all these tasks were performed to her satisfaction, she took off the gloves and apron, folded them up, and put them in the particular corner of the press from which they had been taken, brought out her work-box to her own table in the open window, and sat down, with the green fan between her and the light, to work.

"I wish you'd go up-stairs," said my aunt, as she threaded her needle, "and give my compliments to Mr. Dick, and I'll be glad to know how he gets on with his Memorial."

I rose with all alacrity, to acquit myself of this commission.

"I suppose," said my aunt, eyeing me as narrowly as she had eyed the needle in threading it, "you think Mr. Dick a short name, eh?"

"I thought it was a rather short name, yesterday," I confessed.

"You are not to suppose that he hasn't got a longer name

if he chose to use it," said my aunt, with a loftier air. "Babley—Mr. Richard Babley—that's the gentleman's true name."

I was going to suggest, with a modest sense of my youth and the familiarity I had been already guilty of, that I had better give him the full benefit of that name, when my aunt went on to say:

"But don't you call him by it, whatever you do. He can't bear his name. That's a peculiarity of his. Though I don't know that it's much of a peculiarity, either; for he has been ill-used enough, by some that bear it, to have a mortal antipathy for it, Heaven knows. Mr. Dick is his name here, and everywhere else, now—if he ever went anywhere else, which he don't. So take care, child, you don't call him anything *but* Mr. Dick."

I promised to obey, and went up-stairs with my message; thinking, as I went, that if Mr. Dick had been working at his Memorial long, at the same rate as I had seen him working at it, through the open door, when I came down, he was probably getting on very well indeed. I found him still driving at it with a long pen, and his head almost laid upon the paper. He was so intent upon it, that I had ample leisure to observe the large paper kite in a corner, the confusion of bundles of manuscript, the number of pens, and, above all, the quantity of ink (which he seemed to have in, in half-gallon jars by the dozen), before he observed my being present.

"Ha! Phœbus!" said Mr. Dick, laying down his pen. "How does the world go? I'll tell you what," he added, in a lower tone, "I shouldn't wish it to be mentioned, but it's a"—here he beckoned to me, and put his lips close to my ear—"it's a mad world. Mad as Bedlam, boy!" said Mr. Dick, taking snuff from a round box on the table, and laughing heartily.

Without presuming to give my opinion on this question, I delivered my message.

"Well," said Mr. Dick, in answer, "my compliments to her, and I—I believe I have made a start. I think I have made a start," said Mr. Dick, passing his hand among his grey hair, and casting anything but a confident look at his manuscript. "You have been to school?"

"Yes, sir," I answered; "for a short time."

"Do you recollect the date," said Mr. Dick, looking earnestly at me, and taking up his pen to note it down, "when King Charles the First had his head cut off?"

I said I believed it happened in the year sixteen hundred and forty-nine.

"Well," returned Mr. Dick, scratching his ear with his pen,

and looking dubiously at me. " So the books say; but I don't see how that can be. Because, if it was so long ago, how could the people about him have made that mistake of putting some of the trouble out of *his* head, after it was taken off, into *mine*? "

I was very much surprised by the inquiry; but could give no information on this point.

" It's very strange," said Mr. Dick, with a despondent look upon his papers, and with his hand among his hair again, " that I never can get that quite right. I never can make that perfectly clear. But no matter, no matter! " he said cheerfully, and rousing himself, " there's time enough! My compliments to Miss Trotwood, I am getting on very well indeed."

I was going away, when he directed my attention to the kite.

" What do you think of that for a kite? " he said.

I answered that it was a beautiful one. I should think it must have been as much as seven feet high.

" I made it. We'll go and fly it, you and I " said Mr. Dick. " Do you see this? "

He showed me that it was covered with manuscript, very closely and laboriously written; but so plainly, that as I looked along the lines, I thought I saw some allusion to King Charles the First's head again, in one or two places.

" There's plenty of string," said Mr. Dick, " and when it flies high, it takes the facts a long way. That's my manner of diffusing 'em. I don't know where they may come down. It's according to circumstances, and the wind, and so forth; but I take my chance of that."

His face was so very mild and pleasant, and had something so reverend in it, though it was hale and hearty, that I was not sure but that he was having a good-humoured jest with me. So I laughed, and he laughed, and we parted the best friends possible.

" Well, child," said my aunt, when I went downstairs. " And what of Mr. Dick, this morning? "

I informed her that he sent his compliments, and was getting on very well indeed.

" What do you think of him? " said my aunt.

I had some shadowy idea of endeavouring to evade the question by replying that I thought him a very nice gentleman; but my aunt was not to be so put off, for she laid her work down in her lap, and said, folding her hands upon it:

" Come! Your sister Betsey Trotwood would have told me what she thought of any one, directly. Be as like your sister as you can, and speak out! "

" Is he—is Mr. Dick—I ask because I don't know, aunt—is

he at all out of his mind, then?" I stammered; for I felt I was on dangerous ground.

"Not a morsel," said my aunt.

"Oh, indeed!" I observed faintly.

"If there is anything in the world," said my aunt, with great decision and force of manner, "that Mr. Dick is not, it's that."

I had nothing better to offer, than another timid "Oh, indeed!"

"He has been *called* mad," said my aunt. "I have a selfish pleasure in saying he has been called mad, or I should not have had the benefit of his society and advice for these last ten years and upwards—in fact, ever since your sister, Betsey Trotwood, disappointed me."

"So long as that?" I said.

"And nice people they were, who had the audacity to call him mad," pursued my aunt. "Mr. Dick is a sort of distant connection of mine; it doesn't matter how; I needn't enter into that. If it hadn't been for me, his own brother would have shut him up for life. That's all."

I am afraid it was hypocritical in me, but seeing that my aunt felt strongly on the subject, I tried to look as if I felt strongly too.

"A proud fool!" said my aunt. "Because his brother was a little eccentric—though he is not half so eccentric as a good many people—he didn't like to have him visible about his house, and sent him away to some private asylum-place; though he had been left to his particular care by their deceased father, who thought him almost a natural. And a wise man *he* must have been to think so! Mad himself, no doubt."

Again, as my aunt looked quite convinced, I endeavoured to look quite convinced also.

"So I stepped in," said my aunt, "and made him an offer. I said, 'Your brother's sane—a great deal more sane than you are, or ever will be, it is to be hoped. Let him have his little income, and come and live with me. *I* am not afraid of him, *I* am not proud, *I* am ready to take care of him, and shall not ill-treat him as some people (besides the asylum-folks) have done.' After a good deal of squabbling," said my aunt, "I got him; and he has been here ever since. He is the most friendly and amenable creature in existence; and as for advice!—But nobody knows what that man's mind is, except myself."

My aunt smoothed her dress and shook her head, as if she smoothed defiance of the whole world out of the one, and shook it out of the other.

" He had a favourite sister," said my aunt, " a good creature, and very kind to him. But she did what they all do—took a husband. And *he* did what they all do—made her wretched. It had such an effect upon the mind of Mr. Dick (*that's* not madness, I hope!) that, combined with his fear of his brother, and his sense of his unkindness, it threw him into a fever. That was before he came to me, but the recollection of it is oppressive to him even now. Did he say anything to you about King Charles the First, child? "

" Yes, aunt."

" Ah! " said my aunt, rubbing her nose as if she were a little vexed. " That's his allegorical way of expressing it. He connects his illness with great disturbance and agitation, naturally, and that's the figure, or the simile, or whatever it's called, which he chooses to use. And why shouldn't he, if he thinks proper? "

I said: " Certainly, aunt."

" It's not a business-like way of speaking," said my aunt, " nor a worldly way. I am aware of that; and that's the reason why I insist upon it, that there shan't be a word about it in his Memorial."

" Is it a Memorial about his own history that he is writing, aunt? "

" Yes, child," said my aunt, rubbing her nose again. " He is memorialising the Lord Chancellor, or the Lord Somebody or other—one of those people, at all events, who are paid to *be* memorialised—about his affairs. I suppose it will go in, one of these days. He hasn't been able to draw it up yet, without introducing that mode of expressing himself; but it don't signify; it keeps him employed."

In fact, I found out afterwards that Mr. Dick had been for upwards of ten years endeavouring to keep King Charles the First out of the Memorial; but he had been constantly getting into it, and was there now.

" I say again," said my aunt, " nobody knows what that man's mind is except myself; and he's the most amenable and friendly creature in existence. If he likes to fly a kite sometimes, what of that! Franklin used to fly a kite. He was a Quaker, or something of that sort, if I am not mistaken. And a Quaker flying a kite is a much more ridiculous object than anybody else."

If I could have supposed that my aunt had recounted these particulars for my especial behoof, and as a piece of confidence in me, I should have felt very much distinguished, and should have augured favourably from such a mark of her good opinion. But I could hardly help observing that she had launched into them, chiefly because the question was raised in her own mind, and with very little reference to me, though she had addressed herself to me in the absence of anybody else.

At the same time, I must say that the generosity of her championship of poor harmless Mr. Dick, not only inspired my young breast with some selfish hope for myself, but, warmed it unselfishly towards her. I believe that I began to know that there was something about my aunt, notwithstanding her many eccentricities and odd humours, to be honoured and trusted in. Though she was just as sharp that day as on the day before, and was in and out about the donkeys just as often, and was thrown into a tremendous state of indignation, when a young man, going by, ogled Janet at a window (which was one of the gravest misdemeanours that could be committed against my aunt's dignity), she seemed to me to command more of my respect, if not less of my fear.

The anxiety I underwent, in the interval which necessarily elapsed before a reply could be received to her letter to Mr. Murdstone, was extreme; but I made an endeavour to suppress it, and to be as agreeable as I could in a quiet way, both to my aunt and Mr. Dick. The latter and I would have gone out to fly the great kite; but that I had still no other clothes than the anything but ornamental garments with which I had been decorated on the first day, and which confined me to the house, except for an hour after dark, when my aunt, for my health's sake, paraded me up and down on the cliff outside before going to bed. At length the reply from Mr. Murdstone came, and my aunt informed me, to my infinite terror, that he was coming to speak to her himself on the next day. On the next day, still bundled up in my curious habiliments, I sat counting the time, flushed and heated by the conflict of sinking hopes and rising fears within me; and waiting to be startled by the sight of the gloomy face whose non-arrival startled me every minute.

My aunt was a little more imperious and stern than usual, but I observed no other token of her preparing herself to receive the visitor so much dreaded by me. She sat at work in the window, and I sat by, with my thoughts running astray on all possible and impossible results of Mr. Murdstone's visit, until pretty late in the afternoon. Our dinner had been indefinitely postponed; but it was growing so late, that my aunt had ordered it to be got ready, when she gave me a sudden alarm of donkeys, and to my consternation and amazement, I beheld Miss Murdstone, on a side-saddle, ride deliberately over the sacred piece of green, and stop in front of the house, looking about her.

"Go along with you!" cried my aunt, shaking her head and her fist at the window. "You have no business there. How dare you trespass? Go along! Oh! you bold-faced thing!"

My aunt was so exasperated by the coolness with which Miss Murdstone looked about her, that I really believe she was motionless, and unable for the moment to dart out according to custom. I seized the opportunity to inform her who it was; and that the gentleman now coming near the offender (for the way up was very steep, and he had dropped behind), was Mr. Murdstone himself.

"I don't care who it is!" cried my aunt, still shaking her head, and gesticulating anything but welcome from the bow-window. "I won't be trespassed upon. I won't allow it. Go away! Janet, turn him round. Lead him off!" and I saw, from behind my aunt, a sort of hurried battle-piece, in which the donkey stood resisting everybody, with all his four legs planted different ways, while Janet tried to pull him round by the bridle, Mr. Murdstone tried to lead him on, Miss Murdstone struck at Janet with a parasol, and several boys, who had come to see the engagement, shouted vigorously. But my aunt, suddenly descrying among them the young malefactor who was the donkey's guardian, and who was one of the most inveterate offenders against her, though hardly in his teens, rushed out to the scene of action, pounced upon him, captured him, dragged him, with his jacket over his head and his heels grinding the ground, into the garden, and, calling upon Janet to fetch the constables and justices, that he might be taken, tried, and executed on the spot, held him at bay there. This part of the business, however, did not last long; for the young rascal, being expert at a variety of feints and dodges, of which my aunt had no conception, soon went whooping away, leaving some deep impressions of his nailed boots in the flower-beds, and taking his donkey in triumph with him.

Miss Murdstone, during the latter portion of the contest, had dismounted, and was now waiting with her brother at the bottom of the steps, until my aunt should be at leisure to receive them. My aunt, a little ruffled by the combat, marched past them into the house, with great dignity, and took no notice of their presence, until they were announced by Janet.

"Shall I go away, aunt?" I asked, trembling.

"No, sir," said my aunt. "Certainly not!" With which she pushed me into a corner near her, and fended me in with a chair, as if it were a prison or a bar of justice. This position I continued to occupy during the whole interview, and from it I now saw Mr. and Miss Murdstone enter the room.

" Oh! " said my aunt, " I was not aware at first to whom I had the pleasure of objecting. But I don't allow anybody to ride over that turf. I make no exceptions. I don't allow anybody to do it."

" Your regulation is rather awkward to strangers," said Miss Murdstone.

" Is it? " said my aunt.

Mr. Murdstone seemed afraid of a renewal of hostilities, and interposing began:

" Miss Trotwood! "

" I beg your pardon," observed my aunt with a keen look. " You are the Mr. Murdstone who married the widow of my late nephew, David Copperfield, of Blunderstone Rookery?—Though why Rookery, *I* don't know! "

' I am," said Mr. Murdstone.

" You'll excuse my saying, sir," returned my aunt, " that I think it would have been a much better and happier thing if you had left that poor child alone."

" I so far agree with what Miss Trotwood has remarked," observed Miss Murdstone, bridling, " that I consider our lamented Clara to have been, in all essential respects, a mere child."

" It is a comfort to you and me, ma'am," said my aunt, " who are getting on in life, and are not likely to be made unhappy by our personal attractions, that nobody can say the same of us."

" No doubt! " returned Miss Murdstone, though, I thought, not with a very ready or gracious assent. " And it certainly might have been, as you say, a better and happier thing for my brother if he had never entered into such a marriage. I have always been of that opinion."

" I have no doubt you have," said my aunt. " Janet," ringing the bell, " my compliments to Mr. Dick, and beg him to come down."

Until he came, my aunt sat perfectly upright and stiff, frowning at the wall. When he came, my aunt performed the ceremony of introduction.

" Mr. Dick. An old and intimate friend. On whose judgment," said my aunt, with emphasis, as an admonition to Mr. Dick, who was biting his forefinger and looking rather foolish, " I rely."

Mr. Dick took his finger out of his mouth, on this hint, and stood among the group, with a grave and attentive expression of face. My aunt inclined her head to Mr. Murdstone, who went on:

"Miss Trotwood. On the receipt of your letter, I considered it an act of greater justice to myself, and perhaps of more respect to you—"

"Thank you," said my aunt, still eyeing him keenly. "You needn't mind me."

"To answer it in person, however inconvenient the journey," pursued Mr. Murdstone, "rather than by letter. This unhappy boy who has run away from his friends and his occupation—"

"And whose appearance," interposed his sister, directing general attention to me in my indefinable costume, "is perfectly scandalous and disgraceful."

"Jane Murdstone," said her brother, "have the goodness not to interrupt me. This unhappy boy, Miss Trotwood, has been the occasion of much domestic trouble and uneasiness; both during the lifetime of my late dear wife, and since. He has a sullen, rebellious spirit; a violent temper; and an untoward, intractable disposition. Both my sister and myself have endeavoured to correct his vices, but ineffectually. And I have felt—we both have felt, I may say; my sister being fully in my confidence—that it is right you should receive this grave and dispassionate assurance from our lips."

"It can hardly be necessary for me to confirm anything stated by my brother," said Miss Murdstone; "but I beg to observe, that, of all the boys in the world, I believe this is the worst boy."

"Strong!" said my aunt, shortly.

"But not at all too strong for the facts," returned Miss Murdstone.

"Ha!" said my aunt. "Well, sir?"

"I have my own opinions," resumed Mr. Murdstone, whose face darkened more and more, the more he and my aunt observed each other, which they did very narrowly, "as to the best mode of bringing him up; they are founded, in part, on my knowledge of him, and in part on my knowledge of my own means and resources. I am responsible for them to myself, I act upon them, and I say no more about them. It is enough that I place this boy under the eye of a friend of my own, in a respectable business; that it does not please him; that he runs away from it; makes himself a common vagabond about the country; and comes here, in rags, to appeal to you, Miss Trotwood. I wish to set before you, honourably, the exact consequences—so far as they are within my knowledge—of your abetting him in this appeal."

"But about the respectable business first," said my aunt. "If he had been your own boy, you would have put him to it, just the same, I suppose?"

"If he had been my brother's own boy," returned Miss Murdstone, striking in, "his character, I trust, would have been altogether different."

"Or if the poor child, his mother, had been alive, he would still have gone into the respectable business, would he?" said my aunt.

"I believe," said Mr. Murdstone, with an inclination of his head, "that Clara would have disputed nothing which myself and my sister Jane Murdstone were agreed was for the best."

Miss Murdstone confirmed this with an audible murmur.

"Humph!" said my aunt. "Unfortunate baby!"

Mr. Dick, who had been rattling his money all this time, was rattling it so loudly now, that my aunt felt it necessary to check him with a look, before saying:

"The poor child's annuity died with her?"

"Died with her," replied Mr. Murdstone.

"And there was no settlement of the little property—the house and garden—the what's-its-name Rookery without any rooks in it—upon her boy?"

"It had been left to her, unconditionally, by her first husband," Mr. Murdstone began, when my aunt caught him up with the greatest irascibility and impatience.

"Good Lord, man, there's no occasion to say that. Left to her unconditionally! I think I see David Copperfield looking forward to any condition of any sort or kind, though it stared him point-blank in the face! Of course it was left to her unconditionally. But when she married again—when she took that most disastrous step of marrying you, in short," said my aunt, "to be plain—did no one put in a word for the boy at that time?"

"My late wife loved her second husband, ma'am," said Mr. Murdstone, "and trusted implicitly in him."

"Your late wife, sir, was a most unworldly, most unhappy, most unfortunate baby," returned my aunt, shaking her head at him. "That's what *she* was. And now, what have you got to say next?"

"Merely this, Miss Trotwood," he returned. "I am here to take David back; to take him back unconditionally, to dispose of him as I think proper, and to deal with him as I think right.

I am not here to make any promise, or give any pledge to anybody. You may possibly have some idea, Miss Trotwood, of abetting him in his running away, and in his complaints to you. Your manner, which I must say does not seem intended to propitiate, induces me to think it possible. Now I must caution you that if you abet him once, you abet him for good and all; if you step in between him and me, now, you must step in, Miss Trotwood, for ever. I cannot trifle, or be trifled with. I am here, for the first and last time, to take him away. Is he ready to go? If he is not—and you tell me he is not; on any pretence; it is indifferent to me what—my doors are shut against him henceforth, and yours, I take it for granted, are open to him."

To this address, my aunt had listened with the closest attention, sitting perfectly upright, with her hands folded on one knee, and looking grimly on the speaker. When he had finished, she turned her eyes so as to command Miss Murdstone, without otherwise disturbing her attitude, and said:

"Well, ma'am, have *you* got anything to remark?"

"Indeed, Miss Trotwood," said Miss Murdstone, "all that I could say has been so well said by my brother, and all that I know to be the fact has been so plainly stated by him, that I have nothing to add except my thanks for your politeness. For your very great politeness, I am sure," said Miss Murdstone with an irony which no more affected my aunt than it discomposed the cannon I had slept by at Chatham.

"And what does the boy say?" said my aunt. "Are you ready to go, David?"

I answered no, and entreated her not to let me go. I said that neither Mr. nor Miss Murdstone had ever liked me, or had ever been kind to me. That they had made my mama, who always loved me dearly, unhappy about me, and that I knew it well, and that Peggotty knew it. I said that I had been more miserable than I thought anybody could believe who only knew how young I was. And I begged and prayed my aunt—I forget in what terms now, but I remember that they affected me very much then—to befriend and protect me, for my father's sake.

"Mr. Dick," said my aunt; "what shall I do with this child?"

Mr. Dick considered, hesitated, brightened, and rejoined, "Have him measured for a suit of clothes directly."

"Mr. Dick," said my aunt triumphantly, "give me your hand, for your common sense is invaluable." Having shaken it with great cordiality, she pulled me towards her and said to Mr. Murdstone:

" You can go when you like; I'll take my chance with the boy. If he's all you say he is, at least I can do as much for him then, as you have done. But I don't believe a word of it."

" Miss Trotwood," rejoined Mr. Murdstone, shrugging his shoulders, as he rose, " if you were a gentleman—"

" Bah! Stuff and nonsense! " said my aunt. " Don't talk to me! "

" How exquisitely polite! " exclaimed Miss Murdstone, rising. " Overpowering, really! "

" Do you think I don't know," said my aunt, turning a deaf ear to the sister, and continuing to address the brother, and to shake her head at him with infinite expression, " what kind of life you must have led that poor, unhappy, misdirected baby? Do you think I don't know what a woeful day it was for the soft little creature when *you* first came in her way—smirking and making great eyes at her, I'll be bound, as if you couldn't say boh! to a goose! "

" I never heard anything so elegant! " said Miss Murdstone.

" Do you think I can't understand you as well as if I had seen you," pursued my aunt," now that I *do* see and hear you—which I tell you candidly, is anything but a pleasure to me? Oh yes, bless us! who so smooth and silky as Mr. Murdstone at first! The poor, benighted innocent had never seen such a man. He was made of sweetness. He worshipped her. He doted on her boy —tenderly doted on him! He was to be another father to him, and they were all to live together in a garden of roses, weren't they? Ugh! Get along with you, do! " said my aunt.

" I never heard anything like this person in my life! " exclaimed Miss Murdstone.

" And when you had made sure of the poor little fool," said my aunt—" God forgive me that I should call her so, and she gone where *you* won't go in a hurry—because you had not done wrong enough to her and hers, you must begin to train her, must you? begin to break her, like a poor caged bird, and wear her deluded life away in teaching her to sing *your* notes? "

" This is either insanity or intoxication," said Miss Murdstone, in a perfect agony of not being able to turn the current of my aunt's address towards herself; " and my suspicion is that it's intoxication."

Miss Betsey, without taking the least notice of the interruption, continued to address herself to Mr. Murdstone as if there had been no such thing.

" Mr. Murdstone," she said, shaking her finger at him, " you were a tyrant to the simple baby, and you broke her heart. She was a loving baby—I know that; I knew it years before *you* ever saw her—and through the best part of her weakness you gave her the wounds she died of. There is the truth for your comfort, however you like it. And you and your instruments may make the most of it."

"Allow me to inquire, Miss Trotwood," interposed Miss Murdstone, "whom you are pleased to call, in a choice of words in which I am not experienced, my brother's instruments?"

Still stone-deaf to the voice, and utterly unmoved by it, Miss Betsey pursued her discourse.

"It was clear enough, as I have told you, years before *you* ever saw her—and why, in the mysterious dispensations of Providence, you ever did see her, is more than humanity can comprehend—it was clear enough that the poor soft little thing would marry somebody, at some time or other; but I did hope it wouldn't have been as bad as it has turned out. That was the time, Mr. Murdstone, when she gave birth to her boy here," said my aunt; "to the poor child you sometimes tormented her through afterwards, which is a disagreeable remembrance, and makes the sight of him odious now. Aye, aye! you needn't wince!" said my aunt. "I know it's true without that."

He had stood by the door, all this while, observant of her, with a smile upon his face, though his black eyebrows were heavily contracted. I remarked now, that, though the smile was on his face still, his colour had gone in a moment, and he seemed to breathe as if he had been running.

"Good day, sir," said my aunt, "and good bye! Good day to you, too, ma'am," said my aunt, turning suddenly upon his sister. "Let me see you ride a donkey over *my* green again, and as sure as you have a head upon your shoulders, I'll knock your bonnet off, and tread upon it!"

It would require a painter, and no common painter too, to depict my aunt's face as she delivered herself of this very unexpected sentiment, and Miss Murdstone's face as she heard it. But the manner of the speech, no less than the matter, was so fiery, that Miss Murdstone, without a word in answer, discreetly put her arm through her brother's, and walked haughtily out of the cottage; my aunt remaining in the window looking after them; prepared, I have no doubt, in case of the donkey's re-appearance, to carry her threat into instant execution.

No attempt at defiance being made, however, her face gradually relaxed, and became so pleasant, that I was emboldened to kiss and thank her; which I did with great heartiness, and with both my arms clasped round her neck. I then shook hands with Mr.

Dick, who shook hands with me a great many times, and hailed this happy close of the proceedings with repeated bursts of laughter.

" You'll consider yourself guardian, jointly with me, of this child, Mr. Dick," said my aunt.

" I shall be delighted," said Mr. Dick, " to be the guardian of David's son."

" Very good," returned my aunt, " *that's* settled. I have been thinking, do you know, Mr. Dick, that I might call him Trotwood?'

" Certainly, certainly. Call him Trotwood, certainly," said Mr. Dick. " David's son's Trotwood."

" Trotwood Copperfield, you mean," returned my aunt.

" Yes, to be sure. Yes. Trotwood Copperfield," said Mr. Dick, a little abashed.

My aunt took so kindly to the notion, that some ready-made clothes, which were purchased for me that afternoon, were marked " Trotwood Copperfield," in her own handwriting, and in indelible marking-ink, before I put them on; and it was settled that all the other clothes which were ordered to be made for me (a complete outfit was bespoke that afternoon) should be marked in the same way.

Thus I began my new life, in a new name, and with everything new about me. Now that the state of doubt was over, I felt, for many days, like one in a dream. I never thought that I had a curious couple of guardians, in my aunt and Mr. Dick. I never thought of anything about myself, distinctly. The two things clearest in my mind were, that a remoteness had come upon the old Blunderstone life—which seemed to lie in the haze of an immeasurable distance; and that a curtain had for ever fallen on my life at Murdstone and Grinby's. No one has ever raised that curtain since. I have lifted it for a moment, even in this narrative, with a reluctant hand, and dropped it gladly. The remembrance of that life is fraught with so much pain to me, with so much mental suffering and want of hope, that I have never had the courage even to examine how long I was doomed to lead it. Whether it lasted for a year, or more, or less, I do not know. I only know that it was, and ceased to be; and that I have written, and there I leave it.

15

I MAKE ANOTHER BEGINNING

MR. DICK AND I SOON BECAME THE BEST OF FRIENDS, and very often, when his day's work was done, went out together to fly the great kite. Every day of his life he had a long sitting at the Memorial, which never made the least progress, however hard he laboured, for King Charles the First always strayed into it, sooner or later, and then it was thrown aside, and another one begun. The patience and hope with which he bore these perpetual disappointments, the mild perception he had that there was something wrong about King Charles the First, the feeble efforts he made to keep him out, and the certainty with which he came in, and tumbled the Memorial out of all shape, made a deep impression on me. What Mr. Dick supposed would come of the Memorial, if it were completed; where he thought it was to go, or what he thought it was to do; he knew no more than anybody else, I believe. Nor was it at all necessary that he should trouble himself with such questions, for if anything were certain under the sun, it was certain that the Memorial never would be finished.

It was quite an affecting sight, I used to think, to see him with the kite when it was up a great height in the air. What he had told me, in his room, about his belief in its disseminating the statements pasted on it, which were nothing but old leaves of abortive Memorials, might have been a fancy with him sometimes; but not when he was out, looking up at the kite in the sky, and feeling it pull and tug at his hand. He never looked so serene as he did then. I used to fancy, as I sat by him of an evening, on a green slope, and saw him watch the kite high in the quiet air, that it lifted his mind out of its confusion, and bore it (such was my boyish thought) into the skies. As he wound the string in, and it came lower and lower down out of the beautiful light, until it fluttered to the ground, and lay there like a dead thing, he seemed to wake gradually out of a dream; and I remember to have seen him take it up, and look about him in a lost way, as if they had both come down together, so that I pitied him with all my heart.

While I advanced in friendship and intimacy with Mr. Dick, I did not go backward in the favour of his staunch friend, my aunt. She took so kindly to me, that, in the course of a few weeks, she shortened my adopted name of Trotwood into Trot; and even encouraged me to hope, that if I went on as I had begun, I might take equal rank in her affections with my sister Betsey Trotwood.

"Trot," said my aunt one evening, when the back-gammon-board was placed as usual for herself and Mr. Dick, "we must not forget your education."

This was my only subject of anxiety, and I felt quite delighted by her referring to it.

"Should you like to go to school at Canterbury?" said my aunt.

I replied that I should like it very much, as it was so near her.

"Good," said my aunt. "Should you like to go to-morrow?"

Being already no stranger to the general rapidity of my aunt's evolutions, I was not surprised by the suddenness of the proposal, and said: "Yes."

"Good," said my aunt again. "Janet, hire the grey pony and chaise to-morrow morning at ten o'clock, and pack up Master Trotwood's clothes to-night."

I was greatly elated by these orders; but my heart smote me for my selfishness, when I witnessed their effect on Mr. Dick, who was so low-spirited at the prospect of our separation, and played so ill in consequence, that my aunt, after giving him several admonitory raps on the knuckles with her dice-box, shut up the board, and declined to play with him any more. But, on hearing from my aunt that I should sometimes come over on a Saturday, and that he could sometimes come and see me on a Wednesday, he revived; and vowed to make another kite for those occasions, of proportions greatly surpassing the present one. In the morning he was down-hearted again, and would have sustained himself by giving me all the money he had in his possession, gold and silver too, if my aunt had not interposed, and limited the gift to five shillings, which, at his earnest petition, were afterwards increased to ten. We parted at the garden-gate in a most affectionate manner, and Mr. Dick did not go into the house until my aunt had driven me out of sight of it.

My aunt, who was perfectly indifferent to public opinion, drove the grey pony through Dover in a masterly manner; sitting high and stiff like a state coachman, keeping a steady eye upon him wherever he went, and making a point of not letting him have his own way in any respect. When we came into the country road, she permitted him to relax a little, however; and looking at me down in a valley of cushion by her side, asked me whether I was happy?

"Very happy indeed, thank you, aunt," I said.

She was much gratified; and both her hands being occupied, patted me on the head with her whip.

"Is it a large school, aunt?" I asked.

"Why, I don't know," said my aunt. "We are going to Mr. Wickfield's first."

"Does *he* keep a school?" I asked.

"No, Trot," said my aunt. "He keeps an office."

I asked for no more information about Mr. Wickfield, as she offered none, and we conversed on other subjects until we came to Canterbury, where, as it was market-day, my aunt had a great opportunity for insinuating the grey pony among carts, baskets, vegetables, and hucksters' goods. The hairbreadth turns and twists we made, drew down upon us a variety of speeches from the people standing about, which were not always complimentary; but my aunt drove on with perfect indifference, and I dare say would have taken her own way with as much coolness through an enemy's country.

At length we stopped before a very old house bulging out over the road; a house with long low lattice-windows bulging out still farther, and beams with carved heads on the ends bulging out too, so that I fancied the whole house was leaning forward, trying to see who was passing on the narrow pavement below. It was quite spotless in its cleanliness. The old-fashioned brass knocker on the low arched door, ornamented with carved garlands of fruit and flowers, twinkled like a star; the two stone steps descending to the door were as white as if they had been covered with fair linen; and all the angles and corners, and carvings and mouldings, and quaint little panes of glass, and quainter little windows, though as old as the hills, were as pure as any snow that ever fell upon the hills.

When the pony-chaise stopped at the door, and my eyes were intent upon the house, I saw a cadaverous face appear at a small window on the ground floor (in a little round tower that formed one side of the house), and quickly disappear. The low arched door then opened, and the face came out. It was quite as cadaverous as it had looked in the window, though in the grain of it there was that tinge of red which is sometimes to be observed in the skins of red-haired people. It belonged to a red-haired person

—a youth of fifteen, as I take it now, but looking much older—whose hair was cropped as close as the closest stubble; who had hardly any eyebrows, and no eyelashes, and eyes of a red-brown, so unsheltered and unshaded, that I remember wondering how he went to sleep. He was high-shouldered and bony; dressed in decent black, with a white wisp of a neckcloth; buttoned up to the throat; and had a long, lank, skeleton hand, which particularly attracted my attention, as he stood at the pony's head, rubbing his chin with it, and looking up at us in the chaise.

"Is Mr. Wickfield at home, Uriah Heep?" said my aunt.

"Mr. Wickfield's at home, ma'am," said Uriah Heep, "if you'll please to walk in there:" pointing with his long hand to the room he meant.

We got out; and leaving him to hold the pony, went into a long low parlour looking towards the street, from the window of which I caught a glimpse as I went in, of Uriah Heep breathing into the pony's nostrils, and immediately covering them with his hand, as if he were putting some spell upon him. Opposite to the tall old chimney-piece were two portraits: one of a gentleman with grey hair (though not by any means an old man) and black eyebrows, who was looking over some papers tied together with red tape; the other, of a lady, with a very placid and sweet expression of face, who was looking at me.

I believe I was turning about in search of Uriah's picture, when, a door at the farther end of the room opening, a gentleman entered, at sight of whom I turned to the first-mentioned portrait again, to make quite sure that it had not come out of its frame. But it was stationary; and as the gentleman advanced into the light, I saw that he was some years older than when he had had his picture painted.

"Miss Betsey Trotwood," said the gentleman, "pray walk in. I was engaged for a moment, but you'll excuse my being busy. You know my motive. I have but one in life."

Miss Betsey thanked him, and we went into his room, which was furnished as an office, with books, papers, tin boxes, and so forth. It looked into a garden, and had an iron safe let into the wall; so immediately over the mantelshelf, that I wondered, as I sat down, how the sweeps got round it when they swept the chimney.

"Well, Miss Trotwood," said Mr. Wickfield; for I soon found that it was he, and that he was a lawyer, and steward of the estates of a rich gentleman of the county; "what wind blows you here? Not an ill wind, I hope?"

"No," replied my aunt, "I have not come for any law."

"That's right, ma'am," said Mr. Wickfield, "You had better come for anything else."

His hair was quite white now, though his eyebrows were still black. He had a very agreeable face, and, I thought, was handsome. There was a certain richness in his complexion which I had been long accustomed, under Peggotty's tuition, to connect with port wine; and I fancied it was in his voice too, and referred his growing corpulency to the same cause. He was very cleanly dressed, in a blue coat, striped waistcoat, and nankeen trousers; and his fine frilled shirt and cambric neck-cloth looked unusually soft and white, reminding my strolling fancy (I call to mind) of the plumage on the breast of a swan.

"This is my nephew," said my aunt.

"Wasn't aware you had one, Miss Trotwood," said Mr. Wickfield.

"My grand-nephew, that is to say," observed my aunt.

"Wasn't aware you had a grand-nephew, I give you my word," said Mr. Wickfield.

"I have adopted him," said my aunt, with a wave of her hand, importing that his knowledge and his ignorance were all one to her, "and I have brought him here, to put to a school where he may be thoroughly well taught, and well treated. Now tell me where that school is, and what it is, and all about it."

"Before I can advise you properly," said Mr. Wickfield,—"the old question, you know. What's your motive in this?"

"Deuce take the man!" exclaimed my aunt. "Always fishing, for motives, when they're on the surface! Why, to make the child happy and useful."

"It must be a mixed motive, I think," said Mr. Wickfield, shaking his head and smiling incredulously.

"A mixed fiddlestick," returned my aunt. "You claim to have one plain motive in all you do yourself. You don't suppose, I hope, that you are the only plain dealer in the world?"

"Ay, but I have only one motive in life, Miss Trotwood," he rejoined, smiling. "Other people have dozens, scores, hundreds. I have only one. There's the difference. However, that's beside the question. The best school? Whatever the motive, you want the best?"

My aunt nodded assent.

"At the best we have," said Mr. Wickfield, considering, "your nephew couldn't board just now."

"But he could board somewhere else, I suppose?" suggested my aunt.

Mr. Wickfield thought I could. After a little discussion, he proposed to take my aunt to the school, that she might see it and judge for herself; also, to take her, with the same object, to two or three houses where he thought I could be boarded. My aunt embracing the proposal, we were all three going out together, when he stopped and said:

"Our little friend here might have some motive, perhaps, for objecting to the arrangements. I think we had better leave him behind?"

My aunt seemed disposed to contest the point; but to facilitate matters I said I would gladly remain behind, if they pleased; and returned into Mr. Wickfield's office, where I sat down again, in the chair I had first occupied, to await their return.

It so happened that this chair was opposite a narrow passage, which ended in the little circular room where I had seen Uriah Heep's pale face looking out of window. Uriah, having taken the pony to a neighbouring stable, was at work at a desk in this room, which had a brass frame on the top to hang paper upon, and on which the writing he was making a copy of was then hanging. Though his face was towards me, I thought, for some time, the writing being between us, that he could not see me; but looking that way more attentively, it made me uncomfortable to observe that, every now and then, his sleepless eyes would come below the writing, like two red suns, and stealthily stare at me for I dare say a whole minute at a time, during which his pen went, or pretended to go, as cleverly as ever. I made several attempts to get out of their way—such as standing on a chair to look at a map on the other side of the room, and poring over the columns of a Kentish newspaper—but they always attracted me back again; and whenever I looked towards those two red suns, I was sure to find them, either just rising or just setting.

At length, much to my relief, my aunt and Mr. Wickfield came back, after a pretty long absence. They were not so successful as I could have wished; for though the advantages of the school were undeniable, my aunt had not approved of any of the boarding-houses proposed for me.

"It's very unfortunate," said my aunt. "I don't know what to do, Trot."

"It *does* happen unfortunately," said Mr. Wickfield. "But I'll tell you what you can do, Miss Trotwood."

"What's that?" inquired my aunt.

"Leave your nephew here, for the present. He's a quiet fellow. He won't disturb me at all. It's a capital house for study. As quiet as a monastery, and almost as roomy. Leave him here."

My aunt evidently liked the offer, though she was delicate of accepting it. So did I.

"Come, Miss Trotwood," said Mr. Wickfield. "This is the way out of the difficulty. It's only a temporary arrangement, you know. If it don't act well, or don't quite accord with our mutual convenience, he can easily go to the right-about. There will be time to find some better place for him in the meanwhile. You had better determine to leave him here for the present!"

"I am very much obliged to you," said my aunt; "and so is he, I see; but—"

"Come! I know what you mean," cried Mr. Wickfield. "You shall not be oppressed by the receipt of favours, Miss Trotwood. You may pay for him, if you like. We won't be hard about terms, but you shall pay if you will."

"On that understanding," said my aunt, "though it doesn't lessen the real obligation, I shall be very glad to leave him."

"Then come and see my little housekeeper," said Mr. Wickfield.

We accordingly went up a wonderful old staircase; with a balustrade so broad that we might have gone up that, almost as easily; and into a shady old drawing-room, lighted by some three or four of the quaint windows I had looked up at from the street: which had old oak seats in them, that seemed to have come of the same trees as the shining oak floor, and the great beams in the ceiling. It was a prettily furnished room, with a piano and some lively furniture in red and green, and some flowers. It seemed to be all old nooks and corners; and in every nook and corner there was some queer little table, or cupboard, or bookcase, or seat, or something or other, that made me think there was not such another good corner in the room; until I looked at the next one, and found it equal to it, if not better. On everything there was the same air of retirement and cleanliness that marked the house outside.

Mr. Wickfield tapped at a door in a corner of the panelled wall, and a girl of about my own age came quickly out and kissed him. On her face, I saw immediately the placid and sweet expression of the lady whose picture had looked at me downstairs. It seemed to my imagination as if the portrait had grown womanly, and the original remained a child. Although her face was quite bright and happy, there was a tranquillity about it, and about her—a quiet, good, calm spirit,—that I never have forgotten; that I never shall forget.

This was his little housekeeper, his daughter Agnes, Mr. Wickfield said. When I heard how he said it, and saw how he held her hand, I guessed what the one motive of his life was.

She had a little basket-trifle hanging at her side, with keys in it; and she looked as staid and as discreet a housekeeper as the old house could have. She listened to her father as he told her about me, with a pleasant face; and when he had concluded, proposed to my aunt that we should go up-stairs and see my room. We all went together, she before us. A glorious old room it was, with more oak beams, and diamond panes; and the broad balustrade going all the way up to it.

I cannot call to mind where or when, in my childhood, I had seen a stained glass window in a church. Nor do I recollect its subject. But I know that when I saw her turn round, in the grave light of the old staircase, and wait for us, above, I thought of that window; and I associated something of its tranquil brightness with Agnes Wickfield ever afterwards.

My aunt was as happy as I was in the arrangement made for me, and we went down to the drawing-room again, well pleased and gratified. As she would not hear of staying to dinner, lest she should by any chance fail to arrive at home with the grey pony before dark; and as I apprehend Mr. Wickfield knew her too well to argue any point with her; some lunch was provided for her there, and Agnes went back to her governess, and Mr. Wickfield to his office. So we were left to take leave of one another without any restraint.

She told me that everything would be arranged for me by Mr. Wickfield, and that I should want for nothing, and gave me the kindest words and the best advice.

"Trot," said my aunt in conclusion, "be a credit to yourself, to me, and Mr. Dick, and Heaven be with you!"

I was greatly overcome, and could only thank her again and again, and send my love to Mr. Dick.

"Never," said my aunt, "be mean in anything; never be false; never be cruel. Avoid those three vices, Trot, and I can always be hopeful of you."

I promised, as well as I could, that I would not abuse her kindness or forget her admonition.

"The pony's at the door," said my aunt, "and I am off! Stay here."

With these words she embraced me hastily, and went out of the room, shutting the door after her. At first I was startled by so abrupt a departure, and almost feared I had displeased her; but when I looked into the street, and saw how dejectedly she got into the chaise, and drove away without looking up, I understood her better, and did not do her that injustice.

By five o'clock, which was Mr. Wickfield's dinner-hour, I had mustered up my spirits again, and was ready for my knife and fork. The cloth was only laid for us two; but Agnes was waiting in the drawing-room before dinner, went down with her father, and sat opposite to him at table. I doubted whether he could have dined without her.

We did not stay there, after dinner, but came up-stairs into the drawing-room again: in one snug corner of which, Agnes set glasses for her father, and a decanter of port wine. I thought he would have missed its usual flavour, if it had been put there for him by any other hands.

There he sat, taking his wine, and taking a good deal of it, for two hours; while Agnes played on the piano, worked, and talked to him and me. He was, for the most part, gay and cheerful with us; but sometimes his eyes rested on her, and he fell into a brooding state, and was silent. She always observed this quickly, I thought, and always roused him with a question or caress. Then he came out of his meditation, and drank more wine.

Agnes made the tea, and presided over it; and the time passed away after it, as after dinner, until she went to bed; when her father took her in his arms and kissed her, and, she being gone, ordered candles in his office. Then I went to bed too.

But in the course of the evening I had rambled down to the door, and a little way along the street, that I might have another peep at the old houses, and the grey Cathedral; and might think of my coming through that old city on my journey, and of my passing the very house I lived in, without knowing it. As I came back, I saw Uriah Heep shutting up the office; and, feeling friendly towards everybody, went in and spoke to him, and at parting, gave him my hand. But oh, what a clammy hand his was! as ghostly to the touch as to the sight! I rubbed mine afterwards, to warm it, *and to rub his off.*

It was such an uncomfortable hand, that, when I went to my room, it was still cold and wet upon my memory. Leaning out of window, and seeing one of the faces on the beam-ends looking at me sideways, I fancied it was Uriah Heep got up there somehow, and shut him out in a hurry.

16

I AM A NEW BOY IN MORE SENSES THAN ONE

NEXT MORNING, AFTER BREAKFAST, I ENTERED ON school life again. I went, accompanied by Mr. Wickfield, to the scene of my future studies—a grave building in a courtyard, with a learned air about it that seemed very well suited to the stray rooks and jackdaws who came down from the Cathedral towers to walk with a clerkly bearing on the grass-plot—and was introduced to my new master, Doctor Strong.

Doctor Strong looked almost as rusty, to my thinking, as the tall iron rails and gates outside the house; and almost as stiff and heavy as the great stone urns that flanked them, and were set up, on the top of the red-brick wall, at regular distances all round the court, like sublimated skittles, for Time to play at. He was in his library (I mean Doctor Strong was), with his clothes not particularly well brushed, and his hair not particularly well combed; his knee-smalls unbraced; his long black gaiters unbuttoned; and his shoes yawning like two caverns on the hearth-rug. Turning upon me a lustreless eye, that reminded me of a long-forgotten blind old horse who once used to crop the grass, and tumble over the graves in Blunderstone churchyard, he said he was glad to see me: and then he gave me his hand; which I didn't know what to do with, as it did nothing for itself.

But, sitting at work, not far off from Doctor Strong, was a very pretty young lady—whom he called Annie, and who was his daughter, I supposed—who got me out of my difficulty by kneeling down to put Doctor Strong's shoes on, and button his gaiters, which she did with great cheerfulness and quickness. When she had finished, and we were going out to the schoolroom, I was much surprised to hear Mr. Wickfield, in bidding her good morning, address her as " Mrs. Strong; " and I was wondering could she be Doctor Strong's son's wife, or could she be Mrs. Doctor Strong, when Doctor Strong himself unconsciously enlightened me.

" By-the-by, Wickfield," he said, stopping in a passage with his hand on my shoulder; " you have not found any suitable provision for my wife's cousin yet? "

" No," said Mr. Wickfield. " No. Not yet."

" I could wish it done as soon as it *can* be done, Wickfield," said Doctor Strong, " for Jack Maldon is needy, and idle; and of those two bad things, worse things sometimes come. What does Doctor Watts say," he added, looking at me, and moving his head to the time of his quotation, " ' Satan finds some mischief still, for idle hands to do.' "

" Egad, Doctor," returned Mr. Wickfield, " if Doctor Watts knew mankind, he might have written, with as much truth, ' Satan finds some mischief still, for busy hands to do.' The busy people achieve their full share of mischief in the world, you may rely upon it. What have the people been about, who have been the busiest in getting money, and in getting power, this century or two? No mischief? "

" Jack Maldon will never be very busy in getting either, I expect," said Doctor Strong, rubbing his chin thoughtfully.

" Perhaps not," said Mr. Wickfield; " and you bring me back to the question, with an apology for digressing. No, I have not been able to dispose of Mr. Jack Maldon yet. I believe," he said this with some hesitation, " I penetrate your motive, and it makes the thing more difficult."

" My motive," returned Doctor Strong, " is to make some suitable provision for a cousin, and an old playfellow, of Annie's."

" Yes, I know," said Mr. Wickfield, " at home or abroad."

" Ay! " replied the Doctor, apparently wondering why he emphasised those words so much. " At home or abroad."

" Your own expression, you know," said Mr. Wickfield. " Or abroad."

" Surely," the Doctor answered. " Surely. One or other."

" One or other? Have you no choice? " asked Mr. Wickfield.

" No," returned the Doctor.

" No? " with astonishment.

" Not the least."

" No motive," said Mr. Wickfield, " for meaning abroad, and not at home? "

" No," returned the Doctor.

" I am bound to believe you, and of course I do believe you," said Mr. Wickfield. " It might have simplified my office very much, if I had known it before. But I confess I entertained another impression."

Doctor Strong regarded him with a puzzled and doubting look, which almost immediately subsided into a smile that gave me great encouragement; for it was full of amiability and sweetness, and there was a simplicity in it, and indeed in his whole manner, when the studious, pondering frost upon it was got through, very attractive and hopeful to a young scholar like me. Repeating " no," and " not the least," and other short assurances to the same purport, Doctor Strong jogged on before us, at a queer, uneven pace; and we followed: Mr. Wickfield, looking grave, I observed, and shaking his head to himself, without knowing that I saw him.

The school-room was a pretty large hall, on the quietest side of the house, confronted by the stately stare of some half-dozen of the great urns, and commanding a peep of an old secluded garden belonging to the Doctor, where the peaches were ripening on the sunny south wall. There were two great aloes, in tubs, on the turf outside the windows; the broad hard leaves of which plant (looking as if they were made of painted tin) have ever since, by association, been symbolical to me of silence and retirement. About five-and-twenty boys were studiously engaged at their books when we went in, but they rose to give the Doctor good morning, and remained standing when they saw Mr. Wickfield and me.

" A new boy, young gentlemen," said the Doctor; " Trotwood Copperfield."

One Adams, who was the head-boy, then stepped out of his place and welcomed me. He looked like a young clergyman, in his white cravat, but he was very affable and good-humoured; and he showed me my place, and presented me to the masters, in a gentlemanly way that would have put me at my ease, if anything could.

It seemed to me so long, however, since I had been among such boys, or among any companions of my own age, except Mick Walker and Mealy Potatoes, that I felt as strange as ever I have done in all my life. I was so conscious of having passed through scenes of which they could have no knowledge, and of having acquired experiences foreign to my age, appearance and condition as one of them, that I half believed it was an imposture to come there as an ordinary little schoolboy. I had become, in the Murdstone and Grinby time, however short or long it may have been, so unused to the sports and games of boys, that I knew I was awkward and inexperienced in the commonest things belonging to them. Whatever I had learnt, had so slipped away from me in the sordid cares of my life from day to night, that now, when I was examined about what I knew, I knew nothing, and was put into the lowest form of the school. But, troubled as

I was by my want of boyish skill, and of book-learning too, I was made infinitely more uncomfortable by the consideration that, in what I did know, I was much farther removed from my companions than in what I did not. My mind ran upon what they would think, if they knew of my familiar acquaintance with the King's Bench Prison? Was there anything about me which would reveal my proceedings in connection with the Micawber family—all those pawnings, and sellings, and suppers—in spite of myself? Suppose some of the boys had seen me coming through Canterbury, wayworn and ragged, and should find me out? What would they say, who made so light of money, if they could know how I had scraped my halfpence together, for the purchase of my daily saveloy and beer, or my slices of pudding? How would it affect them, who were so innocent of London life and London streets, to discover how knowing I was (and was ashamed to be) in some of the meanest phases of both? All this ran in my head so much, on that first day at Doctor Strong's, that I felt distrustful of my slightest look and gesture; shrunk within myself whensoever I was approached by one of my new schoolfellows; and hurried off, the minute school was over, afraid of committing myself in my response to any friendly notice or advance.

But there was such an influence in Mr. Wickfield's old house, that when I knocked at it, with my new school-books under my arm, I began to feel my uneasiness softening away. As I went up to my airy old room, the grave shadow of the staircase seemed to fall upon my doubts and fears, and to make the past more indistinct. I sat there, sturdily conning my books, until dinner-time (we were out of school for good at three): and went down, hopeful of becoming a passable sort of boy yet.

Agnes was in the drawing-room, waiting for her father, who was detained by some one in his office. She met me with her pleasant smile, and asked me how I liked the school. I told her I should like it very much, I hoped: but I was a little strange to it at first.

"*You* have never been to school," I said, "have you?"

"Oh yes! Every day."

"Ah, but you mean here, at your own home?"

"Papa couldn't spare me to go anywhere else," she answered, smiling and shaking her head. "His housekeeper must be in his house, you know."

"He is very fond of you, I am sure," I said.

She nodded "Yes," and went to the door to listen for his

coming up, that she might meet him on the stairs. But, as he was not there, she came back again.

"Mama has been dead ever since I was born," she said, in her quiet way. "I only know her picture, down-stairs. I saw you looking at it yesterday. Did you think whose it was?"

I told her yes, because it was so like herself.

"Papa says so, too," said Agnes, pleased. "Hark! That's papa now!"

Her bright calm face lighted up with pleasure as she went to meet him, and as they came in, hand in hand. He greeted me cordially; and told me I should certainly be happy under Doctor Strong, who was one of the gentlest of men.

"There may be some, perhaps—I don't know that there are —who abuse his kindness," said Mr. Wickfield. "Never be one of those, Trotwood, in anything. He is the least suspicious of mankind; and whether that's a merit, or whether it's a blemish, it deserves consideration in all dealings with the Doctor, great or small."

He spoke, I thought, as if he were weary, or dissatisfied with something; but I did not pursue the question in my mind, for dinner was just then announced, and we went down and took the same seats as before.

We had scarcely done so, when Uriah Heep put in his red head and his lank hand at the door, and said:

"Here's Mr. Maldon begs the favour of a word, sir."

"I am but this moment quit of Mr. Maldon," said his master.

"Yes, sir," returned Uriah; "but Mr. Maldon has come back, and he begs the favour of a word."

As he held the door open with his hand, Uriah looked at me, and looked at Agnes, and looked at the dishes, and looked at the plates, and looked at every object in the room, I thought,— yet seemed to look at nothing; he made such an appearance all the while of keeping his red eyes dutifully on his master.

"I beg your pardon. It's only to say, on reflection," observed a voice behind Uriah, as Uriah's head was pushed away, and the speaker's substituted—"pray excuse me for this intrusion—that as it seems I have no choice in the matter, the sooner I go abroad the better. My cousin Annie did say, when we talked of it, that she liked to have her friends within reach rather than to have them banished, and the old Doctor—"

"Doctor Strong, was that?" Mr. Wickfield interposed, gravely.

"Doctor Strong, of course," returned the other: "I call him the old Doctor; it's all the same, you know."

" I *don't* know," returned Mr. Wickfield.

" Well, Doctor Strong," said the other. " Doctor Strong was of the same mind, I believed. But as it appears from the course you take with me he has changed his mind, why there's no more to be said, except that the sooner I am off, the better. Therefore, I thought I'd come back and say, that the sooner I am off the better. When a plunge is to be made into the water, it's no use lingering on the bank."

" There shall be as little lingering as possible, in your case, Mr. Maldon, you may depend upon it," said Mr. Wickfield.

" Thank'ee," said the other. " Much obliged. I don't want to look a gift-horse in the mouth, which is not a gracious thing to do; otherwise, I dare say, my cousin Annie could easily arrange it in her own way. I suppose Annie would only have to say to the old Doctor—"

" Meaning that Mrs. Strong would only have to say to her husband—do I follow you?" said Mr. Wickfield.

" Quite so," returned the other, "—would only have to say, that she wanted such and such a thing to be so and so; and it would be so and so, as a matter of course."

" And why as a matter of course, Mr. Maldon?" asked Mr. Wickfield, sedately eating his dinner.

" Why, because Annie's a charming young girl, and the old Doctor—Doctor Strong, I mean—is not quite a charming young boy," said Mr. Jack Maldon, laughing. " No offence to anybody, Mr. Wickfield. I only mean that some compensation is fair and reasonable in that sort of marriage."

" Compensation to the lady, sir?" asked Mr. Wickfield gravely.

" To the lady, sir," Mr. Jack Maldon answered, laughing. But appearing to remark that Mr. Wickfield went on with his dinner in the same sedate, immovable manner, and that there was no hope of making him relax a muscle of his face, he added:

" However, I have said what I came back to say, and, with another apology for this intrusion, I may take myself off. Of course I shall observe your directions, in considering the matter as one to be arranged between you and me solely, and not to be referred to, up at the Doctor's."

" Have you dined?" asked Mr. Wickfield, with a motion of his hand towards the table.

"Thank'ee. I am going to dine," said Mr. Maldon, " with my cousin Annie. Good-bye!"

Mr. Wickfield, without rising, looked after him thoughtfully as he went out. He was rather a shallow sort of young gentleman,

I thought, with a handsome face, a rapid utterance, and a confident bold air. And this was the first I ever saw of Mr. Jack Maldon; whom I had not expected to see so soon, when I heard the Doctor speak of him that morning.

When we had dined, we went up-stairs again, where everything went on exactly as on the previous day. Agnes set the glasses and decanters in the same corner, and Mr. Wickfield sat down to drink, and drank a good deal. Agnes played the piano to him, sat by him, and worked and talked, and played some games at dominoes with me. In good time she made tea; and afterwards, when I brought down my books, looked into them, and showed me what she knew of them (which was no slight matter, though she said it was), and what was the best way to learn and understand them. I see her, with her modest, orderly, placid manner, and I hear her beautiful calm voice, as I write these words. The influence for all good, which she came to exercise over me at a later time, begins already to descend upon my breast. I love little Em'ly, and I don't love Agnes—no, not at all in that way—but I feel that there are goodness, peace, and truth, wherever Agnes is; and that the soft light of the coloured window in the church, seen long ago, falls on her always, and on me when I am near her, and on everything around.

The time having come for her withdrawal for the night, and she having left us, I gave Mr. Wickfield my hand, preparatory to going away myself. But he checked me and said: "Should you like to stay with us, Trotwood, or to go elsewhere?"

"To stay," I answered, quickly.

"You are sure?"

"If you please. If I may!"

"Why, it's but a dull life that we lead here, boy, I am afraid," he said.

"Not more dull for me than Agnes, sir. Not dull at all!"

"Than Agnes," he repeated, walking slowly to the great chimney-piece, and leaning against it. "Than Agnes!"

He had drank wine that evening (or I fancied it), until his eyes were bloodshot. Not that I could see them now, for they were cast down, and shaded by his hand; but I had noticed them a little while before.

"Now I wonder," he muttered, "whether my Agnes tires of me. When should I ever tire of her! But that's different, that's quite different."

He was musing, not speaking to me; so I remained quiet.

"A dull old house," he said, "and a monotonous life; but I

must have her near me. I must keep her near me. If the thought that I may die and leave my darling, or that my darling may die and leave me, comes like a spectre, to distress my happiest hours, and is only to be drowned in——"

He did not supply the word; but pacing slowly to the place where he had sat, and mechanically going through the action of pouring wine from the empty decanter, set it down and paced back again.

"If it is miserable to bear when she is here," he said, "what would it be, and she away? No, no no. I cannot try that."

He leaned against the chimney-piece, brooding so long that I could not decide whether to run the risk of disturbing him by going, or to remain quietly where I was, until he should come out of his reverie. At length he aroused himself, and looked about the room until his eyes encountered mine.

"Stay with us, Trotwood, eh?" he said in his usual manner, and as if he were answering something I had just said. "I am glad of it. You are company to us both. It is wholesome to have you here. Wholesome for me, wholesome for Agnes, wholesome perhaps for all of us."

"I am sure it is for me, sir," I said. "I am so glad to be here."

"That's a fine fellow!" said Mr. Wickfield. "As long as you are glad to be here, you shall stay here." He shook hands with me upon it, and clapped me on the back; and told me that when I had anything to do at night after Agnes had left us, or when I wished to read for my own pleasure, I was free to come down to his room, if he were there, and if I desired it for company's sake, and to sit with him. I thanked him for his consideration; and, as he went down soon afterwards, and I was not tired, went down too, with a book in my hand, to avail myself, for half-an-hour, of his permission.

But, seeing a light in the little round office, and immediately feeling myself attracted towards Uriah Heep, who had a sort of fascination for me, I went in there instead. I found Uriah reading a great fat book, with such demonstrative attention, that his lank forefinger followed up every line as he read, and made clammy tracks along the page (or so I fully believed) like a snail.

"You are working late to-night, Uriah," says I.

"Yes, Master Copperfield," says Uriah.

As I was getting on the stool opposite, to talk to him more conveniently, I observed that he had not such a thing as a smile about him, and that he could only widen his mouth and make two hard creases down his cheeks, one on each side, to stand for one.

"I am not doing office-work, Master Copperfield," said Uriah.

"What work, then?" I asked.

"I am improving my legal knowledge, Master Copperfield," said Uriah. "I am going through Tidd's Practice. Oh, what a writer Mr. Tidd is, Master Copperfield!"

My stool was such a tower of observation, that as I watched him reading on again, after this rapturous exclamation, and following up the lines with his forefinger, I observed that his nostrils, which were thin and pointed, with sharp dints in them, had a singular and most uncomfortable way of expanding and contracting themselves; that they seemed to twinkle instead of his eyes, which hardly ever twinkled at all.

"I suppose you are quite a great lawyer?" I said, after looking at him for some time.

"Me, Master Copperfield?" said Uriah. "Oh, no! I'm a very umble person."

It was no fancy of mine about his hands, I observed; for he frequently ground the palms against each other as if to squeeze them dry and warm, besides often wiping them, in a stealthy way, on his pocket-handkerchief.

"I am well aware that I am the umblest person going," said Uriah Heep, modestly; "let the other be where he may. My mother is likewise a very umble person. We live in an umble abode, Master Copperfield, but have much to be thankful for. My father's former calling was umble. He was a sexton."

"What is he now?" I asked.

"He is a partaker of glory at present, Master Copperfield," said Uriah Heep, "But we have much to be thankful for. How much have I to be thankful for in living with Mr. Wickfield!"

I asked Uriah if he had been with Mr. Wickfield long?

"I have been with him going on four year, Master Copperfield," said Uriah; shutting up his book, after carefully marking the place where he had left off. "Since a year after my father's death. How much have I to be thankful for, in that! How much have I to be thankful for, in Mr. Wickfield's kind intention to give me my articles, which would otherwise not lay within the umble means of mother and self!"

"Then, when your articled time is over, you'll be a regular lawyer, I suppose?" said I.

"With the blessing of Providence, Master Copperfield," returned Uriah.

"Perhaps you'll be a partner in Mr. Wickfield's business, one of these days," I said, to make myself agreeable; " and it will be Wickfield and Heep, or Heep late Wickfield."

" Oh no, Master Copperfield," returned Uriah, shaking his head, " I am much too umble for that! "

He certainly did look uncommonly like the carved face on the beam outside my window, as he sat, in his humility, eyeing me sideways, with his mouth widened, and the creases in his cheeks.

" Mr. Wickfield is a most excellent man, Master Copperfield," said Uriah. " If you have known him long, you know it, I am sure, much better than I can inform you."

I replied that I was certain he was; but that I had not known him long myself, though he was a friend of my aunt's.

" Oh, indeed, Master Copperfield," said Uriah. " Your aunt is a sweet lady, Master Copperfield! "

He had a way of writhing when he wanted to express enthusiasm, which was very ugly; and which diverted my attention from the compliment he had paid my relation, to the snaky twistings of his throat and body.

" A sweet lady, Master Copperfield! " said Uriah Heep. " She has a great admiration for Miss Agnes, Master Copperfield, I believe? "

I said, " Yes," boldly; not that I knew anything about it, Heaven forgive me!

" I hope you have, too, Master Copperfield," said Uriah. " But I am sure you must have."

" Everybody must have," I returned.

" Oh, thank you, Master Copperfield," said Uriah Heep, " for that remark! It is so true! Umble as I am, I know it is *so* true! Oh, thank you, Master Copperfield! "

He writhed himself quite off his stool in the excitement of his feelings, and, being off, began to make arrangements for going home.

" Mother will be expecting me," he said, referring to a pale, inexpressive-faced watch in his pocket, " and getting uneasy; for though we are very umble, Master Copperfield, we are much attached to one another. If you would come and see us, any afternoon, and take a cup of tea at our lowly dwelling, mother would be as proud of your company as I should be."

I said I should be glad to come.

" Thank you, Master Copperfield," returned Uriah, putting his book away upon the shelf.—" I suppose you stop here, some time, Master Copperfield? "

I said I was going to be brought up there, I believed, as long as I remained at school.

" Oh, indeed! " exclaimed Uriah. " I should think *you* would come into the business at last, Master Copperfield! "

I protested that I had no views of that sort, and that no such scheme was entertained in my behalf by anybody; but Uriah insisted on blandly replying to all my assurances, " Oh, yes, Master Copperfield, I should think you would, indeed! " and, " Oh, indeed, Master Copperfield, I should think you would, certainly! " over and over again. Being, at last, ready to leave the office for the night, he asked me if it would suit my convenience to have the light put out; and on my answering " Yes," instantly extinguished it. After shaking hands with me—his hand felt like a fish—in the dark, he opened the door into the street a very little, and crept out, and shut it, leaving me to grope my way back into the house: which cost me some trouble and a fall over his stool. This was the proximate cause, I suppose, of my dreaming about him, for what appeared to me to be half the night; and dreaming, among other things, that he had launched Mr. Peggotty's house on a piratical expedition, with a black flag at the masthead, bearing the inscription " Tidd's Practice," under which diabolical ensign he was carrying me and little Em'ly to the Spanish Main, to be drowned.

I got a little the better of my uneasiness when I went to school next day, and a good deal the better next day, and so shook it off by degrees, that in less than a fortnight I was quite at home, and happy, among my new companions. I was awkward enough in their games, and backward enough in their studies; but custom would improve me in the first respect, I hoped, and hard work in the second. Accordingly, I went to work very hard, both in play and in earnest, and gained great commendation. And, in a very little while, the Murdstone and Grinby life became so strange to me that I hardly believed in it, while my present life grew so familiar, that I seemed to have been leading it a long time.

Doctor Strong's was an excellent school; as different from Mr. Creakle's as good is from evil. It was very gravely and decorously ordered, and on a sound system; with an appeal, in everything, to the honour and good faith of the boys, and an avowed intention to rely on their possession of those qualities unless they proved themselves unworthy of it, which worked wonders. We all felt that we had a part in the management of the place, and in sustaining its character and dignity. Hence, we soon became warmly attached to it—I am sure I did for one, and I never knew, in all my time, of any other boy being otherwise—and learnt with a good will, desiring to do it credit. We had noble games out of hours, and plenty of liberty; but even then, as I remember, we were well spoken of in the town, and rarely did any disgrace, by our appearance or manner, to the reputation of Doctor Strong and Doctor Strong's boys.

Some of the higher scholars boarded in the Doctor's house, and through them I learned, at second hand, some particulars of the Doctor's history. As, how he had not yet been married twelve months to the beautiful young lady I had seen in the study, whom he had married for love; for she had not a sixpence, and had a world of poor relations (so our fellows said) ready to swarm the Doctor out of house and home. Also, how the Doctor's cogitating manner was attributable to his being always engaged in looking out for Greek roots; which, in my innocence and ignorance, I supposed to be a botanical furor on the Doctor's part, especially as he always looked at the ground when he walked about, until I understood that they were roots of words, with a view to a new Dictionary which he had in contemplation. Adams, our head-boy, who had a turn for mathematics, had made a calculation, I was informed, of the time this Dictionary would take in completing, on the Doctor's plan, and at the Doctor's rate of going. He considered that it might be done in one thousand six hundred and forty-nine years, counting from the Doctor's last, or sixty-second, birthday.

But the Doctor himself was the idol of the whole school: and it must have been a badly-composed school if he had been anything else, for he was the kindest of men; with a simple faith in him that might have touched the stone hearts of the very urns upon the wall. As he walked up and down that part of the court-yard which was at the side of the house, with the stray rooks and jackdaws looking after him with their heads cocked slyly, as if they knew how much more knowing they were in worldly affairs than he, if any sort of vagabond could only get near enough to his creaking shoes to attract his attention to one sentence of a tale of distress, that vagabond was made for the next two days. It was so notorious in the house, that the masters and head-boys took pains to cut these marauders off at angles, and to get out of windows, and turn them out of the court-yard, before they could make the Doctor aware of their presence; which was sometimes happily effected within a few yards of him, without his knowing anything of the matter, as he jogged to and fro. Outside his own domain, and unprotected, he was a very sheep for the shearers. He would have taken his gaiters off his legs, to give away. In fact, there was a story current among us (I have no idea, and never had, on what authority, but I have believed it for so many years that I feel quite certain it is true), that on a frosty day, one winter-time, he actually did bestow his gaiters on a beggar-woman, who occasioned some scandal in the neighbourhood by exhibiting a fine infant from door to door, wrapped in those garments, which were universally recognised, being as well known in the vicinity, as the Cathedral. The legend added that the only person who did not identify them was the Doctor himself, who, when they were shortly afterwards displayed at the door of a little second-hand shop of no very good repute, where such things were taken in exchange for gin, was more than once observed to handle them approvingly, as if admiring some curious novelty in the pattern, and considering them an improvement on his own.

It was very pleasant to see the Doctor with his pretty young wife. He had a fatherly, benignant way of showing his fondness for her, which seemed in itself to express a good man. I often saw them walking in the garden where the peaches were, and I sometimes had a nearer observation of them in the study or the parlour. She appeared to me to take great care of the Doctor, and to like him very much, though I never thought her vitally interested in the Dictionary: some cumbrous fragments of which work the Doctor always carried in his pockets, and in the lining of his hat, and generally seemed to be expounding to her as they walked about.

I saw a good deal of Mrs. Strong, both because she had taken a liking for me on the morning of my introduction to the Doctor, and was always afterwards kind to me, and interested in me; and because she was very fond of Agnes, and was often backwards and forwards at our house. There was a curious constraint between her and Mr. Wickfield, I thought (of whom she seemed to be afraid), that never wore off. When she came there of an evening, she always shrunk from accepting his escort home, and ran away with me instead. And some times, as we were running gaily across the Cathedral yard together, expecting to meet nobody, we would meet Mr. Jack Maldon, who was always surprised to see us.

Mrs. Strong's mama was a lady I took great delight in. Her name was Mrs. Markleham; but our boys used to call her the Old Soldier, on account of her generalship, and the skill with which she marshalled great forces of relations against the Doctor. She was a little, sharp-eyed woman, who used to wear, when she was dressed, one unchangeable cap, ornamented with some artificial flowers, and two artificial butterflies supposed to be hovering over the flowers. There was a superstition among us that this cap had come from France, and could only originate in the workmanship of that ingenious nation: but all I certainly know about it is, that it always made its appearance of an evening, wheresoever Mrs. Markleham made *her* appearance; that it was carried about to friendly meetings in a Hindoo basket; that the butterflies had the gift of trembling constantly; and that they improved the shining hours at Doctor Strong's expense, like busy bees.

I observed the Old Soldier—not to adopt the name disrespectfully—to pretty good advantage, on a night which is made memorable to me by something else I shall relate. It was the night of a little party at the Doctor's, which was given on the occasion of Mr. Jack Maldon's departure for India, whither he was going as a cadet, or something of that kind: Mr. Wickfield having at length arranged the business. It happened to be the Doctor's birthday, too. We had had a holiday, had made presents to him in the morning, had made a speech to him through the head-boy, and had cheered him until we were hoarse, and until he had shed tears. And now, in the evening, Mr. Wickfield, Agnes and I, went to have tea with him in his private capacity.

Mr. Jack Maldon was there, before us. Mrs. Strong, dressed in white, with cherry-coloured ribbons, was playing the piano, when we went in; and he was leaning over her to turn the leaves. The clear red and white of her complexion was not so blooming and flower-like as usual, I thought, when she turned round; but she looked very pretty, wonderfully pretty.

"I have forgotten, Doctor," said Mrs. Strong's mama, when we were seated, "to pay you the compliments of the day: though they are, as you may suppose, very far from being mere compliments in my case. Allow me to wish you many happy returns."

"I thank you, ma'am," replied the Doctor.

"Many, many, many, happy returns," said the Old Soldier. "Not only for your own sake, but for Annie's and John Maldon's, and many other people's. It seems but yesterday to me, John, when you were a little creature, a head shorter than Master Copperfield, making baby love to Annie behind the gooseberry bushes in the back-garden."

"My dear mama," said Mrs. Strong, "never mind that now."

"Annie, don't be absurd," returned her mother. "If you are to blush to hear of such things now you are an old married woman, when are you not to blush to hear of them?"

"Old?" exclaimed Mr. Jack Maldon. "Annie? Come!"

" Yes, John," returned the Soldier. " Virtually, an old married woman. Although not old by years—for when did you ever hear me say, or who has ever heard me say, that a girl of twenty was old by years!—your cousin is the wife of the Doctor, and, as such, what I have described her. It is well for you, John, that your cousin *is* the wife of the Doctor. You have found in him an influential and kind friend, who will be kinder yet, I venture to predict, if you deserve it. I have no false pride. I never hesitate to admit, frankly, that there are some members of our family who want a friend. You were one yourself, before your cousin's influence raised up one for you."

The Doctor, in the goodness of his heart, waved his hand as if to make light of it, and save Mr. Jack Maldon from any further reminder. But Mrs. Markleham changed her chair for one next the Doctor's, and putting her fan on his coat-sleeve, said:

" No, really, my dear Doctor, you must excuse me if I appear to dwell on this rather, because I feel so very strongly. I call it quite my monomania, it is such a subject of mine. You are a blessing to us. You really are a Boon, you know."

" Nonsense, nonsense," said the Doctor.

" No, no, I beg your pardon," retorted the Old Soldier. " With nobody present, but our dear and confidential friend Mr. Wickfield, I cannot consent to be put down. I shall begin to assert the privileges of a mother-in-law, if you go on like that, and scold you. I am perfectly honest and outspoken. What I am saying, is what I said when you first overpowered me with surprise—you remember how surprised I was?—by proposing for Annie. Not that there was anything so very much out of the way, in the mere fact of the proposal—it would be ridiculous to say that!—but because, you having known her poor father and having known her from a baby six months old, I hadn't thought of you in such a light at all, or indeed as a marrying man in any way,—simply that, you know."

" Aye, aye," returned the Doctor, good-humouredly. " Never mind."

" But I *do* mind," said the Old Soldier, laying her fan upon his lips. " I mind very much. I recall these things that I may be contradicted if I am wrong. Well! Then I spoke to Annie, and I told her what had happened. I said, ' My dear, here's Doctor Strong has positively been and made you the subject of a handsome declaration and an offer.' Did I press it in the least? No, I said, ' Now Annie, tell me the truth this moment; is your heart free?' ' Mama,' she said crying, ' I am extremely young '—

which was perfectly true—' and I hardly know if I have a heart at all.' ' Then, my dear,' I said, ' you may rely upon it, it's free. At all events, my love,' said I, ' Doctor Strong is in an agitated state of mind, and must be answered. He cannot be kept in his present state of suspense.' ' Mama,' said Annie, still crying, ' would he be unhappy without me? If he would, I honour and respect him so much, that I think I will have him.' So it was settled. And then, and not till then, I said to Annie, ' Annie, Doctor Strong will not only be your husband, but he will represent your late father: he will represent the head of our family, he will represent the wisdom and station, and I may say the means, of our family; and will be, in short, a Boon to it.' I used the word at the time, and I have used it again, to-day. If I have any merit it is consistency."

The daughter had sat quite silent and still during this speech, with her eyes fixed on the ground; her cousin standing near her, and looking on the ground too. She now said very softly, in a trembling voice:

" Mama, I hope you have finished? "

" No, my dear Annie," returned the Soldier, " I have not quite finished. Since you ask me, my love, I reply that I have *not*. I complain that you really are a little unnatural towards your own family; and, as it is of no use complaining to you, I mean to complain to your husband. Now, my dear Doctor, do look at that silly wife of yours."

As the Doctor turned his kind face, with its smile of simplicity and gentleness, towards her, she drooped her head more. I noticed that Mr. Wickfield looked at her steadily.

" When I happened to say to that naughty thing, the other day," pursued her mother, shaking her head and her fan at her, playfully, " that there was a family circumstance she might mention to you—indeed, I think, was bound to mention—she said, that to mention it was to ask a favour; and that, as you were too generous, and as for her to ask was always to have, she wouldn't."

" Annie, my dear," said the Doctor. " That was wrong. It robbed me of a pleasure."

" Almost the very words I said to her! " exclaimed her mother. " Now really, another time, when I know what she would tell you but for this reason, and won't, I have a great mind, my dear Doctor, to tell you myself."

" I shall be glad if you will," returned the Doctor.

" Shall I? "

" Certainly."

" Well, then, I will! " said the Old Soldier. " That's a bargain." And having, I suppose, carried her point, she tapped the Doctor's hand several times with her fan (which she kissed first), and returned triumphantly to her former station.

Some more company coming in, among whom were the two masters and Adams, the talk became general; and it naturally turned on Mr. Jack Maldon, and his voyage, and the country he was going to, and his various plans and prospects. He was to leave that night, after supper, in a post-chaise, for Gravesend; where the ship, in which he was to make the voyage, lay; and was to be gone—unless he came home on leave, or for his health —I don't know how many years. I recollect it was settled by general consent that India was quite a misrepresented country, and had nothing objectionable in it, but a tiger or two, and a little heat in the warm part of the day. For my own part, I looked on Mr. Jack Maldon as a modern Sinbad, and pictured him the bosom friend of all the Rajahs in the East, sitting under canopies, smoking curly golden pipes—a mile long, if they could be straightened out.

Mrs. Strong was a very pretty singer: as I knew, who often heard her singing by herself. But, whether she was afraid of singing before people, or was out of voice that evening, it was certain that she couldn't sing at all. She tried a duet, once, with her cousin Maldon, but could not so much as begin; and afterwards, when she tried to sing by herself, although she began sweetly, her voice died away on a sudden, and left her quite distressed, with her head hanging down over the keys. The good Doctor said she was nervous, and, to relieve her, proposed a round game at cards; of which he knew as much as of the art of playing the trombone. But I remarked that the Old Soldier took him into custody directly, for her partner; and instructed him, as the first preliminary of initiation, to give her all the silver he had in his pocket.

We had a merry game, not made the less merry by the Doctor's mistakes, of which he committed an innumerable quantity, in spite of the watchfulness of the butterflies, and to their great aggravation. Mrs. Strong had declined to play, on the ground of not feeling very well; and her cousin Maldon had excused himself because he had some packing to do. When he had done it, however, he returned, and they sat together, talking, on the sofa. From time to time she came and looked over the Doctor's hand, and told him what to play. She was very pale, as she bent over him, and I thought her finger trembled as she pointed out the cards; but the Doctor was quite happy in her attention, and took no notice of this, if it were so.

At supper, we were hardly so gay. Every one appeared to feel that a parting of that sort was an awkward thing, and that the nearer it approached, the more awkward it was. Mr. Jack Maldon tried to be very talkative, but was not at his ease, and made matters worse. And they were not improved, as it appeared to me, by the Old Soldier: who continually recalled passages of Mr. Jack Maldon's youth.

The Doctor, however, who felt, I am sure, that he was making everybody happy, was well pleased, and had no suspicion but that we were all at the utmost height of enjoyment.

" Annie, my dear," said he, looking at his watch, and filling his glass, " it is past your cousin Jack's time, and we must not detain him, since time and tide—both concerned in this case—wait for no man. Mr. Jack Maldon, you have a long voyage, and a strange country, before you; but many men have had both, and many men will have both, to the end of time. The winds you are going to tempt have wafted thousands upon thousands to fortune, and brought thousands upon thousands happily back."

" It's an affecting thing," said Mrs. Markleham, " however it's viewed, it's affecting, to see a fine young man one has known from an infant, going away to the other end of the world, leaving all he knows behind, and not knowing what's before him. A young man really well deserves constant support and patronage," looking at the Doctor, " who makes such sacrifices."

" Time will go fast with you, Mr. Jack Maldon," pursued the Doctor, " and fast with all of us. Some of us can hardly expect, perhaps, in the natural course of things, to greet you on your return. The next thing is to hope to do it, and that's my case. I shall not weary you with good advice. You have long had a good model before you, in your cousin Annie. Imitate her virtues as nearly as you can."

Mrs. Markleham fanned herself, and shook her head.

" Farewell, Mr. Jack," said the Doctor, standing up; on which we all stood up. " A prosperous voyage out, a thriving career abroad, and a happy return home! "

We all drank the toast, and all shook hands with Mr. Jack Maldon; after which he hastily took leave of the ladies who were there, and hurried to the door, where he was received, as he got into the chaise, with a tremendous broadside of cheers discharged by our boys, who had assembled on the lawn for the purpose. Running in among them to swell the ranks, I was very near the chaise when it rolled away; and I had a lively impression made upon me, in the midst of the noise and dust, of having seen Mr. Jack Maldon rattle past with an agitated face, and something cherry-coloured in his hand.

After another broadside for the Doctor, and another for the Doctor's wife, the boys dispersed, and I went back into the house, where I found the guests all standing in a group about the Doctor, discussing how Mr. Jack Maldon had gone away, and how he had borne it, and how he had felt it, and all the rest of it. In the midst of these remarks, Mrs. Markleham cried: "Where's Annie?"

No Annie was there; and when they called to her, no Annie replied. But all pressing out of the room, in a crowd, to see what was the matter, we found her lying on the hall floor. There was great alarm at first, until it was found that she was in a swoon, and that the swoon was yielding to the usual means of recovery: when the Doctor, who had lifted her head upon his knee, put her curls aside with his hand, and said, looking around:

"Poor Annie! She's so faithful and tender-hearted! It's the parting from her old playfellow and friend, her favourite cousin, that has done this. Ah! It's a pity! I am very sorry!"

When she opened her eyes, and saw where she was, and that we were all standing about her, she arose with assistance: turning her head, as she did so, to lay it on the Doctor's shoulder—or to hide it, I don't know which. We went into the drawing-room, to leave her with the Doctor and her mother; but she said, it seemed, that she was better than she had been since morning, and that she would rather be brought among us; so they brought her in, looking very white and weak, I thought, and sat her on a sofa.

"Annie, my dear," said her mother, doing something to her dress. "See here! You have lost a bow. Will anybody be so good as find a ribbon; a cherry-coloured ribbon?"

It was the one she had worn at her bosom. We all looked for it; I myself looked everywhere, I am certain; but nobody could find it.

"Do you recollect where you had it last, Annie?" said her mother.

I wondered how I could have thought she looked white, or anything but burning red, when she answered that she had had it safe, a little while ago, she thought, but it was not worth looking for.

Nevertheless, it was looked for again, and still not found. She entreated that there might be no more searching; but it was still sought for in a desultory way, until she was quite well, and the company took their departure.

We walked very slowly home, Mr. Wickfield, Agnes, and I; Agnes and I admiring the moonlight, and Mr. Wickfield scarcely raising his eyes from the ground. When we, at last, reached our own door, Agnes discovered that she had left her little reticule behind. Delighted to be of any service to her, I ran back to fetch it.

I went into the supper-room where it had been left, which was deserted and dark. But a door of communication between that and the Doctor's study, where there was a light, being open, I passed on there, to say what I wanted, and to get a candle.

The Doctor was sitting in his easy-chair by the fireside, and his young wife was on a stool at his feet. The Doctor, with a complacent smile, was reading aloud some manuscript explanation or statement of a theory out of that interminable Dictionary, and she was looking up at him. But with such a face as I never saw. It was so beautiful in its form, it was so ashy pale, it was so fixed in its abstraction, it was so full of a wild, sleep-walking, dreamy horror of I don't know what. The eyes were wide open, and her brown hair fell in two rich clusters on her shoulders, and on her white dress, disordered by the want of the lost ribbon. Distinctly as I recollect her look, I cannot say of what it was expressive, I cannot even say of what it is expressive to me now, rising again before my older judgment. Penitence, humiliation, shame, pride, love, and trustfulness, I see them all; and in them all, I see that horror of I don't know what.

My entrance, and my saying what I wanted, roused her. It disturbed the Doctor too, for when I went back to replace the candle I had taken from the table, he was patting her head, in his fatherly way, and saying he was a merciless drone to let her tempt him into reading on; and he would have her go to bed.

But she asked him, in a rapid, urgent manner, to let her stay —to let her feel assured (I heard her murmur some broken words to this effect) that she was in his confidence that night. And, as she turned again towards him, after glancing at me as I left the room and went out at the door, I saw her cross her hands upon his knee, and look up at him with the same face, something quieted, as he resumed his reading.

It made a great impression on me, and I remembered it a long time afterwards, as I shall have occasion to narrate when the time comes.

17

SOMEBODY TURNS UP

IT HAS NOT OCCURRED TO ME TO MENTION PEGGOTTY since I ran away; but, of course, I wrote her a letter almost as soon as I was housed at Dover, and another and a longer letter, containing all particulars fully related, when my aunt took me formally under her protection. On my being settled at Doctor Strong's I wrote to her again, detailing my happy condition and prospects. I never could have derived anything like the pleasure from spending the money Mr. Dick had given me, that I felt in sending a gold half-guinea to Peggotty, per post, inclosed in this last letter, to discharge the sum I had borrowed of her: in which epistle, not before, I mentioned about the young man with the donkey-cart.

To these communications Peggotty replied as promptly, if not as concisely, as a merchant's clerk. Her utmost powers of expression (which were certainly not great in ink) were exhausted in the attempt to write what she felt on the subject of my journey. Four sides of incoherent and interjectional beginnings of sentences, that had no end, except blots, were inadequate to afford her any relief. But the blots were more expressive to me than the best composition; for they showed me that Peggotty had been crying all over the paper, and what could I have desired more?

I made out, without much difficulty, that she could not take quite kindly to my aunt yet. The notice was too short after so long a prepossession the other way. We never knew a person, she wrote; but to think that Miss Betsey should seem to be so different from what she had been thought to be, was a Moral! That was her word. She was evidently still afraid of Miss Betsey, for she sent her grateful duty to her but timidly; and she was evidently afraid of me, too, and entertained the probability of my running away again soon; if I might judge from the repeated hints she threw out, that the coach-fare to Yarmouth was always to be had of her for the asking.

She gave me one piece of intelligence which affected me very much, namely, that there had been a sale of the furniture at our old home, and that Mr. and Miss Murdstone were gone away, and the house was shut up, to be let or sold. God knows I had no part in it while they remained there, but it pained me to think of the dear old place as altogether abandoned; of the weeds growing tall in the garden, and the fallen leaves lying thick and wet upon the paths. I imagined how the winds of winter would howl round it, how the cold rain would beat upon the window-glass, how the moon would make ghosts on the walls of the empty rooms, watching their solitude all night. I thought afresh of the grave in the churchyard, underneath the tree: and it seemed as if the house were dead too, now, and all connected with my father and mother were faded away.

There was no other news in Peggotty's letters. Mr. Barkis was an excellent husband, she said, though still a little near; but we all had our faults, and she had plenty (though I am sure I don't know what they were); and he sent his duty, and my little bedroom was always ready for me. Mr. Peggotty was well, and Ham was well, and Mrs. Gummidge was but poorly, and little Em'ly wouldn't send her love, but said that Peggotty might send it, if she liked.

All this intelligence I dutifully imparted to my aunt, only reserving to myself the mention of little Em'ly, to whom I instinctively felt that she would not very tenderly incline. While I was yet new at Doctor Strong's, she made several excursions over to Canterbury to see me, and always at unseasonable hours: with the view, I suppose, of taking me by surprise. But, finding me well employed, and bearing a good character, and hearing on all hands that I rose fast in the school, she soon discontinued these visits. I saw her on a Saturday, every third or fourth week, when I went over to Dover for a treat; and I saw Mr. Dick every alternate Wednesday, when he arrived by stage-coach at noon, to stay until next morning.

On these occasions Mr. Dick never travelled without a leathern writing-desk, containing a supply of stationery and the Memorial; in relation to which document he had a notion that time was beginning to press now, and that it really must be got out of hand.

Mr. Dick was very partial to gingerbread. To render his visits the more agreeable, my aunt had instructed me to open a credit for him at a cake-shop, which was hampered with the stipulation that he should not be served with more than one shilling's-worth in the course of any one day. This, and the reference of all his little bills at the county inn where he slept, to my aunt, before they were paid, induced me to suspect that he was only allowed to rattle his money, and not to spend it. I found on further investigation that this was so, or at least there was an agreement between him and my aunt that he should account to her for all his disbursements. As he had no idea of deceiving her, and always desired to please her, he was thus made chary of launching into expense. On this point, as well as on all other possible points, Mr. Dick was convinced that my aunt was the wisest and most wonderful of women; as he repeatedly told me with infinite secrecy, and always in a whisper.

"Trotwood," said Mr. Dick, with an air of mystery, after imparting this confidence to me, one Wednesday; "who's the man that hides near our house and frightens her?"

"Frightens my aunt, sir?"

Mr. Dick nodded. "I thought nothing would have frightened her," he said, "for she's——" here he whispered softly, "don't mention it—the wisest and most wonderful of women." Having said which, he drew back, to observe the effect which this description of her made upon me.

"The first time he came," said Mr. Dick, "was—let me see—sixteen hundred and forty-nine was the date of King Charles's execution. I think you said sixteen hundred and forty-nine?"

"Yes, sir."

"I don't know how it can be," said Mr. Dick, sorely puzzled and shaking his head. "I don't think I am as old as that."

"Was it in that year that the man appeared, sir?" I asked.

"Why, really," said Mr. Dick. "I don't see how it can have been in that year, Trotwood. Did you get that date out of history?"

"Yes, sir."

"I suppose history never lies, does it?" said Mr. Dick, with a gleam of hope.

"Oh dear, no, sir!" I replied, most decisively. I was ingenuous and young, and I thought so.

"I can't make it out," said Mr. Dick, shaking his head. "There's something wrong, somewhere. However, it was very soon after the mistake was made of putting some of the trouble out of King Charles's head into my head, that the man first came. I was walking out with Miss Trotwood after tea, just at dark, and there he was close to our house."

"Walking about?" I inquired.

"Walking about?" repeated Mr. Dick. "Let me see, I must recollect a bit. N—no, no; he was not walking about."

I asked, as the shortest way to get at it, what he *was* doing.

"Well, he wasn't there at all," said Mr. Dick, "until he came up behind her, and whispered. Then she turned round and fainted, and I stood still and looked at him, and he walked away; but that he should have been hiding ever since (in the ground or somewhere), is the most extraordinary thing!"

"*Has* he been hiding, ever since?" I asked.

"To be sure he has," retorted Mr. Dick, nodding his head gravely. "Never came out, till last night! We were walking last night, and he came up behind her again, and I knew him again."

"And did he frighten my aunt again?"

"All of a shiver," said Mr. Dick, counterfeiting that affection and making his teeth chatter. "Held by the palings. Cried. But, Trotwood, come here," getting me close to him, that he might whisper very softly; "why did she give him money, boy, in the moonlight?"

"He was a beggar, perhaps."

Mr. Dick shook his head, as utterly renouncing the suggestion; and having replied a great many times, and with great confidence, "No beggar, no beggar, no beggar, sir!" went on to say, that from his window, he had afterwards, and late at night, seen my aunt give this person money outside the garden rails in the moonlight, who then slunk away—into the ground again, as he thought probable—and was seen no more: while my aunt came hurriedly and secretly back into the house, and had, even that morning, been quite different from her usual self; which preyed on Mr. Dick's mind.

I had not the least belief, in the outset of this story, that the unknown was anything but a delusion of Mr. Dick's, and one of the line of that ill-fated Prince who occasioned him so much difficulty; but after some reflection I began to entertain the question whether an attempt, or threat of an attempt, might have been twice made to take poor Mr. Dick himself from under my aunt's protection, and whether my aunt, the strength of whose kind feeling towards him I knew from herself, might have been induced to pay a price for his peace and quiet. As I was already much attached to Mr. Dick, and very solicitous for his welfare, my fears favoured this supposition; and for a long time his Wednesday hardly ever came round, without my entertaining a misgiving that he would not be on the coach-box as usual. There he always appeared, however, grey-headed, laughing, and happy; and he never had anything more to tell of the man who could frighten my aunt.

These Wednesdays were the happiest days of Mr. Dick's life; they were far from being the least happy of mine. He soon became known to every boy in the school; and though he never took an active part in any game but kite-flying, was as deeply interested in all our sports as any one among us. How often have I seen him, intent upon a match at marbles or pegtop, looking on with a face of unutterable interest, and hardly breathing at the critical times! How often, at hare and hounds, have I seen him mounted on a little knoll, cheering the whole field on to action, and waving his hat above his grey head, oblivious of King Charles the Martyr's head, and all belonging to it! How many a summer-hour have I known to be but blissful minutes to him in the cricket-field! How many winter days have I seen him, standing blue-nosed, in the snow and east wind, looking at the boys going down the long slide, and clapping his worsted gloves in rapture!

He was an universal favourite, and his ingenuity in little things was transcendent. He could cut oranges into such devices as none of us had an idea of. He could make a boat out of anything, from a skewer upwards. He could turn cramp-bones into chess-men; fashion Roman chariots from old court cards; make spoked wheels out of cotton reels, and bird-cages of old wire. But he was greatest of all, perhaps, in the articles of string and straw; with which we were all persuaded he could do anything that could be done by hands.

Mr. Dick's renown was not long confined to us. After a few Wednesdays, Doctor Strong himself made some inquiries of me about him, and I told him all my aunt had told me; which interested the Doctor so much that he requested, on the occasion of his next visit, to be presented to him. This ceremony I performed; and the Doctor begging Mr. Dick, whensoever he should not find me at the coach-office, to come on there, and rest himself until our morning's work was over, it soon passed into a custom for Mr. Dick to come on as a matter of course, and, if we were a little late, as often happened on a Wednesday, to walk about the court-yard, waiting for me. Here he made the acquaintance of the Doctor's beautiful young wife (paler than formerly, all this time; more rarely seen by me or any one, I think; and not so gay, but not less beautiful), and so became more and more familiar by degrees, until, at last, he would come into the school and wait. He always sat in a particular corner, on a particular stool, which was called "Dick," after him; here he would sit, with his grey head bent forward, attentively listening to whatever might be going on, with a profound veneration for the learning he had never been able to acquire.

This veneration Mr. Dick extended to the Doctor, whom he thought the most subtle and accomplished philosopher of any age. It was long before Mr. Dick ever spoke to him otherwise than bareheaded; and even when he and the Doctor had struck up quite a friendship, and would walk together by the hour, on that side of the court-yard which was known among us as The Doctor's Walk, Mr. Dick would pull off his hat at intervals to show his respect for wisdom and knowledge. How it ever came about that the Doctor began to read out scraps of the famous Dictionary, in these walks, I never knew; perhaps he felt it all the same, at first, as reading to himself. However, it passed into a custom too; and Mr. Dick, listening with a face shining with pride and pleasure, in his heart of hearts, believed the Dictionary to be the most delightful book in the world.

As I think of them going up and down before those schoolroom windows—the Doctor reading with his complacent smile, an occasional flourish of the manuscript, or grave motion of his head; and Mr. Dick listening, enchained by interest, with his poor wits calmly wandering God knows where, upon the wings of hard words—I think of it as one of the pleasantest things, in a quiet way, that I have ever seen. I feel as if they might go walking to and fro for ever, and the world might somehow be the better for it. As if a thousand things it makes a noise about, were not one-half so good for it, or me.

Agnes was one of Mr. Dick's friends, very soon; and in often coming to the house, he made acquaintance with Uriah. The friendship between himself and me increased continually, and it was maintained on this odd footing: that, while Mr. Dick came professedly to look after me as my guardian, he always consulted me in any little matter of doubt that arose, and invariably guided himself by my advice; not only having a high respect for my native sagacity, but considering that I inherited a good deal from my aunt.

One Thursday morning, when I was about to walk with Mr. Dick from the hotel to the coach-office before going back to school (for we had an hour's school before breakfast), I met Uriah in the street, who reminded me of the promise I had made to take tea with himself and his mother: adding, with a writhe, "But I didn't expect you to keep it, Master Copperfield, we're so very umble."

I really had not yet been able to make up my mind whether I liked Uriah or detested him; and I was very doubtful about it still, as I stood looking him in the face in the street. But I felt it quite an affront to be supposed proud, and said I only wanted to be asked.

"Oh, if that's all, Master Copperfield," said Uriah, "and it really isn't our umbleness that prevents you, will you come this evening? But if it is our umbleness, I hope you won't mind owning to it, Master Copperfield; for we are well aware of our condition."

I said I would mention it to Mr. Wickfield, and if he approved, as I had no doubt he would, I would come with pleasure. So, at six o'clock that evening, which was one of the early office evenings, I announced myself as ready, to Uriah.

"Mother will be proud, indeed," he said, as we walked away together, "Or she would be proud, if it wasn't sinful, Master Copperfield."

"Yet you didn't mind supposing *I* was proud this morning," I returned.

"Oh dear, no, Master Copperfield!" returned Uriah. "Oh, believe me, no! Such a thought never came into my head! I shouldn't have deemed it at all proud if you had thought *us* too umble for you. Because we are so very umble."

"Have you been studying much law lately?" I asked, to change the subject.

"Oh, Master Copperfield," he said, with an air of self-denial, "my reading is hardly to be called study. I have passed an hour or two in the evening, sometimes, with Mr. Tidd."

"Rather hard, I suppose?" said I.

"He is hard to *me* sometimes," returned Uriah. "But I don't know what he might be to a gifted person."

After beating a little tune on his chin as he walked on, with the two forefingers of his skeleton right hand, he added:

"There are expressions, you see, Master Copperfield—Latin words and terms—in Mr. Tidd, that are trying to a reader of my umble attainments."

"Would you like to be taught Latin?" I said, briskly. "I will teach it you with pleasure, as I learn it."

"Oh, thank you, Master Copperfield," he answered, shaking his head. "I am sure it's very kind of you to make the offer, but I am much too umble to accept it."

"What nonsense, Uriah!"

"Oh, indeed you must excuse me, Master Copperfield! I am greatly obliged, and I should like it of all things, I assure you; but I am far too umble. There are people enough to tread upon me in my lowly state,.without my doing outrage to their feelings by possessing learning. Learning ain't for me. A person like myself had better not aspire. If he is to get on in life, he must get on umbly, Master Copperfield!"

I never saw his mouth so wide, or the creases in his cheeks

so deep, as when he delivered himself of these sentiments: shaking his head all the time, and writhing modestly.

"I think you are wrong, Uriah," I said. "I dare say there are several things that I could teach you, if you would like to learn them."

"Oh, I don't doubt that, Master Copperfield," he answered; "not in the least. But not being umble yourself, you don't judge well, perhaps, for them that are. I won't provoke my betters with knowledge, thank you. I'm much too umble. Here is my umble dwelling, Master Copperfield!"

We entered a low, old-fashioned room, walked straight into from the street, and found there Mrs. Heep, who was the dead image of Uriah, only short. She received me with the utmost humility, and apologised to me for giving her son a kiss, observing that, lowly as they were, they had their natural affections, which they hoped would give no offence to anyone. It was a perfectly decent room, half parlour and half kitchen, but not at all a snug room. The tea-things were set upon the table, and the kettle was boiling on the hob. There was a chest of drawers with an escritoire top, for Uriah to read or write at of an evening; there was Uriah's blue bag lying down and vomiting papers; there was a company of Uriah's books commanded by Mr. Tidd; there was a corner cupboard: and there were the usual articles of furniture. I don't remember that any individual object had a bare, pinched, spare look, but I do remember that the whole place had.

It was perhaps a part of Mrs. Heep's humility, that she still wore weeds. Notwithstanding the lapse of time that had occurred since Mr. Heep's decease, she still wore weeds. I think there was some compromise in the cap; but otherwise she was as weedy as in the early days of her mourning.

"This is a day to be remembered, my Uriah, I am sure," said Mrs. Heep, making the tea, "when Master Copperfield pays us a visit."

"I said you'd think so, mother," said Uriah.

"If I could have wished father to remain among us for any reason," said Mrs. Heep, "it would have been, that he might have known his company this afternoon."

I felt embarrassed by these compliments; but I was sensible, too, of being entertained as an honoured guest, and I thought Mrs. Heep an agreeable woman.

"My Uriah," said Mrs. Heep, "has looked forward to this, sir, a long while. He had his fears that our umbleness stood in the way, and I joined in them myself. Umble we are, umble we have been, umble we shall ever be," said Mrs. Heep.

"I am sure you have no occasion to be so, ma'am," I said, "unless you like."

"Thank you, sir," retorted Mrs. Heep. "We know our station and are thankful in it."

I found that Mrs. Heep gradually got nearer to me, and that Uriah gradually got opposite to me, and that they respectfully plied me with the choicest of the eatables on the table. There was nothing particularly choice there, to be sure; but I took the will for the deed, and felt that they were very attentive. Presently they began to talk about aunts, and then I told them about mine; and about fathers and mothers, and then I told them about mine; and then Mrs. Heep began to talk about fathers-in-law, and then I began to tell her about mine; but stopped, because my aunt had advised me to observe a silence on that subject. A tender young cork, however, would have had no more chance against a pair of corkscrews, or a tender young tooth against a pair of dentists, or a little shuttlecock against two battledores, than I had against Uriah and Mrs. Heep. They did just what they liked with me; and wormed things out of me that I had no desire to tell, with a certainty I blush to think of; the more especially as, in my juvenile frankness, I took some credit to myself for being so confidential and felt that I was quite the patron of my two respectful entertainers.

They were very fond of one another: that was certain. I take it, that had its effect upon me, as a touch of nature; but the skill with which the one followed up whatever the other said, was a touch of art which I was still less proof against. When there was nothing more to be got out of me about myself (for on the Murdstone and Grinby life, and on my journey, I was dumb), they began about Mr. Wickfield and Agnes. Uriah threw the ball to Mrs. Heep, Mrs. Heep caught it and threw it back to Uriah, Uriah kept it up a little while, then sent it back to Mrs. Heep, and so they went on tossing it about until I had no idea who had got it, and was quite bewildered. The ball itself was always changing too. Now it was Mr. Wickfield, now Agnes, now the excellence of Mr. Wickfield, now my admiration of Agnes; now the extent of Mr. Wickfield's business and resources, now our domestic life after dinner; now, the wine that Mr. Wickfield took, the reason why he took it, and the pity that it was he took so much; now one thing, now another, then everything at once; and all the time, without appearing to speak very often, or to do anything but sometimes encourage them a little, for fear they should be overcome by their humility and the honour of my company, I found myself perpetually letting out something or other that I had no business to let out, and seeing the effect of it in the twinkling of Uriah's dinted nostrils.

I had begun to be a little uncomfortable, and to wish myself well out of the visit, when a figure coming down the street passed the door—it stood open to air the room, which was warm, the weather being close for the time of year—came back again, looked in, and walked in, exclaiming loudly, " Copperfield! Is it possible? "

It was Mr. Micawber! It was Mr. Micawber, with his eyeglass, and his walking-stick, and his shirt-collar, and his genteel air, and the condescending roll in his voice, all complete!

" My dear Copperfield," said Mr. Micawber, putting out his hand, " this is indeed a meeting which is calculated to impress the mind with a sense of the instability and uncertainty of all human —in short, it is a most extraordinary meeting. Walking along the street, reflecting upon the probability of something turning up (of which I am at present rather sanguine), I find a young but valued friend turn up, who is connected with the most eventful period of my life; I may say, with the turning-point of my existence. Copperfield, my dear fellow, how do you do? "

I cannot say—I really can*not* say—that I was glad to see Mr. Micawber there; but I was glad to see him too, and shook hands with him, heartily, inquiring how Mrs. Micawber was.

" Thank you," said Mr. Micawber, waving his hand as of old, and settling his chin in his shirt-collar. " She is tolerably convalescent. The twins no longer derive their sustenance from Nature's founts—in short," said Mr. Micawber, in one of his bursts of confidence, " they are weaned—and Mrs. Micawber is, at present, my travelling companion. She will be rejoiced, Copperfield, to renew her acquaintance with one who has proved himself in all respects a worthy minister at the sacred altar of friendship."

I said I should be delighted to see her.

"You are very good," said Mr. Micawber.

Mr. Micawber then smiled, settled his chin again, and looked about him.

" I have discovered my friend Copperfield," said Mr. Micawber genteelly, and without addressing himself particularly to any one, " not in solitude, but partaking of a social meal in company with a widow lady, and one who is apparently her offspring—in short," said Mr. Micawber, in another of his bursts of confidence, " her son. I shall esteem it an honour to be presented."

I could do no less, under these circumstances, than make Mr.

Micawber known to Uriah Heep and his mother; which I accordingly did. As they abased themselves before him, Mr. Micawber took a seat, and waved his hand in his most courtly manner.

"Any friend of my friend Copperfield's," said Mr. Micawber, "has a personal claim upon myself."

"We are too umble, sir," said Mrs. Heep, "my son and me, to be the friends of Master Copperfield. He has been so good as take his tea with us, and we are thankful to him for his company; also to you, sir, for your notice."

"Ma'am," returned Mr. Micawber, with a bow, "you are very obliging; and what are you doing, Copperfield? Still in the wine trade?"

I was excessively anxious to get Mr. Micawber away; and replied, with my hat in my hand, and a very red face, I have no doubt, that I was a pupil at Doctor Strong's.

"A pupil?" said Mr. Micawber, raising his eyebrows. "I am extremely happy to hear it. Although a mind like my friend Copperfield's"—to Uriah and Mrs. Heep—"does not require that cultivation which, without his knowledge of men and things, it would require, still it is a rich soil teeming with latent vegetation—in short," said Mr. Micawber, smiling, in another burst of confidence, "it is an intellect capable of getting up the classics, to any extent."

Uriah, with his long hands slowly twining over one another, made a ghastly writhe from the waist upwards, to express his concurrence in this estimation of me.

"Shall we go and see Mrs. Micawber, sir?" I said, to get Mr. Micawber away.

"If you will do her that favour, Copperfield," replied Mr. Micawber, rising. "I have no scruple in saying, in the presence of our friends here, that I am a man who has, for some years, contended against the pressure of pecuniary difficulties." I knew he was certain to say something of this kind; he always would be so boastful about his difficulties. "Sometimes I have risen superior to my difficulties. Sometimes my difficulties have—in short, have floored me. There have been times when I have administered a succession of facers to them; there have been times when they have been too many for me, and I have given in, and said to Mrs. Micawber, in the words of Cato, 'Plato, thou reasonest well. It's all up now. I can show fight no more.' But at no time of my life," said Mr. Micawber, "have I enjoyed a higher degree of satisfaction than in pouring my griefs (if I may describe difficulties, chiefly arising out of warrants at attorney and promissory notes at two and four months, by that word) into the bosom of my friend Copperfield."

Mr. Micawber closed this handsome tribute by saying, " Mr. Heep! Good evening. Mrs. Heep! Your servant," and then walking out with me in his most fashionable manner, making a good deal of noise on the pavement with his shoes, and humming a tune as we went.

It was a little inn where Mr. Micawber put up, and he occupied a little room in it, partitioned off from the commercial room, and strongly flavoured with tobacco-smoke. I think it was over the kitchen, because a warm greasy smell appeared to come up through the chinks in the floor, and there was a flabby perspiration on the walls. I know it was near the bar, on account of the smell of spirits and jingling of glasses. Here, recumbent on a small sofa, underneath a picture of a race-horse, with her head close to the fire, and her feet pushing the mustard off the dumb-waiter at the other end of the room, was Mrs. Micawber, to whom Mr. Micawber entered first, saying, " My dear, allow me to introduce to you a pupil of Doctor Strong's."

I noticed, by-the-by, that although Mr. Micawber was just as much confused as ever about my age and standing, he always remembered, as a genteel thing, that I was a pupil of Doctor Strong's.

Mrs. Micawber was amazed, but very glad to see me. I was very glad to see her too, and, after an affectionate greeting on both sides, sat down on the small sofa near her.

" My dear," said Mr. Micawber, " if you will mention to Copperfield what our present position is, which I have no doubt he will like to know, I will go and look at the paper the while, and see whether anything turns up among the advertisements."

" I thought you were at Plymouth, ma'am," I said to Mrs. Micawber, as he went out.

" My dear Master Copperfield," she replied, " we went to Plymouth."

" To be on the spot," I hinted.

" Just so," said Mrs. Micawber. " To be on the spot. But the truth is, talent is not wanted in the Custom House. The local influence of my family was quite unavailing to obtain any employment in that department, for a man of Mr. Micawber's abilities. They would rather *not* have a man of Mr. Micawber's abilities. He would only show the deficiency of the others. Apart from which," said Mrs. Micawber, " I will not disguise from you, my dear Master Copperfield, that when that branch of my family which is settled in Plymouth became aware that

Mr. Micawber was accompanied by myself, and by little Wilkins and his sister, and by the twins, they did not receive him with that ardour which he might have expected, being so newly released from captivity. In fact," said Mrs. Micawber, lowering her voice,—" this is between ourselves—our reception was cool."

" Dear me! " I said.

" Yes," said Mrs. Micawber. " It is truly painful to contemplate mankind in such an aspect, Master Copperfield, but our reception was decidedly cool. There is no doubt about it. In fact, that branch of my family which is settled in Plymouth became quite personal to Mr. Micawber, before we had been there a week."

I said, and thought, that they ought to be ashamed of themselves.

" Still, so it was," continued Mrs. Micawber. " Under such circumstances, what could a man of Mr. Micawber's spirit do? But one obvious course was left. To borrow of that branch of my family the money to return to London, and to return at any sacrifice."

" Then you all came back again, ma'am? " I said.

" We all came back again," replied Mrs. Micawber. " Since then, I have consulted other branches of my family on the course which it is most expedient for Mr. Micawber to take—for I maintain that he must take some course, Master Copperfield," said Mrs. Micawber, argumentatively. " It is clear that a family of six, not including a domestic, cannot live upon air."

" Certainly, ma'am," said I.

" The opinion of those other branches of my family," pursued Mrs. Micawber, " is, that Mr. Micawber should immediately turn his attention to coals."

" To what, ma'am? "

" To coals," said Mrs. Micawber. " To the coal trade. Mr. Micawber was induced to think, on inquiry, that there might be an opening for a man of his talent in the Medway Coal Trade. Then, as Mr. Micawber very properly said, the first step to be taken clearly was, to come and *see* the Medway. Which we came, and saw. I say ' we,' Master Copperfield; for I never will," said Mrs. Micawber with emotion, " I never will desert Mr. Micawber."

I murmured my admiration and approbation.

" We came," repeated Mrs. Micawber, " and saw the Medway. My opinion of the coal trade on that river is, that it may require talent, but that it certainly requires capital. Talent, Mr. Micawber has; capital, Mr. Micawber has not. We saw, I think, the greater part of the Medway; and that is my individual conclusion. Being so near here, Mr. Micawber was of opinion that it would be rash not to come on, and see the Cathedral. Firstly, on account of its being so well worth seeing, and our never having seen it; and secondly, on account of the great probability of something turning up in a cathedral town. We have been here," said Mrs. Micawber, "three days. Nothing has, as yet, turned up; and it may not surprise you, my dear Master Copperfield, so much as it would a stranger, to know that we are at present waiting for a remittance from London, to discharge our pecuniary obligations at this hotel. Until the arrival of that remittance," said Mrs. Micawber with much feeling, "I am cut off from my home (I allude to lodgings in Pentonville), from my boy and girl, and from my twins."

I felt the utmost sympathy for Mr. and Mrs. Micawber in this anxious extremity, and said as much to Mr. Micawber, who now returned: adding that I only wished I had money enough, to lend them the amount they needed. Mr. Micawber's answer expressed the disturbance of his mind. He said, shaking hands with me, "Copperfield, you are a true friend; but when the worst comes to the worst, no man is without a friend who is possessed of shaving materials." At this dreadful hint Mrs. Micawber threw her arms round Mr. Micawber's neck and entreated him to be calm. He wept; but so far recovered, almost immediately, as to ring the bell for the waiter, and bespeak a hot kidney pudding and a plate of shrimps for breakfast in the morning.

When I took my leave of them, they both pressed me so much to come and dine before they went away, that I could not refuse. But, as I knew I could not come next day, when I should have a good deal to prepare in the evening, Mr. Micawber arranged that he would call at Doctor Strong's in the course of the morning (having a presentiment that the remittance would arrive by that post), and propose the day after, if it would suit me better. Accordingly I was called out of school next forenoon, and found Mr. Micawber in the parlour; who had called to say that the dinner would take place as proposed. When I asked him if the remittance had come, he pressed my hand and departed.

As I was looking out of window that same evening, it surprised me, and made me rather uneasy, to see Mr. Micawber and Uriah Heep walk past, arm in arm: Uriah humbly sensible of the honour that was done him, and Mr. Micawber taking a bland delight in extending his patronage to Uriah. But I was still more surprised, when I went to the little hotel next day at the appointed dinner-hour, which was four o'clock, to find, from what Mr. Micawber said, that he had gone home with Uriah, and had drunk brandy-and-water at Mrs. Heep's.

"And I'll tell you what, my dear Copperfield," said Mr. Micawber, "your friend Heep is a young fellow who might be attorney-general. If I had known that young man, at the period when my difficulties came to a crisis, all I can say is, that I believe my creditors would have been a great deal better managed than they were."

I hardly understood how this could have been, seeing that Mr. Micawber had paid them nothing at all as it was; but I did not like to ask. Neither did I like to say, that I hoped he had not been too communicative to Uriah; or to inquire if they had talked much about me. I was afraid of hurting Mr. Micawber's feelings, or, at all events, Mrs. Micawber's, she being very sensitive; but I was uncomfortable about it, too, and often thought about it afterwards.

We had a beautiful little dinner. Quite an elegant dish of fish; the kidney-end of a loin of veal, roasted; fried sausage-meat, a partridge, and a pudding. There was wine, and there was strong ale; and after dinner Mrs. Micawber made us a bowl of hot punch with her own hands.

Mr. Micawber was uncommonly convivial. I never saw him such good company. He made his face shine with the punch, so that it looked as if it had been varnished all over. He got cheerfully sentimental about the town, and proposed success to it; observing that Mrs. Micawber and himself had been made extremely snug and comfortable there, and that he never should forget the agreeable hours they had passed in Canterbury. He proposed me afterwards; and he, and Mrs. Micawber, and I, took a review of our past acquaintance, in the course of which, we sold the property all over again. Then I proposed Mrs. Micawber; or, at least, said, modestly, "If you'll allow me, Mrs. Micawber, I shall now have the pleasure of drinking *your* health, ma'am." On which Mr. Micawber delivered an eulogium on Mrs. Micawber's character, and said she had ever been his guide, philosopher, and friend, and that he would recommend me, when I came to a marrying-time of life, to marry such another woman, if such another woman could be found.

As the punch disappeared, Mr. Micawber became still more friendly, and convivial. Mrs. Micawber's spirits becoming elevated, too, we sang "Auld Lang Syne." When we came to "Here's a hand, my trusty frere," we all joined hands round the table; and when we declared we would " take a right gude Willie Waught," and hadn't the least idea what it meant, we were really affected.

In a word, I never saw anybody so thoroughly jovial as Mr. Micawber was, down to the very last moment of the evening, when I took a hearty farewell of himself and his amiable wife. Consequently, I was not prepared, at seven o'clock next morning, to receive the following communication, dated half-past nine in the evening; a quarter of an hour after I had left him:—

" MY DEAR YOUNG FRIEND,

" The die is cast—all is over. Hiding the ravages of care with a sickly mask of mirth, I have not informed you, this evening that there is no hope of the remittance! Under these circumstances, alike humiliating to endure, humiliating to contemplate, and humiliating to relate, I have discharged the pecuniary liability contracted at this establishment, by giving a note of hand, made payable fourteen days after date, at my residence, Pentonville, London. When it becomes due, it will not be taken up. The result is destruction. The bolt is impending, and the tree must fall.

" Let the wretched man who now addresses you, my dear Copperfield, be a beacon to you through life. He writes with that intention, and in that hope. If he could think himself of so much use, one gleam of day might, by possibility, penetrate into the cheerless dungeon of his remaining existence—though his longevity is, at present (to say the least of it), extremely problematical.

" This is the last communication, my dear Copperfield, you will ever receive

" From
" The
" Beggared Outcast,
" WILKINS MICAWBER."

I was so shocked by the contents of this heart-rending letter, that I ran off directly towards the little hotel with the intention of taking it on my way to Doctor Strong's, and trying to soothe Mr. Micawber with a word of comfort. But, half-way there, I met the London coach with Mr. and Mrs. Micawber up behind; Mr. Micawber, the very picture of tranquil enjoyment, smiling at Mrs. Micawber's conversation, eating walnuts out of a paper bag, with a bottle sticking out of his breast pocket. As they did not see me, I thought it best, all things considered, not to see them. So, with a great weight taken off my mind, I turned into a by-street that was the nearest way to school, and felt, upon the whole, relieved that they were gone: though I still liked them very much, nevertheless.

18

A RETROSPECT

MY SCHOOL-DAYS! THE SILENT GLIDING ON OF MY existence—the unseen, unfelt progress of my life—from childhood up to youth! Let me think, as I look back upon that flowing water, now a dry channel overgrown with leaves, whether there are any marks along its course, by which I can remember how it ran.

A moment, and I occupy my place in the Cathedral, where we all went together, every Sunday morning, assembling first at school for that purpose. The earthy smell, the sunless air, the sensation of the world being shut out, the resounding of the organ through the black and white arched galleries and aisles, are wings that take me back, and hold me hovering above those days, in a half-sleeping and half-waking dream.

I am not the last boy in the school. I have risen, in a few months, over several heads. But the first boy seems to me a mighty creature, dwelling afar off, whose giddy height is unattainable. Agnes says " No," but I say, " Yes," and tell her that she little thinks what stores of knowledge have been mastered by the wonderful Being, at whose place she thinks I, even I, weak aspirant, may arrive in time. He is not my private friend and public patron, as Steerforth was; but I hold him in a reverential respect. I chiefly wonder what he'll be, when he leaves Doctor Strong's, and what mankind will do to maintain any place against him.

But who is this that breaks upon me? This is Miss Shepherd, whom I love.

Miss Shepherd is a boarder at the Misses Nettingalls' establishment. I adore Miss Shepherd. She is a little girl, in a spencer, with a round face and curly flaxen hair. The Misses Nettingalls' young ladies come to the Cathedral too. I cannot look upon my book, for I must look upon Miss Shepherd. When the choristers chaunt, I hear Miss Shepherd. In the service I mentally insert Miss Shepherd's name; I put her in among the Royal Family. At home, in my own room, I am sometimes moved to cry out, "Oh, Miss Shepherd!" in a transport of love.

For some time, I am doubtful of Miss Shepherd's feelings, but, at length, Fate being propitious, we meet at the dancing-school. I have Miss Shepherd for my partner. I touch Miss Shepherd's glove, and feel a thrill go up the right arm of my jacket, and come out of my hair. I say nothing tender to Miss Shepherd, but we understand each other. Miss Shepherd and myself live but to be united.

Why do I secretly give Miss Shepherd twelve Brazil nuts for a present, I wonder? They are not expressive of affection, they are difficult to pack into a parcel of any regular shape, they are hard to crack, even in room doors, and they are oily when cracked; yet I feel that they are appropriate to Miss Shepherd. Soft, seedy biscuits, also, I bestow upon Miss Shepherd; and oranges innumerable. Once, I kiss Miss Shepherd in the cloak room. Ecstasy! What are my agony and indignation next day, when I hear a flying rumour that the Misses Nettingall have stood Miss Shepherd in the stocks for turning in her toes!

Miss Shepherd being the one pervading theme and vision of my life, how do I ever come to break with her? I can't conceive. And yet a coolness grows between Miss Shepherd and myself. Whispers reach me of Miss Shepherd having said she wished I wouldn't stare so, and having avowed a preference for Master Jones—for Jones! a boy of no merit whatever! The gulf between me and Miss Shepherd widens. At last, one day, I meet the Misses Nettingalls' establishment out walking. Miss Shepherd makes a face as she goes by, and laughs to her companion. All is over. The devotion of a life—it seems a life, it is all the same—is at an end; Miss Shepherd comes out of the morning service, and the Royal Family know her no more.

I am higher in the school, and no one breaks my peace. I am not at all polite, now, to the Misses Nettingalls' young ladies, and shouldn't dote on any of them, if they were twice as many and twenty times as beautiful. I think the dancing-school a tiresome affair, and wonder why the girls can't dance by themselves and leave us alone. I am growing great in Latin verses, and neglect the laces of my boots. Doctor Strong refers to me in public as a promising young scholar. Mr. Dick is wild with joy, and my aunt remits me a guinea by the next post.

The shade of a young butcher rises, like the apparition of an armed head in Macbeth. Who is this young butcher? He is the terror of the youth of Canterbury. There is a vague belief abroad that the beef suet with which he anoints his hair gives him unnatural strength, and that he is a match for a man. He is a broad-faced, bull-necked, young butcher, with rough red cheeks, an ill-conditioned mind, and an injurious tongue. His main use of this tongue is to disparage Doctor Strong's young gentlemen. He says, publicly, that if they want anything he'll give it 'em. He names individuals among them (myself included), whom he could undertake to settle with one hand, and the other tied behind him. He waylays the smaller boys to punch their unprotected heads, and calls challenges after me in the open streets. For these sufficient reasons I resolve to fight the butcher.

It is a summer evening, down in a green hollow, at the corner of a wall. I meet the butcher by appointment. I am attended by a select body of our boys; the butcher, by two other butchers, a young publican, and a sweep. The preliminaries are adjusted, and the butcher and myself stand face to face. In a moment the butcher lights ten thousand candles out of my left eyebrow. In another moment, I don't know where the wall is, or where I am, or where anybody is. I hardly know which is myself and which the butcher, we are always in such a tangle and tussle, knocking about upon the trodden grass. Sometimes I see the butcher, bloody but confident; sometimes I see nothing, and sit gasping on my second's knee; sometimes I go in at the butcher madly, and cut my knuckles open against his face, without appearing to discompose him at all. At last I awake, very queer about the head, as from a giddy sleep, and see the butcher walking off, congratulated by the two other butchers and the sweep and publican, and putting on his coat as he goes; from which I augur, justly, that the victory is his.

I am taken home in a sad plight, and I have beef-steaks put to my eyes, and am rubbed with vinegar and brandy, and find a great white puffy place bursting out on my upper lip, which swells immoderately. For three or four days I remain at home, a very ill-looking subject, with a green shade over my eyes; and I should be very dull, but that Agnes is a sister to me, and condoles with me, and reads to me, and makes the time light and happy. Agnes has my confidence completely, always; I tell her all about the butcher, and the wrongs he has heaped upon me; she thinks I couldn't have done otherwise than fight the butcher, while she shrinks and trembles at my having fought him.

Time has stolen on unobserved, for Adams is not the head-boy in the days that are come now, nor has he been this many and many a day. Adams has left the school so long, that when he comes back, on a visit to Doctor Strong, there are not many there, besides myself, who know him. Adams is going to be called to the bar almost directly, and is to be an advocate, and to wear a wig. I am surprised to find him a meeker man than I had thought, and less imposing in appearance. He has not staggered the world yet, either; for it goes on (as well as I can make out) pretty much the same is if he had never joined it.

A blank, through which the warriors of poetry and history march on in stately hosts that seem to have no end—and what comes next! *I* am the head-boy, now! I look down on the line of boys below me, with a condescending interest in such of them as bring to my mind the boy I was myself, when I first came there. That little fellow seems to be no part of me; I remember him as something left behind upon the road of life—as something I have passed, rather than have actually been—and almost think of him as of some one else.

And the little girl I saw on that first day at Mr. Wickfield's, where is she? Gone also. In her stead, the perfect likeness of the picture, a child likeness no more, moves about the house; and Agnes, my sweet sister, as I call her in my thoughts, my counsellor and friend, the better angel of the lives of all who come within her calm, self-denying influence, is quite a woman.

What other changes have come upon me, besides the changes in my growth and looks, and in the knowledge I have garnered all this while? I wear a gold watch and chain, a ring upon my little finger, and a long-tailed coat; and I use a great deal of bear's grease—which, taken in conjunction with the ring, looks bad. Am I in love again? I am. I worship the eldest Miss Larkins.

The eldest Miss Larkins is not a little girl. She is a tall, dark, black-eyed, fine figure of a woman. The eldest Miss Larkins is not a chicken; for the youngest Miss Larkins is not that, and the eldest must be three or four years older. Perhaps the eldest Miss Larkins may be about thirty. My passion for her is beyond all bounds.

The eldest Miss Larkins knows officers. It is an awful thing to bear. I see them speaking to her in the street. I see them cross the way to meet her, when her bonnet (she has a bright taste in bonnets) is seen coming down the pavement, accompanied by her sister's bonnet. She laughs and talks, and seems to like it. I spend a good deal of my own spare time in walking up and down to meet her. If I can bow to her once in the day

(I know her to bow to, knowing Mr. Larkins), I am happier. I deserve a bow now and then. The raging agonies I suffer on the night of the Race Ball, where I know the eldest Miss Larkins will be dancing with the military, ought to have some compensation, if there be even-handed justice in the world.

My passion takes away my appetite, and makes me wear my newest silk neckerchief continually. I have no relief but in putting on my best clothes, and having my boots cleaned over and over again. I seem, then, to be worthier of the eldest Miss Larkins. Everything that belongs to her, or is connected with her, is precious to me. Mr. Larkins (a gruff old gentleman with a double chin, and one of his eyes immovable in his head) is fraught with interest to me. When I can't meet his daughter, I go where I am likely to meet him. To say " How do you do, Mr. Larkins? Are the young ladies and all the family quite well? " seems so pointed, that I blush.

I think continually about my age. Say I am seventeen, and say that seventeen is young for the eldest Miss Larkins, what of that? Besides, I shall be one-and-twenty in no time almost. I regularly take walks outside Mr. Larkins's house in the evening, though it cuts me to the heart to see the officers go in, or to hear them up in the drawing-room, where the eldest Miss Larkins plays the harp. I even walk, on two or three occasions, in a sickly, spoony manner, round and round the house after the family are gone to bed, wondering which is the eldest Miss Larkins's chamber (and pitching, I dare say now, on Mr. Larkins's instead); wishing that a fire would burst out; that the assembled crowd would stand appalled; that I, dashing through them with a ladder, might rear it against her window, save her in my arms, go back for something she had left behind, and perish in the flames. For I am generally disinterested in my love, and think I could be content to make a figure before Miss Larkins, and expire. Generally, but not always. Sometimes brighter visions rise before me. When I dress (the occupation of two hours), for a great ball given at the Larkins's (the anticipation of three weeks), I indulge my fancy with pleasing images. I picture myself taking courage to make a declaration to Miss Larkins. I picture Miss Larkins sinking her head upon my shoulder, and saying, " Oh, Mr. Copperfield, can I believe my ears! " I picture Mr. Larkins waiting on me next morning, and saying, " My dear Copperfield, my daughter has told me all. Youth is no objection. Here are twenty thousand pounds. Be happy! " I picture my aunt relenting, and blessing us; and Mr. Dick and Doctor Strong being present at the marriage ceremony. I am a sensible fellow, I believe—I believe, on looking back, I mean—and modest I am sure; but all this goes on notwithstanding.

I repair to the enchanted house, where there are lights, chattering, music, flowers, officers (I am sorry to see), and the eldest Miss Larkins, a blaze of beauty. She is dressed in blue, with blue flowers in her hair—forget-me-nots. As if *she* had any need to wear forget-me-nots! It is the first really grown-up party that I have ever been invited to, and I am a little uncomfortable; for I appear not to belong to anybody, and nobody appears to have anything to say to me, except Mr. Larkins, who asks me how my schoolfellows are, which he needn't do, as I have not come there to be insulted.

But after I have stood in the doorway for some time, and feasted my eyes upon the goddess of my heart, she approaches me—she, the eldest Miss Larkins!—and asks me pleasantly, if I dance?

I stammer, with a bow, " With you, Miss Larkins."

" With no one else? " inquires Miss Larkins.

" I should have no pleasure in dancing with any one else."

Miss Larkins laughs and blushes (or I think she blushes), and says, " Next time but one, I shall be very glad."

The time arrives. " It is a waltz, I think," Miss Larkins doubtfully observes, when I present myself. " Do you waltz? If not, Captain Bailey—"

But I do waltz (pretty well, too, as it happens), and I take Miss Larkins out. I take her sternly from the side of Captain Bailey. He is wretched, I have no doubt; but he is nothing to me. I have been wretched, too. I waltz with the eldest Miss Larkins! I don't know where, among whom, or how long. I only know that I swim about in space, with a blue angel, in a state of blissful delirium, until I find myself alone with her in a little room, resting on a sofa. She admires a flower (pink camellia japonica, price half-a-crown), in my button-hole. I give it her, and say:

" I ask an inestimable price for it, Miss Larkins."

" Indeed! What is that? " returns Miss Larkins.

" A flower of yours, that I may treasure it as a miser does gold."

" You're a bold boy," says Miss Larkins. " There."

She gives it me, not displeased and I put it to my lips, and then into my breast. Miss Larkins, laughing, draws her hand through my arm, and says, " Now take me back to Captain Bailey."

I am lost in the recollection of this delicious interview, and the waltz, when she comes to me again, with a plain elderly gentleman, who has been playing whist all night, upon her arm, and says:

"Oh! here is my bold friend! Mr. Chestle wants to know you, Mr. Copperfield."

I feel at once that he is a friend of the family, and am much gratified.

"I admire your taste, sir," says Mr. Chestle. "It does you credit. I suppose you don't take much interest in hops; but I am a pretty large grower myself and if you ever like to come over to our neighbourhood—neighbourhood of Ashford—and take a run about our place, we shall be glad for you to stop as long as you like."

I thank Mr. Chestle warmly, and shake hands. I think I am in a happy dream. I waltz with the eldest Miss Larkins once again. She says I waltz so well! I go home in a state of unspeakable bliss, and waltz in imagination, all night long, with my arm round the blue waist of my dear divinity. For some days afterwards, I am lost in rapturous reflections but I neither see her in the street, nor when I call. I am imperfectly consoled for this disappointment by the sacred pledge, the perished flower.

"Trotwood," says Agnes, one day after dinner. "Who do you think is going to be married to-morrow? Some one you admire."

"Not you, I suppose, Agnes?"

"Not me!" raising her cheerful face from the music she is copying. "Do you hear him, Papa?—The eldest Miss Larkins."

"To—to Captain Bailey?" I have just enough power to ask.

"No; to no Captain. To Mr. Chestle, a hop-grower."

I am terribly dejected for about a week or two. I take off my ring, I wear my worst clothes, I use no bear's grease, and I frequently lament over the late Miss Larkins's faded flower. Being, by that time, rather tired of this kind of life, and having received new provocation from the butcher, I throw the flower away, go out with the butcher, and gloriously defeat him.

This, and the resumption of my ring, as well as the bear's grease in moderation, are the last marks I can discern, now, in my progress to seventeen.

19

I LOOK ABOUT ME, AND MAKE A DISCOVERY

I AM DOUBTFUL WHETHER I WAS AT HEART GLAD OR sorry, when my school-days drew to an end, and the time came for my leaving Doctor Strong's. I had been very happy there, I had a great attachment for the Doctor, and I was eminent and distinguished in that little world. For these reasons I was sorry to go; but for other reasons, unsubstantial enough, I was glad. Misty ideas of being a young man at my own disposal, of the importance attaching to a young man at his own disposal, of the wonderful things to be seen and done by that magnificent animal, and the wonderful effects he could not fail to make upon society, lured me away. So powerful were these visionary considerations in my boyish mind, that I seem, according to my present way of thinking, to have left school without natural regret. The separation has not made the impression on me that other separations have. I try in vain to recall how I felt about it, and what its circumstances were; but it is not momentous in my recollection. I suppose the opening prospect confused me. I know that my juvenile experiences went for little or nothing then; and that life was more like a great fairy story, which I was just about to begin to read, than anything else.

My aunt and I had held many grave deliberations on the calling to which I should be devoted. For a year or more I had endeavoured to find a satisfactory answer to her often-repeated question, "What I would like to be?" But I had no particular liking, that I could discover, for anything. If I could have been inspired with a knowledge of the science of navigation, taken the command of a fast-sailing expedition, and gone round the world on a triumphant voyage of discovery, I think I might have considered myself completely suited. But in the absence of any such miraculous provision, my desire was to apply myself to some pursuit that would not lie too heavily upon her purse; and to do my duty in it, whatever it might be.

Mr. Dick had regularly assisted at our councils, with a meditative and sage demeanour. He never made a suggestion but once;

and on that occasion (I don't know what put it in his head), he suddenly proposed that I should be "a Brazier." My aunt received this proposal so very ungraciously, that he never ventured on a second; but ever afterwards confined himself to looking watchfully at her for her suggestions, and rattling his money.

"Trot, I tell you what, my dear," said my aunt, one morning in the Christmas season when I left school; "as this knotty point is still unsettled, and as we must not make a mistake in our decision if we can help it, I think we had better take a little breathing-time. In the meanwhile, you must try to look at it from a new point of view, and not as a schoolboy."

"I will, aunt."

"It has occurred to me," pursued my aunt, "that a little change and a glimpse of life out of doors, may be useful, in helping you to know your own mind, and form a cooler judgment. Suppose you were to take a little journey now. Suppose you were to go down into the old part of the country again, for instance, and see that—that out-of-the-way woman with the savagest of names," said my aunt, rubbing her nose, for she could never thoroughly forgive Peggotty for being so called.

"Of all things in the world, aunt, I should like it best!"

"Well," said my aunt, "that's lucky, for I should like it too. But it's natural and rational that you should like it. And I am very well persuaded that whatever you do, Trot, will always be natural and rational."

"I hope so, aunt."

"Your sister, Betsey Trotwood," said my aunt, "would have been as natural and rational a girl as ever breathed. You'll be worthy of her, won't you?"

"I hope I shall be worthy of *you*, aunt. That will be enough for me."

"It's a mercy that poor dear baby of a mother of yours didn't live," said my aunt, looking at me approvingly, "or she'd have been so vain of her boy by this time, that her soft little head would have been completely turned, if there was anything of it left to turn." (My aunt always excused any weakness of her own in my behalf, by transferring it in this way to my poor mother.) "Bless, me Trotwood, how you do remind me of her!"

"Pleasantly, I hope, aunt?" said I.

"He's as like her, Dick," said my aunt, emphatically, "he's as like her, as she was that afternoon, before she began to fret.

Bless my heart, he's as like her, as he can look at me out of his two eyes!"

"Is he indeed?" said Mr. Dick.

"And he's like David, too," said my aunt, decisively.

"He is very like David!" said Mr. Dick.

"But what I want you to be, Trot," resumed my aunt, "—I don't mean physically, but morally; you are very well physically—is, a firm fellow. A fine firm fellow, with a will of your own. With resolution," said my aunt, shaking her cap at me, and clenching her hand. "With determination. With character, Trot. With strength of character that is not to be influenced, except on good reason, by anybody, or by anything. That's what I want you to be. That's what your father and mother might both have been, Heaven knows, and been the better for it."

I intimated that I hoped I should be what she described.

"That you may begin, in a small way, to have a reliance upon yourself, and to act for yourself," said my aunt, "I shall send you upon your trip, alone. I did think, once, of Mr. Dick's going with you; but, on second thoughts, I shall keep him to take care of me."

Mr. Dick for a moment, looked a little disappointed; until the honour and dignity of having to take care of the most wonderful woman in the world, restored the sunshine to his face. "Besides," said my aunt, "there's the Memorial."

"Oh, certainly," said Mr. Dick, in a hurry, "I intend, Trotwood, to get that done immediately—it really must be done immediately! And then it will go in, you know—and then—," said Mr. Dick, after checking himself, and pausing a long time, "there'll be a pretty kettle of fish!"

In pursuance of my aunt's kind scheme, I was shortly afterwards fitted out with a handsome purse of money, and a portmanteau, and tenderly dismissed upon my expedition. At parting, my aunt gave me some good advice, and a good many kisses, and said that as her object was that I should look about me, and should think a little, she would recommend me to stay a few days in London, if I liked it, either on my way down into Suffolk, or in coming back. In a word, I was at liberty to do what I would, for three weeks or a month; and no other conditions were imposed upon my freedom than the before-mentioned thinking and looking about me, and a pledge to write three times a week and faithfully report myself.

I went to Canterbury first, that I might take leave of Agnes and Mr. Wickfield (my old room in whose house I had not yet relinquished), and also of the good Doctor. Agnes was very glad to see me, and told me that the house had not been like itself since I had left it.

"I am sure I am not like myself when I am away," said I. "I seem to want my right hand, when I miss you. Though that's not saying much; for there's no head in my right hand, and no heart. Every one who knows you, consults with you, and is guided by you, Agnes."

"Every one who knows me, spoils me, I believe," she answered, smiling.

"No. It's because you are like no one else. You are so good, and so sweet-tempered. You have such a gentle nature, and you are always right."

"You talk," said Agnes, breaking into a pleasant laugh, as she sat at work, "as if I were the late Miss Larkins."

"Come! It's not fair to abuse my confidence," I answered, reddening at the recollection of my blue enslaver. "But I shall confide in you, just the same Agnes. I can never grow out of that. Whenever I fall into trouble, or fall in love, I shall always tell you, if you'll let me—even when I come to fall in love in earnest."

"Why, you have always been in earnest!" said Agnes, laughing again.

"Oh! that was as a child, or a schoolboy," said I, laughing in my turn, not without being a little shamefaced. "Times are altering now, and I suppose I shall be in a terrible state of earnestness one day or other. My wonder is, that you are not in earnest yourself, by this time, Agnes."

Agnes laughed again, and shook her head.

"Oh, I know you are not!" said I, "because if you had been, you would have told me. Or at least," for I saw a faint blush in her face, "you would have let me find it out for myself. But there is no one that I know of, who deserves to love *you*, Agnes. Some one of a nobler character, and more worthy altogether than any one I have ever seen here, must rise up, before I give *my* consent. In the time to come, I shall have a wary eye on all admirers and shall exact a great deal from the successful one, I assure you."

We had gone on, so far, in a mixture of confidential jest and earnest, that had long grown naturally out of our familiar relations, begun as mere children. But Agnes, now suddenly lifting up her eyes to mine, and speaking in a different manner, said:

"Trotwood, there is something that I want to ask you, and that I may not have another opportunity of asking for a long time, perhaps. Something I would ask, I think, of no one else. Have you observed any gradual alteration in Papa?"

I had observed it, and had often wondered whether she had too. I must have shown as much, now, in my face; for her eyes were in a moment cast down, and I saw tears in them.

"Tell me what it is," she said, in a low voice.

"I think—shall I be quite plain, Agnes, liking him so much?"

"Yes," she said.

"I think he does himself no good by the habit that has increased upon him since I first came here. He is often very nervous, or I fancy so."

"It is not fancy," said Agnes, shaking her head.

"His hand trembles, his speech is not plain, and his eyes look wild. I have remarked that at those times, and when he is least like himself, he is most certain to be wanted on some business."

"By Uriah," said Agnes.

"Yes; and the sense of being unfit for it, or of not having understood it, or of having shown his condition in spite of himself, seems to make him so uneasy, that next day he is worse, and next day worse, and so he becomes jaded and haggard. Do not be alarmed by what I say, Agnes, but in this state I saw him, only the other evening, lay down his head upon his desk, and shed tears like a child."

Her hand passed softly before my lips while I was yet speaking, and in a moment she had met her father at the door of the room, and was hanging on his shoulder. The expression of her face, as they both looked towards me, I felt to be very touching. There was such deep fondness for him, and gratitude to him for all his love and care, in her beautiful look; and there was such a fervent appeal to me to deal tenderly by him, even in my inmost thoughts, and to let no harsh construction find any place against him; she was, at once, so proud of him and devoted to him, yet so compassionate and sorry, and so reliant upon me to be so, too; that nothing she could have said would have expressed more to me, or moved me more.

We were to drink tea at the Doctor's. We went there at the usual hour; and round the study fireside found the Doctor, and his young wife, and her mother. The Doctor, who made as much of my going away as if I were going to China, received me as an honoured guest; and called for a log of wood to be thrown on the fire, that he might see the face of his old pupil reddening in the blaze.

"I shall not see many more new faces in Trotwood's stead,

Wickfield," said the Doctor, warming his hands; "I am getting lazy, and want ease. I shall relinquish all my young people in another six months, and lead a quieter life."

"You have said so, any time these ten years, Doctor," Mr. Wickfield answered.

"But I now mean to do it," returned the Doctor. "My first master will succeed me—I am in earnest at last—so you'll soon have to arrange our contracts, and to bind us firmly to them, like a couple of knaves."

"And to take care," said Mr. Wickfield, "that you're not imposed on, eh? As you certainly would be, in any contract you should make for yourself. Well! I am ready. There are worse tasks than that, in my calling."

"I shall have nothing to think of, then," said the Doctor, with a smile, "but my Dictionary; and this other contract-bargain—Annie."

As Mr. Wickfield glanced towards her, sitting at the tea-table by Agnes, she seemed to me to avoid his look with such unwonted hesitation and timidity, that his attention became fixed upon her, as if something were suggested to his thoughts.

"There is a post come in from India, I observe," he said, after a short silence.

"By-the-by! and letters from Mr. Jack Maldon!" said the Doctor.

"Indeed!"

"Poor dear Jack!" said Mrs. Markleham, shaking her head. "That trying climate! Like living, they tell me, on a sand-heap, underneath a burning-glass! He looked strong, but he wasn't. My dear Doctor, it was his spirit, not his constitution, that he ventured on so boldly. Annie, my dear, I am sure you must perfectly recollect that your cousin never was strong; not what can be called *robust*, you know," said Mrs. Markleham, with emphasis, and looking round upon us generally; "from the time when my daughter and himself were children together, and walking about, arm-in-arm, the livelong day."

Annie, thus addressed, made no reply.

"Do I gather from what you say, ma'am, that Mr. Maldon is ill?" asked Mr. Wickfield.

"Ill!" replied the Old Soldier. "My dear sir, he's all sorts of things."

"Except well?" said Mr. Wickfield.

"Except well, indeed!" said the Old Soldier. "He has had dreadful strokes of the sun, no doubt, and jungle fevers and agues, and every kind of thing you can mention. As to his liver," said the Old Soldier resignedly, " that, of course, he gave up altogether, when he first went out! "

" Does he say all this? " asked Mr. Wickfield.

" Say? My dear sir," returned Mrs. Markleham, shaking her head and her fan, " you little know my poor Jack Maldon when you ask that question. Say? Not he. You might drag him at the heels of four wild horses first."

" Mama! " said Mrs. Strong.

" Annie, my dear," returned her mother, " once for all, I must really beg that you will not interfere with me, unless it is to confirm what I say. You know as well as I do that your cousin Maldon would be dragged at the heels of any number of wild horses—why should I confine myself to four! I *won't* confine myself to four—eight, sixteen, two-and-thirty, rather than say anything calculated to overturn the Doctor's plans."

" Wickfield's plans," said the Doctor, stroking his face, and looking penitently at his adviser. " That is to say, our joint plans for him. I said myself, abroad or at home."

" And I said," added Mr. Wickfield, gravely, " abroad. I was the means of sending him abroad. It's my responsibility."

" Oh! Responsibility! " said the Old Soldier. " Everything was done for the best, my dear Mr. Wickfield; everything was done for the kindest and best, we know. But if the dear fellow can't live there, he can't live there. And if he can't live there, he'll die there, sooner than he'll overturn the Doctor's plans. I know him," said the Old Soldier, fanning herself, in a sort of calm prophetic agony, " and I know he'll die there, sooner than he'll overturn the Doctor's plans."

" Well, well, ma'am," said the Doctor cheerfully, " I am not bigoted to my plans, and I can overturn them myself. I can substitute some other plans. If Mr. Jack Maldon comes home on account of ill health, he must not be allowed to go back, and we must endeavour to make some more suitable and fortunate provision for him in this country."

Mrs. Markleham was so overcome by this generous speech (which, I need not say, she had not at all expected, or led up to) that she could only tell the Doctor it was like himself, and go several times through that operation of kissing the sticks of her fan, and then tapping his hand with it. After which she gently chid her daughter Annie, for not being more demonstrative when such kindnesses were showered, for her sake, on her old playfellow; and entertained us with some particulars concerning other deserving members of her family, whom it was desirable to set on their deserving legs.

All this time, her daughter Annie never once spoke, or lifted up her eyes. All this time, Mr. Wickfield had his glance upon her as she sat by his own daughter's side. It appeared to me that he never thought of being observed by any one; but was so intent upon her, and upon his own thoughts in connection with her, as to be quite absorbed. He now asked what Mr. Jack Maldon had actually written in reference to himself, and to whom he had written it?

" Why, here," said Mrs. Markleham, taking a letter from the chimney-piece above the Doctor's head, " the dear fellow says to the Doctor himself—where is it? Ah!—' I am sorry to inform you that my health is suffering severely, and that I fear I may be reduced to the necessity of returning home for a time, as the only hope of restoration.' That's pretty plain, poor fellow! His only hope of restoration! But Annie's letter is plainer still. Annie, show me that letter again."

" Not now, mama," she pleaded in a low tone.

" My dear, you absolutely are, on some subjects, one of the most ridiculous persons in the world," returned her mother, " and perhaps the most unnatural to the claims of your own family. We never should have heard of the letter at all, I believe, unless I had asked for it myself. Do you call that confidence, my love, towards Doctor Strong? I am surprised. You ought to know better."

The letter was reluctantly produced; and as I handed it to the old lady, I saw how the unwilling hand from which I took it, trembled.

" Now let us see," said Mrs. Markleham, putting her glass to her eye, " where the passage is. ' The remembrance of old times, my dearest Annie '—and so forth—it's not there. ' The amiable old Proctor'—who's he? Dear me, Annie, how illegibly your cousin Maldon writes, and how stupid I am! ' Doctor,' of course. Ah! amiable indeed! " Here she left off, to kiss her fan again, and shake it at the Doctor, who was looking at us in a state of placid satisfaction. " Now, I have found it. ' *You* may not be surprised to hear, Annie,'—no, to be sure, knowing that he never was really strong; what did I say just now?—'that I have undergone so much in this distant place, as to have decided to leave it at all hazards; on sick leave, if I can; on total resignation, if that is not to be obtained. What I have endured, and do endure here, is insupportable.' And but for the promptitude of that best of creatures," said Mrs. Markleham, telegraphing the Doctor as before, and refolding the letter, " it would be insupportable to me to think of."

Mr. Wickfield said not one word, though the old lady looked to him as if for his commentary on this intelligence; but sat severely silent, with his eyes fixed on the ground. Long after the subject was dismissed, and other topics occupied us, he remained so; seldom raising his eyes, unless to rest them for a moment, with a thoughtful frown, upon the Doctor, or his wife, or both.

The Doctor was very fond of music. Agnes sang with great sweetness and expression, and so did Mrs. Strong. They sang together, and played duets together, and we had quite a little concert. But I remarked two things: first, that though Annie soon recovered her composure, and was quite herself, there was a blank between her and Mr. Wickfield which separated them wholly from each other; secondly, that Mr. Wickfield seemed to dislike the intimacy between her and Agnes, and to watch it with uneasiness. And now, I must confess, the recollection of what I had seen on that night when Mr. Maldon went away, first began to return upon me with a meaning it had never had, and to trouble me. The innocent beauty of her face was not as innocent to me as it had been; I mistrusted the natural grace and charm of her manner; and when I looked at Agnes by her side, and thought how good and true Agnes was, suspicions arose within me that it was an ill-assorted friendship.

She was so happy in it herself, however, and the other was so happy too, that they made the evening fly away as if it were but an hour. It closed in an incident which I well remember. They were taking leave of each other, and Agnes was going to embrace her and kiss her, when Mr. Wickfield stepped between them, as if by accident, and drew Agnes quickly away. Then I saw, as though all the intervening time had been cancelled, and I were still standing in the doorway on the night of the departure, the expression of that night in the face of Mrs. Strong, as it confronted his.

I cannot say what an impression this made upon me, or how impossible I found it, when I thought of her afterwards, to separate her from this look, and remember her face in its innocent loveliness again. It haunted me when I got home. I seemed to have left the Doctor's roof with a dark cloud lowering on it. The reverence that I had for his grey head, was mingled with commiseration for his faith in those who were treacherous to him, and with resentment against those who injured him. The impending shadow of a great affliction, and a great disgrace that had no distinct form in it yet, fell like a stain upon the quiet place where I had worked and played as a boy, and did it a cruel wrong. I had no pleasure in thinking, any more, of the grave old broad-leaved aloe-trees which remained shut up in themselves a hundred years together, and of the trim smooth grass-plot, and the stone urns, and the Doctor's walk, and the congenial sound of the Cathedral bell hovering above them all. It was as if the tranquil sanctuary of my boyhood had been sacked before my face, and its peace and honour given to the winds.

But morning brought with it my parting from the old house, which Agnes had filled with her influence; and that occupied my mind sufficiently. I should be there again soon, no doubt; I might sleep again—perhaps often—in my old room; but the days of my inhabiting there were gone, and the old time was past. I was heavier at heart when I packed up such of my books and clothes as still remained there to be sent to Dover, than I cared to show to Uriah Heep; who was so officious to help me, that I uncharitably thought him mighty glad that I was going.

I got away from Agnes and her father, somehow, with an indifferent show of being very manly, and took my seat upon the box of the London coach. I was so softened and forgiving, going through the town, that I had half a mind to nod to my old enemy the butcher, and throw him five shillings to drink. But he looked such a very obdurate butcher as he stood scraping the great block in the shop, and moreover, his appearance was so little improved by the loss of a front tooth which I had knocked out, that I thought it best to make no advances.

The main object on my mind, I remember, when we got fairly on the road, was to appear as old as possible to the coachman, and to speak extremely gruff. The latter point I achieved at great personal inconvenience; but I stuck to it, because I felt it was a grown-up sort of thing.

"You are going through, sir?" said the coachman.

"Yes, William," I said, condescendingly (I knew him); "I am going to London. I shall go down into Suffolk afterwards."

"Shooting, sir?" said the coachman.

He knew as well as I did that it was just as likely, at that time of year, I was going down there whaling; but I felt complimented, too.

"I don't know," I said, pretending to be undecided, "whether I shall take a shot or not."

"Birds is got wery shy, I'm told," said William.

"So I understand," said I.

"Is Suffolk your county, sir?" asked William.

"Yes," I said, with some importance. "Suffolk's my county."

"I'm told the dumplings is uncommon fine down there," said William.

I was not aware of it myself, but I felt it necessary to uphold the institutions of my county, and to evince a familiarity with them; so I shook my head, as much as to say, "I believe you!"

"And the Punches," said William. "There's cattle! A Suffolk Punch, when he's a good un, is worth his weight in gold. Did you ever breed any Suffolk Punches yourself, sir?"

"N—no," I said, "not exactly."

"Here's a gen'lm'n behind me, I'll pound it," said William, "as has bred 'em by wholesale."

The gentleman spoken of was a gentleman with a very unpromising squint, and a prominent chin, who had a tall white hat on with a narrow flat brim, and whose close-fitting drab trousers seemed to button all the way up outside his legs from his boots to his hips. His chin was cocked over the coachman's shoulder, so near to me, that his breath quite tickled the back of my head; and as I looked round at him, he leered at the leaders with the eye with which he didn't squint, in a very knowing manner.

"Ain't you?" asked William.

"Ain't I what?" said the gentleman behind.

"Bred them Suffolk Punches by wholesale?"

"I should think so," said the gentleman. "There ain't no sort of orse that I ain't bred, and no sort of dorg. Orses and dorgs is some men's fancy. They're wittles and drink to me—lodging, wife, and children—reading, writing, and 'rithmetic—snuff, tobacker, and sleep."

"That ain't a sort of man to see sitting behind a coach-box, is it though?" said William in my ear, as he handled the reins.

I construed this remark into an indication of a wish that he should have my place, so I blushingly offered to resign it.

"Well, if you don't mind, sir," said William, "I think it *would* be more correct."

I have always considered this as the first fall I had in life. When I booked my place at the coach-office I had had "Box Seat" written against the entry, and had given the book-keeper half-a-crown. I was got up in a special great-coat and shawl, expressly to do honour to that distinguished eminence; had glorified myself upon it a good deal; and had felt that I was a credit to the coach. And here, in the very first stage, I was supplanted by a shabby man with a squint, who had no other merit than smelling like a livery-stables, and being able to walk across me, more like a fly than a human being, while the horses were at a canter!

A distrust of myself, which has often beset me in life on small occasions, when it would have been better away, was assuredly not stopped in its growth by this little incident outside the Canterbury coach. It was in vain to take refuge in gruffness of speech. I spoke from the pit of my stomach for the rest of the journey, but I felt completely extinguished, and dreadfully young.

It was curious and interesting, nevertheless, to be sitting up there, behind four horses: well educated, well dressed, and with plenty of money in my pocket; and to look out for the places where I had slept on my weary journey. I had abundant occupation for my thoughts, in every conspicuous landmark on the road. When I looked down at the tramps whom we passed, and saw that well-remembered style of face turned up, I felt as if the tinker's blackened hand were in the bosom of my shirt again. When we clattered through the narrow street of Chatham, and I caught a glimpse, in passing, of the lane where the old monster lived who had bought my jacket, I stretched my neck eagerly to look for the place where I had sat, in the sun and in the shade, waiting for my money. When we came, at last, within a stage of London, and passed the veritable Salem House where Mr. Creakle had laid about him with a heavy hand, I would have given all I had, for lawful permission to get down and thrash him, and let all the boys out like so many caged sparrows.

We went to the Golden Cross at Charing Cross, then a mouldy sort of establishment in a close neighbourhood. A waiter showed me into the coffee-room; and a chambermaid introduced me to my small bedchamber, which smelt like a hackney-coach, and was shut up like a family vault. I was still painfully conscious of my youth, for nobody stood in any awe of me at all: the chambermaid being utterly indifferent to my opinions on any subject, and the waiter being familiar with me, and offering advice to my inexperience."

" Well now," said the waiter, in a tone of confidence, " what would you like for dinner? Young gentlemen likes poultry in general: have a fowl! "

I told him, as majestically as I could, that I wasn't in the humour for a fowl.

" Ain't you? " said the waiter. " Young gentlemen is generally tired of beef and mutton: have a weal cutlet! "

I assented to this proposal, in default of being able to suggest anything else.

" Do you care for taters? " said the waiter, with an insinuating smile, and his head on one side. " Young gentlemen generally has been overdosed with taters."

I commanded him, in my deepest voice, to order a veal cutlet and potatoes, and all things fitting; and to inquire at the bar if there were any letters for Trotwood Copperfield, Esquire—which I knew there were not, and couldn't be, but thought it manly to appear to expect.

He soon came back to say that there were none (at which I was much surprised), and began to lay the cloth for my dinner in a box by the fire. While he was so engaged, he asked me what I would take with it; and on my replying " Half a pint of sherry," thought it a favourable opportunity, I am afraid, to extract that measure of wine from the stale leavings at the bottoms of several small decanters. I am of this opinion, because, while I was reading the newspaper, I observed him behind a low wooden partition, which was his private apartment, very busy pouring out of a number of those vessels into one, like a chemist and druggist making up a prescription. When the wine came, too, I thought it flat; and it certainly had more English crumbs in it, than were to be expected in a foreign wine in anything like a pure state; but I was bashful enough to drink it, and say nothing.

Being then in a pleasant frame of mind (from which I infer that poisoning is not always disagreeable in some stages of the process), I resolved to go to the play. It was Covent Garden Theatre that I chose; and there, from the back of a centre box, I saw *Julius Caesar* and the new Pantomime. To have all those noble Romans alive before me, and walking in and out for my entertainment, instead of being the stern taskmasters they had been at school, was a most novel and delightful effect. But the mingled reality and mystery of the whole show, the influence upon me of the poetry, the lights, the music, the company, the smooth stupendous changes of glittering and brilliant scenery, were so dazzling, and opened up such illimitable regions of delight, that when I came out into the rainy street, at twelve o'clock at night, I felt as if I had come from the clouds, where I had been leading a romantic life for ages, to a bawling, splashing, link-lighted, umbrella-struggling, hackney-coach-jostling, patten-clinking, muddy, miserable world.

I had emerged by another door, and stood in the street for a little while, as if I really were a stranger upon earth; but the unceremonious pushing and hustling that I received, soon recalled me to myself, and put me in the road back to the hotel; whither I went, revolving the glorious vision all the way; and where, after some porter and oysters, I sat revolving it still, at past one o'clock, with my eyes on the coffee-room fire.

I was so filled with the play, and with the past—for it was, in a manner, like a shining transparency, through which I saw my earlier life moving along—that I don't know when the figure of a handsome well-formed young man, dressed with a tasteful easy negligence which I have reason to remember very well, became a real presence to me. But I recollect being conscious of his company without having noticed his coming in—and my still sitting, musing, over the coffee-room fire.

At last I rose to go to bed, much to the relief of the sleepy waiter, who had got the fidgets in his legs, and was twisting them, and hitting them, and putting them through all kinds of contortions in his small pantry. In going towards the door, I passed the person who had come in, and saw him plainly. I turned directly, came back, and looked again. He did not know me, but I knew him in a moment.

At another time I might have wanted the confidence or the decision to speak to him, and might have put it off until next day, and might have lost him. But, in the then condition of my mind, where the play was still running high, his former protection of me appeared so deserving of my gratitude, and my old love for him overflowed my breast so freshly and spontaneously, that I went up to him at once, with a fast-beating heart, and said:

"Steerforth! won't you speak to me?"

He looked at me—just as he used to look, sometimes—but I saw no recognition in his face.

"You don't remember me, I am afraid," said I.

"My God!" he suddenly exclaimed. "It's little Copperfield!"

I grasped him by both hands, and could not let them go. But for very shame, and the fear that it might displease him, I could have held him round the neck and cried.

"I never, never, never was so glad! My dear Steerforth, I am so overjoyed to see you!"

"And I am rejoiced, to see you, too!" he said, shaking my hands heartily. "Why, Copperfield, old boy, don't be overpowered!" And yet he was glad, too, I thought, to see how the delight I had in meeting him affected me.

I brushed away the tears that my utmost resolution had not been able to keep back, and I made a clumsy laugh of it, and we sat down together, side by side.

"Why, how do you come to be here?" said Steerforth, clapping me on the shoulder.

"I came here by the Canterbury coach, to-day. I have been adopted by an aunt down in that part of the country, and have just finished my education there. How do *you* come to be here, Steerforth?"

"Well, I am what they call an Oxford man," he returned; "that is to say, I get bored to death down there, periodically—and I am on my way now to my mother's. You're a devilish amiable-looking fellow, Copperfield. Just what you used to be, now I look at you! Not altered in the least!"

"I knew *you* immediately," I said; "but you are more easily remembered."

He laughed as he ran his hand through the clustering curls of his hair, and said gaily:

"Yes, I am on an expedition of duty. My mother lives a little way out of town; and the roads being in a beastly condition, and our house tedious enough, I remained here to-night instead of going on. I have not been in town half-a-dozen hours, and those I have been dozing and grumbling away at the play."

"I have been at the play, too," said I. "At Covent Garden. What a delightful and magnificent entertainment, Steerforth!"

Steerforth laughed heartily.

"My dear young Davy," he said, clapping me on the shoulder again, "you are a very Daisy. The daisy of the field, at sunrise, is not fresher than you are. I have been at Covent Garden, too, and there never was a more miserable business. Hollo, you sir!"

This was addressed to the waiter, who had been very attentive to our recognition, at a distance, and now came forward deferentially.

"Where have you put my friend, Mr. Copperfield?" said Steerforth.

"Beg your pardon, sir?"

"Where does he sleep? What's his number? You know what I mean," said Steerforth.

"Well, sir," said the waiter, with an apologetic air. "Mr. Copperfield is at present in forty-four, sir."

"And what the devil do you mean," retorted Steerforth, "by putting Mr. Copperfield into a little loft over a stable?"

"Why, you see we wasn't aware, sir," returned the waiter, still apologetically, "as Mr. Copperfield was anyways particular. We can give Mr. Copperfield seventy-two, sir, if it would be preferred. Next you, sir."

"Of course it would be preferred," said Steerforth. "And do it at once."

The waiter immediately withdrew to make the exchange. Steerforth, very much amused at my having been put into forty-four, laughed again, and clapped me on the shoulder again, and invited me to breakfast with him next morning at ten o'clock—an invitation I was only too proud and happy to accept. It being now pretty late, we took our candles and went up-stairs, where we parted with friendly heartiness at his door, and where I found my new room a great improvement on my old one, it not being at all musty, and having an immense four-post bedstead in it, which was quite a little landed estate. Here, among pillows enough for six, I soon fell asleep in a blissful condition, and dreamed of ancient Rome, Steerforth, and friendship, until the early morning coaches rumbling out of the archway underneath, made me dream of thunder and the gods.

20

STEERFORTH'S HOME

WHEN THE CHAMBERMAID TAPPED AT MY DOOR AT eight o'clock, and informed me that my shaving-water was outside, I felt severely the having no occasion for it, and blushed in my bed. The suspicion that she laughed too, when she said it, preyed upon my mind all the time I was dressing; and gave me, I was conscious, a sneaking and guilty air when I passed her on the staircase, as I was going down to breakfast. I was so sensitively aware, indeed, of being younger than I could have wished, that for some time I could not make up my mind to pass her at all, under the ignoble circumstances of the case; but, hearing her there with a broom, stood peeping out of window at King Charles on horseback, surrounded by a maze of hackney-coaches, and looking anything but regal in a drizzling rain and a dark-brown fog, until I was admonished by the waiter that the gentleman was waiting for me.

It was not in the coffee-room that I found Steerforth expecting me, but in a snug private apartment, red-curtained and Turkey-carpeted, where the fire burnt bright, and a fine hot breakfast was set forth on a table covered with a clean cloth; and a cheerful miniature of the room, the fire, the breakfast, Steerforth, and all, was shining in the little round mirror over the sideboard. I was rather bashful at first, Steerforth being so self-possessed, and elegant, and superior to me in all respects (age included); but his easy patronage soon put that to rights, and made me quite at home. I could not enough admire the change he had wrought in the Golden Cross; or compare the dull forlorn state I had held yesterday, with this morning's comfort and this morning's entertainment. As to the waiter's familiarity, it was quenched as if it had never been. He attended on us, as I may say, in sackcloth and ashes.

"Now, Copperfield," said Steerforth, when we were alone, "I should like to hear what you are doing, and where you are going, and all about you. I feel as if you were my property."

Glowing with pleasure to find that he had still this interest in me, I told him how my aunt had proposed the little expedition that I had before me, and whither it tended.

"As you are in no hurry, then," said Steerforth, "come home with me to Highgate, and stay a day or two. You will be pleased with my mother—she is a little vain and prosy about me, but that you can forgive her—and she will be pleased with you."

"I should like to be as sure of that, as you are kind enough to say you are," I answered, smiling.

"Oh!" said Steerforth, "every one who likes me, has a claim on her that is sure to be acknowledged."

"Then I think I shall be a favourite," said I.

"Good!" said Steerforth. "Come and prove it. We will go and see the lions for an hour or two—it's something to have a fresh fellow like you to show them to, Copperfield—and then we'll journey out to Highgate by the coach."

I could hardly believe but that I was in a dream, and that I should wake presently in number forty-four, to the solitary box in the coffee-room and the familiar waiter again. After I had written to my aunt and told her of my fortunate meeting with my admired old schoolfellow, and my acceptance of his invitation, we went out in a hackney-chariot, and saw a Panorama and some other sights, and took a walk through the Museum, where I could not help observing how much Steerforth knew, on an infinite variety of subjects, and of how little account he seemed to make his knowledge.

"You'll take a high degree at college, Steerforth," said I, "if you have not done so already; and they will have good reason to be proud of you."

"*I* take a degree!" cried Steerforth. "Not I! my dear Daisy—will you mind my calling you Daisy?"

"Not at all!" said I.

"That's a good fellow! My dear Daisy," said Steerforth, laughing, "I have not the least desire or intention to distinguish myself in that way. I have done quite sufficient for my purpose. I find that I am heavy company enough for myself as I am."

"But the fame——" I was beginning.

"You romantic Daisy!" said Steerforth, laughing still more heartily; "why should I trouble myself, that a parcel of heavy-headed fellows may gape and hold up their hands? Let them do it at some other man. There's fame for him, and he's welcome to it."

I was abashed at having made so great a mistake, and was glad to change the subject. Fortunately it was not difficult to do, for Steerforth could always pass from one subject to another with a carelessness and lightness that were his own.

Lunch succeeded to our sight-seeing, and the short winter day wore away so fast, that it was dusk when the stage-coach stopped with us at an old brick house at Highgate on the summit of the hill. An elderly lady, though not very far advanced in years, with a proud carriage and a handsome face, was in the doorway as we alighted; and greeting Steerforth as "My dearest James," folded him in her arms. To this lady he presented me as his mother, and she gave me a stately welcome.

It was a genteel old-fashioned house, very quiet and orderly. From the windows of my room I saw all London lying in the distance like a great vapour, with here and there some lights twinkling through it. I had only time, in dressing, to glance at the solid furniture, the framed pieces of work (done, I supposed, by Steerforth's mother when she was a girl), and some pictures in crayons of ladies with powdered hair and bodices, coming and going on the walls, as the newly-kindled fire crackled and sputtered, when I was called to dinner.

There was a second lady in the dining-room, of a slight short figure, dark, and not agreeable to look at, but with some appearance of good looks too, who attracted my attention: perhaps because I had not expected to see her: perhaps because I found myself sitting opposite to her: perhaps because of something really remarkable in her. She had black hair and eager black eyes, and was thin, and had a scar upon her lip. It was an old scar—I should rather call it, seam, for it was not discoloured, and had healed years ago—which had once cut through her mouth, downward towards the chin, but was now barely visible across the table, except above and on her upper lip, the shape of which it had altered. I concluded in my own mind that she was about thirty years of age, and that she wished to be married.

She was a little dilapidated—like a house—with having been so long to let; yet had, as I have said, an appearance of good looks. Her thinness seemed to be the effect of some wasting fire within her, which found a vent in her gaunt eyes.

She was introduced as Miss Dartle, and both Steerforth and his mother called her Rosa. I found that she lived there, and had been for a long time Mrs. Steerforth's companion. It appeared to me that she never said anything she wanted to say, outright; but hinted it, and made a great deal more of it by this practice. For example, when Mrs. Steerforth observed, more in jest than earnest, that she feared her son led but a wild life at college, Miss Dartle put in thus:

"Oh, really? You know how ignorant I am, and that I only ask for information, but isn't it always so? I thought that kind of life was on all hands understood to be—eh?"

"It is education for a very grave profession, if you mean that, Rosa," Mrs. Steerforth answered with some coldness.

"Oh! Yes! That's very true," returned Miss Dartle. "But isn't it, though?—I want to be put right, if I am wrong—isn't it, really?"

"Really what?" said Mrs. Steerforth.

"Oh! You mean it's *not*!" returned Miss Dartle. "Well, I'm very glad to hear it! Now, I know what to do! That's the advantage of asking. I shall never allow people to talk before me about wastefulness and profligacy, and so forth, in connection with that life, any more."

"And you will be right," said Mrs. Steerforth. "My son's tutor is a conscientious gentleman; and if I had not implicit reliance on my son, I should have reliance on him."

"Should you?" said Miss Dartle. "Dear me! Conscientious, is he? Really conscientious, now?"

"Yes, I am convinced of it," said Mrs. Steerforth.

"How very nice!" exclaimed Miss Dartle. "What a comfort! Really conscientious? Then he's not—but of course he can't be, if he's really conscientious. Well, I shall be quite happy in my opinion of him, from this time. You can't think how it elevates him in my opinion, to know for certain that he's really conscientious!"

Her own views of every question, and her correction of everything that was said to which she was opposed, Miss Dartle insinuated in the same way: sometimes, I could not conceal from myself, with great power, though in contradiction even of Steerforth. An instance happened before dinner was done. Mrs. Steerforth, speaking to me about my intention of going down into

Suffolk, I said at hazard how glad I should be, if Steerforth wouid only go there with me; and explaining to him that I was going to see my old nurse, and Mr. Peggotty's family, I reminded him of the boatman whom he had seen at school.

"Oh! That bluff fellow!" said Steerforth. "He had a son with him, hadn't he?"

"No. That was his nephew," I replied; "whom he adopted, though, as a son. He has a very pretty little niece too, whom he adopted as a daughter. In short, his house (or rather his boat, for he lives in one, on dry land) is full of people who are objects of his generosity and kindness. You would be delighted to see that household."

"Should I?" said Steerforth. "Well, I think I should. I must see what can be done. It would be worth a journey (not to mention the pleasure of a journey with you, Daisy), to see that sort of people together, and to make one of 'em."

My heart leaped with a new hope of pleasure. But it was in reference to the tone in which he had spoken of "that sort of people," that Miss Dartle, whose sparkling eyes had been watchful of us, now broke in again.

"Oh, but, really? Do tell me. Are they, though?" she said.

"Are they what? And are who what?" said Steerforth.

"That sort of people. Are they really animals and clods, and beings of another order? I want to know *so* much."

"Why, there's a pretty wide separation between them and us," said Steerforth, with indifference. "They are not to be expected to be as sensitive as we are. Their delicacy is not to be shocked, or hurt easily. They are wonderfully virtuous, I dare say. Some people contend for that, at least; and I am sure I don't want to contradict them. But they have not very fine natures, and they may be thankful that, like their coarse rough skins, they are not easily wounded."

"Really!" said Miss Dartle. "Well, I don't know, now, when I have been better pleased than to hear that. It's so consoling! It's such a delight to know that, when they suffer, they don't feel! Sometimes I have been quite uneasy for that sort of people; but now I shall just dismiss the idea of them altogether. Live and learn. I had my doubts, I confess, but now they're cleared up. I didn't know, and now I do know, and that shows the advantage of asking—don't it?"

I believed that Steerforth had said what he had, in jest, or to draw Miss Dartle out; and I expected him to say as much when she was gone, and we two were sitting before the fire. But he merely asked me what I thought of her.

" She is very clever, is she not? " I asked.

" Clever! She brings everything to a grindstone," said Steerforth, " and sharpens it, as she has sharpened her own face and figure these years past. She has worn herself away by constant sharpening. She is all edge."

" What a remarkable scar that is upon her lip! " I said.

Steerforth's face fell, and he paused a moment.

" Why, the fact is," he returned, " *I* did that."

" By an unfortunate accident? "

" No. I was a young boy, and she exasperated me, and I threw a hammer at her. A promising young angel I must have been! "

I was deeply sorry to have touched on such a painful theme, but that was useless now.

" She has borne the mark ever since, as you see," said Steerforth; " and she'll bear it to her grave, if she ever rests in one; though I can hardly believe she will ever rest anywhere. She was the motherless child of a sort of cousin of my father's. He died one day. My mother, who was then a widow, brought her here to be company to her. She has a couple of thousand pounds of her own, and saves the interest of it every year, to add to the principal. There's the history of Miss Rosa Dartle for you."

" And I have no doubt she loves you like a brother? " said I.

" Humph! " retorted Steerforth, looking at the fire. " Some brothers are not loved over much; and some love—but help yourself, Copperfield! We'll drink the daisies of the field, in compliment to you; and the lilies of the valley that toil not, neither do they spin, in compliment to me—the more shame for me! " A moody smile that had overspread his features cleared off as he said this merrily, and he was his own frank, winning self again.

I could not help glancing at the scar with a painful interest when we went in to tea. It was not long before I observed that it was the most susceptible part of her face, and that, when she turned pale, that mark altered first, and became a dull, lead-coloured streak, lengthening out to its full extent, like a mark in invisible ink brought to the fire. There was a little altercation between her and Steerforth about a cast of the dice at backgammon, when I thought her, for one moment, in a storm of rage; and then I saw it start forth like the old writing on the wall.

It was no matter of wonder to me to find Mrs. Steerforth devoted to her son. She seemed to be able to speak or think about nothing else. She showed me his picture as an infant, in a locket, with some of his baby-hair in it; she showed me his picture as he had been when I first knew him; and she wore at her breast his picture as he was now. All the letters he had ever written to her, she kept in a cabinet near her own chair by the fire; and she would have read me some of them, and I should have been very glad to hear them too, if he had not interposed, and coaxed her out of the design.

"It was at Mr. Creakle's, my son tells me, that you first became acquainted," said Mrs. Steerforth, as she and I were talking at one table, while they played backgammon at another. "Indeed, I recollect his speaking, at that time, of a pupil younger than himself who had taken his fancy there; but your name, as you may suppose, has not lived in my memory."

"He was very generous and noble to me in those days, I assure you, ma'am," said I, "and I stood in need of such a friend. I should have been quite crushed without him."

"He is always generous and noble," said Mrs. Steerforth, proudly.

I subscribed to this with all my heart, God knows. She knew I did; for the stateliness of her manner already abated towards me, except when she spoke in praise of him, and then her air was always lofty.

"It was not a fit school generally for my son," said she; "far from it; but there were particular circumstances to be considered at the time, of more importance even than that selection. My son's high spirit made it desirable that he should be placed with some man who felt its superiority, and would be content to bow himself before it; and we found such a man there."

I knew that, knowing the fellow. And yet I did not despise him the more for it, but thought it a redeeming quality in him, if he could be allowed any grace for not resisting one so irresistible as Steerforth.

"My son's great capacity was tempted on, there, by a feeling of voluntary emulation and conscious pride," the fond lady went on to say. "He would have risen against all constraint; but he found himself the monarch of the place, and he haughtily determined to be worthy of his station. It was like himself."

I echoed, with all my heart and soul, that it was like himself.

"So my son took, of his own will, and on no compulsion, to the course in which he can always, when it is his pleasure, outstrip every competitor," she pursued. "My son informs me, Mr. Copperfield, that you were quite devoted to him, and that when you met yesterday you made yourself known to him with tears of joy. I should be an affected woman if I made any pretence of being surprised by my son's inspiring such emotions; but I cannot be indifferent to any one who is so sensible of his merit, and I am very glad to see you here, and can assure you that he feels an unusual friendship for you, and that you may rely on his protection."

Miss Dartle played backgammon as eagerly as she did everything else. If I had seen her, first, at the board, I should have fancied that her figure had got thin, and her eyes had got large, over that pursuit, and no other in the world. But I am very much mistaken if she missed a word of this, or lost a look of mine as I received it with the utmost pleasure, and, honoured by Mrs. Steerforth's confidence, felt older than I had done since I left Canterbury.

When the evening was pretty far spent, and a tray of glasses and decanters came in, Steerforth promised, over the fire, that he would seriously think of going down into the country with me. There was no hurry, he said; a week hence would do; and his mother hospitably said the same. While we were talking, he more than once called me Daisy; which brought Miss Dartle out again.

"But really, Mr. Copperfield," she asked, "is it a nickname? And why does he give it you? Is it—eh?—because he thinks you young and innocent? I am so stupid in these things."

I coloured in replying that I believed it was.

"Oh!" said Miss Dartle. "Now I am glad to know that! I ask for information, and I am glad to know it. He thinks you young and innocent; and so you are his friend? Well, that's quite delightful!"

She went to bed soon after this, and Mrs. Steerforth retired too. Steerforth and I, after lingering for half an hour over the fire, talking about Traddles and all the rest of them at old Salem House, went up-stairs together. Steerforth's room was next to mine, and I went in to look at it. It was a picture of comfort, full of easy-chairs, cushions and footstools, worked by his mother's hand, and with no sort of thing omitted that could help to render it complete. Finally, her handsome features looked down on her darling from a portrait on the wall, as if it were even something to her that her likeness should watch him while he slept.

I found the fire burning clear enough in my room by this time, and the curtains drawn before the windows and round the bed, giving it a very snug appearance. I sat down in a great chair upon the hearth to meditate on my happiness; and had enjoyed the contemplation of it for some time, when I found a likeness of Miss Dartle looking eagerly at me from above the chimney-piece.

It was a startling likeness, and necessarily had a startling look. The painter hadn't made the scar, but *I* made it; and there it was, coming and going: now confined to the upper lip as I had seen it at dinner, and now showing the whole extent of the wound inflicted by the hammer, as I had seen it when she was passionate.

I wondered peevishly why they couldn't put her anywhere else instead of quartering her on me. To get rid of her, I undressed quickly, extinguished my light, and went to bed. But, as I fell asleep, I could not forget that she was still there looking, "Is it really, though? I want to know;" and when I awoke in the night, I found that I was uneasily asking all sorts of people in my dreams whether it really was or not—without knowing what I meant.

21

LITTLE EM'LY

THERE WAS A SERVANT IN THAT HOUSE, A MAN WHO, I understood, was usually with Steerforth, and had come into his service at the University, who was in appearance a pattern of respectability. I believe there never existed in his station a more respectable-looking man. He was taciturn, soft-footed, very quiet in his manner, deferential, observant, always at hand when wanted, and never near when not wanted; but his great claim to consideration was his respectability. He had not a pliant face, he had rather a stiff neck, rather a tight smooth head with short hair clinging to it at the sides, a soft way of speaking, with a peculiar habit of whispering the letter S so distinctly, that he seemed to use it oftener than any other man; but every peculiarity that he had he made respectable. If his nose had been upside-down, he would have made that respectable. He surrounded himself with an atmosphere of respectability, and walked secure in it. It would have been next to impossible to suspect him of anything wrong, he was so thoroughly respectable. Nobody could have thought of putting him in a livery, he was so highly respectable. To have imposed any derogatory work upon him, would have been to inflict a wanton insult on the feelings of a most respectable man. And of this, I noticed the women-servants in the household were so intuitively conscious, that they always did such work themselves, and generally while he read the paper by the pantry fire.

Such a self-contained man I never saw. But in that quality, as in every other he possessed, he only seemed to be the more respectable. Even the fact that no one knew his Christian name, seemed to form a part of his respectability. Nothing could be objected against his surname, Littimer, by which he was known. Peter might have been hanged, or Tom transported; but Littimer was perfectly respectable.

It was occasioned, I suppose, by the reverend nature of respectability in the abstract, but I feel particularly young in this man's presence. How old he was himself, I could not guess. And that again went to his credit on the same score; for in the calmness of respectability he might have numbered fifty years as well as thirty.

Littimer was in my room in the morning before I was up, to bring me that reproachful shaving-water, and to put out my clothes. When I undrew the curtains and looked out of bed, I saw him, in an equable temperature of respectability, unaffected by the east wind of January, and not even breathing frostily, standing my boots right and left in the first dancing position, and blowing specks of dust off my coat as he laid it down like a baby.

I gave him good morning, and asked him what o'clock it was. He took out of his pocket the most respectable hunting-watch I ever saw, and preventing the spring with his thumb from opening far, looked in at the face as if he were consulting an oracular oyster, shut it up again, and said, If I pleased, it was half-past eight.

" Mr. Steerforth will be glad to hear how you have rested, sir."

" Thank you," said I, " very well indeed. Is Mr. Steerforth quite well?"

" Thank you, sir, Mr. Steerforth is tolerably well." Another of his characteristics—no use of superlatives. A cool calm medium always.

" Is there anything more I can have the honour of doing for you, sir? The warning-bell will ring at nine; the family take breakfast at half-past nine."

"Nothing, I thank you."

"I thank *you*, sir, if you please;" and with that, and with a little inclination of his head when he passed the bedside, as an apology for correcting me, he went out, shutting the door as delicately as if I had just fallen into a sweet sleep on which my life depended.

Every morning we held exactly this conversation: never any more, and never any less; and yet, invariably, however far I might have lifted out of myself over-night, and advanced towards maturer years, by Steerforth's companionship, or Mrs. Steerforth's confidence, or Miss Dartle's conversation, in the presence of this most respectable man I became, as our smaller poets sing, "a boy again."

He got horses for us; and Steerforth, who knew everything, gave me lessons in riding. He provided foils for us, and Steerforth gave me lessons in fencing—gloves, and I began, of the same master, to improve in boxing. It gave me no manner of concern that Steerforth should find me a novice in these sciences, but I never could bear to show my want of skill before the respectable Littimer. I had no reason to believe that Littimer understood such arts himself; he never led me to suppose anything of the kind, by so much as the vibration of one of his respectable eyelashes; yet whenever he was by, while we were practising, I felt myself the greenest and most inexperienced of mortals.

I am particular about this man, because he made a particular effect on me at that time, and because of what took place thereafter.

The week passed away in a most delightful manner. It passed rapidly, as may be supposed, to one entranced as I was; and yet it gave me so many occasions for knowing Steerforth better, and admiring him more in a thousand respects, that at its close I seemed to have been with him for a much longer time. A dashing way he had of treating me like a plaything, was more agreeable to me than any behaviour he could have adopted. It reminded me of our old acquaintance; it seemed the natural sequel of it; it showed me that he was unchanged; it relieved me of any uneasiness I might have felt, in comparing my merits with his, and measuring my claims upon his friendship by any equal standard; above all, it was a familiar, unrestrained, affectionate demeanour that he used towards no one else. As he had treated me at school differently from all the rest, I joyfully believed that he treated me in life unlike any other friend he had. I believed that I was nearer to his heart than any other friend, and my own heart warmed with attachment to him.

He made up his mind to go with me into the country, and the day arrived for our departure. He had been doubtful at first whether to take Littimer or not, but decided to leave him at home. The respectable creature, satisfied with his lot whatever it was, arranged our portmanteaus on the little carriage that was to take us into London, as if they were intended to defy the shocks of ages; and received my modestly proffered donation with perfect tranquillity.

We bade adieu to Mrs. Steerforth and Miss Dartle, with many thanks on my part, and much kindness on the devoted mother's. The last thing I saw was Littimer's unruffled eye; fraught, as I fancied, with the silent conviction that I was very young indeed.

What I felt, in returning so auspiciously to the old familiar places, I shall not endeavour to describe. We went down by the Mail. I was so concerned, I recollect, even for the honour of Yarmouth, that when Steerforth said, as we drove through its dark streets to the inn, that, as well as he could make out, it was a good, queer, out-of-the-way kind of hole, I was highly pleased. We went to bed on our arrival (I observed a pair of dirty shoes and gaiters in connection with my old friend the Dolphin as we passed that door), and breakfasted late in the morning. Steerforth, who was in great spirits, had been strolling about the beach before I was up, and had made acquaintance he said, with half the boatmen in the place. Moreover, he had seen, in the distance, what he was sure must be the identical house of Mr. Peggotty, with smoke coming out of the chimney; and had had a great mind, he told me, to walk in and swear he was myself grown out of knowledge.

"When do you propose to introduce me there, Daisy?" he said. "I am at your disposal. Make your own arrangements."

"Why, I was thinking that this evening would be a good time, Steerforth, when they are all sitting round the fire. I should like you to see it when it's snug, it's such a curious place."

"So be it!" returned Steerforth. "This evening."

"I shall not give them any notice that we are here, you know." said I, delighted. "We must take them by surprise."

"Oh, of course! It's no fun," said Steerforth, "unless we take them by surprise. Let us see the natives in their aboriginal condition."

"Though they *are* that sort of people that you mentioned," I returned.

"Aha! What! you recollect my skirmishes with Rosa, do

you?" he exclaimed with a quick look. "Confound the girl, I am half afraid of her. She's like a goblin to me. But never mind her. Now what are you going to do? You are going to see your nurse, I suppose?"

"Why, yes," I said, "I must see Peggotty first of all."

"Well," replied Steerforth, looking at his watch. "Suppose I deliver you up to be cried over for a couple of hours. Is that long enough?"

I answered, laughing, that I thought we might get through it in that time, but that he must come also; for he would find that his renown had preceded him, and that he was almost as great a personage as I was.

"I'll come anywhere you like," said Steerforth, "or do anything you like. Tell me where to come to; and in two hours I'll produce myself in any state you please, sentimental or comical."

I gave him minute directions for finding the residence of Mr. Barkis, carrier to Blunderstone and elsewhere; and, on this understanding, went out alone. There was a sharp bracing air; the ground was dry; the sea was crisp and clear; the sun was diffusing abundance of light, if not much warmth; and everything was fresh and lively. I was so fresh and lively myself, in the pleasure of being there, that I could have stopped the people in the streets and shaken hands with them.

The streets looked small, of course. The streets that we have only seen as children always do, I believe, when we go back to them. But I had forgotten nothing in them, and found nothing changed, until I came to Mr. Omer's shop. OMER AND JORAM was now written up, where OMER used to be; but the inscription, DRAPER, TAILOR, HABERDASHER, FUNERAL FURNISHER. &C., remained as it was.

My footsteps seemed to tend so naturally to the shop-door after I had read these words from over the way, that I went across the road and looked in. There was a pretty woman at the back of the shop, dancing a little child in her arms, while another little fellow clung to her apron. I had no difficulty in recognising either Minnie or Minnie's children. The glass door of the parlour was not open; but in the workshop across the yard I could faintly hear the old tune playing, as if it had never left off.

"Is Mr. Omer at home?" said I, entering. "I should like to see him, for a moment, if he is."

"Oh yes, sir, he is at home," said Minnie; "this weather don't suit his asthma out of doors. Joe, call your grandfather!"

The little fellow, who was holding her apron, gave such a lusty shout, that the sound of it made him bashful, and he buried his face in her skirts, to her great admiration. I heard a heavy puffing and blowing coming towards us, and soon Mr. Omer, shorter-winded than of yore, but not much older-looking, stood before me.

"Servant, sir," said Mr. Omer. "What can I do for you, sir?"

"You can shake hands with me, Mr. Omer, if you please," said I, putting out my own. "You were very good-natured to me once, when I am afraid I didn't show that I thought so."

"Was I though?" returned the old man. "I'm glad to hear it, but I don't remember when. Are you sure it was me?"

"Quite."

"I think my memory has got as short as my breath," said Mr. Omer, looking at me and shaking his head; "for I don't remember you."

"Don't you remember your coming to the coach to meet me, and my having breakfast here, and our riding out to Blunderstone together: you, and I, and Mrs. Joram, and Mr. Joram too—who wasn't her husband then?"

"Why, Lord bless my soul!" exclaimed Mr. Omer, after being thrown by his surprise into a fit of coughing, "you don't say so! Minnie, my dear, you recollect? Dear me, yes; the party was a lady, I think?"

"My mother," I rejoined.

"To—be—sure," said Mr. Omer, touching my waistcoat with his forefinger, "and there was a little child too! There was two parties. The little party was laid along with the other party. Over at Blunderstone it was, of course. Dear me! And how have you been since?"

Very well, I thanked him, as I hoped he had been too.

"Oh! nothing to grumble at, you know," said Mr. Omer. "I find my breath gets short, but it seldom gets longer as a man gets older. I take it as it comes, and make the most of it. That's the best way, ain't it?"

Mr. Omer coughed again, in consequence of laughing, and was assisted out of his fit by his daughter, who now stood close beside us, dancing her smallest child on the counter.

"Dear me!" said Mr. Omer. "Yes, to be sure. Two parties! Why, in that very ride, if you'll believe me, the day was named for my Minnie to marry Joram. 'Do name it, sir,' says Joram. 'Yes, do, father,' says Minnie. And now he's come into the business. And look here! The youngest!"

Minnie laughed, and stroked her banded hair upon her temples, as her father put one of his fat fingers into the hand of the child she was dancing on the counter.

"Two parties, of course!" said Mr. Omer, nodding his head retrospectively. "Ex-actly so! And Joram's at work, at this minute, on a grey one with silver nails, not this measurement"—the measurement of the dancing child upon the counter—"by a good two inches. Will you take something?"

I thanked him, but declined.

"Let me see," said Mr. Omer. "Barkis's the carrier's wife—Peggotty's the boatman's sister—she had something to do with your family? She was in service there, sure?"

My answering in the affirmative gave him great satisfaction.

"I believe my breath will get long next, my memory's getting so much so," said Mr. Omer. "Well, sir, we've got a young relation of hers here, under articles to us, that has as elegant a taste in the dress-making business—I assure you I don't believe there's a Duchess in England can touch her."

"Not little Em'ly?" said I, involuntarily.

"Em'ly's her name," said Mr. Omer, "and she's little too. But if you'll believe me, she has such a face of her own that half the women in this town are mad against her."

"Nonsense, father!" cried Minnie.

"My dear," said Mr. Omer, "I don't say it's the case with you," winking at me, "but I say that half the women in Yarmouth, ah! and in five mile round, are mad against that girl."

"Then she should have kept to her own station in life, father," said Minnie, "and not have given them any hold to talk about her, and then they couldn't have done it."

"Couldn't have done it, my dear!" retorted Mr. Omer. "Couldn't have done it! Is that *your* knowledge of life? What is there that any woman couldn't do, that she shouldn't do—especially on the subject of another woman's good looks?"

I really thought it was all over with Mr. Omer, after he had uttered this libellous pleasantry. He coughed to that extent, and his breath eluded all his attempts to recover it with that obstinacy, that I fully expected to see his head go down behind the counter, and his little black breeches, with the rusty little bunches of ribbons at the knees, come quivering up in a last ineffectual struggle. At length, however, he got better, though he still panted hard, and was so exhausted that he was obliged to sit on the stool of the shop-desk.

"You see," he said, wiping his head, and breathing with difficulty, "she hasn't taken much to any companions here; she hasn't taken kindly to any particular acquaintances and friends, not to mention sweethearts. In consequence, an ill-natured story got about, that Em'ly wanted to be a lady. Now, my opinion is, that it came into circulation principally on account of her sometimes saying at the school, that if she was a lady, she would like to do so-and-so for her uncle—don't you see?—and buy him such-and-such fine things."

"I assure you, Mr. Omer, she has said so to me," I returned eagerly, "when we were both children."

Mr. Omer nodded his head and rubbed his chin. "Just so. Then out of a very little, she could dress herself, you see, better than most others could out of a deal, and *that* made things unpleasant. Moreover, she was rather what might be called wayward. I'll go so far as to say what I should call wayward myself," said Mr. Omer; "didn't know her own mind quite; a little spoiled; and couldn't, at first, exactly bind herself down. No more than that was ever said against her, Minnie?"

"No, father," said Mrs. Joram. "That's the worst, I believe."

"So when she got a situation," said Mr. Omer, "to keep a fractious old lady company, they didn't very well agree, and she didn't stop. At last she came here, apprenticed for three years. Nearly two of 'em are over, and she has been as good a girl as ever was. Worth any six! Minnie, is she worth any six, now?"

"Yes, father," replied Minnie. "Never say *I* detracted from her!"

"Very good," said Mr. Omer. "That's right. And so, young gentleman," he added, after a few moments' further rubbing of his chin, "that you may not consider me long-winded as well as short-breathed, I believe that's all about it."

As they had spoken in a subdued tone, while speaking of Em'ly, I had no doubt that she was near. On my asking now, if that were not so, Mr. Omer nodded yes, and nodded towards the door of the parlour. My hurried inquiry if I might peep in, was answered with a free permission; and, looking through the glass, I saw her sitting at her work. I saw her, a most beautiful little creature, with the cloudless blue eyes, that had looked into my childish heart, turned laughingly upon another child of Minnie's who was playing near her; with enough of wilfulness in her bright face to justify what I had heard; with much of the old capricious coyness lurking in it; but with nothing in her pretty looks, I am sure, but what was meant for goodness and for happiness, and what was on a good and happy course.

The tune across the yard that seemed as if it never had left off—alas! it was the tune that never *does* leave off—was beating, softly, all the while.

" Wouldn't you like to step in," said Mr. Omer, " and speak to her? Walk in and speak to her, sir! Make yourself at home! "

I was too bashful to do so then—I was afraid of confusing her, and I was no less afraid of confusing myself: but I informed myself of the hour at which she left of an evening, in order that our visit might be timed accordingly; and taking leave of Mr. Omer, and his pretty daughter, and her little children, went away to my dear old Peggotty's.

Here she was, in the tiled kitchen, cooking dinner! The moment I knocked at the door she opened it, and asked me what I pleased to want. I looked at her with a smile, but she gave me no smile in return. I had never ceased to write to her, but it must have been seven years since we had met.

" Is Mr. Barkis at home, ma'am? " I said, feigning to speak roughly to her.

" He's at home, sir," returned Peggotty, " but he's bad abed with the rheumatics."

" Don't he go over to Blunderstone now? " I asked.

" When he's well he do," she answered.

" Do *you* ever go there, Mrs. Barkis? "

She looked at me more attentively, and I noticed a quick movement of her hands towards each other.

" Because I want to ask a question about a house there, that they call the—what is it?—the Rookery," said I.

She took a step backward, and put out her hands in an undecided frightened way, as if to keep me off.

" Peggotty! " I cried to her.

She cried, " My darling boy! " and we both burst into tears, and were locked in one another's arms.

What extravagances she committed; what laughing and crying over me; what pride she showed, what joy, what sorrow that she whose pride and joy I might have been could never hold me in a fond embrace; I have not the heart to tell. I was troubled with no misgiving that it was young in me to respond to her emotions. I had never laughed and cried in all my life, I dare say, not even to her, more freely than I did that morning.

" Barkis will be so glad," said Peggotty, wiping her eyes with her apron, " that it'll do him more good than pints of liniment. May I go and tell him you are here? Will you come up and see him, my dear? "

Of course I would. But Peggotty could not get out of the room as easily as she meant to, for as often as she got to the door and looked round at me, she came back again to have another laugh and another cry upon my shoulder. At last, to make the matter easier, I went up-stairs with her; and having waited outside for a minute, while she said a word of preparation to Mr. Barkis, presented myself before that invalid.

He received me with absolute enthusiasm. He was too rheumatic to be shaken hands with, but he begged me to shake the tassel on the top of his nightcap, which I did most cordially. When I sat down by the side of the bed, he said that it did him a world of good to feel as if he was driving me on the Blunderstone road again. As he lay in bed, face upward, and so covered, with that exception, that he seemed to be nothing but a face—like a conventional cherubim—he looked the queerest object I ever beheld.

" What name was it as I wrote up in the cart, sir? " said Mr. Barkis, with a slow rheumatic smile.

" Ah! Mr. Barkis, we had some grave talks about that matter, hadn't we? "

" I was willin' a long time, sir? " said Mr. Barkis.

" A long time," said I.

" And I don't regret it," said Mr. Barkis. " Do you remember what you told me once, about her making all the apple parsties and doing all the cooking? "

" Yes, very well," I returned.

" It was as true," said Mr. Barkis, " as turnips is. It was as true," said Mr. Barkis, nodding his nightcap, which was his only means of emphasis, " as taxes is. And nothing's truer than them."

Mr. Barkis turned his eyes upon me, as if for my assent to this result of his reflections in bed; and I gave it.

" Nothing's truer than them," repeated Mr. Barkis; " a man as poor as I am, finds that out in his mind when he's laid up. I'm a very poor man, sir! "

" I am sorry to hear it, Mr. Barkis."

" A very poor man, indeed I am," said Mr. Barkis.

Here his right hand came slowly and feebly from under the bedclothes, and with a purposeless uncertain grasp took hold of a stick which was loosely tied to the side of the bed. After some poking about with this instrument, in the course of which his face assumed a variety of distracted expressions, Mr. Barkis poked it against a box, an end of which had been visible to me all the time. Then his face became composed.

" Old clothes," said Mr. Barkis.

" Oh! " said I.

" I wish it was Money, sir," said Mr. Barkis.

" I wish it was, indeed," said I.

"But it AIN'T," said Mr. Barkis, opening both his eyes as wide as he possibly could.

I expressed myself quite sure of that, and Mr. Barkis, turning his eyes more gently to his wife, said:

"She's the usefullest and best of women, C. P. Barkis. All the praise that any one can give to C. P. Barkis she deserves, and more! My dear, you'll get a dinner to-day, for company; something good to eat and drink, will you?"

I should have protested against this unnecessary demonstration in my honour, but that I saw Peggotty, on the opposite side of the bed, extremely anxious I should not. So I held my peace.

"I have got a trifle of money somewhere about me, my dear," said Mr. Barkis, "but I'm a little tired. If you and Mr. David will leave me for a short nap, I'll try and find it when I wake."

We left the room, in compliance with this request. When we got outside the door, Peggotty informed me that Mr. Barkis, being now "a little nearer" than he used to be, always resorted to this same device before producing a single coin from his store; and that he endured unheard-of agonies in crawling out of bed alone, and taking it from that unlucky box. In effect, we presently heard him uttering suppressed groans of the most dismal nature, as this magpie proceeding racked him in every joint; but while Peggotty's eyes were full of compassion for him, she said this generous impulse would do him good, and it was better not to check it. So he groaned on, until he had got into bed again, suffering, I have no doubt, a martyrdom; and then called us in, pretending to have just woke up from a refreshing sleep, and to produce a guinea from under his pillow. His satisfaction in which happy imposition on us, and in having preserved the impenetrable secret of the box, appeared to be a sufficient compensation to him for all his tortures.

I prepared Peggotty for Steerforth's arrival and it was not long before he came. I am persuaded she knew no difference between his having been a personal benefactor of hers and a kind friend to me, and that she would have received him with the utmost gratitude and devotion in any case. But his easy, spirited good humour; his genial manner, his handsome looks, his natural gift of adapting himself to whomsoever he pleased, and making direct, when he cared to do it, to the main point of interest in anybody's heart; bound her to him wholly in five minutes. His manner to me alone, would have won her. But, through all these causes combined, I sincerely believe she had a kind of adoration for him before he left the house that night.

He stayed there with me to dinner—if I were to say willingly, I should not half express how readily and gaily. He went into Mr. Barkis's room like light and air, brightening and refreshing it as if he were healthy weather. There was no noise, no effort, no consciousness, in anything he did; but in everything an indescribable lightness, a seeming impossibility of doing anything else, or doing anything better, which was so graceful, so natural and agreeable, that it overcomes me, even now, in the remembrance.

We made merry in the little parlour, where the Book of Martyrs, unthumbed since my time, was laid out upon the desk as of old, and where I now turned over its terrific pictures, remembering the old sensations they had awakened, but not feeling them. When Peggotty spoke of what she called my room, and of its being ready for me at night, and of her hoping I would occupy it, before I could so much as look at Steerforth, hesitating, he was possessed of the whole case.

"Of course," he said. "You'll sleep here, while we stay, and I shall sleep at the hotel."

"But to bring you so far," I returned, "and to separate seems bad companionship, Steerforth."

"Why, in the name of Heaven, where do you naturally belong?" he said. "What is 'seems,' compared to that?" It was settled at once.

He maintained all his delightful qualities to the last, until we started forth, at eight o'clock, for Mr. Peggotty's boat. Indeed, they were more and more brightly exhibited as the hours went on; for I thought even then, and I have no doubt now, that the consciousness of success in his determination to please, inspired him with a new delicacy of perception, and made it, subtle as it was, more easy to him. If any one had told me, then, that all this was a brilliant game, played for the excitement of the moment, for the employment of high spirits, in the thoughtless love of superiority, in a mere wasteful careless course of winning what was worthless to him, and next minute thrown away—I say, if anyone had told me such a lie that night, I wonder in what manner of receiving it my indignation would have found a vent!

Probably only in an increase, had that been possible, of the romantic feelings of fidelity and friendship with which I walked beside him, over the dark wintry sands towards the old boat; the wind sighing around us even more mournfully than it had sighed and moaned upon the night when I first darkened Mr. Peggotty's door.

" This is a wild kind of place, Steerforth, is it not? "

" Dismal enough in the dark," he said: " and the sea roars as if it were hungry for us. Is that the boat, where I see a light yonder? "

" That's the boat," said I.

" And it's the same I saw this morning," he returned. " I came straight to it, by instinct, I suppose."

We said no more as we approached the light, but made softly for the door. I laid my hand upon the latch; and whispering Steerforth to keep close to me, went in.

A murmur of voices had been audible on the outside, and, at the moment of our entrance, a clapping of hands: which latter noise, I was surprised to see, proceeded from the generally disconsolate Mrs. Gummidge. But Mrs. Gummidge was not the only person there who was unusually excited. Mr.Peggotty, his face lighted up with uncommon satisfaction, and laughing with all his might, held his rough arms wide open, as if for little Em'ly to run into them; Ham, with a mixed expression in his face of admiration, exultation, and a lumbering sort of bashfulness that sat upon him very well, held little Em'ly by the hand, as if he were presenting her to Mr. Peggotty; little Em'ly herself, blushing and shy, but delighted with Mr. Peggotty's delight, as her joyous eyes expressed, was stopped by our entrance (for she saw us first) in the very act of springing from Ham to nestle in Mr. Peggotty's embrace. In the first glimpse we had of them all, and at the moment of our passing from the dark cold night into the warm light room, this was the way in which they were all employed: Mrs. Gummidge in the background, clapping her hands like a mad woman.

The little picture was so instantaneously dissolved by our going in, that one might have doubted whether it had ever been. I was in the midst of the astonished family, face to face with Mr. Peggotty, and holding out my hand to him, when Ham shouted:

" Mas'r Davy! It's Mas'r Davy! "

In a moment we were all shaking hands with one another, and asking one another how we did, and telling one another how glad we were to meet, and all talking at once. Mr. Peggotty was so proud and overjoyed to see us, that he did not know what to say or do, but kept over and over again shaking hands, with me, and then with Steerforth, and then with me, and then ruffling his shaggy hair all over his head, and laughing with such glee and triumph, that it was a treat to see him.

" Why, that you two gent'lmen—gent'lmen growed—should come to this here roof to-night, of all nights in my life," said

Mr. Peggotty, "is such a thing as never happened afore, I do rightly believe! Em'ly, my darling, come here! Come here, my little witch! There's Mas'r Davy's friend, my dear! There's the gent'lman as you've heerd on, Em'ly. He comes to see you, along with Mas'r Davy, on the brightest night of your uncle's life as ever was or will be, Gorm the t'other one, and horroar for it!"

After delivering this speech, all in a breath, and with extraordinary animation and pleasure, Mr. Peggotty put one of his large hands rapturously on each side of his niece's face, and kissing it a dozen times, laid it with a gentle pride and love upon his broad chest, and patted it as if his hand had been a lady's. Then he let her go; and as she ran into the little chamber where I used to sleep, looked round upon us, quite hot and out of breath with his uncommon satisfaction.

"If you two gent'lmen—gent'lmen growed now, and such gent'lmen—" said Mr. Peggotty.

"So th' are, so th' are!" cried Ham. "Well said! So th' are. Mas'r Davy bor'—gent'lmen growed—so th' are!"

"If you two gent'lmen, gent'lmen growed," said Mr. Peggotty, "don't ex-cuse me for being in a state of mind, when you understand matters, I'll arks your pardon. Em'ly, my dear!—She knows I'm a going to tell," here his delight broke out again, "and has made off. Would you be so good as look arter her, Mawther, for a minute?"

Mrs. Gummidge nodded and disappeared.

"If this ain't," said Mr. Peggotty, sitting down among us by the fire, "the brightest night o' my life, I'm a shellfish—biled too—and more I can't say. This here little Em'ly, sir," in a low voice to Steerforth, "—her as you see a blushing here just now—"

Steerforth only nodded; but with such a pleased expression of interest, and of participation in Mr. Peggotty's feelings, that the latter answered him as if he had spoken.

"To be sure," said Mr. Peggotty. "That's her, and so she is. Thankee, sir."

Ham nodded to me several times, as if he would have said so too.

"This here little Em'ly of ours," said Mr. Peggotty, "has been, in our house, what I suppose (I'm a ignorant man, but that's my belief) no one but a little bright-eyed creetur *can* be in a house. She ain't my child; I never had one; but I couldn't love her more. You understand! I couldn't do it!"

"I quite understand," said Steerforth.

"I know you do, sir," returned Mr. Peggotty, "and thankee

again. Mas'r Davy, he can remember what she was; you may judge for your own self what she is; but neither of you can't fully know what she has been, is, and will be, to my loving art. I am rough, sir," said Mr. Peggotty, "I am as rough as a Sea Porkypine; but no one, unless, mayhap, it is a woman, can know, I think, what our little Em'ly is to me. And betwixt ourselves," sinking his voice lower yet, "*that* woman's name ain't Missis Gummidge neither, though she has a world of merits."

Mr. Peggotty ruffled his hair again with both hands, as a further preparation for what he was going to say, and went on, with a hand upon each of his knees:

"There was a certain person as had know'd our Em'ly, from the time when her father was drownded; as had seen her constant; when a babby, when a young gal, when a woman. Not much of a person to look at, he warn't," said Mr. Peggotty, "something o' my own build—rough—a good deal o' the sou'-wester in him—wery salt—but, on the whole, a honest sort of a chap, with his art in the right place."

I thought I had never seen Ham grin to anything like the extent to which he sat grinning at us now.

"What does this here blessed tarpaulin go and do," said Mr. Peggotty, with his face one high noon of enjoyment, "but he loses that there art of his to our little Em'ly. He follers her about, he makes hisself a sort o' servant to her, he loses in a great measure his relish for his wittles, and in the long-run he makes it clear to me wot's amiss. Now I could wish myself, you see, that our little Em'ly was in a fair way of being married. I could wish to see her, at all ewents, under articles to a honest man as had a right to defend her. I don't know how long I may live, or how soon I may die; but I know that if I was capsized, any night, in a gale of wind in Yarmouth Roads here, and was to see the town-lights shining for the last time over the rollers as I couldn't make no head against, I could go down quieter for thinking 'There's a man ashore there, iron-true to my little Em'ly, God bless her, and no wrong can touch my Em'ly while so be as that man lives.'"

Mr. Peggotty, in simple earnestness, waved his right arm, as if he were waving it at the town-lights for the last time, and then, exchanging a nod with Ham, whose eye he caught, proceeded as before:

"Well! I counsels him to speak to Em'ly. He's big enough, but he's bashfuller than a little un, and he don't like. So *I* speak. 'What! *Him*!' says Em'ly. '*Him* that I've know'd so intimate so many years, and like so much. Oh, Uncle! I never can have *him.* He's such a good fellow! ' I gives her a kiss, and I says no more to her than ' My dear, you're right to speak out, you're to choose for yourself, you're as free as a little bird.' Then I aways to him, and I says, ' I wish it could have been so, but it can't. But you can both be, as you was, and wot I say to you is, Be as you was with her, like a man,' He says to me, a-shaking of my hand, ' I will! ' he says. And he was—honourable and manful—for two year going on, and we was just the same at home here as afore."

Mr. Peggotty's face, which had varied in its expression with the various stages of his narrative, now resumed all its former triumphant delight, as he laid a hand upon my knee and a hand upon Steerforth's (previously wetting them both, for the greater emphasis of the action), and divided the following speech between us:

" All of a sudden, one evening—as it might be to-night—comes little Em'ly from her work, and him with her! There ain't so much in *that*, you'll say. No, because he takes care on her like a brother, arter dark, and indeed afore dark, and at all times. But this tarpaulin chap, he takes hold of her hand, and he cries out to me, joyful, ' Look here! This is to be my little wife! ' And she says, half bold and half shy, and half a-laughing and half a-crying, ' Yes, Uncle! If you please.'— If I please! " cried Mr. Peggotty, rolling his head in an ecstasy at the idea; " Lord, as if I should do anythink else!—' If you please, I am steadier now, and I have thought better of it, and I'll be as good a little wife as I can to him, for he's a dear, good fellow! ' Then Missis Gummidge, she claps her hands like a play, and you come in. Theer! the murder's out! " said Mr. Peggotty—" You come in! It took place this here present hour; and here's the man that'll marry her, the minute she's out of her time."

Ham staggered, as well he might, under the blow Mr. Peggotty dealt him in his unbounded joy, as a mark of confidence and friendship; but feeling called upon to say something to us, he said, with much faltering and great difficulty:

" She warn't no higher than you was, Mas'r Davy—when you first come—when I thought what she'd grow up to be. I see her grow up—gent'lmen—like a flower. I'd lay down my life for her—Mas'r Davy—Oh! most content and cheerful! She's more to me—gent'lmen—than—she's all to me that ever I can want, and more than ever I—than ever I could say. I—I love her true. There ain't a gent'lman in all the land—nor yet sailing upon all the sea—that can love his lady more than I love her, though there's many a common man—would say better—what he meant."

I thought it affecting to see such a sturdy fellow as Ham was now, trembling in the strength of what he felt for the pretty little creature who had won his heart. I thought the simple confidence reposed in us by Mr. Peggotty and by himself, was, in itself, affecting. I was affected by the story altogether. How far my emotions were influenced by the recollections of my childhood, I don't know. Whether I had come there with any lingering fancy that I was still to love little Em'ly, I don't know. I know that I was filled with pleasure by all this; but, at first, with an indescribably sensitive pleasure, that a very little would have changed to pain.

Therefore, if it had depended upon me to touch the prevailing chord among them with any skill, I should have made a poor hand of it. But it depended upon Steerforth; and he did it with such address, that in a few minutes we were all as easy and as happy as it was possible to be.

" Mr. Peggotty " he said, " you are a thoroughly good fellow, and deserve to be as happy as you are to-night. My hand upon it! Ham, I give you joy, my boy. My hand upon that, too! Daisy, stir the fire, and make it a brisk one! and Mr. Peggotty, unless you can induce your gentle niece to come back (for whom I vacate this seat in the corner), I shall go. Any gap at your fireside on such a night—such a gap least of all—I wouldn't make, for the wealth of the Indies! "

So Mr. Peggotty went into my old room to fetch little Em'ly, At first, little Em'ly didn't like to come, and then Ham went. Presently they brought her to the fireside, very much confused, and very shy,—but she soon became more assured when she found how gently and respectfully Steerforth spoke to her; how skilfully he avoided anything that would embarrass her; how he talked to Mr. Peggotty of boats, and ships, and tides, and fish; how he referred to me about the time when he had seen Mr. Peggotty at Salem House; how delighted he was with the boat and all belonging to it; how lightly and easily he carried on, until he brought us, by degrees, into a charmed circle, and we were all talking away without any reserve.

Em'ly, indeed, said little all the evening; but she looked, and listened, and her face got animated, and she was charming. Steerforth told a story of a dismal shipwreck (which arose out of his talk with Mr. Peggotty), as if he saw it all before him—and little Em'ly's eyes were fastened on him all the time, as if she saw it too. He told us a merry adventure of his own, as a relief to that, with as much gaiety as if the narrative were as fresh to him as it was to us—and little Em'ly laughed until the boat rang with the musical sounds, and we all laughed (Steerforth too), in irresistible sympathy with what was so pleasant and light-hearted. He got Mr. Peggotty to sing, or rather to roar, " When the stormy winds do blow, do blow, do blow; " and he sang a sailor's song himself, so pathetically and beautifully, that I could have almost fancied that the real wind creeping sorrowfully round the house, and murmuring low through our unbroken silence, was there to listen.

As to Mrs. Gummidge, he roused that victim of despondency with a success never attained by any one else (so Mr. Peggotty informed me), since the decease of the old one. He left her so little leisure for being miserable, that she said next day she thought she must have been bewitched.

But he set up no monopoly of the general attention, or the conversation. When little Em'ly grew more courageous, and talked (but still bashfully) across the fire to me, of our old wanderings upon the beach, to pick up shells and pebbles; and when I asked her if she recollected how I used to be devoted to her; and when we both laughed and reddened, casting these looks back on the pleasant old times, so unreal to look at now; he was silent and attentive, and observed us thoughtfully. She sat, at this time, and all the evening, on the old locker in her old little corner by the fire, with Ham beside her, where I used to sit. I could not satisfy myself whether it was in her own little tormenting way, or in a maidenly reserve before us, that she kept quite close to the wall, and away from him; but I observed that she did so, all the evening.

As I remember, it was almost midnight when we took our leave. We had had some biscuit and dried fish for supper, and Steerforth had produced from his pocket a full flask of Hollands, which we men (I may say we men, now, without a blush) had emptied. We parted merrily; and as they all stood crowded round the door to light us as far as they could upon our road, I saw the sweet blue eyes of little Em'ly peeping after us, from behind Ham, and heard her soft voice calling to us to be careful how we went.

" A most engaging little Beauty! " said Steerforth, taking my arm. " Well! It's a quaint place, and they are quaint company; and it's quite a new sensation to mix with them."

" How fortunate we are, too," I returned, " to have arrived to witness their happiness in that intended marriage! I never saw people so happy. How delightful to see it, and to be made the sharers in their honest joy, as we have been!"

"That's rather a chuckle-headed fellow for the girl; isn't he?" said Steerforth.

He had been so hearty with him, and with them all, that I felt a shock in this unexpected and cold reply. But turning quickly upon him, and seeing a laugh in his eyes, I answered, much relieved:

"Ah, Steerforth! It's well for you to joke about the poor! You may skirmish with Miss Dartle, or try to hide your sympathies in jest from me, but I know better. When I see how perfectly you understand them, how exquisitely you can enter into happiness like this plain fisherman's, or humour a love like my old nurse's, I know that there is not a joy or sorrow, not an emotion, of such people, that can be indifferent to you. And I admire and love you for it, Steerforth, twenty times the more!"

He stopped, and looking in my face, said: "Daisy, I believe you are in earnest, and are good. I wish we all were!" Next moment he was gaily singing Mr. Peggotty's song, as we walked at a round pace back to Yarmouth.

22

SOME OLD SCENES, AND SOME NEW PEOPLE

STEERFORTH AND I STAYED FOR MORE THAN A FORTnight in that part of the country. We were very much together, I need not say; but occasionally we were asunder for some hours at a time. He was a good sailor, and I was but an indifferent one; and when he went out boating with Mr. Peggotty, which was a favourite amusement of his, I generally remained ashore. My occupation of Peggotty's spare-room put a constraint upon me, from which he was free: for, knowing how assiduously she attended on Mr. Barkis all day, I did not like to remain out late at night; whereas Steerforth, lying at the Inn, had nothing to consult but his own humour. Thus it came about, that I heard of his making little treats for the fishermen at Mr. Peggotty's house of call, "The Willing Mind," after I was in bed, and of his being afloat, wrapped in fishermen's clothes, whole moonlight nights, and coming back when the morning tide was at flood. By this time, however, I knew that his restless nature and bold spirits delighted to find a vent in rough toil and hard weather, as in any other means of excitement that presented itself freshly to him; so none of his proceedings surprised me.

Another cause of our being sometimes apart was, that I had naturally an interest in going over to Blunderstone, and revisiting the old familiar scenes of my childhood; while Steerforth, after being there once, had naturally no great interest in going there again. Hence, on three or four days that I can at once recall, we went our several ways after an early breakfast, and met again at a late dinner. I had no idea how he employed his time in the interval, beyond a general knowledge that he was very popular in the place, and had twenty means of actively diverting himself where another man might not have found one.

For my own part, my occupation in my solitary pilgrimages was to recall every yard of the old road as I went along it, and to haunt the old spots, of which I never tired. I haunted them, as my memory had often done, and lingered among them as my younger thoughts had lingered when I was far away. The grave beneath the tree, where both my parents lay—on which I had looked out, when it was my father's only, with such curious feelings of compassion, and by which I had stood, so desolate, when it was opened to receive my pretty mother and her baby—the grave which Peggotty's own faithful care had ever since kept neat, and made a garden of, I walked near, by the hour. It lay a little off the churchyard path, in a quiet corner, not so far removed but I could read the names upon the stone as I walked to and fro, startled by the sound of the church-bell when it struck the hour, for it was like a departed voice to me. My reflections at these times were always associated with the figure I was to make in life, and the distinguished things I was to do. My echoing footsteps went to no other tune, but were as constant to that as if I had come home to build my castles in the air at a living mother's side.

There were great changes in my old home. The ragged nests, so long deserted by the rooks, were gone; and the trees were lopped and topped out of their remembered shapes. The garden had run wild, and half the windows of the house were shut up. It was occupied, but only by a poor lunatic gentleman, and the people who took care of him. He was always sitting at my little window, looking out into the churchyard; and I wondered whether his rambling thoughts ever went upon any of the fancies that used to occupy mine, on the rosy mornings when I peeped out of that same little window in my night-clothes, and saw the sheep quietly feeding in the light of the rising sun.

Our old neighbours, Mr. and Mrs. Grayper, were gone to South America, and the rain had made its way through the roof of their empty house, and stained the outer walls. Mr. Chillip was married again to a tall, raw-boned, high-nosed wife; and they had a weazen little baby, with a heavy head that it couldn't hold up, and two weak staring eyes, with which it seemed to be always wondering why it had ever been born.

It was with a singular jumble of sadness and pleasure that I used to linger about my native place, until the reddening winter sun admonished me that it was time to start on my returning walk. But, when the place was left behind, and especially when Steerforth and I were happily seated over our dinner by a blazing fire, it was delicious to think of having been there. So it was, though in a softened degree, when I went to my neat room at night; and, turning over the leaves of the crocodile-book (which was always there, upon a little table), remembered with a grateful heart how blest I was in having such a friend as Steerforth, such a friend as Peggotty, and such a substitute for what I had lost as my excellent and generous aunt.

My nearest way to Yarmouth, in coming back from these long walks, was by a ferry. It landed me on the flat between the town and the sea, which I could make straight across, and so save myself a considerable circuit by the high road. Mr. Peggotty's house being on that waste-place, and not a hundred yards out of my track, I always looked in as I went by. Steerforth was pretty sure to be there expecting me, and we went on together through the frosty air and gathering fog towards the twinkling lights of the town.

One dark evening, when I was later than usual—for I had, that day, been making my parting visit to Blunderstone as we were now about to return home—I found him alone in Mr. Peggotty's house, sitting thoughtfully before the fire. He was so intent upon his own reflections that he was quite unconscious of my approach. This, indeed, he might easily have been if he had been less absorbed, for footsteps fell noiselessly on the sandy ground outside; but even my entrance failed to rouse him. I was standing close to him, looking at him; and still, with a heavy brow, he was lost in his meditations.

He gave such a start when I put my hand upon his shoulder, that he made me start too.

"You come upon me," he said, almost angrily, "like a reproachful ghost!"

"I was obliged to announce myself, somehow," I replied. "Have I called you down from the stars?"

"No," he answered. "No."

"Up from anywhere, then?" said I, taking my seat near him.

"I was looking at the pictures in the fire," he returned.

"But you are spoiling them for me," said I, as he stirred it quickly with a piece of burning wood, striking out of it a train of red-hot sparks that went careering up the little chimney, and roaring out into the air.

"You would not have seen them," he returned. "I detest this mongrel time, neither day nor night. How late you are! Where have you been?"

"I have been taking leave of my usual walk," said I.

"And I have been sitting here," said Steerforth, glancing round the room, "thinking that all the people we found so glad on the night of our coming down, might—to judge from the present wasted air of the place—be dispersed, or dead, or come to I don't know what harm. David, I wish to God I had had a judicious father these last twenty years!"

"My dear Steerforth, what is the matter?"

"I wish with all my soul I had been better guided!" he exclaimed. "I wish with all my soul I could guide myself better!" There was a passionate dejection in his manner that quite amazed me. He was more unlike himself than I could have supposed possible.

"It would be better to be this poor Peggotty, or his lout of a nephew," he said, getting up and leaning moodily against the chimney-piece, with his face towards the fire, "than to be myself, twenty times richer and twenty times wiser, and be the torment to myself that I have been, in this Devil's bark of a boat, within the last half-hour!"

I was so confounded by the alteration in him, that at first I could only observe him in silence, as he stood leaning his head upon his hand, and looking gloomily down at the fire. At length I begged him, with all the earnestness I felt, to tell me what had occurred to cross him so unusually, and to let me sympathise with him, if I could not hope to advise him. Before I had well concluded, he began to laugh—fretfully at first, but soon with returning gaiety.

"Tut, it's nothing Daisy! nothing!" he replied. "I told you

at the inn in London, I am heavy company for myself, sometimes. I have been a nightmare to myself, just now—must have had one, I think. At odd dull times, nursery tales come up into the memory, unrecognised for what they are. I believe I have been confounding myself with the bad boy who 'didn't care,' and became food for lions—a grander kind of going to the dogs, I suppose. What old women call the horrors, have been creeping over me from head to foot. I have been afraid of myself."

"You are afraid of nothing else, I think," said I.

"Perhaps not, and yet may have enough to be afraid of too," he answered. "Well! So it goes by! I am not about to be hipped again, David; but I tell you, my good fellow, once more, that it would have been well for me (and for more than me) if I had had a steadfast and judicious father!"

His face was always full of expression, but I never saw it express such a dark kind of earnestness as when he said these words, with his glance bent on the fire.

"So much for that!" he said, making as if he tossed something light into the air, with his hand.

"'Why, being gone, I am a man again,'

like Macbeth. And now for dinner! If I have not (Macbeth-like) broken up the feast with most admired disorder, Daisy."

"But where are they all, I wonder!" said I.

"God knows," said Steerforth. "After strolling to the ferry looking for you, I strolled in here and found the place deserted. That set me thinking, and you found me thinking."

The advent of Mrs. Gummidge with a basket, explained how the house had happened to be empty. She had hurried out to buy something that was needed, against Mr. Peggotty's return with the tide; and had left the door open in the meanwhile, lest Ham and little Em'ly, with whom it was an early night, should come home while she was gone. Steerforth, after very much improving Mrs. Gummidge's spirit by a cheerful salutation and a jocose embrace, took my arm, and hurried me away.

He had improved his own spirits no less than Mrs. Gummidge's, for they were again at their usual flow, and he was full of vivacious conversation as we went along.

"And so," he said, gaily, "we abandon this buccaneer life to-morrow, do we?"

"So we agreed," I returned. "And our places by the coach are taken, you know."

"Ay! there's no help for it, I suppose," said Steerforth. "I have almost forgotten that there is anything to do in the world but to go out tossing on the sea here. I wish there was not."

"As long as the novelty should last," said I, laughing.

"Like enough," he returned; "though there's a sarcastic meaning in that observation for an amiable piece of innocence like my young friend. Well! I dare say I am a capricious fellow, David. I know I am; but while the iron *is* hot, I can strike it vigorously too. I could pass a reasonably good examination already, as a pilot in these waters, I think."

"Mr. Peggotty says you are a wonder," I returned.

"A nautical phenomenon, eh?" laughed Steerforth.

"Indeed he does, and you know how truly; knowing how ardent you are in any pursuit you follow, and how easily you can master it. And that amazes me most in you, Steerforth—that you should be contented with such fitful uses of your powers."

"Contented?" he answered, merrily. "I am never contented. except with your freshness, my gentle Daisy. As to fitfulness, I have never learnt the art of binding myself to any of the wheels on which the Ixions of these days are turning round and round. I missed it somehow in a bad apprenticeship, and now don't care about it.—You know I have bought a boat down here?"

"What an extraordinary fellow you are, Steerforth!" I exclaimed, stopping—for this was the first I had heard of it. "When you may never care to come near the place again!"

"I don't know that," he returned. "I have taken a fancy to the place. At all events," walking me briskly on, "I have bought a boat that was for sale—a clipper, Mr. Peggotty says; and so she is—and Mr. Peggotty will be master of her in my absence."

"Now I understand you, Steerforth!" said I, exultingly. "You pretend to have bought it for yourself, but you have really done so to confer a benefit on him. I might have known as much at first, knowing you. My dear kind Steerforth, how can I tell you what I think of your generosity?"

"Tush!" he answered, turning red. "The less said, the better."

"Didn't I know?" cried I, "didn't I say that there was not a joy, or sorrow, or any emotion of such honest hearts that was indifferent to you?"

"Aye, aye," he answered, "you told me all that. There let it rest. We have said enough!"

Afraid of offending him by pursuing the subject when he made so light of it, I only pursued it in my thoughts as we went on at even a quicker pace than before.

"She must be newly rigged," said Steerforth, "and I shall leave Littimer behind to see it done, that I may know she is quite complete. Did I tell you Littimer had come down?"

"No."

"Oh yes! came down this morning, with a letter from my mother."

As our looks met, I observed that he was pale even to his lips, though he looked very steadily at me. I feared that some difference between him and his mother might have led to his being in the frame of mind in which I had found him at the solitary fireside. I hinted so.

"Oh no!" he said, shaking his head, and giving a slight laugh. "Nothing of the sort! Yes. He is come down, that man of mine."

"The same as ever?" said I.

"The same as ever," said Steerforth. "Distant and quiet as the North Pole. He shall see to the boat being fresh named. She's the *Stormy Petrel* now. What does Mr. Peggotty care for Stormy Petrels! I'll have her christened again."

"By what name?" I asked.

"The *Little Em'ly*."

As he had continued to look steadily at me, I took it as a reminder that he objected to being extolled for his consideration. I could not help showing in my face how much it pleased me, but I said little, and he resumed his usual smile, and seemed relieved.

"But see here," he said, looking before us, "where the original little Em'ly comes! And that fellow with her, eh? Upon my soul, he's a true knight. He never leaves her!"

Ham was a boat-builder in these days, having improved a natural ingenuity in that handicraft, until he had become a skilled workman. He was in his working-dress, and looked rugged enough, but manly withal, and a very fit protector for the blooming little creature at his side. Indeed, there was a frankness in his face, an honesty, and an undisguised show of his pride in her, and his love for her, which were, to me, the best of good looks. I thought, as they came towards us, that they were well matched even in that particular.

She withdrew her hand timidly from his arm as we stopped to speak to them, and blushed as she gave it to Steerforth and to me. When they passed on, after we had exchanged a few words, she did not like to replace that hand, but, still appearing timid and constrained, walked by herself. I thought all this very pretty and engaging, and Steerforth seemed to think so too, as we looked after them fading away in the light of a young moon.

Suddenly there passed us—evidently following them—a young

woman whose approach we had not observed, but whose face I saw as she went by, and thought I had a faint remembrance of. She was lightly dressed, looked bold, and haggard, and flaunting, and poor; but seemed, for the time, to have given all that to the wind which was blowing, and to have nothing in her mind but going after them. As the dark, distant level, absorbing their figures into itself, left but itself visible between us and the sea and clouds, her figure disappeared in like manner, still no nearer to them than before.

"That is a black shadow to be following the girl," said Steerforth, standing still; "what does it mean?"

He spoke in a low voice that sounded almost strange to me.

"She must have it in her mind to beg of them, I think," said I.

"A beggar would be no novelty," said Steerforth; "but it is a strange thing that the beggar should take that shape to-night."

"Why?" I asked him.

"For no better reason, truly, than because I was thinking," he said, after a pause, "of something like it, when it came by. Where the Devil did it come from, I wonder!"

"From the shadow of this wall, I think," said I, as we emerged upon a road on which a wall abutted.

"It's gone!" he returned, looking over his shoulder. "And all ill go with it. Now for our dinner!"

But he looked again over his shoulder towards the sea-line glimmering afar off; and yet again. And he wondered about it, in some broken expressions, several times, in the short remainder of our walk; and only seemed to forget it when the light of fire and candle shone upon us, seated warm and merry, at table.

Littimer was there, and had his usual effect upon me. When I said to him that I hoped Mrs. Steerforth and Miss Dartle were well, he answered respectfully (and of course respectably), that they were tolerably well, he thanked me, and had sent their compliments. This was all; and yet he seemed to me to say as plainly as a man could say: "You are very young, sir; you are exceedingly young."

We had almost finished dinner, when taking a step or two towards the table, from the corner where he kept watch upon us, or rather upon me, as I felt, he said to his master:

"I beg your pardon, sir. Miss Mowcher is down here."

"Who?" cried Steerforth, much astonished.

"Miss Mowcher, sir."

"Why, what on earth does *she* do here?" said Steerforth.

"It appears to be her native part of the country, sir. She

informs me that she makes one of her professional visits here, every year, sir. I met her in the street this afternoon, and she wished to know if she might have the honour of waiting on you after dinner, sir."

"Do you know the Giantess in question, Daisy?" inquired Steerforth.

I was obliged to confess—I felt ashamed, even of being at this disadvantage before Littimer—that Miss Mowcher and I were wholly unacquainted.

"Then you shall know her," said Steerforth, "for she is one of the seven wonders of the world. When Miss Mowcher comes, show her in."

I felt some curiosity and excitement about this lady, especially as Steerforth burst into a fit of laughing when I referred to her, and positively refused to answer any question of which I made her the subject. I remained, therefore, in a state of considerable expectation until the cloth had been removed some half an hour, and we were sitting over our decanter of wine before the fire, when the door opened, and Littimer, with his habitual serenity quite undisturbed, announced:

"Miss Mowcher!"

I looked at the doorway and saw nothing. I was still looking at the doorway, thinking that Miss Mowcher was a long while making her appearance, when, to my infinite astonishment, there came waddling round a sofa which stood between me and it, a pursy dwarf, of about forty or forty-five, with a very large head and face, a pair of roguish grey eyes, and such extremely little arms, that, to enable herself to lay a finger archly against her snub nose as she ogled Steerforth, she was obliged to meet the finger half-way, and lay her nose against it. Her chin, which was what is called a double-chin, was so fat that it entirely swallowed up the strings of her bonnet, bow and all. Throat she had none; waist she had none; legs she had none, worth mentioning; for though she was more than full-sized down to where her waist would have been, if she had had any, and though she terminated, as human beings generally do, in a pair of feet, she was so short that she stood at a common-sized chair as at a table, resting a bag she carried on the seat. This lady—dressed in an off-hand, easy style; bringing her nose and her forefinger together, with the difficulty I have described; standing with her head necessarily on one side, and, with one of her sharp eyes shut up, making an uncommonly knowing face—after ogling Steerforth for a few moments, broke into a torrent of words.

"What! My flower!" she pleasantly began, shaking her

large head at him. " You're there, are you? Oh, you naughty boy, fie for shame, what do you do so far away from home? Up to mischief, I'll be bound. Oh, you're a downy fellow, Steerforth, so you are, and I'm another, ain't I? Ha, ha, ha! You'd have betted a hundred pound to five, now, that you wouldn't have seen me here, wouldn't you? Bless you, man alive, I'm everywhere. I'm here, and there, and were not, like the conjurer's half-crown in the lady's handkercher. Talking of handkerchers—*and* talking of ladies—what a comfort you are to your blessed mother, ain't you, my dear boy, over one of my shoulders, and I don't say which! "

Miss Mowcher untied her bonnet, at this passage of her discourse, threw back the strings, and sat down, panting, on a footstool in front of the fire—making a kind of arbour of the dining-table, which spread its mahogany shelter above her head.

" Oh my stars and what's-their-names! " she went on, clapping a hand on each of her little knees, and glancing shrewdly at me. " I'm of too full a habit, that's the fact, Steerforth. After a flight of stairs, it gives me as much trouble to draw every breath I want, as if it was a bucket of water. If you saw me looking out of an upper window, you'd think I was a fine woman, wouldn't you? "

" I should think that, wherever I saw you," replied Steerforth.

" Go along, you dog, do! " cried the little creature, making a whisk at him with the handkerchief with which she was wiping her face, " and don't be impudent! But I give you my word and honour I was at Lady Mithers's last week—*there's* a woman! How *she* wears!—and Mithers himself came into the room where I was waiting for her—*there's* a man! How *he* wears! and his wig too, for he's had it these ten years—and he went on at that rate in the complimentary line, that I began to think I should be obliged to ring the bell. Ha! ha! ha! He's a pleasant wretch, but he wants principle.'

" What were you doing for Lady Mithers? " asked Steerforth.

" That's tellings, my blessed infant," she retorted, tapping her nose again, screwing up her face, and twinkling her eyes like an imp of supernatural intelligence. " Never *you* mind! You'd like to know whether I stop her hair from falling off, or dye it, or touch up her complexion, or improve her eyebrows, wouldn't you? And so you shall, my darling—when I tell you! Do you know what my great grandfather's name was? "

" No," said Steerforth.

"It was Walker, my sweet pet," replied Miss Mowcher, "and he came of a long line of Walkers, that I inherit all the Hookey estates from."

I never beheld anything approaching to Miss Mowcher's wink, except Miss Mowcher's self-possession. She had a wonderful way too, when listening to what was said to her, or when waiting for an answer to what she had said herself, of pausing with her head cunningly on one side, and one eye turned up like a magpie's. Altogether I was lost in amazement, and sat staring at her, quite oblivious, I am afraid, of the laws of politeness.

She had by this time drawn the chair to her side, and was busily engaged in producing from the bag (plunging in her short arm to the shoulder, at every dive) a number of small bottles, sponges, combs, brushes, bits of flannel, little pairs of curling-irons, and other instruments, which she tumbled in a heap upon the chair. From this employment she suddenly desisted, and said to Steerforth, much to my confusion:

"Who's your friend?"

"Mr. Copperfield," said Steerforth; "he wants to know you."

"Well, then, he shall! I thought he looked as if he did!" returned Miss Mowcher, waddling up to me, bag in hand, and laughing on me as she came. "Face like a peach!" standing on tiptoe to pinch my cheek as I sat. "Quite tempting! I'm very fond of peaches. Happy to make your acquaintance, Mr. Copperfield, I'm sure."

I said that I congratulated myself on having the honour to make hers, and that the happiness was mutual.

"Oh, my goodness, how polite we are!" exclaimed Miss Mowcher, making a preposterous attempt to cover her large face with her morsel of a hand. "What a world of gammon and spinnage it is, though, ain't it!"

This was addressed confidentially to both of us, as the morsel of a hand came away from the face, and buried itself, arm and all, in the bag again.

"What do you mean, Miss Mowcher?" said Steerforth.

"Ha! ha! ha! What a refreshing set of humbugs we are, to be sure, ain't we, my sweet child?" replied that morsel of a woman, feeling in the bag with her head on one side and her eye in the air. "Look here!" taking something out. "Scraps of the Russian Prince's nails. Prince Alphabet turned topsy-turvy, *I* call him, for his name's got all the letters in it, higgledy-piggledy."

"The Russian Prince is a client of yours, is he?" said Steerforth.

"I believe you, my pet," replied Miss Mowcher. "I keep his nails in order for him. Twice a week! Fingers *and* toes."

"He pays well, I hope?" said Steerforth.

"Pays, as he speaks, my dear child—through the nose," replied Miss Mowcher. "None of your close shavers the Prince ain't. You'd say so, if you saw his moustachios. Red by nature, black by art."

"By your art, of course," said Steerforth.

Miss Mowcher winked assent. "Forced to send for me. Couldn't help it. The climate affected *his* dye; it did very well in Russia, but it was no go here. You never saw such a rusty Prince in all your born days as he was. Like old iron!"

"Is that why you called him a humbug, just now?" inquired Steerforth.

"Oh, you're a broth of a boy, ain't you?" returned Miss Mowcher, shaking her head violently. "I said, what a set of humbugs we were in general, and I showed you the scraps of the Prince's nails to prove it. The Prince's nails do more for me in private families of the genteel sort, than all my talents put together. I always carry 'em about. They're the best introduction. If Miss Mowcher cuts the Prince's nails, she *must* be all right. I give 'em away to the young ladies. They put 'em in albums, I believe. Ha! ha! ha! Upon my life, 'the whole social system' (as the men call it when they make speeches in Parliament) is a system of Prince's nails!" said this least of women, trying to fold her short arms, and nodding her large head.

Steerforth laughed heartily, and I laughed too. Miss Mowcher continuing all the time to shake her head (which was very much on one side), and to look into the air with one eye, and to wink with the other.

"Well, well!" she said, smiting her small knees, and rising, "this is not business. Come, Steerforth, let's explore the polar regions, and have it over."

She then selected two or three of the little instruments, and a little bottle, and asked (to my surprise) if the table would bear. On Steerforth's replying in the affirmative, she pushed a chair against it, and begging the assistance of my hand, mounted up, pretty nimbly, to the top, as if it were a stage.

"If either of you saw my ankles," she said, when she was safely elevated, "say so, and I'll go home and destroy myself."

"*I* did not," said Steerforth.

"*I* did not," said I.

"Well, then" cried Miss Mowcher, "I'll consent to live. Now, ducky, ducky, ducky, come to Mrs. Bond and be killed."

This was an invocation to Steerforth to place himself under her hands; who, accordingly, sat himself down, with his back to the table, and his laughing face towards me, and submitted his head to her inspection, evidently for no other purpose than our entertainment. To see Miss Mowcher standing over him, looking at his rich profusion of brown hair through a large round magnifying glass, which she took out of her pocket, was a most amazing spectacle.

" *You're* a pretty fellow! " said Miss Mowcher, after a brief inspection. " You'd be as bald as a friar on the top of your head in twelve months, but for me. Just half a minute, my young friend, and we'll give you a polishing that shall keep your curls on for the next ten years! "

With this, she tilted some of the contents of the little bottle on to one of the little bits, and, again imparting some of the virtues of that preparation to one of the little brushes, began rubbing and scraping away with both on the crown of Steerforth's head in the busiest manner I ever witnessed, talking all the time.

" There's Charley Pyegrave, the duke's son," she said. " You know Charley? " peeping round into his face.

" A little," said Steerforth.

" What a man *he* is! *There's* a whisker! As to Charley's legs, if they were only a pair (which they ain't), they'd defy competition. Would you believe he tried to do without me—in the Life-Guards, too? "

" Mad! " said Steerforth.

" It looks like it. However, mad or sane, he tried," returned Miss Mowcher. " What does he do, but, lo and behold you, he goes into a perfumer's shop, and wants to buy a bottle of the Madagascar Liquid."

" Charley does? " said Steerforth.

" Charley does. But they haven't got any of the Madagascar Liquid."

" What is it? Something to drink? " asked Steerforth.

" To drink? " returned Miss Mowcher, stopping to slap his cheek. " To doctor his own moustachios with, you *know*. There was a woman in the shop—elderly female—quite a Griffin—who had never even heard of it by name. ' Begging pardon, sir,' said the Griffin to Charley, ' it's not—not—not ROUGE, is it? ' ' Rouge,' said Charley to the Griffin. ' What the unmentionable to ears polite, do you think I want with rouge? ' ' No offence, sir,' said the Griffin; ' we have it asked for by so many names, I thought it might be.' Now that, my child," continued Miss Mowcher, rubbing all the time as busily as ever, "is another instance of the refreshing humbug I was speaking of. *I* do something in that way myself—perhaps a good deal—perhaps a little—sharp's the word, my dear boy—never mind!"

"In what way do you mean? In the rouge way?" said Steerforth.

"Put this and that together, my tender pupil," returned the wary Mowcher, touching her nose, "work it by the rule of Secrets in all trades, and the product will give you the desired result. I say *I* do a little in that way myself. One Dowager, *she* calls it lip-salve. Another, *she* calls it gloves. Another, *she* calls it tucker-edging. Another, *she* calls it a fan. *I* call it whatever *they* call it. I supply it for 'em, but we keep up the trick so, to one another, and make believe with such a face, that they'd as soon think of laying it on before a whole drawing-room, as before me. And when I wait upon 'em, they'll say to me sometimes—*with it on*—thick, and no mistake—'How am I looking, Mowcher? Am I pale?' Ha, ha! ha! ha! Isn't *that* refreshing my young friend!"

I never did in my days behold anything like Mowcher as she stood upon the dining-table, intensely enjoying this refreshment, rubbing busily at Steerforth's head, and winking at me over it.

"Ah!" she said. "Such things are not much in demand hereabouts. That sets me off again! I haven't seen a pretty woman since I've been here, Jemmy."

"No?" said Steerforth.

"Not the ghost of one," replied Miss Mowcher.

"We could show her the substance of one, I think?" said Steerforth, addressing his eyes to mine. "Eh, Daisy?"

"Yes, indeed," said I.

"Aha?" cried the little creature, glancing sharply at my face, and then peeping round at Steerforth's. "Umph?"

The first exclamation sounded like a question put to both of us, and the second like a question put to Steerforth only. She seemed to have found no answer to either, but continued to rub, with her head on one side and her eye turned up, as if she were looking for an answer in the air and were confident of its appearing presently.

"A sister of yours, Mr. Copperfield?" she cried, after a pause, and still keeping the same look-out. "Aye, aye?"

"No," said Steerforth, before I could reply. "Nothing of the sort. On the contrary, Mr. Copperfield used—or I am much mistaken—to have a great admiration for her."

"Why, hasn't he now?" returned Miss Mowcher. "Is he

fickle? oh, for shame! Did he sip every flower, and change every hour, until Polly his passion requited?—Is her name Polly?"

The elfin suddenness with which she pounced upon me with this question, and a searching look, quite disconcerted me for a moment.

"No, Miss Mowcher," I replied. "Her name is Emily."

"Aha?" she cried exactly as before. "Umph? What a rattle I am! Mr. Copperfield, ain't I volatile?"

Her tone and look implied something that was not agreeable to me in connection with the subject. So I said, in a graver manner than any of us had yet assumed:

"She is as virtuous as she is pretty. She is engaged to be married to a most worthy and deserving man in her own station of life. I esteem her for her good sense, as much as I admire her for her good looks."

"Well said!" cried Steerforth. "Hear, hear, hear! Now I'll quench the curiosity of this little Fatima, my dear Daisy, by leaving her nothing to guess at. She is at present apprenticed, Miss Mowcher, or articled, or whatever it may be, to Omer and Joram, Haberdashers, Milliners, and so forth, in this town. Do you observe? Omer and Joram. The promise of which my friend has spoken, is made and entered into with her cousin; Christian name, Ham; surname, Peggotty; occupation, boat-builder; also of this town. She lives with a relative; Christian name, unknown; surname, Peggotty; occupation, seafaring; also of this town. She is the prettiest and most engaging little fairy in the world. I admire her—as my friend does—exceedingly. If it were not that I might appear to disparage her intended, which I know my friend would not like, I would add, that to *me* she seems to be throwing herself away; that I am sure she might do better; and that I swear she was born to be a lady."

Miss Mowcher listened to these words, which were very slowly and distinctly spoken, with her head on one side, and her eye in the air, as if she were still looking for that answer. When he ceased she became brisk again in an instant, and rattled away with surprising volubility.

"Oh! And that's all about it, is it?" she exclaimed, trimming his whiskers with a little restless pair of scissors, that went glancing round his head in all directions. "Very well: *very* well! Quite a long story. Ought to end 'and they lived happy ever afterwards;' oughtn't it? Ah! What's that game at forfeits? I love my love with an E, because she's enticing; I hate her with an E, because she's engaged. I took her to the sign of the exquisite, and treated her with an elopement; her name's Emily, and she lives in the east? Ha! ha! ha! Mr. Copperfield, ain't I volatile?"

Merely looking at me with extravagant slyness, and not waiting for any reply, she continued, without drawing breath:

"There! If ever any scapegrace was trimmed and touched up to perfection, you are, Steerforth. If I understand any noddle in the world, I understand yours. Do you hear me when I tell you that, my darling? I understand yours," peeping down into his face. "Now you may mizzle, Jemmy (as we say at Court), and if Mr. Copperfield will take the chair I'll operate on him."

"What do you say, Daisy?" inquired Steerforth, laughing, and resigning his seat. "Will you be improved?"

"Thank you, Miss Mowcher, not this evening."

"Don't say no," returned the little woman, looking at me with the aspect of a connoisseur; "a little bit more eyebrow?"

"Thank you," I returned, "some other time."

"Have it carried half a quarter of an inch towards the temple," said Miss Mowcher. "We can do it in a fortnight."

"No, I thank you. Not at present."

"Go in for a tip," she urged. "No? Let's get the scaffolding up, then, for a pair of whiskers. Come!"

I could not help blushing as I declined, for I felt we were on my weak point, now. But Miss Mowcher, finding that I was not at present disposed for any decoration within the range of her art, and that I was, for the time being, proof against the blandishments of the small bottle which she held up before one eye to enforce her persuasions, said we would make a beginning on an early day, and requested the aid of my hand to descend from her elevated station. Thus assisted, she skipped down with much agility, and began to tie her double chin into her bonnet.

"The fee," said Steerforth, "is——"

"Five bob," replied Miss Mowcher, "and dirt cheap, my chicken. Ain't I volatile, Mr. Copperfield?"

I replied politely: "Not at all." But I thought she was rather so, when she tossed up his two half-crowns like a goblin pieman, caught them, dropped them in her pocket, and gave it a loud slap.

"That's the till!" observed Miss Mowcher, standing at the chair again, and replacing in the bag a miscellaneous collection of little objects she had emptied out of it. "Have I got all my traps? It seems so. It won't do to be like long Ned Beadwood, when they took him to church 'to marry him to somebody,' as he says, and left the bride behind. Ha! ha! ha! A wicked rascal,

Ned, but droll! Now, I know I'm going to break your hearts, but I am forced to leave you. You must call up all your fortitude, and try to bear it. Good-bye, Mr. Copperfield! Take care of yourself, Jockey of Norfolk! How I *have* been rattling on! It's all the fault of you two wretches. *I* forgive you! 'Bob swore!' —as the Englishman said for 'Good night,' when he first learnt French, and thought it so like English. 'Bob swore,' my ducks!"

With the bag slung over her arm, and rattling as she waddled away, she waddled to the door, where she stopped to inquire if she would leave us a lock of her hair. "Ain't I volatile?" she added, as a commentary on this offer, and, with her finger on her nose, departed.

Steerforth laughed to that degree, that it was impossible for me to help laughing too; though I am not sure I should have done so, but for this inducement. When we had had our laugh quite out, which was after some time, he told me that Miss Mowcher had quite an extensive connection, and made herself useful to a variety of people in a variety of ways. Some people trifled with her as a mere oddity, he said; but she was as shrewdly and sharply observant as any one he knew, and as long-headed as she was short-armed. He told me that what she had said of being here, and there, and everywhere, was true enough; for she made little darts into the provinces, and seemed to pick up customers everywhere, and to know everybody. I asked him what her disposition was: whether it was at all mischievous, and if her sympathies were generally on the right side of things: but, not succeeding in attracting his attention to these questions after two or three attempts, I forbore or forgot to repeat them. He told me instead, with much rapidity, a good deal about her skill, and her profits; and about her being a scientific cupper, if I should ever have occasion for her service in that capacity.

She was the principal theme of our conversation during the evening: and when we parted for the night Steerforth called after me over the banisters, "Bob swore!" as I went downstairs. I was surprised, when I came to Mr. Barkis's house, to find Ham walking up and down in front of it, and still more surprised to learn from him that little Em'ly was inside. I naturally inquired why he was not there too, instead of pacing the streets by himself?

"Why, you see, Mas'r Davy," he rejoined, in a hesitating manner, "Em'ly, she's talking to some 'un in here."

"I should have thought," said I, smiling, "that that was a reason for your being in here too, Ham."

"Well, Mas'r Davy, in a general way, so 't would be," he

returned; " but look'ee here, Mas'r Davy," lowering his voice, and speaking very gravely. " It's a young woman, sir—a young woman, that Em'ly knowed once, and doen't ought to know no more."

When I heard these words, a light began to fall upon the figure I had seen following them, some hours ago.

" It's a poor wurem, Mas'r Davy," said Ham, "as is trod under foot by all the town. Up street and down street. The mowld o' the churchyard don't hold any that the folk shrink away from, more."

" Did I see her to-night, Ham, on the sands, after we met you?"

" Keeping us in sight?" said Ham. " It's like you did, Mas'r Davy. Not that I know'd then, she was theer, sir, but along of her creeping soon afterwards under Em'ly's little winder, when she see the light come, and whisp'ring ' Em'ly, Em'ly, for Christ's sake, have a woman's heart towards me. I was once like you!" Those was solemn words, Mas'r Davy, fur to hear!"

" They were indeed, Ham. What did Em'ly do?"

" Says Em'ly, ' Martha, is it you? Oh, Martha, can it be you?'—for they had sat at work together, many a day, at Mr. Omer's."

" I recollect her now!" cried I, recalling one of the two girls I had seen when I first went there. " I recollect her quite well!"

" Martha Endell," said Ham. " Two or three year older than Em'ly, but was at the school with her."

" I never heard her name," said I. " I didn't mean to interrupt you."

" For the matter o' that, Mas'r Davy," replied Ham, " all's told a'most in them words, ' Em'ly, Em'ly, for Christ's sake, have a woman's heart towards me. I was once like you!' She wanted to speak to Em'ly. Em'ly couldn't speak to her theer, for her loving uncle was come home, and he wouldn't—no, Mas'r Davy," said Ham, with great earnestness, " he couldn't, kind-natur'd, tender-hearted as he is, see them two together, side by side, for all the treasures that's wrecked in the sea."

I felt how true this was. I knew it, on the instant, quite as well as Ham.

" So Em'ly writes in pencil on a bit of paper," he pursued, " and gives it to her out o' winder to bring here. ' Show that,' she says, ' to my aunt, Mrs. Barkis, and she'll set you down by her fire, for the love of me, till uncle is gone out, and I can come.' By-and-by she tells me what I tell you, Mas'r Davy, and asks me to bring her. What can I do? She doen't ought to know any such, but I can't deny her, when the tears is on her face."

He put his hand into the breast of his shaggy jacket, and took out with great care a pretty little purse.

"And if I could deny her when the tears was on her face, Mas'r Davy," said Ham, tenderly adjusting it on the rough palm of his hand, "how could I deny her when she give me this to carry for her—knowing what she brought it for? Such a toy as it is!" said Ham, thoughtfully looking on it. "With such a little money in it, Em'ly, my dear."

I shook him warmly by the hand when he had put it away again—for that was more satisfactory to me than saying anything—and we walked up and down, for a minute or two, in silence. The door opened then, and Peggotty appeared, beckoning to Ham to come in. I would have kept away, but she came after me, entreating me to come in too. Even then, I would have avoided the room where they all were, but for its being the neat-tiled kitchen I have mentioned more than once. The door opening immediately into it, I found myself among them, before I considered whither I was going.

The girl—the same I had seen upon the sands—was near the fire. She was sitting on the ground, with her head and one arm lying on a chair. I fancied, from the disposition of her figure, that Em'ly had but newly arisen from the chair, and that the forlorn head might perhaps have been lying on her lap. I saw but little of the girl's face, over which her hair fell loose and scattered, as if she had been disordering it with her own hands; but I saw that she was young, and of a fair complexion. Peggotty had been crying. So had little Em'ly. Not a word was spoken when we first went in; and the Dutch clock by the dresser seemed, in the silence, to tick twice as loud as usual.

Em'ly spoke first.

"Martha wants," she said to Ham, "to go to London."

"Why to London?" returned Ham.

He stood between them, looking on the prostrate girl with a mixture of compassion for her, and of jealousy of her holding any companionship with her whom he loved so well, which I have always remembered distinctly. They both spoke as if she were ill; in a soft, suppressed tone that was plainly heard, although it hardly rose above a whisper.

"Better there than here," said a third voice aloud—Martha's, though she did not move. "No one knows me there. Everybody knows me here."

"What will she do there?" inquired Ham.

She lifted up her head, and looked darkly round at him for a moment; then laid it down again, and curved her right arm about her neck, as a woman in a fever, or in an agony of pain from a shot, might twist herself.

"She will try to do well," said little Em'ly. "You don't know what she has said to us. Does he—do they—aunt?"

Peggotty shook her head compassionately.

"I'll try," said Martha, "if you'll help me away. I never can do worse than I have done here. I may do better. Oh!" with a dreadful shiver, "take me out of these streets, where the whole town knows me from a child!"

As Em'ly held out her hand to Ham, I saw him put in it a little canvas bag. She took it, as if she thought it were her purse, and made a step or two forward; but finding her mistake, came back to where he had retired near me, and showed it to him.

"It's all yourn, Em'ly," I could hear him say. "I haven't nowt in all the woreld that ain't yourn, my dear. It ain't of no delight to me, except for you!"

The tears rose freshly in her eyes, but she turned away and went to Martha. What she gave her I don't know. I saw her stooping over her, and putting money in her bosom. She whispered something, as she asked was that enough? "More than enough," the other said, and took her hand and kissed it.

Then Martha arose, and gathering her shawl about her, covering her face with it, and weeping aloud, went slowly to the door. She stopped a moment before going out, as if she would have uttered something or turned back; but no word passed her lips. Making the same low, dreary, wretched moaning in her shawl, she went away.

As the door closed, little Em'ly looked at us three in a hurried manner, and then hid her face in her hands, and fell to sobbing.

"Doen't, Em'ly!" said Ham, tapping her gently on the shoulder. "Doen't, my dear! You doen't ought to cry so, pretty!"

"Oh, Ham!" she exclaimed, still weeping pitifully, "I am not so good a girl as I ought to be! I know I have not the thankful heart, sometimes, I ought to have!"

"Yes, yes, you have, I'm sure," said Ham.

"No! no! no!" cried little Em'ly, sobbing, and shaking her head. "I am not as good a girl as I ought to be. Not near! not near!"

And still she cried, as if her heart would break.

"I try your love too much. I know I do!" she sobbed. "I'm often cross to you, and changeable with you, when I ought to be far different. You are never so to me. Why am I ever so to you, when I should think of nothing but how to be grateful, and to make you happy!"

"You always make me so," said Ham, "my dear! I am happy in the sight of you. I am happy, all day long, in the thoughts of you."

"Ah! that's not enough!" she cried. "That is because you are good; not because I am! Oh, my dear, it might have been a better fortune for you, if you had been fond of some one else—of some one steadier and much worthier than me, who was all bound up in you, and never vain and changeable like me!"

"Poor little tender-heart," said Ham, in a low voice. "Martha has overset her, altogether."

"Please, aunt," sobbed Em'ly, "come here, and let me lay my head upon you. Oh, I am very miserable to-night, aunt! Oh, I am not as good a girl as I ought to be. I am not, I know!"

Peggotty had hastened to the chair before the fire. Em'ly with her arms around her neck, kneeled by her, looking up most earnestly into her face.

"Oh, pray, aunt, try to help me! Ham, dear, try to help me! Mr. David, for the sake of old times, do, please, try to help me! I want to be a better girl than I am. I want to feel a hundred times more thankful than I do. I want to feel more, what a blessed thing it is to be the wife of a good man, and to lead a peaceful life. Oh me, oh me! Oh my heart, my heart!"

She dropped her face on my old nurse's breast, and, ceasing this supplication, which in its agony and grief was half a woman's, half a child's, as all her manner was (being, in that, more natural, and better suited to her beauty, as I thought, than any other manner could have been), wept silently, while my old nurse hushed her like an infant.

She got calmer by degrees, and then we soothed her; now talking encouragingly, and now jesting a little with her, until she began to raise her head and speak to us. So we got on, until she was able to smile, and then to laugh, and then to sit up, half ashamed; while Peggotty recalled her stray ringlets, dried her eyes, and made her neat again, lest her uncle should wonder, when she got home, why his darling had been crying.

I saw her do, that night, what I had never seen her do before. I saw her innocently kiss her chosen husband on the cheek, and creep close to his bluff form as if it were her best support. When they went away together, in the waning moonlight, and I looked after them, comparing their departure in my mind with Martha's, I saw that she held his arm with both her hands, and still kept close to him.

23

I CORROBORATE MR. DICK, AND CHOOSE A PROFESSION

WHEN I AWOKE IN THE MORNING I THOUGHT VERY much of little Em'ly, and her emotion last night, after Martha had left. I felt as if I had come into the knowledge of those domestic weaknesses and tendernesses in a sacred confidence, and that to disclose them, even to Steerforth, would be wrong. I had no gentler feeling towards any one than towards the pretty creature who had been my playmate, and whom I have always been persuaded, and shall always be persuaded, to my dying day, I then devotedly loved. The repetition to any ears—even to Steerforth's—of what she had been unable to repress when her heart lay open to me by an accident, I felt would be a rough deed, unworthy of myself, unworthy of the light of our pure childhood, which I always saw encircling her head. I made a resolution, therefore, to keep it in my own breast; and there it gave her image a new grace.

While we were at breakfast, a letter was delivered to me from my aunt. As it contained matter on which I thought Steerforth could advise me as well as any one, and on which I knew I should be delighted to consult him, I resolved to make it a subject of discussion, on our journey home. For the present we had enough to do, in taking leave of all our friends. Mr. Barkis was far from being the last among them, in his regret at our departure; and I believe would even have opened the box again, and sacrificed another guinea, if it would have kept us eight-and-forty hours in Yarmouth. Peggotty and all her family were full of grief at our going. The whole house of Omer and Joram turned out to bid us good-bye; and there were so many seafaring volunteers in attendance on Steerforth, when our portmanteaus went to the coach, that if we had had the baggage of a regiment with us, we should hardly have wanted porters to carry it. In a word, we departed to the regret and admiration of all concerned, and left a great many people very sorry behind us.

"Do you stay long here, Littimer?" said I, as he stood waiting to see the coach start.

"No, sir," he replied; "probably not very long, sir."

"He can hardly say, just now," observed Steerforth, carelessly. "He knows what he has to do, and he'll do it."

"That I am sure he will," said I.

Littimer touched his hat in acknowledgment of my good opinion, and I felt about eight years old. He touched it once more, wishing us a good journey; and we left him standing on the pavement, as respectable a mystery as any pyramid in Egypt.

For some little time we held no conversation, Steerforth being unusually silent, and I being sufficiently engaged in wondering, within myself, when I should see the old places again, and what new changes might happen to me or them in the meanwhile. At length Steerforth, becoming gay and talkative in a moment, as he could become anything he liked at any moment, pulled me by the arm:

"Find a voice, David. What about that letter you were speaking of at breakfast?"

"Oh!" said I, taking it out of my pocket. "It's from my aunt."

"And what does she say, requiring consideration?"

"Why, she reminds me, Steerforth," said I, "that I came out on this expedition to look about me, and to think a little."

"Which, of course, you have done?"

"Indeed I can't say I have, particularly. To tell you the truth, I am afraid I had forgotten it."

"Well! Look about you now, and make up for your negligence," said Steerforth. "Look to the right, and you'll see a flat country, with a good deal of marsh in it; look to the left, and you'll see the same. Look to the front, and you'll find no difference; look to the rear, and there it is still."

I laughed, and replied that I saw no suitable profession in the whole prospect; which was perhaps to be attributed to its flatness.

"What says our aunt on the subject?" inquired Steerforth, glancing at the letter in my hand. "Does she suggest anything?"

"Why, yes," said I. "She asks me, here, if I think I should like to be a proctor? What do you think of it?"

"Well, I don't know," replied Steerforth, coolly. "You may as well do that as anything else, I suppose?"

I could not help laughing again, at his balancing all callings and professions so equally; and I told him so.

"What *is* a proctor, Steerforth?" said I.

"Why, he is a sort of monkish attorney," replied Steerforth. "He is, to some faded courts held in Doctors' Commons—a lazy old nook near St. Paul's Churchyard—what solicitors are to the courts of law and equity. He is a functionary whose existence, in the natural course of things, would have terminated about two hundred years ago. I can tell you best what he is, by telling you what Doctors' Commons is. It's a little out-of-the-way place, where they administer what is called ecclesiastical law, and play all kinds of tricks with obsolete old monsters of acts of Parliament, which three-fourths of the world know nothing about, and the other fourth supposes to have been dug up, in a fossil state, in the days of the Edwards. It's a place that has an ancient monopoly in suits about people's wills and people's marriages, and disputes among ships and boats."

"Nonsense, Steerforth!" I exclaimed. "You don't mean to say that there is any affinity between nautical matters and ecclesiastical matters?"

"I don't, indeed, my dear boy," he returned; "but I mean to say that they are managed and decided by the same set of people, down in that same Doctors' Commons. You shall go there one day, and find them blundering through half the nautical terms in Young's Dictionary, apropos of the *Nancy* having run down the *Sarah Jane*, or Mr. Peggotty and the Yarmouth boatmen having put off in a gale of wind with an anchor and cable to the *Nelson* Indiaman in distress; and you shall go there another day, and find them deep in the evidence, pro and con., respecting a clergyman who has misbehaved himself; and you shall find the judge in the nautical case, the advocate in the clergyman's case, or contrariwise. They are like actors: now a man's a judge, and now he is not a judge; now he's one thing, now he's another; now he's something else, change and change about; but it's always a very pleasant, profitable little affair of private theatricals, presented to an uncommonly select audience."

"But advocates and proctors are not one and the same?" said I, a little puzzled. "Are they?"

"No," returned Steerforth, "the advocates are civilians—men who have taken a doctor's degree at college—which is the first reason of my knowing anything about it. The proctors employ the advocates. Both get very comfortable fees, and altogether they make a mighty snug little party. On the whole, I would recommend you to take to Doctors' Commons kindly, David. They plume themselves on their gentility there, I can tell you, if that's any satisfaction."

I made allowance for Steerforth's light way of treating the subject, and, considering it with reference to the staid air of gravity and antiquity which I associated with that "lazy old nook near St. Paul's Churchyard," did not feel indisposed towards my aunt's suggestion; which she left to my free decision, making no scruple of telling me that it had occurred to her, on her lately visiting her own proctor in Doctors' Commons for the purpose of settling her will in my favour.

"That's a laudable proceeding on the part of your aunt, at all events," said Steerforth, when I mentioned it; "and one deserving of all encouragement. Daisy, my advice is that you take kindly to Doctors' Commons."

I quite made up my mind to do so. I then told Steerforth that my aunt was in town awaiting me (as I found from her letter), and that she had taken lodgings for a week at a kind of private hotel in Lincoln's Inn Fields, where there was a stone staircase, and a convenient door in the roof; my aunt being firmly persuaded that every house in London was going to be burnt down every night.

We achieved the rest of our journey pleasantly, sometimes recurring to Doctors' Commons, and anticipating the distant days when I should be a proctor there, which Steerforth pictured in a variety of humorous and whimsical lights, that made us both merry. When we came to our journey's end, he went home, engaging to call upon me next day but one; and I drove to Lincoln's Inn Fields, where I found my aunt up, and waiting supper.

If I had been round the world since we parted, we could hardly have been better pleased to meet again. My aunt cried outright as she embraced me; and said, pretending to laugh, that if my poor mother had been alive, that silly little creature would have shed tears, she had no doubt.

"So you have left Mr. Dick behind, aunt?" said I. "I am sorry for that. Ah, Janet, how do you do?"

As Janet curtsied, hoping I was well, I observed my aunt's visage lengthen very much.

"I am sorry for it, too," said my aunt, rubbing her nose. "I have had no peace of mind, Trot, since I have been here."

Before I could ask why, she told me.

"I am convinced," said my aunt, laying her hand with melancholy firmness on the table, " that Dick's character is not a character to keep the donkeys off. I am confident he wants strength of purpose. I ought to have left Janet at home, instead, and then my mind might perhaps have been at ease. If ever there was a donkey trespassing on my green," said my aunt, with emphasis, " there was one this afternoon at four o'clock. A cold feeling came over me from head to foot, and I *know* it was a donkey! "

I tried to comfort her on this point, but she rejected consolation.

" It was a donkey," said my aunt; " and it was the one with the stumpy tail which that Murdering sister of a woman rode, when she came to my house." This had been, ever since, the only name my aunt knew for Miss Murdstone. " If there is any Donkey in Dover, whose audacity it is harder to me to bear than another's, that," said my aunt, striking the table, " is the animal! "

Janet ventured to suggest that my aunt might be disturbing herself unnecessarily, and that she believed the donkey in question was then engaged in the sand-and-gravel line of business, and was not available for purposes of trespass. But my aunt wouldn't hear of it.

Supper was comfortably served and hot, though my aunt's rooms were very high up—whether that she might have more stone stairs for her money, or might be nearer to the door in the roof, I don't know—and consisted of a roast fowl, a steak, and some vegetables, to all of which I did ample justice, and which were all excellent. But my aunt had her own ideas concerning London provision, and ate but little.

" I suppose this unfortunate fowl was born and brought up in a cellar," said my aunt, " and never took the air except on a hackney coach-stand. I *hope* the steak may be beef, but I don't believe it. Nothing's genuine in the place, in my opinion, but the dirt."

" Don't you think the fowl may have come out of the country, aunt? " I hinted.

" Certainly not," returned my aunt. " It would be no pleasure to a London tradesman to sell anything which was what he pretended it was."

I did not venture to controvert this opinion, but I made a good supper, which it greatly satisfied her to see me do. When the table was cleared, Janet assisted her to arrange her hair, to put on her nightcap, which was of a smarter construction than usual (" in case of fire," my aunt said), and to fold her gown back over her knees, these being her usual preparations for warming herself before going to bed. I then made her, according to certain established regulations from which no deviation, however slight, could ever be permitted, a glass of hot wine and water, and a slice of toast cut into long thin strips. With these accompaniments we were left alone to finish the evening, my aunt sitting opposite to me drinking her wine and water; soaking her strips of toast in it, one by one, before eating them; and looking benignantly on me, from among the borders of her nightcap.

"Well, Trot," she began, "what do you think of the proctor plan? Or have you not begun to think about it yet?"

"I have thought a good deal about it, my dear aunt, and I have talked a good deal about it with Steerforth. I like it very much indeed. I like it exceedingly."

"Come," said my aunt. "That's cheering."

"I have only one difficulty, aunt."

"Say, what it is Trot," she returned.

"Why, I want to ask, aunt, as this seems, from what I understand, to be a limited profession, whether my entrance into it would not be very expensive?"

"It will cost," returned my aunt, "to article you, just a thousand pounds."

"Now, my dear aunt," said I, drawing my chair nearer, "I am uneasy in my mind about that. It's a large sum of money. You have expended a great deal on my education, and have always been as liberal to me in all things as it was possible to be. You have been the soul of generosity. Surely there are some ways in which I might begin life with hardly any outlay, and yet begin with a good hope of getting on by resolution and exertion. Are you sure that it would not be better to try that course? Are you certain that you can afford to part with so much money, and that it is right that it should be so expended? I only ask you, my second mother, to consider. Are you certain?"

My aunt finished eating the piece of toast on which she was then engaged, looking me full in the face all the while; and then setting her glass on the chimney-piece, and folding her hands upon her folded skirts, replied as follows:

"Trot, my child, if I have any object in life, it is to provide for your being a good, a sensible, and a happy man. I am bent upon it—so is Dick. I should like some people that I know to hear Dick's conversation on the subject. Its sagacity is wonderful. But no one knows the resources of that man's intellect except myself!"

She stopped for a moment to take my hand between hers, and went on:

" It's in vain, Trot, to recall the past, unless it works some influence upon the present. Perhaps I might have been better friends with your poor father. Perhaps I might have been better friends with that poor child your mother, even after your sister Betsey Trotwood disappointed me. When you came to me, a little runaway boy, all dusty and way-worn, perhaps I thought so. From that time until now, Trot, you have ever been a credit to me and a pride and a pleasure. I have no other claim upon my means; at least "—here to my surprise she hesitated, and was confused—" no, I have *no* other claim upon my means—and you are my adopted child. Only be a loving child to me in my age, and bear with my whims and fancies; and you will do more for an old woman whose prime of life was not so happy or conciliating as it might have been, than ever that old woman did for you."

It was the first time I had heard my aunt refer to her past history. There was a magnanimity in her quiet way of doing so, and of dismissing it, which would have exalted her in my respect and affection, if anything could.

" All is agreed and understood between us, now, Trot," said my aunt, " and we need talk of this no more. Give me a kiss, and we'll go to the Commons after breakfast to-morrow."

We had a long chat by the fire before we went to bed. I slept in a room on the same floor with my aunt's, and was a little disturbed in the course of the night by her knocking at my door as often as she was agitated by a distant sound of hackney-coaches or market-carts, and inquiring, " if I heard the engines?" But towards morning she slept better, and suffered me to do so too.

At about midday, we set out for the office of Messrs. Spenlow and Jorkins, in Doctors' Commons. My aunt, who had this other general opinion in reference to London, that every man she saw was a pickpocket, gave me her purse to carry for her, which had ten guineas in it and some silver.

We made a pause at the toy-shop in Fleet Street, to see the giants of Saint Dunstan's strike upon the bells—we had timed our going, so as to catch them at it, at twelve o'clock—and then went on towards Ludgate Hill and St. Paul's Churchyard. We were crossing to the former place, when I found that my aunt greatly accelerated her speed, and looked frightened. I observed, at the same time, that a lowering ill-dressed man who had stopped and stared at us in passing, a little before, was coming so close after us as to brush against her.

"Trot! My dear Trot!" cried my aunt, in a terrified whisper, and pressing my arm. "I don't know what I am to do."

"Don't be alarmed," said I. "There's nothing to be afraid of. Step into a shop, and I'll soon get rid of this fellow."

"No, no. child!" she returned. "Don't speak to him for the world. I entreat, I order you!"

"Good Heaven, aunt!" said I. "He is nothing but a sturdy beggar."

"You don't know what he is!" replied my aunt. "You don't know who he is! You don't know what you say!"

We had stopped in an empty doorway, while this was passing, and he had stopped too.

"Don't look at him!" said my aunt, as I turned my head indignantly, "but get me a coach, my dear, and wait for me in St. Paul's Churchyard."

"Wait for you?" I repeated.

"Yes," rejoined my aunt. "I must go alone. I must go with him."

"With him, aunt? This man?"

"I am in my senses," she replied, "and I tell you I *must*. Get me a coach!"

However much astonished I might be, I was sensible that I had no right to refuse compliance with such a peremptory command. I hurried away a few paces, and called a hackney chariot which was passing empty. Almost before I could let down the steps, my aunt sprang in, I don't know how, and the man followed. She waved her hand to me to go away, so earnestly, that, all confounded as I was, I turned from them at once. In doing so, I heard her say to the coachman, "Drive anywhere! Drive straight on!" and presently the chariot passed me, going up the hill.

What Mr. Dick had told me, and what I had supposed to be a delusion of his, now came into my mind. I could not doubt that this person was the person of whom he had made such mysterious mention, though what the nature of his hold upon my aunt could possibly be, I was quite unable to imagine. After half an hour's cooling in the churchyard, I saw the chariot coming back. The driver stopped beside me, and my aunt was sitting in it alone.

She had not yet sufficiently recovered from her agitation to be quite prepared for the visit we had to make. She desired me to get into the chariot, and to tell the coachman to drive slowly up and down a little while. She said no more, except, "My dear child, never ask me what it was, and don't refer to it," until she had perfectly regained her composure, when she told me she was quite herself now, and we might get out. On her giving me her purse to pay the driver, I found that all the guineas were gone, and only the loose silver remained.

Doctors' Commons was approached by a little low archway. Before we had taken many paces down the street beyond it, the noise of the city seemed to melt, as if by magic, into a softened distance. A few dull courts and narrow ways brought us to the sky-lighted offices of Spenlow and Jorkins; in the vestibule of which temple, accessible to pilgrims without the ceremony of knocking, three or four clerks were at work as copyists. One of these, a little dry man, sitting by himself, who wore a stiff brown wig that looked as if it were made of gingerbread, rose to receive my aunt, and show us into Mr. Spenlow's room.

"Mr. Spenlow's in Court, ma'am," said the dry man; "it's an Arches day; but it's close by, and I'll send for him directly."

As we were left to look about us while Mr. Spenlow was fetched, I availed myself of the opportunity. The furniture of the room was old-fashioned and dusty; and the green baize on the top of the writing-table had lost all its colour, and was as withered and pale as an old pauper. There were a great many bundles of papers on it, some indorsed as Allegations, and some (to my surprise) as Libels, and some as being in the Consistory Court, and some in the Arches Court, and some in the Prerogative Court, and some in the Admiralty Court, and some in the Delegates' Court; giving me occasion to wonder much, how many Courts there might be in the gross, and how long it would take to understand them all. Besides these, there were sundry immense manuscript Books of Evidence taken on affidavit, strongly bound, and tied together in massive sets, a set to each cause, as if every cause were a history in ten or twenty volumes. All this looked tolerably expensive, I thought, and gave me an agreeable notion of a proctor's business. I was casting my eyes with increasing complacency over these and many similar objects, when hasty footsteps were heard in the room outside, and Mr. Spenlow, in a black gown trimmed with white fur, came hurrying in, taking off his hat as he came.

He was a little light-haired gentleman, with undeniable boots, and the stiffest of white cravats and shirt-collars. He was buttoned up mighty trim and tight, and must have taken a great deal of pains with his whiskers, which were accurately curled. His gold watch-chain was so massive, that a fancy came across me, that he ought to have a sinewy golden arm, to draw it out with, like those which are put up over the goldbeaters' shops. He was got up with such care, and was so stiff, that he could hardly bend himself; being obliged, when he glanced at some papers on his desk, after sitting down in his chair, to move his whole body, from the bottom of his spine, like Punch.

I had previously been presented by my aunt, and had been courteously received. He now said:

"And so, Mr. Copperfield, you think of entering into our profession? I casually mentioned to Miss Trotwood, when I had the pleasure of an interview with her the other day,"—with another inclination of his body—Punch again—"that there was a vacancy here. Miss Trotwood was good enough to mention that she had a nephew who was her peculiar care, and for whom she was seeking to provide genteelly, in life. That nephew, I believe, I have now the pleasure of"—Punch again.

I bowed my acknowledgments, and said my aunt had mentioned to me that there was that opening, and that I believed I should like it very much. That I was strongly inclined to like it, and had taken immediately to the proposal. That I could not absolutely pledge myself to like it, until I knew something more about it. That although it was little else than a matter of form, I presumed I should have an opportunity of trying how I liked it, before I bound myself to it irrevocably.

"Oh surely! surely!" said Mr. Spenlow. "We always, in this house, propose a month—an initiatory month. I should be happy, myself, to propose two months—three—an indefinite period, in fact—but I have a partner. Mr. Jorkins."

"And the premium, sir," I returned, "is a thousand pounds?"

"And the premium, Stamp included, is a thousand pounds," said Mr. Spenlow. "As I have mentioned to Miss Trotwood, I am actuated by no mercenary considerations; few men are less so, I believe; but Mr. Jorkins has his opinions on these subjects, and I am bound to respect Mr. Jorkins's opinions. Mr. Jorkins thinks a thousand pounds too little, in short."

"I suppose, sir," said I, still desiring to spare my aunt, "that it is not the custom here, if an articled clerk were particularly useful, and made himself a perfect master of his profession—" I could not help blushing, this looked so like praising myself—"I suppose it is not the custom, in the later years of his time, to allow him any—"

Mr. Spenlow, by a great effort, just lifted his head far enough out of his cravat, to shake it, and answered, anticipating the word "salary"

"No, I will not say what consideration I might give to that point myself, Mr. Copperfield, if I were unfettered. Mr. Jorkins is immovable."

I was quite dismayed by the idea of this terrible Jorkins. But I found out afterwards that he was a mild man of a heavy temperament, whose place in the business was to keep himself in the background, and be constantly exhibited by name as the most obdurate and ruthless of men. If a clerk wanted his salary raised, Mr. Jorkins wouldn't listen to such a proposition. If a client were slow to settle his bill of costs, Mr. Jorkins was resolved to have it paid; and however painful these things might be (and always were) to the feelings of Mr. Spenlow, Mr. Jorkins would have his bond. The heart and hand of the good angel Spenlow would have been always open, but for the restraining demon Jorkins. As I have grown older, I think I have had experience of some other houses doing business on the principle of Spenlow and Jorkins!

It was settled that I should begin my month's probation as soon as I pleased, and that my aunt need neither remain in town nor return at its expiration, as the articles of agreement of which I was to be the subject, could easily be sent to her at home for her signature. When we had got so far, Mr. Spenlow offered to take me into Court then and there, and show me what sort of place it was. As I was willing enough to know, we went out with this object, leaving my aunt behind; who would trust herself, she said, in no such place, and who, I think, regarded all Courts of Law as a sort of powder-mills that might blow up at any time.

Mr. Spenlow conducted me through a paved courtyard formed of grave brick houses, which I inferred, from the Doctors' names upon the doors, to be the official abiding-places of the learned advocates of whom Steerforth had told me; and into a large dull room, not unlike a chapel to my thinking, on the left hand. The upper part of this room was fenced off from the rest; and there, on the two sides of a raised platform of the horse-shoe form, sitting on easy old-fashioned dining-room chairs, were sundry gentlemen in red gowns and grey wigs, whom I found to be the Doctors aforesaid. Blinking over a little desk like a pulpit-desk, in the curve of the horse-shoe, was an old gentleman, whom, if I had seen him in an aviary, I should certainly have taken for an owl, but who, I learned, was the presiding judge. In the space within the horse-shoe, lower than these, that is to say on about the level of the floor, were sundry other gentlemen of Mr. Spenlow's rank, and dressed like him in black gowns with white fur upon them, sitting at a long green table. Their cravats were in general stiff, I thought, and their looks haughty; but in this last respect, I presently conceived I had done them an injustice, for when two or three of them had to rise and answer a question of the presiding dignitary, I never saw anything more sheepish. The public, represented by a boy with a comforter, and a shabby-genteel man secretly eating crumbs out of his coat pockets, was warming itself at a stove in the centre of the Court. The languid stillness of the place was only broken by the chirping of this fire and by the voice of one of the Doctors, who was wandering slowly through a perfect library of evidence, and stopping to put up, from time to time, at little roadside inns of argument on the journey. Altogether, I have never, on any occasion, made one at such a cosey, dosey, old-fashioned, time-forgotten, sleepy-headed little family-party in all my life; and I felt it would be quite a soothing opiate to belong to it in any character—except perhaps as a suitor.

Very well satisfied with the dreamy nature of this retreat, I informed Mr. Spenlow that I had seen enough for that time, and we rejoined my aunt; in company with whom I presently departed from the Commons, feeling very young when I went out of Spenlow and Jorkins's, on account of the clerks poking one another with their pens to point me out.

We arrived at Lincoln's Inn Fields without any new adventures, except encountering an unlucky donkey in a costermonger's cart, who suggested painful associations to my aunt. We had another long talk about my plans, when we were safely housed; and as I knew she was anxious to get home, and, between fire, food, and pickpockets, could never be considered at her ease for half-an-hour in London, I urged her not to be uncomfortable on my account, but to leave me to take care of myself.

"I have not been here a week to-morrow, without considering that too, my dear," she returned. "There is a furnished little set of chambers to be let in the Adelphi, Trot, which ought to suit you to a marvel."

With this brief introduction, she produced from her pocket an advertisement, carefully cut out of a newspaper, setting forth that in Buckingham Street in the Adelphi there was to be let furnished, with a view of the river, a singularly desirable and compact set of chambers, forming a genteel residence for a young gentlemen, a member of one of the Inns of Court, or otherwise, with immediate possession. Terms moderate, and could be taken for a month only, if required.

"Why, this is the very thing, aunt!" said I, flushed with the possible dignity of living in chambers.

"Then come," replied my aunt, immediately resuming the bonnet she had a minute before laid aside. "We'll go and look at 'em."

Away we went. The advertisement directed us to apply to Mrs. Crupp on the premises, and we rung the area bell, which we supposed to communicate with Mrs. Crupp. It was not until we had rung three or four times that we could prevail on Mrs. Crupp to communicate with us, but at last she appeared, being a stout lady with a flounce of flannel petticoat below a nankeen gown.

"Let us see these chambers of yours, if you please, ma'am," said my aunt.

"For this gentleman?" said Mrs. Crupp, feeling in her pocket for her keys.

"Yes, for my nephew," said my aunt.

"And a sweet set they is for sich!" said Mrs. Crupp.

So we went up-stairs.

They were on the top of the house—a great point with my aunt, being near the fire-escape—and consisted of a little half-blind entry where you could see hardly anything, a little stone-blind pantry where you could see nothing at all, a sitting-room, and a bedroom. The furniture was rather faded, but quite good enough for me; and, sure enough, the river was outside the windows.

As I was delighted with the place, my aunt and Mrs. Crupp withdrew into the pantry to discuss the terms, while I remained on the sitting-room sofa, hardly daring to think it possible that I could be destined to live in such a noble residence. After a single combat of some duration they returned, and I saw, to my joy, both in Mrs. Crupp's countenance and in my aunt's, that the deed was done.

"Is it the last occupant's furniture?" inquired my aunt.

"Yes, it is, ma'am," said Mrs. Crupp.

"What's become of him?" asked my aunt.

Mrs. Crupp was taken with a troublesome cough, in the midst of which she articulated with much difficulty. "He was took ill here, ma'am, and—ugh! ugh! ugh! dear me!—and he died!"

"Hey! What did he die of?" asked my aunt.

"Well, ma'am, he died of drink," said Mrs. Crupp, in confidence, "And smoke."

"Smoke? You don't mean chimneys?" said my aunt.

"No, ma'am," returned Mrs. Crupp. "Cigars and pipes."

"*That's* not catching, Trot, at any rate," remarked my aunt, turning to me.

"No, indeed," said I.

In short, my aunt, seeing how enraptured I was with the premises, took them for a month, with leave to remain for twelve months when that time was out. Mrs. Crupp was to find linen, and to cook; every other necessary was already provided; and Mrs. Crupp expressly intimated that she should always yearn towards me as a son. I was to take possession the day after to-morrow, and Mrs. Crupp said, thank Heaven she had now found summun she could care for!

On our way back, my aunt informed me how she confidently trusted that the life I was now to lead would make me firm and self-reliant, which was all I wanted. She repeated this several times next day, in the intervals of our arranging for the transmission of my clothes and books from Mr. Wickfield's; relative to which, and to all my late holiday, I wrote a long letter to Agnes, of which my aunt took charge, as she was to leave on the succeeding day. Not to lengthen these particulars, I need only add, that she made a handsome provision for all my possible wants during my month of trial; that Steerforth, to my great disappointment and hers too, did not make his appearance before she went away; that I saw her safely seated in the Dover coach, exulting in the coming discomfiture of the vagrant donkeys, with Janet at her side; and that when the coach was gone, I turned my face to the Adelphi, pondering on the old days when I used to roam about its subterranean arches, and on the happy changes which had brought me to the surface.

24

MY FIRST DISSIPATION

IT WAS A WONDERFULLY FINE THING TO HAVE THAT lofty castle to myself, and to feel, when I shut my outer door, like Robinson Crusoe, when he had got into his fortification, and pulled his ladder up after him. It was a wonderfully fine thing to walk about town with the key of my house in my pocket, and to know that I could ask any fellow to come home, and make quite sure of its being inconvenient to nobody, if it were not so to me. It was a wonderfully fine thing to let myself in and out, and to come and go without a word to any one, and to ring Mrs. Crupp up, gasping, from the depths of the earth, when I wanted her—and when she was disposed to come. All this, I say, was wonderfully fine; but I must say, too, that there were times when it was very dreary.

It was fine in the morning, particularly in the fine mornings. It looked a very fresh, free life, by daylight: still fresher, and more free, by sunlight. But as the day declined, the life seemed to go down too. I don't know how it was; it seldom looked well by candle-light. I wanted somebody to talk to, then. I missed Agnes. I found a tremendous blank, in the place of that smiling repository of my confidence. Mrs. Crupp appeared to be a long way off. I thought about my predecessor, who had died of drink and smoke; and I could have wished he had been so good as to live, and not bother me with his decease.

After two days and nights, I felt as if I had lived there for a year, and yet I was not an hour older, but was quite as much tormented by my own youthfulness as ever.

Steerforth not yet appearing, which induced me to apprehend that he must be ill, I left the Commons early on the third day, and walked out to Highgate. Mrs. Steerforth was very glad to see me, and said that he had gone away with one of his Oxford friends to see another who lived near St. Albans, but that she expected him to return to-morrow. I was so fond of him, that I felt quite jealous of his Oxford friends.

As she pressed me to stay to dinner, I remained, and I believe we talked about nothing but him all day. I told her how much the people liked him at Yarmouth, and what a delightful companion he had been. Miss Dartle was full of hints and mysterious questions, but took a great interest in all our proceedings there, and said, "Was it really though?" and so forth, so often, that she got everything out of me she wanted to know. Her appearance was exactly what I have described it, when I first saw her; but the society of the two ladies was so agreeable, and came so natural to me, that I felt myself falling a little in love with her. I could not help thinking, several times in the course of the evening, and particularly when I walked home at night, what delightful company she would be in Buckingham Street.

I was taking my coffee and roll in the morning, before going to the Commons—and I may observe in this place that it is surprising how much coffee Mrs. Crupp used, and how weak it was, considering—when Steerforth himself walked in, to my unbounded joy.

"My dear Steerforth," cried I, "I began to think I should never see you again!"

"I was carried off, by force of arms," said Steerforth, "the very next morning after I got home. Why, Daisy, what a rare old bachelor you are here!"

I showed him over the establishment, not omitting the pantry, with no little pride, and he commended it highly. "I tell you what, old boy," he added, "I shall make quite a town-house of this place, unless you give me notice to quit."

This was a delightful hearing. I told him if he waited for that, he would have to wait till doomsday.

"But you shall have some breakfast!" said I, with my hand on the bell-rope, "and Mrs. Crupp shall make you some fresh coffee, and I'll toast you some bacon in a bachelor's Dutch-oven that I have got here."

"No, no!" said Steerforth. "Don't ring! I can't! I am going to breakfast with one of these fellows who is at the Piazza Hotel, in Covent Garden."

"But you'll come back to dinner?" said I.

"I can't, upon my life. There's nothing I should like better, but I *must* remain with these two fellows. We are all three off together to-morrow morning."

"Then bring them here to dinner," I returned. "Do you think they would come?"

"Oh! they would come fast enough," said Steerforth; "but we should inconvenience you. You had better come and dine with us somewhere."

I would not by any means consent to this, for it occurred to me that I really ought to have a little house-warming, and that there never could be a better opportunity. I had a new pride in my rooms after his approval of them, and burned with a desire to develop their utmost resources. I therefore made him promise positively in the names of his two friends, and we appointed six o'clock as the dinner-hour.

When he was gone, I rang for Mrs. Crupp, and acquainted her with my desperate design. Mrs. Crupp said, in the first place, of course it was well known she couldn't be expected to wait, but she knew a handy young man, who she thought could be prevailed upon to do it, and whose terms would be five shillings, and what I pleased. I said, certainly we would have him. Next, Mrs. Crupp said it was clear she couldn't be in two places at once (which I felt to be reasonable), and that "a young gal" stationed in the pantry with a bedroom candle, there never to desist from washing plates, would be indispensable. I said, what would be the expense of this young female? and Mrs. Crupp said she supposed eighteen-pence would neither make nor break me. I said I supposed not; and *that* was settled. Then Mrs. Crupp said, Now about the dinner.

It was a remarkable instance of want of forethought on the part of the ironmonger who had made Mrs. Crupp's kitchen fireplace, that it was capable of cooking nothing but chops and mashed potatoes. As to a fish-kittle, Mrs. Crupp said, well! would I only come and look at the range? She couldn't say fairer than that. Would I come and look at it? As I should not have been much the wiser if I *had* looked at it, I declined, and said, "Never mind fish." But Mrs. Crupp said, Don't say that; oysters was in, why not them? So *that* was settled. Mrs. Crupp then said what she would recommend would be this. A pair of hot roast fowls—from the pastry-cook's; a dish of stewed beef, with vegetables—from the pastry-cook's; two little corner things, as a raised pie and a dish of kidneys—from the pastry-cook's; a tart, and (if I liked) a shape of jelly—from the pastry-cook's. This, Mrs. Crupp said, would leave her at full liberty to concentrate her mind on the potatoes, and to serve up the cheese and celery as she could wish to see it done.

I acted on Mrs. Crupp's opinion, and gave the order at the pastry-cook's myself. Walking along the Strand, afterwards, and observing a hard mottled substance in the window of a ham and beef shop, which resembled marble, but was labelled "Mock Turtle," I went in and bought a slab of it, which I have since seen reason to believe would have sufficed for fifteen people. This preparation, Mrs. Crupp, after some difficulty, consented to warm up; and it shrunk so much in a liquid state, that we found it what Steerforth called "rather a tight fit" for four.

These preparations happily completed, I bought a little dessert in Covent Garden Market, and gave a rather extensive order at a retail wine-merchant's in that vicinity. When I came home in the afternoon, and saw the bottles drawn up in a square on the pantry-floor, they looked so numerous (though there were two missing, which made Mrs. Crupp very uncomfortable), that I was absolutely frightened at them.

One of Steerforth's friends was named Grainger, and the other Markham. They were both very gay and lively fellows; Grainger, something older than Steerforth; Markham, youthful-looking, and I should say not more than twenty. I observed that the latter always spoke of himself indefinitely, as " a man," and seldom or never in the first person singular.

" A man might get on very well here, Mr. Copperfield," said Markham—meaning himself.

" It's not a bad situation," said I, " and the rooms are really commodious."

" I hope you have both brought appetites with you?" said Steerforth.

" Upon my honour," returned Markham, " town seems to sharpen a man's appetite. A man is hungry all day long. A man is perpetually eating."

Being a little embarrassed at first, and feeling much too young to preside, I made Steerforth take the head of the table when dinner was announced, and seated myself opposite to him. Everything was very good; we did not spare the wine; and he exerted himself so brilliantly to make the thing pass off well, that there was no pause in our festivity. I was not quite such good company during dinner as I could have wished to be, for my chair was opposite the door, and my attention was distracted by observing that the handy young man went out of the room very often, and that his shadow always presented itself, immediately afterwards, on the wall of the entry, with a bottle at its mouth. The " young gal " likewise occasioned me some uneasiness: not so much by neglecting to wash the plates, as by breaking them. For being of an inquisitive disposition, and unable to confine herself (as her positive instructions were) to the pantry, she was constantly peering in at us, and constantly imagining herself detected; in which belief, she several times retired upon the plates (with which she had carefully paved the floor), and did a great deal of destruction.

These, however, were small drawbacks, and easily forgotten when the cloth was cleared, and the dessert put on the table; at which period of the entertainment the handy young man was discovered to be speechless. Giving him private directions to seek the society of Mrs. Crupp, and to remove the " young gal " to the basement also, I abandoned myself to enjoyment.

I began, by being singularly cheerful and light-hearted; all sorts of half-forgotten things to talk about, came rushing into my mind, and make me hold forth in a most unwonted manner. I laughed heartily at my own jokes, and everybody else's; called Steerforth to order for not passing the wine; made several engagements to go to Oxford; announced that I meant to have a dinner-party exactly like that, once a week, until further notice; and madly took so much snuff out of Grainger's box, that I was obliged to go into the pantry, and have a private fit of sneezing ten minutes long.

I went on, by passing the wine faster and faster yet, and continually starting up with a corkscrew to open more wine, long before any was needed. I proposed Steerforth's health. I said he was my dearest friend, the protector of my boyhood, and the companion of my prime. I said I was delighted to propose his health. I said I owed him more obligations than I could ever repay, and held him in a higher admiration than I could ever express. I finished by saying, " I'll give you Steerforth! God bless him! Hurrah! " We gave him three times three, and another, and a good one to finish with. I broke my glass in going round the table to shake hands with him, and I said (in two words) "Steerforth, you'retheguidingstarofmyexistence."

I went on, by finding suddenly that somebody was in the middle of a song. Markham was the singer, and he sang " When the heart of a man is depressed with care." He said, when he had sung it, he would give us " Woman! " I took objection to that, and I couldn't allow it. I said it was not a respectful way of proposing the toast, and I would never permit that toast to be drunk in my house otherwise than as " The Ladies! " I was very high with him, mainly I think because I saw Steerforth and Grainger laughing at me—or at him—or at both of us. He said a man was not to be dictated to. I said a man *was*. He said a man was not to be insulted, then. I said he was right there—never under my roof, where the Lares were sacred, and the laws of hospitality paramount. He said it was no derogation from a man's dignity to confess that I was a devilish good fellow. I instantly proposed his health.

Somebody was smoking. We were all smoking, *I* was smoking, and trying to suppress a rising tendency to shudder. Steerforth had made a speech to me, in the course of which I had been affected almost to tears. I returned thanks, and hoped the present company would dine with me to-morrow, and the day after—each day at five o'clock, that we might enjoy the pleasures of conversation and society through a long evening. I felt called upon to propose an individual. I would give them my aunt. Miss Betsey Trotwood, the best of her sex!

Somebody was leaning out of my bedroom window, refreshing his forehead against the cool stone of the parapet, and feeling the air upon his face. It was myself. I was addressing myself as " Copperfield," and saying, " Why did you try to smoke? You might have known you couldn't do it." Now, somebody was unsteadily contemplating his features in the looking-glass. That was I too. I was very pale in the looking-glass; my eyes had a vacant appearance; and my hair—only my hair, nothing else—looked drunk.

Somebody said to me, " Let us go to the theatre, Copperfield! " There was no bedroom before me, but again the jingling table covered with glasses; the lamp; Grainger on my right hand, Markham on my left, and Steerforth opposite—all sitting in a mist, and a long way off. The theatre? To be sure. The very thing. Come along! But they must excuse me if I saw everybody out first, and turned the lamp off—in case of fire.

Owing to some confusion in the dark, the door was gone. I was feeling for it in the window-curtains, when Steerforth, laughing, took me by the arm and led me out. We went downstairs, one behind another. Near the bottom, somebody fell, and rolled down. Somebody else said it was Copperfield. I was angry at that false report, until, finding myself on my back in the passage, I began to think there might be some foundation for it.

A very foggy night, with great rings round the lamps in the streets! There was an indistinct talk of its being wet. *I* considered it frosty. Steerforth dusted me under a lamp-post, and put my hat into shape, which somebody produced from somewhere in a most extraordinary manner, for I hadn't had it on before. Steerforth then said, " You are all right, Copperfield, are you not? " and I told him, " Neverberrer."

A man, sitting in a pigeon-hole-place, looked out of the fog, and took money from somebody, inquiring if I was one of the gentlemen paid for, and appearing rather doubtful (as I remember in the glimpse I had of him) whether to take the money for me or not. Shortly afterwards, we were very high up in a very hot theatre, looking down into a large pit, that seemed to me to smoke; the people with whom it was crammed were so indistinct. There was a great stage, too, looking very clean and smooth after the streets; and there were people upon it, talking about something or other, but not at all intelligibly. There was an abundance of bright lights, and there was music, and there were ladies down in the boxes, and I don't know what more. The whole building looked to me as if it were learning to swim; it conducted itself in such an unaccountable manner, when I tried to steady it.

On somebody's motion, we resolved to go down-stairs to the dress-boxes, where the ladies were. A gentleman lounging, full dressed, on a sofa, with an opera-glass in his hand, passed before my view, and also my own figure at full length in a glass. Then

I was being ushered into one of these boxes, and found myself saying something as I sat down, and people about me crying "Silence!" to somebody, and ladies casting indignant glances at me, and—what! yes!—Agnes, sitting on the seat before me, in the same box, with a lady and gentleman beside her, whom I didn't know. I see her face now, better than I did then, I dare say, with its indelible look of regret and wonder turned upon me.

"Agnes!" I said, thickly, "Lorblessmer! Agnes!"

"Hush! Pray!" she answered, I could not conceive why. "You disturb the company. Look at the stage!"

I tried, on her injunction, to fix it, and to hear something of what was going on there, but quite in vain. I looked at her again by-and-bye, and saw her shrink into her corner, and put her gloved hand to her forehead.

"Agnes!" I said. "I'mafraidyou'renorwell."

"Yes, yes. Do not mind me, Trotwood," she returned. "Listen! Are you going away soon?"

"Amigoarawaysoo?" I repeated.

"Yes."

I had a stupid intention of replying that I was going to wait, to hand her down-stairs. I suppose I expressed it somehow; for, after she had looked at me attentively for a little while, she appeared to understand, and replied in a low tone:

"I know you will do as I ask you, if I tell you I am very earnest in it. Go away now, Trotwood, for my sake, and ask your friends to take you home."

She had so far improved me for the time, that though I was angry with her, I felt ashamed, and with a short "Goori!" (which I intended for "Good-night!") got up and went away. They followed and I stepped at once out of the box-door into my bedroom, where only Steerforth was with me, helping me to undress, and where I was by turns telling him that Agnes was my sister, and adjuring him to bring the corkscrew, that I might open another bottle of wine.

How somebody, lying in my bed, lay saying and doing all this over again, at cross purposes, in a feverish dream all night—the bed a rocking sea that was never still! How, as that somebody slowly settled down into myself, did I begin to parch, and feel as if my outer covering of skin were a hard board; my tongue the bottom of an empty kettle, furred with long service, and burning up over a slow fire; the palms of my hands, hot plates of metal which no ice could cool!

But the agony of mind, the remorse, and shame I felt when I became conscious next day! My horror of having committed a thousand offences I had forgotten, and which nothing could ever expiate—my recollection of that indelible look which Agnes had given me—the torturing impossibility of communicating with her, not knowing, beast that I was, how she came to be in London, or where she stayed—my disgust of the very sight of the room where the revel had been held—my racking head—the smell of smoke, the sight of glasses, the impossibility of going out, or even getting up! Oh what a day it was!

Oh, what an evening, when I sat down by my fire to a basin of mutton broth, dimpled all over with fat, and thought I was going the way of my predecessor, and should succeed to his dismal story as well as to his chambers, and had half a mind to rush express to Dover and reveal all! What an evening, when Mrs. Crupp, coming in to take away the broth-basin, produced one kidney on a cheese-plate as the entire remains of yesterday's feast, and I was really inclined to fall upon her nankeen breast, and say, in heartfelt penitence, "Oh, Mrs. Crupp, Mrs. Crupp, never mind the broken meats! I am very miserable!"—only that I doubted, even at that pass, if Mrs. Crupp were quite the sort of woman to confide in!

25

GOOD AND BAD ANGELS

I WAS GOING OUT AT MY DOOR ON THE MORNING AFTER that deplorable day of headache, sickness, and repentance, with an odd confusion in my mind relative to the date of my dinner-party, as if a body of Titans had taken an enormous lever and pushed the day before yesterday some months back, when I saw a ticket-porter coming up-stairs, with a letter in his hand. He was taking his time about his errand, then; but when he saw me on the top of the staircase, looking at him over the banisters, he swung into a trot, and came up panting, as if he had run himself into a state of exhaustion.

"T. Copperfield, Esquire," said the ticket-porter, touching his hat with his little cane.

I could scarcely lay claim to the name: I was so disturbed by the conviction that the letter came from Agnes. However, I told him I was T. Copperfield, Esquire, and he believed it, and gave me the letter, which he said required an answer. I shut him out on the landing to wait for the answer, and went into my chambers again, in such a nervous state that I was fain to lay the letter down on my breakfast-table, and familiarise myself with the outside of it a little, before I could resolve to break the seal.

I found, when I did open it, that it was a very kind note, containing no reference to my condition at the theatre. All it said was, " My dear Trotwood. I am staying at the house of papa's agent, Mr. Waterbrook, in Ely-place, Holborn. Will you come and see me to-day, at any time you like to appoint? Ever yours affectionately, AGNES."

It took me such a long time to write an answer at all to my satisfaction, that I don't know what the ticket-porter can have thought, unless he thought I was learning to write. I must have written half a dozen answers at least. I began one, " How can I ever hope, my dear Agnes, to efface from your remembrance the disgusting impression'—there I didn't like it, and then I tore it up. I began another, " Shakespeare has observed, my dear Agnes, how strange it is that a man should put an enemy into his mouth"—that reminded me of Markham, and it got no farther. I even tried poetry. I began one note, in a six-syllable line, " Oh, do not remember"—but that associated itself with the fifth of November, and became an absurdity. After many attempts, I wrote, " My dear Agnes. Your letter is like you, and what could I say of it that would be higher praise than that? I will come at four o'clock. Affectionately and sorrowfully, T. C." With this missive (which I was in twenty minds at once about recalling, as soon as it was out of my hands), the ticket-porter at last departed.

If the day were half as tremendous to any other professional gentleman in Doctors' Commons as it was to me, I sincerely believe he made some expiation for his share in that rotten old ecclesiastical cheese. Although I left the office at half-past three, and was prowling about the place of appointment within a few minutes afterwards, the appointed time was exceeded by a full quarter of an hour, according to the clock of St. Andrew's, Holborn, before I could muster up sufficient desperation to pull the private bell-handle let into the left-hand door-post of Mr. Waterbrook's house.

The professional business of Mr. Waterbrook's establishment

was done on the ground floor, and the genteel business (of which there was a good deal) in the upper part of the building. I was shown into a pretty but rather close drawing-room, and there sat Agnes, netting a purse.

She looked so quiet and good, and reminded me so strongly of my airy fresh school days at Canterbury, and the sodden, smoky, stupid wretch I had been the other night, that, nobody being by, I yielded to my self-reproach and shame, and—in short, made a fool of myself. I cannot deny that I shed tears. To this hour I am undecided whether it was upon the whole the wisest thing I could have done, or the most ridiculous.

"If it had been any one but you, Agnes," said I, turning away my head, "I should not have minded it half so much. But that it should have been you who saw me! I almost wish I had been dead, first."

She put her hand—its touch was like no other hand—upon my arm for a moment; and I felt so befriended and comforted, that I could not help moving it to my lips, and gratefully kissing it.

"Sit down," said Agnes, cheerfully. "Don't be unhappy, Trotwood. If you cannot confidently trust me, whom will you trust?"

"Ah, Agnes!" I returned. "You are my good Angel!"

She smiled rather sadly, I thought, and shook her head.

"Yes, Agnes, my good Angel! Always my good Angel!"

"If I were, indeed, Trotwood," she returned, "there is one thing that I should set my heart on very much."

I looked at her inquiringly; but already with a foreknowledge of her meaning.

"On warning you," said Agnes, with a steady glance, "against your bad Angel."

"My dear Agnes," I began, "if you mean Steerforth—"

"I do, Trotwood," she returned.

"Then, Agnes, you wrong him very much. He, my bad Angel, or anyone's! He, anything but a guide, a support, and a friend to me! My dear Agnes! Now, is it not unjust, and unlike you, to judge him from what you saw of me the other night?"

"I do not judge him from what I saw of you the other night," she quietly replied.

"From what, then?"

"From many things—trifles in themselves, but they do not seem to me to be so, when they are put together. I judge him, partly from your account of him, Trotwood, and your character, and the influence he has over you."

There was always something in her modest voice that seemed

to touch a chord within me, answering to that sound alone. It was always earnest; but when it was very earnest, as it was now, there was a thrill in it that quite subdued me. I sat looking at her as she cast her eyes down on her work; I sat seeming still to listen to her; and Steerforth, in spite of all my attachment to him, darkened in that tone.

" It is very bold in me," said Agnes, looking up again, " who have lived in such seclusion, and can know so little of the world, to give you my advice so confidently, or even to have this strong opinion. But I know in what it is engendered, Trotwood,—in how true a remembrance of our having grown up together, and in how true an interest in all relating to you. It is that which makes me bold. I am certain that what I say is right. I am quite sure it is. I feel as if it were some one else speaking to you, and not I, when I caution you that you have made a dangerous friend."

Again I looked at her, again I listened to her after she was silent, and again his image, though it was still fixed in my heart, darkened.

" I am not so unreasonable as to expect," said Agnes, resuming her usual tone, after a little while, " that you will, or that you can, at once, change any sentiment that has become a conviction to you; least of all a sentiment that is rooted in your trusting disposition. You ought not hastily to do that. I only ask you, Trotwood, if you ever think of me—I mean," with a quiet smile, for I was going to interrupt her, and she knew why, " as often as you think of me—to think of what I have said. Do you forgive me for all this? "

" I will forgive you, Agnes," I replied, " when you come to do Steerforth justice, and to like him as well as I do."

" Not until then? " said Agnes.

I saw a passing shadow on her face when I made this mention of him, but she returned my smile, and we were again as unreserved in our mutual confidence as of old.

" And when, Agnes," said I, " will you forgive me the other night? "

" When I recall it," said Agnes.

She would have dismissed the subject so, but I was too full of it to allow that, and insisted on telling her how it happened that I had disgraced myself, and what chain of accidental circumstances had had the theatre for its final link. It was a great relief to me to do this, and to enlarge on the obligation that I owed to Steerforth for his care of me when I was unable to take care of myself.

"You must not forget," said Agnes, calmly changing the conversation as soon as I had concluded, "that you are always to tell me, not only when you fall into trouble, but when you fall in love. Who has succeeded to Miss Larkins, Trotwood?"

"No one, Agnes."

"Some one, Trotwood," said Agnes, laughing, and holding up her finger.

"No, Agnes, upon my word! There is a lady, certainly, at Mrs. Steerforth's house, who is very clever, and whom I like to talk to—Miss Dartle—but I don't adore her."

Agnes laughed again at her own penetration, and told me that if I were faithful to her in my confidence she thought she should keep a little register of my violent attachments, with the date, duration, and termination of each, like the table of the reigns of the kings and queens, in the History of England. Then she asked me if I had seen Uriah.

"Uriah Heep?" said I. "No. Is he in London?"

"He comes to the office down-stairs every day," returned Agnes. "He was in London a week before me. I am afraid on disagreeable business, Trotwood."

"On some business that makes you uneasy, Agnes, I see," said I. "What can that be?"

Agnes laid aside her work, and replied, folding her hands upon one another, and looking pensively at me out of those beautiful soft eyes of hers:

"I believe he is going to enter into partnership with papa."

"What? Uriah? That mean, fawning fellow, worm himself into such promotion!" I cried, indignantly. "Have you made no remonstrance about it, Agnes? Consider what a connection it is likely to be. You must speak out. You must not allow your father to take such a mad step. You must prevent it, Agnes, while there's time."

Still looking at me, Agnes shook her head while I was speaking, with a faint smile at my warmth; and then replied:

"You remember our last conversation about papa? It was not long after that—not more than two or three days—when he gave me the first intimation of what I tell you. It was sad to see him struggling between his desire to represent it to me as a matter of choice on his part, and his inability to conceal that it was forced upon him. I felt very sorry."

"Forced upon him, Agnes! Who forces it upon him?"

"Uriah," she replied, after a moment's hesitation, "has made himself indispensable to papa. He is subtle and watchful. He has mastered papa's weaknesses, fostered them, and taken advantage of them, until—to say all that I mean in a word, Trotwood,—until papa is afraid of him."

There was more that she might have said; more that she knew, or that she suspected; I clearly saw. I could not give her pain by asking what it was, for I knew that she withheld it from me to spare her father. It had long been going on to this, I was sensible: yes, I could not but feel, on the least reflection, that it had been going on to this for a long time. I remained silent.

"His ascendancy over papa," said Agnes, "is very great. He professes humility and gratitude—with truth, perhaps: I hope so—but his position is really one of power, and I fear he makes a hard use of his power."

I said he was a hound, which, at the moment, was a great satisfaction to me.

"At the time I speak of, as the time when papa spoke to me," pursued Agnes, "he had told papa that he was going away; that he was very sorry and unwilling to leave, but that he had better prospects. Papa was very much depressed then, and more bowed down by the care than ever you or I have seen him; but he seemed relieved by this expedient of the partnership, though at the same time he seemed hurt by it and ashamed of it."

"And how did you receive it, Agnes?"

"I did, Trotwood," she replied, "what I hope was right. Feeling sure that it was necessary for papa's peace that the sacrifice should be made, I entreated him to make it. I said it would lighten the load of his life—I hope it will!—and that it would give me increased opportunities of being his companion. Oh, Trotwood!" cried Agnes, putting her hands before her face, as her tears started on it, "I almost feel as if I had been papa's enemy, instead of his loving child. For I know how he has altered, in his devotion to me. I know how he has narrowed the circle of his sympathies and duties, in the concentration of his whole mind upon me. I know what a multitude of things he has shut out for my sake, and how his anxious thoughts of me have shadowed his life, and weakened his strength and energy, by turning them always upon one idea. If I could ever set this right! If I could ever work out his restoration, as I have so innocently been the cause of his decline!"

I had never before seen Agnes cry. I had seen tears in her eyes when I had brought new honours home from school, and I had seen them there when we last spoke about her father, and I had seen her turn her gentle head aside when we took leave of one another; but I had never seen her grieve like this. It made me so sorry that I could only say, in a foolish, helpless manner, " Pray, Agnes, don't! Don't, my dear sister! "

But Agnes was too superior to me in character and purpose, as I know well now, whatever I might know or not know then, to be long in need of my entreaties. The beautiful, calm manner, which makes her so different in my remembrance from everybody else, came back again, as if a cloud had passed from a serene sky.

" We are not likely to remain alone much longer," said Agnes; " and while I have an opportunity, let me earnestly entreat you, Trotwood, to be friendly to Uriah. Don't repel him. Don't resent (as I think you have a general disposition to do) what may be uncongenial to you in him. He may not deserve it, for we know no certain ill of him. In any case, think first of papa and me! "

Agnes had no time to say more, for the room-door opened, and Mrs. Waterbrook, who was a large lady—or who wore a large dress: I don't exactly know which, for I don't know which was dress and which was lady—came sailing in. I had a dim recollection of having seen her at the theatre, as if I had seen her in a pale magic lantern; but she appeared to remember me perfectly, and still to suspect me of being in a state of intoxication.

Finding by degrees, however, that I was sober, and (I hope) that I was a modest young gentleman, Mrs. Waterbrook softened towards me considerably, and inquired, firstly, if I went much into the parks, and secondly, if I went much into society. On my replying to both these questions in the negative, it occurred to me that I fell again in her good opinion; but she concealed the fact gracefully, and invited me to dinner next day. I accepted the invitation, and took my leave, making a call on Uriah in the office as I went out, and leaving a card for him in his absence.

When I went to dinner next day, and on the street-door being opened, plunged into a vapour-bath of haunch of mutton, I divined that I was not the only guest, for I immediately identified the ticket-porter in disguise, assisting the family servant, and waiting at the foot of the stairs to carry up my name. He looked, to the best of his ability, when he asked me for it confidentially, as if he had never seen me before; but well did I know him, and well did he know me. Conscience made cowards of us both.

I found Mr. Waterbrook to be a middle-aged gentleman, with a short throat, and a good deal of shirt-collar, who only wanted a black nose to be the portrait of a pug-dog. He told me he was happy to have the honour of making my acquaintance; and when I had paid my homage to Mrs. Waterbrook, presented me, with much ceremony, to a very awful lady in a black velvet dress, and a great black velvet hat, whom I remember as looking like a near relation of Hamlet's—say his aunt.

Mrs. Henry Spiker was this lady's name; and her husband was there too: so cold a man, that his head, instead of being grey, seemed to be sprinkled with hoar-frost. Immense deference was shown to the Henry Spikers, male and female; which Agnes told me was on account of Mr. Henry Spiker being solicitor to something or somebody, I forget what or which, remotely connected with the Treasury.

I found Uriah Heep among the company, in a suit of black, and in deep humility. He told me, when I shook hands with him, that he was proud to be noticed by me, and that he really felt obliged to me for my condescension. I could have wished he had been less obliged to me, for he hovered about me in his gratitude all the rest of the evening; and whenever I said a word to Agnes, was sure, with his shadowless eyes and cadaverous face, to be looking gauntly down upon us from behind.

There were other guests—all iced for the occasion, as it struck me, like the wine. But there was one who attracted my attention before he came in, on account of my hearing him announced as Mr. Traddles! My mind flew back to Salem House; and could it be Tommy, I thought, who used to draw the skeletons!

I looked for Mr. Traddles with unusual interest. He was a sober, steady-looking young man of retiring manners, with a comic head of hair, and eyes that were rather wide open; and he got into an obscure corner so soon, that I had some difficulty in making him out. At length I had a good view of him, and either my vision deceived me, or it was the old unfortunate Tommy.

I made my way to Mr. Waterbrook, and said, that I believed I had the pleasure of seeing an old schoolfellow there.

"Indeed!" said Mr. Waterbrook, surprised. "You are too young to have been at school with Mr. Henry Spiker?"

"Oh, I don't mean him!" I returned. "I mean the gentleman named Traddles."

"Oh! Aye, aye! Indeed!" said my host, with much diminished interest. "Possibly."

"If it's really the same person," said I, glancing towards him, "it was at a place called Salem House where we were together, and he was an excellent fellow."

"Oh yes. Traddles is a good fellow," returned my host nodding his head with an air of toleration. "Traddles is quite a good fellow."

"It's a curious coincidence," said I.

"It is really," returned my host, "quite a coincidence, that

Traddles should be here at all: as Traddles was only invited this morning, when the place at table intended to be occupied by Mrs. Henry Spiker's brother, became vacant, in consequence of his indisposition. A very gentlemanly man, Mrs. Henry Spiker's brother, Mr. Copperfield."

I murmured an assent, which was full of feeling, considering that I knew nothing at all about him; and I inquired what Mr. Traddles was by profession.

"Traddles," returned Mr. Waterbrook, "is a young man reading for the bar. Yes. He is quite a good fellow—nobody's enemy but his own."

"Is he his own enemy?" said I, sorry to hear this.

"Well," returned Mr. Waterbrook, pursing up his mouth, and playing with his watch-chain, in a comfortable, prosperous sort of way. "I should say he was one of those men who stand in their own light. Yes, I should say he would never, for example, be worth five hundred pound. Traddles was recommended to me by a professional friend. Oh yes. Yes. He has a kind of talent for drawing briefs, and stating a case in writing, plainly. I am able to throw something in Traddles's way, in the course of the years; something—for him—considerable. Oh yes. Yes."

I was much impressed by the extremely comfortable and satisfied manner in which Mr. Waterbrook delivered himself of this little word "Yes," every now and then. There was wonderful expression in it. It completely conveyed the idea of a man who had been born, not to say with a silver spoon, but with a scaling-ladder, and had gone on mounting all the heights of life one after another, until now he looked, from the top of the fortifications, with the eye of a philosopher and a patron, on the people down in the trenches.

My reflections on this theme were still in progress when dinner was announced. Mr. Waterbrook went down with Hamlet's aunt. Mr. Henry Spiker took Mrs. Waterbrook. Agnes, whom I should have liked to take myself, was given to a simpering fellow with weak legs. Uriah, Traddles, and I, as the junior part of the company, went down last, how we could. I was not so vexed at losing Agnes as I might have been, since it gave me an opportunity of making myself known to Traddles on the stairs, who greeted me with great fervour; while Uriah writhed with such obtrusive satisfaction and self-abasement, that I could gladly have pitched him over the banisters.

Traddles and I were separated at table, being billeted in two remote corners: he in the glare of a red velvet lady; I, in the gloom of Hamlet's aunt. The dinner was very long, and the conversation was about the Aristocracy—and Blood. Mrs. Waterbrook repeatedly told us, that if she had a weakness, it was Blood.

It occurred to me several times that we should have got on better, if we had not been quite so genteel. We were so exceedingly genteel, that our scope was very limited. A Mr. and Mrs. Gulpidge were of the party, who had something to do at second-hand (at least, Mr. Gulpidge had) with the law business of the Bank; and what with the Bank, and what with the Treasury, we were as exclusive as the Court Circular. To mend the matter, Hamlet's aunt had the family failing of indulging in soliloquy, and held forth in a desultory manner, by herself, on every topic that was introduced. These were few enough, to be sure; but as we always fell back upon Blood, she had as wide a field for abstract speculation as her nephew himself.

We might have been a party of Ogres, the conversation assumed such a sanguine complexion.

"I confess I am of Mrs. Waterbrook's opinion," said Mr. Waterbrook, with his wine-glass at his eye. "Other things are all very well in their way, but give me Blood!"

"Oh! There is nothing," observed Hamlet's aunt, "so satisfactory to one! There is nothing that is so much one's *beau-ideal* of—of all that sort of thing, speaking generally. There are some low minds (not many, I am happy to believe, but there are *some*) that would prefer to do what *I* should call bow down before idols. Positively Idols! Before service, intellect, and so on. But these are intangible points. Blood is not so. We see Blood in a nose, and we know it. We meet with it in a chin, and we say, 'There it is! That's Blood!' It is an actual matter of fact. We point it out. It admits of no doubt."

The simpering fellow with the weak legs, who had taken Agnes down, stated the question more decisively yet, I thought.

"Oh, you know, deuce take it," said this gentleman, looking round the board with an imbecile smile, "we can't forego Blood, you know. We must have Blood, you know. Some young fellows, you know, may be a little behind their station, perhaps, in point of education and behaviour, and may go a little wrong, you know, and get themselves and other people into a variety of fixes —and all that—but deuce take it, it's delightful to reflect that they've got Blood in 'em! Myself, I'd rather at any time be knocked down by a man who had got Blood in him, than I'd be picked up by a man who hadn't!"

This sentiment, as compressing the general question into a nutshell, gave the utmost satisfaction, and brought the gentleman into great notice until the ladies retired. After that, I observed that Mr. Gulpidge and Mr. Henry Spiker, who had hitherto been very distant, entered into a defensive alliance against us, the common enemy, and exchanged a mysterious dialogue across the table for our defeat and overthrow.

"The affair of the first bond for four thousand five hundred pounds has not taken the course that was expected, Spiker," said Mr. Gulpidge.

"Do you mean the D. of A's?" said Mr. Spiker.

"The C. of B's!" said Mr. Gulpidge.

Mr. Spiker raised his eyebrows, and looked much concerned.

"When the question was referred to Lord—I needn't name him," said Mr. Gulpidge, checking himself—

"I understand," said Mr. Spiker, "N."

Mr. Gulpidge darkly nodded—"was referred to him, his answer was, 'Money, or no release.'"

"Lord bless my soul!" cried Mr. Spiker.

"'Money, or no release,'" repeated Mr. Gulpidge, firmly. "The next in reversion—you understand me?"

"K.," said Mr. Spiker, with an ominous look.

"—K. then positively refused to sign. He was attended at Newmarket for that purpose, and he point-blank refused to do it."

Mr. Spiker was so interested, that he became quite stony.

"So the matter rests at this hour," said Mr. Gulpidge, throwing himself back in his chair. "Our friend Waterbrook will excuse me if I forbear to explain myself generally, on account of the magnitude of the interests involved."

Mr. Waterbrook was only too happy, as it appeared to me, to have such interests, and such names, even hinted at, across his table. He assumed an expression of gloomy intelligence (though I am persuaded he knew no more about the discussion than I did), and highly approved of the discretion that had been observed. Mr. Spiker, after the receipt of such a confidence, naturally desired to favour his friend with a confidence of his own; therefore the foregoing dialogue was succeeded by another, in which it was Mr. Gulpidge's turn to be surprised, and that by another in which the surprise came round to Mr. Spiker's turn again, and so on, turn and turn about. All this time we, the outsiders, remained oppressed by the tremendous interests involved in the conversation; and our host regarded us with pride, as the victims of a salutary awe and astonishment.

I was very glad indeed to get up-stairs to Agnes, and to talk with her in a corner, and to introduce Traddles to her, who was shy, but agreeable, and the same good-natured creature still. As he was obliged to leave early, on account of going away next morning for a month, I had not nearly so much conversation with him as I could have wished; but we exchanged addresses, and promised ourselves the pleasure of another meeting when he should come back to town. He was greatly interested to hear that I knew Steerforth, and spoke of him with such warmth that I made him tell Agnes what he thought of him. But Agnes only looked at me the while, and very slightly shook her head when only I observed her.

As she was not among people with whom I believed she could be very much at home, I was almost glad to hear that she was going away within a few days, though I was sorry at the prospect of parting from her again so soon. This caused me to remain until all the company were gone. Conversing with her, and hearing her sing, was such a delightful reminder to me of my happy life in the grave old house she had made so beautiful, that I could have remained there half the night; but, having no excuse for staying any longer, when the lights of Mr. Waterbrook's society were all snuffed out, I took my leave very much against my inclination. I felt then, more than ever, that she was my better Angel; and if I thought of her sweet face and placid smile, as though they had shone on me from some removed being, like an Angel, I hope I thought no harm.

I have said that the company were all gone; but I ought to have excepted Uriah, whom I don't include in that denomination, and who had never ceased to hover near us. He was close behind me when I went down-stairs. He was close beside me, when I walked away from the house, slowly fitting his long skeleton fingers into the still longer fingers of a great Guy Fawkes pair of gloves.

It was in no disposition for Uriah's company, but in remembrance of the entreaty Agnes had made to me, that I asked him if he would come home to my rooms, and have some coffee.

"Oh, really, Master Copperfield," he rejoined,—"I beg your pardon, Mister Copperfield, but the other comes so natural, I don't like that you should put a constraint upon yourself to ask an umble person like me to your ouse."

"There is no constraint in the case," said I. "Will you come?"

"I should like to, very much," replied Uriah, with a writhe.

"Well, then, come along!" said I.

I could not help being rather short with him, but he appeared not to mind it. We went the nearest way, without conversing much upon the road; and he was so humble in respect of those scarecrow gloves, that he was still putting them on, and seemed to have made no advance in that labour, when we got to my place.

I led him up the dark stairs, to prevent his knocking his head against anything, and really his damp cold hand felt so like a frog in mine, that I was tempted to drop it and run away. Agnes and hospitality prevailed, however, and I conducted him to my fireside. When I lighted my candles, he fell into meek transports with the room that was revealed to him; and when I heated the coffee in an unassuming block-tin vessel in which Mrs. Crupp delighted to prepare it (chiefly, I believe, because it was not intended for the purpose, being a shaving-pot, and because there was a patent invention of great price mouldering away in the pantry), he professed so much emotion, that I could joyfully have scalded him.

" Oh, really, Master Copperfield,—I mean Mister Copperfield," said Uriah, " to see you waiting upon me is what I never could have expected! But, one way and another, so many things happen to me which I never could have expected, I am sure, in my umble station, that it seems to rain blessings on my ed. You have heard something, I des-say, of a change in my expectations, Master Copperfield,—*I* should say, Mister Copperfield? "

As he sat on my sofa, with his long knees drawn up under his coffee-cup, his hat and gloves upon the ground close to him; his spoon going softly round and round, his shadowless red eyes, which looked as if they had scorched their lashes off, turned towards me without looking at me, the disagreeable dints I have formerly described in his nostrils coming and going with his breath, and a snaky undulation pervading his frame from his chin to his boots, I decided in my own mind that I disliked him intensely. It made me very uncomfortable to have him for a guest, for I was young then, and unused to disguise what I so strongly felt.

" You have heard something, I des-say, of a change in my expectations, Master Copperfield,—I should say, Mister Copperfield? " observed Uriah.

" Yes," said I, " something."

" Ah! I thought Miss Agnes would know of it! " he quietly returned. " I'm glad to find Miss Agnes knows of it. Oh, thank you, Master—Mister Copperfield! "

I could have thrown my bootjack at him (it lay ready on the rug), for having entrapped me into the disclosure of anything concerning Agnes, however immaterial. But I only drank my coffee.

"What a prophet you have shown yourself, Mister Copperfield!" pursued Uriah. "Dear me, what a prophet you have proved yourself to be! Don't you remember saying to me once, that perhaps I should be a partner in Mr. Wickfield's business, and perhaps it might be Wickfield and Heep? *You* may not recollect it; but when a person is umble, Master Copperfield, a person treasures such things up!"

"I recollect talking about it," said I, "though I certainly did not think it very likely then."

"Oh! who *would* have thought it likely, Mister Copperfield!" returned Uriah, enthusiastically. "I am sure I didn't myself. I recollect saying with my own lips that I was much too umble. So I considered myself really and truly."

He sat, with that carved grin on his face, looking at the fire, as I looked at him.

"But the umblest persons, Master Copperfield," he presently resumed, "may be the instruments of good. I am glad to think I have been the instrument of good to Mr. Wickfield, and that I may be more so. Oh what a worthy man he is, Mister Copperfield, but how imprudent he has been!"

"I am sorry to hear it," said I. I could not help adding, rather pointedly, "on all accounts."

"Decidedly so, Mister Copperfield," replied Uriah. "On all accounts. Miss Agnes's above all! You don't remember your own eloquent expressions, Master Copperfield; but *I* remember how you said one day that everybody must admire her, and how I thanked you for it! You have forgot that, I have no doubt, Master Copperfield?"

"No," said I, drily.

"Oh how glad I am you have not!" exclaimed Uriah. "To think that you should be the first to kindle the sparks of ambition in my umble breast, and that you've not forgot it! Oh!—Would you excuse me asking for a cup more coffee?"

Something in the emphasis he laid upon the kindling of those sparks, and something in the glance he directed at me as he said it, had made me start as if I had seen him illuminated by a blaze of light. Recalled by his request, preferred in quite another tone of voice, I did the honours of the shaving-pot; but I did them with an unsteadiness of hand, a sudden sense of being no match for him, and a perplexed suspicious anxiety as to what he might be going to say next, which I felt could not escape his observation.

He said nothing at all. He stirred his coffee round and round, he sipped it, he felt his chin softly with his grisly hand, he looked at the fire, he looked about the room, he gasped rather than smiled at me, he writhed and undulated about, in his deferential servility, he stirred and sipped again, but he left the renewal of the conversation to me.

"So, Mr. Wickfield," said I, at last, "who is worth five hundred of you—or me;" for my life, I think, I could not have helped dividing that part of the sentence with an awkward jerk; "has been imprudent, has he, Mr. Heep?"

"Oh, very imprudent indeed, Master Copperfield," returned Uriah, sighing modestly. "Oh, very much so! But I wish you'd call me Uriah, if you please. It's like old times."

"Well! Uriah," said I, bolting it out with some difficulty.

"Thank you," he returned, with fervour. "Thank you, Master Copperfield! It's like the blowing of old breezes or the ringing of old bellses to hear *you* say Uriah. I beg your pardon. Was I making any observation?"

"About Mr. Wickfield," I suggested.

"Oh! Yes, truly," said Uriah. "Ah! Great imprudence, Master Copperfield. It's a topic that I wouldn't touch upon, to any soul but you. Even to you I can only touch upon it, and no more. If any one else had been in my place during the last few years, by this time he would have had Mr. Wickfield (oh, what a worthy man he is, Master Copperfield, too!) under his thumb. Un—der—his thumb," said Uriah, very slowly, as he stretched out his cruel-looking hand above my table, and pressed his own thumb down upon it, until it shook, and shook the room.

If I had been obliged to look at him with his splay foot on Mr. Wickfield's head, I think I could scarcely have hated him more.

"Oh, dear, yes, Master Copperfield," he proceeded, in a soft voice, most remarkably contrasting with the action of his thumb, which did not diminish its hard pressure in the least degree, "there's no doubt of it. There would have been loss, disgrace, I don't know what all. Mr. Wickfield knows it. I am the umble instrument of umbly serving him, and he puts me on an eminence I hardly could have hoped to reach. How thankful should I be!" With his face turned towards me, as he finished, but without looking at me, he took his crooked thumb off the spot where he had planted it, and slowly and thoughtfully scraped his lank jaw with it, as if he were shaving himself.

I recollect well how indignantly my heart beat, as I saw his crafty face, with the appropriately red light of the fire upon it, preparing for something else.

"Master Copperfield," he began—"but am I keeping you up?"

"You are not keeping me up. I generally go to bed late."

"Thank you, Master Copperfield! I have risen from my umble station since first you used to address me, it is true; but I am umble still. I hope I never shall be otherwise than umble. You will not think the worse of my umbleness, if I make a little confidence to you, Master Copperfield? Will you?"

"Oh no," said I, with an effort.

"Thank you!" He took out his pocket-handkerchief, and began wiping the palms of his hands. "Miss Agnes, Master Copperfield—"

"Well, Uriah?"

"Oh, how pleasant to be called Uriah, spontaneously!" he cried; and gave himself a jerk, like a convulsive fish. "You thought her looking very beautiful to-night, Master Copperfield?"

"I thought her looking as she always does: superior, in all respects, to every one around her," I returned.

"Oh, thank you! It's so true!" he cried. "Oh, thank you very much for that!"

"Not at all," I said, loftily. "There is no reason why you should thank me."

"Why that, Master Copperfield," said Uriah, "is, in fact, the confidence that I am going to take the liberty of reposing. Umble as I am," he wiped his hands harder, and looked at them and at the fire by turns, "umble as my mother is, and lowly as our poor but honest roof has ever been, the image of Miss Agnes (I don't mind trusting you with my secret, Master Copperfield, for I have always overflowed towards you since the first moment I had the pleasure of beholding you in a ponyshay) has been in my breast for years. Oh, Master Copperfield, with what a pure affection do I love the ground my Agnes walks on!"

I believe I had a delirious idea of seizing the red-hot poker out of the fire, and running him through with it. It went from me with a shock, like a ball fired from a rifle: but the image of Agnes, outraged by so much as a thought of this red-headed animal's, remained in my mind (when I looked at him, sitting all awry as if his mean soul griped his body), and made me giddy. He seemed to swell and grow before my eyes; the room seemed full of the echoes of his voice; and the strange feeling (to which, perhaps, no one is quite a stranger) that all this had occurred before, at some indefinite time, and that I knew what he was going to say next, took possession of me.

A timely observation of the sense of power that there was in his face, did more to bring back to my remembrance the entreaty of Agnes, in its full force, than any effort I could have made. I asked him, with a better appearance of composure than I could have thought possible a minute before, whether he had made his feelings known to Agnes.

"Oh no, Master Copperfield!" he returned; "oh dear, no! Not to any one but you. You see I am only just emerging from my lowly station. I rest a good deal of hope on her observing how useful I am to her father (for I trust to be very useful to him indeed, Master Copperfield), and how I smooth the way for him, and keep him straight. She's so much attached to her father, Master Copperfield (oh, what a lovely thing it is in a daughter!), that I think she may come, on his account, to be kind to me."

I fathomed the depth of the rascal's whole scheme, and understood why he laid it bare.

"If you'll have the goodness to keep my secret, Master Copperfield," he pursued, "and not, in general, to go against me, I shall take it as a particular favour. You wouldn't wish to make unpleasantness. I know what a friendly heart you've got; but having only known me on my umble footing (on my umblest, I should say, for I am very umble still), you might, unbeknown, go against me rather, with my Agnes. I call her mine, you see, Master Copperfield. There's a song that says, 'I'd crowns resign, to call her mine!' I hope to do it, one of these days,"

Dear Agnes! So much too loving and too good for any one that I could think of, was it possible that she was reserved to be the wife of such a wretch as this!

"There's no hurry at present, you know, Master Copperfield," Uriah proceeded, in his slimy way, as I sat gazing at him, with this thought in my mind. "My Agnes is very young still; and mother and me will have to work our way upwards, and make a good many new arrangements, before it would be quite convenient. So I shall have time gradually to make her familiar with my hopes, as opportunities offer. Oh, I'm so much obliged to you for this confidence! Oh, it's such a relief, you can't think, to know that you understand our situation, and are certain (as you wouldn't wish to make unpleasantness in the family) not to go against me!"

He took the hand which I dared not withhold, and having given it a damp squeeze, referred to his pale-faced watch.

"Dear me!" he said, "it's past one. The moments slip away

so, in the confidence of old times, Master Copperfield, that it's almost half-past one!"

I answered that I had thought it was later. Not that I had really thought so, but because my conversational powers were effectually scattered.

"Dear me!" he said, considering. "The ouse that I am stopping at—a sort of a private hotel and boarding ouse, Master Copperfield, near the New River ed—will have gone to bed these two hours."

"I am sorry," I returned, "that there is only one bed here, and that I—"

"Oh, don't think of mentioning beds, Master Copperfield!" he rejoined ecstatically, drawing up one leg. "But *would* you have any objections to my laying down before the fire?"

"If it comes to that," I said, "pray take my bed, and I'll lie down before the fire."

His repudiation of this offer was almost shrill enough, in the excess of its surprise and humility, to have penetrated to the ears of Mrs. Crupp, then sleeping, I suppose, in a distant chamber, situated at about the level of low-water mark, soothed in her slumbers by the ticking of an incorrigible clock, to which she always referred me when we had any little difference on the score of punctuality, and which was never less than three-quarters of an hour too slow, and had always been put right in the morning by the best authorities. As no arguments I could urge, in my bewildered condition, had the least effect upon his modesty in inducing him to accept my bedroom, I was obliged to make the best arrangements I could, for his repose before the fire. The mattress of the sofa (which was a great deal too short for his lank figure), the sofa pillows, a blanket, the table-cover, a clean breakfast-cloth, and a greatcoat, made him a bed and covering, for which he was more than thankful. Having lent him a night-cap, which he put on at once, and in which he made such an awful figure, that I have never worn one since, I left him to his rest.

I never shall forget that night. I never shall forget how I turned and tumbled; how I wearied myself with thinking about Agnes and this creature; how I considered what could I do, and what ought I to do; how I could come to no other conclusion than that the best course for her peace was to do nothing, and to keep to myself what I had heard. If I went to sleep for a few moments, the image of Agnes with her tender eyes, and of her father looking fondly on her, as I had so often seen him look, arose before me with appealing faces, and filled me with vague terrors.

When I awoke, the recollection that Uriah was lying in the next room, sat heavy on me like a waking nightmare; and oppressed me with a leaden dread, as if I had had some meaner quality of devil for a lodger.

The poker got into my dozing thoughts besides, and wouldn't come out. I thought, between sleeping and waking, that it was still red hot, and I had snatched it out of the fire, and run him through the body. I was so haunted at last by the idea, though I knew there was nothing in it, that I stole into the next room to look at him. There I saw him, lying on his back, with his legs extending to I don't know where, gurglings taking place in his throat, stoppages in his nose, and his mouth open like a post-office. He was so much worse in reality than in my distempered fancy, that afterwards I was attracted to him in very repulsion, and could not help wandering in and out every half-hour or so, and taking another look at him. Still, the long, long night seemed heavy and hopeless as ever, and no promise of day was in the murky sky.

When I saw him going down-stairs early in the morning (for, thank Heaven! he would not stay to breakfast), it appeared to me as if the night was going away in his person. When I went out to the Commons, I charged Mrs. Crupp with particular directions to leave the windows open, that my sitting-room might be aired, and purged of his presence.

26

I FALL INTO CAPTIVITY

I SAW NO MORE OF URIAH HEEP UNTIL THE DAY WHEN Agnes left town. I was at the coach-office to take leave of her and see her go; and there was he, returning to Canterbury by the same conveyance. It was some small satisfaction to me to observe his spare, short-waisted, high-shouldered, mulberry-coloured great-coat perched up, in company with an umbrella like a small tent, on the edge of the back seat on the roof, while Agnes was, of course, inside; but what I underwent in my efforts to be friendly with him, while Agnes looked on, perhaps deserved that little recompense. At the coach-windows, as at the dinner-party, he hovered about us without a moment's intermission, like a great vulture: gorging himself on every syllable that I said to Agnes, or Agnes said to me.

In the state of trouble into which his disclosure by my fire had thrown me, I had thought very much of the words Agnes had used in reference to the partnership: "I did what I hope was right. Feeling sure that it was necessary for papa's peace that the sacrifice should be made, I entreated him to make it." A miserable foreboding that she would yield to, and sustain herself by, the same feeling in reference to any sacrifice for his sake, had oppressed me ever since. I knew how she loved him. I knew what the devotion of her nature was. I knew from her own lips that she regarded herself as the innocent cause of his errors, and as owing him a great debt she ardently desired to pay. I had no consolation in seeing how different she was from this detestable Rufus with the mulberry-coloured great-coat, for I felt that in the very difference between them, in the self-denial of her pure soul and the sordid baseness of his, the greatest danger lay. All this, doubtless, he knew thoroughly, and had, in his cunning, considered well.

Yet I was so certain that the prospect of such a sacrifice afar off, must destroy the happiness of Agnes; and I was so sure, from her manner, of its being unseen by her then, and having cast no shadow on her yet; that I could as soon have injured her, as given her any warning of what impended. Thus it was that we parted without explanation: she waving her hand and smiling farewell from the coach-window; her evil genius writhing on the roof, as if he had her in his clutches and triumphed.

I could not get over this farewell glimpse of them for a long time. When Agnes wrote to tell me of her safe arrival, I was as miserable as when I saw her going away. Whenever I fell into a thoughtful state, this subject was sure to present itself, and all my uneasiness was sure to be redoubled. Hardly a night passed without my dreaming of it. It became a part of my life, and as inseparable from my life as my own head.

I had ample leisure to refine upon my uneasiness: for Steerforth was at Oxford, as he wrote to me, and when I was not at the Commons, I was very much alone. I believe I had at this time some lurking distrust of Steerforth. I wrote to him most affectionately in reply to his, but I think I was glad, upon the whole, that he could not come to London just then. I suspect the truth to be, that the influence of Agnes was upon me, undisturbed by the sight of him; and that it was the more powerful with me, because she had so large a share in my thoughts and interest.

In the meantime, days and weeks slipped away. I was articled to Spenlow and Jorkins. I had ninety pounds a year (exclusive of my house-rent and sundry collateral matters) from my aunt. My rooms were engaged for twelve months certain: and though I still found them dreary of an evening, and the evenings long, I could settle down into a state of equable low spirits, and resign myself to coffee; which I seem, on looking back, to have taken by the gallon at about this period of my existence. At about this time, too, I made three discoveries: first, that Mrs. Crupp was a martyr to a curious disorder called " the spazzums," which was generally accompanied with inflammation of the nose, and required to be constantly treated with peppermint; secondly, that something peculiar in the temperature of my pantry made the brandy-bottles burst; thirdly, that I was alone in the world, and much given to record that circumstance in fragments of English versification.

On the day when I was articled, no festivity took place, beyond my having sandwiches and sherry into the office for the clerks, and going alone to the theatre at night. I went to see " The Stranger " as a Doctors' Commons sort of play, and was so dreadfully cut up, that I hardly knew myself in my own glass when I got home. Mr. Spenlow remarked, on this occasion, when we concluded our business, that he should have been happy to have seen me at his house at Norwood to celebrate our becoming connected, but for his domestic arrangements being in some disorder, on account of the expected return of his daughter from finishing her education at Paris. But he intimated that when she came home he should hope to have the pleasure of entertaining me. I knew that he was a widower with one daughter, and expressed my acknowledgments.

Mr. Spenlow was as good as his word. In a week or two, he referred to this engagement, and said, that if I would do him the favour to come down next Saturday, and stay till Monday, he would be extremely happy. Of course I said I *would* do him the favour; and he was to drive me down in his phaeton, and to bring me back.

When the day arrived, my very carpet-bag was an object of veneration to the stipendiary clerks, to whom the house at Norwood was a sacred mystery. One of them informed me that he had heard that Mr. Spenlow ate entirely off plate and china; and another hinted at champagne being constantly on draught, after the usual custom of table beer. The old clerk with the wig, whose name was Mr. Tiffey, had been down on business several times in the course of his career, and had on each occasion penetrated to the breakfast-parlour. He described it as an apartment of the most sumptuous nature, and said that he had drunk brown East India sherry there, of a quality so precious as to make a man wink.

We had an adjourned cause in the Consistory that day—about excommunicating a baker who had been objecting in a vestry to a paving-rate—and as the evidence was just twice the length of Robinson Crusoe, according to a calculation I made, it was rather late in the day before we finished. However, we got him excommunicated for six weeks, and sentenced in no end of costs; and then the baker's proctor, and the judge, and the advocates on both sides (who were all nearly related), went out of town together, and Mr. Spenlow and I drove away in the phaeton.

The phaeton was a very handsome affair; the horses arched their necks and lifted up their legs as if they knew they belonged to Doctors' Commons. There was a good deal of competition in the Commons on all points of display, and it turned out some very choice equipages then; though I always have considered, and always shall consider, that in my time the great article of competition there was starch: which I think was worn among the proctors to as great an extent as it is in the nature of man to bear.

We were very pleasant, going down, and Mr. Spenlow gave me some hints in reference to my profession. He said it was the genteelest profession in the world, and must on no account be confounded with the profession of a solicitor: being quite another sort of thing, infinitely more exclusive, less mechanical, and more profitable. We took things much more easily in the Commons than they could be taken anywhere else, he observed, and that set us, as a privileged class, apart. He said it was impossible to conceal the disagreeable fact, that we were chiefly employed by solicitors; but he gave me to understand that they were an inferior race of men, universally looked down upon by all proctors of any pretensions.

I asked Mr. Spenlow what he considered the best sort of professional business? He replied, that a good case of a disputed will, where there was a neat little estate of thirty or forty thousand pounds, was, perhaps, the best of all. In such a case, he said, not only were there very pretty pickings, in the way of arguments at every stage of the proceedings, and mountains upon mountains of evidence on interrogatory and counter-interrogatory (to say nothing of an appeal lying, first to the Delegates, and then to the Lords) but, the costs being pretty sure to come out of the estate at last, both sides went at it in a lively and spirited manner, and expense was no consideration. Then, he launched into a general eulogium on the Commons. What was to be particularly admired (he said) in the Commons, was its compactness. It was the most conveniently organised place in the world. It was the complete idea of snugness. It lay in a nut-shell. For example: You brought a divorce case, or a restitution case, into the Consistory. Very good. You tried it in the Consistory. You made a quiet little round game of it, among a family group, and you played it out at leisure. Suppose you were not satisfied with the Consistory, what did you do then? Why, you went into the Arches. What was the Arches? The same court, in the same room, with the same bar, and the same practitioners, but another judge, for there the Consistory judge could plead any court-day as an advocate. Well, you played your round game out again. Still you were not satisfied. Very good. What did you do then? Why, you went to the Delegates. Who were the Delegates? Why, the Ecclesiastical Delegates were the advocates without any business, who had looked on at the round game when it was playing in both courts, and had seen the cards shuffled, and cut, and played, and had talked to all the players about it, and now came fresh, as judges, to settle the matter to the satisfaction of everybody! Discontented people might talk of corruption in the Commons, closeness in the Commons, and the necessity of reforming the Commons, said Mr. Spenlow solemnly, in conclusion; but when the price of wheat per bushel had been highest, the Commons had been busiest; and a man might lay his hand upon his heart, and say this to the whole world,—"Touch the Commons, and down comes the country!"

I listened to all this with attention; and though, I must say, I had my doubts whether the country was quite as much obliged to the Commons as Mr. Spenlow made out, I respectfully deferred to his opinion. That about the price of wheat per bushel, I modestly felt was too much for my strength, and quite settled the question. I have never, to this hour, got the better of that bushel of wheat. It has re-appeared to annihilate me, all through my life, in connection with all kinds of subjects. I don't know now, exactly, what it has to do with me, or what right it has to crush me, on an infinite variety of occasions; but whenever I see my old friend the bushel brought in by the head and shoulders (as he always is, I observe), I give up a subject for lost.

This is a digression. *I* was not the man to touch the Commons, and bring down the country. I submissively expressed by my silence, my acquiescence in all I had heard from my superior in years and knowledge; and we talked about "The Stranger" and the Drama, and the pair of horses, until we came to Mr. Spenlow's gate.

There was a lovely garden to Mr. Spenlow's house; and though that was not the best time of the year for seeing a garden, it was so beautifully kept, that I was quite enchanted. There was a charming lawn, there were clusters of trees, and there were perspective walks that I could just distinguish in the dark, arched over with trellis-work, on which shrubs and flowers grew in the growing season. "Here Miss Spenlow walks by herself," I thought. "Dear me!"

We went into the house, which was cheerfully lighted up, and into a hall where there were all sorts of hats, caps, great-coats, plaids, gloves, whips, and walking-sticks. "Where is Miss Dora?" said Mr. Spenlow to the servant. "Dora!" I thought. "What a beautiful name!"

We turned into a room near at hand (I think it was the identical breakfast-room, made memorable by the brown East Indian sherry), and I heard a voice say, "Mr. Copperfield, my daughter Dora, and my daughter Dora's confidential friend!" It was, no doubt, Mr. Spenlow's voice, but I didn't know it, and I didn't care whose it was. All was over in a moment. I had fulfilled my destiny. I was a captive and a slave. I loved Dora Spenlow to distraction!

She was more than human to me. She was a Fairy, a Sylph, I don't know what she was—anything that no one ever saw, and everything that everybody ever wanted. I was swallowed up in an abyss of love in an instant. There was no pausing on the brink; no looking down, or looking back; I was gone, headlong, before I had sense to say a word to her.

"*I*," observed a well-remembered voice, when I had bowed and murmured something, "have seen Mr. Copperfield before."

The speaker was not Dora. No; the confidential friend, Miss Murdstone!

I don't think I was much astonished. To the best of my judgment, no capacity of astonishment was left in me. There was nothing worth mentioning in the material world, but Dora Spenlow, to be astonished about. I said, "How do you do, Miss Murdstone? I hope you are well." She answered, "Very well." I said, "How is Mr. Murdstone?" She replied, "My brother is robust, I am obliged to you."

Mr. Spenlow, who, I suppose, had been surprised to see us recognise each other, then put in his word.

"I am glad to find," he said, "Copperfield, that you and Miss Murdstone are already acquainted."

"Mr. Copperfield and myself," said Miss Murdstone, with severe composure, "are connections. We were once slightly acquainted. It was in his childish days. Circumstances have separated us since. I should not have known him."

I replied that I should have known her, anywhere. Which was true enough.

"Miss Murdstone has had the goodness," said Mr. Spenlow to me, "to accept the office—if I may so describe it—of my daughter Dora's confidential friend. My daughter Dora having, unhappily, no mother, Miss Murdstone is obliging enough to become her companion and protector."

A passing thought occurred to me that Miss Murdstone, like the pocket instrument called a life-preserver, was not so much designed for purposes of protection as of assault. But as I had none but passing thoughts for any subject save Dora, I glanced at her, directly afterwards, and was thinking that I saw, in her prettily pettish manner, that she was not very much inclined to be particularly confidential to her companion and protector, when a bell rang, which Mr. Spenlow said was the first dinner-bell, and so carried me off to dress.

The idea of dressing one's self, or doing anything in the way of action, in that state of love, was a little too ridiculous. I could only sit down before my fire, biting the key of my carpet-bag, and think of the captivating, girlish, bright-eyed, lovely Dora. What a form she had, what a face she had, what a graceful, variable, enchanting manner!

The bell rang again so soon that I made a mere scramble of my dressing, instead of the careful operation I could have wished under the circumstances, and went downstairs. There was some company. Dora was talking to an old gentleman with a grey head. Grey as he was—and a great-grandfather into the bargain, for he said so—I was madly jealous of him.

What a state of mind I was in! I was jealous of everybody. I couldn't bear the idea of anybody knowing Mr. Spenlow better than I did. It was torturing to me to hear them talk of occurrences in which I had had no share. When a most amiable person, with a highly polished bald head, asked me across the dinner-table, if that were the first occasion of my seeing the grounds, I could have done anything to him that was savage and revengeful.

I don't remember who was there, except Dora. I have not the least idea what we had for dinner, besides Dora. My impression is, that I dined off Dora entirely, and sent away half-a-dozen plates untouched. I sat next to her. I talked to her. She had the most delightful little voice, the gayest little laugh, the pleasantest and most fascinating little ways, that ever led a lost youth into hopeless slavery. She was rather diminutive altogether. So much the more precious, I thought.

When she went out of the room with Miss Murdstone (no other ladies were of the party), I fell into a reverie, only disturbed by the cruel apprehension that Miss Murdstone would disparage me to her. The amiable creature with the polished head told me a long story, which I think was about gardening. I think I heard him say, " my gardener," several times. I seemed to pay the deepest attention to him, but I was wandering in a garden of Eden all the while, with Dora.

My apprehension of being disparaged to the object of my engrossing affection were revived when we went into the drawing-room, by the grim and distant aspect of Miss Murdstone. But I was relieved of them in an unexpected manner.

" David Copperfield," said Miss Murdstone, beckoning me aside into a window. " A word."

I confronted Miss Murdstone alone.

" David Copperfield," said Miss Murdstone, " I need not enlarge upon family circumstances. They are not a tempting subject."

" Far from it, ma'am," I returned.

" Far from it," assented Miss Murdstone. " I do not wish to revive the memory of past differences, or of past outrages. I have received outrages from a person—a female, I am sorry to say, for the credit of my sex—who is not to be mentioned without scorn and disgust; and therefore I would rather not mention her."

I felt very fiery on my aunt's account; but I said it would certainly be better, if Miss Murdstone pleased, *not* to mention her. I could not hear her disrespectfully mentioned, I added, without expressing my opinion in a decided tone.

Miss Murdstone shut her eyes, and disdainfully inclined her head; then, slowly opening her eyes, resumed:

" David Copperfield, I shall not attempt to disguise the fact, that I formed an unfavourable opinion of you in your childhood. It may have been a mistaken one, or you may have ceased to justify it. That is not in question between us now. I belong to a family remarkable, I believe, for some firmness; and I am not the creature of circumstance or change. I may have my opinion of you. You may have your opinion of me."

I inclined my head, in my turn.

"But it is not necessary," said Miss Murdstone, "that these opinions should come into collision here. Under existing circumstances, it is as well on all accounts that they should not. As the chances of life have brought us together again, and may bring us together on other occasions, I would say, let us meet here as distant acquaintances. Family circumstances are a sufficient reason for our only meeting on that footing, and it is quite unnecessary that either of us should make the other the subject of remark. Do you approve of this?"

"Miss Murdstone," I returned, "I think you and Mr. Murdstone used me very cruelly, and treated my mother with great unkindness. I shall always think so, as long as I live. But I quite agree in what you propose."

Miss Murdstone shut her eyes again, and bent her head. Then, just touching the back of my hand with the tips of her cold, stiff fingers, she walked away, arranging the little fetters on her wrists and round her neck; which seemed to be the same set, in exactly the same state, as when I had seen her last. These reminded me, in reference to Miss Murdstone's nature, of the fetters over a jail-door; suggesting on the outside, to all beholders, what was to be expected within.

All I know of the rest of the evening is, that I heard the empress of my heart sing enchanted ballads in the French language, generally to the effect that, whatever was the matter, we ought always to dance, Ta ra la, Ta ra la! accompanying herself on a glorified instrument, resembling a guitar. That I was lost in blissful delirium. That I refused refreshment. That my soul recoiled from punch particularly. That when Miss Murdstone took her into custody and led her away, she smiled and gave me her delicious hand. That I caught a view of myself in a mirror, looking perfectly imbecile and idiotic. That I retired to bed in a most maudlin state of mind, and got up in a crisis of feeble infatuation.

It was a fine morning, and early, and I thought I would go and take a stroll down one of those wire-arched walks, and indulge my passion by dwelling on her image. On my way through the hall, I encountered her little dog, who was called Jip—short for Gipsy. I approached him tenderly, for I loved even him; but he showed his whole set of teeth, got under a chair expressly to snarl, and wouldn't hear of the least familiarity.

The garden was cool and solitary. I walked about, wondering

what my feelings of happiness would be, if I could ever become engaged to this dear wonder. As to marriage, and fortune, and all that, I believe I was almost as innocently undesigning then, as when I loved little Em'ly. To be allowed to call her "Dora," to write to her, to dote upon and worship her, to have reason to think that when she was with other people she was yet mindful of me, seemed to me the summit of human ambition—I am sure it was the summit of mine. There is no doubt whatever that I was a lackadaisical young spooney; but there was a purity of heart in all this, that prevents my having quite a contemptuous recollection of it, let me laugh as I may.

I had not been walking long, when I turned a corner, and met her. I tingle again from head to foot as my recollection turns that corner, and my pen shakes in my hand.

"You—are—out early, Miss Spenlow," said I.

"It's so stupid at home," she replied, "and Miss Murdstone is so absurd! She talks such nonsense about its being necessary for the day to be aired, before I come out. Aired!" (She laughed, here, in the most melodious manner.) "On a Sunday morning, when I don't practise, I must do something. So I told papa last night I *must* come out. Besides, it's the brightest time of the whole day. Don't you think so?"

I hazarded a bold flight, and said (not without stammering) that it was very bright to me then, though it had been very dark to me a minute before.

"Do you mean a compliment?" said Dora, "or that the weather has really changed?"

I stammered worse than before, in replying that I meant no compliment, but in plain truth; though I was not aware of any change having taken place in the weather. It was in the state of my own feelings, I added bashfully: to clench the explanation.

I never saw such curls—how could I, for there never were such curls!—as those she shook out to hide her blushes. As to the straw hat and blue ribbons which was on the top of the curls, if I could only have hung it up in my room in Buckingham Street, what a priceless possession it would have been!"

"You have just come home from Paris," said I.

"Yes," said she. "Have you ever been there?"

"No."

"Oh! I hope you'll go soon! You would like it so much!"

Traces of deep-seated anguish appeared in my countenance. That she should hope I would go, that she should think it possible I *could* go, was insupportable. I depreciated Paris; I depreciated France. I said I wouldn't leave England, under existing circumstances, for any earthly consideration. Nothing should induce me. In short, she was shaking the curls again, when the little dog came running along the walk to our relief.

He was mortally jealous of me, and persisted in barking at me. She took him up in her arms—oh my goodness!—and caressed him, but he persisted upon barking still. He wouldn't let me touch him, when I tried; and then she beat him. It increased my sufferings greatly to see the pats she gave him for punishment on the bridge of his blunt nose, while he winked his eyes, and licked her hand, and still growled within himself like a little double-bass. At length he was quiet—well he might be with her dimpled chin upon his head!—and we walked away to look at a greenhouse.

"You are not very intimate with Miss Murdstone, are you?" said Dora.—"My pet."

(The two last words were to the dog. Oh, if they had only been to me!)

"No," I replied. "Not at all so."

"She is a tiresome creature," said Dora, pouting. "I can't think what papa can have been about, when he chose such a vexatious thing to be my companion. Who wants a protector? I am sure *I* don't want a protector. Jip can protect me a great deal better than Miss Murdstone,—can't you, Jip, dear?"

He only winked lazily, when she kissed his ball of a head.

"Papa calls her my confidential friend, but I am sure she is no such thing—is she, Jip? We are not going to confide in any such cross people, Jip and I. We mean to bestow our confidence where we like, and to find out our own friends, instead of having them found out for us—don't we, Jip?"

Jip made a comfortable noise, in answer, a little like a tea-kettle when it sings. As for me, every word was a new heap of fetters, riveted above the last.

"It is very hard, because we have not a kind Mama, that we are to have, instead, a sulky, gloomy old thing like Miss Murdstone, always following us about—isn't it, Jip? Never mind, Jip. We won't be confidential, and we'll make ourselves as happy as we can in spite of her, and we'll tease her, and not please her—won't we, Jip?"

If it had lasted any longer, I think I must have gone down on my knees on the gravel, with the probability before me of grazing them, and of being presently ejected from the premises besides. But by good fortune the greenhouse was not far off, and these words brought us to it.

It contained quite a show of beautiful geraniums. We loitered along in front of them, and Dora often stopped to admire this one or that one, and I stopped to admire the same one, and Dora, laughing, held the dog up childishly, to smell the flowers; and if we were not all three in Fairyland, certainly *I* was. The scent of a geranium leaf, at this day, strikes me with a half comical, half serious wonder as to what change has come over me in a moment; and then I see a straw hat and blue ribbons, and a quantity of curls, and a little black dog being held up, in two slender arms, against a bank of blossoms and bright leaves.

Miss Murdstone had been looking for us. She found us here; and presented her uncongenial cheek, the little wrinkles in it filled with hair powder, to Dora to be kissed. Then she took Dora's arm in hers, and marched us into breakfast as if it were a soldier's funeral.

How many cups of tea I drank, because Dora made it, I don't know. But I perfectly remember that I sat swilling tea until my whole nervous system, if I had had any in those days, must have gone by the board. By-and-bye we went to church. Miss Murdstone was between Dora and me in the pew; but I heard her sing, and the congregation vanished. A sermon was delivered—about Dora, of course—and I am afraid that is all I know of the service.

We had a quiet day. No company, a walk, a family dinner of four, and an evening of looking over books and pictures; Miss Murdstone with a homily before her, and her eye upon us, keeping guard vigilantly. Ah! little did Mr. Spenlow imagine, when he sat opposite to me after dinner that day, with his pocket-handkerchief over his head, how fervently I was embracing him, in my fancy, as his son-in-law! Little did he think, when I took leave of him at night, that he had just given his full consent to my being engaged to Dora, and that I was invoking blessings on his head!

We departed early in the morning, for we had a Salvage case coming on in the Admiralty Court, requiring a rather accurate knowledge of the whole science of navigation, in which (as we couldn't be expected to know much about those matters in the Commons) the judge had entreated two old Trinity Masters, for charity's sake, to come and help him out. Dora was at the breakfast-table to make the tea again, however; and I had the melancholy pleasure of taking off my hat to her in the phaeton, as she stood on the door-step with Jip in her arms.

What the Admiralty was to me that day; what nonsense I made of our case in my mind, as I listened to it; how I saw "DORA" engraved upon the blade of the silver oar which they lay upon the table, as the emblem of that high jurisdiction; and how I felt when Mr. Spenlow went home without me (I had had an insane hope that he might take me back again), as if I were a mariner myself, and the ship to which I belonged had sailed away and left me on a desert island; I shall make no fruitless effort to describe. If that sleepy old court could rouse itself, and present in any visible form the day-dreams I have had in it about Dora, it would reveal my truth.

I don't mean the dreams that I dreamed on that day alone, but day after day, from week to week, and term to term. I went there, not to attend to what was going on, but to think about Dora. If ever I bestowed a thought upon the cases, as they dragged their slow length before me, it was only to wonder, in the matrimonial cases (remembering Dora), how it was that married people could ever be otherwise than happy; and, in the Prerogative cases, to consider, if the money in question had been left to me, what were the foremost steps I should immediately have taken in regard to Dora. Within the first week of my passion, I bought four sumptuous waistcoats—not for myself; *I* had no pride in them; for Dora—and took to wearing straw-coloured kid gloves in the streets, and laid the foundations of all the corns I have ever had. If the boots I wore at that period could only be produced and compared with the natural size of my feet, they would show what the state of my heart was, in a most affecting manner.

And yet, wretched cripple as I made myself by this act of homage to Dora, I walked miles upon miles daily in the hope of seeing her. Not only was I soon as well known on the Norwood Road as the postmen on the beat, but I pervaded London likewise. I walked about the streets where the best shops for ladies were, I haunted the Bazaar like an unquiet spirit, I fagged through the Park again and again, long after I was quite knocked up. Sometimes, at long intervals and on rare occasions, I saw her. Perhaps I saw her glove waved in a carriage window; perhaps I met her, walked with her and Miss Murdstone a little way, and spoke to her. In the latter case I was always very miserable afterwards, to think that I had said nothing to the purpose; or that she had no idea of the extent of my devotion, or that she cared nothing about me. I was always looking out, as may be supposed, for another invitation to Mr. Spenlow's house. I was always being disappointed, for I got none.

Mrs. Crupp must have been a woman of penetration; for when this attachment was but a few weeks old, and I had not had the courage to write more explicitly even to Agnes, than that I had been to Mr. Spenlow's house, " whose family," I added, " consists of one daughter; "—I say Mrs. Crupp must have been a woman of penetration, for, even in that early stage, she found it out. She came up to me one evening, when I was very low, to ask (she being then afflicted with the disorder I have mentioned) if I could oblige her with a little tincture of cardamums mixed with rhubarb, and flavoured with seven drops of the essence of cloves, which was the best remedy for her complaint;—or, if I had not such a thing by me, with a little brandy, which was the next best. It was not, she remarked, so palatable to her, but it was the next best. As I had never even heard of the first remedy, and always had the second in the closet, I gave Mrs. Crupp a glass of the second, which (that I might have no suspicion of its being devoted to any improper use) she began to take in my presence.

" Cheer up, sir," said Mrs. Crupp. " I can't abear to see you so, sir; I'm a mother myself."

I did not quite perceive the application of this fact to *my*self. but I smiled on Mrs. Crupp, as benignly as was in my power.

" Come, sir," said Mrs. Crupp. " Excuse me. I know what it is, sir. There's a lady in the case."

" Mrs. Crupp? " I returned, reddening.

" Oh, bless you! Keep a good heart, sir! " said Mrs. Crupp, nodding encouragement. " Never say die, sir! If She don't smile upon you, there's a many as will. You are a young gentleman to *be* smiled on, Mr. Copperfull, and you must learn your walue, sir."

Mrs. Crupp always called me Mr. Copperfull: firstly, no doubt, because it was not my name; and secondly, I am inclined to think, in some indistinct association with a washing-day.

" What makes you suppose there is any young lady in the case, Mrs. Crupp? " said I.

" Mr. Copperfull," said Mrs. Crupp, with a great deal of feeling, " I'm a mother myself."

For some time Mrs. Crupp could only lay her hand upon her nankeen bosom, and fortify herself against returning pain with sips of her medicine. At length she spoke again.

" When the present set were took for you by your dear aunt, Mr. Copperfull," said Mrs. Crupp, " my remark were, I had now found summun I could care for. 'Thank Ev'in!' were the expression, 'I have now found summun I can care for!'—You don't eat enough, sir, nor yet drink."

" Is that what you found your supposition on, Mrs. Crupp? " said I.

" Sir," said Mrs. Crupp, in a tone approaching to severity,

"I've laundressed other young gentlemen besides yourself. A young gentleman may be over-careful of himself, or he may be under-careful of himself. He may brush his hair too regular, or too unregular. He may wear his boots much too large for him, or much too small. That is according as the young gentleman has his original character formed. But let him go to which extreme he may, sir, there's a young lady in both of 'em."

Mrs. Crupp shook her head in such a determined manner, that I had not an inch of vantage-ground left.

"It was but the gentleman which died here before yourself," said Mrs. Crupp, "that fell in love—with a barmaid—and had his waistcoasts took in directly, though much swelled by drinking."

"Mrs. Crupp," said I, "I must beg you not to connect the young lady in my case with a barmaid, or anything of that sort, if you please."

"Mr. Copperfull," returned Mrs. Crupp, "I'm a mother myself, and not likely. I ask your pardon, sir, if I intrude. I should never wish to intrude where I were not welcome. But you are a young gentleman, Mr. Copperfull, and my adwice to you is, to cheer up, sir, and keep a good heart, and to know your own walue. If you was to take to something, sir," said Mrs. Crupp, "if you was to take to skittles, now, which is healthy, you might find it divert your mind, and do you good."

With these words, Mrs. Crupp, affecting to be very careful of the brandy—which was all gone—thanked me with a majestic curtsey, and retired. As her figure disappeared into the gloom of the entry, this counsel certainly presented itself to my mind in the light of a slight liberty on Mrs. Crupp's part; but, at the same time, I was content to receive it, in another point of view, as a word to the wise, and a warning in future to keep my secret better.

27

TOMMY TRADDLES

IT MAY HAVE BEEN IN CONSEQUENCE OF MRS. CRUPP'S advice and, perhaps, for no better reason than because there was a certain similarity in the sound of the word skittles and Traddles, that it came into my head, next day, to go and look after Traddles. The time he had mentioned was more than out, and he lived in a little street near the Veterinary College at Camden Town, which was principally tenanted, as one of our clerks who lived in that direction informed me, by gentlemen students, who bought live donkeys, and made experiments on those quadrupeds in their private apartments. Having obtained from this clerk a direction to the academic grove in question, I set out, the same afternoon, to visit my old schoolfellow.

I found that the street was not as desirable a one as I could have wished it to be, for the sake of Traddles. The inhabitants appeared to have a propensity to throw any little trifles they were not in want of, into the road; which not only made it rank and sloppy, but untidy too, on account of the cabbage-leaves. The refuse was not wholly vegetable either, for I myself saw a shoe, a doubled-up saucepan, a black bonnet, and an umbrella, in various stages of decomposition, as I was looking out for the number I wanted.

The general air of the place reminded me forcibly of the days when I lived with Mr. and Mrs. Micawber. An indescribable character of faded gentility that attached to the house I sought, and made it unlike all the other houses in the street—though they were all built on one monotonous pattern, and looked like the early copies of a blundering boy who was learning to make houses, and had not yet got out of his cramped brick-and-mortar pothooks—reminded me still more of Mr. and Mrs. Micawber. Happening to arrive at the door as it was opened to the afternoon milkman, I was reminded of Mr. and Mrs. Micawber more forcibly yet.

"Now," said the milkman to a very youthful servant girl. "Has that there little bill of mine been heerd on?"

"Oh, master says he'll attend to it immediate," was the reply.

"Because," said the milkman, going on as if he had received no answer, and speaking, as I judged from his tone, rather for the edification of somebody within the house, than of the youthful servant—an impression which was strengthened by his manner of glaring down the passage—"because that there little bill has been running so long, that I begin to believe it's run away altogether, and never won't be heerd of. Now, I'm not a going to stand it, you know!" said the milkman, still throwing his voice into the house, and glaring down the passage.

As to his dealing in the mild article of milk, by-the-bye, there never was a greater anomaly. His deportment would have been fierce in a butcher or a brandy-merchant.

The voice of the youthful servant became faint, but she seemed to me, from the action of her lips, again to murmur that it would be attended to immediate.

"I tell you what," said the milkman, looking hard at her for the first time, and taking her by the chin, "are you fond of milk?"

"Yes, I likes it," she replied.

"Good," said the milkman. "Then you won't have none to-morrow. D'ye hear? Not a fragment of milk you won't have to-morrow."

I thought she seemed, upon the whole, relieved by the prospect of having any to-day. The milkman, after shaking his head at her darkly, released her chin, and with anything rather than good-will opened his can, and deposited the usual quantity in the family jug. This done, he went away, muttering, and uttered the cry of his trade next door, in a vindictive shriek.

"Does Mr. Traddles live here?" I then inquired.

A mysterious voice from the end of the passage replied "Yes." Upon which the youthful servant replied "Yes."

"Is he at home?" said I.

Again the mysterious voice replied in the affirmative, and again the servant echoed it. Upon this, I walked in, and in pursuance of the servant's directions walked up-stairs; conscious, as I passed the back parlour-door, that I was surveyed by a mysterious eye, probably belonging to the mysterious voice.

When I got to the top of the stairs—the house was only a story high above the ground floor—Traddles was on the landing to meet me. He was delighted to see me, and gave me welcome, with great heartiness, to his little room. It was in the front of the house, and extremely neat, though sparely furnished. It was his only room, I saw; for there was a sofa-bedstead in it, and his blacking-brushes and blacking were among his books—on the top shelf, behind a dictionary. His table was covered with papers, and he was hard at work in an old coat. I looked at nothing, that I know of, but I saw everything, even to the prospect of a church upon his china inkstand, as I sat down—and this, too, was a faculty confirmed in me in the old Micawber times. Various ingenious arrangements he had made, for the disguise of his chest of drawers, and the accommodation of his boots, his shaving-glass, and so forth, particularly impressed themselves upon me, as evidences of the same Traddles who used to make models of elephants' dens in writing-paper to put flies in; and to comfort himself under ill usage, with the memorable works of art I have so often mentioned.

In a corner of the room was something neatly covered up with a large white cloth. I could not make out what that was.

"Traddles," said I, shaking hands with him again, after I had sat down, "I am delighted to see you."

"I am delighted to see *you*, Copperfield," he returned. "I am very glad indeed to see you. It was because I was thoroughly glad to see you when we met in Ely Place, and was sure you were thoroughly glad to see me, that I gave you this address instead of my address at chambers."

"Oh! You have chambers?" said I.

"Why, I have the fourth of a room and a passage, and the fourth of a clerk," returned Traddles. "Three others and myself unite to have a set of chambers—to look business-like—and we quarter the clerk too. Half-a-crown a week he costs me."

His old simple character and good temper, and something of his old unlucky fortune also, I thought, smiled at me in the smile with which he made this explanation.

"It's not because I have the least pride, Copperfield, you understand," said Traddles, "that I don't usually give my address here. It's only on account of those who come to me, who might not like to come here. For myself, I am fighting my way on in the world against difficulties, and it would be ridiculous if I made a pretence of doing anything else."

"You are reading for the bar, Mr. Waterbrook informed me?" said I.

"Why, yes," said Traddles, rubbing his hands, slowly over one another. "I am reading for the bar. The fact is, I have just begun to keep my terms, after rather a long delay. It's some time since I was articled, but the payment of that hundred pounds was a great pull. A great pull!" said Traddles, with a wince, as if he had had a tooth out.

"Do you know what I can't help thinking of, Traddles, as I sit here looking at you?" I asked him.

"No," said he.

"That sky-blue suit you used to wear."

"Lord, to be sure!" cried Traddles, laughing. "Tight in the arms and legs, you know? Dear me! Well! Those were happy times, weren't they?"

"I think our schoolmaster might have made them happier, without doing any harm to any of us, I acknowledge," I returned.

"Perhaps he might," said Traddles. "But dear me, there was a good deal of fun going on. Do you remember the nights in the bedroom? When we used to have the suppers? And when you used to tell the stories? Ha, ha, ha! And do you remember when I got caned for crying about Mr. Mell? Old Creakle! I should like to see him again, too!"

"He was a brute to you, Traddles," said I, indignantly; for his good-humour made me feel as if I had seen him beaten but yesterday.

"Do you think so?" returned Traddles. "Really? Perhaps he was, rather. But it's all over, a long while. Old Creakle!"

"You were brought up by an uncle, then?" said I.

"Of course I was!" said Traddles. "The one I was always going to write to. And always didn't, eh! Ha, ha, ha! Yes, I had an uncle then. He died soon after I left school."

"Indeed!"

"Yes. He was a retired—what do you call it!—draper—cloth-merchant—and had made me his heir. But he didn't like me when I grew up."

"Do you really mean that?" said I. He was so composed, that I fancied he must have some other meaning.

"Oh dear, yes, Copperfield! I mean it," replied Traddles. "It was an unfortunate thing, but he didn't like me at all. He said I wasn't at all what he expected, and so he married his housekeeper."

"And what did you do?" I asked.

"I didn't do anything in particular," said Traddles. "I lived with them, waiting to be put out in the world, until his gout unfortunately flew to his stomach—and so he died, and so she married a young man, and so I wasn't provided for."

"Did you get nothing, Traddles, after all?"

"Oh dear, yes!" said Traddles. "I got fifty pounds. I had never been brought up to any profession, and at first I was at a loss what to do for myself. However, I began, with the assistance of the son of a professional man, who had been to Salem House

—Yawler, with his nose on one side. Do you recollect him?"

No. He had not been there with me; all the noses were straight in my day.

"It don't matter," said Traddles. "I began, by means of his assistance, to copy law writings. That didn't answer very well; and then I began to state cases for them, and make abstracts, and do that sort of work. For I am a plodding kind of fellow, Copperfield, and had learnt the way of doing such things pithily. Well! That put it in my head to enter myself as a law student; and that ran away with all that was left of the fifty pounds. Yawler recommended me to one or two other offices, however—Mr. Waterbrook's for one—and I got a good many jobs. I was fortunate enough, too, to become acquainted with a person in the publishing way, who was getting up an Encyclopaedia, and he set me to work; and, indeed" (glancing at his table), "I am at work for him at this minute. I am not a bad compiler, Copperfield," said Traddles, preserving the same air of cheerful confidence in all he said, "but I have no invention at all; not a particle. I suppose there never was a young man with less originality than I have."

As Traddles seemed to expect that I should assent to this as a matter of course, I nodded; and he went on, with the same sprightly patience—I can find no better expression—as before.

"So, by little and little, and not living high, I managed to scrape up the hundred pounds at last," said Traddles; "and thank Heaven that's paid—though it was—though it certainly was," said Traddles, wincing again as if he had had another tooth out, "a pull. I am living by the sort of work I have mentioned, still, and I hope, one of these days, to get connected with some newspaper: which would almost be the making of my fortune. Now, Copperfield, you are so exactly what you used to be, with that agreeable face, and it's so pleasant to see you, that I sha'n't conceal anything. Therefore you must know that I am engaged."

Engaged! Oh, Dora!

"She is a curate's daughter," said Traddles; "one of ten, down in Devonshire. Yes!" For he saw me glance, involuntarily, at the prospect of the inkstand. "That's the church! You come round here, to the left, out of this gate," tracing his finger along the inkstand, "and exactly where I hold this pen, there stands the house—facing, you understand, towards the church."

The delight with which he entered into these particulars,

did not fully present itself to me until afterwards; for my selfish thoughts were making a ground-plan of Mr. Spenlow's house and garden at the same moment.

"She is such a dear girl!" said Traddles; "a little older than me, but the dearest girl! I told you I was going out of town? I have been down there. I walked there, and I walked back, and I had the most delightful time! I dare say ours is likely to be a rather long engagement, but our motto is 'Wait and hope!' We always say that. 'Wait and hope,' we always say. And she would wait, Copperfield, till she was sixty—any age you can mention—for me!"

Traddles rose from his chair, and, with a triumphant smile, put his hand upon the white cloth I had observed.

"However," he said, "it's not that we haven't made a beginning towards housekeeping. No, no; we have begun. We must get on by degrees, but we have begun. Here," drawing the cloth off with pride and care, "are two pieces of furniture to commence with. This flower-pot and stand, she bought herself. You put that in a parlour-window," said Traddles, falling a little back from it to survey it with the greater admiration, "with a plant in it, and—and there you are! This little round table with the marble top (it's two feet ten in circumference), *I* bought. You want to lay a book down, you know, or somebody comes to see you or your wife, and wants a place to stand a cup of tea upon, and—and there you are again!" said Traddles. "It's an admirable piece of workmanship—firm as a rock!"

I praised them both, highly, and Traddles replaced the covering as carefully as he had removed it.

"It's not a great deal towards the furnishing," said Traddles, "but it's something. The table-cloths, and pillow-cases and articles of that kind, are what discourage me most, Copperfield. So does the ironmongery—candle-boxes, and gridirons, and that sort of necessaries—because those things tell, and mount up. However, 'wait and hope!' And I assure you she's the dearest girl!"

"I am quite certain of it," said I.

"In the meantime," said Traddles, coming back to his chair; "and this is the end of my prosing about myself, I get on as well as I can. I don't make much, but I don't spend much. In general, I board with people down-stairs, who are very agreeable people indeed. Both Mr. and Mrs. Micawber have seen a good deal of life, and are excellent company."

"My dear Traddles!" I quickly exclaimed. "What are you talking about?"

Traddles looked at me, as if he wondered what *I* was talking about.

"Mr. and Mrs. Micawber!" I repeated. "Why, I am intimately acquainted with them!"

An opportune double knock at the door, which I knew well from old experience in Windsor Terrace, and which nobody but Mr. Micawber could ever have knocked at that door, resolved any doubt in my mind as to their being my old friends. I begged Traddles to ask his landlord to walk up. Traddles accordingly did so, over the banister; and Mr. Micawber, not a bit changed—his tights, his stick, his shirt-collar, and his eye-glass, all the same as ever—came into the room with a genteel and youthful air.,

"I beg your pardon, Mr. Traddles," said Mr. Micawber, with the old roll in his voice, as he checked himself in humming a soft tune. "I was not aware that there was any individual alien to this tenement, in your sanctum."

Mr. Micawber slightly bowed to me, and pulled up his shirt-collar.

"How do you do, Mr. Micawber?" said I.

"Sir," said Mr. Micawber, "you are exceedingly obliging. I am *in statu quo*."

"And Mrs. Micawber?" I pursued.

"Sir," said Mr. Micawber, "she is also, thank God, *in statu quo*."

"And the children, Mr. Micawber?"

"Sir," said Mr. Micawber, "I rejoice to reply that they are, likewise, in the enjoyment of salubrity."

All this time, Mr. Micawber had not known me in the least, though he had stood face to face with me. But now, seeing me smile, he examined my features with more attention, fell back, cried, "Is it possible! Have I the pleasure of again beholding Copperfield!" and shook me by both hands with the utmost fervour.

"Good Heaven, Mr. Traddles!" said Mr. Micawber, "to think that I should find you acquainted with the friend of my youth, the companion of earlier days! My dear!" calling over the banisters to Mrs. Micawber, while Traddles looked (with reason) not a little amazed at this description of me. "Here is a gentleman in Mr. Traddles's apartment, whom he wishes to have the pleasure of presenting to you, my love!"

Mr. Micawber immediately reappeared, and shook hands with me again.

"And how is our good friend the Doctor, Copperfield?" said Mr. Micawber, "and all the circle at Canterbury?"

"I have none but good accounts of them," said I.

"I am most delighted to hear it," said Mr. Micawber. "It was at Canterbury where we last met. Within the shadow, I may figuratively say, of that religious edifice, immortalized by Chaucer, which was anciently the resort of Pilgrims from the remotest corners of—in short," said Mr. Micawber, "in the immediate neighbourhood of the Cathedral."

I replied that it was. Mr. Micawber continued talking as volubly as he could; but not, I thought, without showing, by some marks of concern in his countenance, that he was sensible of sounds in the next room, as of Mrs. Micawber washing her hands, and hurriedly opening and shutting drawers that were uneasy in their action.

"You find us, Copperfield," said Mr. Micawber, with one eye on Traddles, "at present established, on what may be designated as a small and unassuming scale; but, you are aware that I have, in the course of my career, surmounted difficulties, and conquered obstacles. You are no stranger to the fact, that there have been periods of my life, when it has been requisite that I should pause, until certain expected events should turn up; when it has been necessary that I should fall back, before making what I trust I shall not be accused of presumption in terming—a spring. The present is one of those momentous stages in the life of man. You find me, fallen back, *for* a spring; and I have every reason to believe that a vigorous leap will shortly be the result."

I was expressing my satisfaction, when Mrs. Micawber came in; a little more slatternly than she used to be, or so she seemed now, to my unaccustomed eyes, but still with some preparation of herself for company, and with a pair of brown gloves on.

"My dear," said Mr. Micawber, leading her towards me, "here is a gentleman of the name of Copperfield, who wishes to renew his acquaintance with you."

It would have been better, as it turned out, to have led gently up to this announcement, for Mrs. Micawber, being in a delicate state of health, was overcome by it, and was taken so unwell, that Mr. Micawber was obliged, in great trepidation, to run down to the water-butt in the back yard, and draw a basinful to lave her brow with. She presently revived, however, and was really pleased to see me. We had half-an-hour's talk, all together; and I asked her about the twins, who, she said, were "grown great creatures"; and after Master and Miss Micawber, whom she described as " absolute giants," but they were not produced on that occasion.

Mr. Micawber was very anxious that I should stay to dinner. I should not have been averse to do so, but that I imagined I detected trouble, and calculated relative to the extent of the cold meat, in Mrs. Micawber's eye. I therefore pleaded another engagement; and observing that Mrs. Micawber's spirits were immediately lightened, I resisted all persuasion to forego it.

But I told Traddles, and Mr. and Mrs. Micawber, that before I could think of leaving, they must appoint a day when they would come and dine with me. The occupation to which Traddles stood pledged, rendered it necessary to fix a somewhat distant one; but an appointment was made for the purpose, that suited us all, and then I took my leave.

Mr. Micawber, under pretence of showing me a nearer way than that by which I had come, accompanied me to the corner of the street; being anxious (he explained to me) to say a few words to an old friend, in confidence.

" My dear Copperfield," said Mr. Micawber, " I need hardly tell you that to have beneath our roof, under existing circumstances, a mind like that which gleams—if I may be allowed the expression—which gleams—in your friend Traddles, is an unspeakable comfort. With a washerwoman, who exposes hardbake for sale in her parlour-window, dwelling next door, and a Bow-street officer residing over the way, you may imagine that his society is a source of consolation to myself and to Mrs. Micawber. I am at present, my dear Copperfield, engaged in the sale of corn upon commission. It is not an avocation of a remunerative description—in other words, it does *not* pay—and some temporary embarrassments of a pecuniary nature have been the consequence. I am, however, delighted to add that I have now an immediate prospect of something turning up (I am not at liberty to say in what direction), which I trust will enable me to provide, permanently, both for myself and for your friend Traddles, in whom I have an unaffected interest. You may, perhaps, be prepared to hear that Mrs. Micawber is in a state of health which renders it not wholly improbable that an addition may be ultimately made to those pledges of affection which—in short, to the infantine group. Mrs. Micawber's family have been so good as to express their dissatisfaction at this state of things. I have merely to observe, that I am not aware that it is any business of theirs, and that I repel that exhibition of feeling with scorn, and with defiance! "

Mr. Micawber then shook hands with me again, and left me.

28

MR. MICAWBER'S GAUNTLET

UNTIL THE DAY ARRIVED ON WHICH I WAS TO ENTERTAIN my newly-found old friends, I lived principally on Dora and coffee. In my love-lorn condition, my appetite languished; and I was glad of it, for I felt as though it would have been an act of perfidy towards Dora to have a natural relish for my dinner. The quantity of walking exercise I took, was not in this respect attended with its usual consequence, as the disappointment counteracted the fresh air. I have my doubts, too, founded on the acute experience acquired at this period of my life, whether a sound enjoyment of animal food can develop itself freely in any human subject who is always in torment from tight boots. I think the extremities require to be at peace before the stomach will conduct itself with vigour.

On the occasion of this domestic little party, I did not repeat my former extensive preparations. I merely provided a pair of soles, a small leg of mutton, and a pigeon-pie. Mrs. Crupp broke out into rebellion on my first bashful hint in reference to the cooking of the fish and the joint, and said, with a dignified sense of injury, " No! No, sir! You will not ask me sich a thing, for you are better acquainted with me than to suppose me capable of doing what I cannot do with ampial satisfaction to my own feelings! " But, in the end, a compromise was effected; and Mrs. Crupp consented to achieve this feat, on condition that I dined from home for a fortnight afterwards.

And here I may remark, that what I underwent from Mrs. Crupp, in consequence of the tyranny she established over me, was dreadful. I never was so much afraid of any one. We made a compromise of everything. If I hesitated, she was taken with that wonderful disorder which was always lying in ambush in her system, ready, at the shortest notice, to prey upon her vitals. If I rang the bell impatiently, after half-a-dozen unavailing modest pulls, and she appeared at last—which was not by any means to be relied upon—she would appear with a reproachful aspect, sink breathless on a chair near the door, lay her hand upon her nankeen bosom, and become so ill, that I was glad, at any sacrifice of brandy or anything else, to get rid of her. If I objected to having my bed made at five o'clock in the afternoon —which I *do* still think an uncomfortable arrangement—one motion of her hand towards the same nankeen region of wounded sensibility was enough to make me falter an apology. In short, I would have done anything in an honourable way rather than give Mrs. Crupp offence, and she was the terror of my life.

I bought a second-hand dumb-waiter for this dinner-party, in preference to re-engaging the handy young man; against whom I had conceived a prejudice, in consequence of meeting him in the Strand, one Sunday morning, in a waistcoat remarkably like one of mine, which had been missing since the former occasion. The " young gal " was re-engaged; but on the stipulation that she should only bring in the dishes, and then withdraw to the landing-place, beyond the outer door; where a habit of sniffing she had contracted would be lost upon the guests, and where her retiring on the plates would be a physical impossibility.

Having laid in the materials for a bowl of punch, to be compounded by Mr. Micawber; having provided a bottle of lavender-water, two wax candles, a paper of mixed pins, and a pincushion, to assist Mrs. Micawber in her toilette at my dressing-table; having also caused the fire in my bedroom to be lighted for Mrs. Micawber's convenience; and having laid the cloth with my own hands, I awaited the result with composure.

At the appointed time, my three visitors arrived together. Mr. Micawber with more shirt-collar than usual, and a new ribbon to his eye-glass; Mrs. Micawber with her cap in a whitey-brown paper parcel; Traddles carrying the parcel, and supporting Mrs. Micawber on his arm. They were all delighted with my residence. When I conducted Mrs. Micawber to my dressing-table, and she saw the scale on which it was prepared for her, she was in such raptures, that she called Mr. Micawber to come in and look.

" My dear Copperfield," said Mr. Micawber, " this is luxurious. This is a way of life which reminds me of the period when I was myself in a state of celibacy, and Mrs. Micawber had not yet been solicited to plight her faith at the Hymeneal altar."

" He means, solicited by him, Mr. Copperfield," said Mrs. Micawber, archly. " He cannot answer for others."

" My dear," returned Mr. Micawber with sudden seriousness, " I have no desire to answer for others. I am too well aware that when, in the inscrutable decrees of Fate, you were reserved for me, it is possible you may have been reserved for one, destined, after a protracted struggle, at length to fall a victim to pecuniarv involvements of a complicated nature. I understand your allusion, my love. I regret it, but I can bear it."

"Micawber!" exclaimed Mrs. Micawber, in tears. "Have I deserved this! I, who never have deserted you; who never *will* desert you, Micawber!"

"My love," said Mr. Micawber, much affected, "you will forgive, and our old and tried friend Copperfield will, I am sure, forgive, the momentary laceration of a wounded spirit, made sensitive by a recent collision with the Minion of Power—in other words, with a ribald Turncock attached to the waterworks—and will pity, not condemn, its excesses."

Mr. Micawber then embraced Mrs. Micawber, and pressed my hand; leaving me to infer from this broken allusion that his domestic supply of water had been cut off that afternoon in consequence of default in the payment of the company's rates.

To divert his thoughts from this melancholy subject, I informed Mr. Micawber that I relied upon him for a bowl of punch, and led him to the lemons. His recent despondency, not to say despair, was gone in a moment. I never saw a man so thoroughly enjoy himself amid the fragrance of lemon-peel and sugar, the odour of burning rum, and the steam of boiling water, as Mr. Micawber did that afternoon. It was wonderful to see his face shining at us out of a thin cloud of these delicate fumes, as he stirred, and mixed, and tasted, and looked as if he were making, instead of punch, a fortune for his family down to the latest posterity. As to Mrs. Micawber, I don't know whether it was the effect of the cap, or the lavender-water, or the pins, or the fire, or the wax candles, but she came out of my room, comparatively speaking, lovely. And the lark was never gayer than that excellent woman.

I suppose—I never ventured to inquire, but I suppose—that Mrs. Crupp, after frying the soles, was taken ill. Because we broke down at that point. The leg of mutton came up very red within, and very pale without: besides having a foreign substance of a gritty nature sprinkled over it, as if it had had a fall into the ashes of that remarkable kitchen fire-place. But we were not in a condition to judge of this fact from the appearance of the gravy, forasmuch as the "young gal" had dropped it all upon the stairs—where it remained, by-the-bye, in a long train, until it was worn out. The pigeon-pie was not bad, but it was a delusive pie: the crust being like a disappointing head, phrenologically speaking: full of lumps and bumps, with nothing particular underneath. In short, the banquet was such a failure that I should have been quite unhappy—about the failure, I mean, for I was always unhappy about Dora—if I had not been relieved by the great good-humour of my company, and by a bright suggestion from Mr. Micawber.

"My dear friend Copperfield," said Mr. Micawber, "accidents will occur in the best-regulated families; and in families not regulated by that pervading influence which sanctifies while it enhances the—a—I would say, in short, by the influence of Woman, in the lofty character of Wife, they may be expected with confidence, and must be borne with philosophy. If you will allow me to take the liberty of remarking that there are few comestibles better, in their way, than a Devil, and that I believe, with a little division of labour, we could accomplish a good one if the young person in attendance could produce a gridiron, I would put it to you, that this little misfortune may be easily repaired."

There was a gridiron in the pantry, on which my morning rasher of bacon was cooked. We had it in, in a twinkling, and immediately applied ourselves to carrying Mr. Micawber's idea into effect. The division of labour to which he had referred was this:—Traddles cut the mutton into slices; Mr. Micawber (who could do anything of this sort to perfection) covered them with pepper, mustard, salt, and cayenne; I put them on the gridiron, turned them with a fork, and took them off, under Mr. Micawber's direction; and Mrs. Micawber heated, and continually stirred, some mushroom ketchup in a little saucepan. When we had slices enough done to begin upon, we fell-to, with our sleeves still tucked up at the wrist, more slices sputtering and blazing on the fire, and our attention divided between the mutton on our plates, and the mutton then preparing.

What with the novelty of this cookery, the excellence of it, the bustle of it, the frequent starting up to look after it, the frequent sitting down to dispose of it as the crisp slices came off the gridiron hot and hot, the being so busy, so flushed with the fire, so amused, and in the midst of such a tempting noise and savour, we reduced the leg of mutton to the bone. My own appetite came back miraculously. I am ashamed to record it, but I really believe I forgot Dora for a little while. I am satisfied that Mr. and Mrs. Micawber could not have enjoyed the feast more, if they had sold a bed to provide it. Traddles laughed as heartily, almost the whole time, as he ate and worked. Indeed we all did, all at once; and I dare say there never was a greater success.

We were at the height of our enjoyment, and were all busily engaged, in our several departments, endeavouring to bring the last batch of slices to a state of perfection that should crown the feast, when I was aware of a strange presence in the room, and my eyes encountered those of the staid Littimer, standing hat in hand before me.

"What's the matter?" I involuntarily asked.

"I beg your pardon, sir, I was directed to come in. Is my master not here, sir?"

"No."

"Have you not seen him, sir?"

"No; don't you come from him?"

"Not immediately so, sir."

"Did he tell you you would find him here?"

"Not exactly so, sir. But I should think he might be here to-morrow, as he has not been here to-day."

"Is he coming up from Oxford?"

"I beg, sir," he returned respectfully, "that you will be seated, and allow me to do this." With which he took the fork from my unresisting hand, and bent over the gridiron, as if his whole attention were concentrated on it.

We should not have been much discomposed, I dare say, by the appearance of Steerforth himself, but we became in a moment the meekest of the meek before his respectable serving-man. Mr. Micawber, humming a tune, to show that he was quite at ease, subsided into his chair, with the handle of a hastily concealed fork sticking out of the bosom of his coat, as if he had stabbed himself. Mrs. Micawber put on her brown gloves, and assumed a genteel languor, Traddles ran his greasy hands through his hair, and stood it bolt upright, and stared in confusion on the table-cloth. As for me, I was a mere infant at the head of my own table; and hardly ventured to glance at the respectable phenomenon, who had come from Heaven knows where, to put my establishment to rights.

Meanwhile he took the mutton off the gridiron, and gravely handed it round. We all took some, but our appreciation of it was gone, and we merely made a show of eating it. As we severally pushed away our plates, he noiselessly removed them, and set on the cheese. He took that off, too, when it was done with; cleared the table; piled everything on the dumb-waiter; gave us our wine-glasses; and, of his own accord, wheeled the dumb-waiter into the pantry. All this was done in a perfect manner, and he never raised his eyes from what he was about. Yet his very elbows, when he had his back towards me, seemed to teem with the expression of his fixed opinion that I was extremely young.

" Can I do anything more, sir? "

I thanked him and said, No; but would he take no dinner himself?

" None. I am obliged to you, sir."

" Is Mr. Steerforth coming from Oxford? "

" I beg your pardon, sir? "

" Is Mr. Steerforth coming from Oxford? "

" I should imagine that he might be here to-morrow, sir. I rather thought he might have been here to-day, sir. The mistake is mine, no doubt, sir."

" If you should see him first—" said I.

" If you'll excuse me, sir, I don't think I shall see him first."

" In case you do," said I, " pray say that I am sorry he was not here to-day, as an old schoolfellow of his was here."

" Indeed, sir! " and he divided a bow between me and Traddles, with a glance at the latter.

He was moving softly to the door, when, in a forlorn hope of saying something naturally—which I never could, to this man—I said:

" Oh! Littimer! "

" Sir! "

" Did you remain long at Yarmouth, that time? "

" Not particularly so, sir."

" You saw the boat completed? "

" Yes, sir. I remained behind on purpose to see the boat completed."

" I know! " He raised his eyes to mine respectfully. " Mr. Steerforth has not seen it yet, I suppose? "

" I really can't say, sir. I think—but I really can't say, sir. I wish you good night, sir."

He comprehended everybody present, in the respectful bow with which he followed these words, and disappeared. My visitors seemed to breathe more freely when he was gone; but my own relief was very great, for besides the constraint arising from that extraordinary sense of being at a disadvantage which I always had in this man's presence, my conscience had embarrassed me with whispers that I had mistrusted his master, and I could not repress a vague uneasy dread that he might find it out. How was it, having so little in reality to conceal, that I always *did* feel as if this man were finding me out?

Mr. Micawber roused me from this reflection, which was blended with a certain remorseful apprehension of seeing Steerforth himself, by bestowing many encomiums on the absent Littimer as a most respectable fellow, and a thoroughly admirable servant. Mr. Micawber, I may remark, had taken his full share of the general bow, and had received it with infinite condescension.

" But punch, my dear Copperfield," said Mr. Micawber, tasting it, " like time and tide, waits for no man. Ah! it is at the present moment in high flavour. My love, will you give me your opinion? "

Mrs. Micawber pronounced it excellent.

" Then I will drink," said Mr. Micawber, " if my friend Copperfield will permit me to take that social liberty, to the days when my friend Copperfield and myself were younger, and fought our way in the world side by side. I may say, of myself and Copperfield, in words we have sung together before now, that

'We twa hae run about the braes
And pu'd the gowans fine'

—in a figurative point of view—on several occasions. I am not exactly aware," said Mr. Micawber, with the old roll in his voice, and the old indescribable air of saying something genteel, " what gowans may be, but I have no doubt that Copperfield and myself would frequently have taken a pull at them, if it had been feasible."

Mr. Micawber, at the then present moment, took a pull at his punch. So we all did: Traddles evidently lost in wondering at what distant time Mr. Micawber and I could have been comrades in the battle of the world.

" Ahem! " said Mr. Micawber, clearing his throat, and warming with the punch and the fire. " My dear, another glass? "

Mrs. Micawber said it must be very little; but we couldn't allow that, so it was a glassful.

" As we are quite confidential here, Mr. Copperfield," said Mrs. Micawber, sipping her punch, " Mr. Traddles being a part of our domesticity, I should much like to have your opinion on Mr. Micawber's prospects. For corn," said Mrs. Micawber argumentatively, " as I have repeatedly said to Mr. Micawber, may be gentlemanly, but it is not remunerative. Commission to the extent of two and ninepence in a fortnight cannot, however limited our ideas, be considered remunerative."

We were all agreed upon that.

" Then," said Mrs. Micawber, who prided herself on taking a clear view of things, and keeping Mr. Micawber straight by her woman's wisdom, when he might otherwise go a little crooked, "then I ask myself this question. If corn is not to be relied upon, what is? Are coals to be relied upon? Not at all. We have turned our attention to that experiment, on the suggestion of my family, and we find it fallacious."

Mr. Micawber, leaning back in his chair with his hands in his pockets, eyed us aside, and nodded his head, as much as to say that the case was very clearly put.

"The articles of corn and coals," said Mrs. Micawber, still more argumentatively, "being equally out of the question, Mr. Copperfield, I naturally look round the world, and say, 'What is there in which a person of Mr. Micawber's talent is likely to succeed?' And I exclude the doing anything on commission, because commission is not a certainty. What is best suited to a person of Mr. Micawber's peculiar temperament is, I am convinced, a certainty."

Traddles and I both expressed, by a feeling murmur, that this great discovery was no doubt true of Mr. Micawber, and that it did him much credit.

"I will not conceal from you, my dear Mr. Copperfield," said Mrs. Micawber, "that *I* have long felt the Brewing business to be particularly adapted to Mr. Micawber. Look at Barclay and Perkins! Look at Truman, Hanbury, and Buxton! It is on that extensive footing that Mr. Micawber, I know from my own knowledge of him, is calculated to shine; and the profits, I am told, are e-NOR-mous! But if Mr. Micawber cannot get into those firms—which decline to answer his letters, when he offers his services even in an inferior capacity—what is the use of dwelling upon that idea? None. I may have a conviction that Mr. Micawber's manners—"

"Hem! Really, my dear," interposed Mr. Micawber.

"My love, be silent," said Mrs. Micawber, laying her brown glove on his hand. "I may have a conviction, Mr. Copperfield, that Mr. Micawber's manners peculiarly qualify him for the Banking business. I may argue within myself, that if I had a deposit at a banking-house, the manners of Mr. Micawber, as representing that banking-house, would inspire confidence, and must extend the connection. But if the various banking-houses refuse to avail themselves of Mr. Micawber's abilities, or receive the offer of them with contumely, what is the use of dwelling upon *that* idea? None. As to originating a banking-business, I may know that there are members of my family who, if they chose to place their money in Mr. Micawber's hands, might found an establishment of that description. But if they do *not* choose to place their money in Mr. Micawber's hands—which they don't—what is the use of that? Again I contend that we are no farther advanced than we were before."

I shook my head, and said, " Not a bit." Traddles also shook his head, and said, " Not a bit."

" What do I deduce from this? " Mrs. Micawber went on to say, still with the same air of putting a case lucidly. " What is the conclusion, my dear Mr. Copperfield, to which I am irresistibly brought? Am I wrong in saying, it is clear that we must live? "

I answered 'Not at all! " and Traddles answered " Not at all! " and I found myself afterwards sagely adding, alone, that a person must either live or die.

" Just so," returned Mrs. Micawber, " it is precisely that. And the fact is, my dear Mr. Copperfield, that we can *not* live without something widely different from existing circumstances shortly turning up. Now I am convinced, myself, and this I have pointed out to Mr. Micawber several times of late, that things cannot be expected to turn up of themselves. We must, in a measure, assist to turn them up. I may be wrong, but I have formed that opinion."

Both Traddles and I applauded it highly.

" Very well," said Mrs. Micawber. " Then what do I recommend? Here is Mr. Micawber with a variety of qualifications—with great talent—"

" Really, my love," said Mr. Micawber.

" Pray, my dear, allow me to conclude. Here is Mr. Micawber, with a variety of qualifications, with great talent—*I* should say, with genius, but that may be the partiality of a wife—"

Traddles and I both murmured " No."

" And here is Mr. Micawber without any suitable position or employment. Where does that responsibility rest? Clearly on society. Then I would make a fact so disgraceful known, and boldly challenge society to set it right. It appears to me, my dear Mr. Copperfield," said Mrs. Micawber, forcibly, " that what Mr. Micawber has to do, is to throw down the gauntlet to society, and say, in effect, 'Show me who will take that up. Let the party immediately step forward.' "

I ventured to ask Mrs. Micawber how this was to be done.

" By advertising," said Mrs. Micawber—" in all the papers. It appears to me, that what Mr. Micawber has to do, in justice to himself, in justice to his family, and I will even go so far as to say in justice to society, by which he has been hitherto overlooked, is to advertise in all the papers; to describe himself plainly as so-and-so, with such and such qualifications, and to put it thus: '*Now* employ me, on remunerative terms and address, post-paid, to *W. M.*, Post Office, Camden Town.'"

"This idea of Mrs. Micawber's, my dear Copperfield," said Mr. Micawber, making his shirt-collar meet in front of his chin, and glancing at me sideways, "is, in fact, the Leap to which I alluded, when I last had the pleasure of seeing you."

"Advertising is rather expensive," I remarked, dubiously.

"Exactly so!" said Mrs. Micawber, preserving the same logical air. "Quite true, my dear Mr. Copperfield! I have made the identical observation to Mr. Micawber. It is for that reason especially, that I think Mr. Micawber ought (as I have already said, in justice to himself, in justice to his family, and in justice to society) to raise a certain sum of money—on a bill."

Mr. Micawber, leaning back in his chair, trifled with his eye-glass, and cast his eyes up at the ceiling; but I thought him observant of Traddles, too, who was looking at the fire.

"If no member of my family," said Mrs. Micawber, "is possessed of sufficient natural feeling to negotiate that bill—I believe there is a better business-term to express what I mean—"

Mr. Micawber, with his eyes still cast up at the ceiling, suggested "Discount."

"To discount that bill," said Mrs. Micawber, "then my opinion is, that Mr. Micawber should go into the City, should take that bill into the Money Market, and should dispose of it for what he can get. If the individuals in the Money Market oblige Mr. Micawber to sustain a great sacrifice, that is between themselves and their consciences. I view it, steadily, as an investment. I recommend Mr. Micawber, my dear Mr. Copperfield, to do the same; to regard it as an investment which is sure of return, and to make up his mind to *any* sacrifice."

I felt, but I am sure I don't know why, that this was self-denying and devoted in Mrs. Micawber, and I uttered a murmur to that effect. Traddles, who took his tone from me, did likewise, still looking at the fire.

"I will not," said Mrs. Micawber, finishing her punch, and gathering her scarf about her shoulders, preparatory to her withdrawal to my bedroom: "I will not protract these remarks on the subject of Mr. Micawber's pecuniary affairs. At your fireside, my dear Mr. Copperfield, and in the presence of Mr. Traddles, who, though not so old a friend, is quite one of ourselves, I could not refrain from making you acquainted with the course *I* advise Mr. Micawber to take. I feel that the time is arrived when Mr. Micawber should exert himself and—I will add—assert himself, and it appears to me that these are the means. I am aware that I am merely a female, and that a masculine judgment is usually considered more competent to the discussion of such questions; still I must not forget that, when I lived at home with my papa and mama, my papa was in the habit of saying, 'Emma's form is fragile, but her grasp of a subject is inferior to none.' That my papa was too partial, I well know; but that he was an observer of character in some degree, my duty and my reason equally forbid me to doubt."

With these words, and resisting our entreaties that she would grace the remaining circulation of the punch with her presence, Mrs. Micawber retired to my bedroom. And really I felt that she was a noble woman—the sort of woman who might have been a Roman matron, and done all manner of heroic things, in times of public trouble.

In the fervour of this impression, I congratulated Mr. Micawber on the treasure he possessed. So did Traddles. Mr. Micawber extended his hand to each of us in succession, and then covered his face with his pocket-handkerchief, which I think had more snuff upon it than he was aware of. He then returned to the punch, in the highest state of exhilaration.

He was full of eloquence. He gave us to understand that in our children we lived again, and that, under the pressure of pecuniary difficulties, any accession to their number was doubly welcome. He said that Mrs. Micawber had latterly had her doubts on this point, but that he had dispelled them, and re-assured her. As to her family, they were totally unworthy of her, and their sentiments were utterly indifferent to him, and they might—I quote his own expression—go to the Devil.

Mr. Micawber then delivered a warm eulogy on Traddles. He said Traddles's was a character, to the steady virtues of which he (Mr. Micawber) could lay no claim, but which, he thanked Heaven, he could admire. He feelingly alluded to the young lady, unknown, whom Traddles had honoured with his affection, and who had reciprocated that affection by honouring and blessing Traddles with *her* affection. Mr. Micawber pledged her. So did I. Traddles thanked us both, by saying, with a simplicity and honesty I had sense enough to be quite charmed with, "I am very much obliged to you indeed. And I do assure you, she's the dearest girl!—"

Mr. Micawber took an early opportunity, after that, of hinting, with the utmost delicacy and ceremony, at the state of *my* affections. Nothing but the serious assurance of his friend Copperfield to the contrary, he observed, could deprive him of the impression that his friend Copperfield loved and was beloved. After feeling very hot and uncomfortable for some time, and after a good deal of blushing, stammering, and denying, I said, having my glass in my hand, " Well! I would give them D.! " which so excited and gratified Mr. Micawber, that he ran with a glass of punch into my bedroom, in order that Mrs. Micawber might drink D., who drank it with enthusiasm, crying from within, in a shrill voice, " Hear, hear! My dear Mr. Copperfield, I am delighted. Hear! " and tapping at the wall, by way of applause.

Our conversation, afterwards, took a more worldly turn; Mr. Micawber telling us that he found Camden Town inconvenient, and that the first thing he contemplated doing, when the advertisement should have been the cause of something satisfactory turning up, was to move. He mentioned a terrace at the western end of Oxford Street, fronting Hyde Park, on which he had always had his eye, but which he did not expect to attain immediately, as it would require a large establishment. There would probably be an interval, he explained, in which he should content himself with the upper part of a house, over some respectable place of business—say in Piccadilly,—which would be a cheerful situation for Mrs. Micawber; and where, by throwing out a bow window, or carrying up the roof another story, or making some little alteration of that sort, they might live, comfortably and reputably, for a few years. Whatever was reserved for him, he expressly said, or wherever his abode might be, we might rely on this—there would always be a room for Traddles, and a knife and fork for me. We acknowledged his kindness; and he begged us to forgive his having launched into these practical and business-like details, and to excuse it as natural in one who was making entirely new arrangements in life.

Mrs. Micawber, tapping at the wall again, to know if tea were ready, broke up this particular phase of our friendly conversation. She made tea for us in a most agreeable manner; and, whenever I went near her, in handing about the tea-cups and bread-and-butter, asked me, in a whisper, whether D. was fair, or dark, or whether she was short, or tall: or something of that kind; which I think I liked. After tea, we discussed a variety of topics before the fire; and Mrs. Micawber was good enough to sing us (in a small, thin, flat voice, which I remembered to have considered, when I first knew her, the very table-beer of acoustics) the favourite ballads of " The Dashing White Sergeant," and " Little Tafflin." For both of these songs Mrs.

Micawber had been famous when she lived at home with her papa and mama. Mr. Micawber told us, that when he heard her sing the first one, on the first occasion of his seeing her beneath the parental roof, she had attracted his attention in an extraordinary degree; but that when it came to Little Tafflin, he had resolved to win that woman or perish in the attempt.

It was between ten and eleven o'clock when Mrs. Micawber rose to replace her cap in the whitey-brown paper parcel, and to put on her bonnet. Mr. Micawber took the opportunity of Traddles putting on his great-coat, to slip a letter into my hand, with a whispered request that I would read it at my leisure. I also took the opportunity of my holding a candle over the banisters to light them down, when Mr. Micawber was going first, leading Mrs. Micawber, and Traddles was following with the cap, to detain Traddles for a moment on the top of the stairs.

"Traddles," said I, "Mr. Micawber don't mean any harm, poor fellow: but, if I were you, I wouldn't lend him anything."

"My dear Copperfield," returned Traddles, smiling. "I haven't got anything to lend."

"You have got a name, you know," said I.

"Oh! You call *that* something to lend?" returned Traddles, with a thoughtful look.

"Certainly."

"Oh!" said Traddles. "Yes, to be sure! I am very much obliged to you, Copperfield; but—I am afraid I have lent him that already."

"For the bill that is to be a certain investment?" I inquired.

"No," said Traddles. "Not for that one. This is the first I have heard of that one. I have been thinking that he will most likely propose that one, on the way home. Mine's another."

"I hope there will be nothing wrong about it," said I.

"I hope not," said Traddles. "I should think not, though, because he told me, only the other day, that it was provided for. That was Mr. Micawber's expression, 'Provided for.'"

Mr. Micawber looking up at this juncture to where we were standing, I had only time to repeat my caution. Traddles thanked me, and descended. But I was much afraid, when I observed the good-natured manner in which he went down with the cap in his hand, and gave Mrs. Micawber his arm, that he would be carried into the Money Market neck and heels.

I returned to my fireside, and was musing, half gravely and half laughing, on the character of Mr. Micawber and the old relations between us, when I heard a quick step ascending the stairs. At first I thought it was Traddles coming back for something Mrs. Micawber had left behind; but as the step approached, I knew it, and felt my heart beat high, and the blood rush to my face, for it was Steerforth's.

I was never unmindful of Agnes, and she never left that sanctuary in my thoughts—if I may call it so—where I had placed her from the first. But when he entered, and stood before me with his hand out, the darkness that had fallen on him changed to light, and I felt confounded and ashamed of having doubted one I loved so heartily. I loved her none the less; I thought of her as the same benignant, gentle angel in my life; I reproached myself, not her, with having done him an injury; and I would have made him any atonement, if I had known what to make, and how to make it.

"Why, Daisy, old boy, dumb-foundered!" laughed Steerforth, shaking my hand heartily, and throwing it gaily away. "Have I detected you in another feast, you Sybarite! These Doctors' Commons fellows are the gayest men in town, I believe, and beat us sober Oxford people all to nothing!" His bright glance went merrily round the room, as he took the seat on the sofa opposite to me, which Mrs. Micawber had recently vacated, and stirred the fire into a blaze.

"I was so surprised at first," said I, giving him welcome with all the cordiality I felt, "that I had hardly breath to greet you with, Steerforth."

"Well, the sight of me *is* good for sore eyes as the Scotch say," replied Steerforth, "and so is the sight of you, Daisy, in full bloom. How are you, my Bacchanal?"

"I am very well," said I; "and not at all Bacchanalian to-night, though I confess to another party of three."

"All of whom I met in the street, talking loud in your praise," returned Steerforth. "Who's our friend in the tights?"

I gave him the best idea I could, in a few words, of Mr. Micawber. He laughted heartily at my feeble portrait of that gentleman, and said he was a man to know, and he must know him.

"But who do you suppose our other friend is?" said I, in my turn.

"Heaven knows," said Steerforth. "Not a bore, I hope? I thought he looked a little like one."

"Traddles!" I replied, triumphantly.

"Who's he?" asked Steerforth, in his careless way.

"Don't you remember Traddles? Traddles in our room at Salem House?"

"Oh! That fellow!" said Steerforth, beating a lump of coal

on the top of the fire, with the poker. "Is he as soft as ever? And where the deuce did you pick *him* up?"

I extolled Traddles in reply, as highly as I could; but I felt that Steerforth rather slighted him. Steerforth, dismissing the subject with a light nod, and a smile, and the remark that he would be glad to see the old fellow too, for he had always been an odd fish, inquired if I could give him anything to eat? During most of this short dialogue, when he had not been speaking in a wild vivacious manner, he had sat idly beating on the lump of coal with the poker. I observed that he did the same thing while I was getting out the remains of the pigeon-pie, and so forth.

"Why, Daisy, here's a supper for a king!" he exclaimed, starting out of his silence with a burst, and taking his seat at the table. "I shall do it justice, for I have come from Yarmouth."

"I thought you came from Oxford?" I returned

"Not I," said Steerforth. "I have been seafaring—better employed."

"Littimer was here to-day, to inquire for you," I remarked, "and I understood him that you were at Oxford; though, now I think of it, he certainly did not say so."

"Littimer is a greater fool than I thought him, to have been inquiring for me at all," said Steerforth, jovially pouring out a glass of wine, and drinking to me. "As to understanding him, you are a cleverer fellow than most of us, Daisy, if you can do that."

"That's true, indeed," said I, moving my chair to the table. "So you have been at Yarmouth, Steerforth!" interested to know all about it. "Have you been there long?"

"No," he returned. "An *escapade* of a week or so."

"And how are they all? Of course, little Emily is not married yet?"

"Not yet. Going to be, I believe—in so many weeks, or months, or something or other. I have not seen much of 'em. By-the-bye;" he laid down his knife and fork, which he had been using with great diligence, and began feeling in his pockets; "I have a letter for you."

"From whom?"

"Why, from your old nurse," he returned, taking some papers out of his breast pocket. "'J. Steerforth, Esquire, debtor, to The Willing Mind:' that's not it. Patience, and we'll find it presently. Old what's-his-name's in a bad way, and it's about that, I believe."

"Barkis, do you mean?"

"Yes!" still feeling in his pockets, and looking over their contents: "it's all over with poor Barkis, I am afraid. I saw a little apothecary there—surgeon, or whatever he is—who brought your worship into the world. He was mighty learned about the case, to me; but the upshot of his opinion was, that the carrier was making his last journey rather fast.—Put your hand into the breast pocket of my great-coat on the chair yonder, and I think you'll find the letter. Is it there?"

"Here it is!" said I.

"That's right!"

It was from Peggotty; something less legible than usual, and brief. It informed me of her husband's hopeless state, and hinted at his being "a little nearer" than heretofore, and consequently more difficult to manage for his own comfort. It said nothing of her weariness and watching, and praised him highly. It was written with a plain, unaffected, homely piety that I knew to be genuine, and ended with "my duty to my ever darling"—meaning myself.

While I deciphered it, Steerforth continued to eat and drink.

"It's a bad job," he said, when I had done; "but the sun sets every day, and people die every minute, and we mustn't be scared by the common lot. If we failed to hold our own, because that equal foot at all men's doors was heard knocking somewhere, every object in this world would slip from us. No! Ride on! Rough-shod if need be, smooth-shod if that will do, but ride on! Ride on over all obstacles and win the race!"

"And win what race?" said I.

"The race that one has started in," said he. "Ride on!"

I noticed, I remember, as he paused, looking at me with his handsome head a little thrown back, and his glass raised in his hand, that, though the freshness of the sea-wind was on his face, and it was ruddy, there were traces in it, made since I last saw it, as if he had applied himself to some habitual strain of the fervent energy which, when roused, was so passionately roused within him. I had it in my thoughts to remonstrate with him upon his desperate way of pursuing any fancy that he took—such as this buffeting of rough seas, and braving of hard weather, for example—when my mind glanced off to the immediate subject of our conversation again, and pursued that instead.

"I tell you what, Steerforth," said I, "if your high spirits will listen to me—"

"They are potent spirits, and will do whatever you like," he answered, moving from the table to the fireside again.

"Then I tell you what, Steerforth. I think I will go down and see my old nurse. It is not that I can do her any good, or render her any real service; but she is so attached to me that my visit will have as much effect on her, as if I could do both. She will take it so kindly, that it will be a comfort and support to her. It is no great effort to make, I am sure, for such a friend as she has been to me. Wouldn't you go a day's journey, if you were in my place?"

His face was thoughtful, and he sat considering a little before he answered, in a low voice, "Well! Go. You can do no harm."

"You have just come back," said I, "and it would be in vain to ask you to go with me?"

"Quite," he returned. "I am for Highgate to-night. I have not seen my mother this long time, and it lies upon my conscience, for it's something to be loved as she loves her prodigal son.—Bah! Nonsense!—You mean to go to-morrow, I suppose?" he said, holding me out at arm's length, with a hand on each of my shoulders.

"Yes, I think so."

"Well, then, don't go till next day. I wanted you to come and stay a few days with us. Here I am, on purpose to bid you, and you fly off to Yarmouth!"

"You are a nice fellow to talk of flying off, Steerforth, who are always running wild on some unknown expedition or other!"

He looked at me for a moment without speaking, and then rejoined, still holding me as before, and giving me a shake:

"Come! Say the next day, and pass as much of to-morrow as you can with us! Who knows when we may meet again, else? Come! Say the next day! I want you to stand between Rosa Dartle and me, and keep us asunder."

"Would you love each other too much, without me?"

"Yes; or hate," laughed Steerforth; "no matter which. Come! Say the next day!"

I said the next day; and he put on his great-coat and lighted his cigar, and set off to walk home. Finding him in this intention, I put on my own great-coat (but did not light my own cigar, having had enough of that for one while) and walked with him as far as the open road; a dull road, then, at night. He was in great spirits all the way; and when we parted, and I looked after him going so gallantly and airily homeward, I thought of his saying, "Ride on over all obstacles, and win the race!" and wished, for the first time, that he had some worthy race to run.

I was undressing in my own room, when Mr. Micawber's letter tumbled on the floor. Thus reminded of it, I broke the seal and read as follows. It was dated an hour and a half before dinner. I am not sure whether I have mentioned that, when Mr. Micawber was at any particularly desperate crisis, he used a sort of legal phraseology: which he seemed to think equivalent to winding up his affairs.

"SIR—for I dare not say my dear Copperfield,

"It is expedient that I should inform you that the undersigned is Crushed. Some flickering efforts to spare you the premature knowledge of his calamitous position, you may observe in him this day; but hope has sunk beneath the horizon, and the undersigned is Crushed.

"The present communication is penned within the personal range (I cannot call it the society) of an individual, in a state closely bordering on intoxication, employed by a broker. That individual is in legal possession of the premises, under a distress for rent. His inventory includes, not only the chattels and effects of every description belonging to the undersigned, as yearly tenant of this habitation, but also those appertaining to Mr. Thomas Traddles, lodger, a member of the Honourable Society of the Inner Temple.

"If any drop of gloom were wanting in the overflowing cup, which is now 'commended' (in the language of an immortal Writer) to the lips of the undersigned, it would be found in the fact, that a friendly acceptance granted to the undersigned, by the before-mentioned Mr. Thomas Traddles, for the sum of £23 4*s*. 9½*d*. is over due, and is NOT provided for. Also, in the fact that the living responsibilities clinging to the undersigned will, in the course of nature, be increased by the sum of one more helpless victim; whose miserable appearance may be looked for—in round numbers—at the expiration of a period not exceeding six lunar months from the present date.

"After premising thus much, it would be a work of supererogation to add, that dust and ashes are for ever scattered

"On
"The
"Head
"Of
"WILKINS MICAWBER."

Poor Traddles! I knew enough of Mr. Micawber by this time, to foresee that *he* might be expected to recover the blow; but my night's rest was sorely distressed by thoughts of Traddles, and of the curate's daughter, who was one of ten, down in Devonshire, and who was such a dear girl, and who would wait for Traddles (ominous praise!) until she was sixty, or any age that could be mentioned.

29

I VISIT STEERFORTH AT HIS HOME, AGAIN

I MENTIONED TO MR. SPENLOW IN THE MORNING, THAT I wanted leave of absence for a short time; and as I was not in the receipt of any salary, and consequently was not obnoxious to the implacable Jorkins, there was no difficulty about it. I took that opportunity, with my voice sticking in my throat, and my sight failing as I uttered the words, to express my hope that Miss Spenlow was quite well; to which Mr. Spenlow replied, with no more emotion than if he had been speaking of an ordinary human being, that he was much obliged to me, and she was very well.

We articled clerks, as germs of the patrician order of proctors, were treated with so much consideration, that I was almost my own master at all times. As I did not care, however, to get to Highgate before one or two o'clock in the day, and as we had another little excommunication case in court that morning, which was called The office of the Judge promoted by Tipkins against Bullock for his soul's correction, I passed an hour or two in attendance on it with Mr. Spenlow very agreeably. It arose out of a scuffle between two churchwardens, one of whom was alleged to have pushed the other against a pump; the handle of which pump projecting into a school-house, which school-house was under a gable of the church-roof, made the push an ecclesiastical offence. It was an amusing case; and sent me up to Highgate, on the box of the stage-coach, thinking about the Commons, and what Mr. Spenlow had said about touching the Commons and bringing down the country.

Mrs. Steerforth was pleased to see me, and so was Rosa Dartle. I was agreeably surprised to find that Littimer was not there, and that we were attended by a modest little parlourmaid, with blue ribbons in her cap, whose eye it was much more pleasant, and much less disconcerting, to catch by accident than the eye of that respectable man. But what I particularly observed, before I had been half-an-hour in the house, was the close and attentive watch Miss Dartle kept upon me; and the lurking manner in which she seemed to compare my face with Steerforth's, and Steerforth's with mine, and to lie in wait for something to come out between the two. So surely as I looked towards her, did I see that eager visage, with its gaunt black eyes and searching brow, intent on mine; or passing suddenly from mine to Steerforth's; or comprehending both of us at once. In this lynx-like scrutiny she was so far from faltering when she saw I observed it, that at such a time she only fixed her piercing look upon me with a more intent expression still. Blameless as I was, and knew that I was, in reference to any wrong she could possibly suspect me of, I shrunk before her strange eyes, quite unable to endure their hungry lustre.

All day, she seemed to pervade the whole house. If I talked to Steerforth in his room, I heard her dress rustle in the little gallery outside. When he and I engaged in some of our old exercises on the lawn behind the house, I saw her face pass from window to window, like a wandering light, until it fixed itself in one, and watched us. When we all four went out walking in the afternoon, she closed her thin hand on my arm like a spring, to keep me back, while Steerforth and his mother went on out of hearing: and then spoke to me.

" You have been a long time," she said, " without coming here. Is your profession really so engaging and interesting as to absorb your whole attention? I ask because I always want to be informed, when I am ignorant. Is it really, though? "

I replied that I liked it well enough, but that I certainly could not claim so much for it.

" Oh! I am glad to know that, because I always like to be put right when I am wrong," said Rosa Dartle. " You mean it is a little dry, perhaps? "

" Well," I replied; " perhaps it *was* a little dry."

" Oh! and that's a reason why you want relief and change—excitement, and all that? " said she. " Ah! very true! But isn't it a little——Eh?—for him; I don't mean you? "

A quick glance of her eye towards the spot where Steerforth was walking, with his mother leaning on his arm, showing me whom she meant; but beyond that, I was quite lost. And I looked so, I have no doubt.

" Don't it—I don't say that it *does*, mind I want to know—don't it rather engross him? Don't it make him, perhaps, a little more remiss than usual in his visits to his blindly-doting—eh? " With another quick glance at them, and such a glance at me as seemed to look into my innermost thoughts.

" Miss Dartle," I returned, " pray do not think—"

"I don't!" she said. "Oh dear me, don't suppose that I think anything! I am not suspicious. I only ask a question. I don't state any opinion. I want to found an opinion on what you tell me. Then, it's not so? Well! I am very glad to know it."

"It certainly is not the fact," said I, perplexed, "that I am accountable for Steerforth's having been away from home longer than usual—if he has been; which I really don't know at this moment, unless I understand it from you. I have not seen him this long while, until last night."

"No?"

"Indeed, Miss Dartle, no!"

As she looked full at me, I saw her face grow sharper and paler, and the marks of the old wound lengthen out until it cut through the disfigured lip, and deep into the nether lip, and slanted down the face. There was something positively awful to me in this, and in the brightness of her eyes, as she said, looking fixedly at me:

"What is he doing?"

I repeated the words, more to myself than her, being so amazed.

"What is he doing?" she said, with an eagerness that seemed enough to consume her like a fire. "In what is that man assisting him, who never looks at me without an inscrutable falsehood in his eyes? If you are honourable and faithful, I don't ask you to betray your friend. I ask you only to tell me, is it anger, is it hatred, is it pride, is it restlessness, is it some wild fancy, is it love, *what is it*, that is leading him?"

"Miss Dartle," I returned, "how shall I tell you, so that you will believe me, that I know of nothing in Steerforth different from what there was when I first came here? I can think of nothing. I firmly believe there is nothing. I hardly understand even what you mean."

As she still stood looking fixedly at me, a twitching or throbbing, from which I could not dissociate the idea of pain, came into that cruel mark; and lifted up the corner of her lip as if with scorn, or with a pity that despised its object. She put her hand upon it hurriedly—a hand so thin and delicate, that when I had seen her hold it up before the fire to shade her face, I had compared it in my thoughts to fine porcelain—and saying, in a quick, fierce, passionate way, "I swear you to secrecy about this!" said not a word more.

Mrs. Steerforth was particularly happy in her son's society, and Steerforth was, on this occasion, particularly attentive and respectful to her. It was very interesting to me to see them together, not only on account of their mutual affection, but because of the strong personal resemblance between them, and the manner in which what was haughty or impetuous in him was softened by age and sex, in her, to a gracious dignity. I thought, more than once, that it was well no serious cause of division had ever come between them; or two such natures—I ought rather to express it, two such shades of the same nature—might have been harder to reconcile than the two extremest opposites in creation. The idea did not originate in my own discernment, I am bound to confess, but in a speech of Rosa Dartle's.

She said at dinner:

" Oh, but do tell me, though, somebody, because I have been thinking about it all day, and I want to know."

" You want to know what, Rosa?" returned Mrs. Steerforth. " Pray, pray, Rosa, do not be mysterious."

" Mysterious!" she cried. " Oh! really? Do you consider me so?"

" Do I constantly entreat you," said Mrs. Steerforth, " to speak plainly, in your own natural manner?"

" Oh! then this is *not* my natural manner?" she rejoined. " Now you must really bear with me, because I ask for information. We never know ourselves."

" It has become a second nature," said Mrs. Steerforth, without any displeasure; " but I remember,—and so must you, I think,—when your manner was different, Rosa; when it was not so guarded, and was more trustful."

" I am sure you are right" she returned; " and so it is that bad habits grow upon one! Really? Less guarded and more trustful? How *can* I, imperceptibly, have changed, I wonder! Well, that's very odd! I must study to regain my former self."

" I wish you would," said Mrs. Steerforth, with a smile.

" Oh! I really will, you know!" she answered. " I will learn frankness from—let me see—from James."

" You cannot learn frankness, Rosa," said Mrs. Steerforth quickly—for there was always some effect of sarcasm in what Rosa Dartle said, though it was said, as this was, in the most unconscious manner in the world—" in a better school."

" That I am sure of," she answered, with uncommon fervour. " If I am sure of anything, of course, you know, I am sure of that."

Mrs. Steerforth appeared to me to regret having been a little nettled; for she presently said, in a kind tone;

"Well, my dear Rosa, we have not heard what it is that you want to be satisfied about?"

"That I want to be satisfied about?" she replied, with provoking coldness. "Oh! It was only whether people, who are like each other in their moral constitution—is that the phrase?"

"It's as good a phrase as another," said Steerforth.

"Thank you:—whether people, who are like each other in their moral constitution, are in greater danger than people not so circumstanced, supposing any serious cause of variance to arise between them, of being divided angrily and deeply?"

"I should say yes," said Steerforth.

"Should you?" she retorted. "Dear me! Supposing then, for instance—any unlikely thing will do for a supposition—that you and your mother were to have a serious quarrel."

"My dear Rosa," interposed Mrs. Steerforth, laughing good-naturedly, "suggest some other supposition! James and I know our duty to each other better, I pray Heaven!"

"Oh!" said Miss Dartle, nodding her head thoughtfully. "To be sure. *That* would prevent it? Why, of course it would. Exactly. Now, I am glad I have been so foolish as to put the case, for it is so good to know that your duty to each other would prevent it! Thank you very much."

One other little circumstance connected with Miss Dartle I must not omit; for I had reason to remember it thereafter, when all the irremediable past was rendered plain. During the whole of this day, but especially from this period of it, Steerforth exerted himself with his utmost skill, and that was with his utmost ease, to charm this singular creature into a pleasant and pleased companion. That he should succeed, was no matter of surprise to me. That she should struggle against the fascinating influence of his delightful art—delightful nature I thought it then—did not surprise me either; for I knew that she was sometimes jaundiced and perverse. I saw her features and her manner slowly change; I saw her look at him with growing admiration; I saw her try, more and more faintly, but always angrily, as if she condemned a weakness in herself, to resist the captivating power that he possessed; and finally, I saw her sharp glance soften, and her smile become quite gentle, and I ceased to be afraid of her as I had really been all day, and we all sat about the fire, talking and laughing together, with as little reserve as if we had been children.

Whether it was because we had sat there so long, or because Steerforth was resolved not to lose the advantage he had gained, I do not know; but we did not remain in the dining-room more than five minutes after her departure. " She is playing her harp," said Steerforth, softly, at the drawing-room door, " and nobody but my mother has heard her do that, I believe, these three years." He said it with a curious smile, which was gone directly; and we went into the room and found her alone.

" Don't get up," said Steerforth (which she had already done); " my dear Rosa, don't! Be kind for once, and sing us an Irish song."

" What do you care for an Irish song? " she returned.

" Much! " said Steerforth. " Much more than for any other. Here is Daisy, too, loves music from his soul. Sing us an Irish song, Rosa! and let me sit and listen as I used to do."

He did not touch her, or the chair from which she had risen, but sat himself near the harp. She stood beside it for some little while, in a curious way, going through the motion of playing it with her right hand, but not sounding it. At length she sat down, and drew it to her with one sudden action, and played and sang.

I don't know what it was, in her touch or voice, that made that song the most unearthly I have ever heard in my life, or can imagine. There was something fearful in the reality of it. It was as if it had never been written, or set to music, but sprung out of the passion within her; which found imperfect utterance in the low sounds of her voice, and crouched again when all was still. I was dumb when she leaned beside the harp again, playing it, but not sounding it, with her right hand.

A minute more, and this had roused me from my trance:—Steerforth had left his seat, and gone to her, and had put his arm laughingly about her, and had said, " Come, Rosa, for the future we will love each other very much? " And she had struck him, and had thrown him off with the fury of a wild cat, and had burst out of the room.

" What is the matter with Rosa? " said Mrs. Steerforth, coming in.

" She has been an angel, mother," returned Steerforth, " for a little while; and has run into the opposite extreme, since, by way of compensation."

" You should be careful not to irritate her, James. Her temper has been soured, remember, and ought not to be tried."

Rosa did not come back; and no other mention was made of her, until I went with Steerforth into his room to say Good-night. Then he laughed about her, and asked me if I had ever seen such a fierce little piece of incomprehensibility.

I expressed as much of my astonishment as was then capable

of expression, and asked if he could guess what it was that she had taken so much amiss, so suddenly.

" Oh, Heaven knows," said Steerforth. " Anything you like—or nothing! I told you she took everything, herself included, to a grindstone, and sharpened it. She is an edge-tool, and requires great care in dealing with. She is always dangerous. Good-night! "

" Good-night! " said I, " my dear Steerforth! I shall be gone before you wake in the morning. Good-night! "

He was unwilling to let me go; and stood, holding me out, with a hand on each of my shoulders, as he had done in my own room.

" Daisy," he said, with a smile—" for though that's not the name your godfathers and godmothers gave you, it's the name I like best to call you by—and I wish, I wish, I wish, you could give it to me! "

" Why, so I can, if I choose," said I.

" Daisy, if anything should ever separate us, you must think of me at my best, old boy. Come! Let us make that bargain. Think of me at my best, if circumstances should ever part us! "

" You have no best to me, Steerforth," said I, " and no worst. You are always equally loved, and cherished in my heart."

So much compunction for having ever wronged him, even by a shapeless thought, did I feel within me, that the confession of having done so was rising to my lips. But for the reluctance I had to betray the confidence of Agnes, but for my uncertainty how to approach the subject with no risk of doing so, it would have reached them before he said, " God bless you, Daisy, and good-night! " In my doubt, it did *not* reach them; and we shook hands, and we parted.

I was up with the dull dawn, and, having dressed as quietly as I could, looked into his room. He was fast asleep; lying, easily, with his head upon his arm, as I had often seen him lie at school.

The time came in its season, and that was very soon, when I almost wondered that nothing troubled his repose, as I looked at him. But he slept—let me think of him so again—as I had often seen him sleep at school; and thus, in this silent hour, I left him.

—Never more, oh God forgive you, Steerforth! to touch that passive hand in love and friendship. Never, never more!

30

A LOSS

I GOT DOWN TO YARMOUTH IN THE EVENING, AND WENT to the inn. I knew that Peggotty's spare room—my room—was likely to have occupation enough in a little while, if that great Visitor, before whose presence all the living must give place, were not already in the house; so I betook myself to the inn, and dined there, and engaged my bed.

It was ten o'clock when I went out. Many of the shops were shut, and the town was dull. When I came to Omer and Joram's, I found the shutters up, but the shop door standing open. As I could obtain a perspective view of Mr. Omer inside, smoking his pipe by the parlour-door, I entered, and asked him how he was.

"Why, bless my life and soul!" said Mr. Omer, "how do you find yourself? Take a seat.—Smoke not disagreeable, I hope?"

"By no means," said I. "I like it—in somebody else's pipe."

"What, not in your own, eh?" Mr. Omer returned, laughing. "All the better, sir. Bad habit for a young man. Take a seat. I smoke, myself, for the asthma."

Mr. Omer had made room for me, and placed a chair. He now sat down again very much out of breath, gasping at his pipe as if it contained a supply of that necessary, without which he must perish.

"I am sorry to have heard bad news of Mr. Barkis," said I.

Mr. Omer looked at me, with a steady countenance, and shook his head.

"Do you know how he is to-night?" I asked.

"The very question I should have put to you, sir," returned Mr. Omer, "but on account of delicacy. It's one of the drawbacks of our line of business. When a party's ill, we *can't* ask how the party is."

The difficulty had not occurred to me; though I had had my apprehensions too, when I went in, of hearing the old tune. On its being mentioned, I recognised it, however, and said as much.

"Yes, yes, you understand," said Mr. Omer, nodding his head. "We dursn't do it. Bless you, it would be a shock that the generality of parties mightn't recover, to say 'Omer and Joram's compliments, and how do you find yourself this morning?'—or this afternoon—as it may be."

Mr. Omer and I nodded at each other, and Mr. Omer recruited his wind by the aid of his pipe.

"It's one of the things that cut the trade off from attentions they could often wish to show," said Mr. Omer. "Take myself. If I have known Barkis a year, to move to as he went by, I have known him forty years. But *I* can't go and say, 'How is he?'"

I felt it was rather hard on Mr. Omer, and I told him so.

"I'm not more self-interested, I hope, than another man," said Mr. Omer. "Look at me! My wind may fail me at any moment, and it ain't likely that, to my own knowledge, I'd be self-interested under such circumstances. I say it ain't likely, in a man who knows his wind will go, when it *does* go, as if a pair of bellows was cut open; and that man a grandfather," said Mr. Omer.

I said, "Not at all."

"It ain't that I complain of my line of business," said Mr. Omer. "It ain't that. Some good and some bad goes, no doubt, to all callings. What I wish is, that parties was brought up stronger-minded."

Mr. Omer, with a very complacent and amiable face, took several puffs in silence; and then said, resuming his first point:

"Accordingly we're obleeged, in ascertaining how Barkis goes on, to limit ourselves to Em'ly. She knows what our real objects are, and she don't have any more alarms or suspicions about us, than if we was so many lambs. Minnie and Joram have just stepped down to the house, in fact (she's there, after hours, helping her aunt a bit), to ask her how he is to-night; and if you was to please to wait till they come back, they'd give you full partic'lers. Will you take something? A glass of shrub and water, now? I smoke on shrub and water, myself," said Mr. Omer, taking up his glass, "because it's considered softening to the passages, by which this troublesome breath of mine gets into action. But, Lord bless you," said Mr. Omer, huskily, "it ain't the passages that's out of order! 'Give me breath enough,' says I to my daughter Minnie, 'and I'll find passages, my dear.'"

He really had no breath to spare, and it was very alarming to see him laugh. When he was again in a condition to be talked to, I thanked him for the proffered refreshment, which I declined as I had just had dinner; and, observing that I would wait, since he was so good as to invite me, until his daughter and his son-in-law came back, I inquired how little Emily was?

"Well, sir," said Mr. Omer, removing his pipe, that he might rub his chin: "I tell you truly, I shall be glad when her marriage has taken place."

"Why so?" I inquired.

"Well, she's unsettled at present," said Mr. Omer. "It ain't that she's not as pretty as ever, for she's prettier—I do assure you, she is prettier. It ain't that she don't work as well as ever, for she does. She *was* worth any six, and she *is* worth any six. But somehow she wants heart. If you understand," said Mr. Omer, after rubbing his chin again, and smoking a little, "what I mean in a general way by the expression, 'A long pull, and a strong pull, and a pull together, my hearties, hurrah!' I should say to you, that *that* was—in a general way—what I miss in Em'ly."

Mr. Omer's face and manner went for so much, that I could conscientiously nod my head, as divining his meaning. My quickness of apprehension seemed to please him, and he went on:

"Now, I consider this is principally on account of her being in an unsettled state, you see. We have talked it over a good deal, her uncle and myself, and her sweetheart and myself, after business; and I consider it is principally on account of her being unsettled. You must always recollect of Em'ly," said Mr. Omer, shaking his head gently, "that she's a most extraordinary affectionate little thing. The proverb says, 'You can't make a silk purse out of a sow's ear.' Well, I don't know about that. I rather think you may, if you begin early in life. She has made a home out of that old boat, sir, that stone and marble couldn't beat."

"I am sure she has!" said I.

"To see the clinging of that pretty little thing to her uncle," said Mr. Omer; "to see the way she holds on to him, tighter and tighter, and closer and closer, every day, is to see a sight. Now, you know, there's a struggle going on when that's the case. Why should it be made a longer one than is needful?"

I listened attentively to the good old fellow, and acquiesced, with all my heart, in what he said.

"Therefore, I mentioned to them," said Mr. Omer, in a comfortable, easy-going tone, "this. I said. 'Now, don't consider Em'ly nailed down in point of time at all. Make it your own time. Her services have been more valuable than was supposed; her learning has been quicker than was supposed; Omer and Joram can run their pen through what remains; and she's free when you wish. If she likes to make any little arrangement, afterwards, in the way of doing any little thing for us at home, very well. If she don't, very well still. We're no losers, anyhow.' For—don't you see," said Mr. Omer, touching me with his pipe, "it ain't likely that a man so short of breath as myself, and a grandfather too, would go and strain points with a little bit of a blue-eyed blossom, like *her*?"

"Not at all, I am certain," said I.

"Not at all! You're right!" said Mr. Omer. "Well, sir, her cousin—you know it's a cousin she's going to be married to?"

"Oh yes," I replied. "I know him well."

"Of course you do," said Mr. Omer. "Well, sir! Her cousin being, as it appears, in good work, and well to do, thanked me in a very manly sort of manner for this (conducting himself altogether, I must say, in a way that gives me a high opinion of him), and went and took as comfortable a little house as you or I could wish to clap eyes on. That little house is now furnished right through, as neat and complete as a doll's parlour; and but for Barkis's illness having taken this bad turn, poor fellow, they would have been man and wife—I dare say, by this time. As it is, there's a postponement."

"And Emily, Mr. Omer?" I inquired. "Has she become more settled?"

"Why that, you know," he returned, rubbing his double chin again, "can't naturally be expected. The prospect of the change and separation, and all that, is, as one may say, close to her and far away from her, both at once. Barkis's death needn't put it off much, but his lingering might. Anyway, it's an uncertain state of matters, you see."

"I see," said I.

"Consequently," pursued Mr. Omer, "Em'ly's still a little down and a little fluttered; perhaps, upon the whole, she's more so than she was. Every day she seems to get fonder and fonder of her uncle, and more loth to part from all of us. A kind word from me brings the tears into her eyes; and if you was to see her with my daughter Minnie's little girl, you'd never forget it. Bless my heart alive!" said Mr. Omer, pondering, "how she loves that child!"

Having so favourable an opportunity, it occurred to me to ask Mr. Omer, before our conversation should be interrupted by the return of his daughter and her husband, whether he knew anything of Martha.

"Ah!" he rejoined, shaking his head, and looking very much dejected. "No good. A sad story, sir, however you come to know it. I never thought there was harm in the girl. I wouldn't wish to mention it before my daughter Minnie—for she'd take me up directly—but I never did. None of us ever did."

Mr. Omer, hearing his daughter's footstep before I heard it, touched me with his pipe, and shut up one eye, as a caution. She and her husband came in immediately afterwards.

Their report was, that Mr. Barkis was "as bad as bad could be;" that he was quite unconscious; and that Mr. Chillip had mournfully said in the kitchen, on going away just now, that the College of Physicians, the College of Surgeons, and Apothecaries' Hall, if they were all called in together, couldn't help him. He was past both Colleges, Mr. Chillip said, and the Hall could only poison him.

Hearing this, and learning that Mr. Peggotty was there, I determined to go to the house at once. I bade good-night to Mr. Omer, and to Mr. and Mrs. Joram; and directed my steps thither, with a solemn feeling, which made Mr. Barkis quite a new and different creature.

My low tap at the door was answered by Mr. Peggotty. He was not so much surprised to see me as I had expected. I remarked this in Peggotty too, when she came down; and I have seen it since; and I think, in the expectation of that dread surprise, all other changes and surprises dwindle into nothing.

I shook hands with Mr. Peggotty, and passed into the kitchen, while he softly closed the door. Little Emily was sitting by the fire, with her hands before her face. Ham was standing near her.

We spoke in whispers; listening, between whiles, for any sound in the room above. I had not thought of it on the occasion of my last visit, but how strange it was to me now, to miss Mr. Barkis out of the kitchen!

"This is very kind of you, Mas'r Davy," said Mr. Peggotty.

"It's oncommon kind," said Ham.

"Em'ly, my dear," cried Mr. Peggotty. "See here! Here's Mas'r Davy come! What, cheer up, pretty! Not a wured to Mas'r Davy?"

There was a trembling upon her, that I can see now. The coldness of her hand when I touched it, I can feel yet. Its only sign of animation was to shrink from mine; and then she glided from the chair, and, creeping to the other side of her uncle, bowed herself, silently and trembling still, upon his breast.

"It's such a loving art," said Mr. Peggotty, smoothing her rich hair with his great hand, "that it can't abear the sorrer of this. It's nat'ral in young folk, Mas'r Davy, when they're new to these here trials, and timid, like my little bird,—it's nat'ral."

She clung the closer to him, but neither lifted up her face, nor spoke a word.

"It's getting late, my dear," said Mr. Peggotty, "and here's Ham come fur to take you home. Theer! Go along with t'other loving art! What, Em'ly? Eh, my pretty?"

The sound of her voice had not reached me, but he bent his head as if he listened to her, and then said:

"Let you stay with your uncle? Why, you doen't mean to ask me that! Stay with your uncle, Moppet? When your husband that'll be so soon, is here fur to take you home? Now a person wouldn't think it, fur to see this little thing alongside a rough-weather chap like me," said Mr. Peggotty, looking round at both of us, with infinite pride; "but the sea ain't more salt in it than she has fondness in her for her uncle—a foolish little Em'ly."

"Em'ly's in the right in that, Mas'r Davy!" said Ham. "Lookee here! As Em'ly wishes of it, and as she's hurried and frightened, like, besides, I'll leave her till morning. Let me stay too!"

"No, no," said Mr. Peggotty. "You doen't ought—a married man like you—or what's as good—to take and hull away a day's work. And you doen't ought to watch and work both. That won't do. You go home and turn in. You ain't afeerd of Em'ly not being took good care on, *I* know."

Ham yielded to this persuasion, and took his hat to go. Even when he kissed her,—and I never saw him approach her, but I felt that nature had given him the soul of a gentleman,—she seemed to cling closer to her uncle, even to the avoidance of her chosen husband. I shut the door after him, that it might cause no disturbance of the quiet that prevailed; and when I turned back, I found Mr. Peggotty still talking to her.

"Now, I'm a going up-stairs to tell your aunt as Mas'r Davy's here, and that'll cheer her up a bit," he said. "Sit ye down by the fire, the while, my dear, and warm these mortal cold hands. You doen't need to be so fearsome, and take on so much. What? You'll go along with me?—Well! come along with me—come! If her uncle was turned out of house and home, and forced to lay down in a dyke, Mas'r Davy," said Mr. Peggotty, with no less pride than before, "it's my belief she'd go along with him, now! But there'll be some one else, soon,—some one else, soon, Em'ly!"

Afterwards, when I went up-stairs, as I passed the door of my little chamber, which was dark, I had an indistinct impression of her being within it, cast down upon the floor. But, whether it was really she, or whether it was a confusion of the shadows in the room, I don't know now.

I had leisure to think, before the kitchen-fire, of pretty little Em'ly's dread of death—which, added to what Mr. Omer had told me, I took to be the cause of her being so unlike herself—and I had leisure, before Peggotty came down, even to think more leniently of the weakness of it: as I sat counting the ticking of the clock, and deepening my sense of the solemn hush around me. Peggotty took me in her arms, and blessed and thanked me over and over again for being such a comfort to her (that was what she said) in her distress. She then entreated me to come up-stairs, sobbing that Mr. Barkis had always liked me and admired me; that he had often talked of me, before he fell into a stupor; and that she believed, in case of his coming to himself again, he would brighten up at sight of me, if he could brighten up at any earthly thing.

The probability of his ever doing so, appeared to me, when I saw him, to be very small. He was lying with his head and shoulders out of bed, in an uncomfortable attitude, half resting on the box which had cost him so much pain and trouble. I learned that, when he was past creeping out of bed to open it, and past assuring himself of its safety by means of the divining rod I had seen him use, he had required to have it placed on the chair at the bedside, where he had ever since embraced it, night and day. His arm lay on it now. Time and the world were slipping from beneath him, but the box was there; and the last words he had uttered were (in an explanatory tone) " Old clothes! "

" Barkis, my dear! " said Peggotty, almost cheerfully: bending over him, while her brother and I stood at the bed's foot. " Here's my dear boy—my dear boy, Master Davy, who brought us together, Barkis! That you sent messages by, you know! Won't you speak to Master Davy? "

He was as mute and senseless as the box, from which his form derived the only expression it had.

" He's a going out with the tide," said Mr. Peggotty to me, behind his hand.

My eyes were dim, and so were Mr. Peggotty's; but I repeated in a whisper, " With the tide? "

" People can't die, along the coast," said Mr. Peggotty, " except when the tide's pretty nigh out. They can't be born, unless it's pretty nigh in—not properly born, till flood. He's a going out with the tide. It's ebb at half-arter three, slack water half-an-hour. If he lives till it turns, he'll hold his own till past the flood, and go out with the next tide."

We remained there, watching him, a long time—hours. What mysterious influence my presence had upon him in that state of his senses, I shall not pretend to say; but when he at last began to wander feebly, it is certain he was muttering about driving me to school.

" He's coming to himself," said Peggotty.

Mr. Peggotty touched me, and whispered with much awe and reverence, " They are both a-going out fast."

" Barkis, my dear! " said Peggotty.

" C. P. Barkis," he cried faintly. " No better woman anywhere! "

" Look! Here's Master Davy! " said Peggotty. For he now opened his eyes.

I was on the point of asking him if he knew me, when he tried to stretch out his arm, and said to me, distinctly, with a pleasant smile:

" Barkis is willin'! "

And, it being low water, he went out with the tide.

31

A GREATER LOSS

IT WAS NOT DIFFICULT FOR ME, ON PEGGOTTY'S SOLICITATION, to resolve to stay where I was, until after the remains of the poor carrier should have made their last journey to Blunderstone. She had long ago bought, out of her own savings, a little piece of ground in our old churchyard near the grave of " her sweet girl," as she always called my mother; and there they were to rest.

In keeping Peggotty company, and doing all I could for her (little enough at the utmost), I was as grateful, I rejoice to think, as even now I could wish myself to have been. But I am afraid I had a supreme satisfaction, of a personal and professional nature, in taking charge of Mr. Barkis's will, and expounding its contents.

I may claim the merit of having originated the suggestion

that the will should be looked for in the box. After some search, it was found in the box, at the bottom of a horse's nose-bag; wherein (besides hay) there was discovered an old gold watch, with chain and seals, which Mr. Barkis had worn on his wedding-day, and which had never been seen before or since; a silver tobacco-stopper, in the form of a leg; an imitation lemon, full of minute cups and saucers, which I have some idea Mr. Barkis must have purchased to present to me when I was a child, and afterwards found himself unable to part with; eighty-seven guineas and a half, in guineas and half-guineas; two hundred and ten pounds in perfectly clean Bank notes; certain receipts for Bank of England stock; an old horseshoe, a bad shilling, a piece of camphor, and an oyster-shell. From the circumstance of the latter article having been much polished, and displaying prismatic colours on the inside, I conclude that Mr. Barkis had some general ideas about pearls, which never resolved themselves into anything definite.

For years and years, Mr. Barkis had carried this box, on all his journeys, every day. That it might the better escape notice, he had invented a fiction that it belonged to " Mr. Blackboy," and was " to be left with Barkis till called for: " a fable he had elaborately written on the lid, in characters now scarcely legible.

He had hoarded, all these years, I found, to good purpose. His property in money amounted to nearly three thousand pounds. Of this he bequeathed the interest of one thousand to Mr. Peggotty for his life; on his decease, the principal to be equally divided between Peggotty, little Emily, and me, or the survivor or survivors of us, share and share alike. All the rest he died possessed of, he bequeathed to Peggotty; whom he left residuary legatee, and sole executrix of that his last will and testament.

I felt myself quite a proctor when I read this document aloud with all possible ceremony, and set forth its provisions, any number of times, to those whom they concerned. I began to think there was more in the Commons than I had supposed. I examined the will with the deepest attention, pronounced it perfectly formal in all respects, made a pencil-mark or so in the margin, and thought it rather extraordinary that I knew so much.

In this abstruse pursuit; in making an account for Peggotty, of all the property into which she had come; in arranging all the affairs in an orderly manner; and in being her referee and adviser on every point, to our joint delight; I passed the week before the funeral. I did not see little Emily in that interval, but they told me she was to be quietly married in a fortnight.

I did not attend the funeral in character, if I may venture to say so. I mean I was not dressed up in a black cloak and a streamer, to frighten the birds; but I walked over to Blunderstone early in the morning, and was in the churchyard when it came, attended only by Peggotty and her brother. The mad gentleman looked on, out of my little window; Mr. Chillip's baby wagged its heavy head, and rolled its goggle eyes, at the clergyman, over its nurse's shoulder; Mr. Omer breathed short in the background; no one else was there; and it was very quiet. We walked about the churchyard for an hour, after all was over; and pulled some young leaves from the tree above my mother's grave.

A dread falls on me here. A cloud is lowering on the distant town, towards which I retraced my solitary steps. I fear to approach it. I cannot bear to think of what did come, upon that memorable night; of what must come again, if I go on.

It is no worse, because I write of it. It would be no better, if I stopped my most unwilling hand. It is done. Nothing can undo it; nothing can make it otherwise than as it was.

My old nurse was to go to London with me next day, on the business of the will. Little Emily was passing that day at Mr. Omer's. We were all to meet in the old boathouse that night. Ham would bring Emily at the usual hour. I would walk back at my leisure. The brother and sister would return as they had come, and be expecting us, when the day closed in, at the fireside.

I parted from them at the wicket-gate, where visionary Strap had rested with Roderick Random's knapsack in the days of yore; and, instead of going straight back, walked a little distance on the road to Lowestoft. Then I turned, and walked back towards Yarmouth. I stayed to dine at a decent alehouse, some mile or two from the Ferry I have mentioned before; and thus the day wore away, and it was evening when I reached it. Rain was falling heavily by that time, and it was a wild night; but there was a moon behind the clouds, and it was not dark.

I was soon within sight of Mr. Peggotty's house, and of the light within it shining through the window. A little floundering across the sand, which was heavy, brought me to the door, and I went in.

It looked very comfortable indeed. Mr. Peggotty had smoked his evening pipe, and there were preparations for some supper by-and-bye. The fire was bright, the ashes were thrown up, the locker was ready for little Emily in her old place. In her own old place sat Peggotty, once more, looking (but for her dress) as if she had never left it. She had fallen back, already, on the society of the work-box with Saint Paul's upon the lid, a yard-measure in the cottage, and the bit of wax candle: and there they all were, just as if they had never been disturbed. Mrs. Gummidge appeared to be fretting a little, in her old corner; and consequently looked quite natural, too.

"You're first of the lot, Mas'r Davy!" said Mr. Peggotty, with a happy face. "Doen't keep in that coat sir, if it's wet."

"Thank you, Mr. Peggotty," said I, giving him my other coat to hang up. "It's quite dry."

"So 'tis!" said Mr. Peggotty, feeling my shoulders. "As a chip! Sit ye down, sir. It ain't o' no use saying welcome to you, but you're welcome, kind and hearty."

"Thank you, Mr. Peggotty, I am sure of that. Well, Peggotty!" said I, giving her a kiss. "And how are you, old woman?"

"Ha, ha!" laughed Mr. Peggotty, sitting down beside us, and rubbing his hands in his sense of relief from recent trouble, and in the genuine heartiness of his nature; "there's not a woman in the wureld, sir—as I tell her—that need to feel more easy in her mind than her! She done her dooty by the departed, and the departed know'd it; and the departed done what was right by her, as she done what was right by the departed;—and—and—and it's *all* right!"

Mrs. Gummidge groaned.

"Cheer up, my pritty mawther!" said Mr. Peggotty. (But he shook his head aside at us, evidently sensible of the tendency of the late occurrences to recall the memory of the old one.) "Doen't be down! Cheer up, for your own self, on'y a little bit, and see if a good deal more doen't come nat'ral!"

"Not to me, Dan'l," returned Mrs. Gummidge. "Nothink's nat'ral to me but to be lone and lorn."

"No, no," said Mr. Peggotty, soothing her sorrows.

"Yes, yes, Dan'l!" said Mrs. Gummidge. "I ain't a person to live with them as has had money left. Thinks go too contrairy with me. I had better be a riddance."

"Why, how should I ever spend it without you?" said Mr. Peggotty, with an air of serious remonstrance. "What are you a talking on? Doen't I want you more now, than ever I did?"

"I know'd I was never wanted before!" cried Mrs. Gummidge, with a pitiable whimper, "and now I'm told so! How could I expect to be wanted, being so lone and lorn, and so contrairy!"

Mr. Peggotty seemed very much shocked at himself for having made a speech capable of this unfeeling construction, but was prevented from replying, by Peggotty's pulling his sleeve, and shaking her head. After looking at Mrs. Gummidge for some moments, in sore distress of mind, he glanced at the Dutch clock, rose, snuffed the candle, and put it in the window.

"Theer!" said Mr. Peggotty, cheerily. "Theer we are, Missis Gummidge!" Mrs. Gummidge slightly groaned. "Lighted up, accordin' to custom! You're a wonderin, what that's fur, sir! Well, it's fur our little Em'ly. You see, the path ain't over light or cheerful arter dark; and when I'm here at the hour as she's a comin' home, I puts the light in the winder. That, you see," said Mr. Peggotty, bending over me with great glee, "meets two objects. She says, says Em'ly, 'Theer's home!' she says. And likewise, says Em'ly, 'My uncle's theer!' For if I ain't theer, I never have no light showed."

"You're a baby!" said Peggotty; very fond of him for it, if she thought so.

"Well," returned Mr. Peggotty, standing with his legs pretty wide apart, and rubbing his hands up and down them in his comfortable satisfaction, as he looked alternately at us and at the fire, "I doen't know but I am. Not, you see, to look at."

"Not azackly," observed Peggotty.

"No," laughed Mr. Peggotty, "not to look at, but to—to consider on, you know. *I* doen't care, bless you! Now I tell you. When I go a looking and looking about that theer pritty house of our Emly's, I'm—I'm Gormed," said Mr. Peggotty, with sudden emphasis—"theer! I can't say more—if I doen't feel as if the littlest things was her, a'most. I takes 'em up and I puts 'em down, and I touches of 'em as delicate as if they was our Em'ly. So 'tis with her little bonnets and that. I couldn't see one on 'em rough used a purpose—not fur the whole wureld. There's a babby for you, in the form of a great Sea Porkypine!" said Mr. Peggotty, relieving his earnestness with a roar of laughter.

Peggotty and I both laughed, but not so loud.

"It's my opinion, you see," said Mr. Peggotty, with a delighted face, after some further rubbing of his legs, "as this is along of my havin' played with her so much, and made believe as we was Turks, and French, and sharks, and every wariety of forinners—bless you, yes; and lions and whales, and I doen't know what all!—when she warn't no higher than my knee. I've got into the way on it, you know. Why, this here candle, now!" said Mr. Peggotty, gleefully holding out his hand towards it, "*I* know wery well that arter she's married and gone, I shall put that candle theer, just the same as now. I know wery well that when I'm here o' nights (and where else should *I* live, bless your arts, whatever fortun I come into!) and she ain't heer, or I ain't theer, I shall put the candle in the winder, and sit afore the fire, pretending I'm expecting of her, like I'm a doing now. *There's* a babby for you," said Mr. Peggotty, with another roar, "in the form of a Sea Porkypine! Why, at the present minute, when I see the candle sparkle up, I says to myself, 'She's a looking at it! Em'ly's a coming!' *There's* a babby for you, in the form of a Sea Porkypine! Right for all that," said Mr. Peggotty, stopping in his roar, and smiting his hands together; "fur here she is!"

It was only Ham. The night should have turned more wet since I came in, for he had a large sou-wester hat on, slouched over his face.

"Wheer's Em'ly?" said Mr. Peggotty.

Ham made a motion with his head, as if she were outside. Mr. Peggotty took the light from the window, trimmed it, put it on the table, and was busily stirring the fire, when Ham, who had not moved, said:

"Mas'r Davy, will you come out a minute, and see what Em'ly and me has got to show you?"

We went out. As I passed him at the door, I saw, to my astonishment and fright, that he was deadly pale. He pushed me hastily into the open air, and closed the door upon us. Only upon us two.

"Ham! what's the matter?"

"Mas'r Davy!—" Oh, for his broken heart, how dreadfully he wept!

I was paralyzed by the sight of such grief. I don't know what I thought, or what I dreaded. I could only look at him.

"Ham! Poor good fellow! For Heaven's sake, tell me what's the matter!"

"My love, Mas'r Davy—the pride and hope of my art—her that I'd have died for, and would die for now—she's gone!"

"Gone!"

"Em'ly's run away! Oh, Mas'r Davy, think *how* she's run away, when I pray my good and gracious God to kill her (her that is so dear above all things) sooner than let her come to ruin and disgrace!"

The face he turned up to the troubled sky, the quivering of his clasped hands, the agony of his figure, remain associated with that lonely waste, in my remembrance, to this hour. It is always night there, and he is the only object in the scene.

"You're a scholar," he said, hurriedly, "and know what's

right and best. What am I to say, indoors? How am I ever to break it to him, Mas'r Davy?"

I saw the door move, and instinctively tried to hold the latch on the outside, to gain a moment's time. It was too late. Mr. Peggotty thrust forth his face; and never could I forget the change that came upon it when he saw us, if I were to live five hundred years.

I remember a great wail and cry, and the women hanging about him, and we all standing in the room; I with a paper in my hand, which Ham had given me; Mr. Peggotty, with his vest torn open, his hair wild, his face and lips quite white, and blood trickling down his bosom (it had sprung from his mouth, I think), looking fixedly at me.

"Read it, sir," he said, in a low shivering voice. "Slow, please I doen't know as I can understand."

In the midst of the silence of death, I read thus, from a blotted letter:

"'When you, who love me so much better than I ever have deserved, even when my mind was innocent, see this, I shall be far away.'"

"I shall be fur away," he repeated slowly. "Stop! Em'ly fur away. Well!"

"'When I leave my dear home—my dear home—oh, my dear home!—in the morning—'"

the letter bore date on the previous night:

"'—it will be never to come back, unless he brings me back a lady. This will be found at night, many hours after, instead of me. Oh, if you knew how my heart is torn. If even you, that I have wronged so much, that never can forgive me, could only know what I suffer! I am too wicked to write about myself. Oh, take comfort in thinking that I am so bad. Oh, for mercy's sake, tell uncle that I never loved him half so dear as now. Oh, don't remember how affectionate and kind you have all been to me—don't remember we were ever to be married—but try to think as if I died when I was little, and was buried somewhere. Pray Heaven that I am going away from, have compassion on my uncle! Tell him that I never loved him half so dear. Be his comfort. Love some good girl, that will be what I was once to uncle, and be true to you, and worthy of you, and know no shame but me. God bless all! I'll pray for all, often, on my knees. If he don't bring me back a lady, and I don't pray for my own self, I'll pray for all. My parting love to uncle. My last tears, and my last thanks, for uncle!' "

That was all.

He stood, long after I had ceased to read, still looking at me. At length I ventured to take his hand, and to entreat him, as well as I could, to endeavour to get some command of himself. He replied, " I thankee, sir, I thankee! " without moving.

Ham spoke to him. Mr. Peggotty was so far sensible of *his* affliction, that he wrung his hand; but, otherwise, he remained in the same state, and no one dared to disturb him.

Slowly, at last, he moved his eyes from my face, as if he were waking from a vision, and cast them round the room. Then he said, in a low voice:

" Who's the man? I want to know his name."

Ham glanced at me, and suddenly I felt a shock that struck me back.

" There's a man suspected," said Mr. Peggotty. " Who is it? "

" Mas'r Davy! " implored Ham. " Go out a bit, and let me tell him what I must. You doen't ought to hear it, sir."

I felt the shock again. I sank down in a chair, and tried to utter some reply; but my tongue was fettered, and my sight was weak.

" I want to know his name! " I heard said, once more.

" For some time past," Ham faltered, " there's been a servant about here, at odd times. There's been a gen'lm'n too. Both of 'em belonged to one another."

Mr. Peggotty stood fixed as before, but now looking at him.

" The servant," pursued Ham, " was seen along with—our poor girl—last night. He's been in hiding about here, this week or over. He was thought to have gone, but he was hiding. Doen't stay, Mas'r Davy, doen't! "

I felt Peggotty's arm round my neck, but I could not have moved if the house had been about to fall upon me.

" A strange chay and hosses was outside town, this morning, on the Norwich road, a'most afore the day broke," Ham went on. " The servant went to it, and come from it, and went to it again. When he went to it again, Em'ly was nigh him. The t'other was inside. He's the man."

" For the Lord's love," said Mr. Peggotty, falling back, and putting out his hand, as if to keep off what he dreaded. " Doen't tell me his name's Steerforth! "

"Mas'r Davy," exclaimed Ham, in a broken voice, "it ain't no fault of yourn—and I am far from laying of it to you—but his name is Steerforth, and he's a damned villain!"

Mr. Peggotty uttered no cry, and shed no tear, and moved no more, until he seemed to wake again, all at once, and pulled down his rough coat from its peg in a corner.

"Bear a hand with this! I'm struck of a heap, and can't do it," he said, impatiently. "Bear a hand and help me. Well!" when somebody had done so. "Now give me that theer hat!"

Ham asked him whither he was going.

"I'm a going to seek my niece. I'm a going to seek my Em'ly. I'm a going, first, to stave in that theer boat, and sink it where I would have drownded *him*, as I'm a livin' soul, if I had had one thought of what was in him! As he sat afore me," he said, wildly, holding out his clenched right hand, "as he sat afore me, face to face, strike me down dead, but I'd have drownded him, and thought it right!—I'm a going to seek my niece."

"Where?" cried Ham, interposing himself before the door.

"Anywhere! I'm a going to seek my niece through the wureld. I'm a going to find my poor niece in her shame, and bring her back. No one stop me! I tell you I'm a going to seek my niece!"

"No, no!" cried Mrs. Gummidge, coming between them, in a fit of crying. "No, no, Dan'l, not as you are now. Seek her in a little while, my lone lorn Dan'l, and that'll be but right! but not as you are now. Sit ye down, and give me your forgiveness for having ever been a worrit to you, Dan'l—what have *my* contrairies ever been to this!—and let us speak a word about them times when she was first an orphan, and when Ham was too, and when I was a poor widder woman, and you took me in. It'll soften your poor heart, Dan'l," laying her head upon his shoulder, "and you'll bear your sorrow better; for you know the promise, Dan'l, 'As you have done it unto one of the least of these, you have done it unto me'; and that can never fail under this roof, that's been our shelter for so many, many year!"

He was quite passive now; and when I heard him crying, the impulse that had been upon me to go down upon my knees, and ask their pardon for the desolation I had caused, and curse Steerforth, yielded to a better feeling. My overcharged heart found the same relief, and I cried too.

32

THE BEGINNING OF A LONG JOURNEY

WHAT IS NATURAL IN ME, IS NATURAL IN MANY OTHER men, I infer, and so I am not afraid to write that I never had loved Steerforth better than when the ties that bound me to him were broken. In the keen distress of the discovery of his unworthiness, I thought more of all that was brilliant in him, I softened more towards all that was good in him, I did more justice to the qualities that might have made him a man of a noble nature and a great name, than ever I had done in the height of my devotion to him. Deeply as I felt my own unconscious part in his pollution of an honest home, I believed that if I had been brought face to face with him, I could not have uttered one reproach. I should have loved him so well still—though he fascinated me no longer—I should have held in so much tenderness the memory of my affection for him, that I think I should have been as weak as a spirit-wounded child, in all but the entertainment of a thought that we could ever be re-united. That thought I never had. I felt, as he had felt, that all was at an end between us. What his remembrances of me were, I have never known—they were light enough, perhaps, and easily dismissed—but mine of him were as the remembrances of a cherished friend, who was dead.

Yes, Steerforth, long removed from the scenes of this poor history! My sorrow may bear involuntary witness against you at the Judgment Throne; but my angry thoughts or my reproaches never will, I know!

The news of what had happened soon spread through the town; insomuch that as I passed along the streets next morning, I overheard the people speaking of it at their doors. Many were hard upon her, some few were hard upon him, but towards her second father and her lover there was but one sentiment. Among all kinds of people a respect for them in their distress prevailed, which was full of gentleness and delicacy. The seafaring men kept apart, when those two were seen early, walking with slow steps on the beach; and stood in knots, talking compassionately among themselves.

It was on the beach, close down by the sea, that I found them. It would have been easy to perceive that they had not slept all last night, even if Peggotty had failed to tell me of their still sitting just as I left them, when it was broad day. They looked worn; and I thought Mr. Peggotty's head was bowed in one night more than in all the years I had known him. But they were both as grave and steady as the sea itself: then lying beneath a dark sky, waveless—yet with a heavy roll upon it, as if it breathed in its rest—and touched, on the horizon, with a strip of silvery light from the unseen sun.

" We have had a mort of talk, sir," said Mr. Peggotty to me, when we had all three walked a little while in silence, " of what we ought and doen't ought to do. But we see our course now."

I happened to glance at Ham, then looking out to sea upon the distant light, and a frightful thought came into my mind—not that his face was angry, for it was not; I recall nothing but an expression of stern determination in it—that if ever he encountered Steerforth, he would kill him.

" My dooty here, sir," said Mr. Peggotty, " is done. I'm a going to seek my—" he stopped, and went on in a firmer voice: " I'm a going to seek her. That's my dooty evermore."

He shook his head when I asked him where he would seek her, and inquired if I were going to London to-morrow? I told him I had not gone to-day, fearing to lose the chance of being of any service to him; but that I was ready to go when he would.

" I'll go along with you, sir," he rejoined, " if you're agreeable, to-morrow."

We walked again, for a while, in silence.

" Ham," he presently resumed, " he'll hold to his present work, and go and live along with my sister. The old boat yonder —"

" Will you desert the old boat, Mr. Peggotty? " I gently interposed.

" My station, Mas'r Davy," he returned, " ain't there no longer; and if ever a boat foundered, since there was darkness on the face of the deep, that one's gone down. But no, sir, no; I doen't mean as it should be deserted. Fur from that."

We walked again for a while, as before, and until he explained:

" My wishes is, sir, as it shall look, day and night, winter and summer, as it has always looked, since she fust know'd it. If ever she should come a wandering back, I wouldn't have the old place seem to cast her off, you understand, but seem to tempt her to draw nigher to 't, and to peep in, maybe, like a ghost, out of the wind and rain, through the old winder, at the old seat by the fire. Then, maybe, Mas'r Davy, seein' none but Missis Gummidge there, she might take heart to creep in, trembling; and might come to be laid down in her old bed, and rest her weary head where it was once so gay."

I could not speak to him in reply, though I tried.

"Every night," said Mr. Peggotty, "as reg'lar as the night comes, the candle must be stood in its old pane of glass, that if ever she should see it, it may seem to say 'Come back, my child, come back!' If ever there's a knock, Ham (partic'ler a soft knock), arter dark, at your aunt's door, doen't you go nigh it. Let it be her—not you—that sees my fallen child!"

He walked a little in front of us, and kept before us for some minutes. During this interval, I glanced at Ham again, and observing the same expression on his face, and his eye, still directed to the distant light, I touched his arm.

Twice I called him by his name, in the tone in which I might have tried to rouse a sleeper, before he heeded me. When I at last inquired on what his thoughts were so bent, he replied:

"On what's afore me, Mas'r Davy; and over yon."

"On the life before you, do you mean?" He had pointed confusedly out to sea.

"Ay, Mas'r Davy. I doen't rightly know how 'tis, but from over yon there seemed to me to come—the end of it like;" looking at me as if he were waking, but with the same determined face.

"What end?" I asked, possessed by my former fear.

"I doen't know," he said, thoughtfully; "I was calling to mind that the beginning of it all did take place here—and then the end come. But it's gone! Mas'r Davy," he added; answering, as I think, my look; "you han't no call to be afeerd of me; but I'm kiender muddled; I doen't fare to feel no matters,"—which was as much as to say that he was not himself, and quite confounded.

Mr. Peggotty stopping for us to join him: we did so, and said no more. The remembrance of this, in connection with my former thought, however, haunted me at intervals, even until the inexorable end came at its appointed time.

We insensibly approached the old boat, and entered. Mrs. Gummidge, no longer moping in her especial corner, was busy preparing breakfast. She took Mr. Peggotty's hat, and placed his seat for him, and spoke so comfortably and softly, that I hardly knew her.

"Dan'l, my good man," said she, "you must eat and drink,

and keep your strength, for without it you'll do nowt. Try, that's a dear soul! And if I disturb you with my clicketten," she meant her chattering, " tell me so, Dan'l, and I won't."

When she had served us all, she withdrew to the window, where she sedulously employed herself in repairing some shirts and other clothes belonging to Mr. Peggotty, and neatly folding and packing them in an old oilskin bag, such as sailors carry. Meanwhile, she continued talking, in the same quiet manner:

" All times and seasons, you know, Dan'l," said Mrs. Gummidge, " I shall be allus here, and everythink will look accordin' to your wishes. I'm a poor scholar, but I shall write to you, odd times, when you're away, and send my letters to Mas'r Davy. Maybe you'll write to me too, Dan'l, odd times, and tell me how you fare to feel upon your lone lorn journeys.

" You'll be a solitary woman here, I'm afeerd! " said Mr. Peggotty.

" No, no Dan'l," she returned, " I shan't be that. Doen't you mind me. I shall have enough to do to keep a Beein for you." (Mrs. Gummidge meant a home), " again you come back—to keep a Beein here for any that may hap to come back, Dan'l. In the fine time, I shall set outside the door as I used to do. If any *should* come nigh, they shall see the old widder woman true to 'em, a long way off."

What a change in Mrs. Gummidge in a little time! She was another woman. She was so devoted, she had such a quick perception of what it would be well to say, and what it would be well to leave unsaid; she was so forgetful of herself, and so regardful of the sorrow about her, that I held her in a sort of veneration. The work she did that day! There were many things to be brought up from the beach and stored in the outhouse—as oars, nets, sails, cordage, spars, lobster-pots, bags of ballast, and the like; and though there was abundance of assistance rendered, there being not a pair of working hands on all that shore but would have laboured hard for Mr. Peggotty, and been well paid in being asked to do it, yet she persisted, all day long, in toiling under weights that she was quite unequal to, and fagging to and fro on all sorts of unnecessary errands. As to deploring her misfortunes, she appeared to have entirely lost the recollection of ever having had any. She preserved an equable cheerfulness in the midst of her sympathy, which was not the least astonishing part of the change that had come over her. Querulousness was out of the question. I did not even observe her voice to falter, or a tear to escape from her eyes, the whole day through, until twilight; when she and I and Mr. Peggotty being alone together, and he having fallen asleep in perfect exhaustion, she broke into a half-suppressed fit of sobbing and crying, and taking me to the door, said, " Ever bless you, Mas'r Davy, be a friend to him, poor dear! " Then, she immediately ran out of the house to wash her face, in order that she might sit quietly beside him, and be found at work there, when he should awake. In short, I left her, when I went away at night, the prop and staff of Mr. Peggotty's affliction and I could not meditate enough upon the lesson that I read in Mrs. Gummidge, and the new experience she unfolded to me.

It was between nine and ten o'clock when, strolling in a melancholy manner through the town, I stopped at Mr. Omer's door. Mr. Omer had taken it so much to heart, his daughter told me, that he had been very low and poorly all day, and had gone to bed without his pipe.

" A deceitful, bad-hearted girl," said Mrs. Joram. " There was no good in her, ever! "

" Don't say so," I returned. " You don't think so."

" Yes, I do! " cried Mrs. Joram, angrily.

" No, no," said I.

Mrs. Joram tossed her head, endeavouring to be very stern and cross; but she could not command her softer self, and began to cry. I was young, to be sure; but I thought much the better of her for this sympathy, and fancied it became her, as a virtuous wife and mother, very well indeed.

" What will she ever do! " sobbed Minnie. " Where will she go! What will become of her! Oh, how could she be so cruel, to herself and him! "

I remembered the time when Minnie was a young and pretty girl; and I was glad she remembered it too, so feelingly.

" My little Minnie," said Mrs. Joram, " has only just now been got to sleep. Even in her sleep she is sobbing for Em'ly. All day long, little Minnie has cried for her, and asked me, over and over again, whether Em'ly was wicked? What can I say to her, when Em'ly tied a ribbon off her own neck round little Minnie's the last night she was here, and laid her head down on the pillow beside her till she was fast asleep! The ribbon's round my little Minnie's neck now. It ought not to be, perhaps, but what can I do? Em'ly is very bad, but they were fond of one another. And the child knows nothing! "

Mrs. Joram was so unhappy, that her husband came out to take care of her. Leaving them together, I went home to Peggotty's; more melancholy myself, if possible, than I had been yet.

That good creature—I mean Peggotty—all untired by her late

anxieties and sleepless nights, was at her brother's, where she meant to stay till morning. An old woman, who had been employed about the house for some weeks past, while Peggotty had been unable to attend to it, was the house's only other occupant besides myself. As I had no occasion for her services, I sent her to bed, by no means against her will; and sat down before the kitchen fire a little while, to think about all this.

I was blending it with the deathbed of the late Mr. Barkis, and was driving out with the tide towards the distance at which Ham had looked so singularly in the morning, when I was recalled from my wanderings by a knock at the door. There was a knocker upon the door, but it was not that which made the sound. The tap was from a hand, and low down upon the door, as if it were given by a child.

It made me start as much as if it had been the knock of a footman to a person of distinction. I opened the door; and at first looked down, to my amazement, on nothing but a great umbrella that appeared to be walking about of itself. But presently I discovered underneath it, Miss Mowcher.

I might not have been prepared to give the little creature a very kind reception, if, on her removing the umbrella, which her utmost efforts were unable to shut up, she had shown me the "volatile" expression of face which had made so great an impression on me at our first and last meeting. But her face, as she turned it up to mine, was so earnest; and when I relieved her of the umbrella (which would have been an inconvenient one for the Irish giant), she wrung her little hands in such an afflicted manner; that I rather inclined towards her.

"Miss Mowcher!" said I, glancing up and down the empty street, without distinctly knowing what I expected to see besides; "how did you come here? What is the matter?"

She motioned to me with her short right arm, to shut the umbrella for her; and passing me hurriedly, went into the kitchen. When I had closed the door, and followed, with the umbrella in my hand, I found her sitting on the corner of the fender—it was a low iron one, with two flat bars at top to stand plates upon—in the shadow of the boiler, swaying herself backwards and forwards, and chafing her hands upon her knees like a person in pain.

Quite alarmed at being the only recipient of this untimely visit, and the only spectator of this portentous behaviour, I exclaimed again, "Pray tell me, Miss Mowcher, what is the matter! are you ill?"

"My dear young soul," returned Miss Mowcher, squeezing

her hands upon her heart one over the other. "I am ill here, I am very ill. To think that it should come to this, when I might have known it and perhaps prevented it, if I hadn't been a thoughtless fool!"

Again her large bonnet (very disproportionate to her figure) went backwards and forwards, in her swaying of her little body to and fro; while a most gigantic bonnet rocked, in unison with it, upon the wall.

"I am surprised," I began, "to see you so distressed and serious"—when she interrupted me.

"Yes, it's always so!" she said. "They are all surprised, these inconsiderate young people, fairly and full grown, to see any natural feeling in a little thing like me! They make a plaything of me, use me for their amusement, throw me away when they are tired, and wonder that I feel more than a toy horse or a wooden soldier! Yes, yes, that's the way. The old way!"

"It may be, with others," I returned, "but I do assure you it is not with me. Perhaps I ought not to be at all surprised to see you as you are now: I know so little of you. I said, without consideration, what I thought."

"What can I do?" returned the little woman, standing up, and holding out her arms to show herself. "See! What I am, my father was; and my sister is; and my brother is. I have worked for sister and brother these many years—hard, Mr. Copperfield—all day. I must live. I do no harm. If there are people so unreflecting or so cruel, as to make a jest of me, what is left for me to do but to make a jest of myself, them, and everything? If I do so, for the time, whose fault is that? Mine?"

No. Not Miss Mowcher's, I perceived.

"If I had shown myself a sensitive dwarf to your false friend," pursued the little woman, shaking her head at me, with reproachful earnestness, "how much of his help or goodwill do you think *I* should ever have had? If little Mowcher (who had no hand, young gentleman, in the making of herself) addressed herself to him, or the like of him, because of her misfortunes, when do you suppose her small voice would have been heard? Little Mowcher would have as much need to live, if she was the bitterest and dullest of pigmies; but she couldn't do it. No. She might whistle for her bread and butter till she died of Air."

Miss Mowcher sat down on the fender again, and took out her handkerchief, and wiped her eyes.

"Be thankful for me, if you have a kind heart, as I think you have," she said, "that while I know well what I am, I can be cheerful and endure it all. I am thankful for myself, at any rate, that I can find my tiny way through the world, without being beholden to any one; and that in return for all that is thrown at me, in folly or vanity, as I go along, I can throw bubbles back. If I don't brood over all I want, it is the better for me, and not the worse for any one. If I am a plaything for you giants, be gentle with me."

Miss Mowcher replaced her handkerchief in her pocket, looking at me with very intent expression all the while, and pursued:

"I saw you in the street just now. You may suppose I am not able to walk as fast as you, with my short legs and short breath, and I couldn't overtake you; but I guessed where you came, and came after you. I have been here before, to-day, but the good woman wasn't at home."

"Do you know her?" I demanded.

"I know *of* her, and about her," she replied, "from Omer and Joram. I was there at seven o'clock this morning. Do you remember what Steerforth said to me about this unfortunate girl, that time when I saw you both at the inn?"

The great bonnet on Miss Mowcher's head, and the greater bonnet on the wall, began to go backwards and forwards again when she asked this question.

I remembered very well what she referred to, having had it in my thoughts many times that day. I told her so.

"May the Father of all Evil confound him," said the little woman, holding up her forefinger between me and her sparkling eyes; "and ten times more confound that wicked servant; but I believed it was *you* who had a boyish passion for her!"

"I?" I repeated.

"Child, child! In the name of blind ill-fortune," cried Miss Mowcher, wringing her hands impatiently, as she went to and fro again upon the fender, "why did you praise her so, and blush, and look disturbed?"

I could not conceal from myself that I had done this, though for a reason very different from her supposition.

"What did I know?" said Miss Mowcher, taking out her handkerchief again, and giving one little stamp on the ground whenever, at short intervals, she applied it to her eyes with both hands at once. "He was crossing you and wheedling you, I saw; and you were soft wax in his hands, I saw. Had I left the room a minute, when his man told me that 'Young Innocence' (so he called you, and you may call him 'Old Guilt' all the days of your life) had set his heart upon her, and she was giddy and liked him, but his master was resolved that no harm should come of it—more for your sake than for hers—and that that was their business here? How could I *but* believe him? I saw Steerforth soothe and please you by his praise of her! You were the first to mention her name. You owned to an old admiration of her. You were hot and cold, and red and white, all at once when I spoke to you of her. What could I think—what *did* I think—but that you were a young libertine in everything but experience, and had fallen into hands that had experience enough, and could manage you (having the fancy) for your own good? Oh! oh! oh! They were afraid of my finding out the truth," exclaimed Miss Mowcher getting off the fender, and trotting up and down the kitchen with her two short arms distressfully lifted up, "because I am a sharp little thing—I need be, to get through the world at all!—and they deceived me altogether, and I gave the poor unfortunate girl a letter, which I fully believe was the beginning of her ever speaking to Littimer, who was left behind on purpose!"

I stood amazed at the revelation of all this perfidy, looking at Miss Mowcher as she walked up and down the kitchen until she was out of breath: when she sat upon the fender again and, drying her face with her handkerchief, shook her head for a long time, without otherwise moving, and without breaking silence.

"My country rounds," she added at length, "brought me to Norwich, Mr. Copperfield, the night before last. What I happened to find out there, about their secret way of coming and going, without you—which was strange—led to my suspecting something wrong. I got into the coach from London last night, as it came through Norwich, and was here this morning. Oh, oh, oh! too late!"

Poor little Mowcher turned so chilly after all her crying and fretting, that she turned round on the fender, putting her poor little wet feet in among the ashes to warm them, and sat looking at the fire, like a large doll. I sat in a chair on the other side of the hearth, lost in unhappy reflections, and looking at the fire too, and sometimes at her.

"I must go," she said at last, rising as she spoke. "It's late. You don't mistrust me?"

Meeting her sharp glance, which was as sharp as ever when she asked me, I could not on that short challenge answer no, quite frankly.

"Come!" said she, accepting the offer of my hand to help her over the fender, and looking wistfully up into my face, "you know you wouldn't mistrust me, if I was a full-sized woman!"

I felt that there was much truth in this; and I felt rather ashamed of myself.

"You are a young man," she said, nodding. "Take a word of advice, even from three foot nothing. Try not to associate bodily defects with mental, my good friend, except for a solid reason."

She had got over the fender now, and I had got over my suspicion. I told her that I believed she had given me a faithful account of herself, and that we had both been hapless instruments in designing hands. She thanked me, and said I was a good fellow.

"Now, mind!" she exclaimed, turning back on her way to the door, and looking shrewdly at me, with her forefinger up again. "I have some reason to suspect, from what I have heard—my ears are always open; I can't afford to spare what powers I have—that they are gone abroad. But if ever they return, if ever any one of them returns, while I am alive, I am more likely than another, going about as I do, to find it out soon. Whatever I know, you shall know. If ever I can do anything to serve the poor betrayed girl, I will do it faithfully, please Heaven! And Littimer had better have a bloodhound at his back than little Mowcher!"

I placed implicit faith in this last statement, when I marked the look with which it was accompanied.

"Trust me no more, but trust me no less, than you would trust a full-sized woman," said the little creature, touching me appealingly on the wrist. "If ever you see me again, unlike what I am now, and like what I was when you first saw me, observe what company I am in. Call to mind that I am a very helpless and defenceless little thing. Think of me at home with my brother like myself and sister like myself, when my day's work is done. Perhaps you won't, then, be very hard upon me, or surprised if I can be distressed and serious. Good night!"

I gave Miss Mowcher my hand, with a very different opinion of her from that which I had hitherto entertained, and opened the door to let her out. It was not a trifling business to get the great umbrella up, and properly balanced in her grasp; but at last I successfully accomplished this, and saw it go bobbing down the street through the rain, without the least appearance of having anybody underneath it, except when a heavier fall than usual from some over-charged waterspout sent it toppling over, on one side, and discovered Miss Mowcher struggling violently to get it right. After making one or two sallies to her relief, which were rendered futile by the umbrella's hopping on again, like an immense bird, before I could reach it, I came in, went to bed, and slept till morning.

In the morning I was joined by Mr. Peggotty and by my old nurse, and we went at an early hour to the coach-office, where Mrs. Gummidge and Ham were waiting to take leave of us.

"Mas'r Davy," Ham whispered, drawing me aside, while Mr. Peggotty was stowing his bag among the luggage, "his life is quite broke up. He doen't know wheer he's going; he doen't know what's afore him; he's bound upon a voyage that'll last, on and off, all the rest of his days, take my wured for 't, unless he finds what he's a seeking of. I am sure you'll be a friend to him, Mas'r Davy?"

"Trust me, I will indeed," said I, shaking hands with Ham earnestly.

"Thankee. Thankee, very kind, sir. One thing furder. I'm in good employ, you know, Mas'r Davy, and I han't no way now of spending what I gets. Money's of no use to me no more, except to live. If you can lay it out for him, I shall do my work with a better art. Though as to that, sir," and he spoke very steadily and mildly, "you're not to think but I shall work at all times, like a man, and act the best that lays in my power!"

I told him I was well convinced of it; and I hinted that I hoped the time might even come, when he would cease to lead the lonely life he naturally contemplated now.

"No, sir," he said, shaking his head, "all that's past and over with me, sir. No one can never fill the place that's empty. But you'll bear in mind about the money, as theer's at all times some laying by for him?"

Reminding him of the fact that Mr. Peggotty derived a steady, though certainly a very moderate income from the bequest of his late brother-in-law, I promised to do so. We then took leave of each other. I cannot leave him even now, without remembering with a pang, at once his modest fortitude and his great sorrow.

As to Mrs. Gummidge, if I were to endeavour to describe how she ran down the street by the side of the coach, seeing nothing but Mr. Peggotty on the roof, through the tears she tried to repress, and dashing herself against the people who were coming in the opposite direction, I should enter on a task of some difficulty. Therefore I had better leave her sitting on a baker's door-step, out of breath, with no shape at all remaining in her bonnet, and one of her shoes off, lying on the pavement at a considerable distance.

When we got to our journey's end, our first pursuit was to look about for a little lodging for Peggotty, where her brother could have a bed. We were so fortunate as to find one, of a very clean and cheap description, over a chandler's shop, only two streets removed from me. When we had engaged this domicile, I bought some cold meat at an eating-house, and took my fellow-travellers home to tea; a proceeding, I regret to state, which did not meet with Mrs. Crupp's approval, but quite the contrary. I ought to observe, however, in explanation of that lady's state of mind, that she was much offended by Peggotty's tucking up her widow's gown before she had been ten minutes in the place, and setting to work to dust my bedroom. This Mrs. Crupp regarded in the light of a liberty, and a liberty, she said, was a thing she never allowed.

Mr. Peggotty had made a communication to me on the way to London for which I was not unprepared. It was, that he purposed first seeing Mrs. Steerforth. As I felt bound to assist him in this, and also to mediate between them; with the view of sparing the mother's feelings as much as possible, I wrote to her that night. I told her as mildly as I could what his wrong was, and what my own share in his injury. I said he was a man in very common life, but of a most gentle and upright character; and that I ventured to express a hope that she would not refuse to see him in his heavy trouble. I mentioned two o'clock in the afternoon as the hour of our coming, and I sent the letter myself by the first coach in the morning.

At the appointed time, we stood at the door—the door of that house where I had been, a few days since, so happy: where my youthful confidence and warmth of heart had been yielded up so freely: which was closed against me henceforth: which was now a waste, a ruin.

No Littimer appeared. The pleasanter face which had replaced his, on the occasion of my last visit, answered to our summons, and went before us to the drawing-room. Mrs. Steerforth was sitting there. Rosa Dartle glided, as we went in, from another part of the room, and stood behind her chair.

I saw, directly, in his mother's face, that she knew from himself what he had done. It was very pale, and bore the traces of deeper emotion than my letter alone, weakened by the doubts her fondness would have raised upon it, would have been likely to create. I thought her more like him than ever I had thought her; and I felt, rather than saw, that the resemblance was not lost on my companion.

She sat upright in her arm-chair, with a stately, immovable, passionless air, that it seemed as if nothing could disturb. She looked very steadfastly at Mr. Peggotty when he stood before her; and he looked quite as steadfastly at her. Rosa Dartle's keen glance comprehended all of us. For some moments not a word was spoken. She motioned to Mr. Peggotty to be seated. He said, in a low voice, " I shouldn't feel it nat'ral, ma'am, to sit down in this house. I'd sooner stand." And this was succeeded by another silence, which she broke thus:

" I know, with deep regret, what has brought you here. What do you want of me? What do you ask me to do? "

He put his hat under his arm, and feeling in his breast for Emily's letter, took it out, unfolded it, and gave it to her.

" Please to read that, ma'am. That's my niece's hand! "

She read it, in the same stately and impassive way,—untouched by its contents, as far as I could see,—and returned it to him.

" ' Unless he brings me back a lady,' " said Mr. Peggotty, tracing out that part with his finger. " I come to know, ma'am, whether he will keep his wured? "

" No," she returned.

" Why not? " said Mr. Peggotty.

" It is impossible. He would disgrace himself. You cannot fail to know that she is far below him."

" Raise her up! " said Mr. Peggotty.

" She is uneducated and ignorant."

" Maybe she's not; maybe she is," said Mr. Peggotty. " *I* think not, ma'am; but I'm no judge of them things. Teach her better! "

" Since you oblige me to speak more plainly, which I am very unwilling to do, her humble connections would render such a thing impossible, if nothing else did."

" Hark to this, ma'am," he returned slowly and quietly. " You know what it is to love your child. So do I. If she was a hundred times my child, I couldn't love her more. You doen't know what it is to lose your child. I do. All the heaps of riches in the wureld would be nowt to me (if they was mine) to buy her back! But save her from this disgrace, and she shall never be disgraced by us. Not one of us that she's growed up among, not one of us that's lived along with her, and had her for their all in all these many year, will ever look upon her pritty face again. We'll be content to let her be; we'll be content to think of her, far off, as if she was underneath another sun and sky; we'll be content to trust her to her husband,—to her little children, p'raps,—and bide the time when all of us shall be alike in quality afore our God! "

The rugged eloquence with which he spoke, was not devoid

of all effect. She still preserved her proud manner, but there was a touch of softness in her voice, as she answered:

"I justify nothing. I make no counter-accusations. But I am sorry to repeat, it is impossible. Such a marriage would irretrievably blight my son's career, and ruin his prospects. Nothing is more certain than that it never can take place, and never will. If there is any other compensation——"

"I am looking at the likeness of the face," interrupted Mr. Peggotty, with a steady but a kindling eye, "that has looked at me, in my home, at my fireside, in my boat—wheer not?—smiling and friendly, when it was so treacherous, that I go half wild when I think of it. If the likeness of that face don't turn to burning fire, at the thought of offering money to me for my child's blight and ruin, it's as bad. I doen't know, being a lady's, but what it's worse."

She changed now, in a moment. An angry flush overspread her features; and she said, in an intolerant manner, grasping the arm-chair tightly with her hands:

"What compensation can you make to *me* for opening such a pit between me and my son? What is your love to mine? What is your separation to ours?"

Miss Dartle softly touched her, and bent down her head to whisper, but she would not hear a word.

"No, Rosa, not a word! Let the man listen to what I say! My son, who has been the object of my life, to whom its every thought has been devoted, whom I have gratified from a child in every wish, from whom I have had no separate existence since his birth,—to take up in a moment with a miserable girl, and avoid me! To repay my confidence with systematic deception, for her sake, and quit me for her! To set this wretched fancy, against his mother's claims upon his duty, love, respect, gratitude—claims that every day and hour of his life should have strengthened into ties that nothing could be proof against! Is this no injury?"

Again Rosa Dartle tried to soothe her; again ineffectually.

"I say, Rosa, not a word! If he can stake his all upon the lightest object, I can stake my all upon a greater purpose. Let him go where he will, with the means that my love has secured to him! Does he think to reduce me by long absence? He knows his mother very little if he does. Let him put away his whim now, and he is welcome back. Let him not put her away now, and he never shall come near me, living or dying, while I can raise my hand to make a sign against it, unless, being rid of her for ever, he comes humbly to me and begs for my forgiveness. This is my right. This is the acknowledgment I *will have*. This is the separation that there is between us! And is this," she added, looking at her visitor with the proud intolerant air with which she had begun, " no injury? "

While I heard and saw the mother as she said these words, I seemed to hear and see the son, defying them. All that I had ever seen in him of an unyielding, wilful spirit, I saw in her. All the understanding that I had now of his misdirected energy, became an understanding of her character too, and a perception that it was, in its strongest springs, the same.

She now observed to me, aloud, resuming her former restraint, that it was useless to hear more, or to say more, and that she begged to put an end to the interview. She rose with an air of dignity to leave the room, when Mr. Peggotty signified that it was needless.

" Doen't fear me being any hindrance to you, I have no more to say, ma'am," he remarked as he moved towards the door. " I come heer with no hope, and I take away no hope. I have done what I thowt should be done, but I never looked fur any good to come of my stan'ning where I do. This has been too evil a house fur me and mine, fur me to be in my right senses and expect it."

With this, we departed; leaving her standing by her elbow-chair, a picture of a noble presence and a handsome face.

We had, on our way out, to cross a paved hall, with glass sides and roof, over which a vine was trained. Its leaves and shoots were green then, and the day being sunny, a pair of glass doors leading to the garden were thrown open. Rosa Dartle, entering this way with a noiseless step, when we were close to them, addressed herself to me:

" You do well," she said, " indeed, to bring this fellow here! "

Such a concentration of rage and scorn as darkened her face, and flashed in her jet-black eyes, I could not have thought compressible even into that face. The scar made by the hammer was, as usual in this excited state of her features, strongly marked. When the throbbing I had seen before, came into it as I looked at her, she absolutely lifted up her hand and struck it.

" This is a fellow," she said, " to champion and bring here, is he not? You are a true man! "

" Miss Dartle," I returned, " you are surely not so unjust as to condemn *me*! "

" Why do you bring division between these two mad creatures? " she returned. " Don't you know that they are both mad with their own self-will and pride? "

" Is it my doing? " I returned.

" Is it your doing! " she retorted. " Why do you bring this man here? "

" He is a deeply injured man, Miss Dartle," I replied. " You may not know it."

" I know that James Steerforth," she said, with her hand on her bosom as if to prevent the storm that was raging there from being loud, " has a false, corrupt heart, and is a traitor. But what need I know or care about this fellow, and his common niece? "

" Miss Dartle," I returned, " you deepen the injury. It is sufficient already. I will only say, at parting, that you do him a great wrong."

" I do him no wrong," she returned. " They are a depraved, worthless set. I would have her whipped! "

Mr. Peggotty passed on, without a word, and went out at the door.

" Oh, shame, Miss Dartle! shame! " I said indignantly. " How can you bear to trample on his undeserved affliction! "

" I would trample on them all," she answered. " I would have his house pulled down. I would have her branded on the face, dressed in rags, and cast out in the streets to starve. If I had the power to sit in judgment on her, I would see it done. See it done? I would do it! I detest her. If I ever could reproach her with her infamous condition, I would go anywhere to do so. If I could hunt her to her grave, I would. If there was any word of comfort that would be a solace to her in her dying hour, and only I possessed it, I wouldn't part with it for life itself."

The mere vehemence of her words can convey, I am sensible, but a weak impression of the passion by which she was possessed, and which made itself articulate in her whole figure, though her voice, instead of being raised, was lower than usual. No description I could give of her would do justice to my recollection of her, or to her entire deliverance of herself to her anger. I have seen passion in many forms, but I have never seen it in such a form as that.

When I joined Mr. Peggotty, he was walking slowly and thoughtfully down the hill. He told me, as soon as I came up with him, that having now discharged his mind of what he had purposed doing in London, he meant " to set out on his travels," that night. I asked him where he meant to go? He only answered, " I'm a going, sir, to seek my niece."

We went back to the little lodging over the chandler's shop, and there I found an opportunity of repeating to Peggotty what he had said to me. She informed me, in return, that he had said the same to her that morning. She knew no more than I did, where he was going, but she thought he had some project shaped out in his mind.

I did not like to leave him, under such circumstances, and we all three dined together off a beefsteak pie—which was one of the many good things for which Peggotty was famous—and which was curiously flavoured on this occasion, I recollect well, by a miscellaneous taste of tea, coffee, butter, bacon, cheese, new loaves, firewood, candles, and walnut ketchup, continually ascending from the shop. After dinner we sat for an hour or so near the window, without talking much; and then Mr. Peggotty got up, and brought his oilskin bag and his stout stick, and laid them on the table.

He accepted, from his sister's stock of ready money, a small sum on account of his legacy; barely enough, I should have thought, to keep him for a month. He promised to communicate with me, when anything befell him; and he slung his bag about him, took his hat and stick, and bade us both "Goodbye!"

"All good attend you, dear old woman," he said, embracing Peggotty, "and you too, Mas'r Davy!" shaking hands with me. "I'm a-going to seek her, fur and wide. If she should come home while I'm away,—but ah, that ain't like to be!—or if I should bring her back, my meaning is, that she and me shall live and die where no one can't reproach her. If any hurt should come to me, remember that the last words I left for her was, 'My unchanged love is with my darling child, and I forgive her!'"

He said this solemnly, bare-headed; then, putting on his hat, he went down the stairs, and away. We followed to the door. It was a warm, dusty evening, just the time when, in the great main thoroughfare out of which that by-way turned, there was a temporary lull in the eternal tread of feet upon the pavement, and a strong red sunshine. He turned, alone, at the corner of our shady street, into a glow of light, in which we lost him.

Rarely did that hour of the evening come, rarely did I wake at night, rarely did I look up at the moon, or stars, or watch the falling rain, or hear the wind, but I thought of his solitary figure, toiling on, poor pilgrim, and recalled the words:

"I'm a-going to seek her, fur and wide. If any hurt should come to me, remember that the last words I left for her was, 'My unchanged love is with my darling child, and I forgive her!'"

33

BLISSFUL

ALL THIS TIME, I HAD GONE ON LOVING DORA HARDER than ever. Her idea was my refuge in disappointment and distress, and made some amends to me, even for the loss of my friend. The more I pitied myself, or pitied others, the more I sought for consolation in the image of Dora. The greater the accumulation of deceit and trouble in the world, the brighter and the purer shone the star of Dora high above the world. I don't think I had any definite idea where Dora came from, or in what degree she was related to a higher order of beings; but I am quite sure I should have scouted the notion of her being simply human, like any other young lady, with indignation and contempt.

If I may so express it, I was steeped in Dora. I was not merely over head and ears in love with her, but I was saturated through and through. Enough love might have been wrung out of me, metaphorically speaking, to drown anybody in; and yet there would have remained enough within me, and all over me, to pervade my entire existence.

The first thing I did, on my own account, when I came back, was to take a night-walk to Norwood, and, like the subject of a venerable riddle of my childhood, to go " round and round the house, without ever touching the house," thinking about Dora. I believe the theme of this incomprehensible conundrum was the moon. No matter what it was, I, the moon-struck slave of Dora, perambulated round and round the house and garden for two hours, looking through crevices in the palings, getting my chin by dint of violent exertion above the rusty nails on the top, blowing kisses at the lights in the windows, and romantically calling on the night, at intervals, to shield my Dora—I don't exactly know what from, I suppose from fire. Perhaps from mice, to which she had a great objection.

My love was so much on my mind, and it was so natural to me to confide in Peggotty, when I found her again by my side of an evening with the old set of industrial implements, busily making the tour of my wardrobe, that I imparted to her, in a sufficiently roundabout way, my great secret. Peggotty was strongly interested, but I could not get her into my view of the case at all. She was audaciously prejudiced in my favour, and quite unable to understand why I should have any misgivings, or be low-spirited about it. " The young lady might think herself well off," she observed, " to have such a beau. And as to her Pa," she said, " what *did* the gentleman expect, for gracious sake! "

I observed, however, that Mr. Spenlow's proctorial gown and stiff cravat took Peggotty down a little, and inspired her with a greater reverence for the man who was gradually becoming more and more etherealized in my eyes every day, and about whom a reflected radiance seemed to me to beam when he sat erect in Court among his papers, like a little lighthouse in a sea of stationery. And by-the-bye, it used to be uncommonly strange to me to consider, I remember, as I sat in Court too, how those dim old judges and doctors wouldn't have cared for Dora, if they had known her; how they wouldn't have gone out of their senses with rapture, if marriage with Dora had been proposed to them; how Dora might have sung and played upon that glorified guitar, until she led *me* to the verge of madness, yet not have tempted one of those slow-goers an inch out of his road!

I despised them, to a man. Frozen-out old gardeners in the flower-beds of the heart, I took a personal offence against them all. The Bench was nothing to me but an insensible blunderer. The Bar had no more tenderness or poetry in it than the bar of a public-house.

Taking the management of Peggotty's affairs into my own hands, with no little price, I proved the will, and came to a settlement with the Legacy Duty-office, and took her to the Bank, and soon got everything into an orderly train. We varied the legal character of these proceedings by going to see some perspiring Wax-work, in Fleet Street (melted, I should hope, these twenty years); and by visiting Miss Linwood's Exhibition, which I remember as a Mausoleum of needlework, favourable to self-examination and repentance; and by inspecting the Tower of London; and going to the top of St. Paul's. All these wonders afforded Peggotty as much pleasure as she was able to enjoy, under existing circumstances: except, I think, St. Paul's, which, from her long attachment to her work-box, became a rival of the picture on the lid, and was, in some particulars, vanquished, she considered by that work of art.

Peggotty's business, which was what we used to call " common-form business " in the Commons (and very light and lucrative the common-form business was), being settled, I took her down to the office one morning to pay her bill. Mr. Spenlow had stepped out, old Tiffey said, to get a gentleman sworn for a marriage licence; but as I knew he would be back directly, our place lying close to the Surrogate's, and to the Vicar-General's office too, I told Peggotty to wait.

We were a little like undertakers, in the Commons, as regarded Probate transactions; generally making it a rule to look more or less cut up, when we had to deal with clients in mourning. In a similar feeling of delicacy, we were always blithe and light-hearted with the licence clients. Therefore I hinted to Peggotty that she would find Mr. Spenlow much recovered from the shock of Mr. Barkis's decease; and indeed he came in like a bridegroom.

But neither Peggotty nor I had eyes for him, when we saw, in company with him, Mr. Murdstone. He was very little changed. His hair looked as thick, and was certainly as black, as ever; and his glance was as little to be trusted as of old.

"Ah, Copperfield?" said Mr. Spenlow. "You know this gentleman, I believe?"

I made my gentleman a distant bow, and Peggotty barely recognised him. He was, at first, somewhat disconcerted to meet us two together; but quickly decided what to do, and came up to me.

"I hope," he said, "that you are doing well?"

"It can hardly be interesting to you," said I. "Yes, if you wish to know."

We looked at each other, and he addressed himself to Peggotty.

"And you," said he. "I am sorry to observe that you have lost your husband."

"It's not the first loss I have had in my life, Mr. Murdstone," replied Peggotty, trembling from head to foot. "I am glad to hope that there is nobody to blame for this one,—nobody to answer for it."

"Ha!" said he; "that's a comfortable reflection. You have done your duty?"

"I have not worn anybody's life away," said Peggotty, "I am thankful to think! No, Mr. Murdstone, I have not worrited and frightened any sweet creetur to an early grave!"

He eyed her gloomily—remorsefully I thought—for an instant; and said, turning his head towards me, but looking at my feet instead of my face:

"We are not likely to encounter soon again; a source of satisfaction to us both, no doubt, for such meetings as this can never be agreeable. I do not expect that you, who always rebelled against my just authority, exerted for your benefit and reformation, should owe me any good-will now. There is an antipathy between us——"

"An old one, I believe?" said I, interrupting him.

He smiled, and shot as evil a glance at me as could come from his dark eyes.

"It rankled in your baby breast," he said, "It embittered the life of your poor mother. You are right. I hope you may do better, yet; I hope you may correct yourself."

Here he ended the dialogue, which had been carried on in a low voice, in a corner of the outer office, by passing into Mr. Spenlow's room, and saying aloud, in his smoothest manner:

"Gentlemen of Mr. Spenlow's profession are accustomed to family differences, and know how complicated and difficult they always are!" With that, he paid the money for his licence; and, receiving it neatly folded from Mr. Spenlow, together with a shake of the hand, and a polite wish for his happiness and the lady's, went out of the office.

I might have had more difficulty in constraining myself to be silent under his words, if I had had less difficulty in impressing upon Peggotty (who was only angry on my account, good creature!) that we were not in a place for recrimination, and that I besought her to hold her peace. She was so unusually roused, that I was glad to compound for an affectionate hug, elicited by this revival in her mind of our old injuries, and to make the best I could of it, before Mr. Spenlow and the clerks.

Mr. Spenlow did not appear to know what the connection between Mr. Murdstone and myself was; which I was glad of, for I could not bear to acknowledge him, even in my own breast, remembering what I did of the history of my poor mother. Mr. Spenlow seemed to think, if he thought anything about the matter, that my aunt was the leader of the state party in our family, and that there was a rebel party commanded by somebody else—so I gathered at least from what he said, while we were waiting for Mr. Tiffey to make out Peggotty's bill of costs.

"Miss Trotwood," he remarked, "is very firm, no doubt, and not likely to give way to opposition. I have an admiration for her character, and I may congratulate you, Copperfield, on being on the right side. Differences between relations are much to be deplored—but they are extremely general—and the great thing is, to be on the right side:" meaning, I take it, on the side of the moneyed interest.

" Rather a good marriage this, I believe? " said Mr. Spenlow.

I explained that I knew nothing about it.

" Indeed! " he said. "Speaking from the few words Mr. Murdstone dropped—as a man frequently does on these occasions—and from what Miss Murdstone let fall, I should say it was rather a good marriage."

" Do you mean that there is money, sir? " I asked.

" Yes," said Mr. Spenlow, " I understand there's money. Beauty too, I am told."

" Indeed! Is his new wife young? "

" Just of age," said Mr. Spenlow. " So lately, that I should think they have been waiting for that."

" Lord deliver her! " said Peggotty. So very emphatically and unexpectedly, that we were all three discomposed; until Tiffey came in with the bill.

Old Tiffey soon appeared, however, and handed it to Mr. Spenlow, to look over. Mr. Spenlow, settling his chin in his cravat and rubbing it softly, went over the items with a deprecatory air—as if it were all Jorkins's doing—and handed it back to Tiffey with a bland sigh.

" Yes," he said. " That's right. Quite right. I should have been extremely happy, Copperfield, to have limited these charges to the actual expenditure out of pocket, but it is an irksome incident in my professional life, that I am not at liberty to consult my own wishes. I have a partner—Mr. Jorkins."

As he said this with a gentle melancholy, which was the next thing to making no charge at all, I expressed my acknowledgments on Peggotty's behalf, and paid Tiffey in banknotes. Peggotty then retired to her lodging, and Mr. Spenlow and I went into Court, where we had a divorce-suit coming on, under an ingenious little statute (repealed now, I believe, but in virtue of which I have seen several marriages annulled), of which the merits were these. The husband, whose name was Thomas Benjamin, had taken out his marriage licence as Thomas only; suppressing the Benjamin, in case he should not find himself as comfortable as he expected. *Not* finding himself as comfortable as he expected, or being a little fatigued with his wife, poor fellow, he now came forward, by a friend, after being married a year or two, and declared that his name was Thomas Benjamin, and therefore he was not married at all. Which the Court confirmed, to his great satisfaction.

I must say that I had my doubts about the strict justice of this, and was not even frightened out of them by the bushel of wheat which reconciles all anomalies.

But Mr. Spenlow argued the matter with me. He said, Look at the world, there was good and evil in that; look at the ecclesiastical law, there was good and evil in *that*. It was all part of a system. Very good. There you were!

I had not the hardihood to suggest to Dora's father that possibly we might even improve the world a little, if we got up early in the morning, and took off our coats to the work; but I confessed that I thought we might improve the Commons. Mr. Spenlow replied that he would particularly advise me to dismiss that idea from my mind, as not being worthy of my gentlemanly character; but that he would be glad to hear from me of what improvement I thought the Commons susceptible?

Taking that part of the Commons which happened to be nearest to us—for our man was unmarried by this time, and we were out of Court, and strolling past the Prerogative Office—I submitted that I thought the Prerogative Office rather a queerly managed institution. Mr. Spenlow inquired in what respect? I replied, with all due deference to his experience (but with more deference, I am afraid, to his being Dora's father), that perhaps it was a little nonsensical that the Registry of that Court, containing the original wills of all persons leaving effects within the immense province of Canterbury, for three whole centuries, should be an accidental building, never designed for the purpose, leased by the registrars for their own private emolument, unsafe, not even ascertained to be fire-proof, choked with the important documents it held, and positively, from the roof to the basement, a mercenary speculation of the registrars, who took great fees from the public, and crammed the public's wills away anyhow and anywhere, having no other object than to get rid of them cheaply. That, perhaps, it was a little unreasonable that these registrars in the receipt of profits amounting to eight or nine thousand pounds a year (to say nothing of the profits of the deputy registrars, and clerks of seats), should not be obliged to spend a little of that money, in finding a reasonably safe place for the important documents which all classes of people were compelled to hand over to them, whether they would or no. That, perhaps, it was a little unjust, that all the great offices in this great office should be magnificent sinecures, while the unfortunate working-clerks in the cold dark room upstairs were the worst rewarded, and the least considered men, doing important services, in London. That perhaps it was a little indecent that the principal registrar of all, whose duty it was to find the public, constantly resorting to this place, all needful accommodation, should be an enormous sinecurist in virtue of that post (and might be, besides, a clergyman, a pluralist, the holder of a stall in a cathedral, and what not), while the public was put to the inconvenience of which we had a specimen every afternoon when the office was busy, and which we knew to be quite monstrous. That, perhaps, in short, this Prerogative Office of the diocese of Canterbury was altogether such a pestilent job, and such a pernicious absurdity, that but for its being squeezed away in a corner of Saint Paul's Churchyard, which few people knew, it must have been turned completely inside out, and upside down, long ago.

Mr. Spenlow smiled as I became modestly warm on the subject, and then argued this question with me as he had argued the other. He said, what was it after all? It was a question of feeling. If the public felt that their wills were in safe keeping, and took it for granted that the office was not to be made better, who was the worse for it? Nobody. Who was the better for it? All the sinecurists. Very well. Then the good predominated. It might not be a perfect system; nothing *was* perfect; but what he objected to, was, the insertion of the wedge. Under the Prerogative Office, the country had been glorious. Insert the wedge into the Prerogative Office, and the country would cease to be glorious. He considered it the principle of a gentleman to take things as he found them; and he had no doubt the Prerogative Office would last our time. I deferred to his opinion, though I had great doubts of it myself. I find he was right, however; for it has not only lasted to the present moment, but has done so in the teeth of a great parliamentary report made (not too willingly) eighteen years ago, when all these objections of mine were set forth in detail, and when the existing stowage for wills was described as equal to the accumulation of only two years and a half more. What they have done with them since; whether they have lost many, or whether they sell any, now and then, to the butter shops; I don't know. I am glad mine is not there, and I hope it may not go there, yet awhile.

I have set all this down, in my present blissful chapter, because here it comes into its natural place. Mr. Spenlow and I falling into this conversation, prolonged it and our saunter to and fro until we diverged into general topics. And so it came about, in the end, that Mr. Spenlow told me this day week was Dora's birthday, and he would be glad if I would come down and join a little picnic on the occasion. I went out of my senses immediately; became a mere driveller next day, on receipt of a little lace-edged sheet of note-paper, "Favoured by papa. To remind;" and passed the intervening period in a state of dotage.

I think I committed every possible absurdity in the way of preparation for this blessed event. I turn hot when I remember the cravat I bought. My boots might be placed in any collection of instruments of torture. I provided, and sent down by the Norwood coach the night before, a delicate little hamper, amounting in itself, I thought, almost to a declaration. There were crackers in it with the tenderest mottoes that could be got for money. At six in the morning, I was in Covent Garden Market, buying a bouquet for Dora. At ten I was on horseback (I hired a gallant grey, for the occasion), with the bouquet in my hat, to keep it fresh, trotting down to Norwood.

I suppose that when I saw Dora in the garden and pretended not to see her, and rode past the house pretending to be anxiously looking for it, I committed two small fooleries which other young gentlemen in my circumstances might have committed—because they came so very natural to me. But oh! when I *did* find the house, and *did* dismount at the garden gate, and drag those stony-hearted boots across the lawn to Dora sitting on a garden seat under a lilac tree, what a spectacle she was, upon that beautiful morning, among the butterflies, in a white chip bonnet and a dress of celestial blue!

There was a young lady with her—comparatively stricken in years—almost twenty, I should say. Her name was Miss Mills, and Dora called her Julia. She was the bosom friend of Dora. Happy Miss Mills!

Jip was there, and Jip *would* bark at me again. When I presented my bouquet, he gnashed his teeth with jealousy. Well he might. If he had the least idea how I adored his mistress, well he might!

" Oh, thank you, Mr. Copperfield! What dear flowers! " said Dora.

I had had an intention of saying (and had been studying the best form of words for three miles) that I thought them beautiful before I saw them so near *her*. But I couldn't manage it. She was too bewildering. To see her lay the flowers against her little dimpled chin, was to lose all presence of mind and power of language in a feeble ecstasy. I wonder I didn't say, " Kill me, if you have a heart, Miss Mills. Let me die here! "

Then Dora held my flowers to Jip to smell. Then Jip growled, and wouldn't smell them. Then Dora laughed, and held them a little closer to Jip, to make him. Then Jip laid hold of a bit of geranium with his teeth, and worried imaginary cats in it. Then Dora beat him, and pouted, and said, " My poor beautiful flowers!" as compassionately, I thought, as if Jip had laid hold of me. I wished he had!

"You'll be so glad to hear, Mr. Copperfield," said Dora, "that that cross Miss Murdstone is not here. She has gone to her brother's marriage, and will be away at least three weeks. Isn't that delightful?"

I said I was sure it must be delightful to her, and all that was delightful to her was delightful to me. Miss Mills, with an air of superior wisdom and benevolence, smiled upon us.

"She is the most disagreeable thing I ever saw," said Dora. "You can't believe how ill-tempered and shocking she is, Julia."

"Yes, I can, my dear!" said Julia.

"*You* can, perhaps, love," returned Dora, with her hand on Julia's. "Forgive my not excepting you, my dear, at first."

I learnt, from this, that Miss Mills had had her trials in the course of a chequered existence; and that to these, perhaps, I might refer that wise benignity of manner which I had already noticed. I found, in the course of the day, that this was the case: Miss Mills having been unhappy in a misplaced affection, and being understood to have retired from the world on her awful stock of experience, but still to take a calm interest in the unblighted hopes and loves of youth.

But now Mr. Spenlow came out of the house, and Dora went to him, saying, "Look, papa, what beautiful flowers!" And Miss Mills smiled thoughtfully, as who should say, "Ye Mayflies, enjoy your brief existence in the bright morning of life!" And we all walked from the lawn towards the carriage, which was getting ready.

I shall never have such a ride again. I had never had such another. There were only those three, their hamper, my hamper, and the guitar-case, in the phaeton; and, of course, the phaeton was open; and I rode behind it, and Dora sat with her back to the horses, looking towards me. She kept the bouquet close to her on the cushion, and wouldn't allow Jip to sit on that side of her at all, for fear he should crush it. She often carried it in her hand, often refreshed herself with its fragrance. Our eyes at those times often met; and my great astonishment is that I didn't go over the head of my gallant grey into the carriage.

There was dust, I believe. There was a good deal of dust, I believe. I have a faint impression that Mr. Spenlow remonstrated with me for riding in it; but I knew of none. I was sensible of a mist of love and beauty about Dora, but of nothing else. He stood up sometimes, and asked me what I thought of the prospect. I said it was delightful, and I dare say it was; but it was all Dora to me. The sun shone Dora, and the birds sang Dora. The south wind blew Dora, and the wild flowers in the hedges were all Doras, to a bud. My comfort is, Miss Mills understood me. Miss Mills alone could enter into my feelings thoroughly.

I don't know how long we were going, and to this hour I know as little where we went. Perhaps it was near Guildford. Perhaps some Arabian-night magician opened up the place for the day, and shut it up for ever when we came away. It was a green spot, on a hill, carpeted with soft turf. There were shady trees, and heather, and, as far as the eye could see, a rich landscape.

It was a trying thing to find people here, waiting for us; and my jealousy, even of the ladies, knew no bounds. But all of my own sex—especially one imposter, three or four years my elder, with a red whisker, on which he established an amount of presumption not to be endured—were my mortal foes.

We all unpacked our baskets, and employed ourselves in getting dinner ready. Red Whisker pretended he could make a salad (which I don't believe), and obtruded himself on public notice. Some of the young ladies washed the lettuces for him, and sliced them under his directions. Dora was among these. I felt that fate had pitted me against this man, and one of us must fall.

Red Whisker made his salad (I wondered how they could eat it. Nothing should have induced *me* to touch it!) and voted himself into the charge of the wine-cellar, which he constructed, being an ingenious beast, in the hollow trunk of a tree. By-and-by, I saw him, with the majority of a lobster on his plate, eating his dinner at the feet of Dora!

I have but an indistinct idea of what happened for some time after this baleful object presented itself to my view. I was very merry, I know; but it was hollow merriment. I attached myself to a young creature in pink, with little eyes, and flirted with her desperately. She received my attentions with favour; but whether on my account solely, or because she had any designs on Red Whisker, I can't say. Dora's health was drunk. When I drank it, I affected to interrupt my conversation for that purpose, and to resume it immediately afterwards. I caught Dora's eye as I bowed to her, and I thought it looked appealing. But it looked at me over the head of Red Whisker, and I was adamant.

The young creature in pink had a mother in green; and I rather think the latter separated us from motives of policy. Howbeit, there was a general breaking up of the party, while the remnants of the dinner were being put away; and I strolled off by myself among the trees, in a raging and remorseful state.

I was debating whether I should pretend that I was not well, and fly—I don't know where—upon my gallant grey, when Dora and Miss Mills met me.

"Mr. Copperfield," said Miss Mills, "you are dull."

I begged her pardon. Not at all.

"And Dora," said Miss Mills, "*you* are dull."

O dear no! Not in the least.

"Mr. Copperfield and Dora," said Miss Mills, with an almost venerable air. "Enough of this. Do not allow a trivial misunderstanding to wither the blossoms of spring, which, once put forth and blighted, cannot be renewed. I speak," said Miss Mills, "from experience of the past—the remote, irrevocable past. The gushing fountains which sparkle in the sun must not be stopped in mere caprice; the oasis in the desert of Sahara must not be plucked up idly."

I hardly knew what I did, I was burning all over to that extraordinary extent; but I took Dora's little hand and kissed it—and she let me! I kissed Miss Mills's hand; and we all seemed, to my thinking, to go straight up to the seventh heaven.

We did not come down again. We stayed up there all the evening. At first we strayed to and fro among the trees: I with Dora's shy arm drawn through mine: and Heaven knows, folly as it all was, it would have been a happy fate to have been struck immortal with those foolish feelings, and have strayed among the trees for ever!

But, much too soon, we heard the others laughing and talking, and calling "Where's Dora?" So we went back, and they wanted Dora to sing. Red Whisker would have got the guitar-case out of the carriage, but Dora told him nobody knew where it was, but I. So Red Whisker was done for a moment; and *I* got it, and *I* unlocked it, and *I* took the guitar out, and *I* sat by her, and *I* held her handkerchief and gloves, and *I* drank in every note of her dear voice, and she sang to *me* who loved her, and all the others might applaud as much as they liked, but they had nothing to do with it!

I was intoxicated with joy. I was afraid it was too happy to be real, and that I should wake in Buckingham Street presently, and hear Mrs. Crupp clinking the teacups in getting breakfast ready. But Dora sang, and others sang, and Miss Mills sang—about the slumbering echoes in the caverns of Memory; as if she were a hundred years old—and the evening came on; and we had tea, with the kettle boiling gipsy-fashion; and I was still as happy as ever.

I was happier than ever when the party broke up, and the

other people, defeated Red Whisker and all, went their several ways, and we went ours through the still evening and the dying light, with sweet scents rising up around us. Mr. Spenlow being a little drowsy after the champagne—honour to the soil that grew the grape, to the grape that made the wine, to the sun that ripened it, and to the merchant who adulterated it!—and being fast asleep in a corner of the carriage, I rode by the side and talked to Dora. She admired my horse and patted him—oh, what a dear little hand it looked upon a horse!—and her shawl would not keep right, and now and then I drew it round her with my arm; and I even fancied that Jip began to see how it was, and to understand that he must make up his mind to be friends with me.

That sagacious Miss Mills, too; that amiable, though quite used-up, recluse; that little patriarch of something less than twenty, who had done with the world, and mustn't on any account have the slumbering echoes in the caverns of Memory awakened; what a kind thing *she* did!

" Mr. Copperfield," said Miss Mills, " come to this side of the carriage a moment—if you can spare a moment. I want to speak to you."

Behold me, on my gallant grey, bending at the side of Miss Mills, with my hand upon the carriage door!

" Dora is coming to stay with me. She is coming home with me the day after to-morrow. If you would like to call, I am sure papa would be happy to see you."

What could I do but invoke a silent blessing on Miss Mills's head, and store Miss Mills's address in the securest corner of my memory! What could I do but tell Miss Mills, with grateful looks and fervent words, how much I appreciated her good offices, and what an inestimable value I set upon her friendship!

Then Miss Mills benignantly dismissed me, saying, " Go back to Dora! " and I went; and Dora leaned out of the carriage to talk to me, and we talked all the rest of the way; and I rode my gallant grey so close to the wheel that I grazed his near fore leg against it, and " took the bark off," as his owner told me, to the tune of three pun' sivin'—which I paid, and thought extremely cheap for so much joy. What time Miss Mills sat looking at the moon, murmuring verses and recalling, I suppose, the ancient days when she and earth had anything in common.

Norwood was many miles too near, and we reached it many hours too soon; but Mr. Spenlow came to himself a little short of it, and said, " You must come in, Copperfield, and rest! " and I consenting, we had sandwiches and wine-and-water. In the light room, Dora blushing looked so lovely, that I could not tear myself away, but sat there staring, in a dream, until the snoring of Mr. Spenlow inspired me with sufficient consciousness to take my leave. So we parted; I riding all the way to London with the farewell touch of Dora's hand still light on mine, recalling every incident and word ten thousand times; lying down in my own bed at last, as enraptured a young noodle as ever was carried out of his five wits by love.

When I awoke next morning, I was resolute to declare my passion to Dora, and know my fate. Happiness or misery was now the question. There was no other question that I knew of in the world, and only Dora could give the answer to it. I passed three days in a luxury of wretchedness, torturing myself by putting every conceivable variety of discouraging construction on all that ever had taken place between Dora and me. At last, arrayed for the purpose at a vast expense, I went to Miss Mills's fraught with a declaration.

How many times I went up and down the street, and round the square—painfully aware of being a much better answer to the old riddle than the original one—before I could persuade myself to go up the steps and knock, is no matter now. Even when, at last, I had knocked, and was waiting at the door, I had some flurried thought of asking if that were Mr. Blackboy's (in imitation of poor Barkis), begging pardon, and retreating. But I kept my ground.

Mr. Mills was not at home. I did not expect he would be. Nobody wanted *him*. Miss Mills was at home. Miss Mills would do.

I was shown into a room up-stairs, where Miss Mills and Dora were. Jip was there. Miss Mills was copying music (I recollect, it was a new song, called Affection's Dirge), and Dora was painting flowers. What were my feelings when I recognised my own flowers; the identical Covent Garden Market purchase! I cannot say that they were very like, or that they particularly resembled any flowers that have ever come under my observation; but I knew from the paper round them which was accurately copied, what the composition was.

Miss Mills was very glad to see me, and very sorry her papa was not at home: though I thought we all bore that with fortitude. Miss Mills was conversational for a few minutes, and then, laying down her pen upon Affection's Dirge, got up, and left the room.

I began to think I would put it off till tomorrow.

"I hope your poor horse was not tired, when he got home

at night," said Dora, lifting up her beautiful eyes. " It was a long way for him."

I began to think I would do it to-day.

" It was a long way for *him*," said I, " for *he* had nothing to uphold him on the journey."

" Wasn't he fed, poor thing? " asked Dora.

I began to think I would put it off till to-morrow.

" Ye—yes," I said, " he was well taken care of. I mean he had not the unutterable happiness that I had in being so near you."

Dora bent her head over her drawing, and said, after a little while—I had sat, in the interval, in a burning fever, and with my legs in a very rigid state—

" You didn't seem to be sensible of that happiness yourself, at one time of the day."

I saw now that I was in for it, and it must be done on the spot.

" You didn't care for that happiness in the least," said Dora, slightly raising her eyebrows, and shaking her head, " when you were sitting by Miss Kitt."

Kitt, I should observe, was the name of the creature in pink, with the little eyes.

" Though certainly I don't know why you should," said Dora, " or why you should call it a happiness at all. But of course you don't mean what you say. And I am sure no one doubts your being at liberty to do whatever you like. Jip, you naughty boy, come here! "

I don't know how I did it. I did it in a moment. I intercepted Jip. I had Dora in my arms. I was full of eloquence. I never stopped for a word. I told her how I loved her. I told her I should die without her. I told her that I idolised and worshipped her. Jip barked madly all the time.

When Dora hung her head and cried, and trembled, my eloquence increased so much the more. If she would like me to die for her, she had but to say the word, and I was ready. Life without Dora's love was not a thing to have on any terms. I couldn't bear it, and I wouldn't. I had loved her every minute, day and night, since I first saw her. I loved her at that minute to distraction. I should always love her, every minute, to distraction. Lovers had loved before, and lovers would love again; but no lover had ever loved, might, could, would, or should ever love, as I loved Dora. The more I raved, the more Jip barked. Each of us, in his own way, got more mad every moment.

Well, well! Dora and I were sitting on the sofa by-and-by, quiet enough, and Jip was lying in her lap, winking peacefully at me. It was off my mind. I was in a state of perfect rapture. Dora and I were engaged.

I suppose we had some notion that this was to end in marriage. We must have had some, because Dora stipulated that we were never to be married without her papa's consent. But, in our youthful ecstasy, I don't think that we really looked before us or behind us; or had any aspiration beyond the ignorant present. We were to keep our secret from Mr. Spenlow; but I am sure the idea never entered my head, then, that there was anything dishonourable in that.

Miss Mills was more than usually pensive when Dora, going to find her, brought her back;—I apprehend, because there was a tendency in what had passed to awaken the slumbering echoes in the caverns of Memory. But she gave us her blessing, and the assurance of her lasting friendship, and spoke to us, generally, as became a Voice from the Cloister.

What an idle time it was! What an unsubstantial, happy, foolish time it was!

When I measured Dora's finger for a ring that was to be made of Forget-me-nots, and when the jeweller, to whom I took the measure, found me out, and laughed over his order-book and charged me anything he liked for the pretty little toy, with its blue stones—so associated in my remembrance with Dora's hand, that yesterday, when I saw such another, by chance, on the finger of my own daughter, there was a momentary stirring in my heart, like pain!

When I walked about, exalted with my secret, and full of my own interest, and felt the dignity of loving Dora, and of being beloved, so much, that if I had walked the air, I could not have been more above the people not so situated, who were creeping on the earth!

When we had those meetings in the garden of the square, and sat within the dingy summer-house, so happy, that I love the London sparrows, to this hour, for nothing else, and see the plumage of the tropics in their smoky feathers!

When we had our first great quarrel (within a week of our betrothal), and when Dora sent me back the ring, enclosed in a despairing cocked-hat note, wherein she used the terrible expression that "our love had begun in folly, and ended in madness!" which dreadful words occasioned me to tear my hair, and cry that all was over!

When, under cover of the night, I flew to Miss Mills, whom I saw by stealth in a back kitchen where there was a mangle, and implored Miss Mills to interpose between us and avert insanity.

When Miss Mills undertook the office and returned with Dora, exhorting us, from the pulpit of her own bitter youth, to mutual concession, and the avoidance of the Desert of Sahara!

When we cried, and made it up, and were so blest again, that the back kitchen, mangle and all, changed to Love's own temple, where we arranged a plan of correspondence through Miss Mills, always to comprehend at least one letter on each side every day!

What an idle time! What an unsubstantial, happy, foolish time! Of all the times of mine that Time has in his grip, there is none that in one retrospect I can smile at half so much, and think of half so tenderly.

34

MY AUNT ASTONISHES ME

I WROTE TO AGNES AS SOON AS DORA AND I WERE ENgaged. I wrote her a long letter, in which I tried to make her comprehend how blest I was, and what a darling Dora was. I entreated Agnes not to regard this as a thoughtless passion which could ever yield to any other, or had the least resemblance to the boyish fancies that we used to joke about. I assured her that its profundity was quite unfathomable, and expressed my belief that nothing like it had ever been known.

Somehow, as I wrote to Agnes on a fine evening by my open window, and the remembrance of her clear calm eyes and gentle face came stealing over me, it shed such a peaceful influence upon the hurry and agitation in which I had been living lately, and of which my very happiness partook in some degree, that it soothed me into tears. I remember that I sat resting my head upon my hand, when the letter was half done, cherishing a general fancy as if Agnes were one of the elements of my natural home. As if, in the retirement of the house made almost sacred to me by her presence, Dora and I must be happier than anywhere. As if, in love, joy, sorrow, hope, or disappointment; in all emotions; my heart turned naturally there, and found its refuge and best friend.

Of Steerforth I said nothing. I only told her there had been sad grief at Yarmouth, on account of Emily's flight; and that on me it made a double wound, by reason of the circumstances attending it. I knew how quick she always was to divine the truth, and that she would never be the first to breathe his name.

To this letter I received an answer by return of post. As I read it, I seemed to hear Agnes speaking to me. It was like her cordial voice in my ears. What can I say more!

While I had been away from home lately, Traddles had called twice or thrice. Finding Peggotty within, and being informed by Peggotty (who always volunteered that information to whomsoever would receive it), that she was my old nurse, he had established a good-humoured acquaintance with her, and had stayed to have a little chat with her about me. So Peggotty said; but I am afraid the chat was all on her own side, and of immoderate length, as she was very difficult indeed to stop, God bless her! when she had me for her theme.

This reminds me, not only that I expected Traddles on a certain afternoon of his own appointing, which was now come, but that Mrs. Crupp had resigned everything appertaining to her office (the salary excepted) until Peggotty should cease to present herself. Mrs. Crupp, after holding divers conversations respecting Peggotty, in a very high-pitched voice, on the staircase—with some invisible Familiar it would appear, for corporeally speaking she was quite alone at those times—addressed a letter to me, developing her views. Beginning it with that statement of universal application, which fitted every occurrence of her life, namely, that she was a mother herself, she went on to inform me that she had once seen very different days, but that at all periods of her existence she had had a constitutional objection to spies, intruders, and informers. She named no names, she said; let them the cap fitted, wear it; but spies, intruders, and informers, especially in widders' weeds (this clause was underlined), she had ever accustomed herself to look down upon. If a gentleman was the victim of spies, intruders, and informers (but still naming no names), that was his own pleasure. He had a right to please himself; so let him do. All that she, Mrs. Crupp, stipulated for, was, that she should not be "brought in contract" with such persons. Therefore she begged to be excused from any further attendance on the top set, until things were as they formerly was, and as they could be wished to be; and further mentioned that her little book would be found upon the breakfast-table every Saturday morning, when she requested an immediate settlement of the same, with the benevolent view of saving trouble " and an ill-conwenience " to all parties.

After this, Mrs. Crupp confined herself to making pitfalls on the stairs, principally with pitchers, and endeavouring to delude Peggotty into breaking her legs. I found it rather harassing to live in this state of siege, but was too much afraid of Mrs. Crupp to see any way out of it.

" My dear Copperfield," cried Traddles, punctually appearing at my door, in spite of all these obstacles, " how do you do? "

" My dear Traddles," said I, " I am delighted to see you at last, and very sorry I have not been at home before. But I have been so much engaged—"

" Yes, yes, I know," said Traddles, " of course. Yours lives in London, I think."

" What did you say? "

" She—excuse me—Miss D., you know," said Traddles, colouring in his great delicacy, " lives in London, I believe? "

" Oh yes. Near London."

" Mine, perhaps you recollect," said Traddles, with a serious look, " lives down in Devonshire—one of ten. Consequently, I am not so much engaged as you—in that sense."

" I wonder you can bear," I returned, " to see her so seldom."

" Hah! " said Traddles, thoughtfully, " It does seem a wonder. I suppose it is, Copperfield, because there's no help for it? "

" I suppose so," I replied with a smile, and not without a blush. " And because you have so much constancy and patience, Traddles."

" Dear me! " said Traddles, considering about it, " do I strike you in that way, Copperfield? Really I didn't know that I had. But she is such an extraordinarily dear girl herself, that it's possible she may have imparted something of those virtues to me. Now you mention it, Copperfield, I shouldn't wonder at all. I assure you she is always forgetting herself, and taking care of the other nine."

" Is she the eldest? " I inquired.

" Oh dear, no," said Traddles. " The eldest is a Beauty."

He saw, I suppose, that I could not help smiling at the simplicity of this reply; and added, with a smile upon his own ingenuous face:

" Not, of course, but that my Sophy—pretty name, Copperfield, I always think? "

" Very pretty! " said I.

" Not, of course, but that Sophy is beautiful too in my eyes, and would be one of the dearest girls that ever was, in anybody's eyes, I should think. But when I say the eldest is a Beauty, I mean she really is a—" he seemed to be describing clouds about himself, with both hands: "Splendid, you know," said Traddles, energetically.

"Indeed!" said I.

"Oh, I assure you," said Traddles, "something very uncommon, indeed! Then, you know, being formed for society and admiration, and not being able to enjoy much of it in consequence of their limited means, she naturally gets a little irritable and exacting, sometimes. Sophy puts her in good humour!"

"Is Sophy the youngest?" I hazarded.

"Oh dear, no!" said Traddles, stroking his chin. "The two youngest are only nine and ten. Sophy educates 'em."

"The second daughter, perhaps?" I hazarded.

"No," said Traddles. "Sarah's the second. Sarah has something the matter with her spine, poor girl. The malady will wear out by-and-by, the doctors say, but in the meantime she has to lie down for a twelvemonth. Sophy nurses her. Sophy's the fourth."

"Is the mother living?" I inquired.

"Oh yes," said Traddles, "she is alive. She is a very superior woman indeed, but the damp country is not adapted to her constitution, and—in fact, she has lost the use of her limbs."

"Dear me!" said I.

"Very sad, is it not?" returned Traddles. "But in a merely domestic view it is not so bad as it might be, because Sophy takes her place. She is quite as much a mother *to* her mother, as she is to the other nine."

I felt the greatest admiration for the virtues of this young lady and, honestly with the view of doing my best to prevent the good-nature of Traddles from being imposed upon, to the detriment of their joint prospects in life, inquired how Mr. Micawber was?

"He is quite well, Copperfield, thank you," said Traddles. "I am not living with him at present."

"No?"

"No. You see the truth is," said Traddles, in a whisper, "he had changed his name to Mortimer, in consequence of his temporary embarrassments; and he don't come out till after dark —and then in spectacles. There was an execution put into our house, for rent. Mrs. Micawber was in such a dreadful state that I really couldn't resist giving my name to that second bill we spoke of here. You may imagine how delightful it was to my feelings, Copperfield, to see the matter settled with it, and Mrs. Micawber recover her spirits."

"Hum!" said I.

"Not that her happiness was of long duration," pursued Traddles, "for, unfortunately, within a week another execution came in. It broke up the establishment. I have been living in a furnished apartment since then, and the Mortimers have been very private indeed. I hope you won't think it selfish, Copperfield, if I mention that the broker carried off my little round table with the marble top, and Sophy's flower-pot and stand?"

"What a hard thing!" I exclaimed indignantly.

"It was——it was a pull," said Traddles, with his usual wince at that expression. "I don't mention it reproachfully, however, but with a motive. The fact is, Copperfield, I was unable to re-purchase them at the time of their seizure; in the first place, because the broker, having an idea that I wanted them, ran the price up to an extravagant extent; and, in the second place, because I—hadn't any money. Now, I have kept my eye since, upon the broker's shop," said Traddles, with a great enjoyment of his mystery, "which is up at the top of Tottenham Court Road, and, at last, to-day I find them put out for sale. I have only noticed them from over the way, because if the broker saw *me*, bless you, he'd ask any price for them! What has occurred to me, having now the money, is, that perhaps you wouldn't object to ask that good nurse of yours to come with me to the shop—I can show it her from round the corner of the next street—and make the best bargain for them, as if they were for herself, that she can!"

The delight with which Traddles propounded this plan to me, and the sense he had of its uncommon artfulness, are among the freshest things in my remembrance.

I told him that my old nurse would be delighted to assist him, and that we would all three take the field together, but on one condition. That condition was, that he should make a solemn resolution to grant no more loans of his name, or anything else, to Mr. Micawber.

"My dear Copperfield," said Traddles, "I have already done so, because I begin to feel that I have not only been inconsiderate, but that I have been positively unjust to Sophy. My word being passed to myself, there is no longer any apprehension; but I pledge it to you, too, with the greatest readiness. That first unlucky obligation, I have paid. I have no doubt Mr. Micawber would have paid it if he could, but he could not. One thing I ought to mention, which I like very much in Mr. Micawber,

Copperfield. It refers to the second obligation, which is not yet due. He don't tell me that it *is* provided for, but he says it *will be*. Now, I think there is something very fair and honest about that!"

I was unwilling to damp my good friend's confidence, and therefore assented. After a little further conversation, we went round to the chandler's shop, to enlist Peggotty; Traddles declining to pass the evening with me, both because he endured the liveliest apprehensions that his property would be bought by somebody else before he could repurchase it, and because it was the evening he always devoted to writing to the dearest girl in the world.

I never shall forget him peeping round the corner of the street in Tottenham Court Road, while Peggotty was bargaining for the precious articles; or his agitation when she came slowly towards us after vainly offering a price, and was hailed by the relenting broker, and went back again. The end of the negotiation was, that she bought the property on tolerably easy terms, and Traddles was transported with pleasure.

"I am very much obliged to you, indeed," said Traddles, on hearing it was to be sent to where he lived, that night. "If I might ask one other favour, I hope you would not think it absurd, Copperfield?"

I said beforehand, certainly not.

"Then, if you *would* be good enough," said Traddles to Peggotty, "to get the flower-pot now, I think I should like (it being Sophy's, Copperfield) to carry it home myself!"

Peggotty was glad to get it for him, and he overwhelmed her with thanks, and went his way up Tottenham Court Road, carrying the flower-pot affectionately in his arms, with one of the most delighted expressions of countenance I ever saw.

We then turned back towards my chambers. As the shops had charms for Peggotty which I never knew them possess in the same degree for anybody else, I sauntered easily along, amused by her staring in at the windows, and waiting for her as often as she chose. We were thus a good while in getting to the Adelphi.

On our way up-stairs, I called her attention to the sudden disappearance of Mrs. Crupp's pitfalls, and also to the prints of recent footsteps. We were both very much surprised, coming higher up, to find my outer door standing open (which I had shut), and to hear voices inside.

We looked at one another, without knowing what to make of this, and went into the sitting-room. What was my amazement to find, of all people upon earth, my aunt there, and Mr. Dick!

My aunt sitting on a quantity of luggage, with her two birds before her, and her cat on her knee, like a female Robinson Crusoe, drinking tea. Mr. Dick leaning thoughtfully on a great kite, such as we had often been out together to fly, with more luggage piled about him!

"My dear aunt!" cried I. "Why, what an unexpected pleasure!"

We cordially embraced; and Mr. Dick and I cordially shook hands; and Mrs. Crupp, who was busy making tea, and could not be too attentive, cordially said she had knowed well as Mr. Copperfull would have his heart in his mouth, when he see his dear relations.

"Hollo!" said my aunt to Peggotty, who quailed before her awful presence. "How are *you*?"

"You remember my aunt, Peggotty?" said I.

"For the love of goodness, child," exclaimed my aunt, "don't call the woman by that South Sea Island name! If she married and got rid of it, which was the best thing she could do, why don' you give her the benefit of the change? What's your name now,—P?" said my aunt, as a compromise for the obnoxious appellation.

"Barkis, ma'am," said Peggotty, with a curtsey.

"Well! That's human," said my aunt. "It sound less as if you wanted a missionary. How d'ye do, Barkis? I hope you're well?"

Encouraged by these gracious words, and by my aunt's extending her hand, Barkis came forward, and took the hand, and curtseyed her acknowledgments.

"We are older then we were, I see," said my aunt. "We have only met each other once before, you know. A nice business we made of it then! Trot, my dear, another cup."

I handed it dutifully to my aunt, who was in her usual inflexible state of figure; and ventured a remonstrance with her on the subject of her sitting on a box.

"Let me draw the sofa here, or the easy chair, aunt," said I. "Why should you be so uncomfortable?"

"Thank you, Trot," replied my aunt, "I prefer to sit upon my property." Here my aunt looked hard at Mrs. Crupp, and observed, "We needn't trouble you to wait, ma'am."

"Shall I put a little more tea in the pot afore I go, ma'am?" said Mrs. Crupp.

"No, I thank you, ma'am," replied my aunt.

"Would you let me fetch another pat of butter, ma'am?" said Mrs. Crupp. "Or would you be persuaded to try a new-laid hegg? or should I brile a rasher? Ain't there nothing I could do for your dear aunt, Mr. Copperfull?"

"Nothing, ma'am," returned my aunt. "I shall do very well, I thank you."

Mrs. Crupp, who had been incessantly smiling to express sweet temper, and incessantly holding her head on one side, to express a general feebleness of constitution, and incessantly rubbing her hands, to express a desire to be of service to all deserving objects, gradually smiled herself, one-sided herself, and rubbed herself, out of the room.

"Dick!" said my aunt. "You know what I told you about time-servers and wealth-worshippers?"

Mr. Dick—with rather a scared look, as if he had forgotten it—returned a hasty answer in the affirmative.

"Mrs. Crupp is one of them," said my aunt. "Barkis, I'll trouble you to look after the tea, and let me have another cup, for I don't fancy that woman's pouring-out!"

I knew my aunt sufficiently well to know that she had something of importance on her mind, and that there was far more matter in this arrival than a stranger might have supposed. I noticed how her eye lighted on me, when she thought my attention otherwise occupied; and what a curious process of hesitation appeared to be going on within her, while she preserved her outward stiffness and composure. I began to reflect whether I had done anything to offend her; and my conscience whispered me that I had not yet told her about Dora. Could it by any means be that, I wondered!

As I knew she would only speak in her own good time, I sat down near her, and spoke to the birds, and played with the cat, and was as easy as I could be. But I was very far from being really easy; and I should still have been so, even if Mr. Dick, leaning over the great kite behind my aunt, had not taken every secret opportunity of shaking his head darkly at me, and pointing at her.

"Trot," said my aunt at last, when she had finished her tea, and carefully smoothed down her dress, and wiped her lips—"you needn't go, Barkis!—Trot, have you got to be firm and self-reliant?"

"I hope so, aunt."

"What do you think?" inquired Miss Betsey.

"I think so, aunt."

"Then why, my love," said my aunt, looking earnestly at me, "why do you think I prefer to sit upon this property of mine to-night?"

I shook my head, unable to guess.

"Because," said my aunt, "it's all I have. Because I'm ruined, my dear!"

If the house, and every one of us, had tumbled out into the river together, I could hardly have received a greater shock.

"Dick knows it," said my aunt, laying her hand calmly on my shoulder. "I am ruined, my dear Trot! All I have in the world is in this room, except the cottage; and that I have left Janet to let. Barkis, I want to get a bed for this gentleman to-night. To save expense, perhaps you can make up something here for myself. Anything will do. It's only for to-night. We'll talk about this, more, to-morrow."

I was roused from my amazement, and concern for her—I am sure, for her—by her falling on my neck for a moment, and crying that she only grieved for me. In another moment she suppressed this emotion; and said with an aspect more triumphant than dejected:

"We must meet reverses boldly, and not suffer them to frighten us, my dear. We must learn to act the play out. We must live misfortune down, Trot!"

35

DEPRESSION

AS SOON AS I COULD RECOVER MY PRESENCE OF MIND, which quite deserted me in the first overpowering shock of my aunt's intelligence, I proposed to Mr. Dick to come round to the chandler's shop, and take possession of the bed which Mr. Peggotty had lately vacated. The chandler's shop being in Hungerford Market, and Hungerford Market being a very different place in those days, there was a low wooden colonnade before the door (not very unlike that before the house where the little man and woman used to live, in the old weather-glass), which pleased Mr. Dick mightily. The glory of lodging over this structure would have compensated him, I dare say, for many inconveniences; but, as there were really few to bear, beyond the compound of flavours I have already mentioned, and perhaps the want of a little more elbow-room, he was perfectly charmed with his accommodation. Mrs. Crupp had indignantly assured him that there wasn't room to swing a cat there; but, as Mr. Dick justly observed to me, sitting down on the foot of the bed, nursing his leg, " You know, Trotwood, I don't want to swing a cat. I never do swing a cat. Therefore, what does that signify to *me*! "

I tried to ascertain whether Mr. Dick had any understanding of the causes of this sudden and great change in my aunt's affairs. As I might have expected, he had none at all. The only account he could give of it was, that my aunt had said to him, the day before yesterday, " Now, Dick, are you really and truly the philosopher I take you for? " That then he had said, Yes, he hoped so. That then my aunt had said, " Dick, I am ruined." That then he had said, " Oh, indeed! " That then my aunt had praised him highly, which he was very glad of. And that then they had come to me, and had had bottled porter and sandwiches on the road.

Mr. Dick was so very complacent, sitting on the foot of the bed, nursing his leg, and telling me this, with his eyes wide open, and a surprised smile, that I am sorry to say I was provoked into explaining to him that ruin meant distress, want, and starvation; but I was soon bitterly reproved for this harshness, by seeing his face turn pale, and tears course down his lengthened cheeks, while he fixed upon me a look of such unutterable woe, that it might have softened a far harder heart than mine. I took infinitely greater pains to cheer him up again than I had taken to depress him; and I soon understood (as I ought to have known at first) that he had been so confident, merely because of his faith in the wisest and most wonderful of women, and his unbounded reliance on my intellectual resources. The latter, I believe, he considered a match for any kind of disaster not absolutely mortal.

" What can we do, Trotwood? " said Mr. Dick. " There's the Memorial—"

" To be sure there is," said I. " But all we can do just now, Mr. Dick, is to keep a cheerful countenance, and not let my aunt see that we are thinking about it."

He assented to this in the most earnest manner; and implored me, if I should see him wandering an inch out of the right course, to recall him by some of those superior methods which were always at my command. But I regret to state that the fright I had given him proved too much for his best attempts at concealment.

All the evening his eyes wandered to my aunt's face, with an expression of the most dismal apprehension, as if he saw her growing thin on the spot. He was conscious of this, and put a constraint upon his head; but his keeping that immovable, and sitting rolling his eyes like a piece of machinery, did not mend the matter at all. I saw him look at the loaf at supper (which happened to be a small one), as if nothing else stood between us and famine; and when my aunt insisted on his making his customary repast, I detected him in the act of pocketing fragments of his bread and cheese; I have no doubt for the purpose of reviving us with those savings, when we should have reached an advanced stage of attenuation.

My aunt, on the other hand, was in a composed frame of mind, which was a lesson to all of us—to me, I am sure. She was extremely gracious to Peggotty, except when I inadvertently called her by that name; and, strange as I knew she felt in London, appeared quite at home. She was to have my bed, and I was to lie in the sitting-room, to keep guard over her. She made a great point of being so near the river, in case of a conflagration; and I suppose really did find some satisfaction in that circumstance.

"Trot, my dear," said my aunt, when she saw me making preparations for compounding her usual night-draught, "No!"

"Nothing, aunt?"

"Not wine, my dear. Ale."

"But there is wine here, aunt. And you always have it made of wine."

"Keep that, in case of sickness," said my aunt. "We mustn't use it carelessly, Trot. Ale for me. Half a pint."

I thought Mr. Dick would have fallen, insensible. My aunt being resolute, I went out and got the ale myself. As it was growing late, Peggotty and Mr. Dick took that opportunity of repairing to the chandler's shop together. I parted from him, poor fellow, at the corner of the street, with his great kite at his back, a very monument of human misery.

My aunt was walking up and down the room when I returned crimping the borders of her nightcap with her fingers. I warmed the ale and made the toast on the usual infallible principles. When it was ready for her, she was ready for it, with her nightcap on, and the skirt of her gown turned back on her knees.

"My dear," said my aunt, after taking a spoonful of it; "it's a great deal better than wine. Not half so bilious."

I suppose I looked doubtful, for she added:

" Tut, tut, child. If nothing worse than Ale happens to us, we are well off."

" I should think so myself, aunt, I am sure," said I.

" Well, then, why *don't* you think so ? " said my aunt.

" Because you and I are very different people," I returned.

" Stuff and nonsense, Trot! " replied my aunt.

My aunt went on with a quiet enjoyment, in which there was very little affectation, if any; drinking the warm ale with a tea-spoon, and soaking her strips of toast in it.

" Trot," said she, "I don't care for strange faces in general, but I rather like that Barkis of yours, do you know! "

" It's better than a hundred pounds to hear you say so! " said I.

" It's a most extraordinary world," observed my aunt, rubbing her nose; " how that woman ever got into it with that name, is unaccountable to me. It would be much more easy to be born a Jackson, or something of that sort, one would think."

" Perhaps she thinks so, too; it's not her fault," said I.

" I suppose not," returned my aunt, rather grudging the admission; " but it's very aggravating. However, she's Barkis *now*. That's some comfort. Barkis is uncommonly fond of you, Trot."

" There is nothing she would leave undone to prove it," said I.

" Nothing, I believe," returned my aunt. " Here, the poor fool has been begging and praying about handing over some of her money—because she has got too much of it. A simpleton! "

My aunt's tears of pleasure were positively trickling down into the warm ale.

" She's the most ridiculous creature that ever was born," said my aunt. " I knew, from the first moment when I saw her with that poor dear blessed baby of a mother of yours, that she was the most ridiculous of mortals. But there are good points in Barkis! "

Affecting to laugh, she got an opportunity of putting her hand to her eyes. Having availed herself of it, she resumed her toast and her discourse together.

" Ah! Mercy upon us! " sighed my aunt. " I know all about it, Trot! Barkis and myself had quite a gossip while you were out with Dick. I know all about it. I don't know where these wretched girls expect to go to, for my part. I wonder they don't knock out their brains against—against mantelpieces," said my aunt; an idea which was probably suggested to her by her contemplation of mine.

" Poor Emily! " said I.

" Oh, don't talk to me about poor," returned my aunt. " She

should have thought of that, before she caused so much misery! Give me a kiss, Trot, I am sorry for your early experience."

As I bent forward, she put her tumbler on my knee to detain me, and said:

"Oh, Trot, Trot! And so you fancy yourself in love! Do you?"

"Fancy, aunt!" I exclaimed, as red as I could be. "I adore her with my whole soul!"

"Dora, indeed!" returned my aunt. "And you mean to say the little thing is very fascinating, I suppose?"

"My dear aunt," I replied, "no one can form the least idea what she is!"

"Ah! And not silly?" said my aunt.

"Silly, aunt!"

I seriously believe it had never once entered my head for a single moment, to consider whether she was or not. I resented the idea, of course; but I was in a manner struck by it, as a new one altogether.

"Not light-headed?" said my aunt.

"Light-headed, aunt!" I could only repeat this daring speculation with the same kind of feeling with which I had repeated the preceding question.

"Well, well!" said my aunt. "I only ask. I don't depreciate her. Poor little couple! And you think you were formed for one another, and are to go through a party-supper-table kind of life, like two pretty pieces of confectionery, do you, Trot?"

She asked me this so kindly, and with such a gentle air, half playful and half sorrowful, that I was quite touched.

"We are young and inexperienced, aunt, I know," I replied; "and I dare say we say and think a good deal that is rather foolish. But we love one another truly, I am sure. If I thought Dora could ever love anybody else, or cease to love me; or that I could ever love anybody else, or cease to love her; I don't know what I should do—go out of my mind, I think!"

"Ah, Trot!" said my aunt, shaking her head, and smiling gravely, "blind, blind, blind!

"Some one that I know, Trot," my aunt pursued, after a pause, "though of a very pliant disposition, has an earnestness of affection in him that reminds me of poor Baby. Earnestness is what that Somebody must look for, to sustain him and improve him, Trot. Deep, downright, faithful earnestness."

"If you only knew the earnestness of Dora, aunt!" I cried.

"Oh, Trot!" she said again; "blind, blind!" and without knowing why, I felt a vague unhappy loss or want of something overshadow me like a cloud.

"However," said my aunt, "I don't want to put two young creatures out of conceit with themselves, or to make them unhappy; so, though it is a girl and boy attachment, and girl and boy attachments very often—mind! I don't say always!— come to nothing, still we'll be serious about it, and hope for a prosperous issue one of these days. There's time enough for it to come to anything!"

This was not upon the whole very comforting to a rapturous lover; but I was glad to have my aunt in my confidence, and I was mindful of her being fatigued. So I thanked her ardently for this mark of her affection, and for all her other kindnesses towards me; and after a tender good-night, she took her nightcap into my bedroom.

How miserable I was, when I lay down! How I thought and thought about my being poor, in Mr. Spenlow's eyes; about my not being what I thought I was, when I proposed to Dora; about the chivalrous necessity of telling Dora what my worldly condition was, and releasing her from her engagement if she thought fit; about how I should contrive to live, during the long term of my articles, when I was earning nothing; about doing something to assist my aunt, and seeing no way of doing anything; about coming down to have no money in my pocket, and to wear a shabby coat, and to be able to carry Dora no little presents, and to ride no gallant greys, and to show myself in no agreeable light! Sordid and selfish as I knew it was, and as I tortured myself by knowing that it was, to let my mind run on my own distress so much, I was so devoted to Dora that I could not help it. I knew that it was base in me not to think more of my aunt, and less of myself; but, so far, selfishness was inseparable from Dora, and I could not put Dora on one side for any mortal creature. How exceedingly miserable I was, that night!

As to sleep, I had dreams of poverty in all sorts of shapes, but I seemed to dream without the previous ceremony of going to sleep. Now I was ragged, wanting to sell Dora matches, six bundles for a halfpenny; now I was at the office in a nightgown and boots, remonstrated with by Mr. Spenlow on appearing before the clients in that airy attire; now I was hungrily picking up the crumbs that fell from old Tiffey's daily biscuit, regularly eaten when St. Paul's struck one; now I was hopelessly endeavouring to get a licence to marry Dora, having nothing but one of Uriah Heep's gloves to offer in exchange, which the whole Commons rejected; and still, more or less conscious of my own room, I was always tossing about like a distressed ship in a sea of bed-clothes.

My aunt was restless, too, for I frequently heard her walking to and fro. Two or three times in the course of the night, attired in a long flannel wrapper in which she looked seven feet high, she appeared, like a disturbed ghost, in my room, and came to the side of the sofa on which I lay. On the first occasion I started up in alarm, to learn that she inferred from a particular light in the sky, that Westminster Abbey was on fire; and to be consulted in reference to the probability of its igniting Buckingham Street, in case the wind changed. Lying still, after that, I found that she sat down near me, whispering to herself " Poor boy! " And then it made me twenty times more wretched, to know how unselfishly mindful she was of me, and how selfishly mindful I was of myself.

It was difficult to believe that a night so long to me, could be short to anybody else. This consideration set me thinking and thinking of an imaginary party where people were dancing the hours away, until that became a dream too, and I heard the music incessantly playing one tune, and saw Dora incessantly dancing one dance, without taking the least notice of me. The man who had been playing the harp all night, was trying in vain to cover it with an ordinary-sized nightcap, when I awoke; or I should rather say, when I left off trying to go to sleep, and saw the sun shining in through the window at last.

There was an old Roman bath in those days at the bottom of one of the streets out of the Strand—it may be there still—in which I have had many a cold plunge. Dressing myself as quietly as I could, and leaving Peggotty to look after my aunt, I tumbled head foremost into it, and then went for a walk to Hampstead. I had a hope that this brisk treatment might freshen my wits a little; and I think it did them good, for I soon came to the conclusion that the first step I ought to take was to try if my articles could be cancelled and the premium recovered. I got some breakfast on the Heath, and walked back to Doctors' Commons, along the watered roads and through a pleasant smell of summer flowers, growing in gardens and carried into town on hucksters' heads, intent on this first effort to meet our altered circumstances.

I arrived at the office so soon, after all, that I had half an hour's loitering about the Commons, before old Tiffey, who was always first, appeared with his key. Then I sat down in my shady corner, looking up at the sunlight on the opposite chimney-pots, and thinking about Dora; until Mr. Spenlow came in, crisp and curly.

" How are you, Copperfield? " said he. " Fine morning! "

"Beautiful morning, sir," said I. "Could I say a word to you before you go into Court?"

"By all means," said he. "Come into my room."

I followed him into his room, and he began putting on his gown, and touching himself up before a little glass he had, hanging inside a closet door.

"I am sorry to say," said I, "that I have some rather disheartening intelligence from my aunt."

"No!" said he. "Dear me! Not paralysis, I hope?"

"It has no reference to her health, sir," I replied. "She has met with some large losses. In fact, she has very little left, indeed."

"You as-tound me, Copperfield!" cried Mr. Spenlow.

I shook my head. "Indeed, sir," said I, "her affairs are so changed, that I wished to ask you whether it would be possible—at a sacrifice on our part of some portion of the premium, of course," I put in this, on the spur of the moment, warned by the blank expression of his face—"to cancel my articles?"

What it cost me to make this proposal, nobody knows. It was like asking, as a favour, to be sentenced to transportation from Dora.

"To cancel your articles, Copperfield? Cancel?"

I explained with tolerable firmness, that I really did not know where my means of subsistence were to come from, unless I could earn them for myself. I had no fear for the future, I said—and I laid great emphasis on that, as if to imply that I should still be decidedly eligible for a son-in-law one of these days—but, for the present, I was thrown upon my own resources.

"I am extremely sorry to hear this, Copperfield," said Mr. Spenlow. "Extremely sorry. It is not usual to cancel articles for any such reason. It is not a professional course of proceeding. It is not a convenient precedent at all. Far from it. At the same time—"

"You are very good, sir," I murmured, anticipating a concession.

"Not at all. Don't mention it," said Mr. Spenlow. "At the same time, I was going to say, if it had been my lot to have my hands unfettered—if I had not a partner—Mr. Jorkins—"

My hopes were dashed in a moment, but I made another effort.

"Do you think, sir," said I, "if I were to mention it to Mr. Jorkins—"

Mr. Spenlow shook his head discouragingly. "Heaven forbid, Copperfield," he replied, "that I should do any man an injustice: still less, Mr. Jorkins. But I know my partner, Copperfield.

Mr. Jorkins is *not* a man to respond to a proposition of this peculiar nature. Mr. Jorkins is very difficult to move from the beaten track. You know what he is!"

I am sure I knew nothing about him, except that he had originally been alone in the business, and now lived by himself in a house near Montagu Square, which was fearfully in want of painting; that he came very late of a day, and went away very early; that he never appeared to be consulted about anything; and that he had a dingy little black-hole of his own up-stairs, where no business was ever done, and where there was a yellow old cartridge-paper pad upon his desk, unsoiled by ink, and reported to be twenty years of age.

"Would you object to my mentioning it to him, sir?" I asked.

"By no means," said Mr. Spenlow. "But I have some experience of Mr. Jorkins, Copperfield. I wish it were otherwise, for I should be happy to meet your views in any respect. I cannot have the least objection to your mentioning it to Mr. Jorkins, Copperfield, if you think it worth while."

Availing myself of this permission, which was given with a warm shake of the hand, I sat thinking about Dora, and looking at the sunlight stealing from the chimney-pots down the wall of the opposite house, until Mr. Jorkins came. I then went up to Mr. Jorkins's room, and evidently astonished Mr. Jorkins very much by making my appearance there.

"Come in, Mr. Copperfield," said Mr. Jorkins. "Come in!"

I went in, and sat down; and stated my case to Mr. Jorkins pretty much as I had stated it to Mr. Spenlow. Mr. Jorkins was not by any means the awful creature one might have expected, but a large, mild, smooth-faced man of sixty, who took so much snuff that there was a tradition in the Commons that he lived principally on that stimulant, having little room in his system for any other article of diet.

"You have mentioned this to Mr. Spenlow, I suppose?" said Mr. Jorkins; when he had heard me, very restlessly, to an end.

I answered Yes, and told him that Mr. Spenlow had introduced his name.

"He said I should object?" asked Mr. Jorkins.

I was obliged to admit that Mr. Spenlow had considered it probable.

"I am sorry to say, Mr. Copperfield, I can't advance your object," said Mr. Jorkins, nervously. "The fact is—but I have an appointment at the Bank, if you'll have the goodness to excuse me."

With that he rose in a great hurry, and was going out of the room, when I made bold to say that I feared, then, there was no way of arranging the matter?

" No! " said Mr. Jorkins, stopping at the door to shake his head. " Oh, no! I object, you know," which he said very rapidly, and went out. " You must be aware, Mr. Copperfield," he added, looking restlessly in at the door again, " if Mr. Spenlow objects—"

" Personally, he does not object, sir," said I.

" Oh! Personally! " repeated Mr. Jorkins, in an impatient manner. " I assure you there's an objection, Mr. Copperfield. Hopeless! What you wish to be done, can't be done. I—I really have got an appointment at the Bank." With that he fairly ran away; and to the best of my knowledge, it was three days before he showed himself in the Commons again.

Being very anxious to leave no stone unturned, I waited until Mr. Spenlow came in, and then described what had passed; giving him to understand that I was not hopeless of his being able to soften the adamantine Jorkins, if he would undertake the task.

" Copperfield," returned Mr. Spenlow, with a gracious smile, " you have not known my partner, Mr. Jorkins, as long as I have. Nothing is farther from my thoughts than to attribute any degree of artifice to Mr. Jorkins. But Mr. Jorkins has a way of stating his objections which often deceives people. No, Copperfield! " shaking his head. " Mr. Jorkins is not to be moved, believe me! "

I was completely bewildered between Mr. Spenlow and Mr. Jorkins, as to which of them really was the objecting partner; but I saw with sufficient clearness that there was obduracy somewhere in the firm, and that the recovery of my aunt's thousand pounds was out of the question. In a state of despondency, which I remember with anything but satisfaction, for I know it still had too much reference to myself (though always in connection with Dora), I left the office, and went homeward.

I was trying to familiarise my mind with the worst, and to present to myself the arrangements we should have to make for the future in their sternest aspect, when a hackney chariot coming after me, and stopping at my very feet, occasioned me to look up. A fair hand was stretched forth to me from the window; and the face I had never seen without a feeling of serenity and happiness, from the moment when it first turned back on the old oak staircase with the great broad balustrade, and when I associated its softened beauty with the stained glass window in the church, was smiling on me.

"Agnes!" I joyfully exclaimed. "Oh, my dear Agnes, of all people in the world, what a pleasure to see you!"

"Is it, indeed?" she said, in her cordial voice.

"I want to talk to you so much!" said I. "It's such a lightening of my heart, only to look at you! If I had had a conjurer's cap, there is no one I should have wished for but you!"

"What?" returned Agnes.

"Well! perhaps Dora first," I admitted, with a blush.

"Certainly, Dora first, I hope," said Agnes, laughing.

"But you next!" said I. "Where are you going?"

She was going to my rooms to see my aunt. The day being very fine, she was glad to come out of the chariot, which smelt (I had my head in it all this time) like a stable put under a cucumber-frame. I dismissed the coachman, and she took my arm, and we walked on together. She was like Hope embodied, to me. How different I felt in one short minute, having Agnes at my side!

My aunt had written her one of the odd, abrupt notes—very little longer than a Bank note—to which her epistolary efforts were usually limited. She had stated therein that she had fallen into adversity, and was leaving Dover for good, but had quite made up her mind to it, and was so well that nobody need be uncomfortable about her. Agnes had come to London to see my aunt, between whom and herself there had been a mutual liking these many years; indeed, it dated from the time of my taking up my residence in Mr. Wickfield's house. She was not alone, she said. Her papa was with her—and Uriah Heep.

"And now they are partners," said I. "Confound him!"

"Yes," said Agnes. "They have some business here; and I took advantage of their coming, to come too. You must not think my visit all friendly and disinterested, Trotwood, for—I am afraid I may be cruelly prejudiced—I do not like to let papa go away alone, with him."

"Does he exercise the same influence over Mr. Wickfield still, Agnes?"

Agnes shook her head. "There is such a change at home," said she, "that you would scarcely know the dear old house. They live with us now."

"They?" said I.

"Mr. Heep and his mother. He sleeps in your old room." said Agnes, looking up into my face.

"I wish I had the ordering of his dreams," said I. "He wouldn't sleep there long."

"I keep my own little room," said Agnes, "where I used to learn my lessons. How the time goes! You remember? The little panelled room that opens from the drawing-room?"

"Remember, Agnes? When I saw you, for the first time, coming out at the door, with your quaint little basket of keys hanging at your side?"

"It is just the same," said Agnes, smiling. "I am glad you think of it so pleasantly. We were very happy."

"We were, indeed," said I.

"I keep that room to myself still; but I cannot always desert Mrs. Heep, you know. And so," said Agnes, quietly, "I feel obliged to bear her company, when I might prefer to be alone. But I have no other reason to complain of her. If she tires me, sometimes, by her praises of her son, it is only natural in a mother. He is a very good son to her."

I looked at Agnes when she said these words, without detecting in her any consciousness of Uriah's design. Her mild but earnest eyes met mine with their own beautiful frankness, and there was no change in her gentle face.

"The chief evil of their presence in the house," said Agnes, "is that I cannot be as near papa as I could wish—Uriah Heep being so much between us—and cannot watch over him, if that is not too bold a thing to say, as closely as I would. But if any fraud or treachery is practising against him, I hope that simple love and truth will be stronger in the end. I hope that real love and truth are stronger in the end than any evil or misfortune in the world."

A certain bright smile, which I never saw on any other face, died away, even while I thought how good it was, and how familiar it had once been to me; and she asked me, with a quick change of expression (we were drawing very near my street), if I knew how the reverse in my aunt's circumstances had been brought about. On my replying no, she had not told me yet, Agnes became thoughtful, and I fancied I felt her arm tremble in mine.

We found my aunt alone, in a state of some excitement. A difference of opinion had arisen between herself and Mrs. Crupp, on an abstract question (the propriety of chambers being inhabited by the gentler sex); and my aunt, utterly indifferent to spasms on the part of Mrs. Crupp, had cut the dispute short, by informing that lady that she smelt of my brandy, and that she would trouble her to walk out. Both of these expressions Mrs.

Crupp considered actionable, and had expressed her intention of bringing before a "British Judy"—meaning, it was supposed, the bulwark of our national liberties.

My aunt, however, having had time to cool, while Peggotty was out showing Mr. Dick the soldiers at the Horse Guards—and being, besides, greatly pleased to see Agnes—rather plumed herself on the affair than otherwise, and received us with unimpaired good humour. When Agnes laid her bonnet on the table, and sat down beside her, I could not but think, looking on her mild eyes and her radiant forehead, how natural it seemed to have her there: how trustfully, although she was so young and inexperienced, my aunt confided in her; how strong she was, indeed, in simple love and truth.

We began to talk about my aunt's losses, and I told them what I had tried to do that morning.

"Which was injudicious, Trot," said my aunt, "but well meant. You are a generous boy—I suppose I must say, young man, now—and I am proud of you, my dear. So far so good. Now, Trot and Agnes, let us look the case of Betsey Trotwood in the face, and see how it stands."

I observed Agnes turn pale, as she looked very attentively at my aunt. My aunt, patting her cat, looked very attentively at Agnes.

"Betsey Trotwood," said my aunt, who had always kept her money matters to herself: "—I don't mean your sister, Trot, my dear, but myself—had a certain property. It don't matter how much; enough to live on. More; for she had saved a little, and added to it. Betsey funded her property for some time, and then, by the advice of her man of business, laid it out on landed security. That did very well, and returned very good interest, till Betsey was paid off. I am talking of Betsey as if she was a man-of-war. Well! Then, Betsey had to look about her, for a new investment. She thought she was wiser, now, than her man of business, who was not such a good man of business by this time, as he used to be—I am alluding to your father, Agnes—and she took it into her head to lay it out for herself. So she took her pigs," said my aunt, "to a foreign market; and a very bad market it turned out to be. First, she lost in the mining way, and then she lost in the diving way—fishing up treasure, or some such Tom Tiddler nonsense," explained my aunt, rubbing her nose; "and then she lost in the mining way again, and, last of all, to set the thing entirely to rights, she lost in the banking way. I don't know what the Bank shares were worth for a little while," said my aunt; "cent per cent was the lowest of it, I believe; but the Bank was at the other end of the world, and tumbled into space, for what I know; anyhow, it fell to pieces, and never will and never can pay sixpence; and Betsey's sixpences were all there, and there's an end of them. Least said, soonest mended!"

My aunt concluded this philosophical summary, by fixing her eyes with a kind of triumph on Agnes, whose colour was gradually returning.

"Dear Miss Trotwood, is that all the history?" said Agnes.

"I hope it's enough, child," said my aunt. "If there had been more money to lose, it wouldn't have been all, I dare say. Betsey would have contrived to throw that after the rest, and make another chapter, I have little doubt. But there was no more money, and there's no more story."

Agnes had listened at first with suspended breath. Her colour still came and went, but she breathed more freely. I thought I knew why. I thought she had had some fear that her unhappy father might be in some way to blame for what had happened. My aunt took her hand in hers, and laughed.

"Is that all?" repeated my aunt. "Why, yes, that's all, except, 'And she lived happy ever afterwards.' Perhaps I may add that of Betsey yet, one of these days. Now, Agnes, you have a wise head. So have you, Trot, in some things, though I can't compliment you always:" and here my aunt shook her own at me, with an energy peculiar to herself. "What's to be done? Here's the cottage, taking one time with another, will produce, say seventy pounds a year. I think we may safely put it down at that. Well! —That's all we've got," said my aunt; with whom it was an idiosyncrasy, as it is with some horses, to stop very short when she appeared to be in a fair way of going on for a long while.

"Then," said my aunt, after a rest, "there's Dick. He's good for a hundred a year, but of course that must be expended on himself. I would sooner send him away, though I know I am the only person who appreciates him, than have him, and not spend his money on himself. How can Trot and I do best, upon our means? What do you say, Agnes?"

"*I* say, aunt," I interposed, "that I must do something!"

"Go for a soldier, do you mean?" returned my aunt, alarmed; "or go to sea? I won't hear of it. You are to be a proctor. We're not going to have any knockings on the head in *this* family, if you please, sir."

I was about to explain that I was not desirous of introducing that mode of provision into the family, when Agnes inquired if my rooms were held for any long term?

"You come to the point, my dear," said my aunt. "They are

not to be got rid of, for six months at least, unless they could be underlet, and that I don't believe. The last man died here. Five people out of six *would* die—of course—of that woman in nankeen with the flannel petticoat. I have a little ready money; and I agree with you, the best thing we can do, is, to live the term out here, and get Dick a bedroom hard by."

I thought it my duty to hint at the discomfort my aunt would sustain, from living in a continual state of guerilla warfare with Mrs. Crupp; but she disposed of that objection summarily by declaring, that, on the first demonstration of hostilities, she was prepared to astonish Mrs. Crupp for the whole remainder of her natural life.

"I have been thinking, Trotwood," said Agnes, diffidently, "that if you had time—"

"I have a good deal of time, Agnes. I am always disengaged after four or five o'clock, and I have time early in the morning. In one way and another," said I, conscious of reddening a little as I thought of the hours and hours I had devoted to fagging about town, and to and fro upon the Norwood Road, "I have abundance of time."

"I know you would not mind," said Agnes, coming to me, and speaking in a low voice, so full of sweet and hopeful consideration that I hear it now, "the duties of a secretary."

"Mind, my dear Agnes?"

"Because," continued Agnes, "Doctor Strong has acted on his intention of retiring, and has come to live in London; and he asked papa, I know, if he could recommend him one. Don't you think he would rather have his favourite old pupil near him, than anybody else?"

"Dear Agnes!" said I. "What should I do without you! You are always my good angel. I told you so. I never think of you in any other light."

Agnes answered with her pleasant laugh, that one good Angel (meaning Dora) was enough; and went on to remind me that the Doctor had been used to occupy himself in his study, early in the morning, and in the evening—and that probably my leisure would suit his requirements very well. I was scarcely more delighted with the prospect of earning my own bread, than with the hope of earning it under my old master; in short, acting on the advice of Agnes, I sat down and wrote a letter to the Doctor, stating my object, and appointing to call on him next day at ten in the forenoon. This I addressed to Highgate—for in that place, so memorable to me, he lived—and went and posted, myself, without losing a minute.

Wherever Agnes was, some agreeable token of her noiseless presence seemed inseparable from the place. When I came back, I found my aunt's birds hanging, just as they had hung so long in the parlour window of the cottage; and my easy chair imitating my aunt's much easier chair in its position at the open window; and even the round green fan, which my aunt had brought away with her, screwed on to the windowsill. I knew who had done all this, by its seeming to have quietly done itself; and I should have known in a moment who had arranged my neglected books in the old order of my school days, even if I had supposed Agnes to be miles away, instead of seeing her busy with them, and smiling at the disorder into which they had fallen.

My aunt was quite gracious on the subject of the Thames (it really did look very well with the sun upon it, though not like the sea before the cottage), but she could not relent towards the London smoke, which, she said, "peppered everything." A complete revolution, in which Peggotty bore a prominent part, was being effected in every corner of my rooms, in regard of this pepper; and I was looking on, thinking how little even Peggotty seemed to do with a good deal of bustle, and how much Agnes did without any bustle at all, when a knock came at the door.

"I think," said Agnes, turning pale, "it's papa. He promised me that he would come."

I opened the door, and admitted, not only Mr. Wickfield, but Uriah Heep. I had not seen Mr. Wickfield for some time. I was prepared for a great change in him, after what I had heard from Agnes, but his appearance shocked me.

It was not that he looked many years older, though still dressed with the old scrupulous cleanliness; or that there was an unwholesome ruddiness upon his face; or that his eyes were full and bloodshot; or that there was a nervous trembling in his hand, the cause of which I knew, and had for some years seen at work. It was not that he had lost his good looks, or his old bearing of a gentleman—for that he had not—but the thing that struck me most was, that with the evidences of his native superiority still upon him, he should submit himself to that crawling impersonation of meanness, Uriah Heep. The reversal of the two natures, in their relative positions, Uriah's of power and Mr. Wickfield's of dependence, was a sight more painful to me than I can express. If I had seen an Ape taking command of a Man, I should hardly have thought it a more degrading spectacle.

He appeared to be only too conscious of it himself. When he came in, he stood still; and with his head bowed, as if he felt it. This was only for a moment; for Agnes softly said to him, "Papa!

Here is Miss Trotwood—and Trotwood, whom you have not seen for a long while!" and then he approached, and constrainedly gave my aunt his hand, and shook hands more cordially with me. In the moment's pause I speak of, I saw Uriah's countenance form itself into a most ill-favoured smile. Agnes saw it too, I think, for she shrank from him.

What my aunt saw, or did not see, I defy the science of physiognomy to have made out, without her own consent. I believe there never was anybody with such an imperturbable countenance when she chose. Her face might have been a dead wall on the occasion in question, for any light it threw upon her thoughts; until she broke silence with her usual abruptness.

"Well, Wickfield!" said my aunt; and he looked up at her for the first time. "I have been telling your daughter how well I have been disposing of my money for myself, because I couldn't trust it to you, as you were growing rusty in business matters. We have been taking counsel together, and getting on very well, all things considered. Agnes is worth the whole firm, in my opinion."

"If I may umbly make the remark," said Uriah Heep, with a writhe, "I fully agree with Miss Betsey Trotwood, and should be only too appy if Miss Agnes was a partner."

"You're a partner yourself, you know," returned my aunt, "and that's about enough for you, I expect. How do you find yourself, sir?"

In acknowledgment of this question, addressed to him with extraordinary curtness, Mr. Heep, uncomfortably clutching the blue bag he carried, replied that he was pretty well, he thanked my aunt, and hoped she was the same.

"And you, Master—I should say, Mister Copperfield," pursued Uriah, "I hope I see you well! I am rejoiced to see you, Mister Copperfield, even under present circumstances." I believed that; for he seemed to relish them very much. "Present circumstances is not what your friends would wish for you, Mister Copperfield, but it isn't money makes the man: it's—I am really unequal with my umble powers to express what it is," said Uriah, with a fawning jerk, "but it isn't money!"

Here he shook hands with me: not in the common way, but standing at a good distance from me, and lifting my hand up and down like a pump handle, that he was a little afraid of.

"And how do you think we are looking, Master Copperfield, —I should say, Mister?" fawned Uriah. "Don't you find Mr. Wickfield blooming, sir? Years don't tell much in our firm, Master Copperfield, except in raising up the umble, namely, mother and self—and in developing," he added, as an afterthought, " the beautiful, namely, Miss Agnes."

He jerked himself about, after this compliment, in such an intolerable manner, that my aunt, who had sat looking straight at him, lost all patience.

" Deuce take the man! " said my aunt, sternly, " what's he about? Don't be galvanic, sir! "

" I ask your pardon, Miss Trotwood," returned Uriah; " I'm aware you're nervous."

" Go along with you, sir! " said my aunt, anything but appeased. " Don't presume to say so! I am nothing of the sort. If you're an eel, sir, conduct yourself like one. If you're a man, control your limbs, sir! Good God! " said my aunt, with great indignation. " I am not going to be serpentined and corkscrewed out of my senses! "

Mr. Heep was rather abashed, as most people might have been, by this explosion; which derived great additional force from the indignant manner in which my aunt afterwards moved in her chair, and shook her head as if she were making snaps or bounces at him. But he said to me aside in a meek voice:

" I am well aware, Master Copperfield, that Miss Trotwood though an excellent lady, has a quick temper (indeed I think I had the pleasure of knowing her, when I was a umble clerk, before you did, Master Copperfield), and it's only natural, I am sure, that it should be made quicker by present circumstances. The wonder is, that it isn't much worse! I only called to say that if there was anything we could do, in present circumstances, mother or self, or Wickfield and Heep, we should be really glad. I may go so far? " said Uriah, with a sickly smile at his partner.

" Uriah Heep," said Mr. Wickfield, in a monotonous forced way, " is active in the business, Trotwood. What he says, I quite concur in. You know I had an old interest in you. Apart from that, what Uriah says I quite concur in! "

" Oh, what a reward it is," said Uriah, drawing up one leg, at the risk of bringing down upon himself another visitation from my aunt, " to be so trusted in! But I hope I am able to do something to relieve him from the fatigues of business, Master Copperfield! "

" Uriah Heep is a great relief to me," said Mr. Wickfield, in the same dull voice. " It's a load off my mind, Trotwood, to have such a partner."

The red fox made him say all this, I knew, to exhibit him to me in the light he had indicated on the night when he poisoned my rest. I saw the same ill-favoured smile upon his face again, and saw how he watched me.

"You are not going, papa?" said Agnes, anxiously. "Will you not walk back with Trotwood and me?"

He would have looked to Uriah, I believe, before replying, if that worthy had not anticipated him.

"I am bespoke myself," said Uriah, "on business; otherwise I should have been appy to have kept with my friends. But I leave my partner to represent the firm. Miss Agnes, ever yours! I wish you good-day, Master Copperfield, and leave my umble respects for Miss Betsey Trotwood."

With those words, he retired, kissing his great hand, and leering at us like a mask.

We sat there, talking about our pleasant old Canterbury days, an hour or two. Mr. Wickfield, left to Agnes, soon became more like his former self; though there was a settled depression upon him, which he never shook off. For all that, he brightened; and had an evident pleasure in hearing us recall the little incidents of our old life, many of which he remembered very well. He said it was like those times, to be alone with Agnes and me again; and he wished to Heaven they had never changed. I am sure there was an influence in the placid face of Agnes, and in the very touch of her hand upon his arm, that did wonders for him.

My aunt (who was busy nearly all this while with Peggotty, in the inner room) would not accompany us to the place where they were staying, but insisted on my going; and I went. We dined together. After dinner, Agnes sat beside him, as of old, and poured out his wine. He took what she gave him, and no more—like a child—and we all three sat together at a window as the evening gathered in. When it was almost dark, he lay down on a sofa, Agnes pillowing his head and bending over him a little while; and when she came back to the window, it was not so dark but I could see tears glittering in her eyes.

I pray Heaven that I never may forget the dear girl in her love and truth, at that time of my life; for if I should, I must be drawing near the end, and then I would desire to remember her best! She filled my heart with such good resolutions, strengthened my weakness so, by her example, so directed—I know not how, she was too modest and gentle to advise me in many words—the wandering ardour and unsettled purpose within me, that all the little good I have done, and all the harm I have forborne, I solemnly believe I may refer to her.

And how she spoke to me of Dora, sitting at the window in the dark; listened to my praises of her; praised again; and round the little fairy-figure shed some glimpses of her own pure light, that made it yet more precious and more innocent to me! Oh, Agnes, sister of my boyhood, if I had known then, what I knew long afterwards!—

There was a beggar in the street, when I went down; and as I turned my head towards the window, thinking of her calm seraphic eyes, he made me start by muttering, as if he were an echo of the morning:

"Blind! Blind! Blind!"

36

ENTHUSIASM

I BEGAN THE NEXT DAY WITH ANOTHER DIVE INTO THE Roman bath, and then started for Highgate. I was not dispirited now. I was not afraid of the shabby coat, and had no yearnings after gallant greys. My whole manner of thinking of our late misfortune was changed. What I had to do, was, to show my aunt that her past goodness to me had not been thrown away on an insensible, ungrateful object. What I had to do, was, to turn the painful discipline of my younger days to account, by going to work with a resolute and steady heart. What I had to do, was, to take my woodman's axe in my hand, and clear my own way through the forest of difficulty, by cutting down the trees until I came to Dora. And I went on at a mighty rate, as if it could be done by walking.

When I found myself on the familiar Highgate road, pursuing such a different errand from that old one of pleasure, with which it was associated, it seemed as if a complete change had come on my whole life. But that did not discourage me. With the new life, came new purpose, new intention. Great was the labour; priceless the reward. Dora was the reward, and Dora must be won.

I got into such a transport, that I felt quite sorry my coat was not a little shabby already. I wanted to be cutting at those trees in the forest of difficulty, under circumstances that should prove my strength. I had a good mind to ask an old man, in wire spectacles, who was breaking stones upon the road, to lend me his hammer for a little while, and let me begin to beat a path to Dora out of granite. I stimulated myself into such a heat, and got so out of breath, that I felt as if I had been earning I don't know how much. In this state, I went into a cottage that I saw was to let, and examined it narrowly,—for I felt it necessary to be practical. It would do for me and Dora admirably: with a little front garden for Jip to run about in, and bark at the tradespeople through the railings, and a capital room up-stairs for my aunt. I came out again, hotter and faster than ever, and dashed up to Highgate, at such a rate that I was there an hour too early; and, though I had not been, should have been obliged to stroll about to cool myself, before I was at all presentable.

My first care, after putting myself under this necessary course of preparation, was to find the Doctor's house. It was not in that part of Highgate where Mrs. Steerforth lived, but quite on the opposite side of the little town. When I had made this discovery, I went back, in an attraction I could not resist, to a lane by Mrs. Steerforth's, and looked over the corner of the garden wall. His room was shut up close. The conservatory doors were standing open, and Rosa Dartle was walking, bareheaded, with a quick impetuous step, up and down a gravel walk on one side of the lawn. She gave me the idea of some fierce thing, that was dragging the length of its chain to and fro upon a beaten track, and wearing its heart out.

I came softly away from my place of observation, and avoiding that part of the neighbourhood, and wishing I had not gone near it, strolled about until it was ten o'clock. The church with the slender spire, that stands on the top of the hill now, was not there then to tell me the time. An old redbrick mansion, used as a school, was in its place; and a fine old house it must have been to go to school at, as I recollect it.

When I approached the Doctor's cottage—a pretty old place, on which he seemed to have expended some money, if I might judge from the embellishments and repairs that had the look of being just completed—I saw him walking in the garden at the side, gaiters and all, as if he had never left off walking since the days of my pupilage. He had his old companions about him, too; for there were plenty of high trees in the neighbourhood, and two or three rooks were on the grass, looking after him, as if they had been written to about him by the Canterbury rooks, and were observing him closely in consequence.

Knowing the utter hopelessness of attracting his attention from that distance, I made bold to open the gate, and walk after him, so as to meet him when he should turn round. When he did, and came towards me, he looked at me thoughtfully for a few moments, evidently without thinking about me at all; and then his benevolent face expressed extraordinary pleasure, and he took me by both hands.

"Why, my dear Copperfield," said the Doctor, "you are a man! How do you do? I am delighted to see you. My dear Copperfield, how very much you have improved! You are quite—yes—dear me!"

I hoped he was well, and Mrs. Strong too.

"Oh dear, yes!" said the Doctor; "Annie's quite well, and she'll be delighted to see you. You were always her favourite. She said so, last night, when I showed her your letter. And—yes, to be sure—you recollect Mr. Jack Maldon, Copperfield?"

"Perfectly, sir."

"Of course," said the Doctor. "To be sure. *He's* pretty well, too."

"Has he come home, sir?" I inquired.

"From India?" said the Doctor. "Yes. Mr. Jack Maldon couldn't bear the climate, my dear. Mrs. Markleham—you have not forgotten Mrs. Markleham?"

Forgotten the Old Soldier! And in that short time!

"Mrs. Markleham," said the Doctor, "was quite vexed about him, poor thing; so we have got him at home again; and we have bought him a little Patent place, which agrees with him much better."

I knew enough of Mr. Jack Maldon to suspect from this account that it was a place where there was not much to do, and which was pretty well paid. The Doctor, walking up and down with his hand on my shoulder, and his kind face turned encouragingly to mine, went on:

"Now, my dear Copperfield, in reference to this proposal of yours. It's very gratifying and agreeable to me, I am sure; but don't you think you could do better? You achieved distinction, you know, when you were with us. You are qualified for many good things. You have laid a foundation that any edifice may be raised upon; and is it not a pity that you should devote the spring-time of your life to such a poor pursuit as I can offer?"

I became very glowing again, and, expressing myself in a rhapsodical style, I am afraid, urged my request strongly: reminding the Doctor that I had already a profession.

"Well, well," said the Doctor, "that's true. Certainly, your having a profession, and being actually engaged in studying it, makes a difference. But, my good young friend, what's seventy pounds a year?"

"It doubles our income, Doctor Strong," said I.

"Dear me!" replied the Doctor. "To think of that! Not that I mean to say it's rigidly limited to seventy pounds a year, because I have always contemplated making any young friend I might thus employ, a present too. Undoubtedly," said the Doctor, still walking me up and down with his hand on my shoulder. "I have always taken an annual present into account."

"My dear tutor," said I (now, really, without any nonsense), "to whom I owe more obligations already than I ever can acknowledge—"

"No, no," interposed the Doctor. "Pardon me!"

"If you will take such time as I have, and that is my mornings and evenings, and can think it worth seventy pounds a year, you will do me such a service as I cannot express."

"Dear me!" said the Doctor, innocently. "To think that so little should go for so much! Dear, dear! And when you can do better, you will? On your word, now?" said the Doctor,—which he had always made a very grave appeal to the honour of us boys.

"On my word, sir!" I returned, answering in our old school manner.

"Then be it so," said the Doctor, clapping me on the shoulder, and still keeping his hand there, as we still walked up and down.

"And I shall be twenty times happier, sir," said I, with a little—I hope innocent—flattery, "if my employment is to be on the Dictionary."

The Doctor stopped, smilingly clapped me on the shoulder again, and exclaimed, with a triumph most delightful to behold, as if I had penetrated to the profoundest depths of mortal sagacity, "My dear young friend, you have hit it. It is the Dictionary!"

How could it be anything else! His pockets were as full of it as his head. It was sticking out of him in all directions. He told me that since his retirement from scholastic life, he had been advancing with it wonderfully; and that nothing could suit him better than the proposed arrangements for morning and evening work, as it was his custom to walk about in the day-time with his considering cap on. His papers were in a little confusion, in consequence of Mr. Jack Maldon having lately proffered his occasional services as an amanuensis, and not being accustomed to that occupation; but we should soon put right what was amiss, and go on swimmingly. Afterwards, when we were fairly at our work, I found Mr. Jack Maldon's efforts more troublesome to me than I had expected, as he had not confined himself to making numerous mistakes, but had sketched so many soldiers, and ladies' heads, over the Doctor's manuscript, that I often became involved in labyrinths of obscurity.

The Doctor was quite happy in the prospect of our going to work together on that wonderful performance, and we settled to begin next morning at seven o'clock. We were to work two hours every morning, and two or three hours every night, except on Saturdays, when I was to rest. On Sundays, of course, I was to rest also, and I considered these very easy terms.

Our plans being thus arranged to our mutual satisfaction, the Doctor took me into the house to present me to Mrs. Strong, whom we found in the Doctor's new study, dusting his books,—a freedom which he never permitted anybody else to take with those sacred favourites.

They had postponed their breakfast on my account, and we sat down to table together. We had not been seated long, when I saw an approaching arrival in Mrs. Strong's face, before I heard any sound of it. A gentleman on horseback came to the gate, and leading his horse into the little court, with the bridle over his arm, as if he were quite at home, tied him to a ring in the empty coach-house wall, and came into the breakfast parlour, whip in hand. It was Mr. Jack Maldon; and Mr. Jack Maldon was not at all improved by India, I thought. I was in a state of ferocious virtue, however, as to young men who were not cutting down trees in the forest of difficulty; and my impression must be received with due allowance.

"Mr. Jack!" said the Doctor. "Copperfield!"

Mr. Jack Maldon shook hands with me; but not very warmly, I believed; and with an air of languid patronage, at which I secretly took great umbrage. But his languor altogether was quite a wonderful sight; except when he addressed himself to his cousin Annie.

"Have you breakfasted this morning. Mr. Jack?" said the Doctor.

"I hardly ever take breakfast, sir," he replied, with his head thrown back in an easy-chair. "I find it bores me."

"Is there any news to-day?" inquired the Doctor.

"Nothing at all, sir," replied Mr. Maldon. "There's an account about the people being hungry and discontented down in the North, but they are always being hungry and discontented somewhere."

The Doctor looked grave, and said, as though he wished to

change the subject, "Then there's no news at all; and no news, they say, is good news."

"There's a long statement in the papers, sir, about a murder," observed Mr. Maldon. "But somebody is always being murdered, and I didn't read it."

A display of indifference to all the actions and passions of mankind was not supposed to be such a distinguished quality at that time, I think, as I have observed it to be considered since. I have known it very fashionable indeed. I have seen it displayed with such success, that I have encountered some fine ladies and gentlemen who might as well have been born caterpillars. Perhaps it impressed me the more then, because it was new to me, but it certainly did not tend to exalt my opinion of, or to strengthen my confidence in, Mr. Jack Maldon.

"I came out to inquire whether Annie would like to go to the opera to-night," said Mr. Maldon, turning to her. "It's the last good night there will be, this season; and there's a singer there, whom she really ought to hear. She is perfectly exquisite. Besides which, she is so charmingly ugly," relapsing into languor.

The Doctor, ever pleased with what was likely to please his young wife, turned to her and said:

"You must go, Annie. You must go."

"I would rather not," she said to the Doctor. "I prefer to remain at home. I would much rather remain at home."

Without looking at her cousin, she then addressed me, and asked me about Agnes, and whether she should see her, and whether she was not likely to come that day; and was so much disturbed, that I wondered how even the Doctor, buttering his toast, could be blind to what was so obvious.

But he saw nothing. He told her, good-naturedly, that she was young and ought to be amused and entertained, and must not allow herself to be made dull by a dull old fellow. Moreover, he said, he wanted to hear her sing all the new singer's songs to him; and how could she do that well, unless she went? So the Doctor persisted in making the engagement for her, and Mr. Jack Maldon was to come back to dinner. This concluded, he went to his Patent place, I suppose; but at all events went away on his horse, looking very idle.

I was curious to find out next morning, whether she had been. She had not, but had sent into London to put her cousin off; and had gone out in the afternoon to see Agnes, and had prevailed upon the Doctor to go with her; and they had walked home by the fields, the Doctor told me, the evening being delightful. I wondered then, whether she would have gone if Agnes had not been in town, and whether Agnes had some good influence over her too!

She did not look very happy, I thought, but it was a good face, or a very false one. I often glanced at it, for she sat in the window all the time we were at work; and made our breakfast, which we took by snatches as we were employed. When I left, at nine o'clock, she was kneeling on the ground at the Doctor's feet, putting on his shoes and gaiters for him. There was a softened shade upon her face, thrown from some green leaves overhanging the open window of the low room; and I thought all the way to Doctor's Commons, of the night when I had seen it looking at him as he read.

I was pretty busy now; up at five in the morning, and home at nine or ten at night. But I had infinite satisfaction in being so closely engaged, and never walked slowly on any account, and felt enthusiastically that the more I tired myself, the more I was doing to deserve Dora. I had not revealed myself in my altered character to Dora yet, because she was coming to see Miss Mills in a few days, and I deferred all I had to tell her until then; merely informing her in my letters (all our communications were secretly forwarded through Miss Mills), that I had much to tell her. In the meantime, I put myself on a short allowance of bear's grease, wholly abandoned scented soap and lavender water, and sold off three waistcoats at a prodigious sacrifice, as being too luxurious for my stern career.

Not satisfied with all these proceedings, but burning with impatience to do something more, I went to see Traddles, now lodging up behind the parapet of a house in Castle Street, Holborn. Mr. Dick, who had been with me to Highgate twice already, and had resumed his companionship with the Doctor, I took with me.

I took Mr. Dick with me, because, acutely sensitive to my aunt's reverses, and sincerely believing that no galley-slave or convict worked as I did, he had begun to fret and worry himself out of spirits and appetite, as having nothing useful to do. In this condition, he felt more incapable of finishing the Memorial than ever; and the harder he worked at it, the oftener that unlucky head of King Charles the First got into it. Seriously apprehending that his malady would increase, unless we put some innocent deception upon him and caused him to believe that he was useful, or unless we could put him in the way of being really useful (which would be better), I made up my mind to try if Traddles could help us. Before we went, I wrote Traddles a full statement of all that had happened, and Traddles wrote me back a capital answer, expressive of his sympathy and friendship.

We found him hard at work with his inkstand and papers, refreshed by the sight of the flower-pot stand and the little round table in a corner of the small apartment. He received us cordially, and made friends with Mr. Dick in a moment. Mr. Dick professed an absolute certainty of having seen him before, and we both said, "Very likely."

The first subject on which I had to consult Traddles was this. —I had heard that many men distinguished in various pursuits had begun life by reporting the debates in Parliament. Traddles having mentioned newspapers to me, as one of his hopes, I had put the two things together, and told Traddles in my letter that I wished to know how I could qualify myself for this pursuit. Traddles now informed me, as the result of his inquiries, that the mere mechanical acquisition necessary, except in rare cases, for thorough excellence in it, that is to say, a perfect and entire command of the mystery of short-hand writing and reading, was about equal in difficulty to the mastery of six languages; and that it might perhaps be attained, by dint of perseverance, in the course of a few years. Traddles reasonably supposed that this would settle the business; but I, only feeling that here indeed were a few tall trees to be hewn down, immediately resolved to work my way on to Dora through this thicket, axe in hand.

"I am very much obliged to you, my dear Traddles!" said I. "I'll begin to-morrow."

Traddles looked astonished, as he well might; but he had no notion as yet of my rapturous condition.

"I'll buy a book," said I, "with a good scheme of this art in it; I'll work at it at the Commons, where I haven't half enough to do; I'll take down the speeches in our court for practice— Traddles, my dear fellow, I'll master it!"

"Dear me," said Traddles, opening his eyes, "I had no idea you were such a determined character, Copperfield!"

I don't know how he should have had, for it was new enough to me. I passed that off, and brought Mr. Dick on the carpet.

"You see," said Mr. Dick, wistfully, "if I could exert myself, Mr. Traddles—if I could beat a drum—or blow anything!"

Poor fellow! I have little doubt he would have preferred such an employment in his heart to all others. Traddles, who would not have smiled for the world, replied composedly:

"But you are a very good penman, sir. You told me so, Copperfield?"

" Excellent! " said I. And indeed he was. He wrote with extraordinary neatness.

" Don't you think," said Traddles, " you could copy writings, sir, if I got them for you? "

Mr. Dick looked doubtfully at me. " Eh, Trotwood? "

I shook my head. Mr. Dick shook his, and sighed. " Tell him about the Memorial," said Mr. Dick.

I explained to Traddles that there was a difficulty in keeping King Charles the First out of Mr. Dick's manuscripts; Mr. Dick in the meanwhile looking very deferentially and seriously at Traddles, and sucking his thumb.

" But these writings, you know, that I speak of, are already drawn up and finished," said Traddles after a little consideration. " Mr. Dick has nothing to do with them. Wouldn't that make a difference, Copperfield? At all events, wouldn't it be well to try? "

This gave us new hope. Traddles and I laying our heads together apart, while Mr. Dick anxiously watched us from his chair, we concocted a scheme in virtue of which we got him to work next day, with triumphant success.

On a table by the window in Buckingham Street, we set out the work Traddles procured for him—which was to make, I forget how many copies of a legal document about some right of way—and on another table we spread the last unfinished original of the great Memorial. Our instructions to Mr. Dick were that he should copy exactly what he had before him, without the least departure from the original; and that when he felt it necessary to make the slightest allusion to King Charles the First, he should fly to the Memorial. We exhorted him to be resolute in this, and left my aunt to observe him. My aunt reported to us, afterwards, that, at first, he was like a man playing the kettle-drums, and constantly divided his attentions between the two; but that, finding this confuse and fatigue him, and having his copy there, plainly before his eyes, he soon sat at it in an orderly business-like manner, and postponed the Memorial to a more convenient time. In a word, although we took great care that he should have no more to do than was good for him, and although he did not begin with the beginning of a week, he earned by the following Saturday night ten shillings and ninepence; and never, while I live, shall I forget his going about to all the shops in the neighbourhood to change this treasure into sixpences, or his bringing them to my aunt arranged in the form of a heart upon a waiter, with tears of joy and pride in his eyes. He was like one under the propitious influence of a charm, from the moment of his being usefully employed; and if there were a happy man in the world, that Saturday night, it was the grateful creature who thought my aunt the most wonderful woman in existence, and me the most wonderful young man.

" No starving now, Trotwood," said Mr. Dick, shaking hands with me in a corner. " I'll provide for her, sir! " and he flourished his ten fingers in the air, as if they were ten banks.

I hardly know which was the better pleased, Traddles or I. " It really," said Traddles, suddenly, taking a letter out of his pocket, and giving it to me, " put Mr. Micawber quite out of my head! "

The letter (Mr. Micawber never missed any possible opportunity of writing a letter) was addressed to me, " By the kindness of T. Traddles, Esquire, of the Inner Temple." It ran thus:

" MY DEAR COPPERFIELD,

" You may possibly not be unprepared to receive the intimation that something has turned up. I may have mentioned to you on a former occasion that I was in expectation of such an event.

" I am about to establish myself in one of the provincial towns of our favoured island (where the society may be described as a happy admixture of the agricultural and the clerical), in immediate connection with one of the learned professions. Mrs. Micawber and our offspring will accompany me. Our ashes, at a future period, will probably be found commingled in the cemetery attached to a venerable pile, for which the spot to which I refer has acquired a reputation, shall I say from China to Peru?

" In bidding adieu to the modern Babylon, where we have undergone many vicissitudes, I trust not ignobly, Mrs. Micawber and myself cannot disguise from our minds that we part, it may be for years and it may be for ever, with an individual linked by strong associations to the altar of our domestic life. If, on the eve of such a departure, you will accompany our mutual friend, Mr. Thomas Traddles, to our present abode, and there reciprocate the wishes natural to the occasion, you will confer a Boon

" On

" One

" Who

" Is

" Ever yours,

" WILKINS MICAWBER."

I was glad to find that Mr. Micawber had got rid of his dust and ashes, and that something really had turned up at last. Learning from Traddles that the invitation referred to the evening then wearing away, I expressed my readiness to do honour to it; and we went off together to the lodging which Mr. Micawber occupied as Mr. Mortimer, and which was situated near the top of the Gray's Inn Road.

The resources of this lodging were so limited, that we found the twins, now some eight or nine years old, reposing in a turn-up bedstead in the family sitting-room, where Mr. Micawber had prepared, in a wash-hand-stand jug, what he called a "Brew" of the agreeable beverage for which he was famous. I had the pleasure, on this occasion, of renewing the acquaintance of Master Micawber, whom I found a promising boy of about twelve or thirteen, very subject to that restlessness of limb which is not an infrequent phenomenon in youths of his age. I also became once more known to his sister, Miss Micawber, in whom, as Mr. Micawber told us, "her mother renewed her youth, like the Phoenix."

"My dear Copperfield," said Mr. Micawber, "yourself and Mr. Traddles find us on the brink of migration, and will excuse any little discomforts incidental to that position."

Glancing round as I made a suitable reply, I observed that the family effects were already packed, and that the amount of luggage was by no means overwhelming. I congratulated Mrs. Micawber on the approaching change.

"My dear Mr. Copperfield," said Mrs. Micawber, "of your friendly interest in all our affairs, I am well assured. My family may consider it banishment, if they please; but I am a wife and mother, and I never will desert Mr. Micawber."

Traddles, appealed to by Mrs. Micawber's eye, feelingly acquiesced.

"That," said Mrs. Micawber, "that, at least, is my view, my dear Mr. Copperfield and Mr. Traddles, of the obligation which I took upon myself when I repeated the irrevocable words, 'I, Emma, take thee, Wilkins.' I read the service over with a flat-candle on the previous night, and the conclusion I derived from it was, that I never could desert Mr. Micawber. And," said Mrs. Micawber, "though it is possible I may be mistaken in my view of the ceremony, I never will!"

"My dear," said Mr. Micawber, a little impatiently, "I am not conscious that you are expected to do anything of the sort."

"I am aware, my dear Mr. Copperfield," pursued Mrs. Micawber, "that I am now about to cast my lot among strangers; and I am also aware that the various members of my family, to whom Mr. Micawber has written in the most gentlemanly terms, announcing that fact, have not taken the least notice of Mr. Micawber's communication. Indeed I may be superstitious," said Mrs. Micawber, " but it appears to me that Mr. Micawber is destined never to receive any answers whatever to the great majority of the communications he writes. I may augur from the silence of my family, that they object to the resolution I have taken; but I should not allow myself to be swerved from the path of duty, Mr. Copperfield, even by my papa and mama, were they still living."

I expressed my opinion that this was going in the right direction.

" It may be a sacrifice," said Mrs. Micawber, " to immure one's-self in a Cathedral town; but surely, Mr. Copperfield, if it is a sacrifice in me, it is much more a sacrifice in a man of Mr. Micawber's abilities."

" Oh! You are going to a Cathedral town? " said I.

Mr. Micawber, who had been helping us all, out of the wash-hand-stand jug, replied:

" To Canterbury. In fact, my dear Copperfield, I have entered into arrangements, by virtue of which I stand pledged and contracted to our friend Heep, to assist and serve him in the capacity of—and to be—his confidential clerk."

I stared at Mr. Micawber, who greatly enjoyed my surprise.

" I am bound to state to you," he said, with an official air, " that the business habits, and the prudent suggestions, of Mrs. Micawber, have in a great measure conduced to this result. The gauntlet, to which Mrs. Micawber referred upon a former occasion, being thrown down in the form of an advertisement, was taken up by my friend Heep, and led to a mutual recognition. Of my friend Heep," said Mr. Micawber, " who is a man of remarkable shrewdness, I desire to speak with all possible respect. My friend Heep has not fixed the positive remuneration at too high a figure, but he has made a great deal, in the way of extrication from the pressure of pecuniary difficulties, contingent on the value of my services; and on the value of those services I pin my faith. Such address and intelligence as I chance to possess," said Mr. Micawber, boastfully disparaging himself, with the old genteel air, " will be devoted to my friend Heep's service. I have already some acquaintance with the law—as a defendant on civil process—and I shall immediately apply myself to the Commentaries of one of the most eminent and remarkable of our English Jurists. I believe it is unnecessary to add that I allude to Mr. Justice Blackstone."

These observations, and indeed the greater part of the observations made that evening, were interrupted by Mrs. Micawber's discovering that Master Micawber was sitting on his boots, or holding his head on with both arms as if he felt it loose, or accidentally kicking Traddles under the table, or shuffling his feet over one another, or producing them at distances from himself apparently outrageous to nature, or lying sideways with his hair among the wineglasses, or developing his restlessness of limb in some other form incompatible with the general interests of society; and by Master Micawber's receiving those discoveries in a resentful spirit. I sat all the while, amazed by Mr. Micawber's disclosure, and wondering what it meant; until Mrs. Micawber resumed the thread of the discourse, and claimed my attention.

"What I particularly request Mr. Micawber to be careful of, is," said Mrs. Micawber, "that he does not, my dear Mr. Copperfield, in applying himself to this subordinate branch of the law, place out of his power to rise, ultimately, to the top of the tree. I am convinced that Mr. Micawber, giving his mind to a profession so adapted to his fertile resources, and his flow of language, *must* distinguish himself. Now, for example, Mr. Traddles," said Mrs. Micawber, assuming a profound air, "a Judge, or even say a Chancellor. Does an individual place himself beyond the pale of those preferments by entering on such an office as Mr. Micawber has accepted?"

"My dear," observed Mr. Micawber—but glancing inquisitively at Traddles, too; "we have time enough before us, for the consideration of those questions."

"Micawber," she returned, "no! Your mistake in life is, that you do not look forward far enough. You are bound, in justice to your family, if not to yourself, to take in at a comprehensive glance the extremest point in the horizon to which your abilities may lead you."

Mr. Micawber coughed, and drank his punch with an air of exceeding satisfaction—still glancing at Traddles, as if he desired to have his opinion.

"Why, the plain state of the case, Mrs. Micawber," said Traddles, mildly breaking the truth to her. "I mean the real prosaic fact, you know—"

"Just so," said Mrs. Micawber, "my dear Mr. Traddles, I wish to be as prosaic and literal as possible on a subject of so much importance."

"—Is," said Traddles, "that this branch of the law, even if Mr. Micawber were a regular solicitor—"

"Exactly so," returned Mrs. Micawber. ("Wilkins, you are squinting, and will not be able to get your eyes back.")

"—Has nothing," pursued Traddles, "to do with that. Only a barrister is eligible for such preferments; and Mr. Micawber could not be a barrister, without being entered at an inn of court as a student, for five years."

"Do I follow you?" said Mrs. Micawber, with her most affable air of business. "Do I understand, my dear Mr. Traddles, that, at the expiration of that period, Mr. Micawber would be eligible as a Judge or Chancellor?"

"He would be *eligible*," returned Traddles, with a strong emphasis on that word.

"Thank you," said Mrs. Micawber. "That is quite sufficient. If such is the case, and Mr. Micawber forfeits no privilege by entering on these duties, my anxiety is set at rest. I speak," said Mrs. Micawber, "as a female, necessarily; but I have always been of opinion that Mr. Micawber possesses what I have heard my papa call, when I lived at home, the judicial mind; and I hope Mr. Micawber is now entering on a field where that mind will develop itself, and take a commànding station."

I quite believe that Mr. Micawber saw himself, in his judicial mind's eye, on the woolsack. He passed his hand complacently over his bald head, and said with ostentatious resignation:

"My dear, we will not anticipate the decrees of fortune. If I am reserved to wear a wig, I am at least prepared, externally," in allusion to his baldness, "for that distinction. I do not," said Mr. Micawber, "regret my hair, and I may have been deprived of it for a specific purpose. I cannot say. It is my intention, my dear Copperfield, to educate my son for the Church; I will not deny that I should be happy, on his account, to attain to eminence."

"For the Church?" said I, still pondering, between whiles, on Uriah Heep.

"Yes," said Mr. Micawber. "He has a remarkable head-voice, and will commence as a chorister. Our residence at Canterbury, and our local connection, will, no doubt, enable him to take advantage of any vacancy that may arise in the Cathedral corps."

On looking at Master Micawber again, I saw that he had a certain expression of face, as if his voice were behind his eyebrows; where it presently appeared to be, on his singing us (as an alternative between that and bed), "The Wood-Pecker tapping." After many compliments on this performance, we fell into some general conversation; and as I was too full of my desperate intentions to keep my altered circumstances to myself,

I made them known to Mr. and Mrs. Micawber. I cannot express how extremely delighted they both were, by the idea of my aunt's being in difficulties; and how comfortable and friendly it made them.

When we were nearly come to the last round of the punch, I addressed myself to Traddles, and reminded him that we must not separate, without wishing our friends health, happiness, and success in their new career. I begged Mr. Micawber to fill us bumpers, and proposed the toast in due form; shaking hands with him across the table, and kissing Mrs. Micawber, to commemorate that eventful occasion. Traddles immitated me in the first particular, but did not consider himself a sufficiently old friend to venture on the second.

" My dear Copperfield," said Mr. Micawber, rising with one of his thumbs in each of his waistcoat pockets, " the companion of my youth: if I may be allowed the expression—and my esteemed friend Traddles: if I may be permitted to call him so—will allow me, on the part of Mrs. Micawber, myself, and our offspring, to thank them in the warmest and most uncompromising terms for their good wishes. It may be expected that on the event of a migration which will consign us to a perfectly new existence," Mr. Micawber spoke as if they were going five hundred thousand miles, " I should offer a few valedictory remarks to two such friends as I see before me. But all that I have to say in this way, I have said. Whatever station in society I may attain, through the medium of the learned profession of which I am about to become an unworthy member, I shall endeavour not to disgrace, and Mrs. Micawber will be safe to adorn. Under the temporary pressure of pecuniary liabilities, contracted with a view to their immediate liquidation, but remaining unliquidated through a combination of circumstances, I have been under the necessity of assuming a garb from which my natural instincts recoil—I allude to spectacles—and possessing myself of a cognomen, to which I can establish no legitimate pretensions. All I have to say on that score is, that the cloud has passed from the dreary scene, and the God of Day is once more high upon the mountain tops. On Monday next, on the arrival of the four o'clock afternoon coach at Canterbury, my foot will be on my native heath—my name, Micawber! "

Mr. Micawber resumed his seat on the close of these remarks, and drank two glasses of punch in grave succession. He then said with much solemnity:

" One thing more I have to do, before this separation is complete, and that is to perform an act of justice. My friend

Mr. Thomas Traddles has, on two several occasions, 'put his name,' if I may use a common expression, to bills of exchange for my accommodation. On the first occasion Mr. Thomas Traddles was left—let me say, in short, in the lurch. The fulfilment of of the second has not yet arrived. The amount of the first obligation," here Mr. Micawber carefully referred to papers, "was, I believe, twenty-three, four, nine and a half; of the second, according to my entry of that transaction, eighteen, six, two. These sums, united, make a total, if my calculation is correct, amounting to forty-one, ten, eleven and a half. My friend Copperfield will perhaps do me the favour to check that total?"

I did so and found it correct.

"To leave this metropolis," said Mr. Micawber, "and my friend Mr. Thomas Traddles, without acquitting myself of the pecuniary part of this obligation, would weigh upon my mind to an insupportable extent. I have, therefore, prepared for my friend Mr. Thomas Traddles, and I now hold in my hand, a document, which accomplishes the desired object. I beg to hand to my friend Mr. Thomas Traddles my I. O. U. for forty-one, ten, eleven and a half, and I am happy to recover my moral dignity, and to know that I can once more walk erect before my fellow man!"

With this introduction (which greatly affected him), Mr. Micawber placed his I. O. U. in the hands of Traddles, and said he wished him well in every relation of life. I am persuaded, not only that this was quite the same to Mr. Micawber as paying the money, but that Traddles himself hardly knew the difference until he had had time to think about it.

Mr. Micawber walked so erect before his fellow man, on the strength of this virtuous action, that his chest looked half as broad again when he lighted us down-stairs. We parted with great heartiness on both sides; and when I had seen Traddles to his own door, and was going home alone, I thought, among the other odd and contradictory things I mused upon, that, slippery as Mr. Micawber was, I was probably indebted to some compassionate recollection he retained of me as his boy-lodger, for never having been asked by him for money. I certainly should not have had the moral courage to refuse it; and I have no doubt he knew that (to his credit be it written) quite as well as I did.

37

A LITTLE COLD WATER

MY NEW LIFE HAD LASTED FOR MORE THAN A WEEK, AND I was stronger than ever in those tremendous practical resolutions that I felt the crisis required. I continued to walk extremely fast, and to have a general idea that I was getting on. I made it a rule to take as much out of myself as I possibly could, in my way of doing everything to which I applied my energies. I made a perfect victim of myself. I even entertained some idea of putting myself on a vegetable diet, vaguely conceiving that, in becoming a graminivorous animal, I should sacrifice to Dora.

As yet, little Dora was quite unconscious of my desperate firmness, otherwise than as my letters darkly shadowed it forth. But another Saturday came, and on that Saturday evening she was to be at Miss Mills's; and when Mr. Mills had gone to his whist-club (telegraphed to me in the street, by a bird-cage in the drawing-room middle window), I was to go there to tea.

By this time, we were quite settled down in Buckingham Street, where Mr. Dick continued his copying in a state of absolute felicity. My aunt had obtained a signal victory over Mrs. Crupp, by paying her off, throwing the first pitcher she planted on the stairs out of window, and protecting in person, up and down the staircase, a supernumerary whom she engaged from the outer world. These vigorous measures struck such terror to the breast of Mrs. Crupp, that she subsided into her own kitchen, under the impression that my aunt was mad. My aunt being supremely indifferent to Mrs. Crupp's opinion and everybody else's, and rather favouring than discouraging the idea, Mrs. Crupp, of late the bold, became within a few days so faint-hearted, that rather than encounter my aunt upon the staircase, she would endeavour to hide her portly form behind doors—leaving visible, however, a wide margin of flannel petticoat—or would shrink into dark corners. This gave my aunt such unspeakable satisfaction, that I believe she took a delight in prowling up and down, with her bonnet insanely perched on the top of her head, at times when Mrs. Crupp was likely to be in the way.

My aunt, being uncommonly neat and ingenious, made so many little improvements in our domestic arrangements, that I seemed to be richer instead of poorer. Among the rest, she converted the pantry into a dressing-room for me; and purchased and embellished a bedstead for my occupation, which looked as like a bookcase in the daytime as a bedstead could. I was the object of her constant solicitude; and my poor mother herself could not have loved me better, or studied more how to make me happy.

Peggotty had considered herself highly privileged in being allowed to participate in these labours; and, although she still retained something of her old sentiment of awe in reference to my aunt, had received so many marks of encouragement and confidence, that they were the best friends possible. But the time had now come (I am speaking of the Saturday when I was to take tea at Miss Mills's) when it was necessary for her to return home, and enter on the discharge of the duties she had undertaken in behalf of Ham. " So good-bye, Barkis," said my aunt, " and take care of yourself! I am sure I never thought I could be sorry to lose you! "

I took Peggotty to the coach-office and saw her off. She cried at parting, and confided her brother to my friendship as Ham had done. We had heard nothing of him since he went away that sunny afternoon.

" And now, my own dear Davy," said Peggotty, " if, while you're a prentice, you should want any money to spend; or if, when you're out of your time, my dear, you should want any to set you up (and you must do one or other, or both, my darling); who has such a good right to ask leave to lend it you, as my sweet girl's own old stupid me! "

I was not so savagely independent as to say anything in reply, but that if ever I borrowed money of any one, I would borrow it of her. Next to accepting a large sum on the spot, I believe this gave Peggotty more comfort than anything I could have done.

" And, my dear! " whispered Peggotty, " tell the pretty little angel that I should so have liked to see her, only for a minute! And tell her that before she marries my boy, I'll come and make your house so beautiful for you, if you'll let me! "

I declared that nobody else should touch it; and this gave Peggotty such delight, that she went away in good spirits.

I fatigued myself as much as I possibly could in the Commons all day, by a variety of devices, and at the appointed time in the evening repaired to Mr. Mills's street. Mr. Mills, who was a terrible fellow to fall asleep after dinner, had not yet gone out, and there was no bird-cage in the middle window.

He kept me waiting so long, that I fervently hoped the club would fine him for being late. At last he came out; and then I saw my own Dora hang up the bird-cage, and peep into the balcony to look for me, and run in again when she saw I was there, while Jip remained behind, to bark injuriously at an immense butcher's dog in the street, who could have taken him like a pill.

Dora came to the drawing-room door to meet me; and Jip came scrambling out, tumbling over his own growls, under the impression that I was a Bandit; and we all three went in, as happy and loving as could be. I soon carried desolation into the bosom of our joys—not that I meant to do it, but that I was so full of the subject—by asking Dora, without the smallest preparation, if she could love a beggar?

My pretty, little, startled Dora! Her only association with the word was a yellow face and a nightcap, or a pair of crutches, or a wooden leg, or a dog with a decanter-stand in his mouth, or something of that kind; and she stared at me with the most delightful wonder.

"How can you ask me anything so foolish?" pouted Dora. "Love a beggar!"

"Dora, my own dearest!" said I. "*I* am a beggar!"

"How can you be such a silly thing," replied Dora, slapping my hand, "as to sit there, telling such stories? I'll make Jip bite you!"

Her childish way was the most delicious way in the world to me, but it was necessary to be explicit, and I solemnly repeated:

"Dora, my own life, I am your ruined David!"

"I declare I'll make Jip bite you!" said Dora, shaking her curls, "if you are so ridiculous."

But I looked so serious, that Dora left off shaking her curls, and laid her trembling little hand upon my shoulder, and first looked scared and anxious, then began to cry. That was dreadful. I fell upon my knees before the sofa, caressing her, and imploring her not to rend my heart; but, for some time, poor little Dora did nothing but exclaim Oh dear! Oh dear! And oh, she was so frightened! And where was Julia Mills! And oh, take her to Julia Mills, and go away, please! until I was almost beside myself.

At last, after an agony of supplication and protestation, I got Dora to look at me, with a horrified expression of face, which I gradually soothed until it was only loving, and her soft, pretty cheek was lying against mine. Then I told her, with my arms clasped round her, how I loved her, so dearly, and so dearly; how I felt it right to offer to release her from her engagement, because now I was poor; how I never could bear it, or recover it, if I lost her; how I had no fears of poverty, if she had none, my arm being nerved and my heart inspired by her; how I was already working with a courage such as none but lovers knew; how I had begun to be practical, and look into the future; how a crust well-earned was sweeter far than a feast inherited; and much more to the same purpose, which I delivered in a burst of passionate eloquence quite surprising to myself, though I had been thinking about it, day and night, ever since my aunt had astonished me.

"Is your heart mine still, dear Dora?" said I, rapturously, for I knew by her clinging to me that it was.

"Oh, yes!" cried Dora. "Oh, yes, it's all yours. Oh, don't be dreadful!"

I dreadful! To Dora!

"Don't talk about being poor, and working hard!" said Dora, nestling closer to me. "Oh, don't, don't!"

"My dearest love," said I, "the crust well-earned—"

"Oh, yes; but I don't want to hear any more about crusts!" said Dora. "And Jip must have a mutton-chop every day at twelve, or he'll die!"

I was charmed with her childish, winning way. I fondly explained to Dora that Jip should have his mutton-chop with his accustomed regularity. I drew a picture of our frugal home, made independent by my labour—sketching in the little house I had seen at Highgate, and my aunt in her room up-stairs.

"I am not dreadful now, Dora?" said I, tenderly.

"Oh, no, no!" cried Dora. "But I hope your aunt will keep in her own room a good deal. And I hope she's not a scolding old thing!"

If it were possible for me to love Dora more than ever, I am sure I did. But I felt she was a little impracticable. It damped my new-born ardour, to find that ardour so difficult of communication to her. I made another trial. When she was quite herself again, and was curling Jip's ears, as he lay upon her lap, I became grave, and said:

"My own! May I mention something?"

"Oh, please don't be practical!" said Dora coaxingly. "Because it frightens me so!"

"Sweet heart!" I returned; "there is nothing to alarm you in all this. I want you to think of it quite differently. I want to make it nerve you, and inspire you, Dora!"

"Oh, but that's so shocking!" cried Dora.

"My love, no. Perseverance and strength of character will enable us to bear much worse things."

"But I haven't got any strength at all," said Dora, shaking her curls. "Have I, Jip? Oh, do kiss Jip, and be agreeable!"

It was impossible to resist kissing Jip, when she held him up to me for that purpose, putting her own bright, rosy little mouth into kissing form, as she directed the operation, which she insisted should be performed symmetrically, on the centre of his nose. I did as she bade me—rewarding myself afterwards for my obedience—and she charmed me out of my graver character for I don't know how long.

"But, Dora, my beloved!" said I, at last resuming it; "I was going to mention something."

The Judge of the Prerogative Court might have fallen in love with her, to see her fold her little hands and hold them up, begging and praying me not to be dreadful any more.

"Indeed I am not going to be, my darling!" I assured her. "But, Dora, my love, if you will sometimes think—not despondingly, you know; far from that—! but if you will sometimes think—just to encourage yourself—that you are engaged to a poor man—"

"Don't, don't! Pray don't!" cried Dora. "It's so very dreadful!

"My soul, not at all!" said I cheerfully. "If you will sometimes think of that, and look about now and then at your papa's housekeeping, and endeavour to acquire a little habit—of accounts, for instance—"

Poor little Dora received this suggestion with something that was half a sob and half a scream.

"—It would be so useful to us afterwards," I went on. "And if you would promise me to read a little—a little Cookery Book that I would send you, it would be so excellent for both of us. For our path in life, my Dora," said I, warming with the subject, "is stony and rugged now, and it rests with us to smooth it. We must fight our way onward. We must be brave. There are obstacles to be met, and we must meet, and crush them!"

I was going on at a great rate, with a clenched hand, and a most enthusiastic countenance; but it was quite unnecessary to proceed. I had said enough. I had done it again. Oh, she was so frightened! Oh, where was Julia Mills! Oh, take her to Julia

Mills, and go away, please! So that, in short, I was quite distracted, and raved about the drawing-room.

I thought I had killed her, this time. I sprinkled water on her face. I went down on my knees. I plucked at my hair. I denounced myself as a remorseless brute and a ruthless beast. I implored her forgiveness. I besought her to look up. I ravaged Miss Mills's work-box for a smelling-bottle, and in my agony of mind applied an ivory needle-case instead, and dropped all the needles over Dora. I shook my fists at Jip, who was as frantic as myself. I did every wild extravagance that could be done, and was a long way beyond the end of my wits when Miss Mills came into the room.

"Who has done this?" exclaimed Miss Mills, succouring her friend.

I replied, "*I*, Miss Mills! *I* have done it! Behold the destroyer!"—or words to that effect—and hid my face from the light, in the sofa cushion.

At first Miss Mills thought it was a quarrel, and that we were verging on the Desert of Sahara; but she soon found out how matters stood, for my dear affectionate little Dora, embracing her, began exclaiming that I was "a poor labourer;" and then cried for me, and embraced me, and asked me would I let her give me all her money to keep, and then fell on Miss Mills's neck, sobbing as if her tender heart were broken.

Miss Mills must have been born to be a blessing to us. She ascertained from me in a few words what it was all about, comforted Dora, and gradually convinced her that I was not a labourer—from my manner of stating the case I believe Dora concluded that I was a navigator, and went balancing myself up and down a plank all day with a wheelbarrow—and so brought us together in peace. When we were quite composed, and Dora had gone up-stairs to put some rose-water to her eyes, Miss Mills rang for tea. In the ensuing interval, I told Miss Mills that she was evermore my friend, and that my heart must cease to vibrate ere I could forget her sympathy.

I then expounded to Miss Mills what I had endeavoured, so very unsuccessfully, to expound to Dora. Miss Mills replied, on general principles, that the Cottage of content was better than the Palace of cold splendour, and that where love was, all was.

I said to Miss Mills that this was very true, and who should know it better than I, who loved Dora with a love that never mortal had experienced yet? But on Miss Mills observing, with despondency, that it were well indeed for some hearts if this were so, I explained that I begged leave to restrict the observation to mortals of the masculine gender.

I then put it to Miss Mills, to say whether she considered that there was or was not any practical merit in the suggestion I had been anxious to make, concerning the accounts, the housekeeping, and the Cookery Book?

Miss Mills, after some consideration, thus replied:

"Mr. Copperfield, I will be plain with you. Mental suffering and trial supply, in some natures, the place of years, and I will be as plain with you as if I were a Lady Abbess. No. The sugfestion is not appropriate to our Dora. Our dearest Dora is a favourite child of nature. She is a thing of light, and airiness, and joy. I am free to confess that if it could be done, it might be well, but—" And Miss Mills shook her head.

I was encouraged by this closing admission on the part of Miss Mills to ask her, whether, for Dora's sake, if she had any opportunity of luring her attention to such preparations for an earnest life, she would avail herself of it? Miss Mills replied in the affirmative so readily, that I further asked her if she would take charge of the Cookery Book; and, if she ever could insinuate it upon Dora's acceptance, without frightening her, undertake to do me that crowning service. Miss Mills accepted this trust, too; but was not sanguine.

And Dora returned, looking such a lovely little creature, that I really doubted whether she ought to be troubled with anything so ordinary. And she loved me so much, and was so captivating (particularly when she made Jip stand on his hind legs for toast, and when she pretended to hold that nose of his against the hot tea-pot for punishment because he wouldn't), that I felt like a sort of Monster who had got into a Fairy's bower, when I thought of having frightened her, and made her cry.

After tea we had the guitar; and Dora sang those same dear old French songs about the impossibility of ever on any account leaving off dancing, La ra la, La ra la, until I felt a much greater Monster than before.

We had only one check to our pleasure, and that happened a little while before I took my leave, when, Miss Mills chancing to make some allusion to to-morrow morning, I unluckily let out that, being obliged to exert myself now, I got up at five o'clock. Whether Dora had any idea that I was a Private Watchman, I am unable to say; but it made a great impression on her, and she neither played nor sang any more.

It was still on her mind when I bade her adieu; and she said to me, in her pretty coaxing way—as if I were a doll, I used to think:

" Now don't get up at five o'clock, you naughty boy. It's so nonsensical! "

" My love," said I, " I have work to do."

" But don't do it! " returned Dora. " Why should you? "

It was impossible to say to that sweet little surprised face, otherwise than lightly and playfully, that we must work to live.

" Oh! How ridiculous! " cried Dora.

" How shall we live without, Dora? " said I.

" How? Any how! " said Dora.

She seemed to think she had quite settled the question, and gave me such a triumphant little kiss, direct from her innocent heart, that I would hardly have put her out of conceit with her answer, for a fortune.

Well! I loved her, and I went on loving her, most absorbingly, entirely, and completely. But going on, too, working pretty hard, and busily keeping red-hot all the irons I now had in the fire, I would sit sometimes of a night, opposite my aunt, thinking how I had frightened Dora that time, and how I could best make my way with a guitar-case through the forest of difficulty, until I used to fancy that my head was turning quite grey.

38

A DISSOLUTION OF PARTNERSHIP

I DID NOT ALLOW MY RESOLUTION, WITH RESPECT TO the Parliamentary Debates, to cool. It was one of the irons I began to heat immediately, and one of the irons I kept hot, and hammered at, with a perseverance I may honestly admire. I bought an approved scheme of the noble art and mystery of stenography (which cost me ten and sixpence), and plunged into a sea of perplexity that brought me, in a few weeks, to the confines of distraction. The changes that were rung upon dots, which in such a position meant such a thing, and in such another position something else, entirely different; the wonderful vagaries that were played by circles; the unaccountable consequences that resulted from marks like flies' legs; the tremendous effects of a curve in a wrong place; not only troubled my waking hours, but reappeared before me in my sleep. When I had groped my way, blindly, through these difficulties, and had mastered the alphabet, which was an Egyptian Temple in itself, there then appeared a procession of new horrors, called arbitrary characters; the most despotic characters I have ever known; who insisted, for instance, that a thing like the beginning of a cobweb, meant expectation, and that a pen-and-ink sky-rocket stood for disadvantageous. When I had fixed these wretches in my mind, I found that they had driven everything else out of it; then, beginning again, I forgot them; while I was picking them up, I dropped the other fragments of the system; in short, it was almost heart-breaking.

It might have been quite heart-breaking, but for Dora, who was the stay and anchor of my tempest-driven bark. Every scratch in the scheme was a gnarled oak in the forest of difficulty, and I went on cutting them down, one after another, with such vigour, that in three or four months I was in a condition to make an experiment on one of our crack speakers in the Commons. Shall I ever forget how the crack speaker walked off from me before I began, and left my imbecile pencil staggering about the paper as if it were in a fit!

This would not do, it was quite clear. I was flying too high, and should never get on, so. I resorted to Traddles for advice; who suggested that he should dictate speeches to me, at a pace, and with occasional stoppages, adapted to my weakness. Very grateful for this friendly aid, I accepted the proposal; and night after night, almost every night, for a long time, we had a sort of Private Parliament in Buckingham Street, after I came home from the Doctor's.

I should like to see such a Parliament anywhere else! My aunt and Mr. Dick represented the Government or the Opposition (as the case might be), and Traddles, with the assistance of Enfield's Speaker or a volume of parliamentary orations, thundered astonishing invectives against them. Standing by the table, with his finger in the page to keep the place, and his right arm flourishing above his head, Traddles, as Mr. Pitt, Mr. Fox, Mr. Sheridan, Mr. Burke, Lord Castlereagh, Viscount Sidmouth, or Mr. Canning, would work himself into the most violent heats, and deliver the most withering denunciations of the profligacy and corruption of my aunt and Mr. Dick; while I used to sit, at a little distance, with my notebook on my knee, fagging after him with all my might and main. The inconsistency and recklessness of Traddles were not to be exceeded by any real politician. He was for any description of policy, in the compass of a week; and nailed all sorts of colours to every denomination of mast. My aunt, looking very like an immovable Chancellor of the Exchequer, would occasionally throw in an interruption or two, as "Hear!" or "No!" or "Oh!" when the text seemed to require it: which was always a signal to Mr. Dick (a perfect country gentleman) to follow lustily with the same cry. But Mr. Dick got taxed with such things in the course of his Parliamentary career, and was made responsible for such awful consequences, that he became uncomfortable in his mind sometimes. I believe he actually began to be afraid he really had been doing something, tending to the annihilation of the British constitution, and the ruin of the country.

Often and often we pursued these debates until the clock pointed to midnight, and the candles were burning down. The result of so much good practice was, that by-and-by I began to keep pace with Traddles pretty well, and should have been quite triumphant if I had had the least idea what my notes were about. But, as to reading them after I had got them, I might as well have copied the Chinese inscriptions on an immense collection of tea-chests, or the golden characters on all the great red and green bottles in the chemists' shops!

There was nothing for it, but to turn back and begin all over again. It was very hard, but I turned back, though with a heavy heart, and began laboriously and methodically to plod over the same tedious ground at a snail's pace; stopping to examine minutely every speck in the way, on all sides, and making the most desperate efforts to know these elusive characters by sight wherever I met them. I was always punctual at the office; at the Doctor's too; and I really did work, as the common expression is, like a cart-horse.

One day, when I went to the Commons as usual, I found Mr. Spenlow in the doorway looking extremely grave, and talking to himself. As he was in the habit of complaining of pains in his head—he had naturally a short throat, and I do seriously believe he overstarched himself—I was at first alarmed by the idea that he was not quite right in that direction; but he soon relieved my uneasiness.

Instead of returning my "Good morning" with his usual affability, he looked at me in a distant, ceremonious manner, and coldly requested me to accompany him to a certain coffee-house, which, in those days, had a door opening into the Commons, just within the little archway in St. Paul's Churchyard. I complied, in a very uncomfortable state, and with a warm shooting all over me, as if my apprehensions were breaking out into buds. When I allowed him to go on a little before, on account of the narrowness of the way, I observed that he carried his head with a lofty air that was particularly unpromising; and my mind misgave me that he had found out about my darling Dora.

If I had not guessed this, on the way to the coffee-house, I could hardly have failed to know what was the matter when I followed him into an up-stairs room, and found Miss Murdstone there, supported by a background of sideboard, on which were several inverted tumblers sustaining lemons, and two of those extraordinary boxes, all corners and flutings, for sticking knives and forks in, which, happily for mankind, are now obsolete.

Miss Murdstone gave me her chilly finger-nails, and sat severely rigid. Mr. Spenlow shut the door, motioned me to a chair, and stood on the hearth-rug in front of the fire-place.

"Have the goodness to show Mr. Copperfield," said Mr. Spenlow, "what you have in your reticule, Miss Murdstone."

I believe it was the old identical steel-clasped reticule of my childhood, that shut up like a bite. Compressing her lips, in sympathy with the snap, Miss Murdstone opened it—opening her mouth a little at the same time—and produced my last letter to Dora, teeming with expressions of devoted affection.

"I believe that is your writing, Mr. Copperfield?" said Mr. Spenlow.

I was very hot, and the voice I heard was very unlike mine, when I said, "It is, sir!"

"If I am not mistaken," said Mr. Spenlow, as Miss Murdstone brought a parcel of letters out of her reticule, tied round with the dearest bit of blue ribbon, "those are also from your pen, Mr. Copperfield?"

I took them from her with a most desolate sensation; and, glancing at such phrases at the top, as "My ever dearest and own Dora," "My best beloved angel," "My blessed one for ever," and the like, blushed deeply, and inclined my head.

"No, thank you!" said Mr. Spenlow, coldly, as I mechanically offered them back to him. "I will not deprive you of them. Miss Murdstone, be so good as to proceed!"

That gentle creature, after a moment's thoughtful survey of the carpet, delivered herself with much dry unction as follows:

"I must confess to having entertained my suspicions of Miss Spenlow, in reference to David Copperfield, for some time. I observed Miss Spenlow and David Copperfield, when they first met; and the impression made upon me then was not agreeable. The depravity of the human heart is such—"

"You will oblige me, ma'am," interrupted Mr. Spenlow, "by confining yourself to facts."

Miss Murdstone cast down her eyes, shook her head as if protesting against this unseemly interruption, and with frowning dignity resumed:

"Since I am to confine myself to facts, I will state them as dryly as I can. Perhaps that will be considered an acceptable course of proceeding. I have already said, sir, that I have had my suspicions of Miss Spenlow, in reference to David Copperfield, for some time. I have frequently endeavoured to find decisive corroboration of those suspicions, but without effect. I have therefore forborne to mention them to Miss Spenlow's father:" looking severely at him; "knowing how little disposition there usually is in such cases, to acknowledge the conscientious discharge of duty."

Mr. Spenlow seemed quite cowed by the gentlemanly sternness of Miss Murdstone's manner, and deprecated her severity with a conciliatory little wave of his hand.

"On my return to Norwood, after the period of absence occasioned by my brother's marriage," pursued Miss Murdstone in a disdainful voice, "and on the return of Miss Spenlow from her visit to her friend Miss Mills, I imagined that the manner of Miss Spenlow gave me greater occasion for suspicion than before. Therefore I watched Miss Spenlow closely."

Dear, tender little Dora, so unconscious of this Dragon's eye.

"Still," resumed Miss Murdstone, "I found no proof until last night. It appeared to me that Miss Spenlow received too many letters from her friend Miss Mills; but Miss Mills being her friend with her father's full concurrence," another telling blow at Mr. Spenlow, "it was not for me to interfere. If I may not be permitted to allude to the natural depravity of the human heart, at least I may—I must—be permitted, so far to refer to misplaced confidence."

Mr. Spenlow apologetically murmured his assent.

"Last evening after tea," pursued Miss Murdstone, "I observed the little dog starting, rolling, and growling about the drawing-room, worrying something. I said to Miss Spenlow, 'Dora, what is that the dog has in his mouth? It's paper.' Miss Spenlow immediately put her hand to her frock, gave a sudden cry, and ran to the dog. I interposed, and said, 'Dora, my love, you must permit me.'"

Oh Jip, miserable Spaniel, this wretchedness, then, was your work!

" Miss Spenlow endeavoured," said Miss Murdstone, " to bribe me with kisses, work-boxes, and small articles of jewellery —that, of course, I pass over. The little dog retreated under the sofa on my approaching him, and was with great difficulty dislodged by the fire-irons. Even when dislodged, he still kept the letter in his mouth; and on my endeavouring to take it from him, at the imminent risk of being bitten, he kept it between his teeth so pertinaciously as to suffer himself to be held suspended in the air by means of the document. At length I obtained possession of it. After perusing it, I taxed Miss Spenlow with having many such letters in her possession; and ultimately obtained from her the packet which is now in David Copperfield's hand."

Here she ceased; and snapping her reticule again, and shutting her mouth, looked as if she might be broken, but could never be bent.

" You have heard Miss Murdstone," said Mr. Spenlow, turning to me. " I beg to ask, Mr. Copperfield, if you have anything to say in reply? "

The picture I had before me, of the beautiful little treasure of my heart, sobbing and crying all night—of her being alone, frightened, and wretched, then—of her having so piteously begged and prayed that stony-hearted woman to forgive her—of her having vainly offered her those kisses, work-boxes, and trinkets—of her being in such grievous distress, and all for me —very much impaired the little dignity I had been able to muster. I am afraid I was in a tremulous state for a minute or so, though I did my best to disguise it.

" There is nothing I can say, sir," I returned, " except that all the blame is mine. Dora—"

" Miss Spenlow, if you please," said her father, majestically.

"—was induced and persuaded by me," I went on, swallowing that colder designation, " to consent to this concealment, and I bitterly regret it."

" You are very much to blame, sir," said Mr. Spenlow, walking to and fro upon the hearth-rug, and emphasizing what he said with his whole body instead of his head, on account of the stiffness of his cravat and spine. " You have done a stealthy and unbecoming action, Mr. Copperfield. When I take a gentleman to my house, no matter whether he is nineteen, twenty-nine, or ninety, I take him there in a spirit of confidence. If he abuses my confidence, he commits a dishonourable action, Mr. Copperfield."

"I feel it, sir, I assure you," I returned. "But I never thought so, before. Sincerely, honestly, indeed, Mr. Spenlow, I never thought so, before. I love Miss Spenlow to that extent—"

"Pooh! nonsense!" said Mr. Spenlow, reddening. "Pray don't tell me to my face that you love my daughter, Mr. Copperfield!"

"Could I defend my conduct if I did not, sir?" I returned, with all humility.

"Can you defend your conduct if you do, sir?" said Mr. Spenlow, stopping short upon the hearth-rug. "Have you considered your years, and my daughter's years, Mr. Copperfield? Have you considered what it is to undermine the confidence that should subsist between my daughter and myself? Have you considered my daughter's station in life, the projects I may contemplate for her advancement, the testamentary intentions I may have with reference to her? Have you considered anything, Mr. Copperfield?"

"Very little, sir, I am afraid;" I answered, speaking to him as respectfully and sorrowfully as I felt; "but pray believe me, I have considered my own worldly position. When I explained it to you, we were already engaged—"

"I BEG," said Mr. Spenlow, more like Punch than I had ever seen him, as he energetically struck one hand upon the other—I could not help noticing that even in my despair; "that you will NOT talk to me of engagements, Mr. Copperfield!"

The otherwise immovable Miss Murdstone laughed contemptuously in one short syllable.

"When I explained my altered position to you, sir," I began again, substituting a new form of expression for what was so unpalatable to him, "this concealment, into which I am so unhappy as to have led Miss Spenlow, had begun. Since I have been in that altered position, I have strained every nerve, I have exerted every energy, to improve it. I am sure I shall improve it in time. Will you grant me time—any length of time? We are both so young, sir,—"

"You are right," interrupted Mr. Spenlow, nodding his head a great many times, and frowning very much, "you are both very young. It's all nonsense. Let there be an end of the nonsense. Take away those letters, and throw them in the fire. Give me Miss Spenlow's letters to throw in the fire; and although our future intercourse must, you are aware, be restricted to the Commons here, we will agree to make no further mention of the past. Come, Mr. Copperfield, you don't want sense; and this is the sensible course."

No. I couldn't think of agreeing to it. I was very sorry, but there was a higher consideration than sense. Love was above all earthly considerations, and I loved Dora to idolatry, and Dora loved me. I didn't exactly say so; I softened it down as much as I could; but I implied it, and I was resolute upon it. I don't think I made myself very ridiculous, but I know I was resolute.

"Very well, Mr. Copperfield," said Mr. Spenlow, "I must try my influence with my daughter."

Miss Murdstone, by an expressive sound, a long-drawn respiration, which was neither a sigh nor a moan, but was like both, gave it as her opinion that he should have done this at first.

"I must try," said Mr. Spenlow, confirmed by this support, "my influence with my daughter. Do you decline to take those letters, Mr. Copperfield?" For I had laid them on the table.

Yes. I told him I hoped he would not think it wrong, but I couldn't possibly take them from Miss Murdstone.

"Nor from me?" said Mr. Spenlow.

No, I replied with the profoundest respect; nor from him.

"Very well!" said Mr. Spenlow.

A silence succeeding, I was undecided whether to go or stay. At length I was moving quietly towards the door, with the intention of saying that perhaps I should consult his feelings best by withdrawing: when he said, with his hands in his coat pockets, into which it was as much as he could do to get them; and with what I should call, upon the whole, a decidedly pious air:

"You are probably aware, Mr. Copperfield, that I am not altogether destitute of worldly possessions, and that my daughter is my nearest and dearest relative?"

I hurriedly made him a reply to the effect, that I hoped the error into which I had been betrayed by the desperate nature of my love, did not induce him to think me mercenary too?

"I don't allude to the matter in that light," said Mr. Spenlow. "It would be better for yourself, and all of us, if you *were* mercenary, Mr. Copperfield—I mean, if you were more discreet, and less influenced by all this youthful nonsense. No. I merely say, with quite another view, you are probably aware I have some property to bequeath to my child?"

I certainly supposed so.

"And you can hardly think," said Mr. Spenlow, "having experience of what we see, in the Commons here, every day, of the various unaccountable and negligent proceedings of men, in respect of their testamentary arrangements—of all subjects, the one on which perhaps the strangest revelations of human inconsistency are to be met with—but that mine are made?"

I inclined my head in acquiescence.

"I should not allow," said Mr. Spenlow, with an evident increase of pious sentiment, and slowly shaking his head as he poised himself upon his toes and heels alternately, "my suitable provision for my child to be influenced by a piece of youthful folly like the present. It is mere folly. Mere nonsense. In a little while, it will weigh lighter than any feather. But I might—I might—if this silly business were not completely relinquished altogether, be induced in some anxious moment to guard her from, and surround her with protections against, the consequences of any foolish step in the way of marriage. Now, Mr. Copperfield, I hope that you will not render it necessary for me to open, even for a quarter of an hour, that closed page in the book of life, and unsettle, even for a quarter of an hour, grave affairs long since composed."

There was a serenity, a tranquillity, a calm-sunset air about him, which quite affected me. He was so peaceful and resigned —clearly had his affairs in such perfect train, and so systematically wound up—that he was a man to feel touched in the contemplation of. I really think I saw tears rise to his eyes, from the depth of his own feeling of all this.

But what could I do? I could not deny Dora, and my own heart. When he told me I had better take a week to consider of what he had said, how could I say I wouldn't take a week, yet how could I fail to know that no amount of weeks could influence such love as mine?

"In the meantime, confer with Miss Trotwood, or with any person with any knowledge of life," said Mr. Spenlow, adjusting his cravat with both hands. "Take a week, Mr. Copperfield."

I submitted; and, with a countenance as expressive as I was able to make it of dejected and despairing constancy, came out of the room. Miss Murdstone's heavy eyebrows followed me to the door—I say her eyebrows rather than her eyes, because they were much more important in her face—and she looked so exactly as she used to look, at about that hour of the morning, in our parlour at Blunderstone, that I could have fancied I had been breaking down in my lessons again, and that the dead weight on my mind was that horrible old spelling-book with oval woodcuts, shaped, to my youthful fancy, like the glasses out of spectacles.

When I got to the office, and, shutting out old Tiffey and the rest of them with my hands, sat at my desk, in my own particular nook, thinking of this earthquake that had taken place so unexpectedly, and in the bitterness of my spirit cursing

Jip, I fell into such a state of torment about Dora, that I wonder I did not take up my hat and rush insanely to Norwood. The idea of their frightening her, and making her cry, and of my not being there to comfort her, was so excruciating, that it impelled me to write a wild letter to Mr. Spenlow, beseeching him not to visit upon her the consequences of my awful destiny. I implored him to spare her gentle nature—not to crush a fragile flower—and addressed him generally, to the best of my remembrance, as if, instead of being her father, he had been an Ogre, or the Dragon of Wantley. This letter I sealed and laid upon his desk before he returned; and when he came in, I saw him, through the half-opened door of his room, take it up and read it.

He said nothing about it all the morning; but before he went away in the afternoon he called me in, and told me that I need not make myself at all uneasy about his daughter's happiness. He had assured her, he said, that it was all nonsense; and he had nothing more to say to her. He believed he was an indulgent father (as indeed he was), and I might spare myself any solicitude on her account.

"You may make it necessary, if you are foolish or obstinate, Mr. Copperfield," he observed, "for me to send my daughter abroad again, for a term; but I have a better opinion of you. I hope you will be wiser than that, in a few days. As to Miss Murdstone," for I had alluded to her in the letter, "I respect that lady's vigilance, and feel obliged to her; but she has strict charge to avoid the subject. All I desire, Mr. Copperfield, is, that it should be forgotten. All you have got to do, Mr. Copperfield, is to forget it."

All! In the note I wrote to Miss Mills, I bitterly quoted this sentiment. All I had to do, I said, with gloomy sarcasm, was to forget Dora. That was all, and what was that? I entreated Miss Mills to see me, that evening. If it could not be done with Mr. Mills's sanction and concurrence, I besought a clandestine interview in the back kitchen where the mangle was. I informed her that my reason was tottering on its throne, and only she, Miss Mills, could prevent its being deposed. I signed myself, hers distractedly; and I couldn't help feeling, while I read this composition over, before sending it by a porter, that it was something in the style of Mr. Micawber.

However, I sent it. At night I repaired to Miss Mills's street, and walked up and down, until I was stealthily fetched in by Miss Mills's maid, and taken the area way to the back kitchen. I have since seen reason to believe that there was nothing on earth to prevent my going in at the front door, and being shown up into the drawing-room, except Miss Mills's love of the romantic and mysterious.

In the back kitchen I raved as became me. I went there, I suppose, to make a fool of myself, and I am quite sure I did it. Miss Mills had received a hasty note from Dora, telling her that all was discovered, and saying, " Oh pray come to me, Julia, do, do! " But Miss Mills, mistrusting the acceptability of her presence to the higher powers, had not yet gone; and we were all benighted in the Desert of Sahara.

Miss Mills had a wonderful flow of words, and liked to pour them out. I could not help feeling, though she mingled her tears with mine, that she had a dreadful luxury in our afflictions. She petted them, as I may say, and made the most of them. A deep gulf, she observed, had opened between Dora and me, and Love could only span it with its rainbow. Love must suffer in this stern world; it ever had been so, it ever would be so. No matter, Miss Mills remarked. Hearts confined by cobwebs would burst at last, and then Love was avenged.

This was small consolation, but Miss Mills wouldn't encourage fallacious hopes. She made me much more wretched than I was before, and I felt (and told her with the deepest gratitude) that she was indeed a friend. We resolved that she should go to Dora the first thing in the morning, and find some means of assuring her, either by looks or words, of my devotion and misery. We parted, overwhelmed with grief; and I think Miss Mills enjoyed herself completely.

I confided all to my aunt when I got home; and in spite of all she could say to me, went to bed despairing. I got up despairing, and went out despairing. It was Saturday morning, and I went straight to the Commons.

I was surprised, when I came within sight of our office-door, to see the ticket-porters standing outside talking together, and some half-dozen stragglers gazing at the windows which were shut up. I quickened my pace, and, passing among them, wondering at their looks, went hurriedly in.

The clerks were there, but nobody was doing anything. Old Tiffey, for the first time in his life I should think, was sitting on somebody else's stool, and had not hung up his hat.

" This is a dreadful calamity, Mr. Copperfield," said he, as I entered.

" What is? " I exclaimed. " What's the matter? "

" Don't you know? " cried Tiffey, and all the rest of them, coming round me.

" No! " said I, looking from face to face.

"Mr. Spenlow," said Tiffey.

"What about him?"

"Dead!"

I thought it was the office reeling, and not I, as one of the clerks caught hold of me. They sat me down in a chair, untied my neckcloth, and brought me some water. I have no idea whether this took any time.

"Dead?" said I.

"He dined in town yesterday, and drove down in the phaeton by himself," said Tiffey, "having sent his own groom home by the coach, as he sometimes did, you know—"

"Well?"

"The phaeton went home without him. The horses stopped at the stable gate. The man went out with a lantern. Nobody in the carriage."

"Had they run away?"

"They were not hot," said Tiffey, putting on his glasses; "no hotter, I understand, than they would have been, going down at the usual pace. The reins were broken, but they had been dragging on the ground. The house was roused up directly, and three of them went out along the road. They found him a mile off."

"More than a mile off, Mr. Tiffey," interposed a junior.

"Was it? I believe you are right," said Tiffey,—"*more* than a mile off—not far from the church—lying partly on the roadside, and partly on the path, upon his face. Whether he fell out in a fit, or got out, feeling ill before the fit came on—or even whether he was quite dead then, though there is no doubt he was quite insensible—no one appears to know. If he breathed, certainly he never spoke. Medical assistance was got as soon as possible, but it was quite useless."

I cannot describe the state of mind into which I was thrown by this intelligence. The shock of such an event happening so suddenly, and happening to one with whom I had been in any respect at variance—the appalling vacancy in the room he had occupied so lately, where his chair and table seemed to wait for him, and his handwriting of yesterday was like a ghost—the indefinable impossibility of separating him from the place, and feeling, when the door opened, as if he might come in—the lazy hush and rest there was in the office, and the insatiable relish with which our people talked about it, and other people came in and out all day, and gorged themselves with the subject—this is easily intelligible to any one. What I cannot describe is, how, in the innermost recesses of my own heart, I had a lurking jealousy even of Death. How I felt as if its might would push me from my ground in Dora's thoughts. How I was, in a grudging way I have no words for, envious of her grief. How it made me restless to think of her weeping to others, or being consoled by others. How I had a grasping, avaricious wish to shut out everybody from her but myself, and to be all in all to her, at that unseasonable time of all times.

In the trouble of this state of mind—not exclusively my own, I hope, but known to others—I went down to Norwood that night; and finding from one of the servants, when I made my inquiries at the door, that Miss Mills was there, got my aunt to direct a letter to her, which I wrote. I deplored the untimely death of Mr. Spenlow most sincerely, and shed tears in doing so. I entreated her to tell Dora, if Dora were in a state to hea it, that he had spoken to me with the utmost kindness and consideration; and had coupled nothing but tenderness, not a single or reproachful word, with her name. I know I did this selfishly, to have my name brought before her; but I tried to believe it was an act of justice to his memory. Perhaps I did believe it.

My aunt received a few lines next day in reply; addressed, outside, to her; within, to me. Dora was overcome by grief; and when her friend had asked her should she send her love to me, had only cried, as she was always crying, "Oh, dear papa! oh, poor papa!" But she had not said No, and that I made the most of.

Mr. Jorkins, who had been at Norwood since the occurrence, came to the office a few days afterwards. He and Tiffey were closeted together for some few moments, and then Tiffey looked out at the door and beckoned me in.

"Oh!" said Mr. Jorkins. "Mr. Tiffey and myself, Mr. Copperfield, are about to examine the desks, the drawers, and other such repositories of the deceased, with the view of sealing up his private papers, and searching for a Will. There is no trace of any, elsewhere. It may be as well for you to assist us, if you please."

I had been in agony to obtain some knowledge of the circumstances in which my Dora would be placed—as, in whose guardianship, and so forth—and this was something towards it. We began the search at once; Mr. Jorkins unlocking the drawers and desks, and we all taking out the papers. The office-papers we placed on one side, and the private papers (which were not numerous) on the other. We were very grave; and when we came to a stray seal, or pencil-case, or ring, or any little article of that kind which we associated personally with him, we spoke very low.

We had sealed up several packets; and were still going on dustily and quietly, when Mr. Jorkins said to us, applying exactly the same words to his late partner as his late partner had applied to him:

"Mr. Spenlow was very difficult to move from the beaten track. You know what he was! I am disposed to think he had made no will."

"Oh, I know he had!" said I.

They both stopped and looked at me.

"On the very day when I last saw him," said I, "he told me that he had, and that his affairs were long since settled."

Mr. Jorkins and old Tiffey shook their heads with one accord.

"That looks unpromising," said Tiffey.

"Very unpromising," said Mr. Jorkins.

"Surely you don't doubt—" I began.

"My good Mr. Copperfield!" said Tiffey, laying his hand upon my arm, and shutting up both his eyes as he shook his head: "if you had been in the Commons as long as I have, you would know that there is no subject on which men are so inconsistent, and so little to be trusted."

"Why, bless my soul, he made that very remark!" I replied persistently.

"I should call that almost final," observed Tiffey. "My opinion is—no will."

It appeared a wonderful thing to me, but it turned out that there *was* no will. He had never so much as thought of making one, so far as his papers afforded any evidence; for there was no kind of hint, sketch, or memorandum, of any testamentary intention whatever. What was scarcely less astonishing to me was, that his affairs were in a most disordered state. It was extremely difficult, I heard, to make out what he owed, or what he had paid, or of what he died possessed. It was considered likely that for years he could have had no clear opinion on these subjects himself. By little and little it came out, that, in the competition on all points of appearance and gentility then running high in the Commons, he had spent more than his professional income, which was not a very large one, and had reduced his private means, if they ever had been great (which was exceedingly doubtful), to a very low ebb indeed. There was a sale of the furniture and lease, at Norwood; and Tiffey told me, little thinking how interested I was in the story, that paying all the just debts of the deceased, and deducting his share of outstanding bad and doubtful debts due to the firm, he wouldn't give a thousand pounds for all the assets remaining.

This was at the expiration of about six weeks. I had suffered tortures all the time, and thought I really must have laid violent hands upon myself, when Miss Mills still reported to me that my broken-hearted little Dora would say nothing, when I was mentioned, but "Oh, poor papa! Oh, dear papa!" Also, that she had no other relations than two aunts, maiden sisters of Mr. Spenlow, who lived at Putney, and who had not held any other than chance communication with their brother for many years. Not that they had ever quarrelled (Miss Mills informed me); but that having been, on the occasion of Dora's christening, invited to tea, when they considered themselves privileged to be invited to dinner, they had expressed their opinion in writing, that it was "better for the happiness of all parties" that they should stay away. Since which they had gone their road, and their brother had gone his.

These two ladies now emerged from their retirement, and proposed to take Dora to live at Putney. Dora, clinging to them both, and weeping, exclaimed, "O yes, aunts! Please take Julia Mills and me and Jip to Putney!" So they went, very soon after the funeral.

How I found time to haunt Putney, I am sure I don't know; but I contrived, by some means or other, to prowl about the neighbourhood pretty often. Miss Mills, for the more exact discharge of the duties of friendship, kept a journal; and she used to meet me sometimes, on the Common, and read it, or (if she had not time to do that) lend it to me. How I treasured up the entries, of which I subjoin a sample!—

"Monday. My sweet D. still much depressed. Headache. Called attention to J. as being beautifully sleek. D. fondled J. Associations thus awakened, opened floodgates of sorrow. Rush of grief admitted. (Are tears the dewdrops of the heart? J. M.)

"Tuesday. D. weak and nervous. Beautiful in pallor. (Do we not remark this in moon likewise? J. M.) D. J. M. and J. took airing in carriage. J. looking out of window, and barking violently at dustman, occasioned smile to overspread features of D. (Of such slight links is chain of life composed! J. M.)

"Wednesday. D. comparatively cheerful. Sang to her, as congenial melody, Evening Bells. Effect not soothing, but reverse. D. inexpressibly affected. Found sobbing afterwards, in own room. Quoted verses respecting self and young Gazelle. Ineffectually. Also referred to Patience on Monument. (Qy. Why on monument? J. M.)

"Thursday. D. certainly improved. Better night. Slight tinge of damask revisiting cheek. Resolved to mention name of D. C. Introduced same, cautiously, in course of airing. D. immediately overcome. 'Oh, dear, dear Julia! Oh, I have been a naughty and undutiful child!' Soothed and caressed. Drew ideal picture of D. C. on verge of tomb. D. again overcome. 'Oh, what shall I do, what shall I do? Oh, take me somewhere!' Much alarmed. Fainting of D. and glass of water from public-house. (Poetical affinity. Chequered sign on door-post: chequered human life. Alas! J. M.)

"Friday. Day of incident. Man appears in kitchen, with blue bag, 'for lady's boots left out to heel.' Cook replies, 'No such orders.' Man argues point. Cook withdraws to inquire, leaving man alone with J. On Cook's return, man still argues point, but ultimately goes. J. missing. D. distracted. Information sent to police. Man to be identified by broad nose, and legs like balustrades of bridge. Search made in every direction. No J. D. weeping bitterly, and inconsolable. Renewed reference to young Gazelle. Appropriate, but unavailing. Towards evening, strange boy calls. Brought into parlour. Broad nose, but no balustrades. Says he wants a pound, and knows a dog. Declines to explain further, though much pressed. Pound being produced by D. takes Cook to little house, where J. alone tied up to leg of table. Joy of D. who dances round J. while he eats his supper. Emboldened by this happy change, mention D. C. up-stairs. D. weeps afresh, cries piteously, 'Oh, don't don't don't! It is so wicked to think of anything but poor papa!'—embraces J. and sobs herself to sleep. (Must not D. C. confine himself to the broad pinions of Time? J. M.)"

Miss Mills and her journal were my sole consolation at this period. To see her, who had seen Dora but a little while before—to trace the initial letter of Dora's name through her sympathetic pages—to be made more and more miserable by her—were my only comforts. I felt as if I had been living in a palace of cards, which had tumbled down, leaving only Miss Mills and me among the ruins; I felt as if some grim enchanter had drawn a magic circle round the innocent goddess of my heart, which nothing indeed but those same strong pinions, capable of carrying so many people over so much, would enable me to enter!

39

WICKFIELD AND HEEP

MY AUNT, BEGINNING, I IMAGINE, TO BE MADE SERIOUSLY uncomfortable by my prolonged dejection, made a pretence of being anxious that I should go to Dover to see that all was working well at the cottage, which was let; and to conclude an agreement, with the same tenant, for a longer term of occupation. Janet was drafted into the service of Mrs. Strong, where I saw her every day. She had been undecided, on leaving Dover, whether or no to give the finishing touch to that renunciation of mankind in which she had been educated, by marrying a pilot; but she decided against that venture. Not so much for the sake of principle, I believe, as because she happened not to like him.

Although it required an effort to leave Miss Mills, I fell rather willingly into my aunt's pretence, as a means of enabling me to pass a few tranquil hours with Agnes. I consulted the good Doctor relative to an absence of three days; and the Doctor wishing me to take that relaxation,—he wished me to take more; but my energy could not bear that,—I made up my mind to go.

As to the Commons, I had no great occasion to be particular about my duties in that quarter. To say the truth, we were getting in no very good odour among the tip-top proctors, and were rapidly sliding down to but a doubtful position. The business had been indifferent under Mr. Jorkins, before Mr. Spenlow's time; and although it had been quickened by the infusion of new blood, and by the display which Mr. Spenlow made, still it was not established on a sufficiently strong basis to bear, without being shaken, such a blow as the sudden loss of its active manager. It fell off very much. Mr. Jorkins, notwithstanding his reputation in the firm, was an easy-going, incapable sort of man, whose reputation out of doors was not calculated to back it up. I was turned over to him now, and when I saw him take his snuff and let the business go, I regretted my aunt's thousand pounds more than ever.

But this was not the worst of it. There were a number of hangers-on and outsiders about the Commons, who, without being proctors themselves, dabbled in common-form business, and got it done by real proctors, who lent their names in consideration of a share in the spoil;—and there were a good many of these too. As our house now wanted business on any terms, we joined this noble band; and threw out lures to the hangers-on and outsiders, to bring their business to us. Marriage licences and small probates were what we all looked for, and what paid us best; and the competition for these ran very high indeed. Kidnappers and inveiglers were planted in all the avenues of entrance to the Commons, with instructions to do their utmost to cut off all persons in mourning, and all gentlemen with anything bashful in their appearance, and entice them to the offices in which their respective employers were interested; which instructions were so well observed, that I myself, before I was known by sight, was twice hustled into the premises of our principal opponent. The conflicting interests of these touting gentlemen being of a nature to irritate their feelings, personal collisions took place; and the Commons was even scandalised by our principal inveigler (who had formerly been in the wine trade, and afterwards in the sworn brokery line) walking about for some days with a black eye. Any one of these scouts used to think nothing of politely assisting an old lady in black out of a vehicle, killing any proctor whom she inquired for, representing his employer as the lawful successor and representative of that proctor, and bearing the old lady off (sometimes greatly affected) to his employer's office. Many captives were brought to me in this way. As to marriage licences, the competition rose to such a pitch, that a shy gentleman in want of one, had nothing to do but submit himself to the first inveigler, or be fought for, and become the prey of the strongest. One of our clerks, who was an outsider, used, in the height of this contest, to sit with his hat on, that he might be ready to rush out and swear before a surrogate any victim who was brought in. The system of inveigling continues, I believe, to this day. The last time I was in the Commons, a civil able-bodied person in a white apron pounced out upon me from a doorway, and whispering the word "Marriage-licence" in my ear, was with great difficulty prevented from taking me up in his arms and lifting me into a proctor's.

From this digression, let me proceed to Dover.

I found everything in a satisfactory state at the cottage; and was enabled to gratify my aunt exceedingly by reporting that the tenant inherited her feud, and waged incessant war against donkeys. Having settled the little business I had to transact there, and slept there one night, I walked on to Canterbury early in the morning. It was now winter again; and the fresh, cold windy day, and the sweeping downland, brightened up my hopes a little.

Coming into Canterbury, I loitered through the old streets with a sober pleasure that calmed my spirits, and eased my heart. There were the old signs, the old names over the shops, the old people serving in them. It appeared so long, since I had been a schoolboy there, that I wondered the place was so little changed, until I reflected how little I was changed myself. Strange to say, that quiet influence which was inseparable in my mind from Agnes, seemed to pervade even the city where she dwelt. The venerable cathedral towers, and the old jackdaws and rooks whose airy voices made them more retired than perfect silence would have done; the battered gateways, once stuck full with statues, long thrown down, and crumbled away, like the reverential pilgrims who had gazed upon them; the still nooks, where the ivied growth of centuries crept over gabled ends and ruined walls; the ancient houses, the pastoral landscape of field, orchard and garden; everywhere—on everything—I felt the same serener air, the same calm, thoughtful, softening spirit.

Arrived at Mr. Wickfield's house, I found, in the little lower room on the ground floor, where Uriah Heep had been of old accustomed to sit, Mr. Micawber plying his pen with great assiduity. He was dressed in a legal-looking suit of black, and loomed, burly and large, in that small office.

Mr. Micawber was extremely glad to see me, but a little confused too. He would have conducted me immediately into the presence of Uriah, but I declined.

" I know the house of old, you recollect," said I, " and will find my way up-stairs. How do you like the law, Mr. Micawber?"

" My dear Copperfield," he replied. " To a man possessed of the higher imaginative powers, the objection to legal studies is the amount of detail which they involve. Even in our professional correspondence," said Mr. Micawber, glancing at some letters he was writing, " the mind is not at liberty to soar to any exalted form of expression. Still, it is a great pursuit. A great pursuit! "

He then told me that he had become the tenant of Uriah Heep's old house; and that Mrs. Micawber would be delighted to receive me, once more, under her own roof.

" It is humble," said Mr. Micawber, " to quote a favourite expression of my friend Heep; but it may prove the stepping-stone to more ambitious domiciliary accommodation."

I asked him whether he had reason, so far, to be satisfied with his friend Heep's treatment of him? He got up to ascertain if the door were close shut, before he replied, in a lower voice:

"My dear Copperfield, a man who labours under the pressure of pecuniary embarrassments, is, with the generality of people, at a disadvantage. That disadvantage is not diminished, when that pressure necessitates the drawing of stipendiary emoluments, before those emoluments are strictly due and payable. All I can say is, that my friend Heep has responded to appeals to which I need not more particularly refer, in a manner calculated to redound equally to the honour of his head, and of his heart."

"I should not have supposed him to be very free with his money either," I observed.

"Pardon me!" said Mr. Micawber, with an air of constraint, "I speak of my friend Heep as I have experience."

"I am glad your experience is so favourable," I returned.

"You are very obliging, my dear Copperfield," said Mr. Micawber; and hummed a tune.

"Do you see much of Mr. Wickfield?" I asked, to change the subject.

"Not much," said Mr. Micawber, slightingly. "Mr. Wickfield is, I dare say, a man of very excellent intentions; but he is—in short, he is obsolete."

"I am afraid his partner seeks to make him so," said I.

"My dear Copperfield!" returned Mr. Micawber, after some uneasy evolutions on his stool, "allow me to offer a remark! I am here in a capacity of confidence. I am here in a position of trust. The discussion of some topics, even with Mrs. Micawber herself (so long the partner of my various vicissitudes, and a woman of a remarkable lucidity of intellect), is, I am led to consider, incompatible with the functions now devolving on me. I would therefore take the liberty of suggesting that in our friendly intercourse—which I trust will never be disturbed!—we draw a line. On one side of this line," said Mr. Micawber, representing it on the desk with the office ruler, "is the whole range of the human intellect, with a trifling exception; on the other, *is* that exception; that is to say, the affairs of Messrs. Wickfield and Heep, with all belonging and appertaining thereunto. I trust I give no offence to the companion of my youth, in submitting this proposition to his cooler judgement?"

Though I saw an uneasy change in Mr. Micawber, which sat tightly on him, as if his new duties were a misfit, I felt I had no right to be offended. My telling him so, appeared to relieve him; and he shook hands with me.

"I am charmed, Copperfield," said Mr. Micawber, "let me

assure you, with Miss Wickfield. She is a very superior young lady, of very remarkable attractions, graces, and virtues. Upon my honour," said Mr. Micawber, indefinitely kissing his hand and bowing with his genteelist air, "I do Homage to Miss Wickfield! Hem!"

"I am glad of that, at least," said I.

"If you had not assured us, my dear Copperfield, on the occasion of that agreeable afternoon we had the happiness of passing with you, that D. was your favourite letter," said Mr. Micawber, "I should unquestionably have supposed that A. had been so."

We have all some experience of a feeling, that comes over us occasionally, of what we are saying and doing having been said and done before, in a remote time—of our having been surrounded, dim ages ago, by the same faces, objects, and circumstances—of our knowing perfectly what will be said next, as if we suddenly remembered it! I never had this mysterious impression more strongly in my life, than before he uttered those words.

I took my leave of Mr. Micawber, for the time, charging him with my best remembrances to all at home. As I left him, resuming his stool and his pen, and rolling his head in his stock, to get it into easier writing order, I clearly perceived that there was something interposed between him and me, since he had come into his new functions, which prevented our getting at each other as we used to do, and quite altered the character of our intercourse.

There was no one in the quaint old drawing-room, though it presented tokens of Mrs. Heep's whereabout. I looked into the room still belonging to Agnes, and saw her writing by the fire, at a pretty old-fashioned desk she had, writing.

My darkening the light made her look up. What a pleasure to be the cause of that bright change in her attentive face, and the object of that sweet regard and welcome!

"Ah, Agnes!" said I, when we were sitting together, side by side; "I have missed you so much, lately!"

"Indeed?" she replied. "Again! And so soon?"

I shook my head.

"I don't know how it is, Agnes; I seem to want some faculty of mind that I ought to have. You were so much in the habit of thinking of me, in the happy old days here, and I came so naturally to you for counsel and support, that I really think I have missed acquiring it!"

"And what is it?" said Agnes, cheerfully.

"I don't know what to call it," I replied. "I think I am earnest and persevering?"

"I am sure of it," said Agnes.

"And patient, Agnes?" I inquired, with a little hesitation.

"Yes," returned Agnes, laughing. "Pretty well."

"And yet," said I, "I get so miserable and worried, and am so unsteady and irresolute in my power of assuring myself, that I know I must want—shall I call it—reliance, of some kind?"

"Call it so, if you will," said Agnes.

"Well!" I returned. "See here! You come to London, I rely on you, and I have an object and a course at once. I am driven out of it, I come here, and in a moment I feel an altered person. The circumstances that distressed me are not changed, since I came into this room; but an influence comes over me in that short interval that alters me, oh, how much for the better! What is it? What is your secret, Agnes?"

Her head was bent down, looking at the fire.

"It's the old story," said I. "Don't laugh, when I say it was always the same in little things as it is in greater ones. My old troubles were nonsense, and now they are serious; but whenever I have gone away from my adopted sister—"

Agnes looked up—with such a heavenly face!—and gave me her hand, which I kissed.

"Whenever I have not had you, Agnes, to advise and approve in the beginning, I have seemed to go wild, and to get into all sorts of difficulty. When I have come to you, at last (as I have always done), I have come to peace and happiness. I come home, now, like a tired traveller, and find such a blessed sense of rest!"

I felt so deeply what I said, it affected me so sincerely, that my voice failed, and I covered my face with my hand, and broke into tears. I write the truth. Whatever contradictions and inconsistencies there were within me, as there are within so many of us; whatever might have been so different, and so much better; whatever I had done, in which I had perversely wandered away from the voice of my own heart; I knew nothing of. I only knew that I was fervently in earnest, when I felt the rest and peace of having Agnes near me.

In her placid sisterly manner; with her beaming eyes; with her tender voice; and with that sweet composure, which had long ago made the house that held her quite a sacred place to me; she soon won me from this weakness, and led me on to tell all that had happened since our last meeting.

"And there is not another word to tell, Agnes," said I, when

I had made an end of my confidence. " Now, my reliance is on you."

" But it must not be on me, Trotwood," returned Agnes with a pleasant smile. " It must be on some one else."

" On Dora? " said I.

" Assuredly."

" Why, I have not mentioned, Agnes," said I, a little embarrassed, " that Dora is rather difficult to—I would not, for the world, say, to rely upon, because she is the soul of purity and truth—but rather difficult to—I hardly know how to express it, really, Agnes. She is a timid little thing, and easily disturbed and frightened. Some time ago, before her father's death, when I thought it right to mention to her—but I'll tell you, if you will bear with me, how it was."

Accordingly, I told Agnes about my declaration of poverty, about the cookery-book, the housekeeping accounts, and all the rest of it.

" Oh, Trotwood! " she remonstrated, with a smile. " Just your old headlong way! You might have been in earnest in striving to get on in the world, without being so very sudden with a timid, loving, inexperienced girl. Poor Dora! "

I never heard such sweet forbearing kindness expressed in a voice, as she expressed in making this reply. It was as if I had seen her admiringly and tenderly embracing Dora, and tacitly reproving me, by her considerate protection, for my hot haste in fluttering that little heart. It was as if I had seen Dora, in all her fascinating artlessness, caressing Agnes, and thanking her, and coaxingly appealing against me, and loving me with all her childish innocence.

I felt so grateful to Agnes, and admired her so! I saw those two together, in a bright perspective, such well-associated friends, each adorning the other so much!

" What ought I to do then, Agnes? " I inquired, after looking at the fire a little while. " What would it be right to do? "

" I think " said Agnes, " that the honourable course to take, would be to write to those two ladies. Don't you think that any secret course is an unworthy one? "

" Yes. If *you* think so," said I.

" I am poorly qualified to judge of such matters," replied Agnes, with a modest hesitation, " but I certainly feel—in short, I feel that your being secret and clandestine, is not being like yourself."

" Like myself, in the too high opinion you have of me, Agnes, I am afraid." said I.

" Like yourself, in the candour of your nature," she returned; " and therefore I would write to those two ladies. I would relate, as plainly and as openly as possible, all that has taken place; and I would ask their permission to visit sometimes at their house. Considering that you are young and striving for a place in life, I think it would be well to say that you would readily abide by any conditions they might impose upon you. I would entreat them not to dismiss your request, without a reference to Dora; and to discuss it with her when they should think the time suitable. I would not be too vehement," said Agnes, gently, " or propose too much. I would trust to my fidelity and perseverance—and to Dora."

" But if they were to frighten Dora again, Agnes, by speaking to her," said I. " And if Dora were to cry, and say nothing about me! "

" Is that likely? " inquired Agnes, with the same sweet consideration in her face.

" God bless her, she is as easily scared as a bird," said I. " It might be! Or if the two Miss Spenlows (elderly ladies of that sort are odd characters sometimes) should not be likely persons to address in that way! "

" I don't think, Trotwood," returned Agnes, raising her soft eyes to mine, " I should consider that. Perhaps it would be better only to consider whether it is right to do this; and, if it is, to do it."

I had no longer any doubt on the subject. With a lightened heart, though with a profound sense of the weighty importance of my task, I devoted the whole afternoon to the composition of the draft of this letter; for which great purpose, Agnes relinquished her desk to me. But first I went downstairs to see Mr. Wickfield and Uriah Heep.

I found Uriah in possession of a new, plaster-smelling office, built out in the garden; looking extraordinarily mean, in the midst of a quantity of books and papers. He received me in his usual fawning way, and pretended not to have heard of my arrival from Mr. Micawber; a pretence I took the liberty of disbelieving. He accompanied me into Mr. Wickfield's room, which was the shadow of its former self—having been divested of a variety of conveniences, for the accommodation of the new partner—and stood before the fire, warming his back, and shaving his chin with his bony hand, while Mr. Wickfield and I exchanged greetings.

" You stay with us, Trotwood, while you remain in Canterbury?" said Mr. Wickfield, not without a glance at Uriah for his approval.

"Is there room for me?" said I.

"I am sure, Master Copperfield—I should say Mister, but the other comes so natural," said Uriah,—"I would turn out of your old room with pleasure, if it would be agreeable."

"No, no," said Mr. Wickfield. "Why should *you* be inconvenienced? There's another room. There's another room."

"Oh, but you know," returned Uriah, with a grin, "I should really be delighted!"

To cut the matter short, I said I would have the other room or none at all; so it was settled that I should have the other room; and, taking my leave of the firm until dinner, I went up-stairs again.

I had hoped to have no other companion than Agnes. But Mrs. Heep had asked permission to bring herself and her knitting near the fire, in that room; on pretence of its having an aspect more favourable for her rheumatics, as the wind then was, than the drawing-room or dining-parlour. Though I could almost have consigned her to the mercies of the wind on the topmost pinnacle of the Cathedral, without remorse, I made a virtue of necessity, and gave her a friendly salutation.

"I'm umbly thankful to you, sir," said Mrs. Heep, in acknowledgment of my inquiries concerning her health, "but I'm only pretty well. I haven't much to boast of. If I could see my Uriah well settled in life, I couldn't expect much more, I think. How do you think my Ury looking, sir?"

I thought him looking as villainous as ever, and I replied that I saw no change in him.

"Oh, don't you think he's changed?" said Mrs. Heep. "There I must umbly beg leave to differ from you. Don't you see a thinness in him?"

"Not more than usual," I replied.

"*Don't* you though!" said Mrs. Heep. "But you don't take notice of him with a mother's eye!"

His mother's eye was an evil eye to the rest of the world, I thought as it met mine, howsoever affectionate to him; and I believe she and her son were devoted to one another. It passed me, and went on to Agnes.

"Don't *you* see a wasting and a wearing in him, Miss Wickfield?" inquired Mrs. Heep.

"No," said Agnes, quietly pursuing the work on which she was engaged. "You are too solicitous about him. He is very well."

Mrs. Heep, with a prodigious sniff, resumed her knitting.

She never left off, or left us for a moment. I had arrived early in the day, and we had still three or four hours before dinner; but she sat there, plying her knitting-needles as monotonously as an hour-glass might have poured out its sands. She sat on one side of the fire; I sat at the desk in front of it; a little beyond me, on the other side, sat Agnes. Whensoever, slowly pondering over my letter, I lifted up my eyes, and meeting the thoughtful face of Agnes, saw it clear, and beam encouragement upon me, with its own angelic expression, I was conscious presently of the evil eye passing me, and going on to her, and coming back to me again, and dropping furtively upon the knitting. What the knitting was, I don't know, not being learned in that art; but it looked like a net; and as she worked away with those Chinese chopsticks of knitting-needles, she showed in the firelight like an ill-looking enchantress, baulked as yet by the radiant goodness opposite, but getting ready for a cast of her net by-and-by.

At dinner she maintained her watch, with the same unwinking eyes. After dinner, her son took his turn; and when Mr. Wickfield, himself, and I were left alone together, leered at me, and writhed until I could hardly bear it. In the drawing-room, there was the mother knitting and watching again. All the time that Agnes sang and played, the mother sat at the piano. Once she asked for a particular ballad, which she said her Ury (who was yawning in a great chair) doted on; and at intervals she looked round at him, and reported to Agnes that he was in raptures with the music. But she hardly ever spoke—I question if she ever did—without making some mention of him. It was evident to me that this was the duty assigned to her.

This lasted until bedtime. To have seen the mother and son, like two great bats hanging over the whole house, and darkening it with their ugly forms, made me so uncomfortable, that I would rather have remained down-stairs, knitting and all, than gone to bed. I hardly got any sleep. Next day the knitting and watching began again, and lasted all day.

I had not an opportunity of speaking to Agnes, for ten minutes. I could barely show her my letter. I proposed to her to walk out with me; but Mrs. Heep repeatedly complaining that she was worse, Agnes charitably remained within, to bear her company. Towards the twilight I went out by myself, musing on what I ought to do, and whether I was justified in withholding from Agnes, any longer, what Uriah Heep had told me in London: for that began to trouble me again, very much.

I had not walked out far enough to be quite clear of the town, upon the Ramsgate road, where there was a good path, when I was hailed, through the dusk, by somebody behind me. The shambling figure, and the scanty greatcoat, were not to be mistaken. I stopped, and Uriah Heep came up.

"Well?" said I.

"How fast you walk!" said he. "My legs are pretty long, but you've given 'em quite a job."

"Where are you going?" said I.

"I am coming with you, Master Copperfield, if you'll allow me the pleasure of a walk with an old acquaintance." Saying this, with a jerk of his body, which might have been either propitiatory or derisive, he fell into step beside me.

"Uriah!" said I, as civilly as I could, after a silence.

"Master Copperfield!" said Uriah.

"To tell you the truth (at which you will not be offended), I came out to walk alone, because I have had so much company."

He looked at me sideways, and said with his hardest grin,—
"You mean mother."

"Why, yes, I do," said I.

"Ah! But you know we're so very umble," he returned. "And having such a knowledge of our own umbleness, we must really take care that we're not pushed to the wall by them as isn't umble. All stratagems are fair in love, sir."

Raising his great hands until they touched his chin, he rubbed them softly, and softly chuckled; looking as like a malevolent baboon, I thought, as anything human could look.

"You see," he said, still hugging himself in that unpleasant way, and shaking his head at me, "you're quite a dangerous rival, Master Copperfield. You always was, you know."

"Do you set a watch upon Miss Wickfield, and make her home no home, because of me?" said I.

"Oh! Master Copperfield! Those are very arsh words," he replied.

"Put my meaning into any words you like," said I. "You know what it is, Uriah, as well as I do."

"Oh no! You must put it into words," he said. "Oh, really! I couldn't myself."

"Do you suppose," said I, constraining myself to be very temperate and quiet with him, on account of Agnes, "that I regard Miss Wickfield otherwise than as a very dear sister?"

"Well, Master Copperfield," he replied, "you perceive I am not bound to answer that question. You may not, you know. But then, you see, you may!"

Anything to equal the low cunning of his visage, and of his shadowless eyes without the ghost of an eyelash, I never saw.

" Come then! " said I. " For the sake of Miss Wickfield—"

" My Agnes! " he exclaimed, with a sickly, angular contortion of himself. " Would you be so good as call her Agnes, Master Copperfield! "

" For the sake of Agnes Wickfield—Heaven bless her! "

" Thank you for that blessing, Master Copperfield! " he interposed.

" I will tell you what I should, under any other circumstances, as soon have thought of telling to—Jack Ketch."

" To who, sir? " said Uriah, stretching out his neck, and shading his ear with his hand.

" To the hangman," I returned. " The most unlikely person I could think of,"—though his own face had suggested the allusion quite as a natural consequence. " I am engaged to another young lady. I hope that contents you."

" Upon my soul? " said Uriah.

I was about indignantly to give my assertion the confirmation he required, when he caught hold of my hand, and gave it a squeeze.

" Oh, Master Copperfield," he said. " If you had only had the condescension to return my confidence when I poured out the fulness of my art, the night I put you so much out of the way by sleeping before your sitting-room fire, I never should have doubted you. As it is, I'm sure I'll take off mother directly, and only too appy. I know you'll excuse the precautions of affection, won't you? What a pity, Master Copperfield, that you didn't condescend to return my confidence! I'm sure I gave you every opportunity. But you never have condescended to me, as much as I could have wished. I know you have never liked me, as I have liked you! "

All this time he was squeezing my hand with his damp fishy fingers, while I made every effort I decently could to get it away. But I was quite unsuccessful. He drew it under the sleeve of his mulberry-coloured greatcoat, and I walked on, almost upon compulsion, arm in arm with him.

" Shall we turn? " said Uriah, by and by wheeling me face about towards the town, on which the early moon was now shining, silvering the distant windows.

" Before we leave the subject, you ought to understand," said I, breaking a pretty long silence, " that I believe Agnes Wickfield to be as far above *you*, and as far removed from all *your* aspirations, as the moon herself! "

"Peaceful! Ain't she!" said Uriah. "Very! Now confess, Master Copperfield, that you haven't liked me quite as I have liked you. All along you've thought me too umble now, I shouldn't wonder?"

"I am not fond of professions of humility," I returned, "or professions of anything else."

"There now!" said Uriah, looking flabby and lead-coloured in the moonlight. "Didn't I know it! But how little you think of the rightful umbleness of a person in my station, Master Copperfield! Father and me was both brought up at a foundation school for boys; and mother, she was likewise brought up at a public, sort of charitable, establishment. They taught us all a deal of umbleness—not much else that I know of, from morning to night. We was to be umble to this person, and umble to that; and to pull off our caps here, and to make bows there; and always to know our place, and abase ourselves before our betters. And we had such a lot of betters! Father got the monitor-medal by being umble. So did I. Father got made a sexton by being umble. He had the character, among the gentlefolks, of being such a well-behaved man, that they were determined to bring him in. 'Be umble, Uriah,' says father to me, 'and you'll get on. It was what was always being dinned into you and me at school; it's what goes down best. Be umble,' says father, 'and you'll do!' And really it ain't done bad!"

It was the first time it had ever occurred to me, that this detestable cant of false humility might have originated out of the Heep family. I had seen the harvest, but had never thought of the seed.

"When I was quite a young boy," said Uriah, "I got to know what umbleness did, and I took to it. I ate umble pie with an appetite. I stopped at the umble point of my learning, and says I, 'Hold hard!' when you offered to teach me Latin, I knew better 'People like to be above you,' says father, 'keep yourself down.' I am very umble to the present moment, Master Copperfield, but I've got a little power!"

And he said all this—I knew, as I saw his face in the moonlight—that I might understand he was resolved to recompense himself by using his power. I had never doubted his meanness, his craft and malice; but I fully comprehended now, for the first time, what a base, unrelenting, and revengeful spirit, must have been engendered by this early and this long suppression.

His account of himself was so far attended with an agreeable result, that it led to his withdrawing his hand in order that he might have another hug of himself under the chin. Once apart from him, I was determined to keep apart; and we walked back, side by side, saying very little more by the way.

Whether his spirits were elevated by the communication I had made to him, or by his having indulged in this retrospect, I don't know; but they were raised by some influence. He talked more at dinner than was usual with him; asked his mother (off duty from the moment of our re-entering the house) whether he was not growing too old for a bachelor; and once looked at Agnes so, that I would have given all I had for leave to knock him down.

When we three males were left alone after dinner, he got into a more adventurous state. He had taken little or no wine; and I presume it was the mere insolence of triumph that was upon him, flushed perhaps by the temptation my presence furnished to its exhibition.

I had observed yesterday, that he tried to entice Mr. Wickfield to drink; and interpreting the look which Agnes had given me as she went out, had limited myself to one glass, and then proposed that we should follow her. I would have done so again to-day; but Uriah was too quick for me.

"We seldom see our present visitor, sir," he said, addressing Mr. Wickfield, sitting, such a contrast to him, at the end of the table, "and I should propose to give him welcome in another glass or two of wine, if you have no objections. Mr. Copperfield, your elth and appiness!"

I was obliged to make a show of taking the hand he stretched across to me; and then, with very different emotions, I took the hand of the broken gentleman, his partner.

"Come, fellow-partner," said Uriah, "if I may take the liberty,—now, suppose you give us something or another appropriate to Copperfield!"

I pass over Mr. Wickfield's proposing my aunt, his proposing Mr. Dick, his proposing Doctors' Commons, his proposing Uriah, his drinking everything twice; his consciousness of his own weakness, the inffectual effort that he made against it; the struggle between his shame in Uriah's deportment, and his desire to conciliate him; the manifest exultation with which Uriah twisted and turned, and held him up before me. It made me sick at heart to see, and my hand recoils from writing it.

"Come, fellow-partner!" said Uriah, at last, "I'll give you another one, and I umbly ask for bumpers, seeing I intend to make it the divinest of her sex."

Her father had his empty glass in his hand. I saw him set it down, look at the picture she was so like, put his hand to his forehead, and shrink back in his elbow-chair.

"I'm an umble individual to give you her elth," proceeded Uriah, "but I admire—adore her."

No physical pain that her father's grey head could have borne, I think, could have been more terrible to me, than the mental endurance I saw compressed now within both his hands.

"Agnes," said Uriah, either not regarding him, or not knowing what the nature of his action was, "Agnes Wickfield is, I am safe to say, the divinest of her sex. May I speak out, among friends? To be her father is a proud distinction, but to be her usband—"

Spare me from ever again hearing such a cry, as that with which her father rose up from the table!

"What's the matter?" said Uriah, turning of a deadly colour. "You are not gone mad, after all, Mr. Wickfield, I hope? If I say I've an ambition to make your Agnes my Agnes, I have as good a right to it as another man. I have a better right to it than any other man!"

I had my arms round Mr. Wickfield, imploring him by everything that I could think of, oftenest of all by his love for Agnes, to calm himself a little. He was mad for the moment; tearing out his hair, beating his head, trying to force me from him, and to force himself from me, not answering a word, nor looking at or seeing any one; blindly striving for he knew not what, his face all staring and distorted—a frightful spectacle.

I conjured him, incoherently, but in the most impassioned manner, not to abandon himself to this wildness, but to hear me. I besought him to think of Agnes, to connect me with Agnes, to recollect how Agnes and I had grown up together, how I honoured her and loved her, how she was his pride and joy. I tried to bring her idea before him in any form; I even reproached him with not having firmness to spare her the knowledge of such a scene as this. I may have effected something, or his wildness may have spent itself; but by degrees he struggled less, and began to look at me—strangely at first, then with recognition in his eyes. At length he said, "I know, Trotwood! My darling child and you—I know! But look at him!"

He pointed to Uriah, pale and glowering in a corner, evidently very much out in his calculations, and taken by surprise.

"Look at my torturer," he replied. "Before him I have step by step abandoned name and reputation, peace and quiet, house and home."

"I have kept your name and reputation for you, and your

peace and quiet, and your house and home too," said Uriah, with a sulky, hurried, defeated air of compromise. "Don't be foolish, Mr. Wickfield. If I have gone a little beyond what you were prepared for, I can go back, I suppose? There's no harm done."

"I looked for single motives in every one," said Mr. Wickfield, "and I was satisfied I had bound him to me by motives of interest. But see what he is—oh, see what he is!"

"You had better stop him, Copperfield, if you can," cried Uriah, with his long forefinger pointing towards me. "He'll say something presently—mind you!—he'll be sorry to have said afterwards, and you'll be sorry to have heard!"

"I'll say anything!" cried Mr. Wickfield, with a desperate air. "Why should I not be in all the world's power if I am in yours?"

"Mind! I tell you!" said Uriah, continuing to warn me. "If you don't stop his mouth, you're not his friend! Why shouldn't you be in all the world's power, Mr. Wickfield? Because you have got a daughter. You and me know what we know, don't we? Let sleeping dogs lie—who wants to rouse 'em? I don't. Can't you see I am as umble as I can be? I tell you, if I've gone too far, I'm sorry. What would you have, sir?"

"Oh, Trotwood, Trotwood!" exclaimed Mr. Wickfield, wringing his hands. "What I have come down to be, since I first saw you in this house! I was on my downward way then, but the dreary dreary road I have traversed since! Weak indulgence has ruined me. Indulgence in remembrance, and indulgence in forgetfulness. My natural grief for my child's mother turned to disease; my natural love for my child turned to disease. I have infected everything I touched. I have brought misery on what I dearly love, I know—*you* know! I thought it possible that I could truly love one creature in the world, and not love the rest; I thought it possible that I could truly mourn for one creature gone out of the world, and not have some part in the grief of all who mourned. Thus the lessons of my life have been perverted! I have preyed on my own morbid coward heart, and it has preyed on me. Sordid in my grief, sordid in my love, sordid in my miserable escape from the darker side of both, oh see the ruin I am, and hate me, shun me!"

He dropped into a chair, and weakly sobbed. The excitement into which he had been roused was leaving him. Uriah came out of his corner.

"I don't know all I have done, in my fatuity," said Mr. Wickfield, putting out his hands, as if to deprecate my condemnation. "*He* knows best," meaning Uriah Heep, "for he has always been at my elbow, whispering me. You see the millstone that he is about my neck. You find him in my house, you find him in my business. You heard him, but a little time ago. What need have I to say more!"

"You haven't need to say so much, nor half so much, nor anything at all," observed Uriah, half defiant, and half fawning. "You wouldn't have took it up so, if it hadn't been for the wine. You'll think better of it to-morrow, sir. If I have said too much, or more than I meant, what of it? I haven't stood by it!"

The door opened, and Agnes, gliding in, without a vestige of colour in her face, put her arm round his neck, and steadily said, "Papa, you are not well. Come with me!" He laid his head upon her shoulder, as if he were oppressed with heavy shame, and went out with her. Her eyes met mine for but an instant, yet I saw how much she knew of what had passed.

"I didn't expect he'd cut up so rough, Master Copperfield," said Uriah. "But it's nothing. I'll be friends with him to-morrow. It's for his good. I'm umbly anxious for his good."

I gave him no answer, and went up-stairs into the quiet room where Agnes had so often sat beside me at my books. Nobody came near me until late at night. I took up a book and tried to read. I heard the clocks strike twelve, and was still reading, without knowing what I read, when Agnes touched me.

"You will be going early in the morning, Trotwood! Let us say good-bye, now!"

She had been weeping, but her face then was so calm and beautiful!

"Heaven bless you!" she said, giving me her hand.

"Dearest Agnes!" I returned, "I see you ask me not to speak of to-night—but is there nothing to be done?"

"There is God to trust in!" she replied.

"Can *I* do nothing—*I*, who come to you with *my* poor sorrows?"

"And make mine so much lighter," she replied. "Dear Trotwood, no!"

"Dear Agnes," I said, "it is presumptuous for me, who am so poor in all in which you are so rich—goodness, resolution, all noble qualities—to doubt or direct you; but you know how much I love you, and how much I owe to you. You will never sacrifice yourself to a mistaken sense of duty, Agnes?"

More agitated for a moment than I had ever seen her, she took my hand from me, and moved a step back.

"Say you have no such thought, dear Agnes! Much more

than sister! Think of the priceless gift of such a heart as yours, of such a love as yours!"

Oh! long, long afterwards, I saw that face rise up before me, with its momentary look, not wondering, not accusing, not regretting. Oh, long, long afterwards, I saw that look subside, as it did now, into the lovely smile, with which she told me she had no fear for herself—I need have none for her—and parted from me by the name of Brother, and was gone!

It was dark in the morning when I got upon the coach at the inn door. The day was just breaking when we were about to start, and then, as I sat thinking of her, came struggling up the coach side, through the mingled day and night, Uriah's head.

"Copperfield!" said he, in a croaking whisper, as he hung by the iron on the roof. "I thought you'd be glad to hear, before you went off, that there are no squares broke between us. I've been into his room already, and we've made it all smooth. Why, though I'm umble, I'm useful to him, you know; and he understands his interest when he isn't in liquor! What an agreeable man he is, after all, Master Copperfield!"

I obliged myself to say that I was glad he had made his apology.

"Oh, to be sure!" said Uriah. "When a person's umble, you know, what's an apology? So easy! I say! I suppose," with a jerk, "you have sometimes plucked a pear before it was ripe, Master Copperfield?"

"I suppose I have," I replied.

"*I* did that last night," said Uriah; "but it'll ripen yet! It only wants attending to. I can wait!"

Profuse in his farewells, he got down again as the coachman got up. For anything I know, he was eating something to keep the raw morning air out; but he made motions with his mouth as if the pear were ripe already, and he were smacking his lips over it.

40

THE WANDERER

WE HAD A VERY SERIOUS CONVERSATION IN BUCKINGham Street that night, about the domestic occurrence I have detailed in the last chapter. My aunt was deeply interested in them, and walked up and down the room with her arms folded, for more than two hours afterwards. Whenever she was particularly discomposed, she always performed one of these pedestrian feats; and the amount of her discomposure might always be estimated by the duration of her walk. On this occasion she was so much disturbed in mind as to find it necessary to open the bedroom door, and make a course for herself, comprising the full extent of the bedrooms from wall to wall; and while Mr. Dick and I sat quietly by the fire, she kept passing in and out, along this measured track, at an unchanging pace, with the regularity of a clock-pendulum.

When my aunt and I were left to ourselves by Mr. Dick's going out to bed, I sat down to write my letter to the two old ladies. By that time she was tired of walking, and sat by the fire with her dress tucked up as usual. But instead of sitting in her usual manner, holding her glass upon her knee, she suffered it to stand neglected on the chimney-piece; and, resting her left elbow on her right arm, and her chin on her left hand, looked thoughtfully at me. As often as I raised my eyes from what I was about, I met hers. "I am in the lovingest of tempers, my dear," she would assure me with a nod, "but I am fidgeted and sorry!"

I had been too busy to observe, until after she was gone to bed, that she had left her night-mixture, as she always called it, untasted on the chimney-piece. She came to her door, with even more than her usual affection of manner, when I knocked to acquaint her with this discovery; but only said, "I have not the heart to take it, Trot, to-night," and shook her head, and went in again.

She read my letter to the two old ladies, in the morning, and approved of it. I posted it, and had nothing to do then, but wait, as patiently as I could, for the reply. I was still in this state of expectation, and had been, for nearly a week; when I left the Doctor's one snowy night, to walk home.

It had been a bitter day, and a cutting north-east wind had blown for some time. The wind had gone down with the light, and so the snow had come on. It was a heavy, settled fall, I recollect, in great flakes; and it lay thick. The noise of wheels and tread of people were as hushed as if the streets had been strewn that depth with feathers.

My shortest way home,—and I naturally took the shortest way on such a night—was through Saint Martin's Lane. Now, the church which gives its name to the lane, stood in a less free situation at that time; there being no open space before it, and the lane winding down to the Strand. As I passed the steps of the portico, I encountered, at the corner, a woman's face. It looked into mine, passed across the narrow lane, and disappeared. I knew it. I had seen it somewhere. But I could not remember where. I had some association with it, that struck upon my heart directly; but I was thinking of anything else when it came upon me, and was confused.

On the steps of the church, there was the stooping figure of a man, who had put down some burden on the smooth snow, to adjust it; my seeing the face, and my seeing him, were simultaneous. I don't think I had stopped in my surprise; but, in any case, as I went on, he rose, turned, and came down towards me. I stood face to face with Mr. Peggotty!

Then I remembered the woman. It was Martha, to whom Emily had given the money that night in the kitchen. Martha Endell—side by side with whom, he would not have seen his dear niece, Ham had told me, for all the treasures wrecked in the sea.

We shook hands heartily. At first, neither of us could speak a word.

"Mas'r Davy!" he said, gripping me tight, "it do my art good to see you, sir. Well met, well met!"

"Well met, my dear old friend!" said I.

"I had my thowts o' coming to make inquiration for you, sir, to-night," he said, "but knowing as your aunt was living along wi' you—fur I've been down yonder—Yarmouth way—I was afeerd it was too late. I should have come early in the morning, sir, afore going away."

"Again?" said I.

"Yes, sir," he replied, patiently shaking his head, "I'm away to-morrow."

"Where were you going now?" I asked.

"Well!" he replied, shaking the snow out of his long hair, "I was a-going to turn in somewheers."

In those days there was a side-entrance to the stable-yard of the Golden Cross, the inn so memorable to me in connection with his misfortune, nearly opposite to where we stood. I pointed out the gateway, put my arm through his, and we went across. Two or three public-rooms opened out of the stableyard; and looking into one of them, and finding it empty, and a good fire burning, I took him in there.

When I saw him in the light, I observed, not only that his hair was long and ragged, but that his face was burnt dark by the sun. He was greyer, the lines in his face and forehead were deeper, and he had every appearance of having toiled and wandered through all varieties of weather; but he looked very strong, and like a man upheld by steadfastness of purpose, whom nothing could tire out. He shook the snow from his hat and clothes, and brushed it away from his face, while I was inwardly making these remarks. As he sat down opposite to me at a table, with his back to the door by which we had entered, he put out his rough hand again, and grasped mine warmly.

"I'll tell you, Mas'r Davy," he said, "wheer-all I've been, and what-all we've heerd. I've been fur, and we've heerd little; but I'll tell you!"

I rang the bell for something hot to drink. He would have nothing stronger than ale; and while it was being brought, and being warmed at the fire, he sat thinking. There was a fine massive gravity in his face, I did not venture to disturb.

"When she was a child," he said, lifting up his head soon after we were left alone, "she used to talk to me a deal about the sea, and about them coasts wheer the sea got to be dark blue, and to lay a-shining and a-shining in the sun. I thowt, odd times, as her father being drownded made her think on it so much. I doen't know, you see, but maybe she believed—or hoped—he had drifted out to them parts, wheer the flowers is always a-blowing, and the country bright."

"It is likely to have been a childish fancy," I replied.

"When she was—lost," said Mr. Peggotty, "I know'd in my mind, as he would take her to them countries. I know'd in my mind, as he'd have told her wonders of 'em, and how she was to be a lady theer, and how he got her to listen to him fust, along o' sech like. When we see his mother, I know'd quite well as I was right. I went across-channel to France, and landed theer, as if I'd fell down from the sky."

I saw the door move, and the snow drift in. I saw it move a little more, and a hand softly interpose to keep it open.

" I found out an English gen'leman as was in authority," said Mr. Peggotty, " and told him I was a-going to seek my niece. He got me them papers as I wanted fur to carry me through—I doen't rightly know how they're called—and he would have give me money, but that I was thankful to have no need on. I thank him kind, for all he done, I'm sure! ' I've wrote afore you,' he says to me, ' and I shall speak to many as will come that way, and many will know you, fur distant from heer, when you're a-travelling alone.' I told him, best as I was able, what my gratitoode was, and went away through France.'

" Alone, and on foot? " said I.

" Mostly a-foot," he rejoined; " sometimes in carts along with people going to market; sometimes in empty coaches. Many mile a day a-foot, and often with some poor soldier or another, travelling to see his friends. I couldn't talk to him," said Mr. Peggotty, " nor he to me; but we was company for one another, too, along the dusty roads."

I should have known that by his friendly tone.

" When I come to any town," he pursued, " I found the inn, and waited about the yard till some one turned up (some one mostly did) as know'd English. Then I told how that I was on my way to seek my niece, and they told me what manner of gentlefolks was in the house, and I waited to see any as seemed like her, going in or out. When it warn't Em'ly, I went on agen. By little and little, when I come to a new village or that, among the poor people, I found they know'd about me. They would set me down at their cottage doors, and give me what-not fur to eat and drink, and show me wheer to sleep; and many a woman, Mas'r Davy, as has had a daughter of about Em'ly's age, I've found a-waiting fur me, at Our Saviour's Cross outside the village, fur to do me sim'lar kindnesses. Some has had daughters as was dead. And God only knows how good them mothers was to me! "

It was Martha at the door. I saw her haggard, listening face distinctly. My dread was lest he should turn his head, and see her too.

" They would often put their children—partic'lar their little girls," said Mr. Peggotty, " upon my knee; and many a time you might have seen me sitting at their doors, when night was coming in, a'most as if they'd been my Darling's children. Oh, my Darling! "

Overpowered by sudden grief, he sobbed aloud. I laid my

trembling hand upon the hand he put before his face. "Thankee, sir," he said, "doen't take no notice."

In a very little while he took his hand away and put it on his breast, and went on with his story.

"They often walked with me," he said, "in the morning, maybe a mile or two upon my road; and when we parted, and I said, 'I'm very thankful to you! God bless you!' they always seemed to understand, and answered pleasant. At last I come to the sea. It warn't hard, you may suppose, for a seafaring man like me to work his way over to Italy. When I got theer, I wandered on as I had done afore. The people was just as good to me, and I should have gone from town to town, maybe the country through, but that I got news of her being seen among them Swiss mountains yonder. One as know'd his sarvant see 'em theer, all three, and told me how they travelled, and wheer they was. I made fur them mountains, Mas'r Davy, day and night. Ever so fur as I went, ever so fur the mountains seemed to shift away from me. But I come up with 'em, and I crossed 'em. When I got nigh the place as I had been told of, I began to think within my own self, 'What shall I do when I see her?'"

The listening face, insensible to the inclement night, still drooped at the door, and the hands begged me—prayed me—not to cast it forth.

"I never doubted her," said Mr. Peggotty. "No! Not a bit! On'y let her see my face—on'y let her heer my voice—on'y let my stanning still afore her bring to her thoughts the home she had fled away from, and the child she had been—and if she had growed to be a royal lady, she'd have fell down at my feet! I know'd it well! many a time in my sleep had I heerd her cry out, 'Uncle!' and seen her fall like death afore me. Many a time in my sleep had I raised her up, and whispered to her, 'Em'ly, my dear, I am come fur to bring forgiveness, and to take you home!'"

He stopped and shook his head, and went on with a sigh.

"*He* was nowt to me now. Em'ly was all. I bought a country dress to put upon her; and I know'd that, once found, she would walk beside me over them stony roads, go wheer I would, and never, never, leave me more. To put that dress upon her, and to cast off what she wore—to take her on my arm again, and wander towards home—to stop sometimes upon the road, and heal her bruised feet and her worse-bruised heart—was all that I thowt of now. I doen't believe I should have done so much as look at him. But, Mas'r Davy, it warn't to be—not yet! I was too late, and they was gone. Wheer, I couldn't learn. Some said heer, some said theer. I travelled heer, and I travelled theer, but I found no Em'ly, and I travelled home."

"How long ago?" I asked.

"A matter o' fower days," said Mr. Peggotty. "I sighted the old boat arter dark, and the light a-shining in the winder. When I come nigh and looked in through the glass, I see the faithful creetur Missis Gummidge sittin' by the fire, as we had fixed upon, alone. I called out, 'Doen't be afeerd! It's Dan'l!' and I went in. I never could have thowt the old boat would have been so strange!"

From some pocket in his breast he took out, with a very careful hand, a small paper bundle containing two or three letters or little packets, which he laid upon the table.

"This fust one come," he said, selecting it from the rest, "afore I had been gone a week. A fifty pound Bank note, in a sheet of paper, directed to me, and put underneath the door in the night. She tried to hide her writing, but she couldn't hide it from Me!"

He folded up the note again, with great patience and care, in exactly the same form, and laid it on one side.

"This come to Missis Gummidge," he said, opening another, "two or three months ago." After looking at it for some moments, he gave it to me, and added in a low voice, "Be so good as read it, sir."

I read as follows:

"Oh what will you feel when you see this writing, and know it comes from my wicked hand! But try, try—not for my sake, but for uncle's goodness, try to let your heart soften to me, only for a little little time! Try, pray do, to relent towards a miserable girl, and write down on a bit of paper whether he is well, and what he said about me before you left off ever naming me among yourselves—and whether, of a night, when it is my old time of coming home, you ever see him look as if he thought of one he used to love so dear. Oh, my heart is breaking when I think about it! I am kneeling down to you, begging and praying you not to be as hard with me as I deserve—as I well, well know I deserve—but to be so gentle and so good, as to write down something of him, and send it to me. You need not call me Little, you need not call me by the name I have disgraced; but oh, listen to my agony, and have mercy on me so far as to write me some word of uncle, never, never to be seen in this world by my eyes again!

"Dear, if your heart is hard towards me—justly hard, I know—but, listen, if it is hard, dear, ask him I have wronged the most

—him whose wife I was to have been—before you quite decide against my poor prayer! If he should be so compassionate as to say that you might write something for me to read—I think he would, oh, I think he would, if you would only ask him, for he always was so brave and so forgiving—tell him then (but not else), that when I hear the wind blowing at night, I feel as if it was passing angrily from seeing him and uncle, and was going up to God against me. Tell him that if I was to die to-morrow (and oh, if I was fit, I would be so glad to die!) I would bless him and uncle with my last words, and pray for his happy home with my last breath!"

Some money was enclosed in this letter also. Five pounds. It was untouched like the previous sum, and he refolded it in the same way. Detailed instructions were added relative to the address of a reply, which, although they betrayed the intervention of several hands, and made it difficult to arrive at any very probable conclusion in reference to her place of concealment, made it at least not unlikely that she had written from that spot where she was stated to have been seen.

"What answer was sent?" I inquired of Mr. Peggotty.

"Missis Gummidge," he returned, "not being a good scholar, sir, Ham kindly drawed it out, and she made a copy on it. They told her I was gone to seek her, and what my parting words was."

"Is that another letter in your hand?" said I.

"It's money, sir," said Mr. Peggotty, unfolding it a little way. "Ten pound, you see. And wrote inside, 'From a true friend,' like the fust. But the fust was put underneath the door, and this come by the post, day afore yesterday. I'm a-going to seek her at the post-mark."

He showed it to me. It was a town on the Upper Rhine. He had found out, at Yarmouth, some foreign dealers who knew that country, and they had drawn him a rude map on paper, which he could very well understand. He laid it between us on the table; and, with his chin resting on one hand, tracked his course upon it with the other.

I asked him how Ham was? He shook his head.

"He works," he said, "as bold as a man can. His name's as good, in all that part, as any man's is, anywheers in the wureld. Any one's hand is ready to help him, you understand, and his is ready to help them. He's never been heerd fur to complain. But my sister's belief is ('twixt ourselves) as it has cut him deep."

"Poor fellow, I can believe it!"

"He ain't no care, Mas'r Davy," said Mr. Peggotty in a solemn whisper—"keinder no care no-how for his life. When a man's wanted for rough sarvice in rough weather, he's theer. When theer's hard duty to be done with danger in it, he steps for'ard afore all his mates. And yet he's as gentle as any child. Theer ain't a child in Yarmouth that doen't know him."

He gathered up the letters thoughtfully, smoothing them with his hand; put them into their little bundle; and placed it tenderly in his breast again. The face was gone from the door. I still saw the snow drifting in; but nothing else was there.

"Well!" he said, looking to his bag, "having seen you to-night, Mas'r Davy (and that doos me good!), I shall away betimes to-morrow morning. You have seen what I've got heer;" putting his hand on where the little packet lay; "all that troubles me is, to think that any harm might come to me, afore that money was give back. If I was to die, and it was lost, or stole, or elseways made away with, and it was never know'd by him but what I'd took it, I believe the t'other wureld wouldn't hold me! I believe I must come back!"

He rose, and I rose too; we grasped each other by the hand again, before going out.

"I'd go ten thousand mile," he said, "I'd go till I dropped dead, to lay that money down afore him. If I do that, and find my Em'ly, I'm content. If I doen't find her, maybe she'll come to hear, sometime, as her loving uncle only ended his search for her when he ended his life; and if I know her, even that will turn her home at last!"

As he went out into the rigorous night, I saw the lonely figure flit away before us. I turned him hastily on some pretence, and held him in conversation until it was gone.

He spoke of a traveller's house on the Dover Road, where he knew he could find a clean, plain lodging for the night. I went with him over Westminster Bridge, and parted from him on the Surrey shore. Everything seemed, to my imagination, to be hushed in reverence for him, as he resumed his solitary journey through the snow.

I returned to the inn yard, and, impressed by my remembrance of the face, looked awfully around for it. It was not there. The snow had covered our late footprints; my new track was the only one to be seen; and even that began to die away (it snowed so fast) as I looked back over my shoulder.

41

DORA'S AUNTS

AT LAST, AN ANSWER CAME FROM THE TWO OLD LADIES. They presented their compliments to Mr. Copperfield, and informed him that they had given his letter their best consideration, " with a view to the happiness of both parties "—which I thought rather an alarming expression, not only because of the use they had made of it in relation to the family difference beforementioned, but because I had (and have all my life) observed that conventional phrases are a sort of fireworks, easily let o f, and liable to take a great variety of shapes and colours not at all suggested by their original form. The Misses Spenlow added that they begged to forbear expressing, " through the medium of correspondence," an opinion on the subject of Mr. Copperfield's communication; but that if Mr. Copperfield would do them the favour to call, upon a certain day (accompanied, if he thought proper, by a confidential friend), they would be happy to hold some conversation on the subject.

To this favour, Mr. Copperfield immediately replied, with his respectful compliments, that he would have the honour of waiting on the Misses Spenlow, at the time appointed; accompanied, in accordance with their kind permission, by his friend Mr. Thomas Traddles of the Inner Temple. Having dispatched which missive, Mr. Copperfield fell into a condition of strong nervous agitation; and so remained until the day arrived.

It was a great augmentation of my uneasiness to be bereaved, at this eventful crisis, of the inestimable services of Miss Mills. But Mr. Mills, who was always doing something or other to annoy me—or I felt as if he were, which was the same thing—had brought his conduct to a climax, by taking it into his head that he would go to India. Why should he go to India, except to harass me? To be sure he had nothing to do with any other part of the world, and had a good deal to do with that part; being entirely in the Indian trade, whatever that was (I had floating dreams myself concerning golden shawls and elephants' teeth); having been at Calcutta in his youth; and designing now to go out there again, in the capacity of resident partner. But this was nothing to me. However, it was so much to him that for India he was bound, and Julia with him; and Julia went into the country to take leave of her relations; and the house was put into a perfect suit of bills, announcing that it was to be let or sold, and that the furniture (Mangle and all) was to be taken at a valuation. So, here was another earthquake of which I became the sport, before I had recovered from the shock of its predecessor!

I was in several minds how to dress myself on the important day; being divided between my desire to appear to advantage, and my apprehensions of putting on anything that might impair my severely practical character in the eyes of the Misses Spenlow. I endeavoured to hit a happy medium between these two extremes; my aunt approved the result; and Mr. Dick threw one of his shoes after Traddles and me, for luck, as we went downstairs.

Excellent fellow as I knew Traddles to be, and warmly attached to him as I was, I could not help wishing, on that delicate occasion, that he had never contracted the habit of brushing his hair so very upright. It gave him a surprised look—not to say a hearthbroomy kind of expression—which, my apprehensions whispered, might be fatal to us.

I took the liberty of mentioning it to Traddles, as we were walking to Putney; and saying that if he *would* smooth it down a little—

" My dear Copperfield," said Traddles, lifting off his hat, and rubbing his hair all kinds of ways, " nothing would give me greater pleasure. But it won't."

" Won't be smoothed down? " said I.

" No," said Traddles. " Nothing will induce it. If I was to carry a half-hundredweight upon it, all the way to Putney, it would be up again the moment the weight was taken off. You have no idea what obstinate hair mine is, Copperfield. I am quite a fretful porcupine."

I was a little disappointed, I must confess, but thoroughly charmed by his good-nature too. I told him how I esteemed his good-nature; and said that his hair must have taken all the obstinacy out of his character, for *he* had none.

" Oh! " returned Traddles, laughing. " I assure you, it's quite an old story, my unfortunate hair. My uncle's wife couldn't bear it. She said it exasperated her. It stood very much in my way, too, when I first fell in love with Sophy. Very much! "

" Did she object to it? "

"*She* didn't," rejoined Traddles; "but her eldest sister—the one that's the Beauty—quite made game of it, I understand. In fact, all the sisters laugh at it."

"Agreeable!" said I.

"Yes," returned Traddles with perfect innocence, "it's a joke for us. They pretend that Sophy has a lock of it in her desk, and is obliged to shut it in a clasped book, to keep it down. We laugh about it."

"By-the-by, my dear Traddles," said I, "your experience may suggest something to me. When you became engaged to the young lady whom you have just mentioned, did you make a regular proposal to her family? Was there anything like—what we are going through to-day, for instance?" I added, nervously.

"Why," replied Traddles, on whose attentive face a thoughtful shade had stolen, "it was rather a painful transaction, Copperfield, in my case. You see, Sophy being of so much use in the family, none of them could endure the thought of her ever being married. Indeed, they had quite settled among themselves that she never was to be married, and they called her the old maid. Accordingly, when I mentioned it, with the greatest precaution, to Mrs. Crewler—"

"The mama?" said I.

"The mama," said Traddles—"Reverend Horace Crewler—when I mentioned it with every possible precaution to Mrs. Crewler, the effect upon her was such that she gave a scream and became insensible. I couldn't approach the subject again, for months."

"You did at last?" said I.

"Well, the Reverend Horace did," said Traddles. "He is an excellent man, most exemplary in every way; and he pointed out to her that she ought, as a Christian, to reconcile herself to the sacrifice (especially as it was so uncertain), and to bear no uncharitable feeling towards me. As to myself, Copperfield, I give you my word, I felt a perfect bird of prey towards the family."

"The sisters took your part, I hope, Traddles?"

"Why, I can't say they did," he returned. "When we had comparatively reconciled Mrs. Crewler to it, we had to break it to Sarah. You recollect my mentioning Sarah, as the one that has something the matter with her spine?"

"Perfectly!"

"She clenched both her hands," said Traddles, looking at me in dismay; "shut her eyes; turned lead-colour; became perfectly stiff; and took nothing for two days but toast-and-water, administered with a tea-spoon."

"What a very unpleasant girl, Traddles!" I remarked.

"Oh, I beg your pardon, Copperfield!" said Traddles. "She is a very charming girl, but she has a great deal of feeling. In fact, they all have. Sophy told me afterwards, that the self-reproach she underwent while she was in attendance upon Sarah, no words could describe. I know it must have been severe, by my own feelings, Copperfield; which were like a criminal's. After Sarah was restored, we still had to break it to the other eight; and it produced various effects upon them of a most pathetic nature. The two little ones, whom Sophy educates, have only just left off de-testing me."

"At any rate, they are all reconciled to it now, I hope?" said I.

"Ye—yes, I should say they were, on the whole, resigned to it," said Traddles, doubtfully. "The fact is, we avoid mentioning the subject; and my unsettled prospects and indifferent circumstances are a great consolation to them. There will be a deplorable scene, whenever we are married. It will be much more like a funeral than a wedding. And they'll all hate me for taking her away!"

His honest face, as he looked at me with a serio-comic shake of his head, impresses me more in the remembrance than it did in the reality, for I was by this time in a state of such excessive trepidation and wandering of mind, as to be quite unable to fix my attention on anything. On our approaching the house where the Misses Spenlow lived, I was at such a discount in respect of my personal looks and presence of mind, that Traddles proposed a gentle stimulant in the form of a glass of ale. This having been administered at a neighbouring public-house, he conducted me, with tottering steps, to the Misses Spenlow's door.

I had a vague sensation of being, as it were, on view, when the maid opened it; and of wavering, somehow, across a hall with a weather-glass in it, into a quiet little drawing-room on the ground-floor, commanding a neat garden. Also of sitting down here, on a sofa, and seeing Traddles's hair start up, now his hat was removed, like one of those obtrusive little figures made of springs, that fly out of fictitious snuff-boxes when the lid is taken off. Also of hearing an old-fashioned clock ticking away on the chimney-piece, and trying to make it keep time to the jerking of my heart,—which it wouldn't. Also of looking round the room for any sign of Dora, and seeing none. Also of thinking that Jip once barked in the distance, and was instantly choked by somebody. Ultimately I found myself backing Traddles into the fireplace, and bowing in great confusion to two dry little elderly ladies, dressed in black, and each looking wonderfully like a preparation in chip or tan of the late Mr. Spenlow.

"Pray," said one of the two little ladies, "be seated."

When I had done tumbling over Traddles, and had sat upon something which was not a cat—my first seat was—I so far recovered my sight, as to perceive that Mr. Spenlow had evidently been the youngest of the family; that there was a disparity of six or eight years between the two sisters; and that the younger appeared to be the manager of the conference, inasmuch as she had my letter in her hand—so familiar as it looked to me, and yet so odd!—and was referring to it through an eye-glass. They were dressed alike, but this sister wore her dress with a more youthful air than the other; and perhaps had a little more frill, or tucker, or brooch, or bracelet, or some little thing of that kind, which made her look more lively. They were both upright in their carriage, formal, precise, composed, and quiet. The sister who had not my letter, had her arms crossed on her breast, and resting on each other, like an Idol.

"Mr. Copperfield, I believe," said the sister who had got my letter, addressing herself to Traddles.

This was a frightful beginning. Traddles had to indicate that I was Mr. Copperfield, and I had to lay claim to myself, and they had to divest themselves of a preconceived opinion that Traddles was Mr. Copperfield, and altogether we were in a nice condition. To improve it, we all distinctly heard Jip give two short barks, and receive another choke.

"Mr. Copperfield!" said the sister with the letter.

I did something—bowed, I suppose—and was all attention, when the other sister struck in.

"My sister Lavinia," said she, "being conversant with matters of this nature, will state what we consider most calculated to promote the happiness of both parties."

I discovered afterwards that Miss Lavinia was an authority in affairs of the heart, by reason of there having anciently existed a certain Mr. Pidger, who played short whist, and was supposed to have been enamoured of her. My private opinion is, that this was entirely a gratuitous assumption, and that Pidger was altogether innocent of any such sentiments—to which he had never given any sort of expression that I could ever hear of. Both Miss Lavinia and Miss Clarissa had a superstition, however, that he would have declared his passion, if he had not been cut short in his youth (at about sixty) by over-drinking his constitution, and over-doing an attempt to set it right again by swilling

Bath water. They had a lurking suspicion even, that he died of secret love; though I must say there was a picture of him in the house with a damask nose, which concealment did not appear to have ever preyed upon.

"We will not," said Miss Lavinia, "enter on the past history of this matter. Our poor brother Francis's death has cancelled that."

"We had not," said Miss Clarissa, "been in the habit of frequent association with our brother Francis; but there was no decided division or disunion between us. Francis took his road; we took ours. We considered it conducive to the happiness of all parties that it should be so. And it was so."

Each of the sisters leaned a little forward to speak, shook her head after speaking, and became upright again when silent. Miss Clarissa never moved her arms. She sometimes played tunes upon them with her fingers—minuets and marches, I should think—but never moved them.

"Our niece's position, or supposed position, is much changed by our brother Francis's death," said Miss Lavinia; "and therefore we consider our brother's opinions as regarded her position as being changed too. We have no reason to doubt, Mr. Copperfield, that you are a young gentleman possessed of good qualities and honourable character; or that you have an affection—or are fully persuaded that you have an affection—for our niece."

I replied, as I usually did whenever I had a chance, that nobody had ever loved anybody else as I loved Dora. Traddles came to my assistance with a confirmatory murmur.

Miss Lavinia was going on to make some rejoinder, when Miss Clarissa, who appeared to be incessantly beset by a desire to refer to her brother Francis, struck in again:

"If Dora's mama," she said, "when she married our brother Francis, had at once said that there was not room for the family at the dinner-table, it would have been better for the happiness of all parties."

"Sister Clarissa," said Miss Lavinia. "Perhaps we needn't mind that now.'

"Sister Lavinia," said Miss Clarissa, "it belongs to the subject. With our branch of the subject, on which alone you are competent to speak, I should not think of interfering. On this branch of the subject I have a voice and an opinion. It would have been better for the happiness of all parties, if Dora's mama, when she married our brother Francis, had mentioned plainly what her intentions were. We should then have known what we had to expect. We should have said 'Pray do not invite us, at any time;' and all possibility of misunderstanding would have been avoided."

When Miss Clarissa had shaken her head, Miss Lavinia resumed: again referring to my letter through her eye-glass. They both had little bright round twinkling eyes, by the way, which were like birds' eyes. They were not unlike birds, altogether; having a sharp, brisk, sudden manner, and a little short, spruce way of adjusting themselves, like canaries.

Miss Lavinia, as I have said, resumed:

"You ask permission of my sister Clarissa and myself, Mr. Copperfield, to visit here, as the accepted suitor of our niece."

"If our brother Francis," said Miss Clarissa, breaking out again, if I may call anything so calm a breaking out, "wished to surround himself with an atmosphere of Doctors' Commons, and of Doctors' Commons only, what right or desire had we to object? None, I am sure. We have ever been far from wishing to obtrude ourselves on any one. But why not say so? Let our brother Francis and his wife have their society. Let my sister Lavinia and myself have our society. We can find it for ourselves, I hope."

As this appeared to be addressed to Traddles and me, both Traddles and I made some sort of reply. Traddles was inaudible. I think I observed, myself, that it was highly creditable to all concerned. I don't in the least know what I meant.

"Sister Lavinia," said Miss Clarissa, having now relieved her mind, "you can go on, my dear."

Miss Lavinia proceeded:

"Mr. Copperfield, my sister Clarissa and I have been very careful indeed in considering this letter; and we have not considered it without finally showing it to our niece, and discussing it with our niece. We have no doubt that you think you like her very much."

"Think, ma'am," I rapturously began, "Oh!——"

But Miss Clarissa gave me a look (just like a sharp canary), as requesting that I would not interrupt the oracle, I begged pardon.

"Affection," said Miss Lavinia, glancing at her sister for corroboration, which she gave in the form of a little nod to every clause, "mature affection, homage, devotion, does not easily express itself. Its voice is low. It is modest and retiring, it lies in ambush, waits and waits. Such is the mature fruit. Sometimes a life glides away, and finds it still ripening in the shade."

Of course I did not understand then that this was an allusion to her supposed experience of the stricken Pidger; but I saw, from the gravity with which Miss Clarissa nodded her head, that great weight was attached to these words.

"The light—for I call them, in comparison with such sentiments, the light—inclinations of very young people," pursued Miss Lavinia, "are dust, compared to rocks. It is owing to the difficulty of knowing whether they are likely to endure or have any real foundation, that my sister Clarissa and myself have been very undecided how to act, Mr. Copperfield, and Mr. ——"

"Traddles," said my friend, finding himself looked at.

"I beg pardon. Of the Inner Temple, I believe?" said Miss Clarissa, again glancing at my letter.

Traddles said "Exactly so," and became pretty red in the face.

Now, although I had not received any express encouragement as yet, I fancied that I saw in the two little sisters, and particularly in Miss Lavinia, an intensified enjoyment of this new and fruitful subject of domestic interest, a settling down to make the most of it, a disposition to pet it, in which there was a good bright ray of hope. I thought I perceived that Miss Lavinia would have uncommon satisfaction in superintending two young lovers, like Dora and me; and that Miss Clarissa would have hardly less satisfaction in seeing her superintend us, and in chiming in with her own particular department of the subject whenever that impulse was strong upon her. This gave me courage to protest most vehemently that I loved Dora better than I could tell, or any one believe; that all my friends knew how I loved her; that my aunt, Agnes, Traddles, every one who knew me, knew how I loved her, and how earnest my love had made me. For the truth of this, I appealed to Traddles. And Traddles, firing up as if he were plunging into a Parliamentary Debate, really did come out nobly: confirming me in good round terms, and in a plain, sensible, practical manner, that evidently made a favourable impression.

"I speak, if I may presume to say so, as one who has some little experience of such things," said Traddles, "being myself engaged to a young lady—one of ten, down in Devonshire—and seeing no probability, at present, of our engagement coming to a termination."

"You may be able to confirm what I have said, Mr. Traddles," observed Miss Lavinia, evidently taking a new interest in him, "of the affection that is modest and retiring; that waits and waits?"

"Entirely, ma'am," said Traddles.

Miss Clarissa looked at Miss Lavinia, and shook her head

gravely. Miss Lavinia looked consciously at Miss Clarissa, and heaved a little sigh.

"Sister Lavinia," said Miss Clarissa, "take my smelling-bottle."

Miss Lavinia revived herself with a few whiffs of aromatic vinegar—Traddles and I looking on with great solicitude the while; and then went on to say, rather faintly:

"My sister and myself have been in great doubt, Mr. Traddles, what course we ought to take in reference to the likings, or imaginary likings, of such very young people as your friend Mr. Copperfield and our niece."

"Our brother Francis's child," remarked Miss Clarissa. "If our brother Francis's wife had found it convenient in her life-time (though she had an unquestionable right to act as she thought best) to invite the family to her dinner-table, we might have known our brother Francis's child better at the present moment. Sister Lavinia, proceed."

Miss Lavinia turned my letter, so as to bring the superscription towards herself, and referred through her eye-glass to some orderly-looking notes she had made on that part of it.

"It seems to us," said she, "prudent, Mr. Traddles, to bring these feelings to the test of our own observation. At present we know nothing of them, and are not in a situation to judge how much reality there may be in them. Therefore we are inclined so far to accede to Mr. Copperfield's proposal, as to admit his visits here."

"I shall never, dear ladies," I exclaimed, relieved of an immense load of apprehension, "forget your kindness!"

"But," pursued Miss Lavinia,—"but, we would prefer to regard those visits, Mr. Traddles, as made, at present, to us. We must guard ourselves from recognising any positive engagement between Mr. Copperfield and our niece, until we have had an opportunity—"

"Until *you* have had an opportunity, sister Lavinia," said Miss Clarissa.

"Be it so," assented Miss Lavinia, with a sigh—"until I have had an opportunity of observing them."

"Copperfield," said Traddles, turning to me, "you feel, I am sure, that nothing could be more reasonable or considerate."

"Nothing!" cried I. "I am deeply sensible of it."

"In this position of affairs," said Miss Lavinia, again referring to her notes, "and admitting his visits on this understanding only, we must require from Mr. Copperfield a distinct assurance, on his word of honour, that no communication of any kind shall take place between him and our niece without our knowledge. That no project whatever shall be entertained with regard to our niece, without being first submitted to us—"

"To you, sister Lavinia," Miss Clarissa interposed.

"Be it so, Clarissa!" assented Miss Lavinia resignedly—"to me—and receiving our concurrence. We must make this a most express and serious stipulation, not to be broken on any account. We wished Mr. Copperfield to be accompanied by some confidential friend to-day," with an inclination of her head towards Traddles, who bowed, "in order that there might be no doubt or misconception on this subject. If Mr. Copperfield, or if you, Mr. Traddles, feel the least scruple in giving this promise, I beg you to take time to consider it."

I exclaimed, in a state of high ecstatic fervour, that not a moment's consideration could be necessary. I bound myself by the required promise, in a most impassioned manner; called upon Traddles to witness it; and denounced myself as the most atrocious of characters if I ever swerved from it in the least degree.

"Stay!" said Miss Lavinia, holding up her hand; "we resolved, before we had the pleasure of receiving you two gentlemen, to leave you alone for a quarter of an hour, to consider this point. You will allow us to retire."

It was in vain for me to say that no consideration was necessary. They persisted in withdrawing for the specified time. Accordingly, these little birds hopped out with great dignity; leaving me to receive the congratulations of Traddles, and to feel as if I were translated to regions of exquisite happiness. Exactly at the expiration of the quarter of an hour, they reappeared with no less dignity than they had disappeared. They had gone rustling away as if their little dresses were made of autumn-leaves: and they came rustling back in like manner.

I then bound myself once more to the prescribed conditions.

"Sister Clarissa," said Miss Lavinia, "the rest is with you."

Miss Clarissa, unfolding her arms for the first time, took the notes and glanced at them.

"We shall be happy," said Miss Clarissa, "to see Mr. Copperfield to dinner, every Sunday, if it should suit his convenience. Our hour is three."

I bowed.

"In the course of the week," said Miss Clarissa, "we shall be happy to see Mr. Copperfield to tea. Our hour is half-past six."

I bowed again.

" Twice in the week," said Miss Clarissa, " but, as a rule, not oftener."

I bowed again.

" Miss Trotwood," said Miss Clarissa, " mentioned in Mr. Copperfield's letter, will perhaps call upon us. When visiting is better for the happiness of all parties, we are glad to receive visits, and return them. When it is better for the happiness of all parties that no visiting should take place (as in the case of our brother Francis, and his establishment), that is quite different."

I intimated that my aunt would be proud and delighted to make their acquaintance; though I must say I was not quite sure of their getting on very satisfactorily together. The conditions being now closed, I expressed my acknowledgments in the warmest manner; and, taking the hand, first of Miss Clarissa, and then of Miss Lavinia, pressed it, in each case, to my lips.

Miss Lavinia then arose, and begging Mr. Traddles to excuse us for a minute, requested me to follow her. I obeyed, all in a tremble, and was conducted into another room. There I found my blessed darling stopping her ears behind the door, with her dear little face against the wall; and Jip in the plate-warmer with his head tied up in a towel.

Oh! How beautiful she was in her black frock, and how she sobbed and cried at first, and wouldn't come out from behind the door! How fond we were of one another, when she did come out at last; and what a state of bliss I was in, when we took Jip out of the plate-warmer, and restored him to the light, sneezing very much, and were all three reunited!

" My dearest Dora! Now, indeed, my own for ever! "

" Oh, DON'T! " pleaded Dora. " Please! "

" Are you not my own for ever, Dora? "

" Oh yes, of course I am! " cried Dora, " but I am so frightened! "

" Frightened, my own? "

" Oh yes! I don't like him," said Dora. " Why don't he go? "

" Who, my life? "

" Your friend," said Dora. " It isn't any business of his. What a stupid he must be! "

" My love! " (There never was anything so coaxing as her childish ways.) " He is the best creature! "

" Oh, but we don't want any best creatures! " pouted Dora.

" My dear," I argued, " you will soon know him well, and like him of all things. And here is my aunt coming soon: and you'll like her of all things too, when you know her."

"No, please don't bring her!" said Dora, giving me a horrified little kiss, and folding her hands. "Don't. I know she's a naughty, mischief-making old thing! Don't let her come here, Doady!" which was a corruption of David.

Remonstrance was of no use, then; so I laughed, and admired, and was very much in love and very happy; and she showed me Jip's new trick of standing on his hind legs in a corner—which he did for about the space of a flash of lightning, and then fell down—and I don't know how long I should have stayed there, oblivious of Traddles, if Miss Lavinia had not come in to take me away. Miss Lavinia was very fond of Dora (she told me Dora was exactly like what she had been herself at her age—she must have altered a good deal), and she treated Dora just as if she had been a toy. I wanted to persuade Dora to come and see Traddles, but on my proposing it she ran off to her own room, and locked herself in; so I went to Traddles without her, and walked away with him on air.

"Nothing could be more satisfactory," said Traddles; "and they are very agreeable old ladies, I am sure. I shouldn't be at all surprised if you were to be married years before me, Copperfield."

"Does your Sophy play on any instrument, Traddles?" I inquired, in the pride of my heart.

"She knows enough of the piano to teach it to her little sisters," said Traddles.

"Does she sing at all?" I asked.

"Why, she sings ballads, sometimes, to freshen up the others a little when they're out of spirits," said Traddles. "Nothing scientific."

"She doesn't sing to the guitar?" said I.

"Oh dear no!" said Traddles.

"Paint at all?"

"Not at all," said Traddles.

I promised Traddles that he should hear Dora sing, and see some of her flower-painting. He said he should like it very much, and we went home arm in arm in great good humour and delight. I encouraged him to talk about Sophy, on the way; which he did with a loving reliance on her that I very much admired. I compared her in my mind with Dora, with considerable inward satisfaction; but I candidly admitted to myself that she seemed to be an excellent kind of girl for Traddles, too.

Of course my aunt was immediately made acquainted with the successful issue of the conference, and with all that had been said and done in the course of it. She was happy to see me so happy, and promised to call on Dora's aunts without loss of time. But she took such a long walk up and down our rooms that night, while I was writing to Agnes, that I began to think she meant to walk till morning.

My letter to Agnes was a fervent and grateful one, narrating all the good effects that had resulted from my following her advice. She wrote, by return of post, to me. Her letter was hopeful, earnest, and cheerful. She was always cheerful from that time.

I had my hands more full than ever, now. My daily journeys to Highgate considered, Putney was a long way off; and I naturally wanted to go there as often as I could. The proposed tea-drinkings being quite impracticable, I compounded with Miss Lavinia for permission to visit every Saturday afternoon, without detriment to my privileged Sundays. So the close of every week was a delicious time for me; and I got through the rest of the week by looking forward to it.

I was wonderfully relieved to find that my aunt and Dora's aunts rubbed on, all things considered, much more smoothly than I could have expected. My aunt made her promised visit within a few days of the conference; and within a few more days, Dora's aunts called upon her, in due state and form. Similar but more friendly exchanges took place afterwards, usually at intervals of three or four weeks. I know that my aunt distressed Dora's aunts very much, by utterly setting at naught the dignity of fly-conveyance, and walking out to Putney at extraordinary times, as shortly after breakfast or just before tea; likewise by wearing her bonnet in any manner that happened to be comfortable to her head, without at all deferring to the prejudices of civilisation on that subject. But Dora's aunts soon agreed to regard my aunt as an eccentric and somewhat masculine lady, with a strong understanding; and although my aunt occasionally ruffled the feathers of Dora's aunts, by expressing heretical opinions on various points of ceremony, she loved me too well not to sacrifice some of her little peculiarities to the general harmony.

The only member of our small society who positively refused to adapt himself to circumstances, was Jip. He never saw my aunt without immediately displaying every tooth in his head, retiring under a chair, and growling incessantly: with now and then a doleful howl, as if she really were too much for his feelings. All kinds of treatment were tried with him—coaxing, scolding, slapping, bringing him to Buckingham Street (where he instantly dashed at the two cats, to the terror of all beholders); but he never could prevail upon himself to bear my aunt's society. He would sometimes think he had got the better of his objection, and be amiable for a few minutes; and then would put up his snub nose, and howl to that extent, that there was nothing for it but to blind him and put him in the plate-warmer. At length, Dora regularly muffled him in a towel and shut him up there, whenever my aunt was reported at the door.

One thing troubled me much, after we had fallen into this quiet train. It was, that Dora seemed by one consent to be regarded like a pretty toy or plaything. My aunt, with whom she gradually became familiar, always called her Little Blossom; and the pleasure of Miss Lavinia's life was to wait upon her, curl her hair, make ornaments for her, and treat her like a pet child. What Miss Lavinia did, her sister did as a matter of course. It was very odd to me; but they all seemed to treat Dora, in her degree, much as Dora treated Jip in his.

I made up my mind to speak to Dora about this; and one day when we were out walking (for we were licensed by Miss Lavinia, after a while, to go out walking by ourselves), I said to her that I wished she could get them to behave towards her differently.

"Because you know, my darling," I remonstrated, "you are not a child."

"There!" said Dora. "Now you're going to be cross!"

"Cross, my love?"

"I am sure they're very kind to me," said Dora, "and I am very happy."

"Well! But, my dearest life!" said I, "you might be very happy, and yet be treated rationally."

Dora gave me a reproachful look—the prettiest look!—and then began to sob, saying, if I didn't like her, why had I ever wanted so much to be engaged to her? And why didn't I go away now, if I couldn't bear her?

What could I do, but kiss away her tears, and tell her how I doted on her, after that!

"I am sure I am very affectionate," said Dora: "you oughtn't to be cruel to me, Doady!"

"Cruel, my precious love! As if I would—or could—be cruel to you, for the world!"

"Then don't find fault with me," said Dora, making a rose-bud of her mouth; "and I'll be good."

I was charmed by her presently asking me, of her own accord, to give her that cookery-book I had once spoken of, and to show her how to keep accounts, as I had once promised I would. I brought the volume with me on my next visit (I got it prettily bound, first, to make it look less dry and more inviting); and as we strolled about the Common, I showed her an old housekeeping-book of my aunt's, and gave her a set of tablets, and a pretty little pencil-case, and box of leads, to practise housekeeping with.

But the cookery-book made Dora's head ache, and the figures made her cry. They wouldn't add up, she said. So she rubbed them out, and drew little nosegays, and likenesses of me and Jip, all over the tablets.

Then I playfully tried verbal instruction in domestic matters, as we walked about on a Saturday afternoon. Sometimes, for example, when we passed a butcher's shop, I would say:

"Now suppose, my pet, that we were married, and you were going to buy a shoulder of mutton for dinner, would you know how to buy it?"

My pretty little Dora's face would fall, and she would make her mouth into a bud again, as if she would very much prefer to shut mine with a kiss.

"Would you know how to buy it, my darling?" I would repeat, perhaps, if I were very inflexible.

Dora would think a little, and then reply, perhaps, with great triumph:

"Why, the butcher would know how to sell it, and what need *I* know? Oh, you silly boy!"

So, when I once asked Dora, with an eye to the cookery-book, what she would do, if we were married, and I were to say I should like a nice Irish stew, she replied that she would tell the servant to make it: and then clapped her little hands together across my arm, and laughed in such a charming manner that she was more delightful than ever.

Consequently, the principal use to which the cookery-book was devoted, was being put down in the corner for Jip to stand upon. But Dora was so pleased, when she had trained him to stand upon it without offering to come off, and at the same time to hold the pencil-case in his mouth, that I was very glad I had bought it.

And we fell back on the guitar-case, and the flower-painting, and the songs about never leaving off dancing, Ta ra la! and were as happy as the week was long. I occasionally wished I could venture to hint to Miss Lavinia, that she treated the darling of my heart a little too much like a plaything; and I sometimes awoke, as it were, wondering to find that I had fallen into the general fault, and treated her like a plaything too—but not often.

42

MISCHIEF

I FEEL AS IF IT WERE NOT FOR ME TO RECORD, EVEN though this manuscript is intended for no eyes but mine, how hard I worked at that tremendous shorthand, and all improvement appertaining to it, in my sense of responsibility to Dora and her aunts. I will only add, to what I have already written of my perseverance at this time of my life, and of a patient and continuous energy which then began to be matured within me, and which I know to be the strong part of my character, if it have any strength at all, that there, on looking back, I find the source of my success. I have been very fortunate in worldly matters; many men have worked much harder, and not succeeded half so well; but I never could have done what I have done, without the habits of punctuality, order, and diligence, without the determination to concentrate myself on one object at a time, no matter how quickly its successor should come upon its heels, which I then formed. Heaven knows I write this in no spirit of self-laudation. The man who reviews his own life, as I do mine, in going on here, from page to page, had need to have been a good man indeed, if he would be spared the sharp consciousness of many talents neglected, many opportunities wasted, many erratic and perverted feelings constantly at war within his breast, and defeating him. I do not hold one natural gift, I dare say, that I have not abused. My meaning simply is, that whatever I have tried to do in life, I have tried with all my heart to do well; that whatever I have devoted myself to, I have devoted myself to completely; that in great aims and in small, I have always been thoroughly in earnest. I have never believed it possible that any natural or improved ability can claim immunity from the companionship of the steady, plain, hard-working qualities, and hope to gain its end. There is no such thing as such fulfilment on this earth. Some happy talent, and some fortunate opportunity, may form the two sides of the ladder on which some men mount, but the rounds of that ladder must be made of stuff to stand wear and tear; and there is no substitute for thorough-going, ardent, and sincere earnestness. Never to put one hand to anything on which I could throw my whole self; and never to affect depreciation of my work, whatever it was; I find, now, to have been my golden rules.

How much of the practice I have just reduced to precept, I owe to Agnes, I will not repeat here. My narrative proceeds to Agnes, with a thankful love.

She came on a visit of a fortnight to the Doctor's. Mr. Wickfield was the Doctor's old friend, and the Doctor wished to talk with him, and do him good. It had been matter of conversation with Agnes when she was last in town, and this visit was the result. She and her father came together. I was not much surprised to hear from her that she had engaged to find a lodging in the neighbourhood for Mrs. Heep, whose rheumatic complaint required change of air, and who would be charmed to have it in such company. Neither was I surprised when, on the very next day, Uriah, like a dutiful son, brought his worthy mother to take possession.

"You see, Master Copperfield," said he, as he forced himself upon my company for a turn in the Doctor's garden, "where a person loves, a person is a little jealous—leastways, anxious to keep an eye on the beloved one."

"Of whom are you jealous, now?" said I.

"Thanks to you, Master Copperfield," he returned, "of no one in particular just at present—no male person, at least."

"Do you mean that you are jealous of a female person?"

He gave me a sidelong glance out of his sinister red eyes, and laughed.

"Really, Master Copperfield," he said, "—I should say Mister, but I know you'll excuse the abit I've got into—you're so insinuating, that you draw me like a corkscrew! Well, I don't mind telling you," putting his fish-like hand on mine, "I'm not a lady's man in general, sir, and I never was, with Mrs. Strong."

His eyes looked green now, as they watched mine with a rascally cunning.

"What do you mean?" said I.

"Why, though I am a lawyer, Master Copperfield," he replied, with a dry grin, "I mean, just at present, what I say."

"And what do you mean by your look?" I retorted, quietly.

"By my look? Dear me, Copperfield, that's sharp practice! What do I mean by my look?"

"Yes," said I. "By your look."

He seemed very much amused, and laughed as heartily as it was in his nature to laugh. After some scraping of his chin with his hand, he went on to say, with his eyes cast downward—still scraping, very slowly:

"When I was but an umble clerk, she always looked down upon me. She was for ever having my Agnes backwards and forwards at her ouse, and she was for ever being a friend to you, Master Copperfield; but I was too far beneath her, myself, to be noticed."

"Well?" said I; "suppose you were!"

"And beneath him too," pursued Uriah, very distinctly, and in a meditative tone of voice, as he continued to scrape his chin.

"Don't you know the Doctor better," said I, "than to suppose him conscious of your existence, when you were not before him?"

He directed his eyes at me in that sidelong glance again, and he made his face very lantern-jawed, for the greater convenience of scraping, as he answered:

"Oh, dear I am not referring to the Doctor! Oh no, poor man! I mean Mr. Maldon!"

My heart quite died within me. All my old doubts and apprehensions on that subject, all the Doctor's happiness and peace, all the mingled possibilities of innocence and compromise, that I could not unravel, I saw, in a moment, at the mercy of this fellow's twisting.

"He never could come into the office, without ordering and shoving me about," said Uriah. "One of your fine gentlemen he was! I was very meek and umble—and I am. But I didn't like that sort of thing—and I don't!"

He left off scraping his chin, and sucked in his cheeks until they seemed to meet inside; keeping his sidelong glance upon me all the while.

"She is one of your lovely women, she is," he pursued, when he had slowly restored his face to its natural form; "and ready to be no friend to such as me, *I* know. She's just the person as would put my Agnes up to higher sort of game. Now, I ain't one of your lady's men, Master Copperfield; but I've had eyes in my ed, a pretty long time back. We umble ones have got eyes, mostly speaking—and we look out of 'em."

I endeavoured to appear unconscious and not disquieted, but, I saw in his face, with poor success.

"Now, I'm not a-going to let myself be run down, Copperfield," he continued, raising that part of his countenance, where his red eyebrows would have been if he had had any, with malignant triumph, "and I shall do what I can to put a stop to this friendship. I don't approve of it. I don't mind acknowledging to you that I've got rather a grudging disposition, and want to keep off all intruders. I ain't a-going, if I know it, to run the risk of being plotted against."

"You are always plotting, and delude yourself into the belief that everybody else is doing the like, I think," said I.

"Perhaps so, Master Copperfield," he replied. "But I've got a motive, as my fellow-partner used to say; and I go at it tooth and nail. I mustn't be put upon, as an umble person, too much. I can't allow people in my way. Really they must come out of the cart, Master Copperfield!"

"I don't understand you," said I.

"Don't you, though?" he returned, with one of his jerks. "I'm astonished at that, Master Copperfield, you being usually so quick! I'll try to be plainer, another time.—Is that Mr. Maldon a-norseback, ringing at the gate, sir?"

"It looks like him," I replied, as carelessly as I could.

Uriah stopped short, put his hands between his great knobs of knees, and doubled himself up with laughter. With perfectly silent laughter. Not a sound escaped from him. I was so repelled by his odious behaviour, particularly by this concluding instance, that I turned away without any ceremony; and left him doubled up in the middle of the garden, like a scarecrow in want of support.

It was not on that evening; but, as I well remember, on the next evening but one, which was a Saturday; that I took Agnes to see Dora. I had arranged the visit, beforehand, with Miss Lavinia; and Agnes was expected to tea.

I was in a flutter of pride and anxiety; pride in my dear little betrothed, and anxiety that Agnes should like her. All the way to Putney, Agnes being inside the stage coach, and I outside, I pictured Dora to myself in every one of the pretty looks I knew so well; now making up my mind that I should like her to look exactly as she looked at such a time, and then doubting whether I should not prefer her looking as she looked at such another time; and almost worrying myself into a fever about it.

I was troubled by no doubt of her being very pretty, in any case; but it fell out that I had never seen her look so well. She was not in the drawing-room when I presented Agnes to her little aunts, but was shyly keeping out of the way. I knew where to look for her, now; and sure enough I found her stopping her ears again, behind the same dull old door.

At first she wouldn't come at all; and then she pleaded for

five minutes by my watch. When at length she put her arm through mine, to be taken to the drawing-room, her charming little face was flushed, and had never been so pretty. But when we went into the room, and it turned pale, she was ten thousand times prettier yet.

Dora was afraid of Agnes. She had told me that she knew Agnes was " too clever." But when she saw her looking at once so cheerful and so earnest, and so thoughtful, and so good, she gave a faint little cry of pleased surprise, and just put her affectionate arms round Agnes's neck, and laid her innocent cheek against her face.

I never was so happy. I never was so pleased as when I saw those two sit down together, side by side. As when I saw my little darling looking up so naturally to those cordial eyes. As when I saw the tender, beautiful regard which Agnes cast upon her.

Miss Lavinia and Miss Clarissa partook, in their way, of my joy. It was the pleasantest tea-table in the world. Miss Clarissa presided. I cut and handed the sweet seed-cake—the little sisters had a bird-like fondness for picking up seeds and pecking at sugar; Miss Lavinia looked on with benignant patronage, as if our happy love were all her work; and we were perfectly contented with ourselves and one another.

The gentle cheerfulness of Agnes went to all their hearts. Her quiet interest in everything that interested Dora; her manner of making acquaintance with Jip (who responded instantly); her pleasant way, when Dora was ashamed to come over to her usual seat by me; her modest grace and ease, eliciting a crowd of blushing little marks of confidence from Dora; seemed to make our circle quite complete.

" I am so glad," said Dora, after tea, " that you like me. I didn't think you would; and I want, more than ever, to be liked, now Julia Mills is gone."

I have omitted to mention it, by-the-by. Miss Mills had sailed, and Dora and I had gone aboard a great East Indiaman at Gravesend to see her; and we had had preserved ginger, and guava, and other delicacies of that sort for lunch; and we had left Miss Mills weeping on a camp-stool on the quarterdeck, with a large new diary under her arm, in which the original reflections awakened by the contemplation of Ocean were to be recorded under lock and key.

Agnes said she was afraid I must have given her an unpromising character; but Dora corrected that directly.

" Oh no! " she said, shaking her curls at me: " it was all

praise. He thinks so much of your opinion, that I was quite afraid of it."

"My good opinion cannot strengthen his attachment to some people whom he knows," said Agnes, with a smile; "it is not worth their having."

"But please let me have it," said Dora, in her coaxing way, "if you can!"

We made merry about Dora's wanting to be liked, and Dora said I was a goose, and she didn't like me at any rate, and the short evening flew away on gossamer-wings. The time was at hand when the coach was to call for us. I was standing alone before the fire, when Dora came stealing softly in, to give me that usual precious little kiss before I went.

"Don't you think, if I had had her for a friend a long time ago, Doady," said Dora, her bright eyes shining very brightly, and her little right hand idly busying itself with one of the buttons of my coat, "I might have been more clever perhaps?"

"My love!" said I, "what nonsense!"

"Do you think it is nonsense?" returned Dora, without looking at me. "Are you sure it is?"

"Of course I am!"

"I have forgotten," said Dora, still turning the button round and round, "what relation Agnes is to you, you dear bad boy."

"No blood-relation," I replied; "but we were brought up together, like brother and sister."

"I wonder why you ever fell in love with me?" said Dora, beginning on another button of my coat.

"Perhaps because I couldn't see you, and not love you, Dora!"

"Suppose you had never seen me at all," said Dora, going to another button.

"Suppose we had never been born!" said I, gaily.

I wondered what she was thinking about, as I glanced in admiring silence at the little soft hand travelling up the row of buttons on my coat, and at the clustering hair that lay against my breast, and at the lashes of her downcast eyes, slightly rising as they followed her idle fingers. At length her eyes were lifted up to mine, and she stood on tiptoe to give me, more thoughtfully than usual, that precious little kiss—once, twice, three times—and went out of the room.

They all came back together within five minutes afterwards, and Dora's unusual thoughtfulness was quite gone then. She was laughingly resolved to put Jip through the whole of his performances, before the coach came. They took some time (not so much on account of their variety, as Jip's reluctance), and were still unfinished when it was heard at the door. There was a hurried but affectionate parting between Agnes and herself; and Dora was to write to Agnes (who was not to mind her letters being foolish, she said), and Agnes was to write to Dora; and they had a second parting at the coach-door, and a third when Dora, in spite of the remonstrances of Miss Lavinia, would come running out once more to remind Agnes at the coach-window about writing, and to shake her curls at me on the box.

The stage-coach was to put us down near Covent Garden, where we were to take another stage-coach for Highgate. I was impatient for the short walk in the interval, that Agnes might praise Dora to me. Ah! what praise it was! How lovingly and fervently did it commend the pretty creature I had won, with all her artless graces best displayed, to my most gentle care! How thoughtfully remind me, yet with no pretence of doing so, of the trust in which I held the orphan child!

Never, never, had I loved Dora so deeply and truly, as I loved her that night. When we had again alighted, and were walking in the starlight along the quiet road that led to the Doctor's house, I told Agnes it was her doing.

" When you were sitting by her," said I, " you seemed to be no less *her* guardian angel than mine; and you seem so now, Agnes."

" A poor angel," she returned, " but faithful."

The clear tone of her voice going straight to my heart, made it natural to me to say:

" The cheerfulness that belongs to you, Agnes (and to no one else that ever I have seen), is so restored, I have observed to-day, that I have begun to hope you are happier at home? "

" I am happier in myself," she said; " I am quite cheerful and light-hearted."

I glanced at the serene face looking upward, and thought it was the stars that made it seem so noble.

" There has been no change at home," said Agnes, after a few moments.

" No fresh reference," said I, " to—I wouldn't distress you, Agnes, but I cannot help asking—to what we spoke of, when we parted last? "

" No, none," she answered.

" I have thought so much about it."

" You must think less about it. Remember that I confide in simple love and truth at last. Have no apprehensions for me,

Trotwood," she added, after a moment; " the step you dread my taking, I shall never take."

Although I think I had never really feared it, in any season of cool reflection, it was an unspeakable relief to me to have this assurance from her own truthful lips. I told her so, earnestly.

" And when this visit is over," said I,—" for we may not be alone another time,—how long is it likely to be, my dear Agnes, before you come to London again? "

" Probably a long time," she replied; " I think it will be best—for papa's sake—to remain at home. We are not likely to meet often, for some time to come; but I shall be a good correspondent of Dora's, and we shall frequently hear of one another that way."

We were now within the little court-yard of the Doctor's cottage It was growing late. There was a light in the window of Mrs Strong's chamber, and Agnes, pointing to it, bade me good-night.

" Do not be troubled," she said, giving me her hand, " by our misfortunes and anxieties. I can be happier in nothing than in your happiness. If you can ever give me help, rely upon it I will ask you for it. God bless you always! "

In her beaming smile, and in these last tones of her cheerful voice, I seemed again to see and hear my little Dora in her company. I stood awhile, looking through the porch at the stars, with a heart full of love and gratitude, and then walked slowly forth. I had engaged a bed at a decent alehouse close by, and was going out at the gate, when, happening to turn my head, I saw a light in the Doctor's study. A half-reproachful fancy came into my mind, that he had been working at the Dictionary without my help. With the view of seeing if this were so, and, in any case, of bidding him good night, if he were yet sitting among his books, I turned back, and going softly across the hall, and gently opening the door, looked in.

The first person whom I saw, to my surprise, by the sober light of the shaded lamp, was Uriah. He was standing close beside it, with one of his skeleton hands over his mouth, and the other resting on the Doctor's table. The Doctor sat in his study chair, covering his face with his hands. Mr. Wickfield, sorely troubled and distressed, was leaning forward, irresolutely touching the Doctor's arm.

For an instant, I supposed that the Doctor was ill. I hastily advanced a step under that impression, when I met Uriah's eye, and saw what was the matter. I would have withdrawn, but the Doctor made a gesture to detain me, and I remained.

" At any rate," observed Uriah, with a writhe of his ungainly person, " we may keep the door shut. We needn't make it known to ALL the town."

Saying which, he went on his toes to the door, which I had left open, and carefully closed it. He then came back, and took up his former position. There was an obtrusive show of compassionate zeal in his voice and manner, more intolerable—at least to me—than any demeanour he could have assumed.

" I have felt it incumbent upon me, Master Copperfield," said Uriah, " to point out to Doctor Strong what you and me have already talked about. You didn't exactly understand me, though? "

I gave him a look, but no other answer; and, going to my good old master, said a few words that I meant to be words of comfort and encouragement. He put his hand upon my shoulder, as it had been his custom to do when I was quite a little fellow, but did not lift his grey head.

" As you didn't understand me, Master Copperfield," resumed Uriah in the same officious manner, " I may take the liberty of umbly mentioning, being among friends, that I have called Doctor Strong's attention to the goings-on of Mrs. Strong. It's much against the grain with me, I assure you, Copperfield, to be concerned in anything so unpleasant; but really, as it is, we're all mixing ourselves up with what oughtn't to be. That was what my meaning was, sir, when you didn't understand me."

I wonder now, when I recall this leer, that I did not collar him, and try to shake the breath out of his body.

" I dare say I didn't make myself very clear," he went on, " nor you neither. Naturally, we was both of us inclined to give such a subject a wide berth. Hows'ever, at last I have made up my mind to speak plain; and I have mentioned to Doctor Strong that—did you speak, sir? "

This was to the Doctor, who had moaned. The sound might have touched any heart, I thought, but it had no effect upon Uriah's.

" —mentioned to Doctor Strong," he proceeded, " that any one may see that Mr. Maldon, and the lovely and agreeable lady as is Doctor Strong's wife, are too sweet on one another. Really the time is come (we being at present all mixing ourselves up with what oughtn't to be), when Doctor Strong must be told that this was full as plain to everybody as the sun, before Mr. Maldon went to India; that Mr. Maldon made excuses to come back, for nothing else; and that he's always here, for nothing else. When you come in, sir, I was just putting it to my fellow-partner," towards whom he turned, " to say to Doctor Strong upon his word and honour, whether he'd ever been of this opinion long ago, or not. Come, Mr. Wickfield, sir! Would you be so good as tell us? Yes or no, sir? Come, partner! "

" For God's sake, my dear Doctor," said Mr. Wickfield, again laying his irresolute hand upon the Doctor's arm, " don't attach too much weight to any suspicions I may have entertained."

" There! " cried Uriah, shaking his head. " What a melancholy confirmation: ain't it? Him! Such an old friend! Bless your soul, when I was nothing but a clerk in his office, Copperfield, I've seen him twenty times, if I've seen him once, quite in a taking about it—quite put out, you know (and very proper in him as a father: I'm sure *I* can't blame him), to think that Miss Agnes was mixing herself up with what oughtn't to be."

" My dear Strong," said Mr. Wickfield in a tremulous voice, " my good friend, I needn't tell you that it has been my vice to look for some one master motive in everybody, and to try all actions by one narrow test. I may have fallen into such doubts as I have had, through this mistake."

" You have had doubts, Wickfield," said the Doctor, without lifting up his head. " You have had doubts."

" Speak up, fellow-partner," urged Uriah.

" I had, at one time, certainly," said Mr. Wickfield, " I—God forgive me—I thought *you* had."

" No, no, no! " returned the Doctor, in a tone of most pathetic grief.

" I thought, at one time," said Mr. Wickfield, " that you wished to send Maldon abroad to effect a desirable separation."

" No, no, no! " returned the Doctor. " To give Annie pleasure, by making some provision for the companion of her childhood. Nothing else."

" So I found," said Mr. Wickfield. " I couldn't doubt it, when you told me so. But I thought—I implore you to remember the narrow construction which has been my besetting sin—that, in a case where there was so much disparity in point of years—"

" That's the way to put it, you see, Master Copperfield! " observed Uriah, with fawning and offensive pity.

"—a lady of such youth, and such attractions, however real her respect for you, might have been influenced in marrying, by worldly considerations only. I make no allowance for innumerable feelings and circumstances that may have all tended to good. For Heaven's sake remember that! "

"How kind he puts it!" said Uriah, shaking his head.

"Always observing her from one point of view," said Mr. Wickfield; "but by all that is dear to you, my old friend, I entreat you to consider what it was; I am forced to confess now, having no escape—"

"No! There's no way out of it, Mr. Wickfield, sir," observed Uriah, "when it's got to this."

"—that I did," said Mr. Wickfield, glancing helplessly and distractedly at his partner, "that I did doubt her, and think her wanting in her duty to you; and that I did sometimes, if I must say all, feel averse to Agnes being in such a familiar relation towards her, as to see what I saw, or in my diseased theory fancied that I saw. I never mentioned this to any one. I never meant it to be known to any one. And though it is terrible to you to hear," said Mr. Wickfield, quite subdued, "if you knew how terrible it is for me to tell, you would feel compassion for me!"

The Doctor, in the perfect goodness of his nature, put out his hand. Mr. Wickfield held it for a little while in his, with his head bowed down.

"I am sure," said Uriah, writhing himself into the silence like a conger-eel, "that this is a subject full of unpleasantness to everybody. But since we have got so far, I ought to take the liberty of mentioning that Copperfield has noticed it too."

I turned upon him, and asked him how he dared refer to me!

"Oh! it's very kind of you Copperfield," returned Uriah, undulating all over, "and we all know what an amiable character yours is; but you know that the moment I spoke to you the other night, you knew what I meant. You know you knew what I meant, Copperfield. Don't deny it! You deny it with the best intentions; but don't do it, Copperfield."

I saw the mild eye of the good old Doctor turned upon me for a moment, and I felt that the confession of my old misgivings and remembrances was too plainly written in my face to be overlooked. It was of no use raging. I could not undo that. Say what I would, I could not unsay it.

We were silent again, and remained so, until the Doctor rose and walked twice or thrice across the room. Presently he returned to where his chair stood; and, leaning on the back of it, and occasionally putting his handkerchief to his eyes, with a simple honesty that did him more honour, to my thinking, than any disguise he could have effected, said:

"I have been much to blame. I believe I have been very much to blame. I have exposed one whom I hold in my heart, to trials and aspersions—I call them aspersions, even to have been conceived in anybody's inmost mind—of which she never, but for me, could have been the object."

Uriah Heep gave a kind of snivel. I think to express sympathy.

"Of which my Annie," said the Doctor, "never, but for me, could have been the object. Gentlemen, I am old now, as you know; I do not feel, to-night, that I have much to live for. But my life—my life—upon the truth and honour of the dear lady who has been the subject of this conversation!"

I do not think that the best embodiment of chivalry, the realisation of the handsomest and most romantic figure ever imagined by painter could have said this with a more impressive and affecting dignity than the plain old Doctor did.

"But I am not prepared" he went on "to deny—perhaps I may have been without knowing it in some degree prepared to admit—that I may have unwittingly ensnared that lady into an unhappy marriage. I am a man quite unaccustomed to observe; and I cannot but believe that the observation of several people, of different ages and positions, all too plainly tending in one direction (and that so natural), is better than mine."

I had often admired, as I have elsewhere described, his benignant manner towards his youthful wife; but the respectful tenderness he manifested in every reference to her on this occasion, and the almost reverential manner in which he put away from him the lightest doubt of her integrity, exalted him, in my eyes, beyond description.

"I married that lady," said the Doctor, "when she was extremely young. I took her to myself when her character was scarcely formed. So far as it was developed, it had been my happiness to form it. I knew her father well. I knew her well. I had taught her what I could, for the love of all her beautiful and virtuous qualities. If I did her wrong; as I fear I did, in taking advantage (but I never meant it) of her gratitude and her affection; I ask pardon of that lady, in my heart!"

He walked across the room, and came back to the same place; holding the chair with a grasp that trembled, like his subdued voice, in its earnestness.

"I regarded myself as a refuge, for her, from the dangers and vicissitudes of life. I persuaded myself that, unequal though we were in years, she would live tranquilly and contentedly with me. I did not shut out of my consideration the time when I should leave her free, and still young and still beautiful, but with her judgment more matured—no, gentlemen—upon my truth!"

His homely figure seemed to be lightened up by his fidelity and generosity. Every word he uttered had a force that no other grace could have imparted to it.

"My life with this lady has been very happy. Until to-night, I have had uninterrupted occasion to bless the day on which I did her great injustice."

His voice, more and more faltering in the utterance of these words, stopped for a few moments; then he went on:

"Once awakened from my dream—I have been a poor dreamer, in one way or other, all my life—I see how natural it is that she should have some regretful feeling towards her old companion and her equal. That she does regard him with some innocent regret, with some blameless thoughts of what might have been, but for me, is, I fear, too true. Much that I have seen, but not noted, has come back upon me with new meaning, during this last trying hour. But, beyond this, gentlemen, the dear lady's name never must be coupled with a word, a breath, of doubt."

For a little while, his eye kindled and his voice was firm; for a little while he was again silent. Presently, he proceeded as before:

"It only remains for me to bear the knowledge of the unhappiness I have occasioned, as submissively as I can. It is she who should reproach; not I. To save her from misconstruction, cruel misconstruction, that even my friends have not been able to avoid, becomes my duty. The more retired we live, the better I shall discharge it. And when the time comes—may it come soon, if it be His merciful pleasure!—when my death shall release her from constraint, I shall close my eyes upon her honoured face, with unbounded confidence and love; and leave her, with no sorrow then, to happier and brighter days."

I could not see him for the tears which his earnestness and goodness, so adorned by, and so adorning, the perfect simplicity of his manner, brought into my eyes. He had moved to the door, when he added:

"Gentlemen, I have shown you my heart. I am sure you will respect it. What we have said to-night is never to be said more. Wickfield, give me an old friend's arm up-stairs!"

Mr. Wickfield hastened to him. Without interchanging a word they went slowly out of the room together, Uriah looking after them.

"Well, Master Copperfield!" said Uriah, meekly turning to me. "The thing hasn't took quite the turn that might have been expected, for the old Scholar—what an excellent man!—is as blind as a brickbat: but *this* family's out of the cart, I think!"

I needed but the sound of his voice to be so madly enraged as I never was before, and never have been since:

"You villain," said I, "what do you mean by entrapping me into your schemes? How dare you appeal to me just now, you false rascal, as if we had been in discussion together?"

As we stood, front to front, I saw so plainly, in the stealthy exultation of his face, what I already so plainly knew; I mean that he forced his confidence upon me, expressly to make me miserable, and had set a deliberate trap for me in this very matter; that I couldn't bear it. The whole of his lank cheek was invitingly before me, and I struck it with my open hand with that force that my fingers tingled as if I had burnt them.

He caught the hand in his, and we stood in that connection, looking at each other. We stood so a long time; long enough for me to see the white marks of my fingers die out of the deep red of his cheek, and leave it a deeper red.

"Copperfield," he said at length, in a breathless voice, "have you taken leave of your senses?"

"I have taken leave of you," said I, wresting my hand away. "You dog, I'll know no more of you."

"Won't you?" said he, constrained by the pain of his cheek to put his hand there. "Perhaps you won't be able to help it. Isn't this ungrateful of you, now?"

"I have shown you often enough," said I, "that I despise you. I have shown you now, more plainly, that I do. Why should I dread your doing your worst to all about you? What else do you ever do?"

He perfectly understood this allusion to the considerations that had hitherto restrained me in my communications with him. I rather think that neither the blow, nor the allusion, would have escaped me, but for the assurance I had had from Agnes that night. It is no matter.

There was another long pause. His eyes, as he looked at me, seemed to take every shade of colour that could make eyes ugly.

"Copperfield," he said, removing his hand from his cheek, "you have always gone against me. I know you always used to be against me at Mr. Wickfield's."

"You may think what you like," said I, still in a towering rage. "If it is not true, so much the worthier you."

"And yet I always liked you, Copperfield!" he rejoined.

I deigned to make him no reply; and, taking up my hat, was going out to bed, when he came between me and the door.

"Copperfield," he said, "there must be two parties to a quarrel. I won't be one."

" You may go to the devil! " said I.

" Don't say that! " he replied. " I know you'll be sorry afterwards. How can you make yourself so inferior to me, as to show such a bad spirit? But I forgive you."

" You forgive me! " I repeated disdainfully.

" I do, and you can't help yourself," replied Uriah. " To think of your going and attacking *me*, that have always been a friend to you! But there can't be a quarrel without two parties, and I won't be one. I will be a friend to you, in spite of you. So now you know what you've got to expect."

The necessity of carrying on this dialogue (his part in which was very slow; mine very quick) in a low tone, that the house might not be disturbed at an unseasonable hour, did not improve my temper; though my passion was cooling down. Merely telling him that I should expect from him what I always had expected, and had never yet been disappointed in, I opened the door upon him, as if he had been a great walnut put there to be cracked, and went out of the house. But he slept out of the house too, at his mother's lodging; and before I had gone many hundred yards, came up with me.

" You know, Copperfield," he said, in my ear (I did not turn my head), "you're in quite a wrong position; " which I felt to be true, and that made me chafe the more; " you can't make this a brave thing, and you can't help being forgiven. I don't intend to mention it to mother, nor to any living soul. I'm determined to forgive you. But I do wonder that you should lift your hand against a person that you knew to be so umble! "

I felt only less mean than he. He knew me better than I knew myself. If he had retorted or openly exasperated me, it would have been a relief and a justification; but he had put me on a slow fire, on which I lay tormented half the night.

In the morning, when I came out, the early church bell was ringing, and he was walking up and down with his mother. He addressed me as if nothing had happened, and I could do no less than reply. I had struck him hard enough to give him the toothache, I suppose. At all events his face was tied up in a black silk handkerchief, which, with his hat perched on the top of it, was far from improving his appearance. I heard that he went to a dentist's in London on the Monday morning, and had a tooth out. I hope it was a double one.

The Doctor gave out that he was not quite well; and remained alone, for a considerable part of every day, during the remainder of the visit. Agnes and her father had been gone a week, before we resumed our usual work. On the day preceding its resumption, the Doctor gave me with his own hands a folded note, not sealed. It was addressed to myself; and laid an injunction on me, in a few affectionate words, never to refer to the subject of that evening. I had confided it to my aunt, but to no one else. It was not a subject I could discuss with Agnes, and Agnes certainly had not the least suspicion of what had passed.

Neither, I felt convinced, had Mrs. Strong then. Several weeks elapsed before I saw the least change in her. It came on slowly, like a cloud when there is no wind. At first, she seemed to wonder at the gentle compassion with which the Doctor spoke to her, and at his wish that she should have her mother with her, to relieve the dull monotony of her life. Often, when we were at work, and she was sitting by, I could see her pausing and looking at him with that memorable face. Afterwards, I sometimes observed her rise, with her eyes full of tears, and go out of the room. Gradually, an unhappy shadow fell upon her beauty, and deepened every day. Mrs. Markleham was a regular inmate of the cottage then; but she talked and talked, and saw nothing.

As this change stole on Annie, once like sunshine in the Doctor's house, the Doctor became older in appearance, and more grave; but the sweetness of his temper, the placid kindness of his manner, and his benevolent solicitude for her, if they were capable of any increase, were increased. I saw him once, early on the morning of her birthday, when she came to sit in the window while we were at work (which she had always done, but now began to do with a timid and uncertain air that I thought very touching), take her forehead between his hands, kiss it, and go hurriedly away, too much moved to remain. I saw her stand where he had left her, like a statue; and then bend down her head, and clasp her hands, and weep, I cannot say how sorrowfully.

Sometimes, after that, I fancied that she tried to speak, even to me, in intervals when we were left alone. But she never uttered a word. The Doctor always had some new project for her participating in amusements away from home, with her mother; and Mrs. Markleham, who was very fond of amusements, and very easily dissatisfied with anything else, entered into them with great good will, and was loud in her commendations. But Annie, in a spiritless unhappy way, only went whither she was led, and seemed to have no care for anything.

I did not know what to think. Neither did my aunt; who must have walked, at various times, a hundred miles in her uncertainty. What was strangest of all was, that the only real relief which seemed to make its way into the secret region of this domestic unhappiness, made its way there in the person of Mr. Dick.

What his thoughts were on the subject, or what his observation was, I am as unable to explain, as I dare say he would have been to assist me in the task. But, as I have recorded in the narrative of my school days, his veneration for the Doctor was unbounded; and there is a subtlety of perception in real attachment, even when it is borne towards man by one of the lower animals, which leaves the highest intellect behind. To this mind of the heart, if I may call it so, in Mr. Dick, some bright ray of the truth shot straight.

He had proudly resumed his privilege, in many of his spare hours, of walking up and down the garden with the Doctor; as he had been accustomed to pace up and down The Doctor's Walk at Canterbury. But matters were no sooner in this state, than he devoted all his spare time (and got up earlier to make it more) to these perambulations. If he had never been so happy as when the Doctor read that marvellous performance, the Dictionary, to him; he was now quite miserable unless the Doctor pulled it out of his pocket, and began. When the Doctor and I were engaged, he now fell into the custom of walking up and down with Mrs. Strong, and helping her to trim her favourite flowers, or weed the beds. I dare say he rarely spoke a dozen words in an hour: but his quiet interest, and his wistful face, found immediate response in both their breasts; each knew that the other liked him, and that he loved both; and he became what no one else could be—a link between them.

When I think of him, with his impenetrably wise face, walking up and down with the Doctor, delighted to be battered by the hard words in the Dictionary; when I think of him carrying huge watering-pots after Annie; kneeling down, in very paws of gloves, at patient microscopic work among the little leaves; expressing as no philosopher could have expressed, in everything he did, a delicate desire to be her friend; showering sympathy, trustfulness, and affection, out of every hole in the watering-pot; when I think of him never wandering in that better mind of his to which unhappiness addressed itself, never bringing the unfortunate King Charles into the garden, never wavering in his grateful service, never diverted from his knowledge that there was something wrong, or from his wish to set it right—I really feel almost ashamed of having known that he was not quite in his wits, taking account of the utmost I have done with mine.

"Nobody but myself, Trot, knows what that man is!" my aunt would proudly remark, when we conversed about it. "Dick will distinguish himself yet!"

I must refer to one other topic before I close this chapter. While the visit at the Doctor's was still in progress, I observed that the postman brought two or three letters every morning for Uriah Heep, who remained at Highgate until the rest went back, it being a leisure time; and that these were always directed in a business-like manner by Mr. Micawber, who now assumed a round legal hand. I was glad to infer, from these slight premises, that Mr. Micawber was doing well; and consequently was much surprised to receive, about this time, the following letter from his amiable wife:—

"CANTERBURY, *Monday Evening.*

"You will doubtless be surprised, my dear Mr. Copperfield, to receive this communication. Still more so, by its contents. Still more so, by the stipulation of implicit confidence which I beg to impose. But my feelings as a wife and mother require relief; and as I do not wish to consult my family (already obnoxious to the feelings of Mr. Micawber), I know no one of whom I can better ask advice than my friend and former lodger.

"You may be aware, my dear Mr. Copperfield, that between myself and Mr. Micawber (whom I will never desert), there has always been preserved a spirit of mutual confidence. Mr. Micawber may have occasionally given a bill without consulting me, or he may have misled me as to the period when that obligation would become due. This has actually happened. But, in general, Mr. Micawber has had no secrets from the bosom of affection—I allude to his wife—and has invariably, on our retirement to rest, recalled the events of the day.

"You will picture to yourself, my dear Mr. Copperfield, what the poignancy of my feelings must be, when I inform you that Mr. Micawber is entirely changed. He is reserved. He is secret. His life is a mystery to the partner of his joys and sorrows—I again allude to his wife—and if I should assure you that beyond knowing that it is passed from morning to night at the office, I now know less of it than I do of the man in the south, connected with whose mouth the thoughtless children repeat an idle tale respecting cold plum porridge, I should adopt a popular fallacy to express an actual fact.

"But this is not all. Mr. Micawber is morose. He is severe. He is estranged from our eldest son and daughter, he has no pride in his twins, he looks with an eye of coldness even on the unoffending stranger who last became a member of our circle. The pecuniary means of meeting our expenses, kept down to the utmost farthing, are obtained from him with great difficulty, and even under fearful threats that he will Settle himself (the exact expression); and he inexorably refuses to give any explanation whatever of this distracting policy.

"This is hard to bear. This is heart-breaking. If you will advise me, knowing my feeble powers such as they are, how you think it will be best to exert them in a dilemma so unwonted, you will add another friendly obligation to the many you have already rendered me. With loves from the children, and a smile from the happily-unconscious stranger, I remain, dear Mr. Copperfield,

"Your afflicted

"EMMA MICAWBER."

I did not feel justified in giving a wife of Mrs. Micawber's experience any other recommendation, than that she should try to reclaim Mr. Micawber by patience and kindness (as I knew she would in any case); but the letter set me thinking about him very much.

43

ANOTHER RETROSPECT

ONCE, AGAIN LET ME PAUSE UPON A MEMORABLE PERIOD of my life. Let me stand aside, to see the phantoms of those days go by me, accompanying the shadow of myself, in dim procession.

Weeks, months, seasons, pass along. They seem little more than a summer day and a winter evening. Now, the Common where I walk with Dora is all in bloom, a field of bright gold, and now the unseen heather lies in mounds and bunches underneath a covering of snow. In a breath, the river that flows through our Sunday walks is sparkling in the summer sun, is ruffled by the winter wind, or thickened with drifting heaps of ice. Faster than ever river ran towards the sea, it flashes, darkens, and rolls away.

Not a thread changes in the house of the two little bird-like ladies. The clock ticks over the fireplace, the weather-glass hangs in the hall. Neither clock nor weather-glass is ever right; but we believe in both, devoutly.

I have come legally to man's estate. I have attained the dignity of twenty-one. But this is a sort of dignity that may be thrust upon one. Let me think what I have achieved.

I have tamed that savage stenographic mystery. I make a respectable income by it. I am in high repute for my accomplishment in all pertaining to the art, and am joined with eleven others in reporting the debates in Parliament for a Morning Newspaper. Night after night, I record predictions that never come to pass, professions that are never fulfilled, explanations that are only meant to mystify. I wallow in words. Britannia, that unfortunate female, is always before me, like a trussed fowl: skewered through and through with office-pens, and bound hand and foot with red tape. I am sufficiently behind the scenes to know the worth of political life. I am quite an Infidel about it, and shall never be converted.

My dear old Traddles has tried his hand at the same pursuit, but it is not Traddles's way. He is perfectly good-humoured respecting his failure, and reminds me that he always did consider himself slow. He has occasional employment on the same newspaper, in getting up the facts of dry subjects, to be written about and embellished by more fertile minds. He is called to the bar; and with admirable industry and self-denial has scraped another hundred pounds together, to a fee conveyancer whose chambers he attends. A great deal of very hot port wine was consumed at his call; and, considering the figure, I should think the Inner Temple must have made a profit by it.

I have come out in another way. I have taken with fear and trembling to authorship. I wrote a little something, in secret, and sent it to a magazine, and it was published in the magazine. Since then, I have taken heart to write a good many trifling pieces. Now, I am regularly paid for them. Altogether, I am well off; when I tell my income on the fingers of my left hand, I pass the third finger and take in the fourth to the middle joint.

We have removed from Buckingham Street, to a pleasant little cottage very near the one I looked at, when my enthusiasm first came on. My aunt, however (who has sold the house at Dover, to good advantage), is not going to remain here, but intends removing herself to a still more tiny cottage close at hand. What does this portend? My marriage? Yes!

Yes! I am going to be married to Dora! Miss Lavinia and Miss Clarissa have given their consent; and if ever canary birds were in a flutter, they are. Miss Lavinia, self-charged with the superintendence of my darling's wardrobe, is constantly cutting out brown-paper cuirasses, and differing in opinion from a highly respectable young man, with a long bundle, and a yard measure under his arm. A dressmaker, always stabbed in the breast with a needle and thread, boards and lodges in the house; and seems to me, eating, drinking, or sleeping, never to take her thimble off. They make a lay-figure of my dear. They are always sending for her to come and try something on. We can't be happy together for five minutes in the evening, but some intrusive female knocks at the door, and says, "Oh, if you please, Miss Dora, would you step up-stairs!"

Miss Clarissa and my aunt roam all over London, to find out articles of furniture for Dora and me to look at. It would be better for them to buy the goods at once, without this ceremony of inspection; for, when we go to see a kitchen fender and meat-screen, Dora sees a Chinese house for Jip, with little bells on the top, and prefers that. And it takes a long time to accustom Jip to his new residence, after we have bought it; whenever he goes in or out, he makes all the little bells ring, and is horribly frightened.

Peggotty comes up to make herself useful, and falls to work immediately. Her department appears to be, to clean everything over and over again. She rubs everything that can be rubbed, until it shines, like her own honest forehead, with perpetual friction. And now it is, that I begin to see her solitary brother passing through the dark streets at night, and looking, as he goes, among the wandering faces. I never speak to him at such an hour. I know too well, as his grave figure passes onward, what he seeks, and what he dreads.

Why does Traddles look so important when he calls upon me this afternoon in the Commons—where I still occasionally attend, for form's sake, when I have time? The realisation of my boyish day-dream is at hand. I am going to take out the licence.

It is a little document to do so much; and Traddles contemplates it, as it lies upon my desk, half in admiration, half in awe, There are the names in the sweet old visionary connection, David Copperfield and Dora Spenlow; and there, in the corner, is that Parental Institution, the Stamp Office, which is so benignantly interested in the various transactions of human life, looking down upon our Union; and there is the Archbishop of Canterbury invoking a blessing on us in print, and doing it as cheap as could possibly be expected.

Nevertheless, I am in a dream, a flustered, happy, hurried dream. I can't believe that it is going to be; and yet I can't believe but that every one I pass in the street must have some kind of perception, that I am to be married the day after to-morrow. The Surrogate knows me, when I go down to be sworn, and disposes of me easily, as if there were a Masonic understanding between us. Traddles is not at all wanted, but is in attendance as my general backer.

" I hope the next time you come here, my dear fellow," I say to Traddles, " it will be on the same errand for yourself. And I hope it will be soon."

" Thank you for your good wishes, my dear Copperfield," he replies. " I hope so too. It's a satisfaction to know that she'll wait for me any length of time, and that she really is the dearest girl— "

" When are you to meet her at the coach ? " I ask.

" At seven," says Traddles, looking at his plain old silver watch —the very watch he once took a wheel out of, at school, to make a water-mill. " That is about Miss Wickfield's time, is it not ? "

" A little earlier. Her time is half-past eight."

" I assure you, my dear boy," says Traddles, " I am almost as pleased as if I were going to be married myself, to think that this event is coming to such a happy termination. And really the great friendship and consideration of personally associating Sophy with the joyful occasion, and inviting her to be a bridesmaid in conjunction with Miss Wickfield, demands my warmest thanks. I am extremely sensible of it."

I hear him, and shake hands with him; and we talk, and walk, and dine, and so on; but I don't believe it. Nothing is real.

Sophy arrives at the house of Dora's aunts, in due course. She has the most agreeable of faces,—not absolutely beautiful, but extraordinarily pleasant,—and is one of the most genial, unaffected, frank, engaging creatures I have ever seen. Traddles presents her to us with great pride; and rubs his hands for ten minutes by the clock, with every individual hair upon his head standing on tiptoe, when I congratulate him in a corner on his choice.

I have brought Agnes from the Canterbury coach, and her cheerful and beautiful face is among us for the second time. Agnes has a great liking for Traddles, and it is capital to see them meet, and to observe the glory of Traddles as he commends the dearest girl in the world to her acquaintance.

Still I don't believe it. We have a delightful evening, and are supremely happy: but I don't believe it yet. I can't collect myself. I can't check off my happiness as it takes place. I feel in a misty and unsettled kind of state; as if I had got up very early in the morning a week or two ago, and had never been to bed since. I can't make out when yesterday was. I seem to have been carrying the licence about, in my pocket, many months.

Next day, too, when we all go in a flock to see the house—our house—Dora's and mine—I am quite unable to regard myself as its master. I seem to be there, by permission of somebody else. I half expect the real master to come home presently, and say he is glad to see me. Such a beautiful little house as it is, with everything so bright and new; with the flowers on the carpets looking as if freshly gathered, and the green leaves on the paper as if they had just come out: with the spotless muslin curtains, and the blushing rose-coloured furniture, and Dora's garden hat with the blue ribbon—do I remember, now, how I loved her in such another hat when I first knew her!—already hanging on its little peg; the guitar-case quite at home on its heels in a corner; and everybody tumbling over Jip's pagoda, which is much too big for the establishment.

Another happy evening, quite as unreal as all the rest of it, and I steal into the usual room before going away. Dora is not there. I suppose they have not done trying on yet. Miss Lavinia peeps in, and tells me mysteriously that she will not be long. She is rather long, notwithstanding; but by-and-by I hear a rustling at the door, and some one taps.

I say, "Come in!" but some one taps again.

I go to the door, wondering who it is; there, I meet a pair of bright eyes, and a blushing face; they are Dora's eyes and face, and Miss Lavinia has dressed her in to-morrow's dress, bonnet and all, for me to see. I take my little wife to my heart; and Miss Lavinia gives a little scream because I tumble the bonnet, and Dora laughs and cries at once, because I am so pleased; and I believe it less than ever.

"Do you think it pretty, Doady?" says Dora.

Pretty! I should rather think I did.

"And are you sure you like me very much?" says Dora.

The topic is fraught with such danger to the bonnet, that Miss Lavinia gives another little scream, and begs me to understand that Dora is only to be looked at, and on no account to be touched. So Dora stands in a delightful state of confusion for a minute or two, to be admired; and then takes off her bonnet—looking so natural without it!—and runs away with it in her hand; and comes dancing down again in her own familiar dress, and asks Jip if I have got a beautiful little wife, and whether he'll forgive her for being married, and kneels down to make him stand upon the cookery-book, for the last time in her single life.

I go home, more incredulous than ever, to a lodging that I have hard by; and get up very early in the morning, to ride to the Highgate road and fetch my aunt.

I have never seen my aunt in such state. She is dressed in lavender-coloured silk, and has a white bonnet on, and is amazing. Janet has dressed her, and is there to look at me. Peggotty is ready to go to church, intending to behold the ceremony from the gallery. Mr. Dick, who is to give my darling to me at the altar, has had his hair curled. Traddles, whom I have taken up by appointment at the turnpike, presents a dazzling combination of cream colour and light blue; and both he and Mr. Dick have a general effect about them of being all gloves.

No doubt I see this, because I know it is so; but I am astray, and seem to see nothing. Nor do I believe anything whatever. Still, as we drive along in an open carriage, this fairy marriage is real enough to fill me with a sort of wondering pity for the unfortunate people who have no part in it, but a sweeping out the shops, and going to their daily occupations.

My aunt sits with my hand in hers all the way. When we stop a little way short of the church, to put down Peggotty, whom we have brought on the box, she gives it a squeeze, and me a kiss.

" God bless you, Trot! My own boy never could be dearer. I think of poor dear Baby this morning."

" So do I. And of all I owe to you, dear aunt."

" Tut, child! " says my aunt; and gives her hand in overflowing cordiality to Traddles, who then gives his to Mr. Dick, who then gives his to me, who then gives mine to Traddles, and then we come to the church door.

The church is calm enough, I am sure; but it might be a steam-power loom in full action, for any sedative effect it has on me. I am too far gone for that.

The rest is all a more or less incoherent dream.

A dream of their coming in with Dora; of the pew-opener arranging us, like a drill-sergeant, before the altar rails; of my wondering, even then, why pew-openers must always be the most disagreeable females procurable, and whethere there is any religious dread of a disastrous infection of good humour which renders it indispensable to set those vessels of vinegar upon the road to Heaven.

Of the clergyman and clerk appearing; of a few boatmen and some other people strolling in; of an ancient mariner behind me, strongly flavouring the church with rum; of the service beginning in a deep voice, and our all being very attentive.

Of Miss Lavinia, who acts as a semi-auxiliary bridesmaid, being the first to cry, and of her doing homage (as I take it) to the memory of Pidger, in sobs; of Miss Clarissa applying a smelling-bottle; of Agnes taking care of Dora; of my aunt endeavouring to represent herself as a model of sternness, with tears rolling down her face; of little Dora trembling very much, and making her responses in faint whispers.

Of our kneeling down together, side by side; of Dora's trembling less and less, but always clasping Agnes by the hand; of the service being got through, quietly and gravely; of our all looking at each other in an April state of smiles and tears, when it is over; of my young wife being hysterical in the vestry, and crying for her poor papa, her dear papa.

Of her soon cheering up again, and our signing the register all round. Of my going into the gallery for Peggotty to bring *her* to sign it; of Peggotty's hugging me in a corner, and telling me she saw my own dear mother married; of its being over, and our going away.

Of my walking so proudly and lovingly down the aisle with my sweet wife upon my arm, through a mist of half-seen people, pulpits, monuments, pews, fonts, organs, and church-windows, in which there flutter faint airs of association with my childish church at home, so long ago.

Of their whispering, as we pass, what a youthful couple we are, and what a pretty little wife she is. Of our all being so merry and talkative in the carriage going back. Of Sophy telling us that when she saw Traddles (whom I had entrusted with the licence) asked for it, she almost fainted, having been convinced that he would contrive to lose it, or to have his pocket picked. Of Agnes laughing so gaily; and of Dora being so fond of Agnes that she will not be separated from her, but still keeps her hand.

Of there being a breakfast, with abundance of things, pretty and substantial, to eat and drink, whereof I partake, as I should do in any other dream, without the least perception of their flavour; eating and drinking, as I may say, nothing but love and marriage, and no more believing in the viands than in anything else.

Of my making a speech in the same dreamy fashion, without having any idea of what I want to say, beyond such as may be comprehended in the full conviction that I haven't said it. Of our being very sociably and simply happy (always in a dream though); and of Jip's having wedding cake, and its not agreeing with him afterwards.

Of the pair of hired post-horses being ready, and of Dora's going away to change her dress. Of my aunt and Miss Clarissa remaining with us; and our walking in the garden; and my aunt, who has made quite a speech at breakfast touching Dora's aunts, being mightily amused with herself, but a little proud of it too.

Of Dora's being ready, and of Miss Lavinia's hovering about her, loth to lose the pretty toy that has given her so much pleasant occupation. Of Dora's making a long series of surprised discoveries that she has forgotten all sorts of little things; and of everybody's running everywhere to fetch them.

Of their all closing about Dora, when at last she begins to say good-bye, looking, with their bright colours and ribbons, like a bed of flowers. Of my darling being almost smothered among the flowers, and coming out, laughing and crying both together, to my jealous arms.

Of my wanting to carry Jip (who is to go along with us), and Dora's saying, No, that she must carry him, or else he'll think she don't like him any more, now she is married, and will break his heart. Of our going, arm in arm, and Dora stopping and looking back, and saying, "If I have ever been cross or ungrateful to anybody, don't remember it!" and bursting into tears.

Of her waving her little hand, and our going away once more. Of her once more stopping and looking back, and hurrying to Agnes, and giving Agnes, above all the others, her last kisses and farewells.

We drive away together, and I awake from the dream. I believe it at last. It is my dear, dear, little wife beside me, whom I love so well!

"Are you happy now, you foolish boy?" says Dora, "and sure you don't repent?"

I have stood aside to see the phantoms of those days go by me. They are gone, and I resume the journey of my story.

44

OUR HOUSEKEEPING

IT WAS A STRANGE CONDITION OF THINGS, THE HONEYMOON being over, and the bridesmaids gone home, when I found myself sitting down in my own small house with Dora; quite thrown out of employment, as I may say, in respect of the delicious old occupation of making love.

It seemed such an extraordinary thing to have Dora always there. It was so unaccountable not to be obliged to go out to see her, not to have any occasion to be tormenting myself about her, not to have to write to her, not to be scheming and devising opportunities of being alone with her. Sometimes of an evening, when I looked up from my writing, and saw her seated opposite, I would lean back in my chair, and think how queer it was that there we were, alone together as a matter of course—nobody's business any more—all the romance of our engagement put away upon a shelf, to rust—no one to please but one another—one another to please, for life.

When there was a debate, and I was kept out very late, it seemed so strange to me, as I was walking home, to think that Dora was at home! It was such a wonderful thing, at first, to have her coming softly down to talk to me as I ate my supper. It was such a stupendous thing to know for certain that she put her hair in papers. It was altogether such an astonishing event to see her do it!

I doubt whether two young birds could have known less about keeping house, than I and my pretty Dora did. We had a servant, of course. She kept house for us. I have still a latent belief that she must have been Mrs. Crupp's daughter in disguise, we had such an awful time of it with Mary Anne.

Her name was Paragon. Her nature was represented to us, when we engaged her, as being feebly expressed in her name. She had a written character, as large as a proclamation; and, according to this document, could do everything of a domestic nature that ever I heard of, and a great many things that I never did hear of. She was a woman in the prime of life; of a severe countenance; and subject (particularly in the arms) to a sort of perpetual measles or fiery rash. She had a cousin in the Life Guards, with such long legs that he looked like the afternoon shadow of somebody else. His shell-jacket was as much too little for him as he was too big for the premises. He made the cottage smaller than it need have been, by being so very much out of proportion to it. Besides which, the walls were not thick, and whenever he passed the evening at our house, we always knew of it by hearing one continual growl in the kitchen.

Our treasure was warranted sober and honest. I am therefore willing to believe that she was in a fit when we found her under the boiler; and that the deficient tea-spoons were attributable to the dustman.

But she preyed upon our minds dreadfully. We felt our inexperience, and were unable to help ourselves. We should have been at her mercy, if she had had any; but she was a remorseless woman, and had none. She was the cause of our first little quarrel.

"My dearest life," I said one day to Dora, "do you think Mary Anne has any idea of time?"

"Why, Doady?" inquired Dora, looking up, innocently, from her drawing.

"My love, because it's five. and we were to have dined at four."

Dora glanced wistfully at the clock, and hinted that she thought it was too fast.

"On the contrary, my love," said I, referring to my watch, "it's a few minutes too slow."

My little wife came and sat upon my knee, to coax me to be quiet, and drew a line with her pencil down the middle of my nose; but I couldn't dine off that, though it was very agreeable.

"Don't you think, my dear," said I, "it would be better for you to remonstrate with Mary Anne?"

"Oh no, please! I couldn't, Doady!" said Dora.

"Why not, my love?" I gently asked.

"Oh, because I am such a little goose," said Dora, "and she knows I am!"

I thought this sentiment so incompatible with the establishment of any system of check on Mary Anne, that I frowned a little.

"Oh, what ugly wrinkles in my bad boy's forehead!" said Dora, and still being on my knee, she traced them with her pencil; putting it to her rosy lips to make it mark blacker, and working at my forehead with a quaint little mockery of being industrious, that quite delighted me in spite of myself.

"There's a good child," said Dora, "it makes its face so much prettier to laugh."

"But, my love," said I.

"No, no! please!" cried Dora, with a kiss, "don't be a naughty Blue Beard! Don't be serious!"

"My precious wife," said I, "we must be serious sometimes. Come! Sit down on this chair, close beside me! Give me the pencil! There! Now let us talk sensibly. You know, dear;" what a little hand it was to hold, and what a tiny wedding-ring it was to see! "You know, my love, it is not exactly comfortable to have to go out without one's dinner. Now, is it?"

"N—n—no!" replied Dora, faintly.

"My love, how you tremble!"

"Because I KNOW you're going to scold me," exclaimed Dora, in a piteous voice.

"My sweet, I am only going to reason."

"Oh, but reasoning is worse than scolding!" exclaimed Dora, in despair. "I didn't marry to be reasoned with. If you meant to reason with such a poor little thing as I am, you ought to have told me so, you cruel boy!"

I tried to pacify Dora, but she turned away her face, and shook her curls from side to side, and said, "You cruel, cruel boy!" so many times, that I really did not exactly know what to do: so I took a few turns up and down the room in my uncertainty, and came back again.

"Dora, my darling!"

"No, I am not your darling. Because you *must* be sorry that you married me, or else you wouldn't reason with me!" returned Dora.

I felt so injured by the inconsequential nature of this charge, that it gave me courage to be grave.

"Now, my own Dora," said I, "you are very childish, and are talking nonsense. You must remember, I am sure, that I was obliged to go out yesterday when dinner was half over; and that, the day before, I was made quite unwell by being obliged to eat underdone veal in a hurry; to-day, I don't dine at all—and I am afraid to say how long we waited for breakfast—and *then* the water didn't boil. I don't mean to reproach you, my dear, but this is not comfortable."

"Oh, you cruel, cruel boy, to say I am a disagreeable wife!" cried Dora.

"Now, my dear Dora, you must know that I never said that!"

"You said I wasn't comfortable!" cried Dora.

"I said the housekeeping was not comfortable!"

"It's exactly the same thing!" cried Dora. And she evidently thought so, for she wept most grievously.

I took another turn across the room, full of love for my pretty wife, and distracted by self-accusatory inclinations to knock my head against the door. I sat down again, and said:

"I am not blaming you, Dora. We have both a great deal to learn. I am only trying to show you, my dear, that you must—you really must" (I was resolved not to give this up) "accustom yourself to look after Mary Anne. Likewise to act a little for yourself, and me."

"I wonder, I do, at your making such ungrateful speeches," sobbed Dora. "When you know that the other day, when you said you would like a little bit of fish, I went out myself, miles and miles, and ordered it, to surprise you."

"And it was very kind of you, my own darling," said I. "I felt it so much that I wouldn't on any account have even mentioned that you bought a Salmon—which was too much for two. Or that it cost one pound six—which was more than we can afford."

"You enjoyed it very much," sobbed Dora. "And you said I was a Mouse."

"And I'll say so again, my love," I returned, "a thousand times!"

But I had wounded Dora's soft little heart, and she was not to be comforted. She was so pathetic in her sobbing and bewailing, that I felt as if I had said I don't know what to hurt her. I was obliged to hurry away; I was kept out late; and I felt all night such pangs of remorse as made me miserable. I had the conscience of an assassin, and was haunted by a vague sense of enormous wickedness.

It was two or three hours past midnight when I got home. I found my aunt, in our house, sitting up for me.

"Is anything the matter, aunt?" said I, alarmed.

"Nothing, Trot," she replied. "Sit down, sit down. Little Blossom has been rather out of spirits, and I have been keeping her company. That's all."

I leaned my head upon my hand; and felt more sorry and downcast, as I sat looking at the fire, than I could have supposed possible so soon after the fulfilment of my brightest hopes. As I sat thinking, I happened to meet my aunt's eyes, which were resting on my face. There was an anxious expression in them, but it cleared directly.

"I assure you, aunt," said I, "I have been quite unhappy myself all night, to think of Dora's being so. But I had no other intention than to speak to her tenderly and lovingly about our home-affairs."

My aunt nodded encouragement.

"You must have patience, Trot," said she.

"Of course. Heaven knows I don't mean to be unreasonable, aunt!"

"No, no," said my aunt, "But Little Blossom is a very tender little blossom, and the wind must be gentle with her."

I thanked my good aunt, in my heart, for her tenderness towards my wife; and I was sure that she knew I did.

"Don't you think, aunt," said I, after some further contemplation of the fire, "that you could advise and counsel Dora a little, for our mutual advantage, now, and then?"

"Trot," returned my aunt, with some emotion, "no! Don't ask me such a thing."

Her tone was so very earnest that I raised my eyes in surprise.

"I look back on my life, child," said my aunt, "and I think of some who are in their graves, with whom I might have been on kinder terms. If I judged harshly of other people's mistakes in marriage, it may have been because I had bitter reason to judge harshly of my own. Let that pass. I have been a grumpy, frumpy, wayward sort of a woman, a good many years. I am still, and I always shall be. But you and I have done one another some good, Trot—at all events, you have done me good, my dear; and division must not come between us, at this time of day."

"Division between *us*!" cried I.

"Child, child!" said my aunt, smoothing her dress, "how soon it might come between us, or how unhappy I might make our Little Blossom, if I meddled in anything, a prophet couldn't say. I want our pet to like me, and be as gay as a butterfly. Remember your own home, in that second marriage; and never do both me and her the injury you have hinted at!"

I comprehended, at once, that my aunt was right; and I comprehended the full extent of her generous feeling towards my dear wife.

"These are early days, Trot," she pursued, "and Rome was not built in a day, nor in a year. You have chosen freely for yourself;" a cloud passed over her face for a moment, I thought; "and you have chosen a very pretty and a very affectionate creature. It will be your duty, and it will be your pleasure too —of course I know that; I am not delivering a lecture—to estimate her (as you chose her) by the qualities she has, and not by the qualities she may not have. The latter you must develop in her, if you can. And if you cannot, child," here my aunt rubbed her nose, " you must just accustom yourself to do without'em. But remember, my dear, your future is between you two. No one can assist you; you are to work it out for yourselves. This is marriage, Trot; and Heaven bless you both in it, for a pair of babes in the wood as you are! "

My aunt said this in a sprightly way, and gave me a kiss to ratify the blessing.

" Now," said she, " light my little lantern, and see me into my bandbox by the garden path; " for there was a communication between our cottages in that direction. " Give Betsy Trotwood's love to Blossom, when you come back; and whatever you do, Trot, never dream of setting Betsey up as a scarecrow, for if *I* ever saw her in the glass, she's quite grim enough and gaunt enough in her private capacity! "

With this my aunt tied her head up in a handkerchief, with which she was accustomed to make a bundle of it on such occasions; and I escorted her home. As she stood in her garden, holding up her little lantern to light me back, I thought her observation of me had an anxious air again; but I was too much occupied in pondering on what she had said, and too much impressed—for the first time, in reality—by the conviction that Dora and I had indeed to work out our future for ourselves, and that no one could assist us, to take much notice of it.

Dora came stealing down in her little slippers, to meet me, now that I was alone; and cried upon my shoulder, and said I had been hard-hearted and she had been naughty; and I said much the same thing in effect, I believe; and we made it up, and agreed that our first little difference was to be our last, and that we were never to have another if we lived a hundred years.

The next domestic trial we went through, was the Ordeal of Servants. Mary Anne's cousin deserted into our coal-hole, and was brought out, to our great amazement, by a piquet of his companions in arms, who took him away handcuffed in a procession that covered our front-garden with ignominy. This nerved me to get rid of Mary Anne, who went so mildly, on receipt of wages, that I was surprised, until I found out about the teaspoons, and also about the little sums she had borrowed in my name of the tradespeople without authority. After an interval of Mrs. Kidgerbury—the oldest inhabitant of Kentish Town, I believe, who went out charing, but was too feeble to execute her conceptions of that art—we found another treasure, who was one of the most amiable of women, but who generally made a point of falling either up or down the kitchen stairs with the tray, and almost plunged into the parlour, as into a bath, with the tea-things. The ravages committed by this unfortunate rendering her dismissal necessary, she was succeeded (with intervals of Mrs. Kidgerbury) by a long line of Incapables; terminating in a young person of genteel appearance, who went to Greenwich Fair in Dora's bonnet. After whom I remember nothing but an average equality of failure.

Everybody we had anything to do with seemed to cheat us. Our appearance in a shop was a signal for the damaged goods to be brought out immediately. If we bought a lobster, it was full of water. All our meat turned out to be tough, and there was hardly any crust to our loaves. In search of the principle on which joints ought to be roasted, to be roasted enough, and not too much, I myself referred to the Cookery Book, and found it there established as the allowance of a quarter of an hour to every pound, and say a quarter over. But the principle always failed us by some curious fatality, and we never could hit any medium between redness and cinders.

I had reason to believe that in accomplishing these failures we incurred a far greater expense than if we had achieved a series of triumphs. It appeared to me, on looking over the tradesmen's books, as if we might have kept the basement storey paved with butter, such was the extensive scale of our consumption of that article. I don't know whether the Excise returns of the period may have exhibited any increase in the demand for pepper; but if our performances did not affect the market, I should say several families must have left off using it. And the most wonderful fact of all was, that we never had anything in the house.

As to the washerwoman pawning the clothes, and coming in a state of penitent intoxication to apologise, I suppose that might have happened several times to anybody. Also the chimney on fire, the parish engine, and perjury on the part of the Beadle. But I apprehend that we were personally fortunate in engaging a servant with a taste for cordials, who swelled our running account for porter at the public-house by such inexplicable items as "Quartern rum shrub (Mrs. C.);" "Half-quartern gin and cloves (Mrs. C.);" "Glass rum and peppermint (Mrs. C.)"—the parentheses always referring to Dora, who was supposed, it appeared on explanation, to have imbibed the whole of these refreshments.

One of our first feats in the housekeeping way was a little dinner to Traddles. I met him in town, and asked him to walk out with me that afternoon. He readily consenting, I wrote to Dora, saying I would bring him home. It was pleasant weather, and on the road we made my domestic happiness the theme of conversation. Traddles was very full of it; and said, that, picturing himself with such a home, and Sophy waiting and preparing for him, he could think of nothing wanting to complete his bliss.

I could not have wished for a prettier little wife at the opposite end of the table, but I certainly could have wished, when we sat down, for a little more room. I did not know how it was, but though there were only two of us, we were at once always cramped for room, and yet had always room enough to lose everything in. I suspect it may have been because nothing had a place of its own, except Jip's pagoda, which invariably blocked up the main thoroughfare. On the present occasion, Traddles was so hemmed in by the pagoda and the guitar-case, and Dora's flower-painting, and my writing-table, that I had serious doubts of the possibility of his using his knife and fork; but he protested, with his own good-humour. " Oceans of room, Copperfield! I assure you. Oceans! "

There was another thing I could have wished; namely, that Jip had never been encouraged to walk about the table-cloth during dinner. I began to think there was something disorderly in his being there at all, even if he had not been in the habit of putting his foot in the salt or the melted-butter. On this occasion he seemed to think he was introduced expressly to keep Traddles at bay; and he barked at my old friend, and made short runs at his plate, with such undaunted pertinacity, that he may be said to have engrossed the conversation.

However, as I knew how tender-hearted my dear Dora was, and how sensitive she would be to any slight upon her favourite, I hinted no objection. For similar reasons I made no allusion to the skirmishing plates upon the floor; or to the disreputable appearance of the casters, which were all at sixes and sevens, and looked drunk; or to the further blockade of Traddles by wandering vegetable dishes and jugs. I could not help wondering in my own mind, as I contemplated the boiled leg of mutton before me, previous to carving it, how it came to pass that our joints of meat were of such extraordinary shapes—and whether our butcher contracted for all the deformed sheep that came into the world; but I kept my reflections to myself.

" My love," said I to Dora, " what have you got in that dish? "

I could not imagine why Dora had been making tempting little faces at me, as if she wanted to kiss me.

" Oysters, dear," said Dora, timidly.

" Was that *your* thought? " said I, delighted.

" Ye-yes, Doady," said Dora.

"There never was a happier one!" I exclaimed, laying down the carving-knife and fork. "There is nothing Traddles likes so much!"

"Ye-yes, Doady," said Dora, "and so I bought a beautiful little barrel of them, and the man said they were very good. But I—I am afraid there's something the matter with them. They don't seem right." Here Dora shook her head, and diamonds twinkled in her eyes.

"They are only opened in both shells," said I. "Take the top one off, my love."

"But it won't come off," said Dora, trying very hard, and looking very much distressed.

"Do you know, Copperfield," said Traddles, cheerfully examining the dish, "I think it is in consequence—they are capital oysters, but I *think* it is in consequence—of their never having been opened."

They never had been opened; and we had no oyster-knives—and couldn't have used them if we had; so we looked at the oysters and ate the mutton. At least we ate as much of it as was done, and made up with capers. If I had permitted him, I am satisfied that Traddles would have made a perfect savage of himself, and eaten a plateful of raw meat, to express enjoyment of the repast; but I would hear of no such immolation on the altar of friendship; and we had a course of bacon instead; there happening, by good fortune, to be cold bacon in the larder.

My poor little wife was in such affliction when she thought I should be annoyed, and in such a state of joy when she found I was not, that the discomfiture I had subdued very soon vanished, and we passed a happy evening; Dora sitting with her arm on my chair while Traddles and I discussed a glass of wine, and taking every opportunity of whispering in my ear that it was so good of me not to be a cruel, cross old boy. By-and-by she made tea for us; which it was so pretty to see her do, as if she was busying herself with a set of doll's tea-things, that I was not particular about the quality of the beverage. Then Traddles and I played a game or two at cribbage; and Dora singing to the guitar the while, it seemed to me as if our courtship and marriage were a tender dream of mine, and the night when I first listened to her voice were not yet over.

When Traddles went away, and I came back into the parlour from seeing him out, my wife planted her chair close to mine, and sat down by my side.

"I am very sorry," she said. "Will you try to teach me, Doady?"

"I must teach myself first, Dora," said I. "I am as bad as you, love."

"Ah! But you can learn," she returned: "and you are a clever, clever man!"

"Nonsense, mouse!" said I.

"I wish," resumed my wife, after a long silence, "that I could have gone down into the country for a whole year, and lived with Agnes!"

Her hands were clasped upon my shoulder, and her chin rested on them, and her blue eyes looked quietly into mine.

"Why so?" I asked.

"I think she might have improved me, and I think I might have learned from *her*," said Dora.

"All in good time, my love. Agnes has had her father to take care of for these many years, you should remember. Even when she was quite a child, she was the Agnes whom we know," said I.

"Will you call me a name I want you to call me?" inquired Dora, without moving.

"What is it?" I asked with a smile.

"It's a stupid name," she said, shaking her curls for a moment. "Child-wife."

I laughingly asked my child-wife what her fancy was in desiring to be so called. She answered without moving, otherwise than as the arm I twined about her may have brought her blue eyes nearer to me:

"I don't mean, you silly fellow, that you should use the name instead of Dora. I only mean that you should think of me that way. When you are going to be angry with me, say to yourself, 'it's only my child-wife!' When I am very disappointing, say, 'I knew, a long time ago, that she would make but a child-wife!' When you miss what I should like to be, and I think can never be, say, 'still my foolish child-wife loves me!' For indeed I do."

I had not been serious with her; having no idea, until now, that she was serious herself. But her affectionate nature was so happy in what I now said to her with my whole heart, that her face became a laughing one before her glittering eyes were dry. She was soon my child-wife indeed; sitting down on the floor outside the Chinese House, ringing all the little bells one after another, to punish Jip for his recent bad behaviour; while Jip lay blinking in the doorway with his head out, even too lazy to be teased.

This appeal of Dora's made a strong impression on me. I

look back on the time I write of; I invoke the innocent figure that I dearly loved, to come out from the mists and shadows of the past, and turn its gentle head towards me once again; And I can still declare that this one little speech was constantly in my memory. I may not have used it to the best account; I was young and inexperienced; but I never turned a deaf ear to its artless pleading.

Dora told me, shortly afterwards, that she was going to be a wonderful housekeeper. Accordingly, she polished the tablets, pointed the pencil, bought an immense account-book, carefully stitched up with a needle and thread all the leaves of the Cookery Book which Jip had torn, and made quite a desperate little attempt "to be good," as she called it. But the figures had the old obstinate propensity—they *would not* add up. When she had entered two or three laborious items in the account-book, Jip would walk over the page, wagging his tail, and smear them all out. Her own little right-hand middle finger got steeped to the very bone in ink; and I think that was the only decided result obtained.

Sometimes, of an evening, when I was at home and at work —for I wrote a good deal now, and was beginning in a small way to be known as a writer—I would lay down my pen, and watch my child-wife trying to be good. First of all, she would bring out the immense account-book, and lay it down upon the table, with a deep sigh. Then she would open it at the place where Jip had made it illegible last night, and call Jip up to look at his misdeeds. This would occasion a diversion in Jip's favour, and some inking of his nose, perhaps, as a penalty. Then she would tell Jip to lie down on the table instantly, "like a lion"—which was one of his tricks, though I cannot say the likeness was striking—and, if he were in an obedient humour, he would obey. Then she would take up a pen, and begin to write, and find a hair in it. Then she would take up another pen, and begin to write, and find that it spluttered. Then she would take up another pen, and begin to write, and say in a low voice, "Oh, it's a talking pen, and will disturb Doady!" And then she would give it up as a bad job, and put the account-book away, after pretending to crush the lion with it.

Or, if she were in a very sedate and serious state of mind, she would sit down with the tablets, and a little basket of bills and other documents, which looked more like curl-papers than anything else, and endeavour to get some result out of them. After severely comparing one with another, and making entries on the tablets, and blotting them out, and counting all the fingers of her left hand over and over again, backwards and forwards, she would be so vexed and discouraged, and would look so unhappy, that it gave me pain to see her bright face clouded—and for me!—and I would go softly to her, and say:

"What's the matter, Dora?"

Dora would look up hopelessly, and reply, "They won't come right. They make my head ache so. And they won't do anything I want!"

Then I would say, "Now let us try together. Let me show you, Dora."

Then I would commence a practical demonstration, to which Dora would pay profound attention, perhaps for five minutes; when she would begin to be dreadfully tired, and would lighten the subject by curling my hair, or trying the effect of my face with my shirt-collar turned down. If I tacitly checked this playfulness, and persisted, she would look so scared and disconsolate, as she became more and more bewildered, that the remembrance of her natural gaiety when I first strayed into her path, and of her being my child-wife, would come reproachfully upon me; and I would lay the pencil down, and call for the guitar.

I had a great deal of work to do, and had many anxieties, but the same considerations made me keep them to myself. I am far from sure, now, that it was right to do this, but I did it for my child-wife's sake. I search my breast, and I commit its secrets, if I know them, without any reservation to this paper. The old unhappy loss or want of something had, I am conscious, some place in my heart; but not to the embitterment of my life. When I walked alone in the fine weather, and thought of the summer days when all the air had been filled with my boyish enchantment, I did miss something of the realisation of my dreams; but I thought it was a softened glory of the Past, which nothing could have thrown upon the present time. I did feel, sometimes, for a little while, that I could have wished my wife had been my counsellor; had had more character and purpose, to sustain me, and improve me by; had been endowed with power to fill up the void which somewhere seemed to be about me; but I felt as if this were an unearthly consummation of my happiness, that never had been meant to be, and never could have been.

I was a boyish husband as to years. I had known the softening influence of no other sorrows or experiences than those recorded in these leaves. If I did any wrong, as I may have done much, I did it in mistaken love, and in my want of wisdom. I write the exact truth. It would avail me nothing to extenuate it now.

Thus it was that I took upon myself the toils and cares of our life, and had no partner in them. We lived much as before, in reference to our scrambling household arrangements; but I had got used to those, and Dora I was pleased to see was seldom vexed now. She was bright and cheerful in the old childish way, loved me dearly, and was happy with her old trifles.

When the debates were heavy—I mean as to length, not quality, for in the last respect they were not often otherwise—and I went home late, Dora would never rest when she heard my footsteps, but would always come down-stairs to meet me. When my evenings were unoccupied by the pursuit for which I had qualified myself with so much pains, and I was engaged in writing at home, she would sit quietly near me, however late the hour, and be so mute, that I would often think she had dropped asleep. But generally, when I raised my head, I saw her blue eyes looking at me with the quiet attention of which I have already spoken.

"Oh, what a weary boy!" said Dora one night, when I met her eyes as I was shutting up my desk.

"What a weary girl!" said I. "That's more to the purpose. You must go to bed another time, my love. It's far too late for you."

"No, don't send me to bed!" pleaded Dora, coming to my side. "Pray, don't do that!"

"Dora!"

To my amazement she was sobbing on my neck.

"Not well, my dear! not happy!"

"Yes! quite well, and very happy!" said Dora. "But say you'll let me stop, and see you write."

"Why, what a sight for such bright eyes at midnight!" I replied.

"Are they bright, though?" returned Dora, laughing. "I'm so glad they're bright."

"Little Vanity!" said I.

But it was not vanity; it was only harmless delight in my admiration. I knew that very well, before she told me so.

"If you think them pretty, say I may always stop, and see you write!" said Dora. "*Do* you think them pretty?"

"Very pretty."

"Then let me always stop and see you write."

"I am afraid that won't improve their brightness, Dora."

"Yes, it will! Because, you clever boy, you'll not forget me then, while you are full of silent fancies. Will you mind it, if I say something very, very silly?—more than usual?" inquired Dora, peeping over my shoulder into my face.

"What wonderful thing is that?" said I.

"Please let me hold the pens," said Dora. "I want to have something to do with all those many hours when you are so industrious. May I hold the pens?"

The remembrance of her pretty joy when I said Yes, brings tears into my eyes. The next time I sat down to write, and regularly afterwards, she sat in her old place, with a spare bundle of pens at her side. Her triumph in this connection with my work, and her delight when I wanted a new pen—which I very often feigned to do—suggested to me a new way of pleasing my child-wife. I occasionally made a pretence of wanting a page or two of manuscript copied. Then Dora was in her glory. The preparations she made for this great work, the aprons she put on, the bibs she borrowed from the kitchen to keep off the ink, the time she took, the innumerable stoppages she made to have a laugh with Jip as if he understood it all, her conviction that her work was incomplete unless she signed her name at the end, and the way in which she would bring it to me, like a school-copy, and then, when I praised it, clasp me round the neck, are touching recollections to me, simple as they might appear to other men.

She took possession of the keys soon after this, and went jingling about the house with the whole bunch in a little basket, tied to her slender waist. I seldom found that the places to which they belonged were locked, or that they were of any use except as a plaything for Jip—but Dora was pleased, and that pleased me. She was quite satisfied that a good deal was effected by this make-belief of housekeeping; and was as merry as if we had been keeping a baby-house, for a joke.

So we went on. Dora was hardly less affectionate to my aunt than to me, and often told her of the time when she was afraid she was "a cross old thing." I never saw my aunt unbend more systematically to any one. She courted Jip, though Jip never responded; listened, day after day, to the guitar, though I am afraid she had no taste for music; never attacked the Incapables, though the temptation must have been severe; went wonderful distances on foot to purchase, as surprises, any trifles that she found out Dora wanted; and never came in by the garden, and missed her from the room, but she would call out, at the foot of the stairs, in a voice that sounded cheerfully all over the house:

"Where's Little Blossom?"

45

MR. DICK FULFILS MY AUNT'S PREDICTIONS

IT WAS SOME TIME NOW, SINCE I HAD LEFT THE DOCTOR. Living in his neighbourhood, I saw him frequently; and we all went to his house on two or three occasions to dinner or tea. The Old Soldier was in permanent quarters under the Doctor's roof. She was exactly the same as ever, and the same immortal butterflies hovered over her cap.

Like some other mothers, whom I have known in the course of my life, Mrs. Markleham was far more fond of pleasure than her daughter was. She required a great deal of amusement, and, like a deep old soldier, pretended, in consulting her own inclinations, to be devoting herself to her child. The Doctor's desire that Annie should be entertained, was therefore particularly acceptable to this excellent parent; who expressed unqualified approval of his discretion.

I have no doubt, indeed, that she probed the Doctor's wound without knowing it. Meaning nothing but a certain matured frivolity and selfishness, not always inseparable from full-blown years, I think she confirmed him in his fear that he was a constraint upon his young wife, and that there was no congeniality of feeling between them, by so strongly commending his design of lightening the load of her life.

" My dear soul," she said to him one day when I was present, " you know there is no doubt it would be a little pokey for Annie to be always shut up here."

The Doctor nodded his benevolent head.

" When she comes to her mother's age," said Mrs. Markleham, with a flourish of her fan, " then it'll be another thing. You might put ME into a Jail, with genteel society and a rubber, and I should never care to come out. But I am not Annie, you know; and Annie is not her mother."

" Surely, surely," said the Doctor.

" You are the best of creatures—no, I beg your pardon! " for the Doctor made a gesture of deprecation, " I must say before your face, as I always say behind your back, you are the best of creatures; but of course you don't—now do you?—enter into the same pursuits and fancies as Annie."

"No," said the Doctor, in a sorrowful tone.

"No, of course not," retorted the Old Soldier. "Take your Dictionary, for example. What a useful work a Dictionary is! What a necessary work! The meanings of words! Without Doctor Johnson, or somebody of that sort, we might have been at this present moment calling an Italian-iron a bedstead. But we can't expect a Dictionary—especially when it's making—to interest Annie, can we?"

The Doctor shook his head.

"And that's why I *so* much approve," said Mrs. Markleham, tapping him on the shoulder with her shut-up fan, "of your thoughtfulness. It shows that you don't expect, as many elderly people do expect, old heads on young shoulders. You have studied Annie's character, and you understand it. *That's* what I find so charming!"

Even the calm and patient face of Doctor Strong expressed some little sense of pain, I thought, under the infliction of these compliments.

"Therefore, my dear Doctor," said the Soldier, giving him several affectionate taps, "you may command me, at all times and seasons. Now, do understand that I am entirely at your service. I am ready to go with Annie to operas, concerts, exhibitions, all kinds of places; and you shall never find that I am tired. Duty, my dear Doctor, before every consideration in the universe!"

She was as good as her word. She was one of those people who can bear a great deal of pleasure, and she never flinched in her perseverance in the cause. She seldom got hold of the newspaper (which she settled herself down in the softest chair in the house to read through an eye-glass, every day, for two hours), but she found out something that she was certain Annie would like to see. It was in vain for Annie to protest that she was weary of such things. Her mother's remonstrance always was, "Now, my dear Annie, I am sure you know better; and I must tell you, my love, that you are not making a proper return for the kindness of Doctor Strong."

This was usually said in the Doctor's presence, and appeared to me to constitute Annie's principal inducement for withdrawing her objections when she made any. But in general she resigned herself to her mother, and went where the Old Soldier would.

It rarely happened now that Mr. Maldon accompanied them.

Sometimes my aunt and Dora were invited to do so, and accepted the invitation. Sometimes Dora only was asked. The time had been when I should have been uneasy in her going; but reflection on what had passed that former night in the Doctor's study, had made a change in my mistrust. I believed that the Doctor was right, and I had no worse suspicions.

My aunt rubbed her nose sometimes when she happened to be alone with me, and said she couldn't make it out; she wished they were happier; she didn't think our military friend (so she always called the Old Soldier) mended the matter at all. My aunt further expressed her opinion, " that if our military friend would cut off those butterflies, and give 'em to the chimney-sweepers for May-day, it would look like the beginning of something sensible on her part."

But her abiding reliance was on Mr. Dick. That man had evidently an idea in his head, she said; and if he could only once pen it up into a corner, which was his great difficulty, he would distinguish himself in some extraordinary manner.

Unconscious of this prediction, Mr. Dick continued to occupy precisely the same ground in reference to the Doctor and to Mrs. Strong. He seemed neither to advance nor to recede. He appeared to have settled into his original foundation, like a building; and I must confess that my faith in his ever moving, was not much greater than if he had been a building.

But one night, when I had been married some months, Mr. Dick put his head into the parlour, where I was writing alone (Dora having gone out with my aunt to take tea with the two little birds), and said, with a significant cough:

" You couldn't speak to me without inconveniencing yourself, Trotwood, I am afraid?"

" Certainly, Mr. Dick," said I; " come in!"

" Trotwood," said Mr. Dick, laying his finger on the side of his nose, after he had shaken hands with me. " Before I sit down, I wish to make an observation. You know your aunt?"

" A little," I replied.

" She is the most wonderful woman in the world, sir!"

After the delivery of this communication, which he shot out of himself as if he were loaded with it, Mr. Dick sat down with greater gravity than usual, and looked at me.

" Now, boy," said Mr. Dick, " I am going to put a question to you."

" As many as you please," said I.

" What do you consider me, sir?" asked Mr. Dick, folding his arms.

"A dear old friend," said I.

"Thank you, Trotwood," returned Mr. Dick, laughing, and reaching across in high glee to shake hands with me. "But I mean, boy," resuming his gravity, "what do you consider me in this respect?" touching his forehead.

I was puzzled how to answer, but he helped me with a word.

"Weak?" said Mr. Dick.

"Well," I replied, dubiously. "Rather so."

"Exactly!" cried Mr. Dick, who seemed quite enchanted by my reply. "That is, Trotwood, when they took some of the trouble out of you-know-who's head, and put it you know where, there was a——" Mr. Dick made his two hands revolve very fast about each other a great number of times, and then brought them into collision, and rolled them over and over one another, to express confusion. "There was that sort of thing done to me somehow. Eh?"

I nodded at him, and he nodded back again.

"In short, boy," said Mr. Dick, dropping his voice to a whisper, "I am simple."

I would have qualified that conclusion, but he stopped me.

"Yes, I am! She pretends I am not. She won't hear of it; but I am. I know I am. If she hadn't stood my friend, sir, I should have been shut up, to lead a dismal life these many years. But I'll provide for her! I never spend the copying money. I put it in a box. I have made a will. I'll leave it all to her. She shall be rich—noble!"

Mr. Dick took out his pocket-handkerchief and wiped his eyes. He then folded it up with great care, pressed it smooth between his two hands, put it in his pocket, and seemed to put my aunt away with it.

"Now you are a scholar, Trotwood," said Mr. Dick. "You are a fine scholar. You know what a learned man, what a great man, the Doctor is. You know what honour he has always done me. Not proud in his wisdom. Humble, humble—condescending even to poor Dick, who is simple and knows nothing. I have sent his name up, on a scrap of paper, to the kite, along the string, when it has been in the sky, among the larks. The kite has been glad to receive it, sir, and the sky has been brighter with it."

I delighted him by saying, most heartily, that the Doctor was deserving of our best respect and highest esteem.

"And his beautiful wife is a star," said Mr. Dick. "A shining star. I have seen her shine, sir. But," bringing his chair nearer, and laying one hand upon my knee—"clouds, sir—clouds."

I answered the solicitude which his face expressed, by conveying the same expression into my own, and shaking my head.

"What clouds?" said Mr. Dick.

He looked so wistfully into my face, and was so anxious to understand, that I took great pains to answer him slowly and distinctly, as I might have entered on an explanation to a child.

"There is some unfortunate division between them," I replied. "Some unhappy cause of separation. A secret. It may be inseparable from the discrepancy in their years. It may have grown up out of almost nothing."

Mr. Dick, who told off every sentence with a thoughtful nod, paused when I had done, and sat considering, with his eyes upon my face, and his hand upon my knee.

"Doctor not angry with her, Trotwood?" he said, after some time.

"No. Devoted to her."

"Then, I have got it, boy!" said Mr. Dick.

The sudden exultation with which he slapped me on the knee, and leaned back in his chair, with his eyebrows lifted up as high as he could possibly lift them, made me think him farther out of his wits than ever. He became as suddenly grave again, and leaning forward as before, said—first respectfully taking out his pocket-handkerchief, as if it really did represent my aunt:

"Most wonderful woman in the world, Trotwood. Why has *she* done nothing to set things right?"

"Too delicate and difficult a subject for such interference," I replied.

"Fine scholar," said Mr. Dick, touching me with his finger. "Why has *he* done nothing?"

"For the same reason," I returned.

"Then I have got it, boy!" said Mr. Dick. And he stood up before me, more exultingly than before, nodding his head, and striking himself repeatedly upon the breast, until one might have supposed that he had nearly nodded and struck all the breath out of his body.

"A poor fellow with a craze, sir," said Mr. Dick, "a simpleton, a weak-minded person—present company, you know!" striking himself again, "may do what wonderful people may not do. I'll bring them together, boy. I'll try. They'll not blame *me*. They'll not object to *me*. They'll not mind what *I* do, if it's wrong. I'm only Mr. Dick. And who minds Dick? Dick's nobody! Whoo!" He blew a slight, contemptuous breath, as if he blew himself away.

It was fortunate he had proceeded so far with his mystery,

for we heard the coach stop at the little garden gate, which brought my aunt and Dora home.

"Not a word, boy!" he pursued in a whisper; "leave all the blame with Dick—simple Dick—mad Dick. I have been thinking, sir, for some time, that I was getting it, and now I have got it. After what you have said to me, I am sure I have got it. All right!"

Not another word did Mr. Dick utter on the subject; but he made a very telegraph of himself for the next half-hour (to the great disturbance of my aunt's mind), to enjoin inviolable secrecy on me.

To my surprise, I heard no more about it for some two or three weeks, though I was sufficiently interested in the result of his endeavours; descrying a strange gleam of good sense—I say nothing of good feeling, for that he always exhibited—in the conclusion to which he had come. At last I began to believe, that, in the flighty and unsettled state of his mind, he had either forgotten his intention or abandoned it.

One fair evening, when Dora was not inclined to go out, my aunt and I strolled up to the Doctor's cottage. It was autumn, when there were no debates to vex the evening air; and I remember how the leaves smelt like our garden at Blunderstone as we trod them under foot, and how the old, unhappy feeling seemed to go by, on the sighing wind.

It was twilight when we reached the cottage. Mrs. Strong was just coming out of the garden, where Mr. Dick yet lingered. busy with his knife, helping the gardener to point some stakes. The Doctor was engaged with some one in his study; but the visitor would be gone directly, Mrs. Strong said, and begged us to remain and see him. We went into the drawing-room with her, and sat down by the darkening window. There was never any ceremony about the visits of such old friends and neighbours as we were.

We had not sat here many minutes, when Mrs. Markleham, who usually contrived to be in a fuss about something, came bustling in, with her newspaper in her hand, and said, out of breath, "My goodness gracious, Annie, why didn't you tell me there was some one in the Study!"

"My dear mama," she quietly returned, "how could I know that you desired the information?"

"Desired the information!" said Mrs. Markleham, sinking on the sofa. "I never had such a turn in all my life!"

"Have you been to the Study, then, mama?" asked Annie.

"*Been* to the Study, my dear!" she returned emphatically.

"Indeed I have! I came upon the amiable creature—if you'll imagine my feelings, Miss Trotwood and David—in the act of making his will."

Her daughter looked round from the window quickly.

"In the act, my dear Annie," repeated Mrs. Markleham, spreading the newspaper on her lap like a table-cloth, and patting her hands upon it, "of making his last Will and Testament. The foresight and affection of the dear! I must tell you how it was. I really must, in justice to the darling—for he is nothing less! —tell you how it was. Perhaps you know, Miss Trotwood, that there is never a candle lighted in this house, until one's eyes are literally falling out of one's head with being stretched to read the paper. And that there is not a chair in this house, in which a paper can be what *I* call, read, except one in the Study. This took me to the Study, where I saw a light. I opened the door. In company with the dear Doctor were two professional people, evidently connected with the law, and they were all three standing at the table: the darling Doctor pen in hand. 'This simply expresses then' said the Doctor—Annie, my love, attend to the very words—'this simply expresses then, gentlemen, the confidence I have in Mrs. Strong, and gives her all unconditionally?' One of the professional people replied. 'And gives her all unconditionally.' Upon that, with the natural feelings of a mother, I said, 'Good God, I beg your pardon!' fell over the door-step, and came away through the little back passage where the pantry is."

Mrs. Strong opened the window, and went out into the verandah, where she stood leaning against a pillar.

"But now isn't it, Miss Trotwood, isn't it, David, invigorating," said Mrs. Markleham, mechanically following her with her eyes, "to find a man at Doctor Strong's time of life, with the strength of mind to do this kind of thing? It only shows how right I was. I said to Annie, when Doctor Strong paid a very flattering visit to myself, and made her the subject of a declaration and an offer, I said, 'My dear, there is no doubt whatever, in my opinion, with reference to a suitable provision for you, that Doctor Strong will do more than he binds himself to do.'"

Here the bell rang, and we heard the sound of the visitors' feet as they went out.

"It's all over, no doubt," said the Old Soldier, after listening; "the dear creature has signed, sealed, and delivered, and his mind's at rest. Well it may be! What a mind! Annie, my love, I am going to the Study with my paper, for I am a poor creature without news. Miss Trotwood, David, pray come and see the Doctor."

I was conscious of Mr. Dick's standing in the shadow of the room, shutting up his knife, when we accompanied her to the Study; and of my aunt's rubbing her nose violently, by the way, as a mild vent for her intolerance of our military friend; but who got first into the Study, or how Mrs. Markleham settled herself in a moment in her easy chair, or how my aunt and I came to be left together near the door (unless her eyes were quicker than mine, and she held me back), I have forgotten if I ever knew. But this I know,—that we saw the Doctor before he saw us, sitting at his table, among the folio volumes in which he delighted, resting his head calmly on his hand. That, in the same moment, we saw Mrs. Strong glide in, pale and trembling. That Mr. Dick supported her on his arm. That he laid his other hand upon the Doctor's arm, causing him to look up with an abstracted air. That, as the Doctor moved his head, his wife dropped down on one knee at his feet, and, with her hands imploringly lifted, fixed upon his face the memorable look I had never forgotten. That at this sight Mrs. Markleham dropped the newspaper, and stared more like a figure-head intended for a ship to be called The Astonishment, than anything else I can think of.

The gentleness of the Doctor's manner and surprise, the dignity that mingled with the supplicating attitude of his wife, the amiable concern of Mr. Dick, and the earnestness with which my aunt said to herself, "*That* man mad!" (triumphantly expressive of the misery from which she had saved him)—I see and hear, rather than remember, as I write about it.

"Doctor!" said Mr. Dick. "What is it that's amiss? Look here!"

"Annie!" cried the Doctor. "Not at my feet, my dear!"

"Yes!" she said. "I beg and pray that no one will leave the room! Oh, my husband and father, break this long silence. Let us both know what it is that has come between us!"

Mrs. Markleham, by this time recovering the power of speech, and seeming to swell with family pride and motherly indignation, here exclaimed, "Annie, get up immediately, and don't disgrace everybody belonging to you by humbling yourself like that, unless you wish to see me go out of my mind on the spot!"

"Mama!" returned Annie. "Waste no words on me, for my appeal is to my husband, and even you are nothing here."

"Nothing!" exclaimed Mrs. Markleham. "Me, nothing! The child has taken leave of her senses. Please to get me a glass of water!"

I was too attentive to the Doctor and his wife, to give any heed to this request; and it made no impression on anybody else; so Mrs. Markleham panted, stared, and fanned herself.

"Annie!" said the Doctor, tenderly taking her in his hands. "My dear! If any unavoidable change has come, in the sequence of time, upon our married life, you are not to blame. The fault is mine, and only mine. There is no change in my affection, admiration, and respect. I wish to make you happy. I truly love and honour you. Rise, Annie, pray!"

But she did not rise. After looking at him for a little while, she sank down closer to him, laid her arm across his knee, and dropping her head upon it, said:

"If I have any friend here, who can speak one word for me, or for my husband in this matter; if I have any friend here, who can give a voice to any suspicion that my heart has sometimes whispered to me; if I have any friend here, who honours my husband, or has ever cared for me, and has anything within his knowledge, no matter what it is, that may help to mediate between us,—I implore that friend to speak!"

There was a profound silence. After a few moments of painful hesitation, I broke the silence.

"Mrs. Strong," I said, "there is something within my knowledge, which I have been earnestly entreated by Doctor Strong to conceal, and have concealed until to-night. But I believe the time has come when it would be mistaken faith and delicacy to conceal it any longer, and when your appeal absolves me from his injunction."

She turned her face towards me for a moment, and I knew that I was right. I could not have resisted its entreaty, if the assurance that it gave me had been less convincing.

"Our future peace," she said, "may be in your hands. I trust it confidently to your not suppressing anything. I know beforehand that nothing you, or any one, can tell me, will show my husband's noble heart in any other light than one. Howsoever it may seem to you to touch me, disregard that. I will speak for myself, before him, and before God afterwards."

Thus earnestly besought, I made no reference to the Doctor for his permission, but, without any other compromise of the truth than a little softening of the coarseness of Uriah Heep, related plainly what had passed in that same room that night. The staring of Mrs. Markleham during the whole narration, and the shrill, sharp interjections with which she occasionally interrupted it, defy description.

When I had finished, Annie remained, for some few moments,

silent, with her head bent down as I have described. Then, she took the Doctor's hand (he was sitting in the same attitude as when we had entered the room), and pressed it to her breast, and kissed it. Mr. Dick softly raised her; and she stood, when she began to speak, leaning on him, and looking down upon her husband—from whom she never turned her eyes.

"All that has ever been in my mind, since I was married," she said in a low, submissive, tender voice, "I will lay bare before you. I could not live and have one reservation, knowing what I know now."

"Nay, Annie," said the Doctor, mildly, "I have never doubted you, my child. There is no need; indeed there is no need, my dear."

"There is great need," she answered, in the same way, "that I should open my whole heart before the soul of generosity and truth, whom, year by year, and day by day, I have loved and venerated more and more, as Heaven knows!"

"Really," interrupted Mrs. Markleham, "if I have any discretion at all—"

("Which you haven't, you Marplot," observed my aunt, in an indignant whisper.)

"—I must be permitted to observe that it cannot be requisite to enter into these details."

"No one but my husband can judge of that, mama," said Annie without removing her eyes from his face, "and he will hear me. If I say anything to give you pain, mama, forgive me. I have borne pain first, often and long, myself."

"Upon my word!" gasped Mrs. Markleham.

"When I was very young," said Annie, "quite a little child, my first associations with knowledge of any kind were inseparable from a patient friend and teacher—the friend of my dead father—who was always dear to me. I can remember nothing that I know, without remembering him. He stored my mind with its first treasures, and stamped his character upon them all. They never could have been, I think, as good as they have been to me, if I had taken them from any other hands."

"Makes her mother nothing!" exclaimed Mrs. Markleham.

"Not so mama," said Annie; "but I make him what he was. I must do that. As I grew up, he occupied the same place still. I was proud of his interest: deeply, fondly, gratefully attached to him. I looked up to him, I can hardly describe how—as a father, as a guide, as one whose praise was different from all other praise, as one in whom I could have trusted and confided, if I had doubted all the world. You know, mama, how young and inexperienced I was, when you presented him before me, of a sudden, as a lover."

"I have mentioned the fact, fifty times at least, to everybody here!" said Mrs. Markleham.

("Then hold your tongue, for the Lord's sake, and don't mention it any more!" muttered my aunt.)

"It was so great a change: so great a loss, I felt it at first," said Annie, still preserving the same look and tone, "that I was agitated and distressed. I was but a girl; and when so great a change came in the character in which I had so long looked up to him, I think I was sorry. But nothing could have made him what he used to be again; and I was proud that he should think me so worthy, and we were married."

"—At Saint Alphage, Canterbury," observed Mrs. Markleham.

("Confound the woman!" said my aunt, "she *won't* be quiet!")

"I never thought," proceeded Annie, with a heightened colour, "of any worldly gain that my husband would bring to me. My young heart had no room in its homage for any such poor reference. Mama, forgive me when I say that it was *you* who first presented to my mind the thought that any one could wrong me, and wrong him, by such a cruel suspicion."

"Me!" cried Mrs. Markleham.

("Ah! You, to be sure!" observed my aunt, "and you can't fan it away, my military friend!")

"It was the first unhappiness of my new life," said Annie. "It was the first occasion of every unhappy moment I have known. These moments have been more, of late, than I can count; but not—my generous husband!—not for the reason you suppose; for in my heart there is not a thought, a recollection, or a hope, that any power could separate from you!"

She raised her eyes, and clasped her hands, and looked as beautiful and true, I thought, as any Spirit. The Doctor looked on her, henceforth, as steadfastly as she on him.

"Mama is blameless," she went on, "of having ever urged you for herself, and she is blameless in intention every way, I am sure,—but when I saw how many importunate claims were pressed upon you in my name; how you were traded on in my name; how generous you were, and how Mr. Wickfield, who had your welfare very much at heart, resented it; the first sense of my exposure to the mean suspicion that my tenderness was bought—and sold to you, of all men on earth—fell upon me like unmerited disgrace, in which I forced you to participate. I cannot tell you what it was—mama cannot imagine what it was —to have this dread and trouble always on my mind, yet know in my own soul that on my marriage-day I crowned the love and honour of my life!"

"A specimen of the thanks one gets," cried Mrs. Markleham, in tears, "for taking care of one's family! I wish I was a Turk!"

("I wish you were, with all my heart—and in your native country!" said my aunt.)

"It was at that time that mama was most solicitous about my Cousin Maldon. I had liked him:" she spoke softly, but without any hesitation: "very much. We had been little lovers once. If circumstances had not happened otherwise, I might have come to persuade myself that I really loved him, and might have married him, and been most wretched. There can be no disparity in marriage like unsuitability of mind and purpose."

I pondered on those words, even while I was studiously attending to what followed, as if they had some particular interest, or some strange application that I could not divine. "There can be no disparity in marriage like unsuitability of mind and purpose"—"no disparity in marriage like unsuitability of mind and purpose."

"There is nothing," said Annie, "that we have in common. I have long found that there is nothing. If I were thankful to my husband for no more, instead of for so much, I should be thankful to him for having saved me from the first mistaken impulse of my undisciplined heart."

She stood quite still, before the Doctor, and spoke with an earnestness that thrilled me. Yet her voice was just as quiet as before.

"When he was waiting to be the object of your munificence, so freely bestowed for my sake, and when I was unhappy in the mercenary shape I was made to wear, I thought it would have become him better to have worked his own way on. I thought that if I had been he, I would have tried to do it, at the cost of almost any hardship. But I thought no worse of him, until the night of his departure for India. That night I knew he had a false and thankless heart. I saw a double meaning, then, in Mr. Wickfield's scrutiny of me. I perceived, for the first time, the dark suspicion that shadowed my life."

"Suspicion, Annie!" said the Doctor. "No, no, no!"

"In your mind there was none, I know, my husband!" she returned. "And when I came to you, that night, to lay down all my load of shame and grief, and knew that I had to tell that, underneath your roof, one of my own kindred, to whom you had been a benefactor, for the love of me, had spoken to me words that should have found no utterance, even if I had been the weak and mercenary wretch he thought me—my mind revolted from the taint the very tale conveyed. It died upon my lips, and from that hour till now has never passed them."

Mrs. Markleham, with a short groan, leaned back in her easy chair; and retired behind her fan, as if she were never coming out any more.

"I have never, but in your presence, interchanged a word with him from that time; then, only when it has been necessary for the avoidance of this explanation. Years have passed since he knew from me what his situation here was. The kindnesses you have secretly done for his advancement, and then disclosed to me, for my surprise and pleasure, have been, you will believe, but aggravations of the unhappiness and burden of my secret."

She sunk down gently at the Doctor's feet, though he did his utmost to prevent her; and said, looking up, tearfully, into his face:

"Do not speak to me yet! Let me say a little more! Right or wrong, if this were to be done again, I think I should do just the same. You never can know what it was to be devoted to you, with those old associations; to find that any one could be so hard as to suppose that the truth of my heart was bartered away, and to be surrounded by appearances confirming that belief. I was very young, and had no adviser. Between mama and me, in all relating to you, there was a wide division. If I shrunk into myself, hiding the disrespect I had undergone, it was because I honoured you so much, and so much wished that you should honour me!"

"Annie, my pure heart!" said the Doctor, "my dear girl!"

"A little more! a very few words more! I used to think there were so many whom you might have married, who would not have brought such charge and trouble on you, and who would have made your home a worthier home. I used to be afraid that I had better have remained your pupil, and almost your child. I used to fear that I was so unsuited to your learning and wisdom. If all this made me shrink within myself (as indeed it did), when I had that to tell, it was still because I honoured you so much, and hoped that you might one day honour me."

"That day has shone this long time, Annie," said the Doctor, "and can have but one long night, my dear."

"Another word! I afterwards meant—steadfastly meant, and purposed to myself—to bear the whole weight of knowing the unworthiness of one to whom you had been so good. And now a last word, dearest and best of friends! The cause of the late change in you, which I have seen with so much pain and sorrow, and have sometimes referred to my old apprehension—at other times to lingering suppositions nearer to the truth—has been made clear to-night; and by an accident I have also come to know, to-night, the full measure of your noble trust in me, even under that mistake. I do not hope that any love and duty I may render in return, will ever make me worthy of your priceless confidence; but with all this knowledge fresh upon me, I can lift my eyes to this dear face, revered as a father's, loved as a husband's, sacred to me in my childhood as a friend's, and solemnly declare that in my lightest thought I have never wronged you; never wavered in the love and the fidelity I owe you!"

She had her arms around the Doctor's neck, and he leant his head down over her, mingling his grey hair with her dark brown tresses.

"Oh, hold me to your heart, my husband! Never cast me out! Do not think or speak of disparity between us, for there is none, except in all my many imperfections. Every succeeding year I have known this better, as I have esteemed you more and more. Oh, take me to your heart, my husband, for my love was founded on a rock, and it endures!"

In the silence that ensued, my aunt walked gravely up to Mr. Dick, without at all hurrying herself, and gave him a hug and a sounding kiss. And it was very fortunate, with a view to his credit, that she did so; for I am confident that I detected him at that moment in the act of making preparations to stand on one leg, as an appropriate expression of delight.

"You are a very remarkable man, Dick!" said my aunt, with an air of unqualified approbation; "and never pretend to be anything else, for I know better!"

With that, my aunt pulled him by the sleeve, and nodded to me; and we three stole quietly out of the room, and came away.

"That's a settler for our military friend, at any rate," said my aunt, on the way home. "I should sleep the better for that, if there was nothing else to be glad of!"

"She was quite overcome, I am afraid," said Mr. Dick, with great commiseration.

"What! Did you ever see a crocodile overcome?" inquired my aunt.

"I don't think I ever saw a crocodile," returned Mr. Dick, mildly.

"There never would have been anything the matter, if it hadn't been for that old Animal," said my aunt, with strong emphasis. "It's very much to be wished that some mothers would leave their daughters alone after marriage, and not be so violently affectionate. They seem to think the only return that can be made them for bringing an unfortunate young woman into the world—God bless my soul, as if she asked to be brought, or wanted to come!—is full liberty to worry her out of it again. What are you thinking of, Trot?"

I was thinking of all that had been said. My mind was still running on some of the expressions used. "There can be no disparity in marriage like unsuitability of mind and purpose." "The first mistaken impulse of an undisciplined heart." "My love was founded on a rock." But we were at home; and the trodden leaves were lying underfoot, and the autumn wind was blowing.

46

INTELLIGENCE

I MUST HAVE BEEN MARRIED, IF I MAY TRUST TO MY imperfect memory for dates, about a year or so, when one evening, as I was returning from a solitary walk, thinking of the book I was then writing—for my success had steadily increased with my steady application, and I was engaged at that time upon my first work of fiction—I came past Mrs. Steerforth's house. I had often passed it before, during my residence in that neighbourhood, though never when I could choose another road. Howbeit, it did sometimes happen that it was not easy to find another, without making a long circuit; and so I had passed that way, upon the whole, pretty often.

I had never done more than glance at the house, as I went by with a quickened step. It had been uniformly gloomy and dull. None of the best rooms abutted on the road; and the narrow, heavily-framed old-fashioned windows, never cheerful under any circumstances, looked very dismal, close shut, and with their blinds always drawn down. There was a covered way across a little paved court, to an entrance that was never used; and there was one round staircase window, at odds with all the rest, and the only one unshaded by a blind, which had the same unoccupied blank look. I do not remember that I ever saw a light in all the house. If I had been a casual passer-by, I should have probably supposed that some childless person lay dead in it. If I had happily possessed no knowledge of the place, and had seen it often in that changeless state, I should have pleased my fancy with many ingenious speculations, I dare say.

As it was, I thought as little of it as I might. But my mind could not go by it and leave it, as my body did; and it usually awakened a long train of meditations. Coming before me on this particular evening that I mention, mingled with the childish recollections and later fancies, the ghosts of half-formed hopes, the broken shadows of disappointments dimly seen and understood, the blending of experience and imagination, incidental to the occupation with which my thoughts had been busy, it was more than commonly suggestive. I fell into a brown study as I walked on, and a voice at my side made me start.

It was a woman's voice, too. I was not long in recollecting Mrs. Steerforth's little parlour-maid, who had formerly worn blue ribbons in her cap. She had taken them out now, to adapt herself, I suppose, to the altered character of the house; and wore but one or two disconsolate bows of sober brown.

"If you please, sir, would you have the goodness to walk in, and speak to Miss Dartle?"

"Has Miss Dartle sent you for me?" I inquired.

"Not to-night, sir, but it's just the same. Miss Dartle saw you pass a night or two ago, and I was to sit at work on the staircase, and when I saw you pass again, to ask you to step in and speak to her."

I turned back, and inquired of my conductor, as we went along, how Mrs. Steerforth was. She said her lady was but poorly, and kept her own room a good deal.

When we arrived at the house, I was directed to Miss Dartle in the garden, and left to make my presence known to her myself. She was sitting on a seat at one end of a kind of terrace, overlooking the great city. It was a sombre evening, with a lurid light in the sky; and as I saw the prospect scowling in the distance, with here and there some larger object starting up into the sullen glare, I fancied it was no inapt companion to the memory of this fierce woman.

She saw me as I advanced, and rose for a moment to receive me. I thought her, then, still more colourless and thin than when I had seen her last; the flashing eyes still brighter, and the scar still plainer.

Our meeting was not cordial. We had parted angrily on the

last occasion; and there was an air of disdain about her, which she took no pains to conceal.

"I am told you wish to speak to me, Miss Dartle," said I, standing near her, with my hand upon the back of the seat, and declining her gesture of invitation to sit down.

"If you please," said she. "Pray has this girl been found?"

"No."

"And yet she has run away!"

I saw her thin lips working while she looked at me, as if they were eager to load her with reproaches.

"Run away?" I repeated.

"Yes! From him," she said, with a laugh. "If she is not found, perhaps she never will be found. She may be dead!"

The vaunting cruelty with which she met my glance, I never saw expressed in any other face that ever I have seen.

"To wish her dead," said I, "may be the kindest wish that one of her own sex could bestow upon her. I am glad that time has softened you so much, Miss Dartle."

She condescended to make no reply, but, turning on me with another scornful laugh, said:

"The friends of this excellent and much-injured young lady are friends of yours. You are their champion, and assert their rights. Do you wish to know what is known of her?"

"Yes," said I.

She rose with an ill-favoured smile, and taking a few steps towards a wall of holly that was near at hand, dividing the lawn from a kitchen-garden, said, in a louder voice, "Come here!" —as if she were calling to some unclean beast.

"You will restrain any demonstrative championship or vengeance in this place, of course, Mr. Copperfield?" said she, looking over her shoulder at me with the same expression.

I inclined my head, without knowing what she meant; and she said, "Come here!" again; and returned, followed by the respectable Mr. Littimer, who, with undiminished respectability, made me a bow, and took up his position behind her. The air of wicked grace: of triumph, in which, strange to say, there was yet something feminine and alluring: with which she reclined upon the seat between us, and looked at me, was worthy of a cruel princess in a legend.

"Now," said she, imperiously, without glancing at him, and touching the old wound as it throbbed; perhaps, in this instance, with pleasure rather than pain. "Tell Mr. Copperfield about the flight."

"Mr. James and myself, ma'am——"

"Don't address yourself to me!" she interrupted with a frown.

"Mr. James and myself, sir——"

"Nor to me, if you please," said I.

Mr. Littimer, without being at all discomposed, signified by a slight obeisance, that anything that was most agreeable to us was most agreeable to him; and began again:

"Mr. James and myself have been abroad with the young woman, ever since she left Yarmouth under Mr. James's protection. We have been in a variety of places, and seen a deal of foreign country. We have been in France, Switzerland, Italy—in fact, almost all parts."

He looked at the back of the seat, as if he were addressing himself to that; and softly played upon it with his hands, as if he were striking chords upon a dumb piano.

"Mr. James took quite uncommonly to the young woman; and was more settled, for a length of time, than I have known him to be since I have been in his service. The young woman was very improvable, and spoke the languages; and wouldn't have been known for the same country-person. I noticed that she was much admired wherever we went."

Miss Dartle put her hand upon her side. I saw him steal a glance at her, and slightly smile to himself.

"Very much admired, indeed, the young woman was. What with her dress; what with the air and sun; what with being made so much of; what with this, that, and the other; her merits really attracted general notice."

He made a short pause. Her eyes wandered restlessly over the distant prospect, and she bit her nether lip to stop that busy mouth.

Taking his hands from the seat, and placing one of them within the other, as he settled himself on one leg, Mr. Littimer proceeded, with his eyes cast down, and his respectable head a little advanced, and a little on one side:

"The young woman went on in this manner for some time, being occasionally low in her spirits, until I think she began to weary Mr. James by giving way to her low spirits and tempers of that kind; and things were not so comfortable. Mr. James he began to be restless again. The more restless he got, the worse she got; and I must say, for myself, that I had a very difficult time of it indeed between the two. Still matters were patched up here, and made good there, over and over again; and altogether lasted, I am sure, for a longer time than anybody could have expected."

Recalling her eyes from the distance, she looked at me again now, with her former air. Mr. Littimer, clearing his throat behind his hand with a respectable short cough, changed legs, and went on:

"At last, when there had been, upon the whole, a good many words and reproaches, Mr. James he set off one morning, from the neighbourhood of Naples, where we had a villa (the young woman being very partial to the sea), and, under pretence of coming back in a day or so, left it in charge with me to break it out, that, for the general happiness of all concerned, he was" —here an interruption of the short cough—"gone. But Mr. James, I must say, certainly did behave extremely honourable; for he proposed that the young woman should marry a very respectable person, who was fully prepared to overlook the past, and who was, at least, as good as anybody the young woman could have aspired to in a regular way: her connections being very common."

He changed legs again, and wetted his lips. I was convinced that the scoundrel spoke of himself, and I saw my conviction reflected in Miss Dartle's face.

"This I also had it in charge to communicate. I was willing to do anything to relieve Mr. James from his difficulty, and to restore harmony between himself and an affectionate parent, who has undergone so much on his account. Therefore I undertook the commission. The young woman's violence when she came to, after I broke the fact of his departure, was beyond all expectations. She was quite mad, and had to be held by force; or, if she couldn't have got to a knife, or got to the sea, she'd have beaten her head against the marble floor."

Miss Dartle, leaning back upon the seat, with a light of exultation in her face, seemed almost to caress the sounds this fellow had uttered.

"But when I came to the second part of what had been entrusted to me," said Mr. Littimer, rubbing his hands uneasily, "which anybody might have supposed would have been, at all events, appreciated as a kind intention, then the young woman came out in her true colours. A more outrageous person I never did see. Her conduct was surprisingly bad. She had no more gratitude, no more feeling, no more patience, no more reason in her, than a stock or a stone. If I hadn't been upon my guard, I am convinced she would have had my blood."

"I think the better of her for it," said I, indignantly.

Mr. Littimer bent his head, as much as to say, "Indeed, sir? But, you're young!" and resumed his narrative.

"It was necessary, in short, for a time, to take away everything nigh her, that she could do herself, or anybody else, an injury with, and to shut her up close. Notwithstanding which, she got out in the night; forced the lattice of a window, that I had nailed up myself; dropped on a vine that was trailed below; and never has been seen or heard of, to my knowledge, since."

"She is dead, perhaps," said Miss Dartle, with a smile, as if she could have spurned the body of the ruined girl.

"She may have drowned herself, miss," returned Mr. Littimer, catching at an excuse for addressing himself to somebody. "It's very possible. Or she may have had assistance from the boatmen, and the boatmen's wives and children. Being given to low company, she was very much in the habit of talking to them on the beach, Miss Dartle, and sitting by their boats. I have known her do it, when Mr. James has been away, whole days. Mr. James was far from pleased to find out once, that she had told the children she was a boatman's daughter, and that in her own country, long ago, she had roamed about the beach, like them."

Oh, Emily! Unhappy beauty! What a picture rose before me of her sitting on the far-off shore, among the children like herself when she was innocent, listening to little voices such as might have called her Mother had she been a poor man's wife; and to the great voice of the sea, with its eternal "Never more!"

"When it was clear that nothing could be done, Miss Dartle—"

"Did I tell you not to speak to me?" she said, with stern contempt.

"You spoke to me, miss," he replied. "I beg your pardon. But it is my service to obey."

"Do your service," she returned. "Finish your story, and go!"

"When it was clear," he said, with infinite respectability, and an obedient bow, "that she was not to be found, I went to Mr. James, at the place where it had been agreed that I should write to him, and informed him of what had occurred. Words passed between us in consequence, and I felt it due to my character to leave him. I could bear, and I have borne, a great deal from Mr. James; but he insulted me too far. He hurt me. Knowing the unfortunate difference between himself and his mother, and what her anxiety of mind was likely to be, I took the liberty of coming home to England, and relating—"

"For money which I paid him," said Miss Dartle to me.

"Just so, ma'am—and relating what I knew. I am not aware,"

said Mr. Littimer, after a moment's reflection, "that there is anything else. I am at present out of employment, and should be happy to meet with a respectable situation."

Miss Dartle glanced at me, as though she would inquire if there were anything that I desired to ask. As there was something which had occurred to my mind, I said in reply:

"I could wish to know from this—creature," I could not bring myself to utter any more conciliatory word, "whether they intercepted a letter that was written to her from home, or whether he supposes that she received it."

He remained calm and silent, with his eyes fixed on the ground, and the tip of every finger of his right hand delicately poised against the tip of every finger of his left.

Miss Dartle turned her head disdainfully towards him.

"I beg your pardon, miss," he said, awakening from his abstraction, "but, however submissive to you, I have my position, though a servant. Mr. Copperfield and you, miss, are different people. If Mr. Copperfield wishes to know anything from me, I take the liberty of reminding Mr. Copperfield that he can put a question to me. I have a character to maintain."

After a momentary struggle with myself, I turned my eyes upon him, and said, "You have heard my question. Consider it addressed to yourself, if you choose. What answer do you make?"

"Sir," he rejoined, with an occasional separation and reunion of those delicate tips, "my answer must be qualified; because, to betray Mr. James's confidence to his mother, and to betray it to you, are two different actions. It is not probable, I consider, that Mr. James would encourage the receipt of letters likely to increase low spirits and unpleasantness; but further than that, sir, I should wish to avoid going."

"Is that all?" inquired Miss Dartle of me.

I indicated that I had nothing more to say. "Except," I added, as I saw him moving off, "that I understand this fellow's part in the wicked story, and that, as I shall make it known to the honest man who has been her father from her childhood, I would recommend him to avoid going too much into public."

He had stopped the moment I began, and had listened with his usual repose of manner.

"Thank you, sir. But you'll excuse me if I say, sir, that there are neither slaves nor slave-drivers in this country, and that people are not allowed to take the law into their own hands. If they do, it is more to their own peril, I believe, than to other people's. Consequently speaking, I am not at all afraid of going wherever I may wish, sir."

With that, he made a polite bow; and, with another to Miss Dartle, went away through the arch in the wall of holly by which he had come. Miss Dartle and I regarded each other for a little while in silence; her manner being exactly what it was, when she had produced the man.

"He says besides," she observed, with a slow curling of her lip, "that his master, as he hears, is coasting Spain; and this done, is away to gratify his seafaring tastes till he is weary. But this is of no interest to you. Between these two proud persons, mother and son, there is a wider breach than before, and little hope of its healing, for they are one at heart, and time makes each more obstinate and imperious. Neither is this of any interest to you; but it introduces what I wish to say. This devil whom you make an angel of, I mean this low girl whom he picked out of the tide-mud," with her black eyes full upon me, and her passionate finger up, "may be alive,—for I believe some common things are hard to die. If she is, you will desire to have a pearl of such price found and taken care of. We desire that, too; that he may not by any chance be made her prey again. So far, we are united in one interest; and that is why I, who would do her any mischief that so coarse a wretch is capable of feeling, have sent for you to hear what you have heard."

I saw, by the change in her face, that someone was advancing behind me. It was Mrs. Steerforth, who gave me her hand more coldly than of yore, and with an augmentation of her former stateliness of manner; but still, I perceived—and I was touched by it—with an ineffaceable remembrance of my old love for her son. She was greatly altered. Her fine figure was far less upright, her handsome face was deeply marked, and her hair was almost white. But when she sat down on the seat, she was a handsome lady still; and well I knew the bright eye with its lofty look, that had been a light in my very dreams at school.

"Is Mr. Copperfield informed of everything, Rosa?"

"Yes."

"And has he heard Littimer himself?"

"Yes; I have told him why you wished it."

"You are a good girl. I have had some slight correspondence with your former friend, sir," addressing me, "but it has not restored his sense of duty or natural obligation. Therefore I have no other object in this, than what Rosa has mentioned. If, by the course which may relieve the mind of the decent man you brought here (for whom I am sorry—I can say no more), my son may be saved from again falling into the snares of a designing enemy, well! "

She drew herself up, and sat looking straight before her, far away.

" Madam," I said respectfully, " I understand. I assure you I am in no danger of putting any strained construction on your motives. But I must say, even to you, having known this injured family from childhood, that if you suppose the girl, so deeply wronged, has not been cruelly deluded, and would not rather die a hundred deaths than take a cup of water from your son's hand now, you cherish a terrible mistake."

" Well, Rosa, well! " said Mrs. Steerforth, as the other was about to interpose, " it is no matter. Let it be. You are married, sir, I am told? "

I answered that I had been some time married.

" And are doing well? I hear little in the quiet life I lead, but I understand you are beginning to be famous."

" I have been very fortunate," I said, " and find my name connected with some praise."

" You have no mother? "—in a softened voice.

" No."

" It is a pity," she returned. " She would have been proud of you. Good night! "

I took the hand she held out with a dignified, unbending air, and it was as calm in mine as if her breast had been at peace. Her pride could still its very pulses, it appeared, and draw the placid veil before her face, through which she sat looking straight before her on the far distance.

As I moved away from them along the terrace, I could not help observing how steadily they both sat gazing on the prospect, and how it thickened and closed around them. Here and there, some early lamps were seen to twinkle in the distant city; and in the eastern quarter of the sky the lurid light still hovered. But, from the greater part of the broad valley interposed, a mist was rising like a sea, which, mingling with the darkness, made it seem as if the gathering waters would encompass them. I have reason to remember this, and think of it with awe; for before I looked upon those two again, a stormy sea had risen to their feet.

Reflecting on what had been thus told me, I felt it right that it should be communicated to Mr. Peggotty. On the following evening I went into London in quest of him. He was always wandering about from place to place, with his own object of recovering his niece before him; but was more in London than elsewhere. Often and often, now, had I seen him in the dead of night passing along the streets, searching, among the few who loitered out of doors at those untimely hours, for what he dreaded to find.

He kept a lodging over the little chandler's shop in Hungerford Market, which I have had occasion to mention more than once, and from which he first went forth upon his errand of mercy. Hither I directed my walk. On making inquiry for him, I learned from the people of the house that he had not gone out yet, and I should find him in his room up-stairs.

He was sitting reading by a window in which he kept a few plants. The room was very neat and orderly. I saw in a moment that it was always kept prepared for her reception, and that he never went out but he thought it possible he might bring her home. He had not heard my tap at the door, and only raised his eyes when I laid my hand upon his shoulder.

"Mas'r Davy! Thankee, sir! thankee hearty, for this visit! Sit ye down. You're kindly welcome, sir!"

"Mr. Peggotty," said I, taking the chair he handed me, "don't expect much! I have heard some news."

"Of Em'ly!"

He put his hand, in a nervous manner, on his mouth, and turned pale, as he fixed his eyes on mine.

"It gives no clue to where she is; but she is not with him."

He sat down, looking intently at me, and listened in profound silence to all I had to tell. I well remember the sense of dignity, beauty even, with which the patient gravity of his face impressed me, when, having gradually removed his eyes from mine, he sat looking downward, leaning his forehead on his hand. He offered no interruption, but remained throughout perfectly still. He seemed to pursue her figure through the narrative, and to let every other shape go by him, as if it were nothing.

When I had done, he shaded his face, and continued silent. I looked out of the window for a little while, and occupied myself with the plants.

"How do you fare to feel about it, Mas'r Davy?" he inquired at length.

"I think that she is living," I replied.

"I doen't know. Maybe the first shock was too rough, and in the wildness of her art——! That there blue water as she used to speak on. Could she have thowt o' that so many year, because it was to be her grave!"

He said this, musing, in a low, frightened voice; and walked across the little room.

"And yet," he added, "Mas'r Davy, I have felt so sure as she was living—I have know'd, awake and sleeping, as it was so trew that I should find her—I have been so led on by it, and held up by it—that I doen't believe I can have been deceived. No! Em'ly's alive!"

He put his hand down firmly on the table, and set his sunburnt face into a resolute expression.

"My niece, Em'ly, is alive, sir!" he said, steadfastly. "I doen't know wheer it comes from, or how 'tis, but *I am told* as she's alive!"

He looked almost like a man inspired, as he said it. I waited for a few moments, until he could give me his undivided attention; and then proceeded to explain the precaution, that, it had occurred to me last night, it would be wise to take.

"Now, my dear friend—" I began.

"Thankee, thankee, kind sir," he said, grasping my hand in both of his.

"If she should make her way to London, which is likely—for where could she lose herself so readily as in this vast city; and what would she wish to do, but lose and hide herself, if she does not go home?—"

"And she won't go home," he interposed, shaking his head mournfully. "If she had left of her own accord, she might: not as 'twas, sir."

"If she should come here," said I, "I believe there is one person, here, more likely to discover her than any other in the world. Do you remember—hear what I say, with fortitude—think of your great object!—do you remember Martha?"

"Of our town?"

I needed no other answer than his face.

"Do you know that she is in London?"

"I have seen her in the streets," he answered with a shiver.

"But you don't know," said I, "that Emily was charitable to her, with Ham's help, long before she fled from home. Nor, that, when we met one night, and spoke together in the room yonder, over the way, she listened at the door."

"Mas'r Davy!" he replied in astonishment. "That night when it snew so hard?"

"That night. I have never seen her since. I went back, after parting from you, to speak to her, but she was gone. I was unwilling to mention her to you then, and I am now; but she is the person of whom I speak, and with whom I think we should communicate. Do you understand?"

"Too well, sir," he replied. We had sunk our voices, almost to a whisper, and continued to speak in that tone.

"You say you have seen her. Do you think that you could find her? I could only hope to do so by chance."

"I think, Mas'r Davy, I know wheer to look."

"It is dark. Being together, shall we go out now, and try to find her to-night?"

He assented, and prepared to accompany me. Without appearing to observe what he was doing, I saw how carefully he adjusted the little room, put a candle ready and the means of lighting it, arranged the bed, and finally took out of a drawer one of her dresses (I remember to have seen her wear it), neatly folded with some other garments, and a bonnet, which he placed upon a chair. He made no allusion to these clothes, neither did I. There they had been waiting for her, many and many a night, no doubt.

"The time was, Mas'r Davy," he said, as we came downstairs, "when I thowt this girl, Martha, almost like the dirt underneath my Em'ly's feet. God forgive me, theer's a difference now!"

As we went along, partly to hold him in conversation, and partly to satisfy myself, I asked him about Ham. He said, almost in the same words as formerly, that Ham was just the same, "wearing away his life with kiender no care nohow for't; but never murmuring, and liked by all."

I asked him what he thought Ham's state of mind was, in reference to the cause of their misfortunes? Whether he believed it was dangerous? What he supposed, for example, Ham would do, if he and Steerforth ever should encounter?

"I doen't know, sir," he replied. "I have thowt of it oftentimes, but I can't arrize myself of it, no matters."

I recalled to his remembrance the morning after her departure, when we were all three on the beach. "Do you recollect," said I, "a certain wild way in which he looked out to sea, and spoke about 'the end of it'?"

"Sure I do!" said he.

"What do you suppose he meant?"

"Mas'r Davy," he replied, "I've put the question to myself a mort o' times, and never found no answer. And theer's one curious thing—that, though he is so pleasant, I wouldn't fare to feel comfortable to try and get his mind upon 't. He never said a wured to me as warn't as dootiful as dootiful could be, and it ain't likely as he'd begin to speak any other ways now; but it's fur from being fleet water in his mind, wheer them thowts lays. It's deep, sir, and I can't see down."

"You are right," said I, "and that has sometimes made me anxious."

"And me too, Mas'r Davy," he rejoined. "Even more so, I do assure you, than his ventersome ways, though both belongs to the alteration in him. I doen't know as he'd do violence under any circumstances, but I hope as them two may be kep asunders."

We had come, through Temple Bar, into the city. Conversing no more now, and walking at my side, he yielded himself up to the one aim of his devoted life, and went on, with that hushed concentration of his faculties which would have made his figure solitary in a multitude. We were not far from Blackfriars Bridge, when he turned his head and pointed to a solitary female figure flitting along the opposite side of the street. I knew it, readily, to be the figure that we sought.

We crossed the road, and were pressing on towards her, when it occurred to me that she might be more disposed to feel a woman's interest in the lost girl, if we spoke to her in a quieter place, aloof from the crowd, and where we should be less observed. I advised my companion, therefore, that we should not address her yet, but follow her; consulting in this, likewise, an indistinct desire I had, to know where she went.

He acquiescing, we followed at a distance: never losing sight of her, but never caring to come very near, as she frequently looked about. Once she stopped to listen to a band of music: and then we stopped too.

She went on a long way. Still we went on. It was evident, from the manner in which she held her course, that she was going to some fixed destination; and this, and her keeping in the busy streets, and I suppose the strange fascination in the secrecy and mystery of so following any one, made me adhere to my first purpose. At length she turned into a dull, dark street, where the noise and crowd were lost; and I said, "We may speak to her now;" and, mending our pace, we went after her.

47

MARTHA

WE WERE NOW DOWN IN WESTMINSTER. WE HAD TURNED back to follow her, having encountered her coming towards us; and Westminster Abbey was the point at which she passed from the lights and noise of the leading streets. She proceeded so quickly, when she got free of the two currents of passengers setting towards and from the bridge, that, between this and the advance she had of us when she struck off, we were in the narrow waterside street by Millbank before we came up with her. At that moment she crossed the road, as if to avoid the footsteps that she heard so close behind; and, without looking back, passed on even more rapidly.

A glimpse of the river through a dull gateway, where some waggons were housed for the night, seemed to arrest my feet. I touched my companion without speaking, and we both forbore to cross after her, and both followed on that opposite side of the way; keeping as quietly as we could in the shadow of the houses, but keeping very near her.

There was, and is when I write, at the end of that low-lying street, a dilapidated little wooden building, probably an obsolete old ferry-house. Its position is just at that point where the street ceases, and the road begins to lie between a row of houses and the river. As soon as she came here, and saw the water, she stopped as if she had come to her destination; and presently went slowly along by the brink of the river, looking intently at it.

All the way here, I had supposed that she was going to some house; indeed, I had vaguely entertained the hope that the house might be in some way associated with the lost girl. But that one dark glimpse of the river, through the gateway, had instinctively prepared me for her going no farther.

The neighbourhood was a dreary one at that time; as oppressive, sad, and solitary by night, as any about London. There were neither wharves nor houses on the melancholy waste of road near the great blank Prison. A sluggish ditch deposited its mud at the prison walls. Coarse grass and rank weeds straggled over all the marshy land in the vicinity. In one part, carcases of houses, inauspiciously begun and never finished, rotted away. In another, the ground was cumbered with rusty iron monsters of steam-boilers, wheels, cranks, pipes, furnaces, paddles, anchors, diving-bells, windmill-sails, and I know not what strange objects, accumulated by some speculator, and grovelling in the dust, underneath which—having sunk into the soil of their own weight in wet weather—they had the appearance of vainly trying to hide themselves. The clash and glare of sundry fiery Works upon the river-side, arose by night to disturb everything except the heavy and unbroken smoke that poured out of their chimneys. Slimy gaps and causeways, winding among old wooden piles, with a sickly substance clinging to the latter, like green hair, and the rags of last year's handbills offering rewards for drowned men fluttering above high-water mark, led down through the ooze and slush to the ebb-tide. There was a story that one of the pits dug for the dead in the time of the Great Plague was hereabout; and a blighting influence seemed to have proceeded from it over the whole place. Or else it looked as if it had gradually decomposed into that nightmare condition, out of the overflowings of the polluted stream.

As if she were a part of the refuse it had cast out, and left to corruption and decay, the girl we had followed strayed down to the river's brink, and stood in the midst of this night-picture, lonely and still, looking at the water.

There were some boats and barges astrand in the mud, and these enabled us to come within a few yards of her without being seen. I then signed to Mr. Peggotty to remain where he was, and emerged from their shade to speak to her. I did not approach her solitary figure without trembling; for this gloomy end to her determined walk, and the way in which she stood, almost within the cavernous shadow of the iron bridge, looking at the lights crookedly reflected in the strong tide, inspired a dread within me.

I think she was talking to herself. I am sure, although absorbed in gazing at the water, that her shawl was off her shoulders, and that she was muffling her hands in it, in an unsettled and bewildered way, more like the action of a sleep-walker than a waking person. I know, and never can forget, that there was that in her wild manner which gave me no assurance but that she would sink before my eyes, until I had her arm within my grasp.

At the same moment I said "Martha!"

She uttered a terrified scream, and struggled with me with such strength that I doubt if I could have held her alone. But a stronger hand than mine was laid upon her; and when she raised her frightened eyes and saw whose it was, she made but one more effort and dropped down between us. We carried her away from the water to where there were some dry stones, and there laid her down, crying and moaning. In a little while she sat among the stones, holding her wretched head with both her hands.

" Oh, the river! " she cried passionately, " Oh, the river! "

" Hush, hush! " said I. " Calm yourself."

But she still repeated the same words, continually exclaiming, " Oh, the river! " over and over again.

" I know it's like me! " she exclaimed. " I know that I belong to it. I know that it's the natural company of such as I am! It comes from country places, where there was once no harm in it —and it creeps through the dismal streets, defiled and miserable —and it goes away, like my life, to a great sea, that is always troubled—and I feel that I must go with it! "

I have never known what despair was, except in the tone of those words.

" I can't keep away from it. I can't forget it. It haunts me day and night. It's the only thing in all the world that I am fit for, or that's fit for me. Oh, the dreadful river! "

The thought passed through my mind that in the face of my companion, as he looked upon her without speech or motion, I might have read his niece's history, if I had known nothing of it. I never saw, in any painting or reality, horror and compassion so impressively blended. He shook as if he would have fallen; and his hand—I touched it with my own, for his appearance alarmed me—was deadly cold.

" She is in a state of frenzy," I whispered to him. " She will speak differently in a little time."

I don't know what he would have said in answer. He made some motion with his mouth, and seemed to think he had spoken; but he had only pointed to her with his outstretched hand.

A new burst of crying came upon her now, in which she once more hid her face among the stones, and lay before us, a prostrate image of humiliation and ruin. Knowing that this state must pass, before we could speak to her with any hope, I ventured to restrain him when he would have raised her, and we stood by in silence until she became more tranquil.

" Martha," said I then, leaning down, and helping her to rise—she seemed to want to rise as if with the intention of going away, but she was weak, and leaned against a boat. "Do you know who this is, who is with me?"

She said faintly, "Yes."

"Do you know that we have followed you a long way to-night?"

She shook her head. She looked neither at him nor at me, but stood in a humble attitude, holding her bonnet and shawl in one hand, without appearing conscious of them, and pressing the other, clenched, against her forehead.

"Are you composed enough," said I, "to speak on the subject which so interested you—I hope Heaven may remember it!—that snowy night?"

Her sobs broke out afresh, and she murmured some inarticulate thanks to me for not having driven her away from the door.

"I want to say nothing for myself," she said, after a few moments. "I am bad, I am lost. I have no hope at all. But tell him, sir," she had shrunk away from him, "if you don't feel too hard to me to do it, that I never was in any way the cause of his misfortune."

"It has never been attributed to you," I returned, earnestly responding to her earnestness.

"It was you, if I don't deceive myself," she said, in a broken voice, "that came into the kitchen, the night she took such pity on me; was so gentle to me; didn't shrink away from me like all the rest, and gave me such kind help! Was it you, sir?"

"It was," said I.

"I should have been in the river long ago," she said, glancing at it with a terrible expression, "if any wrong to her had been upon my mind. I never could have kept out of it a single winter's night, if I had not been free of any share in that!"

"The cause of her flight is too well understood," I said. "You are innocent of any part in it, we thoroughly believe,—we know."

"Oh, I might have been much the better for her, if I had had a better heart!" exclaimed the girl, with most forlorn regret; "for she was always good to me! She never spoke a word to me but what was pleasant and right. Is it likely I would try to make her what I am myself, knowing what I am myself so well? When I lost everything that makes life dear, the worst of all my thoughts was that I was parted for ever from her!"

Mr. Peggotty, standing with one hand on the gunwale of the boat, and his eyes cast down, put his disengaged hand before his face.

"And when I heard what had happened before that snowy night, from some belonging to our town," cried Martha, "the bitterest thought in all my mind was, that the people would remember she once kept company with me, and would say I had corrupted her! When, Heaven knows, I would have died to have brought back her good name! "

Long unused to any self-control, the piercing agony of her remorse and grief was terrible.

" To have died, would not have been much—what can I say? —I would have lived! " she cried. " I would have lived to be old, in the wretched streets—and to wander about, avoided, in the dark—and to see the day break on the ghastly line of houses, and remember how the same sun used to shine into my room, and wake me once—I would have done even that to save her! "

Sinking on the stones, she took some in each hand, and clenched them up, as if she would have ground them. She writhed into some new posture constantly: stiffening her arms, twisting them before her face, as though to shut out from her eyes the little light there was, and drooping her head, as if it were heavy with insupportable recollections.

" What shall I ever do! " she said, fighting thus with her despair. " How can I go on as I am, a solitary curse to myself, a living disgrace to every one I come near! " Suddenly she turned to my companion. " Stamp upon me, kill me! When she was your pride, you would have thought I had done her harm if I had brushed against her in the street. You can't believe—why should you?—a syllable that comes out of my lips. It would be a burning shame upon you, even now, if she and I exchanged a word. I don't complain. I don't say she and I are alike. I know there is a long, long way between us. I only say, with all my guilt and wretchedness upon my head, that I am grateful to her from my soul, and love her. Oh, don't think that all the power I had of loving anything is quite worn out! Throw me away, as all the world does. Kill me for being what I am, and having ever known her; but don't think that of me! "

He looked upon her, while she made this supplication, in a wild distracted manner; and, when she was silent, gently raised her.

" Martha," said Mr. Peggotty, " God forbid as I should judge you. Forbid as I, of all men, should do that, my girl! You doen't know half the change that's come, in course of time, upon me, when you think it likely. Well! " he paused a moment, then went on. " You doen't understand how 'tis that this here gentleman and me has wished to speak to you. You doen't understand what 'tis we has afore us. Listen now! "

His influence upon her was complete. She stood, shrinkingly, before him, as if she were afraid to meet his eyes; but her passionate sorrow was quite hushed and mute.

"If you heerd," said Mr. Peggotty, "owt of what passed between Mas'r Davy and me, th' night when it snew so hard, you know as I have been—wheer not—fur to seek my dear niece. My dear niece," he repeated steadily. "Fur she's more dear to me now, Martha, than ever she was dear afore."

She put her hands before her face; but otherwise remained quiet.

"I have heerd her tell," said Mr. Peggotty, "as you was early left fatherless and motherless, with no friend fur to take, in a rough seafaring-way, their place. Maybe you can guess that if you'd had such a friend, you'd have got into a way of being fond of him in course of time, and that my niece was kiender daughter-like to me."

As she was silently trembling, he put her shawl carefully about her, taking it up from the ground for that purpose.

"Whereby," said he, "I know, both as she would go to the wureld's furdest end with me, if she could once see me again; and that she would fly to the wureld's furdest end to keep off seeing me. For though she ain't no call to doubt my love, and doen't—and doen't," he repeated, with a quiet assurance of the truth of what he said, "there's shame steps in, and keeps betwixt us."

I read, in every word of his plain impressive way of delivering himself, new evidence of his having thought of this one topic, in every feature it presented.

"According to our reckoning," he proceeded, "Mas'r Davy's here, and mine, she is like, one day, to make her own poor solitary course to London. We believe—Mas'r Davy, me, and all of us—that you are as innocent of everything that has befell her, as the unborn child. You've spoke of her being pleasant, kind, and gentle to you. Bless her, I knew she was! I knew she always was, to all. You're thankful to her, and you love her. Help us all you can to find her, and may Heaven reward you!"

She looked at him hastily, and for the first time, as if she were doubtful of what he had said.

"Will you trust me?" she asked, in a low voice of astonishment.

"Full and free!" said Mr. Peggotty.

"To speak to her, if I should ever find her; shelter her, if I have any shelter to divide with her; and then, without her knowledge, come to you, and bring you to her?" she asked hurriedly.

We both replied together, "Yes!"

She lifted up her eyes, and solemnly declared that she would devote herself to this task, fervently and faithfully. That she would never waver in it, never be diverted from it, never relinquish it while there was any chance of hope. If she were not true to it, might the object she now had in life, which bound her to something devoid of evil, in its passing away from her, leave her more forlorn and more despairing, if that were possible, than she had been upon the river's brink that night; and then might all help, human and Divine, renounce her evermore!

She did not raise her voice above her breath, or address us, but said this to the night sky; then stood profoundly quiet, looking at the gloomy water.

We judged it expedient, now, to tell her all we knew; which I recounted at length. She listened with great attention, and with a face that often changed, but had the same purpose in all its varying expressions. Her eyes occasionally filled with tears, but those she repressed. It seemed as if her spirit were quite altered, and she could not be too quiet.

She asked, when all was told, where we were to be communicated with, if occasion should arise. Under a dull lamp in the road, I wrote our two addresses on a leaf of my pocket-book, which I tore out and gave to her, and which she put in her poor bosom. I asked her where she lived herself. She said, after a pause, in no place long. It were better not to know.

Mr. Peggotty suggesting to me, in a whisper, what had already occurred to myself, I took out my purse; but I could not prevail upon her to accept any money, nor could I exact any promise from her that she would do so at another time. I represented to her that Mr. Peggotty could not be called, for one in his condition, poor; and that the idea of her engaging in this search, while depending on her own resources, shocked us both. She continued steadfast. In this particular, his influence upon her was equally powerless with mine. She gratefully thanked him but remained inexorable.

"There may be work to be got," she said. "I'll try."

"At least take some assistance," I returned, "until you have tried."

"I could not do what I have promised, for money," she replied. "I could not take it, if I was starving. To give me money would be to take away your trust, to take away the object that you have given me, to take away the only certain thing that saves me from the river."

"In the name of the great Judge," said I, "before whom you and all of us must stand at His dread time, dismiss that terrible idea! We can all do some good, if we will."

She trembled, and her lip shook, and her face was paler as she answered:

"It has been put into your hearts, perhaps, to save a wretched creature for repentance. I am afraid to think so; it seems too bold. If any good should come of me, I might begin to hope; for nothing but harm has ever come of my deeds yet. I am to be trusted, for the first time in a long while, with my miserable life, on account of what you have given me to try for. I know no more, and I can say no more."

Again she repressed the tears that had begun to flow; and, putting out her trembling hand, and touching Mr. Peggotty, as if there was some healing virtue in him, went away along the desolate road. She had been ill, probably for a long time. I observed, upon that closer opportunity of observation, that she was worn and haggard, and that her sunken eyes expressed privation and endurance.

We followed her at a short distance, our way lying in the same direction, until we came back into the lighted and populous streets. I had such implicit confidence in her declaration, that I then put it to Mr. Peggotty, whether it would not seem, in the onset, like distrusting her, to follow her any farther. He being of the same mind, and equally reliant on her, we suffered her to take her own road, and took ours, which was towards Highgate. He accompanied me a good part of the way; and when we parted, with a prayer for the success of this fresh effort, there was a new and thoughtful compassion in him that I was at no loss to interpret.

It was midnight when I arrived at home. I had reached my own gate, and was standing listening for the deep bell of Saint Paul's, the sound of which I thought had been borne towards me among the multitude of striking clocks, when I was rather surprised to see that the door of my aunt's cottage was open, and that a faint light in the entry was shining out across the road.

Thinking that my aunt might have relapsed into one of her old alarms, and might be watching the progress of some imaginary conflagration in the distance, I went to speak to her. It was with very great surprise that I saw a man standing in her little garden.

He had a glass and bottle in his hand, and was in the act of drinking. I stopped short, among the thick foliage outside, for the moon was up now, though obscured; and I recognised the man whom I had once supposed to be a delusion of Mr. Dick's, and had once encountered with my aunt in the streets of the city.

He was eating as well as drinking, and seemed to eat with a hungry appetite. He seemed curious regarding the cottage, too, as if it were the first time he had seen it. After stooping to put the bottle on the ground, he looked up at the windows, and looked about; though with a covert and impatient air, as if he was anxious to be gone.

The light in the passage was obscured for a moment, and my aunt came out. She was agitated, and told some money into his hand. I heard it chink.

"What's the use of this?" he demanded.

"I can spare no more," returned my aunt.

"Then I can't go," said he. "Here! You may take it back!"

"You bad man," returned my aunt, with great emotion; "how can you use me so? But why do I ask? It is because you know how weak I am! What have I to do, to free myself for ever of your visits, but to abandon you to your deserts?"

"And why don't you abandon me to my deserts?" said he.

"*You* ask me why!" returned my aunt. "What a heart you must have!"

He stood moodily rattling the money, and shaking his head, until at length he said:

"Is this all you mean to give me, then?"

"It is all I *can* give you," said my aunt. "You know I have had losses, and am poorer than I used to be. I have told you so. Having got it, why do you give me the pain of looking at you for another moment, and seeing what you have become?"

"I have become shabby enough, if you mean that," he said. "I lead the life of an owl."

"You stripped me of the greater part of all I ever had," said my aunt. "You closed my heart against the whole world, years and years. You treated me falsely, ungratefully, and cruelly. Go, and repent of it. Don't add new injuries to the long, long list of injuries you have done me!"

"Aye!" he returned. "It's all very fine!—Well! I must do the best I can, for the present, I suppose."

In spite of himself, he appeared abashed by my aunt's indignant tears, and came slouching out of the garden. Taking two or three quick steps, as if I had just come up, I met him at the gate, and went in as he came out. We eyed one another narrowly in passing, and with no favour.

"Aunt," said I, hurriedly. "This man alarming you again! Let me speak to him. Who is he?"

"Child," returned my aunt, taking my arm, "come in, and don't speak to me for ten minutes."

We sat down in her little parlour. My aunt retired behind the round green fan of former days, which was screwed on the back of a chair, and occasionally wiped her eyes, for about a quarter of an hour. Then she came out, and took a seat beside me.

"Trot," said my aunt, calmly, "it's my husband."

"Your husband, aunt? I thought he had been dead!"

"Dead to me," returned my aunt, "but living."

I sat in silent amazement.

"Betsey Trotwood don't look a likely subject for the tender passion," said my aunt, composedly, "but the time was, Trot, when she believed in that man most entirely. When she loved him, Trot, right well. When there was no proof of attachment and affection that she would not have given him. He repaid her by breaking her fortune, and nearly breaking her heart. So she put all that sort of sentiment, once and for ever, in a grave, and filled it up, and flattened it down."

"My dear good aunt!"

"I left him," my aunt proceeded, laying her hand as usual on the back of mine, "generously. I may say at this distance of time, Trot, that I left him generously. He had been so cruel to me, that I might have effected a separation on easy terms for myself; but I did not. He soon made ducks and drakes of what I gave him, sank lower and lower, married another woman, I believe, became an adventurer, a gambler, and a cheat. What he is now, you see. But he was a fine-looking man when I married him," said my aunt, with an echo of her old pride and admiration in her tone; "and I believed him—I was a fool!—to be the soul of honour!"

She gave my hand a squeeze, and shook her head.

"He is nothing to me now, Trot, less than nothing. But, sooner than have him punished for his offences (as he would be if he prowled about in this country), I give him more money than I can afford, at intervals when he reappears, to go away. I was a fool when I married him; and I am so far an incurable fool on that subject, that, for the sake of what I once believed him to be, I wouldn't have even this shadow of my idle fancy hardly dealt with. For I was in earnest, Trot, if ever a woman was."

My aunt dismissed the matter with a heavy sigh, and smoothed her dress.

"There, my dear!" she said. "Now you know the beginning, middle, and end, and all about it. We won't mention the subject to one another any more; neither, of course, will you mention it to anybody else. This is my grumpy, frumpy story, and we'll keep it to ourselves, Trot!"

48

DOMESTIC

I LABOURED HARD AT MY BOOK, WITHOUT ALLOWING IT to interfere with the punctual discharge of my newspaper duties; and it came out and was very successful. I was not stunned by the praise which sounded in my ears, notwithstanding that I was keenly alive to it, and thought better of my own performance, I have little doubt, than anybody else did. It has always been in my observation of human nature, that a man who has any good reason to believe in himself never flourishes himself before the faces of other people in order that they may believe in him. For this reason, I retained my modesty in very self-respect; and the more praise I got, the more I tried to deserve.

It is not my purpose, in this record, though in all other essentials it is my written memory, to pursue the history of my own fictions. They express themselves, and I leave them to themselves. When I refer to them, incidentally, it is only as a part of my progress.

Having some foundation for believing, by this time, that nature and accident had made me an author, I pursued my vocation with confidence. Without such assurance I should certainly have left it alone, and bestowed my energy on some other endeavour. I should have tried to find out what nature and accident really had made me, and to be that, and nothing else.

I had been writing, in the newspaper and elsewhere, so prosperously, that when my new success was achieved, I considered myself reasonably entitled to escape from the dreary debates.

One joyful night, therefore, I noted down the music of the parliamentary bagpipes for the last time, and I have never heard it since; though I still recognise the old drone in the newspapers, without any substantial variation (except, perhaps, that there is more of it) all the livelong session.

I now write of the time when I had been married, I suppose, about a year and a half. After several varieties of experiment, we had given up the housekeeping as a bad job. The house kept itself, and we kept a page. The principal function of this retainer was to quarrel with the cook; in which respect he was a perfect Whittington, without his cat, or the remotest chance of being made Lord Mayor.

He appears to me to have lived in a hail of saucepan-lids. His whole existence was a scuffle. He would shriek for help on the most improper occasions,—as when we had a little dinner party, of a few friends in the evening,—and would come tumbling out of the kitchen, with iron missiles flying after him. We wanted to get rid of him, but he was very much attached to us, and wouldn't go. He was a tearful boy, and broke into such deplorable lamentations, when a cessation of our connection was hinted at, that we were obliged to keep him. He had no mother—no anything in the way of a relative, that I could discover, except a sister, who fled to America the moment we had taken him off her hands; and he became quartered on us like a horrible young changeling. He had a lively perception of his own unfortunate state, and was always rubbing his eyes with the sleeve of his jacket, or stooping to blow his nose on the extreme corner of a little pocket-handkerchief, which he never *would* take completely out of his pocket, but always economised and secreted.

This unlucky page, engaged in an evil hour at six pounds ten per annum, was a source of continual trouble to me. I watched him as he grew—and he grew like scarlet beans—with painful apprehensions of the time when he would begin to shave; even of the days when he would be bald or grey. I saw no prospect of ever getting rid of him; and, projecting myself into the future, used to think what an inconvenience he would be when he was an old man.

I never expected anything less, than this unfortunate's manner of getting me out of my difficulty. He stole Dora's watch, which, like everything else belonging to us, had no particular place of its own; and, converting it into money, spent the produce (he was always a weak-minded boy) in incessantly riding up and down between London and Uxbridge outside the coach. He was taken to Bow Street, as well as I remember, on the completion of his fifteenth journey; when four-and-sixpence, and a second-hand fife which he couldn't play, were found upon his person.

The surprise and its consequences would have been much less disagreeable to me if he had not been penitent. But he was very penitent indeed, and in a peculiar way—not in the lump, but by instalments. For example: the day after that on which I was obliged to appear against him, he made certain revelations touching a hamper in the cellar, which we believed to be full of wine, but which had nothing in it except bottles and corks. We supposed he had now eased his mind, and told the worst he knew of the cook; but, a day or two afterwards, his conscience sustained a new twinge, and he disclosed how she had a little girl, who, early every morning, took away our bread; and also how he himself had been suborned to maintain the milkman in coals. In two or three days more, I was informed by the authorities of his having led to the discovery of sirloins of beef among the kitchen-stuff, and sheets in the rag-bag. A little while afterwards, he broke out in an entirely new direction, and confessed to a knowledge of burglarious intentions as to our premises, on the part of the pot-boy, who was immediately taken up. I got to be so ashamed of being such a victim, that I would have given him any money to hold his tongue, or would have offered a round bribe for his being permitted to run away. It was an aggravating circumstance in the case that he had no idea of this, but conceived that he was making me amends in every new discovery: not to say, heaping obligations on my head.

At last I ran away myself, whenever I saw an emissary of the police approaching with some new intelligence; and lived a stealthy life until he was tried and ordered to be transported. Even then he couldn't be quiet, but was always writing us letters; and wanted so much to see Dora before he went away, that Dora went to visit him, and fainted when she found herself inside the iron bars. In short, I had no peace of my life until he was expatriated, and made (as I afterwards heard) a shepherd of, "up the country" somewhere; I have no geographical idea where.

All this led me into some serious reflections, and presented our mistakes in a new aspect; as I could not help communicating to Dora one evening, in spite of my tenderness for her.

"My love," said I, "it is very painful to me to think that our want of system and management involves not only ourselves (which we have got used to), but other people."

"You have been silent for a long time, and now you are going to be cross!" said Dora.

"No, my dear, indeed! Let me explain to you what I mean."

"I think I don't want to know," said Dora.

"But I want you to know, my love. Put Jip down."

Dora put his nose to mine, and said "Boh!" to drive my seriousness away; but, not succeeding, ordered him into his Pagoda, and sat looking at me, with her hands folded, and a most resigned little expression of countenance.

"The fact is, my dear," I began, "there is contagion in us. We infect every one about us."

I might have gone on in this figurative manner, if Dora's face had not admonished me that she was wondering with all her might whether I was going to propose any new kind of vaccination, or other medical remedy, for this unwholesome state of ours. Therefore I checked myself, and made my meaning plainer.

"It is not merely, my pet," said I, "that we lose money and comfort, and even temper sometimes, by not learning to be more careful; but that we incur the serious responsibility of spoiling every one who comes into our service, or has any dealings with us. I begin to be afraid that the fault is not entirely on one side, but that these people all turn out ill because we don't turn out very well ourselves."

"Oh, what an accusation," exclaimed Dora, opening her eyes wide; "to say that you ever saw me take gold watches! Oh!"

"My dearest," I remonstrated, "don't talk preposterous nonsense! Who has made the least allusion to gold watches?"

"You did," returned Dora. "You know you did. You said I hadn't turned out well, and compared me to him."

"To whom?" I asked.

"To the page," sobbed Dora. "Oh, you cruel fellow, to compare your affectionate wife to a transported page! Why didn't you tell me your opinion of me before we were married? Why didn't you say, you hard-hearted thing, that you were convinced I was worse than a transported page? Oh, what a dreadful opinion to have of me! Oh, my goodness!"

"Now, Dora, my love," I returned, gently trying to remove the handkerchief she pressed to her eyes, "this is not only very ridiculous of you, but very wrong. In the first place, it's not true."

"You always said he was a story-teller," sobbed Dora. "And now you say the same of me! Oh, what shall I do! What shall I do!"

"My darling girl," I retorted, "I really must entreat you to be reasonable, and listen to what I did say, and do say. My dear Dora, unless we learn to do our duty to those whom we employ, they will never learn to do their duty to us. I am afraid we present opportunities to people to do wrong, that never ought to be presented. Even if we were as lax as we are, in all our arrangements, by choice—which we are not—even if we liked it, and found it agreeable to do so—which we don't—I am persuaded we should have no right to go on in this way. We are positively corrupting people. We are bound to think of that. I can't help thinking of it, Dora. It is a reflection I am unable to dismiss, and it sometimes makes me very uneasy. There, dear, that's all. Come now. Don't be foolish!"

Dora would not allow me, for a long time, to remove the handkerchief. She sat sobbing and murmuring behind it, that, if I was uneasy, why had I ever been married? Why hadn't I said, even the day before we went to church, that I knew I should be uneasy, and I would rather not? If I couldn't bear her, why didn't I send her away to her aunts at Putney, or to Julia Mills in India? Julia would be glad to see her, and would not call her a transported page; Julia never had called her anything of the sort. In short, Dora was so afflicted, and so afflicted me by being in that condition, that I felt it was of no use repeating this kind of effort, though never so mildly, and I must take some other course.

What other course was left to take? To "form her mind"? This was a common phrase of words which had a fair and promising sound, and I resolved to form Dora's mind.

I began immediately. When Dora was very childish, and I would have infinitely preferred to humour her, I tried to be grave—and disconcerted her, and myself too. I talked to her on the subjects which occupied my thoughts; and I read Shakespeare to her—and fatigued her to the last degree. I accustomed myself to giving her, as it were quite casually, little scraps of useful information, or sound opinion—and she started from them when I let them off, as if they had been crackers. No matter how incidentally or naturally I endeavoured to form my little wife's mind, I could not help seeing that she always had an instinctive perception of what I was about, and became a prey to the keenest apprehensions. In particular, it was clear to me, that she thought Shakespeare a terrible fellow. The formation went on very slowly.

I pressed Traddles into the service without his knowledge; and whenever he came to see us, exploded my mines upon him for the edification of Dora at second hand. The amount of practical wisdom I bestowed upon Traddles in this manner was immense, and of the best quality; but it had no other effect upon Dora than to depress her spirits, and make her always nervous with the dread that it would be her turn next. I found myself in the condition of a schoolmaster, a trap, a pitfall; of always playing spider to Dora's fly, and always pouncing out of my hole to her infinite disturbance.

Still, looking forward through this intermediate stage, to the time when there should be a perfect sympathy between Dora and me, and when I should have " formed her mind " to my entire satisfaction, I persevered, even for months. Finding at last, however, that, although I had been all this time a very porcupine or hedgehog, bristling all over with determination, I had effected nothing, it began to occur to me that perhaps Dora's mind was already formed.

On further consideration this appeared so likely, that I abandoned my scheme, which had had a more promising appearance in words than in action; resolving henceforth to be satisfied with my child-wife, and to try to change her into nothing else by any process. I was heartily tired of being sagacious and prudent by myself, and of seeing my darling under restraint; so I bought a pretty pair of ear-rings for her, and a collar for Jip, and went home one day to make myself agreeable.

Dora was delighted with the little presents, and kissed me joyfully; but there was a shadow between us, however slight, and I had made up my mind that it should not be there. If there must be such a shadow anywhere, I would keep it for the future in my own breast.

I sat down by my wife on the sofa, and put the ear-rings in her ears; and then I told her that I feared we had not been quite as good company lately, as we used to be, and that the fault was mine. Which I sincerely felt, and which indeed it was.

" The truth is, Dora, my life," I said, " I have been trying to be wise."

" And to make me wise too," said Dora, timidly. " Haven't you, Doady? "

I nodded assent to the pretty inquiry of the raised eyebrows, and kissed the parted lips.

" It's not a bit of use," said Dora, shaking her head, until the ear-rings rang again. " You know what a little thing I am, and what I wanted you to call me from the first. If you can't do so, I am afraid you'll never like me. Are you sure you don't think, sometimes, it would have been better to have—"

" Done what, my dear? " For she made no effort to proceed.

" Nothing! " said Dora.

" Nothing? " I repeated.

She put her arms round my neck, and laughed, and called

herself by her favourite name of a goose, and hid her face on my shoulder in such a profusion of curls that it was quite a task to clear them away and see it.

" Don't I think it would have been better to have done nothing, than to have tried to form my little wife's mind? " said I, laughing at myself. " Is that the question? Yes, indeed, I do."

" Is that what you have been trying? " cried Dora. " Oh what a shocking boy! "

" But I shall never try any more," said I. " For I love her dearly as she is."

" Without a story—really? " inquired Dora, creeping closer to me.

" Why should I seek to change," said I, " what has been so precious to me for so long? You never can show better than as your own natural self, my sweet Dora; and we'll try no conceited experiments, but go back to our old way, and be happy."

" And be happy! " returned Dora. " Yes! All day! And you won't mind things going a tiny morsel wrong, sometimes? "

" No, no," said I. " We must do the best we can."

" And you won't tell me, any more, that we make other people bad," coaxed Dora; " will you? Because you know it's so dreadfully cross! "

" No, no," said I.

" It's better for me to be stupid than uncomfortable, isn't it? " said Dora.

" Better to be naturally Dora than anything else in the world."

" In the world! Ah, Doady, it's a large place! "

She shook her head, turned her delighted bright eyes up to mine, kissed me, broke into a merry laugh, and sprang away to put on Jip's new collar.

So ended my last attempt to make any change in Dora. I had been unhappy in trying it; I could not endure my own solitary wisdom; I could not reconcile it with her former appeal to me as my child-wife. I resolved to do what I could, in a quiet way, to improve our proceedings myself; but I foresaw that my utmost would be very little, or I must degenerate into the spider again, and be for ever lying in wait.

And the shadow I have mentioned, that was not to be between us any more, but was to rest wholly on my own heart? How did that fall?

The old unhappy feeling pervaded my life. It was deepened, if it were changed at all; but it was as undefined as ever, and addressed me like a strain of sorrowful music faintly heard in the night. I loved my wife dearly, and I was happy; but the happiness I had vaguely anticipated, once, was not the happiness I enjoyed, and there was always something wanting.

In fulfilment of the compact I have made with myself, to reflect my mind on this paper, I again examine it, closely, and bring its secrets to the light. What I missed, I still regarded—I always regarded—as something that had been a dream of my youthful fancy; that was incapable of realisation; that I was now discovering to be so, with some natural pain, as all men did. But that it would have been better for me if my wife could have helped me more, and shared the many thoughts in which I had no partner; and that this might have been; I knew.

Between these two irreconcilable conclusions: the one, that what I felt was general and unavoidable; the other, that it was particular to me, and might have been different: I balanced curiously, with no distinct sense of their opposition to each other. When I thought of the airy dreams of youth that are incapable of realisation, I thought of the better state preceding manhood that I had outgrown. And then the contented days with Agnes, in the dear old house, arose before me, like spectres of the dead, that might have some renewal in another world, but never more could be reanimated here.

Sometimes, the speculation came into my thoughts, What might have happened, or what would have happened, if Dora and I had never known each other? But she was so incorporated with my existence, that it was the idlest of all fancies, and would soon rise out of my reach and sight, like gossamer floating in the air.

I always loved her. What I am describing, slumbered, and half awoke, and slept again, in the innermost recesses of my mind. There was no evidence of it in me; I know of no influence it had in anything I said or did. I bore the weight of all our little cares, and all my projects; Dora held the pens; and we both felt that our shares were adjusted as the case required. She was truly fond of me, and proud of me; and when Agnes wrote a few earnest words in her letters to Dora, of the pride and interest with which my old friends heard of my growing reputation, and read my book as if they heard me speaking its contents, Dora read them out to me with tears of joy in her bright eyes, and said I was a dear old clever, famous boy.

"The first mistaken impulse of an undisciplined heart." Those words of Mrs. Strong's were constantly recurring to me, at this time; were almost always present to my mind. I awoke with them, often, in the night; I remember to have even read them, in dreams, inscribed upon the walls of houses. For I knew, now, that my own heart was undisciplined when it first loved Dora; and that if it had been disciplined, it never could have felt, when we were married, what it had felt in its secret experience.

" There can be no disparity in marriage, like unsuitability of mind and purpose." Those words I remembered too. I had endeavoured to adapt Dora to myself, and found it impracticable. It remained for me to adapt myself to Dora; to share with her what I could, and be happy; to bear on my own shoulders what I must, and be still happy. This was the discipline to which I tried to bring my heart, when I began to think. It made my second year much happier than my first; and, what was better still, made Dora's life all sunshine.

But, as that year wore on, Dora was not strong. I had hoped that lighter hands than mine would help to mould her character, and that a baby-smile upon her breast might change my child-wife to a woman. It was not to be. The spirit fluttered for a moment on the threshold of its little prison, and, unconscious of captivity, took wing.

" When I can run about again, as I used to do, aunt," said Dora, " I shall make Jip race. He is getting quite slow and lazy."

" I suspect, my dear," said my aunt, quietly working by her side, " he has a worse disorder than that. Age, Dora."

" Do you think he is old? " said Dora, astonished. " Oh, how strange it seems that Jip should be old! "

" It's a complaint we are all liable to, Little One, as we get on in life," said my aunt, cheerfully; " I don't feel more free from it than I used to be, I assure you"'

" But Jip," said Dora, looking at him with compassion, "even little Jip! Oh, poor fellow! "

" I dare say he'll last a long time yet, Blossom," said my aunt, patting Dora on the cheek, as she leaned out of her couch to look at Jip, who responded by standing on his hind legs, and baulking himself in various asthmatic attempts to scramble up by the head and shoulders. " He must have a piece of flannel in his house this winter, and I shouldn't wonder if he came out quite fresh again, with the flowers in the spring. Bless the little dog! " exclaimed my aunt. " If he had as many lives as a cat, and was on the point of losing 'em all, he'd bark at me with his last breath, I believe! "

Dora had helped him up on the sofa; where he really was defying my aunt to such a furious extent, that he couldn't keep straight, but barked himself sideways. The more my aunt looked at him, the more he reproached her; for she had lately taken to spectacles, and for some inscrutable reason he considered the glasses personal.

Dora made him lie down by her, with a good deal of persuasion; and when he was quiet, drew one of his long ears through and through her hand, repeating thoughtfully, "Even little Jip! Oh, poor fellow!"

"His lungs are good enough," said my aunt, gaily, "and his dislikes are not at all feeble. He has a good many years before him, no doubt. But if you want a dog to race with, Little Blossom, he has lived too well for that, and I'll give you one."

"Thank you, aunt," said Dora, faintly. "But don't please!"

"No?" said my aunt, taking off her spectacles.

"I couldn't have any other dog but Jip," said Dora. "It would be so unkind to Jip! Besides, I couldn't be such friends with any other dog but Jip; because he wouldn't have known me before I was married, and wouldn't have barked at Doady when he first came to our house. I couldn't care for any other dog but Jip, I am afraid, aunt."

"To be sure!" said my aunt, patting her cheek again. "You are right."

"You are not offended," said Dora, "are you?"

"Why, what a sensitive pet it is!" cried my aunt, bending over her affectionately. "To think that I could be offended!"

"No, no, I didn't really think so," returned Dora; "but I am a little tired, and it made me silly for a moment—I am always a silly little thing, you know; but it made me more silly—to talk about Jip. He has known me in all that has happened to me, haven't you, Jip? And I couldn't bear to slight him, because he was a little altered—could I, Jip?"

Jip nestled closer to his mistress, and lazily licked her hand.

"You are not so old, Jip, are you, that you'll leave your mistress yet?" said Dora. "We may keep one another company a little longer!"

My pretty Dora! When she came down to dinner on the ensuing Sunday, and was so glad to see old Traddles (who always dined with us on Sunday), we thought she would be "running about as she used to do," in a few days. But they said, wait a few days more, and then, wait a few days more; and still she neither ran nor walked. She looked very pretty, and was very merry; but the little feet that used to be so nimble when they danced round Jip, were dull and motionless.

I began to carry her downstairs every morning, and upstairs every night. She would clasp me round the neck and laugh, the while, as if I did it for a wager. Jip would bark and caper round us, and go on before, and look back on the landing, breathing short, to see that we were coming. My aunt, the best and most cheerful of nurses, would trudge after us, a moving mass of shawls and pillows. Mr. Dick would not have relinquished his post of candle-bearer to any one alive. Traddles would be often at the bottom of the staircase, looking on, and taking charge of sportive messages from Dora to the dearest girl in the world. We made quite a gay procession of it, and my child-wife was the gayest there.

But, sometimes, when I took her up, and felt that she was lighter in my arms, a dead blank feeling came upon me, as if I were approaching to some frozen region yet unseen, that numbed my life. I avoided the recognition of this feeling by any name, or by any communing with myself; until one night, when it was very strong upon me, and my aunt had left her with a parting cry of " Good night, Little Blossom," I sat down at my desk alone, and cried to think, Oh what a fatal name it was, and how the blossom withered in its bloom upon the tree!

49

I AM INVOLVED IN MYSTERY

I RECEIVED ONE MORNING BY THE POST, THE FOLLOWING letter, dated Canterbury, and addressed to me at Doctors' Commons; which I read with some surprise:

" MY DEAR SIR,

" Circumstances beyond my individual control have, for a considerable lapse of time, effected a severance of that intimacy which, in the limited opportunities conceded to me in the midst of my professional duties, of contemplating the scenes and events of the past, tinged by the prismatic hues of memory, has ever afforded me, as it ever must continue to afford, gratifying emotions of no common description. This fact, my dear sir, combined with the distinguished elevation to which your talents have raised you, deters me from presuming to aspire to the liberty of addressing the companion of my youth, by the familiar appellation of Copperfield! It is sufficient to know that the name to which I do myself the honour to refer, will ever be treasured among the muniments of our house (I allude to the archives connected with our former lodgers, preserved by Mrs. Micawber), with sentiments of personal esteem amounting to affection.

"It is not for one situated, through his original errors and a fortuitous combination of unpropitious events, as is the foundered Bark (if he may be allowed to assume so maritime a denomination), who now takes up the pen to address you—it is not, I repeat, for one so circumstanced, to adopt the language of compliment, or of congratulation. That he leaves to abler and to purer hands.

"If your more important avocations should admit of your ever tracing these imperfect characters thus far—which may be, or may not be, as circumstances arise—you will naturally inquire by what object am I influenced, then, in inditing the present missive? Allow me to say that I fully defer to the reasonable character of that inquiry, and proceed to develop it: promising that it is *not* an object of a pecuniary nature.

"Without more directly referring to any latent ability that may possibly exist on my part, of wielding the thunderbolt, or directing the devouring and avenging flame in any quarter, I may be permitted to observe, in passing, that my brightest visions are for ever dispelled—that my peace is shattered and my power of enjoyment destroyed—that my heart is no longer in the right place—and that I no more walk erect before my fellow-man. The canker is in the flower. The cup is bitter to the brim. The worm is at his work, and will soon dispose of his victim. The sooner the better. But I will not digress.

"Placed in a mental position of peculiar painfulness, beyond the assuaging reach even of Mrs. Micawber's influence, though exercised in the tripartite character of woman, wife, and mother, it is my intention to fly from myself for a short period, and devote a respite of eight-and-forty hours to revisiting some metropolitan scenes of past enjoyment. Among other havens of domestic tranquillity and peace of mind, my feet will naturally tend towards the King's Bench Prison. In stating that I shall be (D. V.) on the outside of the south wall of that place of incarceration on civil process, the day after to-morrow, at seven in the evening, precisely, my object in this epistolary communication is accomplished.

"I do not feel warranted in soliciting my former friend Mr.

Copperfield, or my former friend Mr. Thomas Traddles of the Inner Temple, if that gentleman is still existent and forthcoming, to condescend to meet me, and renew (so far as may be) our past relations of the olden time. I confine myself to throwing out the observation, that, at the hour and place I have indicated, may be found such ruined vestiges as yet

"Remain,
"Of
"A
"Fallen Tower,
"WILKINS MICAWBER.

"P.S. It may be advisable to superadd to the above, the statement that Mrs. Micawber is *not* in confidential possession of my intentions."

I read the letter over several times. Making due allowance for Mr. Micawber's lofty style of composition, and for the extraordinary relish with which he sat down and wrote long letters on all possible and impossible occasions, I still believed that something important lay hidden at the bottom of this roundabout communication. I put it down, to think about it; and took it up again, to read it once more; and was still pursuing it, when Traddles found me in the height of my perplexity.

"My dear fellow," said I, "I never was better pleased to see you. You come to give me the benefit of your sober judgment at a most opportune time. I have received a very singular letter, Traddles, from Mr. Micawber."

"No?" cried Traddles. "You don't say so? And I have received one from Mrs. Micawber!"

With that, Traddles, who was flushed with walking, and whose hair, under the combined effects of exercise and excitement, stood on end as if he saw a cheerful ghost, produced his letter and made an exchange with me. I watched him into the heart of Mr. Micawber's letter, and returned the elevation of eyebrows with which he said "'Wielding the thunderbolt, or directing the devouring and avenging flame!' Bless me, Copperfield!"—and then entered on the perusal of Mrs. Micawber's epistle.

It ran thus:

"My best regards to Mr. Thomas Traddles, and if he should still remember one who formerly had the happiness of being well acquainted with him, may I beg a few moments of his leisure time? I assure Mr. T. T. that I would not intrude upon his kindness, were I in any other position than on the confines of distraction.

"Though harrowing to myself to mention, the alienation of Mr. Micawber (formerly so domesticated) from his wife and family, is the cause of my addressing my unhappy appeal to Mr. Traddles, and soliciting his best indulgence. Mr. T. can form no adequate idea of the change in Mr. Micawber's conduct, of his wildness, of his violence. It has gradually augmented, until it assumes the appearance of aberration of intellect. Scarcely a day passes, I assure Mr. Traddles, on which some paroxysm does not take place. Mr. T. will not require me to depict my feelings, when I inform him that I have become accustomed to hear Mr. Micawber assert that he has sold himself to the D. Mystery and secrecy have long been his principal characteristic, have long replaced unlimited confidence. The slightest provocation, even being asked if there is anything he would prefer for dinner, causes him to express a wish for a separation. Last night, on being childishly solicited for twopence, to buy 'lemon-stunners'—a local sweetmeat—he presented an oyster-knife at the twins!

"I entreat Mr. Traddles to bear with me in entering into these details. Without them, Mr. T. would indeed find it difficult to form the faintest conception of my heart-rending situation.

"May I now venture to confide to Mr. T. the purport of my letter? Will he now allow me to throw myself on his friendly consideration? Oh yes, for I know his heart!

"The quick eye of affection is not easily blinded, when of the female sex. Mr. Micawber is going to London. Though he studiously concealed his hand, this morning before breakfast, in writing the direction-card which he attached to the little brown valise of happier days, the eagle-glance of matrimonial anxiety detected, d, o, n, distinctly traced. The West-End destination of the coach is the Golden Cross. Dare I fervently implore Mr. T. to see my misguided husband, and to reason with him! Dare I ask Mr. T. to endeavour to step in between Mr. Micawber and his agonised family? Oh no, for that would be too much!

"If Mr. Copperfield should yet remember one unknown to fame, will Mr. T. take charge of my unalterable regards and similar entreaties? In any case, he will have the benevolence *to consider this communication strictly private, and on no account whatever to be alluded to, however distantly, in presence of Mr. Micawber*. If Mr. T. should ever reply to it (which I cannot but feel to be *most* improbable), a letter addressed to M. E., Post

Office, Canterbury, will be fraught with less painful consequences than any addressed immediately to one, who subscribes herself, in extreme distress,

"Mr. Thomas Traddles's respectful friend and suppliant,

"EMMA MICAWBER."

"What do you think of that letter?" said Traddles, casting his eyes upon me, when I had read it twice.

"What do you think of the other?" said I. For he was still reading it with knitted brows.

"I think that the two together, Copperfield," replied Traddles, "mean more than Mr. and Mrs. Micawber usually mean in their correspondence—but I don't know what. They are both written in good faith, I have no doubt, and without any collusion. Poor thing!" he was now alluding to Mrs. Micawber's letter, and we were standing side by side comparing the two; "it will be a charity to write to her, at all events, and tell her that we will not fail to see Mr. Micawber."

I acceded to this the more readily, because I now reproached myself with having treated her former letter rather lightly. It had set me thinking a good deal at the time, as I have mentioned in its place; but my absorption in my own affairs, my experience of the family, and my hearing nothing more, had gradually ended in my dismissing the subject. I had often thought of the Micawbers, but chiefly to wonder what "pecuniary liabilities" they were establishing in Canterbury, and to recall how shy Mr. Micawber was of me when he became clerk to Uriah Heep.

However, I now wrote a comforting letter to Mrs. Micawber in our joint names, and we both signed it. As we walked into town to post it, Traddles and I held a long conference, and launched into a number of speculations, which I need not repeat. We took my aunt into our counsels in the afternoon; but our only decided conclusion was, that we would be very punctual in keeping Mr. Micawber's appointment.

Although we appeared at the stipulated place a quarter of an hour before the time, we found Mr. Micawber already there. He was standing with his arms folded, over against the wall, looking at the spikes on the top, with a sentimental expression, as if they were the interlacing boughs of trees that had shaded him in his youth.

When we accosted him, his manner was something more confused, and something less genteel than of yore. He had relinquished his legal suit of black for the purposes of this excursion, and wore the old surtout and tights, but not quite with the old air.

He gradually picked up more and more of it as we conversed with him; but his very eye-glass seemed to hang less easily, and his shirt-collar, though still of the old formidable dimensions, rather drooped.

"Gentlemen!" said Mr. Micawber, after the first salutations, "you are friends in need, and friends indeed. Allow me to offer my inquiries with reference to the physical welfare of Mrs. Copperfield *in esse*, and Mrs. Traddles *in posse*,—presuming, that is to say, that my friend Mr. Traddles is not yet united to the object of his affections, for weal and for woe."

We acknowledged his politeness, and made suitable replies. He then directed our attention to the wall, and was beginning, "I assure you, gentlemen," when I ventured to object to that ceremonious form of address, and to beg that he would speak to us in the old way.

"My dear Copperfield," he returned, pressing my hand, "your cordiality overpowers me. This reception of a shattered fragment of the Temple once called Man—if I may be permitted so to express myself—bespeaks a heart that is an honour to our common nature. I was about to observe that I again behold the serene spot where some of the happiest hours of my existence fleeted by."

"Made so, I am sure, by Mrs. Micawber," said I. "I hope she is well?"

"Thank you," returned Mr. Micawber, whose face clouded at this reference, "she is but so-so. And this," said Mr. Micawber, nodding his head sorrowfully, "is the Bench! Where, for the first time in many revolving years, the overwhelming pressure of pecuniary liabilities was not proclaimed, from day to day, by importunate voices declining to vacate the passage; where there was no knocker on the door for any creditor to appeal to; where personal service of process was not required, and detainers were merely lodged at the gate! Gentlemen," said Mr. Micawber, "when the shadow of that iron-work on the summit of the brick structure has been reflected on the gravel of the Parade, I have seen my children thread the mazes of the intricate pattern, avoiding the dark marks. I have been familiar with every stone in the place. If I betray weakness, you will know how to excuse me."

"We have all got on in life since then, Mr. Micawber," said I.

"Mr. Copperfield," returned Mr. Micawber, bitterly, "when I was an inmate of that retreat, I could look my fellow-man in the face, and punch his head if he offended me. My fellow-man and myself are no longer on those glorious terms!"

Turning from the building in a downcast manner, Mr. Micawber accepted my proffered arm on one side, and the proffered arm of Traddles on the other, and walked away between us.

"There are some landmarks," observed Mr. Micawber, looking fondly back over his shoulder, "on the road to the tomb, which, but for the impiety of the aspiration, a man would wish never to have passed. Such is the Bench in my chequered career"

"Oh, you are in low spirits, Mr. Micawber," said Traddles.

"I am, sir," interposed Mr. Micawber.

"I hope," said Traddles, "it is not because you have conceived a dislike to the law—for I am a lawyer myself, you know."

Mr. Micawber answered not a word.

"How is our friend Heep, Mr. Micawber?" said I, after a silence.

"My dear Copperfield," returned Mr. Micawber, bursting into a state of much excitement, and turning pale, "if you ask after my employer as *your* friend, I am sorry for it; if you ask after him as *my* friend, I sardonically smile at it. In whatever capacity you ask after my employer, I beg, without offence to you, to limit my reply to this—that whatever his state of health may be, his appearance is foxy: not to say diabolical. You will allow me, as a private individual, to decline pursuing a subject which has lashed me to the utmost verge of desperation in my professional capacity."

I expressed my regret for having innocently touched upon a theme that roused him so much. "May I ask," said I, "without any hazard of repeating the mistake, how my old friends Mr. and Miss Wickfield are?"

"Miss Wickfield," said Mr. Micawber, now turning red, "is, as she always is, a pattern, and a bright example. My dear Copperfield, she is the only starry spot in a miserable existence. My respect for that young lady, my admiration of her character, my devotion to her for her love and truth, and goodness!—Take me," said Mr. Micawber, "down a turning, for, upon my soul, in my present state of mind I am not equal to this!"

We wheeled him off into a narrow street, where he took out his pocket-handkerchief, and stood with his back to a wall. If I looked as gravely at him as Traddles did, he must have found our company by no means inspiriting.

"It is my fate," said Mr. Micawber, unfeignedly sobbing, but doing even that, with a shadow of the old expression of doing something genteel; "it is my fate, gentlemen, that the finer feelings of our nature have become reproaches to me. My homage to Miss Wickfield is a flight of arrows in my bosom. You had better leave me, if you please, to walk the earth as a vagabond. The worm will settle *my* business in double-quick time."

Without attending to this invocation, we stood by, until he put up his pocket-handkerchief, pulled up his shirt-collar, and, to delude any person in the neighbourhood who might have been observing him, hummed a tune with his hat very much on one side. I then mentioned—not knowing what might be lost if we lost sight of him yet—that it would give me great pleasure to introduce him to my aunt, if he would ride out to Highgate, where a bed was at his service.

"You shall make us a glass of your own punch, Mr. Micawber," said I, "and forget whatever you have on your mind, in pleasanter reminiscences."

"Or, if confiding anything to friends will be more likely to relieve you, you shall impart it to us, Mr. Micawber," said Traddles, prudently.

"Gentlemen," returned Mr. Micawber, "do with me as you will! I am a straw upon the surface of the deep, and am tossed in all directions by the elephants—I beg your pardon; I should have said the elements."

We walked on, arm-in-arm, again; found the coach in the act of starting; and arrived at Highgate without encountering any difficulties by the way. I was very uneasy and very uncertain in my mind what to say or do for the best—so was Traddles, evidently. Mr. Micawber was for the most part plunged into deep gloom. He occasionally made an attempt to smarten himself, and hum the fag-end of a tune; but his relapses into profound melancholy were only made the more impressive by the mockery of a hat exceedingly on one side, and a shirt-collar pulled up to his eyes.

We went to my aunt's house rather than to mine, because of Dora's not being well. My aunt presented herself on being sent for, and welcomed Mr. Micawber with gracious cordiality. Mr. Micawber kissed her hand, retired to the window, and pulling out his pocket-handkerchief, had a mental wrestle with himself.

Mr. Dick was at home. He was by nature so exceedingly compassionate of any one who seemed to be ill at ease, and was so quick to find any such person out, that he shook hands with Mr. Micawber, at least half-a-dozen times in five minutes. To Mr. Micawber, in his trouble, this warmth, on the part of a stranger, was so extremely touching, that he could only say, on the occasion of each successive shake, "My dear sir, you overpower me!" Which gratified Mr. Dick so much, that he went at it again with greater vigour than before.

"The friendliness of this gentleman," said Mr. Micawber to my aunt, "if you will allow me, ma'am, to cull a figure of speech from the vocabulary of our coarser national sports—floors me. To a man who is struggling with a complicated burden of perplexity and disquiet, such a reception is trying, I assure you."

"My friend Mr. Dick," replied my aunt, proudly, "is not a common man."

"That I am convinced of," said Mr. Micawber. "My dear sir!" for Mr. Dick was shaking hands with him again; "I am deeply sensible of your cordiality!"

"How do you find yourself?" said Mr. Dick, with an anxious look.

"Indifferent, my dear sir," returned Mr. Micawber, sighing.

"You must keep up your spirits," said Mr. Dick, "and make yourself as comfortable as possible."

Mr. Micawber was quite overcome by these friendly words, and by finding Mr. Dick's hand again within his own. "It has been my lot," he observed, "to meet, in the diversified panorama of human existence, with an occasional oasis, but never with one so green, so gushing, as the present!"

At another time I should have been amused by this; but I felt that we were all constrained and uneasy, and I watched Mr. Micawber so anxiously, in his vacillations between an evident disposition to reveal something, and a counter-disposition to reveal nothing, that I was in a perfect fever. Traddles, sitting on the edge of his chair, with his eyes wide open, and his hair more emphatically erect than ever, stared by turns at the ground and at Mr. Micawber, without so much as attempting to put in a word. My aunt, though I saw that her shrewdest observation was concentrated on her new guest, had more useful possession of her wits than either of us; for she held him in conversation, and made it necessary for him to talk, whether he liked it or not.

"You are a very old friend of my nephew's, Mr. Micawber," said my aunt. "I wish I had had the pleasure of seeing you before."

"Madam," returned Mr. Micawber, "I wish I had had the honour of knowing you at an earlier period. I was not always the wreck you at present behold."

"I hope Mrs. Micawber and your family are well, sir," said my aunt.

Mr. Micawber inclined his head. "They are as well, ma'am," he desperately observed, after a pause, "as Aliens and Outcasts can ever hope to be."

"Lord bless you, sir!" exclaimed my aunt in her abrupt way. "What are you talking about?"

"The subsistence of my family, ma'am," returned Mr. Micawber, "trembles in the balance. My employer——"

Here Mr. Micawber provokingly left off; and began to peel the lemons that had been under my directions set before him, together with all the other appliances he used in making punch.

"Your employer, you know," said Mr. Dick, jogging his arm as a gentle reminder.

"My good sir," returned Mr. Micawber, "you recall me. I am obliged to you." They shook hands again. "My employer, ma'am—Mr. Heep—once did me the favour to observe to me, that if I were not in the receipt of the stipendiary emoluments appertaining to my engagement with him, I should probably be a mountebank about the country, swallowing a sword-blade, and eating the devouring element. For anything that I can perceive to the contrary, it is still probable that my children may be reduced to seek a livelihood by personal contortion, while Mrs. Micawber abets their unnatural feats by playing the barrel-organ."

Mr. Micawber, with a random but expressive flourish of his knife, signified that these performances might be expected to take place after he was no more; then resumed his peeling with a desperate air.

My aunt leaned her elbow on the little round table that she usually kept beside her, and eyed him attentively. Notwithstanding the aversion with which I regarded the idea of entrapping him into any disclosure he was not prepared to make voluntarily, I should have taken him up at this point, but for the strange proceedings in which I saw him engaged; whereof his putting the lemon-peel into the kettle, the sugar into the snuffer-tray, the spirit into the empty jug, and confidently attempting to pour boiling water out of a candle-stick, were among the most remarkable. I saw that a crisis was at hand, and it came. He clattered all his means and implements together, rose from his chair, pulled out his pocket-handkerchief, and burst into tears.

"My dear Copperfield," said Mr. Micawber, behind his handkerchief, "this is an occupation, of all others, requiring an untroubled mind, and self-respect. I cannot perform it. It is out of the question."

"Mr. Micawber," said I, "what is the matter? Pray speak out. You are among friends."

"Among friends, sir!" repeated Mr. Micawber, and all he

had reserved came breaking out of him. " Good heavens, it is principally because I *am* among friends that my state of mind is what it is. What is the matter, gentlemen? What is *not* the matter? Villainy is the matter; baseness is the matter; deception, fraud, conspiracy, are the matter; and the name of the whole atrocious mass is—HEEP! "

My aunt clapped her hands, and we all started up as if we were possessed.

" The struggle is over! " said Mr. Micawber, violently gesticulating with his pocket-handkerchief, and fairly striking out from time to time with both arms, as if he were swimming under superhuman difficulties. " I will lead this life no longer. I am a wretched being, cut off from everything that makes life tolerable. I have been under a Taboo in that infernal scoundrel's service. Give me back my wife, give me back my family, substitute Micawber for the petty wretch who walks about in the boots at present on my feet, and call upon me to swallow a sword to-morrow, and I'll do it. With an appetite! "

I never saw a man so hot in my life. I tried to calm him, that we might come to something rational; but he got hotter and hotter, and wouldn't hear a word.

" I'll put my hand in no man's hand," said Mr. Micawber, gasping, puffing, and sobbing, to that degree that he was like a man fighting with cold water, " until I have—blown to fragments—the—a—detestable—serpent—HEEP! I'll partake of no one's hospitality, until I have—a—moved Mount Vesuvius—to eruption—on—a—the abandoned rascal—HEEP! Refreshment—a—underneath this roof—particularly punch—would—a—choke me—unless—I had—previously—choked the eyes—out of the head—a—of—interminable cheat, and liar—HEEP! I—a I'll know nobody—and—a—say nothing—and—a—live nowhere—until I have crushed—to—a—undiscoverable atoms—the—transcendent and immortal hypocrite and perjurer—HEEP! "

I really had some fear of Mr. Micawber's dying on the spot. The manner in which he struggled through these inarticulate sentences, and, whenever he found himself getting near the name of Heep, fought his way on to it, dashed at it in a fainting state, and brought it out with a vehemence little less than marvellous, was frightful; but now, when he sank into a chair, steaming, and looked at us, with every possible colour in his face that had no business there, and an endless procession of lumps following one another in hot haste up his throat, whence they seemed to shoot into his forehead, he had the appearance of being in the last extremity. I would have gone to his assistance, but he waved me off, and wouldn't hear a word.

"No, Copperfield!—No communication—a—until—Miss Wickfield—a—redress from wrongs inflicted by consummate scoundrel—HEEP!" (I am quite convinced he could not have uttered three words, but for the amazing energy with which this word inspired him when he felt it coming.) "Inviolable secret—a—from the whole world—a—no exceptions—this day week—a—at breakfast time—a—everybody present—including aunt—a—and extremely friendly gentleman—to be at the hotel at Canterbury—a—where—Mrs. Micawber and myself—Auld Lang Syne in chorus—and—a—will expose intolerable ruffian—HEEP! No more to say—a—or listen to persuasion—go immediately—not capable—a—bear society—upon the track of devoted and doomed traitor—HEEP!"

With this last repetition of the magic word that had kept him going at all, and in which he surpassed all his previous efforts, Mr. Micawber rushed out of the house; leaving us in a state of excitement, hope, and wonder, that reduced us to a condition little better than his own. But even then his passion for writing letters was too strong to be resisted; for while we were yet in the height of our excitement, hope, and wonder, the following pastoral note was brought to me from a neighbouring tavern, at which he had called to write it:—

"Most secret and confidential.

"MY DEAR SIR,

"I beg to be allowed to convey, through you, my apologies to your excellent aunt for my late excitement. An explosion of a smouldering volcano long suppressed, was the result of an internal contest more easily conceived than described.

"I trust I rendered tolerably intelligible my appointment for the morning of this day week, at the house of public entertainment at Canterbury, where Mrs. Micawber and myself had once the honour of uniting our voices to yours, in the well-known strain of the Immortal exciseman nurtured beyond the Tweed.

"The duty done, and act of reparation performed, which can alone enable me to contemplate my fellow-mortal, I shall be known no more. I shall simply require to be deposited in that place of universal resort, where

"Each in his narrow cell for ever laid,
"The rude forefathers of the hamlet sleep,

"—With the plain Inscription,

"WILKINS MICAWBER."

50

MR. PEGGOTTY'S DREAM COMES TRUE

BY THIS TIME, SOME MONTHS HAD PASSED SINCE OUR interview on the bank of the river with Martha. I had never seen her since, but she had communicated with Mr. Peggotty on several occasions. Nothing had come of her zealous intervention; nor could I infer, from what he told me, that any clue had been obtained, for a moment, to Emily's fate. I confess that I began to despair of her recovery, and gradually to sink deeper and deeper into the belief that she was dead.

His conviction remained unchanged. So far as I know—and I believe his honest heart was transparent to me—he never wavered again, in his solemn certainty of finding her. His patience never tired. And, although I trembled for the agony it might one day be to him to have his strong assurance shivered at a blow, there was something so religious in it, so affectingly expressive of its anchor being in the purest depths of his fine nature, that the respect and honour in which I held him were exalted every day.

His was not a lazy trustfulness that hoped, and did no more. He had been a man of sturdy action all his life, and he knew that in all things wherein he wanted help he must do his own part faithfully, and help himself. I have known him set out in the night, on a misgiving that the light might not be, by some accident, in the window of the old boat, and walk to Yarmouth. I have known him, on reading something in the newspaper, that might apply to her, take up his stick, and go forth on a journey of three or four score miles. He made his way by sea to Naples and back, after hearing the narrative to which Miss Dartle had assisted me. All his journeys were ruggedly performed; for he was always steadfast in a purpose of saving money for Emily's sake, when she should be found. In all this long pursuit, I never heard him repine; I never heard him say he was fatigued, or out of heart.

Dora had often seen him since our marriage, and was quite fond of him. I fancy his figure before me now, standing near her sofa, with his rough cap in his hand, and the blue eyes of my child-wife raised, with a timid wonder, to his face. Sometimes of an evening, about twilight, when he came to talk with me, I would induce him to smoke his pipe in the garden, as we slowly paced to and fro together; and then the picture of his deserted home, and the comfortable air it used to have in my childish eyes of an evening when the fire was burning, and the wind moaning round it, came most vividly into my mind.

One evening, at this hour, he told me that he had found Martha waiting near his lodging on the preceding night when he came out, and that she had asked him not to leave London on any account, until he should have seen her again.

"Did she tell you why?" I inquired.

"I asked her, Mas'r Davy," he replied, "but it is but few words as she ever says, and she on'y got my promise and so went away."

"Did she say when you might expect to see her again?" I demanded.

"No, Mas'r Davy," he returned, drawing his hand thoughtfully down his face. "I asked that too; but it was more (she said) than she could tell."

As I had long forborne to encourage him with hopes that hung on threads, I made no other comment on this information than that I supposed he would see her soon. Such speculations as it engendered within me I kept to myself, and those were faint enough.

I was walking alone in the garden, one evening, about a fortnight afterwards. I remember that evening well. It was the second in Mr. Micawber's week of suspense. There had been rain all day, and there was a damp feeling in the air. The leaves were thick upon the trees and heavy with wet; but the rain had ceased, though the sky was still dark; and the hopeful birds were singing cheerfully. As I walked to and fro in the garden, and the twilight began to close around me, their little voices were hushed; and that peculiar silence which belongs to such an evening in the country when the lightest trees are quite still, save for the occasional droppings from their boughs, prevailed.

There was a little green perspective of trellis-work and ivy at the side of our cottage, through which I could see, from the garden where I was walking, into the road before the house. I happened to turn my eyes towards this place, as I was thinking of many things; and I saw a figure beyond, dressed in a plain cloak. It was bending eagerly towards me, and beckoning.

"Martha!" said I, going to it.

"Can you come with me?" she inquired, in an agitated whisper. "I have been to him, and he is not at home. I wrote down where he was to come, and left it on his table with my own hand. They said he would not be out long. I have tidings for him. Can you come directly?"

My answer was to pass out at the gate immediately. She made a hasty gesture with her hand, as if to entreat my patience and my silence, and turned towards London, whence, as her dress betokened, she had come expeditiously on foot.

I asked her if that were not our destination? On her motioning Yes, with the same hasty gesture as before, I stopped an empty coach that was coming by, and we got into it. When I asked her where the coachman was to drive, she answered, "Anywhere near Golden Square! And quick!"—then shrunk into a corner, with one trembling hand before her face, and the other making the former gesture, as if she could not bear a voice.

Now much disturbed, and dazzled with conflicting gleams of hope and dread, I looked at her for some explanation. But seeing how strongly she desired to remain quiet, and feeling that it was my own natural inclination too, at such a time, I did not attempt to break the silence. We proceeded without a word being spoken. Sometimes she glanced out of the window, as though she thought we were going slowly, though indeed we were going fast; but otherwise remained exactly as at first.

We alighted at one of the entrances to the Square she had mentioned, where I directed the coach to wait, not knowing but that we might have some occasion for it. She laid her hand on my arm, and hurried me on to one of the sombre streets, of which there are several in that part, where the houses were once fair dwellings in the occupation of single families, but have, and had, long degenerated into poor lodgings let off in rooms. Entering at the open door of one of these, and releasing my arm, she beckoned me to follow her up the common staircase, which was like a tributary channel to the street.

The house swarmed with inmates. As we went up, doors of rooms were opened and people's heads put out; and we passed other people on the stairs, who were coming down. In glancing up from the outside, before we entered, I had seen women and children lolling at the windows over flowerpots; and we seemed to have attracted their curiosity, for these were principally the observers who looked out of their doors. It was a broad panelled staircase, with massive balustrades of some dark wood; cornices above the doors, ornamented with carved fruit and flowers; and broad seats in the windows. But all these tokens of past grandeur were miserably decayed and dirty; rot, damp, and age, had weakened the flooring, which in many places was unsound and even unsafe. Some attempts had been made, I noticed, to infuse new blood into this dwindling frame, by repairing the costly old wood-work here and there with common deal; but it was like the marriage of a reduced old noble to a plebeian pauper, and each party to the ill-assorted union shrunk away from the other. Several of the back windows on the staircase had been darkened or wholly blocked up. In those that remained, there was scarcely any glass; and, through the crumbling frames by which the bad air seemed always to come in, and never to go out, I saw, through other glassless windows, into other houses in a similar condition, and looked giddily down into a wretched yard, which was the common dust-heap of the mansion.

We proceeded to the top-storey of the house. Two or three times, by the way, I thought I observed in the indistinct light the skirts of a female figure going up before us. As we turned to ascend the last flight of stairs between us and the roof, we caught a full view of this figure pausing for a moment, at a door. Then it turned the handle, and went in.

" What's this! " said Martha, in a whisper. " She has gone into my room. I don't know her! "

I knew her. I had recognised her with amazement, for Miss Dartle.

I said something to the effect that it was a lady whom I had seen before, in a few words, to my conductress; and had scarcely done so when we heard her voice in the room, though not, from where we stood, what she was saying. Martha, with an astonished look, repeated her former action, and softly led me up the stairs; and then, by a little back door which seemed to have no lock, and which she pushed open with a touch, into a small empty garret with a low sloping roof: little better than a cupboard. Between this, and the room she had called hers, there was a small door of communication, standing partly open. Here we stopped, breathless with our ascent, and she placed her hand lightly on my lips. I could only see, of the room beyond, that it was pretty large; that there was a bed in it; and that there were some common pictures of ships upon the walls. I could not see Miss Dartle, or the person whom we had heard her address. Certainly, my companion could not, for my position was the best.

A dead silence prevailed for some moments. Martha kept one hand on my lips, and raised the other in a listening attitude.

" It matters little to me her not being at home," said Rosa

Dartle, haughtily, "I know nothing of her. It is you I come to see."

"Me?" replied a soft voice.

At the sound of it, a thrill went through my frame For it was Emily's!

"Yes," returned Miss Dartle, "I have come to look at you. What? You are not ashamed of the face that has done so much?"

The resolute and unrelenting hatred of her tone, its cold stern sharpness, and its mastered rage, presented her before me, as if I had seen her standing in the light. I saw the flashing black eyes, and the passion-wasted figure; and I saw the scar, with its white track cutting through her lips, quivering and throbbing as she spoke.

"I have come to see," she said, "James Steerforth's fancy; the girl who ran away with him, and is the town-talk of the commonest people of her native place; the bold, flaunting, practised companion of persons like James Steerforth. I want to know what such a thing is like."

There was a rustle, as if the unhappy girl, on whom she heaped these taunts, ran towards the door, and the speaker swiftly interposed herself before it. It was succeeded by a moment's pause.

When Miss Dartle spoke again, it was through her set teeth, and with a stamp upon the ground.

"Stay there!" she said, "or I'll proclaim you to the house, and the whole street! If you try to evade *me*, I'll stop you, if it's by the hair, and raise the very stones against you!"

A frightened murmur was the only reply that reached my ears. A silence succeeded. I did not know what to do. Much as I desired to put an end to the interview, I felt that I had no right to present myself; but it was for Mr. Peggotty alone to see her and recover her. Would he never come? I thought, impatiently.

"So!" said Rosa Dartle, with a contemptuous laugh, "I see her at last! Why, he was a poor creature to be taken by that delicate mock-modesty, and that hanging head!"

"Oh, for Heaven's sake, spare me!" exclaimed Emily. "Whoever you are, you know my pitiable story, and for Heaven's sake spare me, if you would be spared yourself!"

"If *I* would be spared!" returned the other fiercely; "what is there in common between *us*, do you think!"

"Nothing but our sex," said Emily, with a burst of tears.

"And that," said Rosa Dartle, "is so strong a claim, preferred by one so infamous, that if I had any feeling in my breast but scorn and abhorrence of you, it would freeze it up. Our sex! You are an honour to our sex!"

"I have deserved this," said Emily, "but it's dreadful! Dear, dear lady, think what I have suffered, and how I am fallen! Oh, Martha, come back! Oh, home, home!"

Miss Dartle placed herself in a chair, within view of the door, and looked downward, as if Emily were crouching on the floor before her. Being now between me and the light, I could see her curled lip, and her cruel eyes intently fixed on one place, with a greedy triumph.

"Listen to what I say!" she said; "and reserve your false arts for your dupes. Do you hope to move *me* by your tears? No more than you could charm me by your smiles, you purchased slave."

"Oh, have some mercy on me!" cried Emily. "Show me some compassion, or I shall die mad!"

"It would be no great penance," said Rosa Dartle, "for your crimes. Do you know what you have done? Do you ever think of the home you have laid waste?"

"Oh, is there ever night or day, when I don't think of it!" cried Emily; and now I could just see her, on her knees, with her head thrown back, her pale face looking upwards, her hands wildly clasped and held out, and her hair streaming about her. "Has there ever been a single minute, waking or sleeping, when it hasn't been before me, just as it used to be in the lost days when I turned my back upon it for ever and for ever! Oh, home, home! Oh dear, dear uncle, if you ever could have known the agony your love would cause me when I fell away from good, you never would have shown it to me so constant, much as you felt it; but would have been angry to me, at least once in my life, that I might have had some comfort! I have none, none, no comfort upon earth, for all of them were always fond of me!" She dropped on her face, before the imperious figure in the chair, with an imploring effort to clasp the skirt of her dress.

Rosa Dartle sat looking down upon her, as inflexible as a figure of brass. Her lips were tightly compressed, as if she knew that she must keep a strong constraint upon herself—I write what I sincerely believe—or she would be tempted to strike the beautiful form with her foot. I saw her, distinctly, and the whole power of her face and character seemed forced into that expression.—Would he never come?

"The miserable vanity of these earth-worms!" she said, when she had so far controlled the angry heavings of her breast, that she could trust herself to speak. "*Your* home! Do you imagine that I bestow a thought on it, or suppose you could do any harm to that low place, which money would not pay for, and handsomely? *Your* home! You were a part of the trade of your home, and were bought and sold like any other vendible thing your people dealt in."

"Oh, not that!" cried Emily. "Say anything of me; but don't visit my disgrace and shame, more than I have done, on folks who are as honourable as you! Have some respect for them, as you are a lady, if you have no mercy for me."

"I speak," she said, not deigning to take any heed of this appeal, and drawing away her dress from the contamination of Emily's touch, "I speak of *his* home—where I live. Here," she said, stretching out her hand with a contemptuous laugh, and looking down upon the prostrate girl, "is a worthy cause of division between lady-mother and gentleman-son; of grief in a house where she wouldn't have been admitted as a kitchen-girl; of anger, and repining, and reproach. This piece of pollution, picked up from the waterside, to be made much of for an hour, and then tossed back to her original place!"

"No! no!" cried Emily, clasping her hands together. "When he first came into my way—that the day had never dawned upon me, and he had met me being carried to my grave!—I had been brought up as virtuous as you or any lady, and was going to be the wife of as good a man as you or any lady in the world can ever marry. If you live in his home and know him, you know, perhaps, what his power with a weak, vain girl might be. I don't defend myself, but I know well, and he knows well, or he will know when he comes to die, and his mind is troubled with it, that he used all his power to deceive me, and that I believed him, trusted him, and loved him!"

Rosa Dartle sprang up from her seat; recoiled; and in recoiling struck at her, with a face of such malignity, so darkened and disfigured by passion, that I had almost thrown myself between them. The blow, which had no aim, fell upon the air. As she now stood panting, looking at her with the utmost detestation that she was capable of expressing, and trembling from head to foot with rage and scorn, I thought I had never seen such a sight, and never could see such another.

"*You* love him? *You*?" she cried, with her clenched hand, quivering as if it only wanted a weapon to stab the object of her wrath.

Emily had shrunk out of my view. There was no reply.

"And tell that to *me*," she added, "with your shameful lips?

Why don't they whip these creatures? If I could order it to be done, I would have this girl whipped to death."

And so she would, I have no doubt. I would not have trusted her with the rack itself, while that furious look lasted.

She slowly, very slowly, broke into a laugh, and pointed at Emily with her hand, as if she were a sight of shame for gods and men.

"*She* love!" she said. "That carrion! And he ever cared for her, she'd tell me. Ha, ha! The liars that these traders are!"

Her mockery was worse than her undisguised rage. Of the two, I would have much preferred to be the object of the latter. But, when she suffered it to break loose, it was only for a moment. She had chained it up again, and however it might tear her within, she subdued it to herself.

"I came here, you pure fountain of love," she said, "to see —as I began by telling you—what such a thing as you was like. I was curious. I am satisfied. Also to tell you, that you had best seek that home of yours, with all speed, and hide your head among those excellent people who are expecting you, and whom your money will console. When it's all gone, you can believe and trust, and love again, you know! I thought you a broken toy that had lasted its time; a worthless spangle that was tarnished, and thrown away. But, finding you true gold, a very lady, and an ill-used innocent, with a fresh heart full of love and trustfulness—which you look like, and is quite consistent with your story!—I have something more to say. Attend to it; for what I say I'll do. Do you hear me, you fairy spirit? What I say, I mean to do!"

Her rage got the better of her again, for a moment; but it passed over her face like a spasm, and left her smiling.

"Hide yourself," she pursued, "if not at home, somewhere. Let it be somewhere beyond reach; in some obscure life—or, better still, in some obscure death. I wonder, if your loving heart will not break, you have found no way of helping it to be still! I have heard of such means sometimes. I believe they may be easily found."

A low crying, on the part of Emily, interrupted her here. She stopped, and listened to it as if it were music.

"I am of a strange nature, perhaps," Rosa Dartle went on; "but I can't breathe freely in the air you breathe. I find it sickly. Therefore, I will have it cleared; I will have it purified of you. If you live here to-morrow, I'll have your story and your character proclaimed on the common stair. There are decent women in the house, I am told; and it is a pity such a light as you should be among them, and concealed. If, leaving here, you seek any refuge in this town in any character but your true one (which you are welcome to bear, without molestation from me), the same service shall be done you, if I hear of your retreat. Being assisted by a gentleman who not long ago aspired to the favour of your hand, I am sanguine as to that."

Would he never, never come? How long was I to bear this? How long could I bear it?

"Oh me, oh me!" exclaimed the wretched Emily, in a tone that might have touched the hardest heart, I should have thought; but there was no relenting in Rosa Dartle's smile. "What, what, shall I do!"

"Do?" returned the other. "Live happy in your own reflections! Consecrate your existence to the recollection of James Steerforth's tenderness—he would have made you his serving-man's wife, would he not?—or to feeling grateful to the upright and deserving creature who would have taken you as his gift. Or, if those proud remembrances, and the consciousness of your own virtues, and the honourable position to which they have raised you in the eyes of everything that wears the human shape, will not sustain you, marry that good man, and be happy in his condescension. If this will not do either, die! There are doorways and dust-heaps for such deaths, and such despair—find one, and take your flight to Heaven!"

I heard a distant foot upon the stairs. I knew it, I was certain. It was his, thank God!

She moved slowly from before the door when she said this, and passed out of my sight.

"But mark!" she added, slowly and sternly, opening the other door to go away, "I am resolved, for reasons that I have and hatreds that I entertain, to cast you out, unless you withdraw from my reach altogether, or drop your pretty mask. This is what I had to say; and what I say, I mean to do!"

The foot upon the stairs came nearer—nearer—passed her as she went down—rushed into the room!

"Uncle!"

A fearful cry followed the word. I paused a moment, and, looking in, saw him supporting her insensible figure in his arms. He gazed for a few seconds in the face; then stooped to kiss it—oh, how tenderly!—and drew a handkerchief before it.

"Mas'r Davy," he said in a low tremulous voice, when it was covered. "I thank my Heav'nly Father as my dream's come true! I thank Him hearty for having guided of me, in His own ways, to my darling!"

With those words he took her up in his arms; and, with the veiled face lying on his bosom, and addressed towards his own, carried her, motionless and unconscious, down the stairs.

51

THE BEGINNING OF A LONGER JOURNEY

IT WAS YET EARLY IN THE MORNING OF THE FOLLOWING day, when, as I was walking in my garden with my aunt (who took little other exercise now, being so much in attendance on my dear Dora), I was told that Mr. Peggotty desired to speak with me. He came into the garden to meet me half-way, on my going towards the gate; and bared his head, as it was always his custom to do when he saw my aunt, for whom he had a high respect. I had been telling her all that had happened overnight. Without saying a word, she walked up with a cordial face, shook hands with him, and patted him on the arm. It was so expressively done, that she had no need to say a word. Mr. Peggotty understood her quite as well as if she had said a thousand.

"I'll go in now, Trot," said my aunt, "and look after Little Blossom, who will be getting up presently."

"Not along of my being heer, ma'am, I hope?" said Mr. Peggotty. "Unless my wits is gone a bahd's neezing"—by which Mr. Peggotty meant to say, bird's-nesting—"this morning, 'tis along of me as you're a-going to quit us?"

"You have something to say, my good friend," returned my aunt, "and will do better without me."

"By your leave, ma'am," returned Mr. Peggotty, "I should take it kind, perviding you doen't mind my clicketten, if you'd bide heer."

"Would you?" said my aunt, with short good-nature. "Then I am sure I will!"

So she drew her arm through Mr. Peggotty's, and walked with him to a leafy little summer-house there was at the bottom of the garden, where she sat down on a bench, and I beside her. There was a seat for Mr. Peggotty too, but he preferred to stand, leaning his hand on the small rustic table. As he stood, looking at his cap for a little while before beginning to speak, I could not help observing what power and force of character his sinewy hand expressed, and what a good and trusty companion it was to his honest brow and iron-grey hair.

"I took my dear child away last night," Mr. Peggotty began, as he raised his eyes to ours, "to my lodging, wheer I have a long time been expecting of her and preparing fur her. It was hours afore she knowed me right; and when she did, she kneeled down at my feet, and kiender said to me, as if it was her prayers, how it all come to be. You may believe me, when I heerd her voice, as I had heerd at home so playful—and see her humbled, as it might be in the dust our Saviour wrote in with his blessed hand—I felt a wownd go to my 'art, in the midst of all its thankfulness."

He drew his sleeve across his face, without any pretence of concealing why; and then cleared his voice.

"It warn't for long as I felt that; for she was found. I had on'y to think as she was found, and it was gone. I doen't know why I do so much as mention of it now, I'm sure. I didn't have it in my mind a minute ago, to say a word about myself; but it come up so nat'ral, that I yielded to it afore I was aweer."

"You are a self-denying soul," said my aunt, "and will have your reward."

Mr. Peggotty, with the shadows of the leaves playing athwart his face, made a surprised inclination of the head towards my aunt, as an acknowledgment of her good opinion; then took up the thread he had relinquished.

"When my Em'ly took flight," he said, in stern wrath for the moment, "from the house wheer she was made a pris'ner by that theer spotted snake as Mas'r Davy see,—and his story's trew, and may God confound him!—she took flight in the night. It was a dark night, with a many stars a-shining. She was wild. She ran along the sea beach, believing the old boat was theer; and calling out to us to turn away our faces, for she was a-coming by. She heerd herself a-crying out, like as if it was another person; and cut herself on them sharp-pinted stones and rocks, and felt it no more than if she had been rock herself. Ever so fur she run, and there was fire afore her eyes, and roarings in her ears. Of a sudden—or so she thowt, you unnerstand—the day broke, wet and windy, and she was lying b'low a heap of stone upon the shore, and a woman was a-speaking to her, saying, in the language of that country, what was it as had gone so much amiss?"

He saw everything he related. It passed before him, as he spoke, so vividly, that, in the intensity of his earnestness, he presented what he described to me, with greater distinctness than I can express. I can hardly believe, writing now long afterwards, but that I was actually present in these scenes; they are impressed upon me with such an astonishing air of fidelity.

"As Em'ly's eyes—which was heavy—see this woman better," Mr. Peggotty went on, "she know'd as she was one of them as she had often talked to on the beach. Fur though she had run (as I have said) ever so fur in the night, she had oftentimes wandered long ways, partly afoot, partly in boats and carriages, and know'd all that country, 'long the coast, miles and miles. She hadn't no children of her own, this woman, being a young wife; but she was a-looking to have one afore long. And may my prayers go up to Heaven that 'twill be a happ'ness to her, and a comfort, and a honour, all her life! May it love her and be dootiful to her, in her old age; helpful of her at the last; a Angel to her heer, and heerafter!"

"Amen!" said my aunt.

"She had been summat timorous and down," said Mr. Peggotty, "and had sat, at first, a little way off, at her spinning, or such work as it was, when Em'ly talked to the children. But Em'ly had took notice of her, and had gone and spoke to her; and as the young woman was partial to the children herself, they had soon made friends. Sermuchser, that when Em'ly went that way, she always giv Em'ly flowers. This was her as now asked what it was that had gone so much amiss. Em'ly told her, and she—took her home. She did indeed. She took her home," said Mr. Peggotty, covering his face.

He was more affected by this act of kindness, than I had ever seen him affected by anything since the night she went away. My aunt and I did not attempt to disturb him.

"It was a little cottage, you may suppose," he said, presently, "but she found space for Em'ly in it,—her husband was away at sea,—and she kep it secret, and prevailed upon such neighbours as she had (they was not many near) to keep it secret too. Em'ly was took bad with fever, and what is very strange to me is,—maybe 'tis not so strange to scholars,—the language of that country went out of her head, and she could only speak her own, that no one unnerstood. She recollects, as if she had dreamed it, that she lay theer, always a-talking her own tongue. always believing as the old boat was round the next pint in the bay, and begging and imploring of 'em to send theer and tell how she was dying, and bring back a message of forgiveness, if it was on'y a wured. A'most the whole time, she thowt,—now, that him as I made mention on just now was lurking for her unnerneath the winder: now, that him as had brought her to this was in the room,—and cried to the good young woman not to give her up, and know'd at the same time, that she couldn't unnerstand, and dreaded that she must be took away. Likewise the fire was afore her eyes, and the roarings in her ears; and theer was no to-day, nor yesterday, nor yet to-morrow; but everything in her life as ever had been, or as ever could be, and everything as never had been, and as never could be, was a-crowding on her all at once, and nothing clear nor welcome, and yet she sang and laughed about it! How long this lasted, I doen't know; but then theer come a sleep; and in that sleep, from being a many times stronger than her own self, she fell into the weakness of the littlest child."

Here he stopped, as if for relief from the terrors of his own description. After being silent for a few moments, he pursued his story.

"It was a pleasant arternoon when she awoke; and so quiet, that theer warn't a sound but the rippling of that blue sea without a tide, upon the shore. It was her belief, at first, that she was at home upon a Sunday morning; but the vine leaves as she see at the winder, and the hills beyond, warn't home, and contradicted of her. Then come in her friend to watch alongside of her bed; and then she know'd as the old boat warn't round that next pint in the bay no more, but was fur off; and know'd wheer she was, and why; and broke out a-crying on that good young woman's bosom, wheer I hope her baby is a lying now, a-cheering of her with its pretty eyes!"

He could not speak of this good friend of Emily's without a flow of tears. It was in vain to try. He broke down again, endeavouring to bless her!

"That done my Em'ly good," he resumed, after such emotion as I could not behold without sharing in; and as to my aunt, she wept with all her heart; "that done Em'ly good, and she begun to mend. But the language of that country was quite gone from her, and she was forced to make signs. So she went on, getting better from day to day, slow, but sure, and trying to learn the names of common things—names as she seemed never to have heerd in all her life—till one evening come, when she was a-setting at her winder, looking at a little girl at play upon the beach. And of a sudden this child held out her hand,

and said, what would be in English, ' Fisherman's daughter here's a shell! '—for you are to unnerstand that they used at first to call her ' Pretty lady,' as the general way in that country is, and that she had taught 'em to call her ' Fisherman's daughter ' instead. The child says of a sudden, ' Fisherman's daughter, here's a shell! ' Then Em'ly unnerstands her; and she answers, bursting out a-crying; and it all comes back!

" When Em'ly got strong again," said Mr. Peggotty, after another short interval of silence, " she casts about to leave that good young creetur, and get to her own country. The husband was come home, then; and the two together put her aboard a small trader bound to Leghorn, and from that to France. She had a little money, but it was less than little as they would take for all they done. I'm a'most glad on it, though they was so poor. What they done, is laid up wheer neither moth nor rust doth corrupt, and wheer thieves do not break through nor steal. Mas'r Davy, it'll outlast all the treasure in the wureld.

" Em'ly got to France, and took service to wait on travelling ladies at a inn in the port. Theer, theer come, one day, that snake.—Let him never come nigh me. I doen't know what hurt I might do him!—Soon as she see him, without him seeing her, all her fear and wildness returned upon her, and she fled afore the very breath he draw'd. She come to England, and was set ashore at Dover.

" I doen't know," said Mr. Peggotty, " for sure, when her 'art begun to fail her; but all the way to England she had thowt to come to her dear home. Soon as she got to England she turned her face tow'rds it. But fear of not being forgiv, fear of being pinted at, fear of some of us being dead along of her, fear of many things, turned her from it, kiender by force, upon the road: ' Uncle, uncle,' she says to me, ' the fear of not being worthy to do what my torn and bleeding breast so longed to do, was the most fright'ning fear of all! I turned back, when my 'art was full of prayers that I might crawl to the old doorstep, in the night, kiss it, lay my wicked face upon it, and theer be found dead in the morning.'

" She come," said Mr. Peggotty, dropping his voice to an awe-stricken whisper, " to London. She—as had never seen it in her life—alone—without a penny—young—so pretty—come to London. A'most the moment as she lighted heer, all so desolate, she found (as she believed) a friend; a decent woman as spoke to her about the needlework as she had been brought up tc do, about finding plenty of it fur her, about a lodging fur the night, and making secret inquiration concerning of me and all at home, to-morrow. When my child," he said aloud, and with an energy of gratitude that shook him from head to foot, " stood upon the brink of more than I can say or think on—Martha, trew to her promise, saved her."

I could not repress a cry of joy.

" Mas'r Davy! " said he, gripping my hand in that strong hand of his, " it was you as first made mention of her to me. I thankee, sir! She was arnest. She had know'd of her bitter knowledge wheer to watch and what to do. She had done it. And the Lord was above all! She come, white and hurried, upon Em'ly in her sleep. She says to her, ' Rise up from worse than death, and come with me! ' Them belonging to the house would have stopped her, but they might as soon have stopped the sea. ' Stand away from me,' she says, ' I am a ghost that calls her from beside her open grave! ' She told Em'ly she had seen me, and know'd I loved her, and forgive her. She wrapped her, hasty, in her clothes. She took her, faint and trembling, on her arm. She heeded no more what they said, than if she had had no ears. She walked among 'em with my child, minding only her; and brought her safe out, in the dead of the night, from that black pit of ruin!

" She attended on Em'ly," said Mr. Peggotty, who had released my hand, and put his own hand on his heaving chest; " she attended to my Em'ly, lying wearied out, and wandering betwixt whiles, till late next day. Then she went in search of me; then in search of you, Mas'r Davy. She didn't tell Em'ly what she come out fur, lest her 'art should fail, and she should think of hiding of herself. How the cruel lady know'd of her being theer, I can't say. Whether him as I have spoke so much of, chanced to see 'em going theer, or whether (which is most like to my thinking) he had heerd it from the woman, I doen't greatly ask myself. My niece is found.

" All night long," said Mr. Peggotty, " we have been together, Em'ly and me. 'Tis little (considering the time) as she has said, in wureds, through them broken-hearted tears; 'tis less as I have seen of her dear face, as grow'd into a woman's at my hearth. But, all night long, her arms has been about my neck; and her head has laid heer; and we knows full well, as we can put our trust in one another ever more."

He ceased to speak, and his hand upon the table rested there in perfect repose, with a resolution in it that might have conquered lions.

" It was a gleam of light upon me, Trot," said my aunt, drying her eyes, " when I formed the resolution of being godmother to your sister Betsey Trotwood, who disappointed me; but, next to that, hardly anything would have given me greater pleasure, than to be godmother to that good young creature's baby!"

Mr. Peggotty nodded his understanding of my aunt's feelings, but could not trust himself with any verbal reference to the subject of her commendation. We all remained silent, and occupied with our own reflections (my aunt drying her eyes, and now sobbing convulsively, and now laughing and calling herself a fool), until I spoke.

"You have quite made up your mind," said I to Mr. Peggotty, "as to the future, good friend? I need scarcely ask you."

"Quite, Mas'r Davy," he returned; "and told Em'ly. Theer's mighty countries, fur from heer. Our future life lays over the sea."

"They will emigrate together, aunt," said I.

"Yes!" said Mr. Peggotty, with a hopeful smile. "No one can't reproach my darling in Australia. We will begin a new life over theer!"

I asked him if he yet proposed to himself any time for going away.

"I was down at the Docks early this morning, sir," he returned, "to get information concerning of them ships. In about six weeks or two months from now, theer'll be one sailing—I see her this morning—went aboard—and we shall take our passage in her."

"Quite alone?" I asked.

"Aye, Mas'r Davy!" he returned. "My sister, you see, she's that fond of you and yourn, and that accustomed to think on'y of her own country, that it wouldn't be hardly fair to let her go. Besides which, theer's one she has in charge, Mas'r Davy, as doen't ought to be forgot."

"Poor Ham!" said I.

"My good sister takes care of his house, you see, ma'am, and he takes kindly to her," Mr. Peggotty explained for my aunt's better information. "He'll set and talk to her with a calm spirit, wen it's like he couldn't bring himself to open his lips to another. Poor fellow!" said Mr. Peggotty, shaking his head, "theer's not so much left him, that he could spare the little as he has!"

"And Mrs. Gummidge?" said I.

"Well, I've had a mort of con-sideration, I do tell you," returned Mr. Peggotty, with a perplexed look which gradually cleared as he went on, "concerning of Missis Gummidge. You see, wen Missis Gummidge falls a-thinking of the old 'un, she an't what you may call good company. Betwixt you and me,

Mas'r Davy—and you, ma'am—wen Mrs. Gummidge takes to wimicking,"—our old country word for crying,—" she's liable to be considered to be, by them as didn't know the old 'un, peevish-like. Now I *did* know the old 'un," said Mr. Peggotty, " and I know'd his merits, so I unnerstan' her; but 'tan't entirely so, you see, with others—nat'rally can't be! "

My aunt and I both acquiesced.

" Wheerby," said Mr. Peggotty, " my sister might—I doen't say she would, but might—find Missis Gummidge give her a leetle trouble now and again. Theerful 'tan't my intentions to moor Missis Gummidge 'long with them, but to find a Bein' fur her wheer she can fisherate for herself." (A Bein' signifies, in that dialect, a home, and to fisherate is to provide,) " Fur which purpose," said Mr. Peggotty, " I means to make her a 'lowance afore I go, as'll leave her pretty comfort'ble. She's the faithfullest of creeturs. 'Tan't to be expected, of course, at her time of life, and being lone and lorn, as the good old mawther is, to be knocked about aboardship, and in the woods and wilds of a new and fur-away country. So that's what I'm a-going to do with *her*."

He forgot nobody. He thought of everybody's claims and strivings, but his own.

" Em'ly," he continued, " will keep along with me—poor child, she's sore in need of peace and rest!—until such time as we goes upon our voyage. She'll work at them clothes, as must be made; and I hope her troubles will begin to seem longer ago than they was, wen she finds herself once more by her rough but loving uncle."

My aunt nodded confirmation of this hope, and imparted great satisfaction to Mr. Peggotty.

" There's one thing furder, Mas'r Davy," said he, putting his hand in his breast-pocket, and gravely taking out the little paper bundle I had seen before, which he unrolled on the table. " Theer's these heer bank-notes—fifty pound, and ten. To them I wish to add the money as she come away with. I've asked her about that (but not saying why), and have added of it up; I an't a scholar. Would you be so kind as see how 'tis? "

He handed me, apologetically for his scholarship, a piece of paper, and observed me while I looked it over. It was quite right.

" Thankee, sir," he said, taking it back. " This money, if you doen't see objections, Mas'r Davy, I shall put up jest afore I go, in a cover d'rected to him; and put that up in another, d'rected to his mother. I shall tell her, in no more wureds than

I speak to you, what it's the price on; and that I'm gone, and past receiving of it back."

I told him that I thought it would be right to do so—that I was thoroughly convinced it would be, since he felt it to be right.

"I said that theer was on'y one thing furder," he proceeded with a grave smile, when he had made up his little bundle again, and put it in his pocket; "but theer was two. I warn't sure in my mind, wen I come out this morning, as I could go and break to Ham, of my own self, what had so thankfully happened. So I writ a letter while I was out, and put it in the post-office, telling of 'em how all was as 'tis, and that I should come down to-morrow to unload my mind of what little needs a-doing of down theer, and, mostlike, take my farewell leave of Yarmouth."

"And do you wish me to go with you?" said I, seeing that he left something unsaid.

"If you could do me that kind favour, Mas'r Davy," he replied. "I know the sight on you would cheer 'em up a bit."

My little Dora being in good spirits, and very desirous that I should go—as I found on talking it over with her—I readily pledged myself to accompany him in accordance with his wish. Next morning, consequently, we were on the Yarmouth coach, and again travelling over the old ground.

As we passed along the familiar street at night—Mr. Peggotty, in despite of all my remonstrances, carrying my bag—I glanced into Omer and Joram's shop, and saw my old friend Mr. Omer there, smoking his pipe. I felt reluctant to be present, when Mr. Peggotty first met his sister and Ham; and made Mr. Omer my excuse for lingering behind.

"How is Mr. Omer after this long time?" said I, going in.

He fanned away the smoke of his pipe, that he might get a better view of me, and soon recognised me with great delight.

"I should get up, sir, to acknowledge such an honour as this visit," said he, "only my limbs are rather out of sorts, and I am wheeled about. With the exception of my limbs and my breath, hows'ever, I am as hearty as a man can be, I'm thankful to say."

I congratulated him on his contented looks and his good spirits, and saw, now, that his easy-chair went on wheels.

"It's an ingenious thing, ain't it?" he inquired, following the direction of my glance, and polishing the elbow with his arm. "It runs as light as a feather, and tracks as true as a mail-coach. Bless you, my little Minnie—my grand-daughter you know, Minnie's child—puts her little strength against the back, gives it a shove, and away we go, as clever and merry as ever you see anything! And I tell you what—it's a most uncommon chair to smoke a pipe in."

I never saw such a good old fellow to make the best of a thing, and find out the enjoyment of it, as Mr. Omer. He was as radiant as if his chair, his asthma, and the failure of his limbs, were the various branches of a great invention for enhancing the luxury of a pipe.

"I see more of the world, I can assure you," said Mr. Omer, "in this chair, than ever I see out of it. You'd be surprised at the number of people that looks in of a day to have a chat. You really would! There's twice as much in the newspaper, since I've taken to this chair, as there used to be. As to general reading, dear me, what a lot of it I do get through! That's what I feel so strong, you know! If it had been my eyes, what should I have done? If it had been my ears, what should I have done? Being my limbs, what does it signify? Why, my limbs only made my breath shorter when I used 'em. And now, if I want to go out into the street or down to the sands, I've only got to call Dick, Joram's youngest 'prentice, and away I go in my own carriage, like the Lord Mayor of London."

He half suffocated himself with laughing here.

"Lord bless you!" said Mr. Omer, resuming his pipe, "a man must take the fat with the lean; that's what he must make up his mind to, in this life. Joram does a fine business. Ex-cellent business!"

"I am very glad to hear it," said I.

"I knew you would be," said Mr. Omer, "And Joram and Minnie are like valentines. What more can a man expect? What's his limbs to *that*!"

His supreme contempt for his own limbs, as he sat smoking, was one of the pleasantest oddities I have ever encountered.

"And since I've took to general reading, you've took to general writing, eh, sir?" said Mr. Omer, surveying me admiringly. "What a lovely work that was of yours! What expressions in it! I read it every word—every word. And as to feeling sleepy! Not at all!"

I laughingly expressed my satisfaction, but I must confess that I thought this association of ideas significant.

"I give you my word of honour, sir," said Mr. Omer, "that when I lay that book upon the table, and look at it outside; compact in three separate and indiwidual wollumes—one, two, three; I am as proud as Punch to think that I once had the honour of being connected with your family. And dear me, it's a long time ago, now, ain't it? Over at Blunderstone. With a pretty little party laid along with the other party. And you quite a small party then, yourself. Dear, dear!"

I changed the subject by referring to Emily. After assuring him that I did not forget how interested he had always been in her, and how kindly he had always treated her, I gave him a general account of her restoration to her uncle by the aid of Martha; which I knew would please the old man. He listened with the utmost attention, and said, feelingly, when I had done:

"I am rejoiced at it, sir! It's the best news I have heard for many a day. Dear, dear, dear! And what's going to be undertook for that unfortunate young woman, Martha, now?"

"You touch a point that my thoughts have been dwelling on since yesterday," said I, "but on which I can give you no information yet, Mr. Omer. Mr. Peggotty has not alluded to it, and I have a delicacy in doing so. I am sure he has not forgotten it. He forgets nothing that is disinterested and good."

"Because you know," said Mr. Omer, taking himself up, where he had left off, "whatever *is* done, I should wish to be a member of. Put me down for anything you may consider right, and let me know. I never could think the girl all bad, and I am glad to find she's not. So will my daughter Minnie be. Young women are contradictory creatures in some things—her mother was just the same as her—but their hearts are soft and kind. It's all show with Minnie, about Martha. Why she should consider it necessary to make any show, I don't undertake to tell you. But it's all show, bless you. She'd do her any kindness in private. So put me down for whatever you may consider right, will you be so good? and drop me a line where to forward it. Dear me!" said Mr. Omer, "when a man is drawing on to a time of life, where the two ends of life meet; when he finds himself, however hearty he is, being wheeled about for the second time, in a speeches of go-cart; he should be over-rejoiced to do a kindness if he can. He wants plenty. And I don't speak of myself, particular," said Mr. Omer, "because, sir, the way I look at it is, that we are all drawing on to the bottom of the hill, whatever age we are, on account of time never standing still for a single moment. So let us always do a kindness, and be over-rejoiced. To be sure!"

He knocked the ashes out of his pipe, and put it on a ledge in the back of his chair, expressly made for its reception.

"There's Em'ly's cousin, him that she was to have been married to," said Mr. Omer, rubbing his hands feebly, "as fine a fellow as there is in Yarmouth! He'll come and talk or read to me, in the evening, for an hour together sometimes. That's a kindness, I should call it! All his life's a kindness."

"I am going to see him now," said I.

"Are you?" said Mr. Omer. "Tell him I was hearty, and sent my respects. Minnie and Joram's at a ball. They would be as proud to see you as I am, if they was at home. Minnie won't hardly go out at all, you see, 'on account of father,' as she says. So I swore to-night, that if she didn't go, I'd go to bed at six. In consequence of which," Mr. Omer shook himself and his chair with laughter at the success of his device, "she and Joram's at a ball."

I shook hands with him, and wished him good-night.

"Half a minute, sir," said Mr. Omer. "If you was to go without seeing my little elephant, you'd lose the best of sights. You never see such a sight! Minnie!"

A musical little voice answered, from somewhere upstairs, "I am coming, grandfather!" and a pretty little girl with long, flaxen, curling hair, soon came running into the shop.

"This is my little elephant, sir," said Mr. Omer, fondling the child. "Siamese breed, sir. Now, little elephant!"

The little elephant set the door of the parlour open, enabling me to see that, in these latter days, it was converted into a bedroom for Mr. Omer, who could not be easily conveyed upstairs; and then hid her pretty forehead, and tumbled her long hair, against the back of Mr. Omer's chair.

"The elephant butts, you know, sir," said Mr. Omer, winking, "when he goes at a object. Once, elephant. Twice. Three times!"

At this signal, the little elephant, with a dexterity that was next to marvellous in so small an animal, whisked the chair round with Mr. Omer in it, and rattled it off, pell-mell, into the parlour, without touching the doorpost; Mr. Omer indescribably enjoying the performance, and looking back at me on the road as if it were the triumphant issue of his life's exertions.

After a stroll about the town I went to Ham's house. Peggotty had now removed here for good; and had let her own house to the successor of Mr. Barkis in the carrying business, who had paid her very well for the goodwill, cart, and horse. I believe the very same slow horse that Mr. Barkis drove was still at work.

I found them in the neat kitchen, accompanied by Mrs. Gummidge, who had been fetched from the old boat by Mr. Peggotty himself. I doubt if she could have been induced to desert her post by any one else. He had evidently told them all. Both

Peggotty and Mrs. Gummidge had their aprons to their eyes, and Ham had just stepped out "to take a turn on the beach." He presently came home, very glad to see me; and I hope they were all the better for my being there. We spoke, with some approach to cheerfulness of Mr. Peggotty's growing rich in a new country, and of the wonders he would describe in his letters. We said nothing of Emily by name, but distantly referred to her more than once. Ham was the serenest of the party.

But Peggotty told me, when she lighted me to a little chamber where the Crocodile book was lying ready for me on the table, that he always was the same. She believed (she told me, crying) that he was broken-hearted; though he was as full of courage as of sweetness, and worked harder and better than any boat-builder in any yard in all that part. There were times, she said, of an evening, when he talked of their old life in the boat-house; and then he mentioned Emily as a child. But he never mentioned her as a woman.

I thought I had read in his face that he would like to speak to me alone. I therefore resolved to put myself in his way next evening, as he came home from his work. Having settled this with myself, I fell asleep. That night, for the first time in all those many nights, the candle was taken out of the window, Mr. Peggotty swung in his old hammock in the old boat, and the wind murmured with the old sound round his head.

All next day he was occupied in disposing of his fishing-boat and tackle; in packing up, and sending to London by waggon, such of his little domestic possessions as he thought would be useful to him; and in parting with the rest, or bestowing them on Mrs. Gummidge. She was with him all day. As I had a sorrowful wish to see the old place once more, before it was locked up, I engaged to meet them there in the evening. But I so arranged it, as that I should meet Ham first.

It was easy to come in his way, as I knew where he worked. I met him at a retired part of the sands, which I knew he would cross, and turned back with him, that he might have leisure to speak to me if he really wished. I had not mistaken the expression of his face. We had walked but a little way together, when he said, without looking at me:

"Mas'r Davy, have you seen her?"

"Only for a moment, when she was in a swoon," I softly answered.

We walked a little farther, and he said:

"Mas'r Davy, shall you see her, d'ye think?"

"It would be too painful to her, perhaps," said I.

"I have thowt of that," he replied. "So 'twould, sir, so 'twould."

"But, Ham," said I, gently, "if there is anything that I could write to her, for you, in case I could not tell it; if there is anything you would wish to make known to her through me; I should consider it a sacred trust."

"I am sure on't. I thankee, sir, most kind! I think theer is something I could wish said or wrote."

"What is it?"

We walked a little farther in silence, and then he spoke.

"'Tan't that I forgive her. 'Tan't that so much. 'Tis more as I beg of her to forgive me, for having pressed my affections upon her. Odd times, I think that if I hadn't had her promise fur to marry me, sir, she was that trustful of me, in a friendly way, that she'd have told me what was struggling in her mind, and would have counselled with me, and I might have saved her."

I pressed his hand. "Is that all?"

"Theer's yet a something else," he returned, "if I can say it, Mas'r Davy."

We walked on, farther than we had walked yet, before he spoke again. He was not crying when he made the pauses I shall express by lines. He was merely collecting himself to speak very plainly.

"I loved her—and I love the mem'ry of her—too deep—to be able to lead her to believe of my own self as I'm a happy man. I could only be happy—by forgetting of her—and I'm afeerd I couldn't hardly bear as she should be told I done that. But if you, being so full of learning, Mas'r Davy, could think of anything to say as might bring her to believe I wasn't greatly hurt: still loving of her, and mourning for her: anything as might bring her to believe as I was not tired of my life, and yet was hoping fur to see her without blame, wheer the wicked cease from troubling and the weary are at rest—anything as would ease her sorrowful mind, and yet not make her think as I could ever marry, or as 'twas possible that any one could ever be to me what she was—I should ask of you to say that—with my prayers for her—that was so dear."

I pressed his manly hand again, and told him I would charge myself to do this as well as I could.

"I thankee, sir," he answered. "'Twas kind of you to meet me. 'Twas kind of you to bear him company down. Mas'r Davy, I unnerstan' very well, though my aunt will come to Lon'on afore they sail, and they'll unite once more, that I am not like to see him agen. I fare to feel sure on't. We doen't say so, but so 'twill be, and better so. The last you see on him—the very last—will you give him the lovingest duty and thanks of the orphan, as he was ever more than a father to?"

This I also promised faithfully.

"I thankee agen, sir," he said heartily shaking hands. "I know wheer you're a-going. Good-bye!"

With a slight wave of his hand, as though to explain to me that he could not enter the old place, he turned away. As I looked after his figure, crossing the waste in the moonlight, I saw him turn his face towards the strip of silvery light upon the sea, and pass on, looking at it, until he was a shadow in the distance.

The door of the boat-house stood open when I approached; and, on entering, I found it emptied of all its furniture, saving one of the old lockers, on which Mrs. Gummidge, with a basket on her knee, was seated, looking at Mr. Peggotty. He leaned his elbow on the rough chimney-piece, and gazed upon a few expiring embers in the grate; but he raised his head, hopefully, on my coming in, and spoke in a cheery manner.

"Come, according to promise, to bid farewell to 't, eh, Mas'r Davy?" he said, taking up the candle. "Bare enough, now, an't it?"

"Indeed you have made good use of the time," said I.

"Why, we have not been idle, sir. Missis Gummidge has worked like a—I doen't know what Missis Gummidge an't worked like," said Mr. Peggotty, looking at her, at a loss for a sufficiently approving simile.

Mrs. Gummidge, leaning on her basket, made no observation.

"Theer's the very locker that you used to sit on, 'long with Em'ly!" said Mr. Peggotty, in a whisper. "I'm a-going to carry it away with me, last of all. And heer's your old little bedroom, see, Mas'r Davy? A'most as bleak to-night, as 'art could wish!"

In truth, the wind, though it was low, had a solemn sound, and crept around the deserted house with a whispered wailing that was very mournful. Everything was gone, down to the little mirror with the oyster-shell frame. I thought of myself, lying here, when that first great change was being wrought at home. I thought of the blue-eyed child who had enchanted me. I thought of Steerforth: and a foolish, fearful fancy came upon me of his being near at hand, and liable to be met at any turn.

"'Tis like to be long," said Mr. Peggotty, in a low voice, "afore the boat finds new tenants. They look upon 't down heer, as being unfort'nate now!"

"Does it belong to anybody in the neighbourhood?" I asked.

"To a mast-maker up town," said Mr. Peggotty. "I'm a-going to give the key to him to-night."

We looked into the other little room, and came back to Mrs. Gummidge, sitting on the locker, whom Mr. Peggotty, putting the light on the chimney-piece, requested to rise, that he might carry it outside the door before extinguishing the candle.

"Dan'l," said Mrs. Gummidge, suddenly deserting her basket, and clinging to his arm, "my dear Dan'l, the parting words I speak in this house is, I mustn't be left behind. Doen't ye think of leaving me behind, Dan'l! Oh, doen't ye ever do it!"

Mr. Peggotty, taken aback, looked from Mrs. Gummidge to me, and from me to Mrs. Gummidge, as if he had been awakened from a sleep.

"Doen't ye, dearest Dan'l, doen't ye!" cried Mrs. Gummidge, fervently. "Take me 'long with you, Dan'l, take me 'long with you and Em'ly! I'll be your servant, constant and trew. If there's slaves in them parts where you're a-going, I'll be bound to you for one, and happy, but doen't ye leave me behind, Dan'l, that's a deary dear!"

"My good soul," said Mr. Peggotty, shaking his head, "you doen't know what a long voyage, and what a hard life 'tis!"

"Yes, I do, Dan'l! I can guess!" cried Mrs. Gummidge. "But my parting words under this roof is, I shall go into the house and die, if I am not took. I can dig, Dan'l. I can work. I can live hard. I can be loving and patient now—more than you think, Dan'l, if you'll on'y try me. I wouldn't touch the 'lowance, not if I was dying of want, Dan'l Peggotty; but I'll go with you and Em'ly, if you'll on'y let me, to the world's end! I know how 'tis; I know you think that I am lone and lorn; but, deary love, 'tan't so no more! I ain't sat here, so long, a-watching, and a-thinking of your trials without some good being done me. Mas'r Davy, speak to him for me! I knows his ways, and Em'ly's, and I knows their sorrows, and can be a comfort to 'em, some odd times, and labour for 'em allus! Dan'l, deary Dan'l, let me go 'long with you!"

And Mrs. Gummidge took his hand, and kissed it with a homely pathos and affection, in a homely rapture of devotion and gratitude, that he well deserved.

We brought the locker out, extinguished the candle, fastened the door on the outside, and left the old boat close shut up, a dark speck in the cloudy night. Next day, when we were returning to London outside the coach, Mrs. Gummidge and her basket were on the seat behind, and Mrs. Gummidge was happy.

52

I ASSIST AT AN EXPLOSION

WHEN THE TIME MR. MICAWBER HAD APPOINTED SO mysteriously was within four-and-twenty hours of being come, my aunt and I consulted how we should proceed; for my aunt was very unwilling to leave Dora. Ah! how easily I carried Dora up and down stairs, now!

We were disposed, notwithstanding Mr. Micawber's stipulation for my aunt's attendance, to arrange that she should stay at home, and be represented by Mr. Dick and me. In short, we had resolved to take this course, when Dora again unsettled us by declaring that she never would forgive herself, and never would forgive her bad boy, if my aunt remained behind, on any pretence.

"I won't speak to you," said Dora, shaking her curls at my aunt. "I'll be disagreeable! I'll make Jip bark at you all day. I shall be sure that you really are a cross old thing, if you don't go!"

"Tut, Blossom!" laughed my aunt. "You know you can't do without me!"

"Yes, I can," said Dora. "You are no use to me at all. You never run up and down stairs for me, all day long. You never sit and tell me stories about Doady, when his shoes were worn out, and he was covered with dust—oh, what a poor little mite of a fellow! You never do anything at all to please me, do you, dear?" Dora made haste to kiss my aunt, and say, "Yes, you do! I'm only joking!"—lest my aunt should think she really meant it.

"But, aunt," said Dora, coaxingly, "now listen. You must go. I shall tease you, till you let me have my own way about it. I shall lead my naughty boy *such* a life, if he don't make you go. I shall make myself *so* disagreeable—and so will Jip! You'll wish you had gone, like a good thing, for ever and ever so long, if you don't go. Besides, "said Dora, putting back her hair, and looking wonderingly at my aunt and me, "why shouldn't you both go? I am not very ill indeed. Am I?"

"Why, what a question!" cried my aunt.

"What a fancy!" said I.

"Yes! I know I am a silly little thing!" said Dora, slowly looking from one of us to the other, and then putting up her pretty lips to kiss us as she lay upon her couch. "Well, then, you must both go, or I shall not believe you; and then I shall cry!"

I saw, in my aunt's face, that she began to give way now, and Dora brightened again, as she saw it too.

"You'll come back with so much to tell me, that it'll take at least a week to make me understand!" said Dora. "Because I *know* I shan't understand, for a length of time, if there's any business in it. And there's sure to be some business in it! If there's anything to add up, besides, I don't know when I shall make it out; and my bad boy will look *so* miserable all the time. There! Now you'll go, won't you? You'll only be gone one night, and Jip will take care of me while you are gone. Doady will carry me up-stairs before you go, and I won't come down again till you come back; and you shall take Agnes a dreadfully scolding letter from me, because she has never been to see us!"

We agreed, without any more consultation, that we would both go, and that Dora was a little impostor, who feigned to be rather unwell, because she liked to be petted. She was greatly pleased, and very merry; and we four, that is to say, my aunt, Mr. Dick, Traddles, and I, went down to Canterbury by the Dover mail that night.

At the hotel where Mr. Micawber had requested us to await him, which we got into, with some trouble, in the middle of the night, I found a letter, importing that he would appear in the morning punctually at half-past nine. After which, we went shivering, at that uncomfortable hour, to our respective beds, through various close passages; which smelt as if they had been steeped for ages in a solution of soup and stables.

Early in the morning, I sauntered through the dear old tranquil streets, and again mingled with the shadows of the venerable gateways and churches. The rooks were sailing about the cathedral towers; and the towers themselves, overlooking many a long unaltered mile of the rich country and its pleasant streams, were cutting the bright morning air, as if there were no such thing as change on earth. Yet the bells, when they sounded, told me sorrowfully of change in everything; told me of their own age, and my pretty Dora's youth; and of the many, never old, who had lived and loved and died, while the reverberations of the bells had hummed through the rusty armour of the Black Prince hanging up within, and, motes upon the deep of Time, had lost themselves in air, as circles do in water.

I looked at the old house, from the corner of the street, but did not go nearer to it, lest, being observed, I might unwittingly do any harm to the design I had come to aid. The early sun was striking edgewise on its gables and lattice-windows, touching them with gold; and some beams of its old peace seemed to touch my heart.

I strolled into the country for an hour or so, and then returned by the main street, which in the interval had shaken off its last night's sleep. Among those who were stirring in the shops, I saw my ancient enemy, the butcher, now advanced to top-boots and a baby, and in business for himself. He was nursing the baby, and appeared to be a benignant member of society.

We all became very anxious and impatient, when we sat down to breakfast. As it approached nearer and nearer to half-past nine o'clock, our restless expectation of Mr. Micawber increased. At last we made no more pretence of attending to the meal, which except with Mr. Dick, had been a mere form from the first; but my aunt walked up and down the room, Traddles sat upon the sofa affecting to read the paper with his eyes on the ceiling; and I looked out of the window to give early notice of Mr. Micawber's coming. Nor had I long to watch, for, at the first chime of the half-hour, he appeared in the street.

"Here he is," said I, "and not in his legal attire!"

My aunt tied the strings of her bonnet (she had come down to breakfast in it), and put on her shawl, as if she were ready for anything that was resolute and uncompromising. Traddles buttoned his coat with a determined air. Mr. Dick, disturbed by these formidable appearances, but feeling it necessary to imitate them, pulled his hat, with both hands, as firmly over his ears as he possibly could; and instantly took it off again, to welcome Mr. Micawber.

"Gentlemen, and madam," said Mr. Micawber, "good morning! My dear sir," to Mr. Dick, who shook hands with him violently, "you are extremely good."

"Have you breakfasted?" said Mr. Dick. "Have a chop!"

"Not for the world, my good sir!" cried Mr. Micawber, stopping him on his way to the bell; "appetite and myself, Mr. Dixon, have long been strangers."

Mr. Dixon was so well pleased with his new name, and appeared to think it so very obliging in Mr. Micawber to confer it upon him, that he shook hands with him again, and laughed rather childishly.

"Dick," said my aunt, "attention!"

Mr. Dick recovered himself, with a blush.

" Now, sir," said my aunt to Mr. Micawber, as she put on her gloves, " we are ready for Mount Vesuvius, or anything else, as soon as *you* please."

" Madam," returned Mr. Micawber, " I trust you will shortly witness an eruption. Mr. Traddles, I have your permission, I believe, to mention here that we have been in communication together? "

" It is undoubtedly the fact, Copperfield," said Traddles, to whom I looked in surprise. " Mr. Micawber has consulted me, in reference to what he has in contemplation; and I have advised him to the best of my judgment."

" Unless I deceive myself, Mr. Traddles," pursued Mr. Micawber, " what I contemplate is a disclosure of an important nature."

" Highly so," said Traddles.

" Perhaps, under such circumstances, madam and gentlemen," said Mr. Micawber, " you will do me the favour to submit yourselves, for the moment, to the direction of one who, however unworthy to be regarded in any other light but as Waif and Stray upon the shore of human nature, is still your fellow-man, though crushed out of his original form by individual errors, and the accumulative force of a combination of circumstances? "

" We have perfect confidence in you, Mr. Micawber," said I, " and will do what you please."

" Mr. Copperfield," returned Mr. Micawber, " your confidence is not, at the existing juncture, ill-bestowed. I would beg to be allowed a start of five minutes by the clock; and then to receive the present company, inquiring for Miss Wickfield, at the office of Wickfield and Heep, whose Stipendiary I am."

My aunt and I looked at Traddles, who nodded his approval.

" I have no more," observed Mr. Micawber, " to say at present."

With which, to my infinite surprise, he included us all in a comprehensive bow, and disappeared; his manner being extremely distant, and his face extremely pale.

Traddles only smiled, and shook his head (with his hair standing upright on the top of it), when I looked to him for an explanation; so I took out my watch, and, as a last resource, counted off the five minutes. My aunt, with her own watch in her hand, did the like. When the time was expired, Traddles gave her his arm; and we all went out together to the old house without saying one word on the way.

We found Mr. Micawber at his desk, in the turret office on

the ground floor, either writing, or pretending to write, hard. The large office-ruler was stuck into his waistcoat, and was not so well concealed but that a foot or more of that instrument protruded from his bosom, like a new kind of shirt-frill.

As it appeared to me that I was expected to speak, I said aloud:

"How do you do, Mr. Micawber?"

"Mr. Copperfield," said Mr. Micawber, gravely, "I hope I see you well?"

"Is Miss Wickfield at home?" said I.

"Mr. Wickfield is unwell in bed, sir, of a rheumatic fever," he returned; "but Miss Wickfield, I have no doubt, will be happy to see old friends. Will you walk in, sir?"

He preceded us to the dining-room—the first room I had entered in that house—and flinging open the door of Mr. Wickfield's former office, said, in a sonorous voice:

"Miss Trotwood, Mr. David Copperfield, Mr. Thomas Traddles, and Mr. Dixon!"

I had not seen Uriah Heep since the time of the blow. Our visit astonished him, evidently; not the less, I dare say, because it astonished ourselves. He did not gather his eyebrows together, for he had none worth mentioning; but he frowned to that degree that he almost closed his small eyes, while the hurried raising of his grisly hand to his chin betrayed some trepidation or surprise. This was only when we were in the act of entering his room, and when I caught a glance of him over my aunt's shoulder. A moment afterwards, he was as fawning and as humble as ever.

"Well, I am sure," he said. "This is indeed an unexpected pleasure! To have, as I may say, all friends round Saint Paul's at once, is a treat unlooked for! Mr. Copperfield, I hope I see you well, and—if I may umbly express myself so—friendly towards them as is ever your friends, whether or not. Mrs. Copperfield, sir, I hope she's getting on. We have been made quite uneasy by the poor accounts we have had of her state, lately, I do assure you."

I felt ashamed to let him take my hand, but I did not know yet what else to do.

"Things are changed in this office, Miss Trotwood, since I was an umble clerk, and held your pony; ain't they?" said Uriah, with his sickliest smile. "But *I* am not changed, Miss Trotwood."

"Well, sir," returned my aunt, "to tell you the truth, I think you are pretty constant to the promise of your youth; if that's any satisfaction to you."

" Thank you, Miss Trotwood," said Uriah, writhing in his ungainly manner, " for your good opinion! Micawber, tell 'em to let Miss Agnes know—and mother. Mother will be quite in a state, when she sees the present company! " said Uriah, setting chairs.

" You are not busy, Mr. Heep? " said Traddles, whose eye the cunning red eye accidentally caught, as it at once scrutinised and evaded us.

" No, Mr. Traddles," replied Uriah, resuming his official seat, and squeezing his bony hands, laid palm to palm, between his bony knees. " Not so much so as I could wish. But lawyers, sharks, and leeches, are not easily satisfied, you know! Not but what myself and Micawber have our hands pretty full in general, on account of Mr. Wickfield's being hardly fit for any occupation, sir. But it's a pleasure as well as a duty, I am sure, to work for *him*. You've not been intimate with Mr. Wickfield, I think, Mr. Traddles? I believe I've only had the honour of seeing you once myself? "

" No, I have not been intimate with Mr. Wickfield," returned Traddles; " or I might perhaps have waited on you long ago, Mr. Heep."

There was something in the tone of this reply, which made Uriah look at the speaker again, with a very sinister and suspicious expression. But, seeing only Traddles, with his good-natured face, simple manner, and hair on end, he dismissed it as he replied, with a jerk of his whole body, but especially his throat:

" I am sorry for that, Mr. Traddles. You would have admired him as much as we all do. His little failings would only have endeared him to you the more. But if you would like to hear my fellow-partner eloquently spoken of, I should refer you to Copperfield. The family is a subject he's very strong upon, if you never heard him."

I was prevented from disclaiming the compliment (if I should have done so, in any case), by the entrance of Agnes, now ushered in by Mr. Micawber. She was not quite so self-possessed as usual, I thought; and had evidently undergone anxiety and fatigue. But her earnest cordiality, and her quiet beauty, shone with the gentler lustre for it.

I saw Uriah watch her while she greeted us; and he reminded me of an ugly and rebellious genie watching a good spirit. In the meanwhile, some slight sign passed between Mr. Micawber and Traddles; and Traddles, unobserved except by me, went out.

" Don't wait, Micawber," said Uriah.

Mr. Micawber, with his hand upon the ruler in his breast,

stood erect before the door, most unmistakably contemplating one of his fellow-men, and that man his employer.

"What are you waiting for?" said Uriah. "Micawber! did you hear me tell you not to wait?"

"Yes!" replied the immovable Mr. Micawber.

"Then why *do* you wait?" said Uriah.

"Because I—in short, choose," replied Mr. Micawber, with a burst.

Uriah's cheeks lost colour, and an unwholesome paleness, still faintly tinged by his pervading red, overspread them. He looked at Mr. Micawber attentively, with his whole face breathing short and quick in every feature.

"You are a dissipated fellow, as all the world knows," he said, with an effort at a smile, "and I am afraid you'll oblige me to get rid of you. Go along! I'll talk to you presently."

"If there is a scoundrel on this earth," said Mr. Micawber, suddenly breaking out again with the utmost vehemence, "with whom I have already talked too much, that scoundrel's name is —HEEP!"

Uriah fell back, as if he had been struck or stung. Looking slowly round upon us with the darkest and wickedest expression that his face could wear, he said, in a lower voice:

"Oho! This is a conspiracy! You have met here by appointment! You are playing Booty with my clerk, are you, Copperfield? Now, take care. You'll make nothing of this. We understand each other, you and me. There's no love between us. You were always a puppy with a proud stomach, from your first coming here; and you envy me my rise, do you? None of your plots against me; I'll counterplot you! Micawber, you be off. I'll talk to you presently."

"Mr. Micawber," said I, "there is a sudden change in this fellow, in more respects than the extraordinary one of his speaking the truth in one particular, which assures me that he is brought to bay. Deal with him as he deserves!"

"You are a precious set of people, ain't you?" said Uriah, in the same low voice, and breaking out into a clammy heat, which he wiped from his forehead with his long lean hand, "to buy over my clerk, who is the very scum of society,—as you yourself were, Copperfield, you know it, before any one had charity on you,—to defame me with his lies? Miss Trotwood, you had better stop this; or I'll stop your husband shorter than will be pleasant to you. I won't know your story professionally, for nothing, old lady! Miss Wickfield, if you have any love for your father, you had better not join that gang. I'll ruin him, if you do.

Now, come! I have got some of you under the harrow. Think twice, before it goes over you. Think twice, you, Micawber, if you don't want to be crushed. I recommend you to take yourself off, and be talked to presently, you fool! while there's time to retreat! Where's mother?" he said, suddenly appearing to notice, with alarm, the absence of Traddles, and pulling down the bell-rope. "Fine doings in a person's own house!"

"Mrs. Heep is here, sir," said Traddles, returning with that worthy mother of a worthy son. "I have taken the liberty of making myself known to her."

"Who are you to make yourself known?" retorted Uriah. "And what do you want here?"

"I am the agent and friend of Mr. Wickfield, sir," said Traddles, in a composed and business-like way. "And I have a power of attorney from him in my pocket, to act for him in all matters."

"The old ass has drunk himself into a state of dotage," said Uriah, turning uglier than before, "and it has been got from him by fraud!"

"Something has been got from him by fraud, I know," returned Traddles quietly; "and so do you, Mr. Heep. We will refer that question, if you please, to Mr. Micawber."

"Ury—!" Mrs. Heep began, with an anxious gesture.

"You hold your tongue, mother," he returned; "least said, soonest mended."

"But, my Ury—"

"Will you hold your tongue, mother, and leave it to me?"

Though I had long known that his servility was false, and all his pretences knavish and hollow, I had had no adequate conception of the extent of his hypocrisy, until I now saw him with his mask off. The suddenness with which he dropped it, when he perceived that it was useless to him; the malice, insolence, and hatred he revealed; the leer with which he exulted, even at this moment, in the evil he had done—all this time being desperate too, and at his wits' end for the means of getting the better of us—though perfectly consistent with the experience I had of him, at first took even me by surprise, who had known him so long, and disliked him so heartily.

I say nothing of the look he conferred on me, as he stood eyeing us, one after another; for I had always understood that he hated me, and I remembered the marks of my hand upon his cheek. But when his eyes passed on to Agnes, and I saw the rage with which he felt his power over her slipping away, and the exhibition, in their disappointment, of the odious passions that had led him to aspire to one whose virtues he could never appreciate or care for, I was shocked by the mere thought of her having lived, an hour, within sight of such a man.

After some rubbing of the lower part of his face, and some looking at us with those bad eyes, over his grisly fingers, he made one more address to me, half whining, and half abusive.

"You think it justifiable, do you, Copperfield, you who pride yourself so much on your honour and all the rest of it, to sneak about my place, eaves-dropping with my clerk? If it had been *me*, I shouldn't have wondered; for I don't make myself out a gentleman (though I never was in the streets either, as you were, according to Micawber), but being *you*!—And you're not afraid of doing this, either? You don't think at all of what I shall do, in return; or of getting yourself into trouble for conspiracy and so forth? Very well. We shall see! Mr. What's-your-name, you were going to refer some question to Micawber. There's your referee. Why don't you make him speak? He has learnt his lesson, I see."

Seeing that what he said had no effect on me or any of us, he sat on the edge of his table with his hands in his pockets, and one of his splay feet twisted round the other leg, waiting doggedly for what might follow.

Mr. Micawber, whose impetuosity I had restrained thus far with the greatest difficulty, and who had repeatedly interposed with the first syllable of SCOUN-drel! without getting to the second, now burst forward, drew the ruler from his breast (apparently as a defensive weapon), and produced from his pocket a foolscap document, folded in the form of a large letter. Opening this packet, with his old flourish, and glancing at the contents, as if he cherished an artistic admiration of their style of composition, he began to read as follows:

"'Dear Miss Trotwood and gentlemen——'"

"Bless and save the man!" exclaimed my aunt in a low voice. "He'd write letters by the ream, if it was a capital offence!"

Mr. Micawber, without hearing her, went on.

"'In appearing before you to denounce probably the most consummate Villain that has ever existed,'" Mr. Micawber, without looking off the letter, pointed the ruler, like a ghostly truncheon, at Uriah Heep, "'I ask no consideration for myself. The victim, from the cradle, of pecuniary liabilities to which I have been unable to respond, I have ever been the sport and toy of debasing circumstances. Ignominy, Want, Despair, and Madness, have, collectively or separately, been the attendants of my career.' "

The relish with which Mr. Micawber described himself as a prey to these dismal calamities was only to be equalled by the emphasis with which he read his letter; and the kind of homage he rendered to it with a roll of his head, when he thought he had hit a sentence very hard indeed.

" ' In an accumulation of Ignominy, Want, Despair, and Madness, I entered the office—or, as our lively neighbour the Gaul would term it, the Bureau—of the Firm, nominally conducted under the appellation of Wickfield and—HEEP, but, in reality, wielded by—HEEP alone. HEEP and only HEEP, is the mainspring of that machine. HEEP, and only HEEP, is the Forger and the Cheat.' "

Uriah, more blue than white at these words, made a dart at the letter, as if to tear it in pieces. Mr. Micawber, with a perfect miracle of dexterity or luck, caught his advancing knuckles with the ruler, and disabled his right hand. It dropped at the wrist, as if it were broken. The blow sounded as if it had fallen on wood.

" The Devil take you! " said Uriah, writhing in a new way with pain. " I'll be even with you."

" Approach me again, you—you—you HEEP of infamy," gasped Mr. Micawber, " and if your head is human, I'll break it. Come on, come on! "

I think I never saw anything more ridiculous—I was sensible of it, even at the time—than Mr. Micawber making broadsword guards with the ruler, and crying, " Come on! " while Traddles and I pushed him back into a corner, from which, as often as we got him into it, he persisted in emerging again.

His enemy, muttering to himself, after wringing his wounded hand for some time, slowly drew off his neckerchief and bound it up; then held it in his other hand, and sat upon his table with his sullen face looking down.

Mr. Micawber, when he was sufficiently cool, proceeded with his letter.

" ' The stipendiary and emoluments in consideration of which I entered into the service of—HEEP,' " always pausing before that word and uttering it with astonishing vigour, " ' were not defined, beyond the pittance of twenty-two shillings and six per week. The rest was left contingent on the value of my professional exertions; in other and more expressive words, on the baseness of my nature, the cupidity of my motives, the poverty of my family, the general moral (or rather immoral) resemblance between myself and—HEEP. Need I say that it soon became necessary for me to solicit from—HEEP—pecuniary advances towards the support of Mrs. Micawber, and our blighted but rising family? Need I say that this necessity had been foreseen by—HEEP? That those advances were secured by I O U's and other similar acknowledgments, known to the legal institutions of this country? And that I thus became immeshed in the web he had spun for my reception?' "

Mr. Micawber's enjoyment of his epistolary powers, in describing this unfortunate state of things, really seemed to outweigh any pain or anxiety that the reality could have caused him. He read on:

" 'Then it was that—HEEP—began to favour me with just so much of his confidence as was necessary to the discharge of his infernal business. Then it was that I began, if I may so Shakespearianly express myself, to dwindle, peak, and pine. I found that my services were constantly called into requisition for the falsification of business, and the mystification of an individual whom I will designate as Mr. W. That Mr. W. was imposed upon, kept in ignorance, and deluded, in every possible way; yet, that all this while, the ruffian—HEEP—was professing unbounded gratitude to, and unbounded friendship for, that much-abused gentleman. This was bad enough; but, as the philosophic Dane observes, with that universal applicability which distinguishes the illustrious ornament of the Elizabethan Era, worse remains behind!' "

Mr. Micawber was so very much struck by this happy rounding off with a quotation, that he indulged himself, and us, with a second reading of the sentence, under pretence of having lost his place.

" 'It is not my intention,' " he continued, reading on, " 'to enter on a detailed list, within the compass of the present epistle (though it is ready elsewhere), of the various malpractices of a minor nature, affecting the individual whom I have denominated Mr. W., to which I have been a tacitly consenting party. My object, when the contest within myself between stipend and no stipend, baker and no baker, existence and non-existence, ceased, was to take advantage of my opportunities to discover and expose the major malpractices committed, to that gentleman's grievous wrong and injury, by—HEEP. Stimulated by the silent monitor within, and by a no less touching and appealing monitor without—to whom I will briefly refer as Miss W.—I entered on a not unlaborious task of clandestine investigation, protracted now, to the best of my knowledge, information, and belief, over a period exceeding twelve calendar months.' "

He read this passage as if it were from an Act of Parliament; and appeared majestically refreshed by the sound of the words.

" 'My charges against—HEEP,' " he read on, glancing at him, and drawing the ruler into a convenient position under his left arm, in case of need, " 'are as follows.' "

We all held our breath, I think. I am sure Uriah held his.

" 'First,' " said Mr. Micawber. " 'When Mr. W.'s faculties and memory for business became, through causes into which it is not necessary or expedient for me to enter, weakened and confused,—HEEP—designedly perplexed and complicated the whole of the official transactions. When Mr. W. was least fit to enter on business,—HEEP was always at hand to force him to enter on it. He obtained Mr. W.'s signature under such circumstances to documents of importance, representing them to be other documents of no importance. He induced Mr. W. to empower him to draw out, thus, one particular sum of trust-money, amounting to twelve six fourteen, two and nine, and employed it to meet pretended business charges and deficiencies which were either already provided for, or had never really existed. He gave this proceeding, throughout, the appearance of having originated in Mr. W.'s own dishonest intention, and of having been accomplished by Mr. W.'s own dishonest act: and has used it, ever since, to torture and constrain him.' "

"You shall prove this, you Copperfield!" said Uriah, with a threatening shake of the head. "All in good time!"

"Ask—HEEP—Mr. Traddles, who lived in his house after him," said Mr. Micawber, breaking off from the letter; "will you?"

"The fool himself—and lives there now," said Uriah, disdainfully.

"Ask—HEEP—if he ever kept a pocket-book in that house," said Mr. Micawber; "will you?"

I saw Uriah's lank hand stop, involuntarily, in the scraping of his chin.

"Or ask him," said Mr. Micawber, "if he ever burnt one there. If he says Yes, and asks you where the ashes are, refer him to Wilkins Micawber, and he will hear of something not at all to his advantage!"

The triumphant flourish with which Mr. Micawber delivered himself of these words, had a powerful effect in alarming the mother; who cried out in much agitation:

"Ury, Ury! Be umble, and make terms, my dear!"

"Mother!" he retorted, "will you keep quiet? You're in a

fright, and don't know what you say or mean. Umble!" he repeated, looking at me, with a snarl; "I've umbled some of 'em for a pretty long time back, umble as I was!"

Mr. Micawber, genteelly adjusting his chin in his cravat, presently proceeded with his composition.

"'Second. HEEP has, on several occasions, to the best of my knowledge, information, and belief—'"

"But *that* won't do," muttered Uriah, relieved. "Mother, you keep quiet."

"We will endeavour to provide something that WILL do, and do for you finally, sir, very shortly," replied Mr. Micawber.

"'Second. HEEP has, on several occasions, to the best of my knowledge, information, and belief, systematically forged, to various entries, books, and documents, the signature of Mr. W.; and has distinctly done so in one instance, capable of proof by me. To wit, in manner following, that is to say:'"

Again, Mr. Micawber had a relish in this formal piling up of words, which, however ludicrously displayed in his case, was, I must say, not at all peculiar to him. I have observed it, in the course of my life, in numbers of men. It seems to me to be a general rule. In the taking of legal oaths, for instance, deponents seem to enjoy themselves mightily when they come to several good words in succession, for the expression of one idea; as, that they utterly detest, abominate, and abjure, or so forth; and the old anathemas were made relishing on the same principle. We talk about the tyranny of words, but we like to tyrannise over them too; we are fond of having a large superfluous establishment of words to wait upon us on great occasions; we think it looks important, and sounds well. As we are not particular about the meaning of our liveries on state occasions, if they be but fine and numerous enough, so the meaning or necessity of our words is a secondary consideration, if there be but a great parade of them. And as individuals get into trouble by making too great a show of liveries, or as slaves when they are too numerous rise against their masters, so I think I could mention a nation that has got into many great difficulties, and will get into many greater, from maintaining too large a retinue of words.

Mr. Micawber read on, almost smacking his lips:

"'To wit, in manner following, that is to say. Mr. W. being infirm, and it being within the bounds of probability that his decease might lead to some discoveries, and to the downfall of—HEEP's—power over the W. family,—as I, Wilkins Micawber, the undersigned, assume—unless the filial affection of his daughter could be secretly influenced from allowing any investigation of the partnership affairs to be ever made, the said—HEEP—deemed it expedient to have a bond ready by him, as from Mr. W., for the before-mentioned sum of twelve six fourteen, two and nine, with interest, stated therein to have been advanced by—HEEP—to Mr. W. to save Mr. W. from dishonour; though really the sum was never advanced by him, and has long been replaced. The signatures to this instrument purporting to be executed by Mr. W. and attested by Wilkins Micawber, are forgeries by—HEEP. I have, in my possession, in his hand and pocket-book, several similar imitations of Mr. W.'s signature, here and there defaced by fire, but legible to any one. I never attested any such document. And I have the document itself, in my possession.' "

Uriah Heep, with a start, took out of his pocket a bunch of keys, and opened a certain drawer; then, suddenly bethought himself of what he was about, and turned again towards us, without looking in it.

" 'And I have the document,' " Mr. Micawber read again, looking about as if it were the text of a sermon, " 'in my possession,'—that is to say, I had, early this morning, when this was written, but have since relinquished it to Mr. Traddles."

"It is quite true," assented Traddles.

"Ury, Ury!" cried the mother, "be umble and make terms. I know my son will be umble, gentlemen, if you'll give him time to think. Mr. Copperfield, I'm sure you know that he was always very umble, sir!"

It was singular to see how the mother still held to the old trick, when the son had abandoned it as useless.

"Mother," he said, with an impatient bite at the handkerchief in which his hand was wrapped, "you had better take and fire a loaded gun at me."

"But I love you, Ury," cried Mrs. Heep. And I have no doubt she did; or that he loved her, however strange it may appear; though, to be sure, they were a congenial couple. "And I can't bear to hear you provoking the gentlemen, and endangering of yourself more. I told the gentleman at first, when he told me up-stairs it was come to light, that I would answer for your being umble, and making amends. Oh, see how umble, *I* am, gentlemen, and don't mind him!"

"Why, there's Copperfield, mother," he angrily retorted, pointing his lean finger at me, against whom all his animosity was levelled, as the prime mover in the discovery; and I did not undeceive him; "there's Copperfield, would have given you a hundred pound to say less than you've blurted out!"

"I can't help it, Ury," cried his mother. "I can't see you running into danger, through carrying your head so high. Better be umble, as you always was."

He remained for a little, biting the handkerchief, and then said to me with a scowl:

"What more have you got to bring forward? If anything, go on with it. What do you look at me for?"

Mr. Micawber promptly resumed his letter, glad to revert to a performance with which he was so highly satisfied.

"'Third. And last. I am now in a condition to show, by—HEEP's—false books, and—HEEP's—real memoranda, beginning with the partially destroyed pocket-book (which I was unable to comprehend, at the time of its accidental discovery by Mrs. Micawber, on our taking possession of our present abode, in the locker or bin devoted to the reception of the ashes calcined on our domestic hearth), that the weaknesses, the faults, the very virtues, the parental affections, and the sense of honour, of the unhappy Mr. W. have been for years acted on by, and warped to the base purposes of—HEEP. That Mr. W. has been for years deluded and plundered, in every conceivable manner, to the pecuniary aggrandisement of the avaricious, false, and grasping—HEEP. That the engrossing object of—HEEP—was, next to gain, to subdue Mr. and Miss W. (of his ulterior views in reference to the latter I say nothing) entirely to himself. That his last act, completed but a few months since, was to induce Mr. W. to execute a relinquishment of his share in the partnership, and even a bill of sale on the very furniture of his house, in consideration of a certain annunity, to be well and truly paid by—HEEP—on the four common quarter-days in each and every year. That these meshes; beginning with alarming and falsified accounts of the estate of which Mr. W. is the receiver, at a period when Mr. W. had launched into imprudent and ill-judged speculations, and may not have had the money, for which he was morally and legally responsible, in hand; going on with pretended borrowings of money at enormous interest, really coming from—HEEP—and by—HEEP—fraudulently obtained or withheld from Mr. W. himself, on pretence of such speculations or otherwise; perpetuated by a miscellaneous catalogue of unscrupulous chicaneries—gradually thickened, until the unhappy Mr. W. could see no world beyond. Bankrupt, as he believed, alike in circumstances, in all other hope, and in honour, his sole reliance was upon the monster in the garb of man,'"—Mr. Micawber made a good deal of this, as a new turn of expression,—"'who, by making himself necessary to him, had achieved his destruction. All this I undertake to show. Probably much more!"

I whispered a few words to Agnes, who was weeping, half joyfully, half sorrowfully, at my side; and there was a movement among us, as if Mr. Micawber had finished. He said, with exceeding gravity, "Pardon me," and proceeded, with a mixture of the lowest spirits and the most intense enjoyment to the peroration of his letter.

"'I have now concluded. It merely remains for me to substantiate these accusations; and then, with my ill-starred family, to disappear from the landscape on which we appear to be an incumbrance. That is soon done. It may be reasonably inferred that our baby will first expire of inanition, as being the frailest member of our circle; and that our twins will follow next in order. So be it! For myself, my Canterbury Pilgrimage has done much; imprisonment on civil process, and want, will soon do more. I trust that the labour and hazard of an investigation—of which the smallest results have been slowly pieced together, in the pressure of arduous avocations, under grinding penurious apprehensions, at rise of morn, at dewy eve, in the shadows of night, under the watchful eye of one whom it were superfluous to call Demon—combined with the struggle of parental Poverty to turn it, when completed, to the right account, may be as the sprinkling of a few drops of sweet water on my funeral pyre. I ask no more. Let it be, in justice, merely said of me, as of a gallant and eminent naval Hero, with whom I have no pretensions to cope, that what I have done, I did, in despite of mercenary and selfish objects,

"For England, home and Beauty."

"'Remaining always, &c. &c., WILKINS MICAWBER.'"

Much affected, but still intensely enjoying himself, Mr. Micawber folded up his letter, and handed it with a bow to my aunt, as something she might like to keep.

There was, as I had noticed on my first visit long ago, an iron safe in the room. The key was in it. A hasty suspicion seemed to strike Uriah; and, with a glance at Mr. Micawber, he went to it, and threw the doors clanking open. It was empty.

"Where are the books?" he cried, with a frightful face. "Some thief has stolen the books!"

Mr. Micawber tapped himself with the ruler. "*I* did, when I got the key from you as usual—but a little earlier—and opened it this morning."

"Don't be uneasy," said Traddles. "They have come into my

possession. I will take care of them, under the authority I mentioned."

"You receive stolen goods, do you?" cried Uriah.

"Under such circumstances," answered Traddles, "yes."

What was my astonishment when I beheld my aunt, who had been profoundly quiet and attentive, make a dart at Uriah Heep, and seize him by the collar with both hands!

"You know what *I* want?" said my aunt.

"A strait-waistcoat," said he.

"No. My property!" returned my aunt. "Agnes, my dear, as long as I believed it had been really made away with by your father, I wouldn't—and, my dear, I didn't, even to Trot, as he knows—breathe a syllable of its having been placed here for investment. But now I know this fellow's answerable for it, and I'll have it! Trot, come and take it away from him!"

Whether my aunt supposed, for the moment, that he kept her property in his neckerchief, I am sure I don't know; but she certainly pulled at it as if she thought so. I hastened to put myself between them, and to assure her that we would all take care that he should make the utmost restitution of everything he had wrongfully got. This, and a few moments' reflection, pacified her; but she was not at all disconcerted by what she had done (though I cannot say as much for her bonnet), and resumed her seat composedly.

During the last few minutes, Mrs. Heep had been clamouring to her son to be 'umble'; and had been going down on her knees to all of us in succession, and making the wildest promises. Her son sat her down in his chair; and, standing sulkily by her, holding her arm with his hand, but not rudely, said to me, with a ferocious look:

"What do you want done?"

"I will tell you what must be done," said Traddles.

"Has that Copperfield no tongue?" muttered Uriah. "I would do a good deal for you if you could tell me, without lying, that somebody had cut it out."

"My Uriah means to be umble!" cried his mother. "Don't mind what he says, good gentlemen!"

"What must be done," said Traddles, "is this. First, the deed of relinquishment, that we have heard of, must be given over to me now—here."

"Suppose I haven't got it," he interrupted.

"But you have," said Traddles; "therefore, you know, we won't suppose so." And I cannot help avowing that this was the first occasion on which I really did justice to the clear head, and the plain, patient, practical good sense, of my old schoolfellow. "Then," said Traddles, "you must prepare to disgorge all that your rapacity has become possessed of, and to make restoration to the last farthing. All the partnership books and papers must remain in our possession; all your books and papers; all money accounts and securities, of both kinds. In short, everything here."

"Must it? I don't know that," said Uriah. "I must have time to think about that."

"Certainly," replied Traddles; "but in the meanwhile, and, until everything is done to our satisfaction, we shall maintain possession of these things; and beg you—in short, compel you—to keep your own room, and hold no communication with any one."

"I won't do it!" said Uriah, with an oath.

"Maidstone Jail is a safer place of detention," observed Traddles; "and though the law may be longer in righting us, and may not be able to right us so completely as you can, there is no doubt of its punishing *you*. Dear me, you know that quite as well as I! Copperfield, will you go round to the Guildhall, and bring a couple of officers?"

Here, Mrs. Heep broke out again, crying on her knees to Agnes to interfere in their behalf, exclaiming that he was very humble, and it was all true, and if he didn't do what we wanted, she would, and much more to the same purpose; being half frantic with fears for her darling. To inquire what he might have done, if he had had any boldness, would be like inquiring what a mongrel cur might do, if it had the spirit of a tiger. He was a coward, from head to foot; and showed his dastardly nature through his sullenness and mortification, as much as at any time of his mean life.

"Stop!" he growled to me; and wiped his hot face with his hand. "Mother, hold your noise. Well! Let 'em have that deed. Go and fetch it!"

"Do you help her, Mr. Dick," said Traddles, "if you please."

Proud of his commission, and understanding it, Mr. Dick accompanied her as a shepherd's dog might accompany a sheep. But Mrs. Heep gave him little trouble; for she not only returned with the deed, but with the box in which it was, where we found a banker's book and some other papers that were afterwards serviceable.

"Good!" said Traddles, when this was brought. "Now, Mr. Heep, you can retire to think: particularly observing, if you please, that I declare to you, on the part of all present, that there is only one thing to be done; that it is what I have explained; and that it must be done without delay."

Uriah, without lifting his eyes from the ground, shuffled across the room with his hand to his chin, and pausing at the door, said:

"Copperfield, I have always hated you. You've always been an upstart, and you've always been against me."

"As I think I told you once before," said I, "it is you who have been, in your greed and cunning, against all the world. It may be profitable to you to reflect, in future, that there never were greed and cunning in the world yet, that did not do too much, and over-reach themselves. It is as certain as death."

"Or as certain as they used to teach at school (the same school where I picked up so much umbleness), from nine o'clock to eleven, that labour was a curse; and from eleven o'clock to one, that it was a blessing and a cheerfulness, and a dignity, and I don't know what all, eh?" said he with a sneer. "You preach about as consistent as they did. Won't umbleness go down? I shouldn't have got round my gentleman fellow-partner without it, I think.—Micawber, you old bully, I'll pay *you*!"

Mr. Micawber, supremely defiant of him and his extended finger, and making a great deal of his chest until he had slunk out at the door, then addressed himself to me, and proffered me the satisfaction of "witnessing the re-establishment of mutual confidence between himself and Mrs. Micawber." After which, he invited the company generally to the contemplation of that affecting spectacle.

"The veil that has long been interposed between Mrs. Micawber and myself, is now withdrawn," said Mr. Micawber; "and my children and the Author of their Being can once more come in contact on equal terms."

As we were all very grateful to him, and all desirous to show that we were, as well as the hurry and disorder of our spirits would permit, I dare say we should all have gone, but that it was necessary for Agnes to return to her father, as yet unable to bear more than the dawn of hope; and for some one else to hold Uriah in safe keeping. So Traddles remained for the latter purpose, to be presently relieved by Mr. Dick; and Mr. Dick, my aunt, and I, went home with Mr. Micawber. As I parted hurriedly from the dear girl to whom I owed so much, and thought from what she had been saved, perhaps, that morning —her better resolution notwithstanding—I felt devoutly thankful for the miseries of my younger days which had brought me to the knowledge of Mr. Micawber.

His house was not far off; and as the street-door opened into the sitting-room, and he bolted in with a precipitation quite his own, we found ourselves at once in the bosom of the family. Mr. Micawber exclaiming, " Emma! my life! " rushed into Mrs. Micawber's arms. Mrs. Micawber shrieked, and folded Mr. Micawber in her embrace. Miss Micawber, nursing the unconscious stranger of Mrs. Micawber's last letter to me, was sensibly affected. The stranger leaped. The twins testified their joy by several inconvenient but innocent demonstrations. Master Micawber, whose disposition appeared to have been soured by early disappointment, and whose aspect had become morose, yielded to his better feelings, and blubbered.

" Emma! " said Mr. Micawber. " The cloud is passed from my mind. Mutual confidence, so long preserved between us once, is restored, to know no further interruption. Now, welcome poverty! " cried Mr. Micawber, shedding tears. " Welcome misery, welcome houselessness, welcome hunger, rags, tempest, and beggary! Mutual confidence will sustain us to the end! "

With these expressions, Mr. Micawber placed Mrs. Micawber in a chair, and embraced the family all round; welcoming a variety of bleak prospects, which appeared, to the best of my judgment, to be anything but welcome to them; and calling upon them to come out into Canterbury and sing a chorus, as nothing else was left for their support.

But Mrs. Micawber having, in the strength of her emotions, fainted away, the first thing to be done, even before the chorus could be considered complete, was to recover her. This my aunt and Mr. Micawber did; and then my aunt was introduced, and Mrs. Micawber recognised me.

" Excuse me, dear Mr. Copperfield," said the poor lady, giving me her hand, " but I am not strong; and the removal of the late misunderstanding between Mr. Micawber and myself was at first too much for me."

" Is this all your family, ma'am? " said my aunt.

" There are no more at present," returned Mrs. Micawber.

" Good gracious, I didn't mean that, ma'am," said my aunt. " I mean, are all these yours? "

" Madam," replied Mr. Micawber, " it is a true bill."

" And that eldest young gentleman, now," said my aunt, musing, " what has *he* been brought up to? "

" It was my hope when I came here," said Mr. Micawber, " to have got Wilkins into the Church: or perhaps I shall express my meaning more strictly, if I say the Choir. But there was no vacancy for a tenor in the venerable Pile for which this city is so justly eminent; and he has—in short, he has contracted a habit of singing in public-houses, rather than in sacred edifices."

"But he means well," said Mrs. Micawber, tenderly.

"I dare say, my love," rejoined Mr. Micawber, "that he means particularly well; but I have not yet found that he carries out his meaning, in any given direction whatsoever."

Master Micawber's moroseness of aspect returned upon him again, and he demanded, with some temper, what he was to do? Whether he had been born a carpenter, or a coach-painter, any more than he had been born a bird? Whether he could go into the next street, and open a chemist's shop? Whether he could rush to the next assizes, and proclaim himself a lawyer? Whether he could come out by force at the opera, and succeed by violence? Whether he could do anything, without being brought up to something?

My aunt mused a little while, and then said:

"Mr. Micawber, I wonder you have never turned your thoughts to emigration."

"Madam," returned Mr. Micawber, "it was the dream of my youth, and the fallacious aspiration of my riper years." I am thoroughly persuaded, by-the-by, that he had never thought of it in his life.

"Aye?" said my aunt, with a glance at me. "Why, what a thing it would be for yourselves and your family, Mr. and Mrs. Micawber, if you were to emigrate now."

"Capital, madam, capital," urged Mr. Micawber, gloomily.

"That is the principal, I may say the only difficulty, my dear Mr. Copperfield," assented his wife.

"Capital?" cried my aunt. "But you are doing us a great service—have done us a great service, I may say, for surely much will come out of the fire—and what could we do for you, that would be half so good as to find the capital?"

"I could not receive it as a gift," said Mr. Micawber, full of fire and animation, "but if a sufficient sum could be advanced, say at five per cent. interest per annum, upon my personal liability—say my notes of hand, at twelve, eighteen, and twenty-four months, respectively, to allow time for something to turn up——"

"Could be? Can be and shall be, on your own terms," returned my aunt, "if you say the word. Think of this now, both of you. Here are some people David knows, going out to Australia shortly. If you decide to go, why shouldn't you go in the same ship? You may help each other. Think of this now, Mr. and Mrs. Micawber. Take your time, and weigh it well."

"There is but one question, my dear ma'am, I could wish to ask," said Mrs. Micawber. "The climate, I believe, is healthy?"

"Finest in the world!" said my aunt.

"Just so," returned Mrs. Micawber. "Then my question arises. Now, *are* the circumstances of the country such, that a man of Mr. Micawber's abilities would have a fair chance of rising in the social scale? I will not say, at present, might he aspire to be Governor, or anything of that sort; but would there be a reasonable opening for his talents to develop themselves—that would be amply sufficient—and find their own expansion?"

"No better opening anywhere," said my aunt, "for a man who conducts himself well, and is industrious."

"For a man who conducts himself well," repeated Mrs. Micawber, with her clearest business manner, "and is industrious. Precisely. It is evident to me that Australia is the legitimate sphere of action for Mr. Micawber!"

"I entertain the conviction, my dear madam," said Mr. Micawber, "that it is, under existing circumstances, the land, the only land, for myself and family; and that something of an extraordinary nature will turn up on that shore. It is no distance—comparatively speaking; and though consideration is due to the kindness of your proposal, I assure you that is a mere matter of form."

Shall I ever forget how, in a moment, he was the most sanguine of men, looking on to fortune; or how Mrs. Micawber presently discoursed about the habits of the kangaroo! Shall I ever recall that street of Canterbury on a market day, without recalling him, as he walked back with us; expressing, in the hardy roving manner he assumed, the unsettled habits of a temporary sojourner in the land; and looking at the bullocks, as they came by, with the eye of an Australian farmer!

53

ANOTHER RETROSPECT

I MUST PAUSE YET ONCE AGAIN. OH, MY CHILD-WIFE, there is a figure in the moving crowd before my memory, quiet and still, saying in its innocent love and childish beauty, Stop to think of me—turn to look upon the Little Blossom, as it flutters to the ground!

I do. All else grows dim, and fades away. I am again with Dora, in our cottage. I do not know how long she has been ill. I am so used to it in feeling, that I cannot count the time. It is not really long, in weeks or months; but, in my usage and experience, it is a weary, weary while.

They have left off telling me to "wait a few days more." I have begun to fear, remotely, that the day may never shine, when I shall see my child-wife running in the sunlight with her old friend Jip.

He is, as it were suddenly, grown very old. It may be that he misses in his mistress something that enlivened him and made him younger; but he mopes, and his sight is weak, and his limbs are feeble, and my aunt is sorry that he objects to her no more, but creeps near her as he lies on Dora's bed—she sitting at the bedside—and mildly licks her hand.

Dora lies smiling on us, and is beautiful, and utters no hasty or complaining word. She says that we are very good to her; that her dear old careful boy is tiring himself out, she knows; that my aunt has no sleep, yet is always wakeful, active, and kind. Sometimes, the little bird-like ladies come to see her; and then we talk about our wedding-day, and all that happy time.

What a strange rest and pause in my life there seems to be—and in all life, within doors and without—when I sit in the quiet, shaded, orderly room, with the blue eyes of my child-wife turned towards me, and her little fingers twining round my hand! Many and many an hour I sit thus; but, of all those times, three times come the freshest on my mind.

It is morning; and Dora, made so trim by my aunt's hands,

shows me how her pretty hair *will* curl upon the pillow yet, and how long and bright it is, and how she likes to have it loosely gathered in that net she wears.

" Not that I am vain of it, now, you mocking boy," she says, when I smile; " but because you used to say you thought it so beautiful; and because, when I first began to think about you, I used to peep in the glass, and wonder whether you would like very much to have a lock of it. Oh what a foolish fellow you were, Doady, when I gave you one! "

" That was on the day when you were painting the flowers I had given you, Dora, and when I told you how much in love I was."

" Ah! but I didn't like to tell *you*," says Dora, " *then*, how I had cried over them, because I believed you really liked me! When I can run about again as I used to do, Doady, let us go and see those places where we were such a silly couple, shall we? And take some of the old walks? And not forget poor papa? "

" Yes, we will, and have some happy days. So you must make haste to get well, my dear."

" Oh, I shall soon do that! I am so much better, you don't know! "

It is evening; and I sit in the same chair, by the same bed, with the same face turned towards me. We have been silent, and there is a smile upon her face. I have ceased to carry my light burden up and down stairs now. She lies here all the day.

" Doady! "

" My dear Dora! "

" You won't think what I am going to say, unreasonable, after what you told me, such a little while ago, of Mr. Wickfield's not being well? I want to see Agnes. Very much I want to see her."

" I will write to her, my dear."

" Will you? "

" Directly."

" What a good, kind boy! Doady, take me on your arm. Indeed, my dear, it's not a whim. It's not a foolish fancy. I want, very much indeed, to see her! "

" I am certain of it. I have only to tell her so, and she is sure to come."

" You are very lonely when you go down-stairs, now? " Dora whispers, with her arm about my neck.

" How can I be otherwise, my own love, when I see your empty chair? "

"My empty chair!" She clings to me for a little while, in silence. "And you really miss me, Doady?" looking up, and brightly smiling. "Even poor, giddy, stupid me?"

"My heart, who is there upon earth that I could miss so much?"

"Oh, husband! I am so glad, yet so sorry!" creeping closer to me, and folding me in both her arms. She laughs and sobs, and then is quiet, and quite happy.

"Quite!" she says. "Only give Agnes my dear love, and tell her that I want very, very much to see her; and I have nothing left to wish for."

"Except to get well again, Dora."

"Ah, Doady! Sometimes I think—you know I always was a silly little thing!—that that will never be!"

"Don't say so, Dora! Dearest love, don't think so!"

"I won't, if I can help it, Doady. But I am very happy; though my dear boy is so lonely by himself, before his child-wife's empty chair!"

It is night; and I am with her still. Agnes has arrived; has been among us for a whole day and an evening. She, my aunt, and I, have sat with Dora since the morning, all together. We have not talked much, but Dora has been perfectly contented and cheerful. We are now alone.

Do I know, now, that my child-wife will soon leave me? They have told me so; they have told me nothing new to my thoughts; but I am far from sure that I have taken that truth to heart. I cannot master it. I have withdrawn by myself, many times to-day, to weep. I have remembered Who wept for a parting between the living and the dead. I have bethought me of all that gracious and compassionate history. I have tried to resign myself, and to console myself; and that, I hope, I may have done imperfectly; but what I cannot firmly settle in my mind is, that the end will absolutely come. I hold her hand in mine, I hold her heart in mind, I see her love for me, alive in all its strength. I cannot shut out a pale lingering shadow of belief that she will be spared.

"I am going to speak to you, Doady. I am going to say something I have often thought of saying, lately. You won't mind?" with a gentle look.

"Mind, my darling?"

"Because I don't know what you will think, or what you may have thought sometimes. Perhaps you have often thought the same. Doady, dear, I am afraid I was too young."

I lay my face upon the pillow by her, and she looks into my eyes, and speaks very softly. Gradually, as she goes on, I feel, with a stricken heart, that she is speaking of herself as past.

" I am afraid, dear, I was too young. I don't mean in years only, but in experience, and thoughts, and everything. I was such a silly little creature! I am afraid it would have been better, if we had only loved each other as a boy and girl, and forgotten it. I have begun to think I was not fit to be a wife."

I try to stay my tears, and to reply, " Oh, Dora, love, as fit as I to be a husband! "

" I don't know," with the old shake of her curls. " Perhaps! But if I had been more fit to be married, I might have made you more so, too. Besides, you are very clever, and I never was."

" We have been very happy, my sweet Dora."

" I was very happy, very. But, as years went on, my dear boy would have wearied of his child-wife. She would have been less and less a companion for him. He would have been more and more sensible of what was wanting in his home. She wouldn't have improved. It is better as it is."

" Oh, Dora, dearest, dearest, do not speak to me so. Every word seems a reproach! "

" No, not a syllable! " she answers, kissing me. " Oh, my dear, you never deserved it, and I loved you far too well to say a reproachful word to you, in earnest—it was all the merit I had, except being pretty—or you thought me so. Is it lonely, downstairs, Doady? "

" Very! Very! "

" Don't cry! Is my chair there? "

" In its old place."

" Oh, how my poor boy cries! Hush, hush! Now, make me one promise. I want to speak to Agnes. When you go downstairs, tell Agnes so, and send her up to me; and while I speak to her, let no one come—not even aunt. I want to speak to Agnes by herself. I want to speak to Agnes, quite alone."

I promise that she shall, immediately; but I cannot leave her, for my grief.

" I said that it was better as it is! " she whispers, as she holds me in her arms. " Oh, Doady, after more years, you never could have loved your child-wife better than you do; and, after more years, she would so have tried and disappointed you, that you might not have been able to love her half so well! I know I was too young and foolish. It is much better as it is! "

Agnes is down-stairs, when I go into the parlour; and I give her the message. She disappears, leaving me alone with Jip. His Chinese house is by the fire; and he lies within it, on his bed of flannel, querulously trying to sleep. The bright moon is high and clear. As I look out on the night, my tears fall fast, and my undisciplined heart is chastened heavily—heavily.

I sit down by the fire, thinking with a blind remorse of all those secret feelings I have nourished since my marriage. I think of every little trifle between me and Dora, and feel the truth, that trifles make the sum of life. Ever rising from the sea of my remembrance, is the image of the dear child as I knew her first, graced by my young love, and by her own, with every fascination wherein such love is rich. Would it, indeed, have been better if we had loved each other as a boy and girl, and forgotten it? Undisciplined heart, reply!

How the time wears, I know not; until I am recalled by my child-wife's old companion. More restless than he was, he crawls out of his house, and looks at me, and wanders to the door, and whines to go up-stairs.

"Not to-night, Jip! Not to-night!"

He comes very slowly back to me, licks my hand, and lifts his dim eyes to my face.

"Oh, Jip! It may be, never again!"

He lies down at my feet, stretches himself out as if to sleep, and with a plaintive cry, is dead.

"Oh, Agnes! Look, look, here!"

—That face, so full of pity, and of grief, that rain of tears, that awful mute appeal to me, that solemn hand upraised towards Heaven!

"Agnes?"

It is over. Darkness comes before my eyes; and, for a time, all things are blotted out of my remembrance.

54

MR. MICAWBER'S TRANSACTIONS

THIS IS NOT THE TIME AT WHICH I AM TO ENTER ON THE state of my mind beneath its load of sorrow. I came to think that the Future was walled up before me, that the energy and action of my life were at an end, that I never could find any refuge but in the grave. I came to think so, I say, but not in the first shock of my grief. It slowly grew to that. If the events I go on to relate, had not thickened around me, in the beginning to confuse, and in the end to augment, my affliction, it is possible (though I think not probable), that I might have fallen at once into this condition. As it was, an interval occurred before I fully knew my own distress; an interval in which I even supposed that its sharpest pangs were past; and when my mind could soothe itself by resting on all that was most innocent and beautiful, in the tender story that was closed for ever.

When it was first proposed that I should go abroad, or how it came to be agreed among us that I was to seek the restoration of my peace in change and travel, I do not, even now, distinctly know. The spirit of Agnes so pervaded all we thought, and said, and did, in that time of sorrow, that I assume I may refer the project to her influence. But her influence was so quiet that I know no more.

And now, indeed, I began to think that in my old association of her with the stained-glass window in the church, a prophetic foreshadowing of what she would be to me, in the calamity that was to happen in the fulness of time, had found a way into my mind. In all that sorrow, from the moment, never to be forgotten, when she stood before me with her upraised hand, she was like a sacred presence in my lonely house. When the Angel of Death alighted there, my child-wife fell asleep—they told me so when I could bear to hear it—on her bosom, with a smile. From my swoon, I first awoke to a consciousness of her compassionate tears, her words of hope and peace, her gentle face bending down as from a purer region nearer Heaven, over my undisciplined heart, and softening its pain.

Let me go on.

I was to go abroad. That seemed to have been determined among us from the first. The ground now covering all that could perish of my departed wife, I waited only for what Mr. Micawber called the "final pulverisation of Heep;" and for the departure of the emigrants.

At the request of Traddles, most affectionate and devoted of friends in my trouble, we returned to Canterbury: I mean my aunt, Agnes, and I. We proceeded by appointment straight to Mr. Micawber's house; where, and at Mr. Wickfield's, my friend had been labouring ever since our explosive meeting. When poor Mrs. Micawber saw me come in, in my black clothes, she was sensibly affected. There was a great deal of good in Mrs. Micawber's heart, which had not been dunned out of it in all those many years.

"Well, Mr. and Mrs. Micawber," was my aunt's first salutation after we were seated. "Pray, have you thought about that emigration proposal of mine?"

"My dear madam," returned Mr. Micawber, "perhaps I cannot better express the conclusion at which Mrs. Micawber, your humble servant, and I may add our children, have jointly and severally arrived, than by borrowing the language of an illustrious poet, to reply that our Boat is on the shore, and our Bark is on the sea."

"That's right," said my aunt. "I augur all sorts of good from your sensible decision."

"Madam, you do us a great deal of honour," he rejoined. He then referred to a memorandum. "With respect to the pecuniary assistance enabling us to launch our frail canoe on the ocean of enterprise, I have reconsidered that important business point; and would beg to propose my notes of hand—drawn, it is needless to stipulate, on stamps of the amounts respectively required by the various Acts of Parliament applying to such securities—at eighteen, twenty-four, and thirty months. The proposition I originally submitted, was twelve, eighteen, and twenty-four; but I am apprehensive that such an arrangement might not allow sufficient time for the requisite amount of —Something—to turn up. We might not," said Mr. Micawber, looking round the room as if it represented several hundred acres of highly cultivated land, "on the first responsibility becoming due, have been successful in our harvest, or we might not have got our harvest in. Labour, I believe, is sometimes difficult to obtain in that portion of our colonial possessions where it will be our lot to combat with the teeming soil."

"Arrange it in any way you please, sir," said my aunt.

"Madam," he replied, "Mrs. Micawber and myself are deeply sensible of the very considerate kindness of our friends and patrons. What I wish is, to be perfectly business-like, and perfectly punctual. Turning over, as we are about to turn over, an entirely new leaf; and falling back, as we are now in the act of falling back, for a Spring of no common magnitude; it is important to my sense of self-respect, besides being an example to my son, that these arrangements should be concluded as between man and man."

I don't know that Mr. Micawber attached any meaning to this last phrase; I don't know that anybody ever does, or did; but he appeared to relish it uncommonly, and repeated, with an impressive cough, "as between man and man."

"I propose," said Mr. Micawber, "Bills—a convenience to the mercantile world, for which, I believe, we are originally indebted to the Jews, who appear to me to have had a devilish deal too much to do with them ever since—because they are negotiable. But if a Bond, or any other description of security, would be preferred, I should be happy to execute any such instrument. As between man and man."

My aunt observed, that in a case where both parties were willing to agree to anything, she took it for granted there would be no difficulty in settling this point. Mr. Micawber was of her opinion.

"In reference to our domestic preparations, madam," said Mr. Micawber, with some pride, "for meeting the destiny to which we are now understood to be self-devoted, I beg to report them. My eldest daughter attends at five every morning in a neighbouring establishment, to acquire the process—if process it may be called—of milking cows. My younger children are instructed to observe, as closely as circumstances will permit, the habits of pigs and poultry maintained in the poorer parts of this city: a pursuit from which they have, on two occasions, been brought home, within an inch of being run over. I have myself directed some attention, during the past week, to the art of baking; and my son Wilkins has issued forth with a walking-stick and driven cattle, when permitted, by the rugged hirelings who had them in charge, to render any voluntary service in that direction—which I regret to say, for the credit of our nature, was not often; he being generally warned, with imprecations, to desist."

"All very right indeed," said my aunt, encouragingly. "Mrs. Micawber has been busy, too, I have no doubt."

"My dear madam," returned Mrs. Micawber, with her business-like air. "I am free to confess that I have not been actively engaged in pursuits immediately connected with cultivation or with stock, though well aware that both will claim my attention on a foreign shore. Such opportunities as I have been enabled to alienate from my domestic duties, I have devoted to corresponding at some length with my family. For I own it seems to me, my dear Mr. Copperfield," said Mrs. Micawber, who always fell back on me (I suppose from old habit) to whomsoever else she might address her discourse at starting, "that the time is come when the past should be buried in oblivion; when my family should take Mr. Micawber by the hand, and Mr. Micawber should take my family by the hand; when the lion should lie down with the lamb, and my family be on terms with Mr. Micawber."

I said I thought so too.

"This, at least, is the light, my dear Mr. Copperfield," pursued Mrs. Micawber, "in which *I* view the subject. When I lived at home with my papa and mama, my papa was accustomed to ask, when any point was under discussion in our limited circle, 'In what light does my Emma view the subject?' That my papa was too partial, I know; still, on such a point as the frigid coldness which has ever subsisted between Mr. Micawber and my family, I necessarily have formed an opinion, delusive though it may be."

"No doubt. Of course you have, ma'am." said my aunt.

"Precisely so," assented Mrs. Micawber. "Now, I may be wrong in my conclusions; it is very likely that I am, but my individual impression is, that the gulf between my family and Mr. Micawber may be traced to an apprehension, on the part of my family, that Mr. Micawber would require pecuniary accommodation. I cannot help thinking," said Mrs. Micawber, with an air of deep sagacity, "that there are members of my family who have been apprehensive that Mr. Micawber would solicit them for their names.—I do not mean to be conferred in Baptism upon our children, but to be inscribed on Bills of Exchange, and negotiated in the Money Market."

The look of penetration with which Mrs. Micawber announced this discovery, as if no one had ever thought of it before, seemed rather to astonish my aunt; who abruptly replied, "Well, ma'am, upon the whole, I shouldn't wonder if you were right!"

"Mr. Micawber being now on the eve of casting off the pecuniary shackles that have so long enthralled him," said Mrs.

Micawber, "and of commencing a new career in a country where there is sufficient range for his abilities,—which, in my opinion, is exceedingly important; Mr. Micawber's abilities peculiarly requiring space,—it seems to me that my family should signalise the occasion by coming forward. What I could wish to see, would be a meeting between Mr. Micawber and my family at a festive entertainment, to be given at my family's expense; where Mr. Micawber's health and prosperity being proposed by some leading member of my family, Mr. Micawber might have an opportunity of developing his views."

"My dear," said Mr. Micawber, with some heat, "it may be better for me to state distinctly, at once, that if I were to develop my views to that assembled group, they would possibly be found of an offensive nature; my impression being that your family are, in the aggregate, impertinent Snobs; and, in detail, unmitigated Ruffians."

"Micawber," said Mrs. Micawber, shaking her head, "no! You have never understood them, and they have never understood you."

Mr. Micawber coughed.

"They have never understood you, Micawber," said his wife. "They may be incapable of it. If so, that is their misfortune. I can pity their misfortune."

"I am extremely sorry, my dear Emma," said Mr. Micawber, relenting, "to have been betrayed into any expressions that might, even remotely, have the appearance of being strong expressions. All I would say is, that I can go abroad without your family coming forward to favour me,—in short, with a parting Shove of their cold shoulders; and that, upon the whole, I would rather leave England with such impetus as I possess, than derive any acceleration of it from that quarter. At the same time, my dear, if they should condescend to reply to your communications—which our joint experience renders most improbable—far be it from me to be a barrier to your wishes."

The matter being thus amicably settled, Mr. Micawber gave Mrs. Micawber his arm, and glancing at the heap of books and papers lying before Traddles on the table, said they would leave us to ourselves; which they ceremoniously did.

"My dear Copperfield," said Traddles, leaning back in his chair when they were gone, and looking at me with an affection that made his eyes red, and his hair all kinds of shapes, "I don't make any excuse for troubling you with business, because I know you are deeply interested in it, and it may divert your thoughts. My dear boy, I hope you are not worn out?"

"I am quite myself," said I, after a pause. "We have more cause to think of my aunt than of any one. You know how much she has done."

"Surely, surely," answered Traddles. "Who can forget it!"

"But even that is not all," said I. "During the last fortnight, some new trouble has vexed her; and she has been in and out of London every day. Several times she has gone out early, and been absent until evening. Last night, Traddles, with this journey before her, it was almost midnight before she came home. You know what her consideration for others is. She will not tell me what has happened to distress her."

My aunt, very pale, and with deep lines in her face, sat immovable until I had finished; when some stray tears found their way to her cheeks, and she put her hand on mine.

"It's nothing, Trot; it's nothing. There will be no more of it. You shall know by-and-by. Now, Agnes, my dear, let us attend to these affairs."

"I must do Mr. Micawber the justice to say," Traddles began, "that although he would appear not to have worked to any good account for himself, he is a most untiring man when he works for other people. I never saw such a fellow. If he always goes on in the same way, he must be, virtually, about two hundred years old at present. The heat into which he has been continually putting himself; and the distracted and impetuous manner in which he has been diving, day and night, among papers and books; to say nothing of the immense number of letters he has written me between this house and Mr. Wickfield's, and often across the table when he has been sitting opposite, and might much more easily have spoken; is quite extraordinary."

"Letters!" cried my aunt. "I believe he dreams in letters!"

"There's Mr. Dick, too," said Traddles, "has been doing wonders! As soon as he was released from overlooking Uriah Heep, whom he kept in such charge as *I* never saw exceeded, he began to devote himself to Mr. Wickfield. And really his anxiety to be of use in the investigations we have been making, and his real usefulness in extracting, and copying, and fetching, and carrying, have been quite stimulating to us."

"Dick is a very remarkable man," exclaimed my aunt; "and I always said he was. Trot, you know it."

"I am happy to say, Miss Wickfield," pursued Traddles, at once with great delicacy and with great earnestness, "that in your absence Mr. Wickfield has considerably improved. Relieved of the incubus that had fastened upon him for so long a time, and of the dreadful apprehensions under which he had lived, he is hardly the same person. At times, even his impaired power of concentrating his memory and attention on particular points of business, has recovered itself very much; and he has been able to assist us in making some things clear, that we should have found very difficult indeed, if not hopeless, without him. But what I have to do is to come to results, which are short enough; not to gossip on all the hopeful circumstances I have observed, or I shall never have done."

His natural manner and agreeable simplicity made it transparent that he said this to put us in good heart, and to enable Agnes to hear her father mentioned with greater confidence; but it was not the less pleasant for that.

"Now, let me see," said Traddles, looking among the papers on the table. "Having counted our funds, and reduced to order a great mass of unintentional confusion in the first place, and of wilful confusion and falsification in the second, we take it to be clear that Mr. Wickfield might now wind up his business, and his agency-trust, and exhibit no deficiency or defalcation whatever."

"Oh, thank Heaven!" cried Agnes fervently.

"But," said Traddles, "the surplus that would be left as his means of support—and I suppose the house to be sold, even in saying this—would be so small, not exceeding in all probability some hundreds of pounds, that perhaps, Miss Wickfield, it would be best to consider whether he might not retain his agency of the estate to which he has so long been receiver. His friends might advise him, you know; now he is free. You yourself, Miss Wickfield—Copperfield—I—"

"I have considered it, Trotwood," said Agnes, looking to me, "and I feel that it ought not to be, and must not be; even on the recommendation of a friend to whom I am so grateful, and owe so much."

"I will not say that I recommend it," observed Traddles. "I think it right to suggest it. No more."

"I am happy to hear you say so," answered Agnes, steadily, "for it gives me hope, almost assurance, that we think alike. Dear Mr. Traddles and dear Trotwood, papa once free with honour, what could I wish for! I have always aspired, if I could have released him from the toils in which he was held, to render back some little portion of the love and care I owe him, and to devote my life to him. It has been, for years, the utmost height of my hopes. To take our future on myself, will be the next great happiness—the next to his release from all trust and responsibility—that I can know."

"Have you thought how, Agnes?"

"Often! I am not afraid, dear Trotwood. I am certain of success. So many people know me here, and think kindly of me, that I am certain. Don't mistrust me. Our wants are not many. If I rent the dear old house, and keep a school, I shall be useful and happy."

The calm fervour of her cheerful voice brought back so vividly first the dear old house itself, and then my solitary home, that my heart was too full for speech. Traddles pretended for a little while to be busy looking among the papers.

"Next, Miss Trotwood," said Traddles, "that property of yours."

"Well, sir," sighed my aunt. "All I have got to say about it is, that if it's gone, I can bear it; and if it's not gone, I shall be glad to get it back."

"It was originally, I think, eight thousand pounds, Consols?" said Traddles.

"Right!" replied my aunt.

"I can't account for more than five," said Traddles, with an air of perplexity.

"—thousand, do you mean?" inquired my aunt, with uncommon composure, "or pounds?"

"Five thousand pounds," said Traddles.

"It was all there was," returned my aunt. "I sold three, myself. One, I paid for your articles, Trot, my dear; and the other two I have by me. When I lost the rest, I thought it wise to say nothing about that sum, but to keep it secretly for a rainy day. I wanted to see how you would come out of the trial, Trot; and you came out nobly—persevering, self-reliant, self-denying! So did Dick. Don't speak to me, for I find my nerves a little shaken!"

Nobody would have thought so, to see her sitting upright, with her arms folded; but she had wonderful self-command.

"Then I am delighted to say," cried Traddles, beaming with joy, "that we have recovered the whole money!"

"Don't congratulate me, anybody!" exclaimed my aunt. "How so, sir?"

"You believed it had been misappropriated by Mr. Wickfield?" said Traddles.

"Of course I did," said my aunt, "and was therefore easily silenced. Agnes, not a word!"

"And indeed," said Traddles, "it was sold, by virtue of the power of management he held from you; but I needn't say by whom sold, or on whose actual signature. It was afterwards pretended to Mr. Wickfield, by that rascal,—and proved, too, by figures,—that he had possessed himself of the money (on general instructions, *he* said) to keep other deficiencies and difficulties from the light. Mr. Wickfield, being so weak and helpless in his hands as to pay you, afterwards, several sums of interest on a pretended principal which he knew did not exist, made himself, unhappily, a party to the fraud."

"And at last took the blame upon himself," added my aunt; "and wrote me a mad letter, charging himself with robbery, and wrong unheard of. Upon which I paid him a visit early one morning, called for a candle, burnt the letter, and told him if he ever could right me and himself, to do it; and if he couldn't, to keep his own counsel for his daughter's sake.—If anybody speaks to me, I'll leave the house!"

We all remained quiet; Agnes covering her face.

"Well, my dear friend," said my aunt, after a pause, "and you have really extorted the money back from him?"

"Why, the fact is," returned Traddles, "Mr. Micawber had so completely hemmed him in, and was always ready with so many new points if an old one failed, that he could not escape from us. A most remarkable circumstance is, that I really don't think he grasped this sum even so much for the gratification of his avarice, which was inordinate, as in the hatred he felt for Copperfield. He said so to me, plainly. He said he would even have spent as much, to baulk or injure Copperfield."

"Ha!" said my aunt, knitting her brows thoughtfully, and glancing at Agnes. "And what's become of him?"

"I don't know. He left here," said Traddles, "with his mother, who had been clamouring, and beseeching, and disclosing, the whole time. They went away by one of the London night coaches, and I know no more about him; except that his malevolence to me at parting was audacious. He seemed to consider himself hardly less indebted to me than to Mr. Micawber; which I consider (as I told him) quite a compliment."

"Do you suppose he has any money, Traddles?" I asked.

"Oh dear, yes, I should think so," he replied, shaking his head, seriously. "I should say he must have pocketed a good deal, in one way or other. But I think you would find, Copperfield, if you had an opportunity of observing his course, that money would never keep that man out of mischief. He is such an incarnate hypocrite, that whatever object he pursues, he must pursue crookedly. It's his only compensation for the outward restraints he puts upon himself. Always creeping along the ground to some small end or other, he will always magnify every object in the way; and consequently will hate and suspect everybody that comes, in the most innocent manner, between him and it. So the crooked courses will become crookeder, at any moment, for the least reason, or for none. It's only necessary to consider his history here," said Traddles, "to know that."

"He's a monster of meanness!" said my aunt.

"Really, I don't know about that," observed Traddles, thoughtfully. "Many people can be very mean, when they give their minds to it."

"And now, touching Mr. Micawber," said my aunt.

"Well, really," said Traddles, cheerfully, "I must, once more, give Mr. Micawber high praise. But for his having been so patient and persevering for so long a time, we never could have hoped to do anything worth speaking of. And I think we ought to consider that Mr. Micawber did right, for right's sake, when we reflect what terms he might have made with Uriah Heep himself, for his silence."

"I think so too," said I.

"Now, what would you give him?" inquired my aunt.

"Oh! Before you come to that," said Traddles, a little disconcerted, "I am afraid I thought it discreet to omit (not being able to carry everything before me) two points, in making this lawless adjustment—for it's perfectly lawless from beginning to end—of a difficult affair. Those I.O.U.'s, and so forth, which Mr. Micawber gave him for the advances he had—"

"Well! They must be paid," said my aunt.

"Yes, but I don't know when they may be proceeded on, or where they are," rejoined Traddles, opening his eyes; "and I anticipate that, between this time and his departure, Mr. Micawber will be constantly arrested, or taken in execution."

"Then he must be constantly set free again, and taken out of execution," said my aunt. "What's the amount altogether?"

"Why, Mr. Micawber has entered the transactions—he calls them transactions—with great form, in a book," rejoined Traddles, smiling; "and he makes the amount a hundred and three pounds, five."

"Now, what shall we give him, that sum included?" said my aunt. "Agnes, my dear, you and I can talk about division of it afterwards. What should it be? Five hundred pounds?"

Upon this, Traddles and I both struck in at once. We both recommended a small sum in money, and the payment, without stipulation to Mr. Micawber, of the Uriah claims as they came in. We proposed that the family should have their passage and their outfit, and a hundred pounds; and that Mr. Micawber's arrangement for the repayment of the advances should be gravely entered into, as it might be wholesome for him to suppose himself under that responsibility. To this, I added the suggestion, that I should give some explanation of his character and history to Mr. Peggotty, who I knew could be relied on; and that to Mr. Peggotty should be quietly entrusted the discretion of advancing another hundred. I further proposed to interest Mr. Micawber in Mr. Peggotty, by confiding so much of Mr. Peggotty's story to him as I might feel justified in relating, or might think expedient; and to endeavour to bring each of them to bear upon the other, for the common advantage. We all entered warmly into these views; and I may mention at once, that the principals themselves did so, shortly afterwards, with perfect good will and harmony.

Seeing that Traddles now glanced anxiously at my aunt again, I reminded him of the second and last point to which he had adverted.

"You and your aunt will excuse me, Copperfield, if I touch upon a painful theme, as I greatly fear I shall," said Traddles, hesitating; "but I think it necessary to bring it to your recollection. On the day of Mr. Micawber's memorable denunciation, a threatening allusion was made by Uriah Heep to your aunt's—husband."

My aunt, retaining her stiff position, and apparent composure, assented with a nod.

"Perhaps," observed Traddles, "it was mere purposeless impertinence?"

"No," returned my aunt.

"There was—pardon me—really such a person, and at all in his power?" hinted Traddles.

"Yes, my good friend," said my aunt.

Traddles, with a perceptible lengthening of his face, explained that he had not been able to approach this subject; that it had shared the fate of Mr. Micawber's liabilities, in not being comprehended in the terms he had made; that we were no longer of any authority with Uriah Heep; and that if he could do us, or any of us, any injury or annoyance, no doubt he would.

My aunt remained quiet; until again some stray tears found their way to her cheeks.

"You are quite right," she said. "It was very thoughtful to mention it."

"Can I—or Copperfield—do anything?" asked Traddles, gently.

"Nothing," said my aunt. "I thank you many times. Trot, my dear, a vain threat! Let us have Mr. and Mrs. Micawber back. And don't any of you speak to me!" With that she smoothed her dress, and sat, with her upright carriage, looking at the door.

"Well, Mr. and Mrs. Micawber!" said my aunt, when they entered. "We have been discussing your emigration, with many apologies to you for keeping you out of the room so long; and I'll tell you what arrangements we propose."

These she explained to the unbounded satisfaction of the family,—children and all being then present,—and so much to the awakening of Mr. Micawber's punctual habits in the opening stage of all bill transactions, that he could not be dissuaded from immediately rushing out, in the highest spirits, to buy the stamps for his notes of hand. But his joy received a sudden check; for within five minutes he returned in the custody of a sheriff's officer, informing us, in a flood of tears, that all was lost. We, being quite prepared for this event, which was of course a proceeding of Uriah Heep's, soon paid the money; and in five minutes more Mr. Micawber was seated at the table, filling up the stamps with an expression of perfect joy, which only that congenial employment, or the making of punch, could impart in full completeness to his shining face. To see him at work on the stamps, with the relish of an artist, touching them like pictures, looking at them sideways, taking weighty notes of dates and amounts in his pocket-book, and contemplating them when finished, with a high sense of their precious value, was a sight indeed.

"Now, the best thing you can do, sir, if you'll allow me to advise you," said my aunt, after silently observing him "is to abjure that occupation for evermore."

"Madam," replied Mr. Micawber, "it is my intention to register such a vow on the virgin page of the future. Mrs. Micawber will attest it. I trust," said Mr. Micawber, solemnly, "that my son Wilkins will ever bear in mind, that he had infinitely better put his fist in the fire, than use it to handle the serpents that have poisoned the life-blood of his unhappy parent!" Deeply affected, and changed in a moment to the image of despair, Mr. Micawber regarded the serpents with a look of gloomy abhorrence (in which his late admiration of them was not quite subdued), folded them up and put them in his pocket.

This closed the proceedings of the evening. We were weary with sorrow and fatigue, and my aunt and I were to return to London on the morrow. It was arranged that the Micawbers should follow us, after effecting a sale of their goods to a broker: that Mr. Wickfield's affairs should be brought to a settlement, with all convenient speed, under the direction of Traddles; and that Agnes should also come to London, pending those arrangements. We passed the night at the old house, which, freed from the presence of the Heeps, seemed purged of a disease; and I lay in my old room, like a shipwrecked wanderer come home.

We went back next day to my aunt's house—not to mine; and when she and I sat alone, as of old, before going to bed, she said:

"Trot, do you really wish to know what I have had upon my mind lately?"

"Indeed I do, aunt. If there ever was a time when I felt unwilling that you should have a sorrow or anxiety which I could not share, it is now."

"You have had sorrow enough, child," said my aunt, affectionately, "without the addition of *my* little miseries. I could have no other motive, Trot, in keeping anything from you."

"I know that well," said I. "But tell me now."

"Would you ride with me a little way to-morrow morning?" asked my aunt.

"Of course."

"At nine," said she. "I'll tell you then, my dear."

At nine, accordingly, we went out in a little chariot, and drove to London. We drove a long way through the streets until we came to one of the large hospitals. Standing hard by the building was a plain hearse. The driver recognised my aunt, and in obedience to a motion of her hand at the window, drove slowly off; we following.

"You understand it now, Trot," said my aunt. "He is gone!"

"Did he die in the hospital?"

"Yes."

She sat immovable beside me; but again I saw the stray tears on her face.

"He was there once before," said my aunt presently. "He was ailing a long time—a shattered, broken man, these many years. When he knew his state in this last illness, he asked them to send for me. He was sorry then. Very sorry."

"You went, I know, aunt."

"I went. I was with him a good deal afterwards."

"He died the night before we went to Canterbury?" said I.

My aunt nodded. "No one can harm him now," she said. "It was a vain threat."

We drove away, out of town, to the churchyard at Hornsey. "Better here than in the streets," said my aunt. "He was born here."

We alighted; and followed the plain coffin to a corner I remember well, where the service was read consigning it to the dust.

"Six-and-thirty years ago, this day, my dear," said my aunt, as we walked back to the chariot, "I was married. God forgive us all!"

We took our seats in silence; and so she sat beside me for a long time, holding my hand. At length she suddenly burst into tears, and said:

"He was a fine-looking man when I married him, Trot—and he was sadly changed!"

It did not last long. After the relief of tears, she soon became composed, and even cheerful. Her nerves were a little shaken, she said, or she would not have given way to it. God forgive us all!

So we rode back to her little cottage at Highgate, where we found the following short note, which had arrived by that morning's post from Mr. Micawber:

"Canterbury,
"Friday.

"My dear Madam, and Copperfield,

"The fair land of promise lately looming on the horizon is again enveloped in impenetrable mists, and for ever withdrawn from the eyes of a drifting wretch whose Doom is sealed!

"Another writ has been issued (in His Majesty's High Court of King's Bench at Westminster), in another cause of HEEP *v.* MICAWBER, and the defendant in that cause is the prey of the sheriff having legal jurisdiction in this bailiwick.

"Now's the day, and now's the hour,
See the front of battle lower,
See approach proud EDWARD's power—
Chains and slavery!

Consigned to which, and to a speedy end (for mental torture is not supportable beyond a certain point, and that point I feel I have attained), my course is run. Bless you, bless you! Some future traveller, visiting, from motives of curiosity, not unmingled, let us hope, with sympathy, the place of confinement allotted to debtors in this city, may, and I trust will, Ponder, as he traces on its wall, inscribed with a rusty nail,

"The obscure initials,
"W. M.

"P.S. I re-open this to say that our common friend, Mr.

Thomas Traddles (who has not yet left us, and is looking extremely well), has paid the debt and costs, in the noble name of Miss Trotwood; and that myself and family are at the height of earthly bliss."

55

TEMPEST

I NOW APPROACH AN EVENT IN MY LIFE, SO INDELIBLE, so awful, so bound by an infinite variety of ties to all that has preceded it in these pages, that, from the beginning of my narrative, I have seen it growing larger and larger as I advanced, like a great tower in a plain, and throwing its fore-cast shadow even on the incidents of my childish days.

For years after it occurred, I dreamed of it often. I have started up so vividly impressed by it, that its fury has yet seemed raging in my quiet room, in the still night. I dream of it sometimes, though at lengthened and uncertain intervals, to this hour. I have an association between it and a stormy wind, or the lightest mention of a sea-shore, as strong as any of which my mind is conscious. As plainly as I behold what happened, I will try to write it down. I do not recall it, but see it done; for it happens again before me.

The time drawing on rapidly for the sailing of the emigrant-ship, my good old nurse (almost broken-hearted for me, when we first met) came up to London. I was constantly with her, and her brother, and the Micawbers (they being very much together): but Emily I never saw.

One evening when the time was close at hand, I was alone with Peggotty and her brother. Our conversation turned on Ham. She described to us how tenderly he had taken leave of her, and how manfully and quietly he had borne himself. Most of all, of late, when she believed he was most tried. It was a subject of which the affectionate creature never tired; and our interest in hearing the many examples which she, who was so much with him, had to relate, was equal to hers in relating them.

My aunt and I were at that time vacating the two cottages at

Highgate; I intending to go abroad, and she to return to her house at Dover. We had a temporary lodging in Covent Garden. As I walked home to it, after this evening's conversation, reflecting on what had passed between Ham and myself when I was last at Yarmouth, I wavered in the original purpose I had formed, of leaving a letter for Emily when I should take leave of her uncle on board the ship, and thought it would be better to write to her now. She might desire, I thought, after receiving my communication, to send some parting word by me to her unhappy lover. I ought to give her the opportunity.

I therefore sat down in my room, before going to bed, and wrote to her. I told her that I had seen him, and that he had requested me to tell her what I have already written in its place in these sheets. I faithfully repeated it. I had no need to enlarge upon it, if I had had the right. Its deep fidelity and goodness were not to be adorned by me or any man. I left it out, to be sent round in the morning; with a line to Mr. Peggotty, requesting him to give it to her; and went to bed at daybreak.

I was weaker than I knew then; and, not falling asleep until the sun was up, lay late, and unrefreshed, next day. I was roused by the silent presence of my aunt at my bedside. I felt it in my sleep, as I suppose we all do feel such things.

"Trot, my dear," she said, when I opened my eyes, "I couldn't make up my mind to disturb you, Mr. Peggotty is here; shall he come up?"

I replied yes, and he soon appeared.

"Mas'r Davy," he said, when we had shaken hands, "I giv Em'ly your letter, sir, and she writ this heer; and begged of me fur to ask you to read it, and if you see no hurt in't, to be so kind as take charge on't."

"Have you read it?" said I.

He nodded sorrowfully. I opened it, and read as follows:

"I have got your message. Oh, what can I write, to thank you for your good and blessed kindness to me!

"I have put the words close to my heart. I shall keep them till I die. They are sharp thorns, but they are such comfort. I have prayed over them, oh, I have prayed so much. When I find what you are, and what uncle is, I think what God must be, and can cry to him.

"Good-bye for ever. Now, my dear, my friend, good-bye for ever in this world. In another world, if I am forgiven, I may wake a child and come to you. All thanks and blessings. Farewell, evermore."

This, blotted with tears, was the letter.

"May I tell her as you doen't see no hurt in't, and as you'll be so kind as take charge on't, Mas'r Davy?" said Mr. Peggotty, when I had read it.

"Unquestionably," said I—"but I am thinking—"

"Yes, Mas'r Davy?"

"I am thinking," said I, "that I'll go down again to Yarmouth. There's time, and to spare, for me to go and come back before the ship sails. My mind is constantly running on him, in his solitude; to put this letter of her writing in his hand at this time, and to enable you to tell her, in the moment of parting, that he has got it, will be a kindness to both of them. I solemnly accepted his commission, dear good fellow, and cannot discharge it too completely. The journey is nothing to me. I am restless, and shall be better in motion. I'll go down to-night."

Though he anxiously endeavoured to dissuade me, I saw that he was of my mind; and this, if I had required to be confirmed in my intention, would have had the effect. He went round to the coach-office, at my request, and took the box-seat for me on the mail. In the evening I started, by that conveyance, down the road I had traversed under so many vicissitudes.

"Don't you think that," I asked the coachman, in the first stage out of London, "a very remarkable sky? I don't remember to have seen one like it."

"Nor I—not equal to it," he replied. "That's wind, sir. There'll be mischief done at sea, I expect, before long."

It was a murky confusion—here and there blotted with a colour like the colour of the smoke from damp fuel—of flying clouds tossed up into most remarkable heaps, suggesting greater heights in the clouds than there were depths below them to the bottom of the deepest hollows in the earth, through which the wild moon seemed to plunge headlong, as if, in a dread disturbance of the laws of nature, she had lost her way and were frightened. There had been a wind all day; and it was rising then, with an extraordinary great sound. In another hour it had much increased, and the sky was more overcast, and blew hard.

But as the night advanced, the clouds closing in and densely overspreading the whole sky, then very dark, it came on to blow, harder and harder. It still increased, until our horses could scarcely face the wind. Many times, in the dark part of the night (it was then late in September, when the nights were not short), the leaders turned about, or came to a dead stop; and we were often in serious apprehension that the coach would be blown over. Sweeping gusts of rain came up before this storm, like showers of steel; and, at those times, when there was any shelter of trees or lee walls to be got, we were fain to stop, in a sheer impossibility of continuing the struggle.

When the day broke, it blew harder and harder. I had been in Yarmouth when the seamen said it blew great guns, but I had never known the like of this, or anything approaching to it. We came to Ipswich—very late, having had to fight every inch of ground since we were ten miles out of London; and found a cluster of people in the market-place, who had risen from their beds in the night, fearful of falling chimneys. Some of these, congregating about the inn-yard while we changed horses, told us of great sheets of lead having been ripped off a high church-tower, and flung into a by-street, which they then blocked up. Others had to tell of country people, coming in from neighbouring villages, who had seen great trees lying torn out of the earth, and whole ricks scattered about the roads and fields. Still there was no abatement in the storm, but it blew harder.

As we struggled on, nearer and nearer to the sea, from which this mighty wind was blowing dead on shore, its force became more and more terrific. Long before we saw the sea, its spray was on our lips, and showered salt rain upon us. The water was out, over miles and miles of the flat country adjacent to Yarmouth; and every sheet and puddle lashed its banks, and had its stress of little breakers setting heavily towards us. When we came within sight of the sea, the waves on the horizon, caught at intervals above the rolling abyss, were like glimpses of another shore with towers and buildings. When at last we got into the town, the people came out to their doors, all aslant, and with streaming hair, making a wonder of the mail that had come through such a night.

I put up at the old inn, and went down to look at the sea; staggering along the street, which was strewn with sand and sea-weed, and with flying blotches of sea-foam; afraid of falling slates and tiles; and holding by people I met, at angry corners. Coming near the beach, I saw, not only the boatmen, but half the people of the town, lurking behind buildings; some, now and then braving the fury of the storm to look away to sea, and blown sheer out of their course in trying to get zigzag back.

Joining these groups, I found bewailing women whose husbands were away in herring or oyster boats, which there was too much reason to think might have foundered before they could run in anywhere for safety. Grizzled old sailors were among the people, shaking their heads, as they looked from water to sky, and muttering to one another; ship-owners, excited and uneasy;

children, huddling together, and peering into older faces; even stout mariners, disturbed and anxious, levelling their glasses at the sea from behind places of shelter, as if they were surveying an enemy.

The tremendous sea itself, when I could find sufficient pause to look at it, in the agitation of the blinding wind, the flying stones and sand, and the awful noise, confounded me. As the high watery walls came rolling in, and, at their highest, tumbled into surf, they looked as if the least would engulf the town. As the receding wave swept back with a hoarse roar, it seemed to scoop out deep caves in the beach, as if its purpose were to undermine the earth. When some white-headed billows thundered on, and dashed themselves to pieces before they reached the land, every fragment of the late whole seemed possessed by the full might of its wrath, rushing to be gathered to the composition of another monster. Undulating hills were changed to valleys, undulating valleys (with a solitary stormbird sometimes skimming through them) were lifted up to hills; masses of water shivered and shook the beach with a booming sound; every shape tumultuously rolled on, as soon as made, to change its shape and place, and beat another shape and place away; the ideal shore on the horizon, with its towers and buildings, rose and fell; the clouds fell fast and thick; I seemed to see a rending and upheaving of all nature.

Not finding Ham among the people whom this memorable wind—for it is still remembered down there, as the greatest ever known to blow upon that coast—had brought together, I made my way to his house. It was shut; and as no one answered to my knocking, I went, by back ways and by-lanes, to the yard where he worked. I learned, there, that he had gone to Lowestoft, to meet some sudden exigency of ship-repairing in which his skill was required; but that he would be back to-morrow morning, in good time.

I went back to the inn; and when I had washed and dressed, and tried to sleep, but in vain, it was five o'clock in the afternoon. I had not sat five minutes by the coffee-room fire, when the waiter coming to stir it, as an excuse for talking, told me that two colliers had gone down, with all hands, a few miles away; and that some other ships had been seen labouring hard in the Roads, and trying, in great distress, to keep off shore. Mercy on them, and on all poor sailors, said he, if we had another night like the last!

I was very much depressed in spirits; very solitary; and felt an uneasiness in Ham's not being there, disproportionate to the occasion. I was seriously affected, without knowing how much, by late events; and my long exposure to the fierce wind had confused me. There was that jumble in my thoughts and recollections, that I had lost the clear arrangement of time and distance. Thus, if I had gone out into the town, I should not have been surprised, I think, to encounter some one who I knew must be then in London. So to speak, there was in these respects a curious inattention in my mind. Yet it was busy, too, with all the remembrances the place naturally awakened; and they were particularly distinct and vivid.

In this state, the waiter's dismal intelligence about the ships immediately connected itself, without any effort of my volition, with my uneasiness about Ham. I was persuaded that I had an apprehension of his returning from Lowestoft by sea, and being lost. This grew so strong with me, that I resolved to go back to the yard before I took my dinner, and ask the boat-builder if he thought his attempting to return by sea at all likely? If he gave me the least reason to think so, I would go over to Lowestoft and prevent it by bringing him with me.

I hastily ordered my dinner, and went back to the yard. I was none too soon; for the boat-builder, with a lantern in his hand, was locking the yard-gate. He quite laughed when I asked him the question, and said there was no fear; no man in his senses, or out of them, would put off in such a gale of wind, least of all Ham Peggotty, who had been born to seafaring.

So sensible of this, beforehand, that I had really felt ashamed of doing what I was nevertheless impelled to do. I went back to the inn. If such a wind could rise, I think it was rising. The howl and roar, the rattling of the doors and windows, the rumbling in the chimneys, the apparent rocking of the very house that sheltered me, and the prodigious tumult of the sea, were more fearful than in the morning. But there was now a great darkness besides; and that invested the storm with new terrors, real and fanciful.

I could not eat, I could not sit still, I could not continue steadfast to anything. Something within me, faintly answering to the storm without, tossed up the depths of my memory and made a tumult of them. Yet, in all the hurry of my thoughts, wild running with the thundering sea,—the storm and my uneasiness regarding Ham were always in the foreground.

My dinner went away almost untasted, and I tried to refresh myself with a glass or two of wine. In vain. I fell into a dull slumber before the fire, without losing my consciousness, either of the uproar out of doors, or of the place in which I was. Both became overshadowed by a new and indefinable horrror; and when I awoke—or rather when I shook off the lethargy that bound me in my chair—my whole frame thrilled with objectless and unintelligible fear.

I walked to and fro, tried to read an old gazetteer, listened to the awful noises; looked at faces, scenes, and figures in the fire. At length, the steady ticking of the undisturbed clock on the wall tormented me to that degree that I resolved to go to bed.

It was reassuring, on such a night, to be told that some of the inn-servants had agreed together to sit up until morning. I went to bed, exceedingly weary and heavy; but, on my lying down, all such sensations vanished, as if by magic, and I was broad awake, with every sense refined.

For hours I lay there, listening to the wind and water; imagining, now, that I heard shrieks out at sea; now, that I distinctly heard the firing of signal guns; and now, the fall of houses in the town. I got up several times, and looked out; but could see nothing, except the reflection in the window-panes of the faint candle I had left burning, and of my own haggard face looking in at me from the black void.

At length, my restlessness attained to such a pitch, that I hurried on my clothes, and went down-stairs. In the large kitchen, where I dimly saw bacon and ropes of onions hanging from the beams, the watchers were clustered together, in various attitudes, about a table, purposely moved away from the great chimney, and brought near the door. A pretty girl, who had her ears stopped with her apron, and her eyes upon the door, screamed when I appeared, supposing me to be a spirit; but the others had more presence of mind, and were glad of an addition to their company. One man, referring to the topic they had been discussing, asked me whether I thought the souls of the collier-crews who had gone down, were out in the storm?

I remained there, I dare say, two hours. Once, I opened the yard-gate, and looked into the empty street. The sand, the sea-weed, and the flakes of foam, were driving by; and I was obliged to call for assistance before I could shut the gate again, and make it fast against the wind.

There was a dark gloom in my solitary chamber, when I at length returned to it; but I was tired now, and, getting into bed again, fell—off a tower and down a precipice—into the depths of sleep. I have an impression that for a long time, though I dreamed of being elsewhere and in a variety of scenes, it was always blowing in my dream. At length, I lost that feeble hold upon reality, and was engaged with two dear friends, but who they were I don't know, at the siege of some town in a roar of cannonading.

The thunder of the cannon was so loud and incessant, that I could not hear something I much desired to hear, until I made a great exertion and awoke. It was broad day—eight or nine o'clock; the storm raging, in lieu of the batteries; and some one knocking and calling at my door.

"What is the matter?" I cried.

"A wreck! Close by!"

I sprung out of bed, and asked, what wreck?

"A schooner, from Spain or Portugal, laden with fruit and wine. Make haste, sir, if you want to see her! It's thought, down on the beach, she'll go to pieces every moment."

The excited voice went clamouring along the staircase; and I wrapped myself in my clothes as quickly as I could, and ran into the street.

Numbers of people were there before me, all running in one direction to the beach. I ran the same way, outstripping a good many, and soon came facing the wild sea.

The wind might by this time have lulled a little, though not more sensibly than if the cannonading I had dreamed of had been diminished by the silencing of half-a-dozen guns out of hundreds. But the sea having upon it the additional agitation of the whole night, was infinitely more terrific than when I had seen it last. Every appearance it had then presented, bore the expression of being *swelled*; and the height to which the breakers rose, and, looking over one another, bore one another down, and rolled in, in interminable hosts, was most appalling.

In the difficulty of hearing anything but wind and waves, and in the crowd, and the unspeakable confusion, and my first breathless efforts to stand against the weather, I was so confused that I looked out to sea for the wreck, and saw nothing but the foaming heads of the great waves. A half-dressed boatman, standing next me, pointed with his bare arm (a tattoo'd arrow on it, pointing in the same direction) to the left. Then, O great Heaven, I saw it, close in upon us!

One mast was broken short off, six or eight feet from the deck, and lay over the side, entangled in a maze of sail and rigging; and all that ruin, as the ship rolled and beat—which she did without a moment's pause, and with a violence quite inconceivable—beat the side as if it would stave it in. Some efforts were even then being made, to cut this portion of the wreck away; for as the ship, which was broadside on, turned towards us in her rolling, I plainly descried her people at work with axes, especially one active figure with long curling hair, conspicuous among the rest. But a great cry, which was audible even above the wind and water, rose from the shore at this moment; the sea, sweeping over the rolling wreck, made a clean breach, and carried men, spars, casks, planks, bulwarks, heaps of such toys, into the boiling surge.

The second mast was yet standing, with the rags of a rent sail, and a wild confusion of broken cordage flapping to and fro. The ship had struck once, the same boatman hoarsely said in my ear, and then lifted in and struck again. I understood him to add that she was parting amidships, and I could readily suppose so, for the rolling and beating were too tremendous for any human work to suffer long. As he spoke, there was another great cry of pity from the beach; four men arose with the wreck out of the deep, clinging to the rigging of the remaining mast: uppermost, the active figure with the curling hair.

There was a bell on board; and as the ship rolled and dashed, like a desperate creature driven mad, now showing us the whole sweep of her deck, as she turned on her beam-ends, towards the shore, now nothing but her keel, as she sprung wildly over and turned towards the sea, the bell rang; and its sound, the knell of those unhappy men, was borne towards us on the wind. Again we lost her, and again she rose. Two men were gone. The agony on shore increased. Men groaned, and clasped their hands; women shrieked, and turned away their faces. Some ran wildly up and down along the beach, crying for help where no help could be. I found myself one of these, frantically imploring a knot of sailors whom I knew, not to let those two lost creatures perish before our eyes.

They were making out to me, in an agitated way—I don't know how, for the little I could hear I was scarcely composed enough to understand—that the lifeboat had been bravely manned an hour ago, and could do nothing; and that as no man would be so desperate as to attempt to wade off with a rope, and establish a communication with the shore, there was nothing left to try; when I noticed that some new sensation moved the people on the beach, and saw them part, and Ham come breaking through them to the front.

I ran to him—as well as I know—to repeat my appeal for help. But, distracted though I was by a sight so new to me and terrible, the determination in his face, and his look out to sea—exactly the same look as I remembered in connection with the morning after Emily's flight—awoke me to a knowledge of his danger. I held him back with both arms; and implored the men with whom I had been speaking, not to listen to him, not to do murder, not to let him stir from off that sand!

Another cry arose on shore; and looking to the wreck, we saw the cruel sail, with blow on blow, beat off the lower of the two men, and fly up in triumph round the active figure left alone upon the mast.

Against such a sight, and against such determination as that of the calmly desperate man who was already accustomed to lead half the people present, I might as hopefully have entreated the wind. "Mas'r Davy," he said, cheerily grasping me by both hands, "if my time is come, 'tis come. If 'tan't, I'll bide it. Lord above bless you, and bless all! Mates, make me ready! I'm a-going off!"

I was swept away, but not unkindly, to some distance, where the people around me made me stay; urging, as I confusedly perceived, that he was bent on going, with help or without, and that I should endanger the precautions for his safety by troubling those with whom they rested. I don't know what I answered, or what they rejoined; but I saw hurry on the beach, and men running with ropes from a capstan that was there, and penetrating into a circle of figures that hid him from me. Then I saw him standing alone, in a seaman's frock and trousers: a rope in his hand, or slung to his wrist: another round his body; and several of the best men holding, at a little distance, to the latter, which he laid out himself, slack upon the shore, at his feet.

The wreck, even to my unpractised eye, was breaking up. I saw that she was parting in the middle, and that the life of the solitary man upon the mast hung by a thread. Still, he clung to it. He had a singular red cap on,—not like a sailor's cap, but of a finer colour; and as the few yielding planks between him and destruction rolled and bulged, and his anticipative deathknell rung, he was seen by all of us to wave it. I saw him do it now, and thought I was going distracted, when his action brought an old remembrance to my mind of a once dear friend.

Ham watched the sea, standing alone, with the silence of suspended breath behind him, and the storm before, until there was a great retiring wave, when, with a backward glance at those who held the rope which was made fast round his body, he dashed in after it, and in a moment was buffeting with the water; rising with the hills, falling with the valleys, lost beneath the foam; then drawn again to land. They hauled in hastily.

He was hurt. I saw blood on his face, from where I stood; but he took no thought of that. He seemed hurriedly to give them some directions for leaving him more free—or so I judged from the motion of his arm—and was gone as before.

And now he made for the wreck, rising with the hills, falling with the valleys, lost beneath the rugged foam, borne in towards the shore, borne on towards the ship, striving hard and valiantly. The distance was nothing, but the power of the sea and the wind made the strife deadly. At length he neared the wreck. He was so near, that with one more of his vigorous strokes he would be clinging to it,—when a high, green, vast hill-side of water, moving on shoreward, from beyond the ship, he seemed to leap up into it with a mighty bound, and the ship was gone!

Some eddying fragments I saw in the sea, as if a mere cask had been broken, in running to the spot where they were hauling in. Consternation was in every face. They drew him to my very feet—insensible—dead. He was carried to the nearest house; and, no one preventing me now, I remained near him, busy, while every means of restoration were tried; but he had been beaten to death by the great wave, and his generous heart was stilled for ever.

As I sat beside the bed, when hope was abandoned, and all was done, a fisherman, who had known me when Emily and I were children, and ever since, whispered my name at the door.

"Sir," said he, with tears starting to his weather-beaten face, which, with his trembling lips, was ashy pale, "will you come over yonder?"

The old remembrance that had been recalled to me, was in his look. I asked him, terror-stricken, leaning on the arm he held out to support me:

"Has a body come ashore?"

He said, "Yes."

"Do I know it?" I asked then.

He answered nothing.

But he led me to the shore. And on that part of it where she and I had looked for shells, two children—on that part of it where some lighter fragments of the old boat, blown down last night, had been scattered by the wind—among the ruins of the home he had wronged—I saw him lying with his head upon his arm, as I had often seen him lie at school.

56

THE NEW WOUND, AND THE OLD

NO NEED, O STEERFORTH, TO HAVE SAID, WHEN WE LAST spoke together, in that hour which I so little deemed to be our parting-hour—no need to have said, "Think of me at my best!" I had done that ever; and could I change now, looking on this sight?

They brought a hand-bier, and laid him on it, and covered him with a flag, and took him up and bore him on towards the houses. All the men who carried him had known him, and gone sailing with him, and seen him merry and bold. They carried him through the wild roar, a hush in the midst of all the tumult; and took him to the cottage where Death was already.

But when they set the bier down on the threshold, they looked at one another, and at me, and whispered. I knew why. They felt as if it were not right to lay him down in the same quiet room.

We went into the town, and took our burden to the inn. So soon as I could at all collect my thoughts, I sent for Joram, and begged him to provide me a conveyance in which it could be got to London in the night. I knew that the care of it, and the hard duty of preparing his mother to receive it, could only rest with me; and I was anxious to discharge that duty as faithfully as I could.

I chose the night for the journey, that there might be less curiosity when I left the town. But, although it was nearly midnight when I came out of the yard in a chaise, followed by what I had in charge, there were many people waiting. At intervals, along the town, and even a little way out upon the road, I saw more; but at length only the bleak night and the open country were around me, and the ashes of my youthful friendship.

Upon a mellow autumn day, about noon, when the ground was perfumed by fallen leaves, and many more, in beautiful tints of yellow, red, and brown, yet hung upon the trees, through which the sun was shining, I arrived at Highgate. I walked the last mile, thinking as I went along of what I had to do; and left the carriage that had followed me all through the night, awaiting orders to advance.

The house, when I came up to it, looked just the same. Not a blind was raised; no sign of life was in the dull paved court, with its covered way leading to the disused door. The wind had quite gone down, and nothing moved.

I had not, at first, the courage to ring at the gate; and when I did ring, my errand seemed to me to be expressed in the very sound of the bell. The little parlour-maid came out, with the key in her hand; and looking earnestly at me as she unlocked the gate, said:

"I beg your pardon, sir. Are you ill?"

"I have been much agitated, and am fatigued."

"Is anything the matter, sir?—Mr. James?——"

"Hush!" said I. "Yes, something has happened, that I have to break to Mrs. Steerforth. She is at home?"

The girl anxiously replied that her mistress was very seldom out now, even in a carriage; that she kept her room; that she saw no company, but would see me. Her mistress was up, she said, and Miss Dartle was with her. What message should she take up-stairs?

Giving her a strict charge to be careful of her manner, and only to carry in my card and say I waited, I sat down in the drawing-room (which we had now reached) until she should come back. Its former pleasant air of occupation was gone, and the shutters were half closed. The harp had not been used for many and many a day. His picture, as a boy, was there. The cabinet in which his mother had kept his letters was there. I wondered if she ever read them now; if she would ever read them more!

The house was so still that I heard the girl's light step up-stairs. On her return, she brought a message, to the effect that Mrs. Steerforth was an invalid and could not come down; but that if I would excuse her being in her chamber, she would be glad to see me. In a few moments I stood before her.

She was in his room; not in her own. I felt, of course, that she had taken to occupy it, in remembrance of him; and that the many tokens of his old sports and accomplishments, by which she was surrounded, remained there, just as he had left them, for the same reason. She murmured, however, even in her reception of me, that she was out of her own chamber because its aspect was unsuited to her infirmity; and with her stately look repelled the least suspicion of the truth.

At her chair, as usual, was Rosa Dartle. From the first

moment of her dark eyes resting on me, I saw she knew I was the bearer of evil tidings. The scar sprung into view that instant. She withdrew herself a step behind the chair, to keep her own face out of Mrs. Steerforth's observation; and scrutinised me with a piercing gaze that never faltered, never shrunk.

"I am sorry to observe you are in mourning, sir," said Mrs. Steerforth.

"I am unhappily a widower," said I.

"You are very young to know so great a loss," she returned. "I am grieved to hear it. I am grieved to hear it. I hope Time will be good to you."

"I hope Time," said I, looking at her, "will be good to all of us. Dear Mrs. Steerforth, we must all trust to that, in our heaviest misfortunes."

The earnestness of my manner, and the tears in my eyes, alarmed her. The whole course of her thoughts appeared to stop, and change.

I tried to command my voice, in gently saying his name, but it trembled. She repeated it to herself, two or three times, in a low tone. Then, addressing me, she said, with enforced calmness:

"My son is ill?"

"Very ill."

"You have seen him?"

"I have."

"Are you reconciled?"

I could not say Yes, I could not say No. She slightly turned her head towards the spot where Rosa Dartle had been standing at her elbow, and in that moment I said, by the motion of my lips, to Rosa, "Dead!"

That Mrs. Steerforth might not be induced to look behind her, and read, plainly written, what she was not yet prepared to know, I met her look quickly; but I had seen Rosa Dartle throw her hands up in the air with vehemence of despair and horror, and then clasp them on her face.

The handsome lady—so like, oh so like!—regarded me with a fixed look, and put her hand to her forehead. I besought her to be calm, and prepare herself to bear what I had to tell; but I should rather have entreated her to weep, for she sat like a stone figure.

"When I was last here," I faltered, "Miss Dartle told me he was sailing here and there. The night before last was a dreadful one at sea. If he were at sea that night, and near a dangerous coast, as it is said he was; and if the vessel that was seen should really be the ship which——"

"Rosa!" said Mrs. Steerforth, "come to me!"

She came, but with no sympathy or gentleness. Her eyes gleamed like fire as she confronted his mother, and broke into a frightful laugh.

"Now," she said, "is your pride appeased, you madwoman? *Now* has he made atonement to you——with his life! Do you hear?—His life!"

Mrs. Steerforth, fallen back stiffly in her chair, and making no sound but a moan, cast her eyes upon her with a wide stare.

"Aye!" cried Rosa, smiting herself passionately on the breast, "look at me! Moan, and groan, and look at me! Look here!" striking the scar, "at your dead child's handiwork!"

The moan the mother uttered, from time to time, went to my heart. Always the same. Always inarticulate and stifled. Always accompanied with an incapable motion of the head, but with no change of face. Always proceeding from a rigid mouth and closed teeth, as if the jaw were locked and the face frozen up in pain.

"Do you remember when he did this?" she proceeded. "Do you remember when, in his inheritance of your nature, and in your pampering of his pride and passion, he did this, and disfigured me for life? Look at me, marked until I die with his high displeasure; and moan and groan for what you made him!"

"Miss Dartle," I entreated her. "For Heaven's sake——"

"I *will* speak!" she said, turning on me with her lightning eyes. "Be silent, you! Look at me, I say, proud mother of a proud false son! Moan for your nurture of him, moan for your corruption of him, moan for your loss of him, moan for mine!"

She clenched her hand, and trembled through her spare, worn figure, as if her passion were killing her by inches.

"YOU, resent his self-will!" she exclaimed. "YOU, injured by his haughty temper! YOU, who opposed to both, when your hair was grey, the qualities which made both when you gave him birth! YOU, who from his cradle reared him to be what he was, and stunted what he should have been! Are you rewarded, *now*, for your years of trouble?"

"Oh, Miss Dartle, shame! Oh, cruel!"

"I tell you," she returned, "I *will* speak to her. No power on earth should stop me, while I was standing here! Have I been silent all these years, and shall I not speak now? I loved him better than you ever loved him!" turning on her fiercely. "I could have loved him, and asked no return. If I had been his wife, I could have been the slave of his caprices for a word of love a year. I should have been. Who knows it better than I? You were exacting, proud, punctilious, selfish. My love would have been devoted—would have trod your paltry whimpering under foot!"

With flashing eyes, she stamped upon the ground as if she actually did it.

"Look here!" she said, striking the scar again, with a relentless hand. "When he grew into the better understanding of what he had done, he saw it, and repented of it! I could sing to him, and talk to him, and show the ardour that I felt in all he did, and attain with labour to such knowledge as most interested him; and I attracted him. When he was freshest and truest, he loved *me*. Yes, he did! Many a time, when you were put off with a slight word, he has taken Me to his heart!"

She said it with a taunting pride in the midst of her frenzy—for it was little less—yet with an eager remembrance of it, in which the smouldering embers of a gentler feeling kindled for the moment.

"I descended—as I might have known I should, but that he fascinated me with his boyish courtship—into a doll, a trifle for the occupation of an idle hour, to be dropped, and taken up, and trifled with, as the inconstant humour took him. When he grew weary, I grew weary. As his fancy died out, I would no more have tried to strengthen any power I had, than I would have married him on his being forced to take me for his wife. We fell away from one another without a word. Perhaps you saw it, and were not sorry. Since then, I have been a mere disfigured piece of furniture between you both; having no eyes, no ears, no feelings, no remembrances. Moan? Moan for what you made him; not for your love. I tell you that the time was, when I loved him better than you ever did!"

She stood with her bright angry eyes confronting the wide stare, and the set face; and softened no more, when the moaning was repeated, than if the face had been a picture.

"Miss Dartle," said I, "if you can be so obdurate as not to feel for this afflicted mother——"

"Who feels for me?" she sharply retorted. "She has sown this. Let her moan for the harvest that she reaps to-day!"

"And if his faults——" I began.

"Faults!" she cried, bursting into passionate tears. "Who dares malign him? He had a soul worth millions of the friends to whom he stooped!"

"No one can have loved him better, no one can hold him in

dearer remembrance than I," I replied. "I meant to say, if you have no compassion for his mother; or if his faults—you have been bitter on them——"

"It's false," she cried, tearing her black hair; "I loved him!"

"—if his faults cannot," I went on, "be banished from your remembrance, in such an hour; look at that figure, even as one you have never seen before, and render it some help!"

All this time, the figure was unchanged, and looked unchangeable. Motionless, rigid, staring; moaning in the same dumb way from time to time, with the same helpless motion of the head; but giving no other sign of life. Miss Dartle suddenly kneeled down before it, and began to loosen the dress.

"A curse upon you!" she said, looking round at me, with a mingled expression of rage and grief. "It was in an evil hour that you ever came here! A curse upon you! Go!"

After passing out of the room, I hurried back to ring the bell, the sooner to alarm the servants. She had then taken the impassive figure in her arms, and, still upon her knees, was weeping over it, kissing it, calling to it, rocking it to and fro upon her bosom like a child, and trying every tender means to rouse the dormant senses. No longer afraid of leaving her, I noiselessly turned back again; and alarmed the house as I went out.

Later in the day, I returned, and we laid him in his mother's room. She was just the same, they told me; Miss Dartle never left her; doctors were in attendance, many things had been tried; but she lay like a statue, except for the low sound now and then.

I went through the dreary house, and darkened the windows. The windows of the chamber where he lay, I darkened last. I lifted up the leaden hand, and held it to my heart; and all the world seemed death and silence, broken only by his mother's moaning.

57

THE EMIGRANTS

ONE THING MORE I HAD TO DO, BEFORE YIELDING MYSELF to the shock of these emotions. It was, to conceal what had occurred, from those who were going away; and to dismiss them on their voyage in happy ignorance. In this, no time was to be lost.

I took Mr. Micawber aside that same night, and confided to him the task of standing between Mr. Peggotty and intelligence of the late catastrophe. He zealously undertook to do so, and to intercept any newspaper through which it might, without such precautions, reach him.

"If it penetrates to him, sir," said Mr. Micawber, striking himself on the breast, "it shall first pass through this body!"

Mr. Micawber, I must observe, in his adaptation of himself to a new state of society, had acquired a bold buccaneering air, not absolutely lawless, but defensive and prompt. One might have supposed him a child of the wilderness, long accustomed to live out of the confines of civilisation, and about to return to his native wilds.

He had provided himself, among other things, with a complete suit of oil-skin, and a straw hat with a very low crown, pitched or caulked on the outside. In this rough clothing, with a common mariner's telescope under his arm, and a shrewd trick of casting up his eye at the sky as looking out for dirty weather, he was far more nautical, after his manner, than Mr. Peggotty. His whole family, if I may so express it, were cleared for action. I found Mrs. Micawber in the closest and most uncompromising of bonnets, made fast under the chin; and in a shawl which tied her up (as I had been tied up, when my aunt first received me) like a bundle, and was secured behind at the waist, in a strong knot. Miss Micawber I found made snug for stormy weather, in the same manner; with nothing superfluous about her. Master Micawber was hardly visible in a Guernsey shirt, and the shaggiest suit of slops I ever saw; and the children were done up, like preserved meats, in impervious cases. Both Mr. Micawber and his eldest son wore their sleeves loosely turned back at the wrists, as being ready to lend a hand in any direction, and to "tumble up," or sing out, "Yeo—Heave—Yeo!" on the shortest notice.

Thus Traddles and I found them at nightfall, assembled on the wooden steps, at that time known as Hungerford Stairs, watching the departure of a boat with some of their property on board. I had told Traddles of the terrible event, and it had greatly shocked him; but there could be no doubt of the kindness of keeping it a secret, and he had come to help me in this last service. It was here that I took Mr. Micawber aside, and received his promise.

The Micawber family were lodged in a little, dirty, tumble-down public-house, which in those days was close to the stairs, and whose protruding wooden rooms overhung the river. The family, as emigrants, being objects of some interest in and about Hungerford, attracted so many beholders, that we were glad to take refuge in their room. It was one of the wooden chambers up-stairs, with the tide flowing underneath. My aunt and Agnes were there, busily making some little extra comforts, in the way of dress, for the children. Peggotty was quietly assisting, with the old insensible work-box, yard measure, and bit of wax candle before her, that had now outlived so much.

It was not easy to answer her inquiries; still less to whisper Mr. Peggotty, when Mr. Micawber brought him in, that I had given the letter, and all was well. But I did both, and made them happy. If I showed any trace of what I felt, my own sorrows were sufficient to account for it.

"And when does the ship sail, Mr. Micawber?" asked my aunt.

Mr. Micawber considered it necessary to prepare either my aunt or his wife, by degrees, and said, sooner than he had expected yesterday.

"The boat brought you word, I suppose?" said my aunt.

"It did, ma'am," he returned.

"Well?" said my aunt. "And she sails—"

"Madam," he replied, "I am informed that we must positively be on board before seven to-morrow morning."

"Heyday!" said my aunt, "that's soon. Is it a sea-going fact, Mr. Peggotty?"

"'Tis so, ma'am. She'll drop down the river with that theer tide. If Mas'r Davy and my sister comes aboard at Gravesen', arternoon o' next day, they'll see the last on us."

"And that we shall do," said I, "be sure!"

"Until then, and until we are at sea," observed Mr. Micawber, with a glance of intelligence at me, "Mr. Peggotty and myself will constantly keep a double look-out together, on our goods and chattels. Emma, my love," said Mr. Micawber, clearing his throat in his magnificent way, "my friend Mr. Thomas Traddles is so obliging as to solicit, in my ear, that he should have the privilege of ordering the ingredients necessary to the composition of a moderate portion of that Beverage which is peculiarly associated, in our minds, with the Roast Beef of Old England. I allude to—in short, Punch. Under ordinary circumstances, I should scruple to entreat the indulgence of Miss Trotwood and Miss Wickfield, but—"

"I can only say for myself," said my aunt, "that I will drink all happiness and success to you, Mr. Micawber, with the utmost pleasure."

"And I too!" said Agnes, with a smile.

Mr. Micawber immediately descended to the bar, where he appeared to be quite at home; and in due time returned with a steaming jug. I could not but observe that he had been peeling the lemons with his own clasp-knife, which, as became the knife of a practical settler, was about a foot long; and which he wiped, not wholly without ostentation, on the sleeve of his coat. Mrs. Micawber and the two elder members of the family I now found to be provided with similar formidable instruments, while every child had its own wooden spoon attached to its body by a strong line. In a similar anticipation of life afloat, and in the Bush, Mr. Micawber, instead of helping Mrs. Micawber and his eldest son and daughter to punch, in wine-glasses, which he might easily have done, for there was a shelf-full in the room, served it out to them in a series of villainous little tin pots; and I never saw him enjoy anything so much as drinking out of his own particular pint pot, and putting it in his pocket at the close of the evening.

"The luxuries of the old country," said Mr. Micawber, with an intense satisfaction in their renouncement, "we abandon. The denizens of the forest cannot, of course, expect to participate in the refinements of the land of the Free."

Here, a boy came in to say that Mr. Micawber was wanted down-stairs.

"I have a presentiment," said Mrs. Micawber, setting down her tin pot, "that it is a member of my family!"

"If so, my dear," observed Mr. Micawber, with his usual suddenness of warmth on that subject, "as the member of your family—whoever he, she, or it, may be—has kept *us* waiting for a considerable period, perhaps the Member may now wait my convenience."

"Micawber," said his wife, in a low tone, "at such a time as this—"

"'It is not meet,'" said Mr. Micawber, rising, "'that every nice offence should bear its comment?' Emma, I stand reproved."

"The loss, Micawber," observed his wife, "has been my family's, not yours. If my family are at length sensible of the deprivation to which their own conduct has, in the past exposed them, and now desire to extend the hand of fellowship, let it not be repulsed."

"My dear," he returned, "so be it!"

"If not for their sakes; for mine, Micawber," said his wife.

"Emma," he returned, "that view of the question is, at such a moment, irresistible. I cannot, even now, distinctly pledge myself to fall upon your family's neck; but the member of your family, who is now in attendance, shall have no genial warmth frozen by me."

Mr. Micawber withdrew, and was absent some little time; in the course of which Mrs. Micawber was not wholly free from an apprehension that words might have arisen between him and the Member. At length the same boy re-appeared, and presented me with a note written in pencil, and headed, in a legal manner, "Heep *v.* Micawber," From this document, I learned that Mr. Micawber being again arrested, was in a final paroxysm of despair; and that he begged me to send him his knife and pint pot, by bearer, as they might prove serviceable during the brief remainder of his existence in jail. He also requested, as a last act of friendship, that I would see his family to the Parish Workhouse, and forget that such a Being ever lived.

Of course I answered this note by going down with the boy to pay the money, where I found Mr. Micawber sitting in a corner, looking darkly at the Sheriff's Officer who had effected the capture. On his release, he embraced me with the utmost fervour; and made an entry of the transaction in his pocket-book—being very particular, I recollect, about a halfpenny I inadvertently omitted from my statement of the total.

This momentous pocket-book was a timely reminder to him of another transaction. On our return to the room up-stairs (where he accounted for his absence by saying that it had been occasioned by circumstances over which he had no control), he took out of it a large sheet of paper, folded small, and quite covered with long sums, carefully worked. From the glimpse

I had of them, I should say that I never saw such sums out of a school ciphering-book. These, it seemed, were calculations of compound interest on what he called " the principal amount of forty-one, ten, eleven and a half," for various periods. After a careful consideration of these, and an elaborate estimate of his resources, he had come to the conclusion to select that sum which represented the amount with compound interest to two years, fifteen calendar months, and fourteen days, from that date. For this he had drawn a note-of-hand with great neatness, which he handed over to Traddles on the spot, a discharge of his debt in full (as between man and man), with many acknowledgments.

" I have still a presentiment," said Mrs. Micawber, pensively shaking her head, " that my family will appear on board, before we finally depart."

Mr. Micawber evidently had his presentiment on the subject too, but he put it in his tin pot and swallowed it.

" If you have any opportunity of sending letters home, on your passage, Mrs. Micawber," said my aunt, " you must let us hear from you, you know."

" My dear Miss Trotwood," she replied, " I shall only be too happy to think that any one expects to hear from us. I shall not fail to correspond. Mr. Copperfield, I trust, as an old and familiar friend, will not object to receive occasional intelligence, himself, from one who knew him when the twins were yet unconscious? "

I said that I should hope to hear, whenever she had an opportunity of writing.

" Please Heaven, there will be many such opportunities," said Mr. Micawber. " The ocean, in these times, is a perfect fleet of ships; and we can hardly fail to encounter many, in running over. It is merely crossing," said Mr. Micawber, trifling with his eye-glass, " merely crossing. The distance is quite imaginary."

I think, now, how odd it was, but how wonderfully like Mr. Micawber, that, when he went from London to Canterbury, he should have talked as if he were going to the farthest limits of the earth; and, when he went from England to Australia, as if he were going for a little trip across the channel.

" On the voyage, I shall endeavour," said Mr. Micawber, " occasionally to spin them a yarn; and the melody of my son Wilkins will, I trust, be acceptable at the galley-fire. When Mrs. Micawber has her sea-legs on—an expression in which I hope there is no conventional impropriety—she will give them, I dare say, Little Tafflin. Porpoises and dolphins, I believe, will be frequently observed athwart our bows, and, either on the starboard or the larboard quarter, objects of interest will be continually described. In short," said Mr. Micawber, with the old genteel air, " the probability is, all will be found so exciting, alow and aloft, that when the lookout, stationed in the main-top cries Land-oh! we shall be very considerably astonished! "

With that he flourished off the contents of his little tin pot, as if he had made the voyage, and had passed a first-class examination before the highest naval authorities.

" What *I* chiefly hope, my dear Mr. Copperfield," said Mrs. Micawber, " is, that in some branches of our family we may live again in the old country. Do not frown, Micawber! I do not now refer to my own family, but to our children's children. However vigorous the sapling," said Mrs. Micawber, shaking her head, " I cannot forget the parent-tree; and when our race attains to eminence and fortune, I own I should wish that fortune to flow into the coffers of Britannia."

" My dear," said Mr. Micawber, " Britannia must take her chance. I am bound to say that she has never done much for me, and that I have no particular wish upon the subject."

" Micawber," returned Mrs. Micawber, " there you are wrong. You are going out, Micawber, to this distant clime, to strengthen, not to weaken, the connection between yourself and Albion."

" The connection in question, my love," rejoined Mr. Micawber, " has not laid me, I repeat, under that load of personal obligation, that I am at all sensitive as to the formation of another connection."

" Micawber," returned Mrs. Micawber, " there, I again say, you are wrong. You do not know your power, Micawber. It is that which will strengthen, even in this step you are about to take, the connection between yourself and Albion."

Mr. Micawber sat in his elbow-chair, with his eyebrows raised; half receiving and half repudiating Mrs. Micawber's views as they were stated, but very sensible of their foresight.

" My dear Mr. Copperfield," said Mrs. Micawber, " I wish Mr. Micawber to feel his position. It appears to me highly important that Mr. Micawber should, from the hour of his embarkation, feel his position. Your old knowledge of me, my dear Mr. Copperfield, will have told you that I have not the sanguine disposition of Mr. Micawber. My disposition is, if I may say so, eminently practical. I know that this is a long voyage. I know that it will involve many privations and inconveniences.

I cannot shut my eyes to those facts. But I also know what Mr. Micawber is. I know the latent power of Mr. Micawber. And therefore I consider it vitally important that Mr. Micawber should feel his position."

"My love," he observed, "perhaps you will allow me to remark that it is barely possible that I *do* feel my position at the present moment."

"I think not, Micawber," she rejoined. "Not fully. My dear Mr. Copperfield, Mr. Micawber's is not a common case. Mr. Micawber is going to a distant country expressly in order that he may be fully understood and appreciated for the first time. I wish Mr. Micawber to take his stand upon that vessel's prow, and firmly say, 'This country I am come to conquer! Have you honours? Have you riches? Have you posts of profitable pecuniary emolument? Let them be brought forward. They are mine!'"

Mr. Micawber, glancing at us all, seemed to think there was a good deal in this idea.

"I wish Mr. Micawber, if I make myself understood," said Mrs. Micawber, in her argumentative tone, "to be the Caesar of his own fortunes. That, my dear Mr. Copperfield, appears to me to be his true position. From the first moment of this voyage, I wish Mr. Micawber to stand upon that vessel's prow and say, 'Enough of delay: enough of disappointment: enough of limited means. That was in the old country. This is the new. Produce your reparation. Bring it forward?."

Mr. Micawber folded his arms in a resolute manner, as if he were then stationed on the figure-head.

"And doing that," said Mrs. Micawber, "—feeling his position—am I not right in saying that Mr. Micawber will strengthen, and not weaken, his connection with Britain? An important public character arising in that hemisphere, shall I be told that its influence will not be felt at home? Can I be so weak as to imagine that Mr. Micawber, wielding the rod of talent and of power in Australia, will be nothing in England? I am but a woman; but I should be unworthy of myself, and of my papa, if I were guilty of such absurd weakness."

Mrs. Micawber's conviction that her arguments were unanswerable, gave a moral elevation to her tone which I think I had never heard in it before.

"And therefore it is," said Mrs. Micawber, "that I the more wish, that, at a future period, we may live again on the parent soil. Mr. Micawber may be—I cannot disguise from myself that the probability is, Mr. Micawber will be—a page of History;

and he ought then to be represented in the country which gave him birth, and did *not* give him employment!"

"My love," observed Mr. Micawber, "it is impossible for me not to be touched by your affection. I am always willing to defer to your good sense. What will be—will be. Heaven forbid that I should grudge my native country any portion of the wealth that may be accumulated by our descendants!"

"That's well," said my aunt, nodding towards Mr. Peggotty, "and I drink my love to you all, and every blessing and success attend you!"

Mr. Peggotty put down the two children he had been nursing, one on each knee, to join Mr. and Mrs. Micawber in drinking to all of us in return; and when he and the Micawbers cordially shook hands as comrades, and his brown face brightened with a smile, I felt that he would make his way, establish a good name, and be beloved, go where he would.

Even the children were instructed, each to dip a wooden spoon into Mr. Micawber's pot, and pledge us in its contents. When this was done, my aunt and Agnes rose, and parted from the emigrants. It was a sorrowful farewell. They were all crying; the children hung about Agnes to the last; and we left poor Mrs. Micawber in a very distressed condition, sobbing and weeping by a dim candle, that must have made the room look, from the river, like a miserable lighthouse.

I went down again next morning to see that they were away. They had departed, in a boat, as early as five o'clock. It was a wonderful instance to me of the gap such partings make, that although my association of them with the tumble-down public-house and the wooden stairs dated only from last night, both seemed dreary and deserted, now that they were gone.

In the afternoon of the next day, my old nurse and I went down to Gravesend. We found the ship in the river, surrounded by a crowd of boats; a favourable wind blowing; the signal for sailing at her mast-head. I hired a boat directly, and we put off to her; and getting through the little vortex of confusion of which she was the centre, went on board.

Mr. Peggotty was waiting for us on deck. He told me that Mr. Micawber had just now been arrested again (and for the last time) at the suit of Heep, and that, in compliance with a request I had made to him, he had paid the money: which I repaid him. He then took us down between decks; and there, any lingering fears I had of his having heard any rumours of what had happened, were dispelled by Mr. Micawber's coming out of the gloom, taking his arm with an air of friendship and protection, and telling me that they had scarcely been asunder for a moment, since the night before last.

It was such a strange scene to me, and so confined and dark, that, at first, I could make out hardly anything; but, by degrees, it cleared, as my eyes became more accustomed to the gloom, and I seemed to stand in a picture by OSTADE. Among the great beams, bulks, and ringbolts of the ship, and the emigrant-berths, and chests, and bundles, and barrels, and heaps of miscellaneous baggage—lighted up, here and there, by dangling lanterns; and elsewhere by the yellow daylight straying down a windsail or a hatchway—were crowded groups of people, making new friendships, taking leave of one another, talking, laughing, crying, eating and drinking; some, already settled down into the possession of their few feet of space, with their little households arranged, and tiny children established on stools, or in dwarf elbow-chairs; others, despairing of a resting-place, and wandering disconsolately. From babies who had but a week or two of life behind them, to crooked old men and women who seemed to have but a week or two of life before them; and from ploughmen bodily carrying out soil of England on their boots, to smiths taking away samples of its soot and smoke upon their skins; every age and occupation appeared to be crammed into the narrow compass of the 'tween decks.

As my eye glanced round this place, I thought I saw sitting, by an open port, with one of the Micawber children near her, a figure like Emily's; it first attracted my attention, by another figure parting from it with a kiss; and as it glided calmly away through the disorder, reminding me of—Agnes! But in the rapid motion and confusion, and in the unsettlement of my own thoughts, I lost it again; and only knew that the time was come when all visitors were being warned to leave the ship; that my nurse was crying on a chest beside me; and that Mrs. Gummidge, assisted by some younger stooping woman in black, was busily arranging Mr. Peggotty's goods.

"Is there any last wured, Mas'r Davy?" said he. "Is there any one forgotten thing afore we parts?"

"One thing!" said I. "Martha!"

He touched the younger woman I have mentioned on the shoulder, and Martha stood before me.

"Heaven bless you, you good man!" cried I. "You take her with you!"

She answered for him, with a burst of tears. I could speak no more at that time, but I wrung his hand; and if ever I have loved and honoured any man, I loved and honoured that man in my soul.

The ship was clearing fast of strangers. The greatest trial that I had, remained. I told him what the noble spirit that was gone, had given me in charge to say at parting. It moved him deeply. But when he charged me, in return, with many messages of affection and regret for those deaf ears, he moved me more.

The time was come, I embraced him, took my weeping nurse upon my arm, and hurried away. On deck, I took leave of poor Mrs. Micawber. She was looking distractedly about for her family, even then; and her last words to me were, that she never would desert Mr. Micawber.

We went over the side into our boat, and lay at a little distance to see the ship wafted on her course. It was then calm, radiant sunset. She lay between us and the red light; and every taper line and spar was visible against the glow. A sight at once so beautiful, so mournful, and so hopeful, as the glorious ship, lying still on the flushed water, with all the life on board her crowded at the bulwarks, and there clustering, for a moment, bare-headed and silent, I never saw.

Silent only for a moment. As the sails rose to the wind, and the ship began to move, there broke from all the boats three resounding cheers, which those on board took up, and echoed back, and which were echoed and re-echoed. My heart burst out when I heard the sound, and beheld the waving of the hats and handkerchiefs—and then I saw her!

Then I saw her, at her uncle's side, and trembling on his shoulder. He pointed to us with an eager hand; and she saw us, and waved her last good-bye to me. Aye, Emily, beautiful and drooping, cling to him with the utmost trust of thy bruised heart; for he has clung to thee with all the might of his great love!

Surrounded by the rosy light, and standing high upon the deck, apart together, she clinging to him, and he holding her, they solemnly passed away. The night had fallen on the Kentish hills when we were rowed ashore—and fallen darkly upon me.

58

ABSENCE

IT WAS A LONG AND GLOOMY NIGHT THAT GATHERED on me, haunted by the ghosts of many hopes, of many dear remembrances, many errors, many unavailing sorrows and regrets.

I went away from England; not knowing, even then, how great the shock was that I had to bear. I left all who were dear to me, and went away; and believed that I had borne it, and it was past. As a man upon a field of battle will receive a mortal hurt, and scarcely know that he is struck, so I, when I was left alone with my undisciplined heart, had no conception of the wound with which it had to strive.

The knowledge came upon me, not quickly, but little by little, and grain by grain. The desolate feeling with which I went abroad, deepened and widened hourly. At first it was a heavy sense of loss and sorrow, wherein I could distinguish little else. By imperceptible degrees, it became a hopeless consciousness of all that I had lost—love, friendship, interest; of all that had been shattered—my first trust, my first affection, the whole airy castle of my life; of all that remained—a ruined blank and waste, lying wide around me, unbroken, to the dark horizon.

If my grief were selfish, I did not know it to be so. I mourned for my child-wife, taken from her blooming world, so young. I mourned for him who might have won the love and admiration of thousands, as he had won mine long ago. I mourned for the broken heart that had found rest in the stormy sea; and for the wandering remnants of the simple home, where I had heard the night-wind blowing when I was a child.

From the accumulated sadness into which I fell, I had at length no hope of ever issuing again. I roamed from place to place, carrying my burden with me everywhere. I felt its whole weight now; and I drooped beneath it, and I said in my heart that it could never be lightened.

When this despondency was at its worst, I believed that I should die. Sometimes, I thought that I would like to die at home; and actually turned back on my road, that I might get there soon. At other times, I passed on farther away, from city to city, seeking I know not what, and trying to leave I know not what behind.

It is not in my power to retrace, one by one, all the weary phases of distress of mind through which I passed. There are some dreams that can only be imperfectly and vaguely described; and when I oblige myself to look back on this time of my life, I seem to be recalling such a dream. I see myself passing on among the novelties of foreign towns, palaces, cathedrals, temples, pictures, castles, tombs, fantastic streets—the old abiding places of History and Fancy—as a dreamer might; bearing my painful load through all, and hardly conscious of the objects as they fade before me. Listlessness to everything, but brooding sorrow, was the night that fell on my undisciplined heart. Let me look up from it—as at last I did, thank Heaven!—and from its long, sad, wretched dream, to dawn.

For many months I travelled with this ever-darkening cloud upon my mind. Some blind reasons that I had for not returning home—reasons then struggling within me, vainly, for more distinct expression—kept me on my pilgrimage. Sometimes, I had proceeded restlessly from place to place, stopping nowhere; sometimes, I had lingered long in one spot. I had had no purpose, no sustaining soul within me, anywhere.

I was in Switzerland. I had come out of Italy, over one of the great passes of the Alps, and had since wandered with a guide among the by-ways of the mountains. If those awful solitudes had spoken to my heart, I did not know it. I had found sublimity and wonder in the dread heights and precipices, in the roaring torrents, and the wastes of ice and snow; but as yet, they had taught me nothing else.

I came, one evening before sunset, down into a valley, where I was to rest. In the course of my descent to it, by the winding track along the mountain-side, from which I saw it shining far below, I think some long-unwonted sense of beauty and tranquillity, some softening influence awakened by its peace, moved faintly in my breast. I remember pausing once, with a kind of sorrow that was not all oppressive, not quite despairing. I remember almost hoping that some better change was possible within me.

I came into the valley, as the evening sun was shining on the remote heights of snow, that closed it in like eternal clouds. The bases of the mountains forming the gorge in which the little village lay, were richly green; and high above this gentler vegetation, grew forests of dark fir, cleaving the wintry snow-drift, wedge-like, and stemming the avalanche. Above these, were range upon range of craggy steeps, grey rock, bright ice, and smooth verdure-specks of pasture, all gradually blending with the crowning snow. Dotted here and there on the mountain's side, each tiny dot a home, were lonely wooden cottages, so dwarfed by the towering heights that they appeared too small for toys. So did even the clustered village in the valley, with its wooden bridge across the stream, where the stream tumbled over broken rocks, and roared away among the trees. In the quiet air, there was a sound of distant singing—shepherd voices; but, as one bright evening cloud floated midway along the mountain's side, I could almost have believed it came from there, and was not earthly music. All at once, in this serenity, great Nature spoke to me; and soothed me to lay down my weary head upon the grass, and weep as I had not wept yet, since Dora died!

I had found a packet of letters awaiting me but a few minutes before, and had strolled out of the village to read them while my supper was making ready. Other packets had missed me, and I had received none for a long time. Beyond a line or two, to say that I was well, and had arrived at such a place, I had not had fortitude or constancy to write a letter since I left home.

The packet was in my hand. I opened it, and read the writing of Agnes.

She was happy and useful, was prospering as she had hoped. That was all she told me of herself. The rest referred to me.

She gave me no advice; she urged no duty on me; she only told me, in her own fervent manner, what her trust in me was. She knew (she said) how such a nature as mine would turn affliction to good. She knew how trial and emotion would exalt and strengthen it. She was sure that in my every purpose I should gain a firmer and a higher tendency, through the grief I had undergone. She, who so gloried in my fame, and so looked forward to its augmentation, well knew that I would labour on. She knew that in me, sorrow could not be weakness, but must be strength. As the endurance of my childish days had done its part to make me what I was, so greater calamities would nerve me on, to be yet better than I was; and so, as they had taught me, would I teach others. She commended me to God, who had taken my innocent darling to His rest; and in her sisterly affection cherished me always, and was always at my side go where I would; proud of what I had done, but infinitely prouder yet of what I was reserved to do.

I put the letter in my breast, and thought what had I been an hour ago! When I heard the voices die away, and saw the quiet evening cloud grow dim, and all the colours in the valley fade, and the golden snow upon the mountain tops become a remote part of the pale night sky, yet felt that the night was passing from my mind, and all its shadows clearing, there was no name for the love I bore her, dearer to me, henceforward, than ever until then.

I read her letter, many times. I wrote to her before I slept. I told her that I had been in sore need of her help; that without her I was not, and I never had been, what she thought me; but that she inspired me to be that, and I would try.

I did try. In three months more, a year would have passed since the beginning of my sorrow. I determined to make no resolutions until the expiration of those three months, but to try. I lived in that valley, and its neighbourhood, all the time.

The three months gone, I resolved to remain away from home for some time longer; to settle myself for the present in Switzerland, which was growing dear to me in the remembrance of that evening; to resume my pen; to work.

I resorted humbly whither Agnes had commended me; I sought out Nature, never sought in vain; and I admitted to my breast the human interest I had lately shrunk from. It was not long, before I had almost as many friends in the valley as in Yarmouth: and when I left it, before the winter set in, for Geneva, and came back in the spring, their cordial greetings had a homely sound to me, although they were not conveyed in English words.

I worked early and late, patiently and hard. I wrote a Story, with a purpose growing, not remotely, out of my experience, and sent it to Traddles, and he arranged for its publication very advantageously for me; and the tidings of my growing reputation began to reach me from travellers whom I encountered by chance. After some rest and change, I fell to work, in my old ardent way, on a new fancy, which took strong possession of me. As I advanced in the execution of this task, I felt it more and more, and roused my utmost energies to do it well. This was my third work of fiction. It was not half written, when, in an interval of rest, I thought of returning home.

For a long time, though studying and working patiently, I had accustomed myself to robust exercise. My health, severely impaired when I left England, was quite restored. I had seen much. I had been in many countries, and I hope I had improved my store of knowledge.

I have now recalled all that I think it needful to recall here, of this term of absence—with one reservation. I have made it, thus far, with no purpose of suppressing any of my thoughts; for, as I have elsewhere said, this narrative is my written memory. I have desired to keep the most secret current of my mind apart, and to the last. I enter on it now.

I cannot so completely penetrate the mystery of my own heart, as to know when I began to think that I might have set its earliest and brightest hopes on Agnes. I cannot say at what stage of my grief it first became associated with the reflection that, in my wayward boyhood, I had thrown away the treasure of her love. I believe I may have heard some whisper of that distant thought, in the old unhappy loss or want of something never to be realised, of which I had been sensible. But the thought came into my mind as a new reproach and new regret, when I was left so sad and lonely in the world.

If, at that time, I had been much with her, I should, in the weakness of my desolation, have betrayed this. It was what I remotely dreaded when I was first impelled to stay away from England. I could not have borne to lose the smallest portion of her sisterly affection; yet, in that betrayal, I should have set a constraint between us hitherto unknown.

I could not forget that the feeling with which she now regarded me had grown up in my own free choice and course. That if she had ever loved me with another love—and I sometimes thought the time was when she might have done so—I had cast it away. It was nothing, now, that I had accustomed myself to think of her, when we were both mere children, as one who was far removed from my wild fancies. I had bestowed my passionate tenderness upon another object; and what I might have done, I had not done; and what Agnes was to me, I and her own noble heart had made her.

In the beginning of the change that gradually worked in me, when I tried to get a better understanding of myself and be a better man, I did glance, through some indefinite probation, to a period when I might possibly hope to cancel the mistaken past, and to be so blessed as to marry her. But, as time wore on, this shadowy prospect faded, and departed from me. If she had ever loved me, then, I should hold her the more sacred, remembering the confidences I had reposed in her, her knowledge of my errant heart, the sacrifice she must have made to be my friend and sister, and the victory she had won. If she had never loved me, could I believe that she would love me now?

I had always felt my weakness, in comparison with her constancy and fortitude; and now I felt it more and more.

Whatever I might have been to her, or she to me, if I had been more worthy of her long ago, I was not now, and she was not. The time was past. I had let it go by, and had deservedly lost her.

That I suffered much in these contentions, that they filled me with unhappiness and remorse, and yet that I had a sustaining sense that it was required of me, in right and honour, to keep away from myself, with shame, the thought of turning to the dear girl in the withering of my hopes, from whom I had frivolously turned when they were bright and fresh—which consideration was at the root of every thought I had concerning her—is all equally true. I made no effort to conceal from myself, now, that I loved her, that I was devoted to her; but I brought the assurance home to myself, that it was now too late, and that our long-subsisting relation must be undisturbed.

I had thought, much and often, of my Dora's shadowing out to me what might have happened, in those years that were destined not to try us. I had considered how the things that never happen, are often as much realities to us, in their effects, as those that are accomplished. The very years she spoke of, were realities now, for my correction; and would have been, one day, a little later perhaps, though we had parted in our earliest folly. I endeavoured to convert what might have been between myself and Agnes, into a means of making me more self-denying, more resolved, more conscious of myself, and my defects and errors. Thus, through the reflection that it might have been, I arrived at the conviction that it could never be.

These, with their perplexities and inconsistencies, were the shifting quicksands of my mind, from the time of my departure to the time of my return home, three years afterwards. Three years had elapsed since the sailing of the emigrant ship; when, at the same hour of sunset, and in the same place, I stood on the deck of the packet vessel that brought me home, looking on the rosy water where I had seen the image of that ship reflected.

Three years. Long in the aggregate, thought short as they went by. And home was very dear to me, and Agnes too—but she was not mine—she was never to be mine. She might have been, but that was past!

59

RETURN

I LANDED IN LONDON ON A WINTRY AUTUMN EVENING. It was dark and raining, and I saw more fog and mud in a minute than I had seen in a year. I walked from the Custom House to the Monument before I found a coach; and although the very house-fronts, looking on the swollen gutters, were like old friends to me, I could not but admit that they were very dingy friends.

I have often remarked—I suppose everybody has—that one's going away from a familiar place, would seem to be the signal for change in it. As I looked out of the coach-window, and observed that an old house on Fish-street Hill, which had stood untouched by painter, carpenter, or bricklayer, for a century, had been pulled down in my absence; and that a neighbouring street, of time-honoured insalubrity and inconvenience, was being drained and widened; I half expected to find St. Paul's Cathedral looking older.

For some changes in the fortunes of my friends, I was prepared. My aunt had long been re-established at Dover, and Traddles had begun to get into some little practice at the Bar, in the very first term after my departure. He had chambers in Gray's Inn, now; and had told me, in his last letters, that he was not without hopes of being soon united to the dearest girl in the world.

They expected me home before Christmas; but had no idea of my returning so soon. I had purposely misled them, that I might have the pleasure of taking them by surprise. And yet, I was perverse enough to feel a chill and disappointment in receiving no welcome, and rattling, alone and silent, through the misty streets.

The well-known shops, however, with their cheerful lights, did something for me; and when I alighted at the door of the Gray's Inn Coffee-house, I had recovered my spirits. It recalled, at first, that so-different time when I had put up at the Golden

Cross, and reminded me of the changes that had come to pass since then; but that was natural.

"Do you know where Mr. Traddles lives in the Inn?" I asked the waiter, as I warmed myself by the coffee-room fire.

"Holborn Court, sir. Number two."

"Mr. Traddles has a rising reputation among the lawyers, I believe?" said I.

"Well, sir," returned the waiter, "probably he has, sir; but I am not aware of it myself."

This waiter, who was middle-aged and spare, looked for help to a waiter of more authority—a stout, potential old man, with a double-chin, in black breeches and stockings, who came out of a place like a churchwarden's pew, at the end of the coffee-room, where he kept company with a cash-box, a Directory, a Law-list, and other books and papers.

"Mr. Traddles," said the spare waiter. "Number two in the Court."

The potential waiter waved him away, and turned, gravely, to me.

"I was inquiring," said I, "whether Mr. Traddles, at number two in the Court, has not a rising reputation among the lawyers?"

"Never heard his name," said the waiter, in a rich husky voice.

I felt quite apologetic for Traddles.

"He's a young man, sure?" said the portentous waiter, fixing his eyes severely on me. "How long has he been in the Inn?"

"Not above three years," said I.

The waiter, who I supposed had lived in his churchwarden's pew for forty years, could not pursue such an insignificant subject. He asked me what I would have for dinner.

I felt I was in England again, and really was quite cast down on Traddles's account. There seemed to be no hope for him. I meekly ordered a bit of fish and a steak, and stood before the fire musing on his obscurity.

As I followed the chief waiter with my eyes, I could not help thinking that the garden in which he had gradually blown to be the flower he was, was an arduous place to rise in. It had such a prescriptive, stiff-necked, long-established, solemn, elderly air. I glanced about the room, which had had its sanded floor sanded, no doubt, in exactly the same manner when the chief waiter was a boy—if he ever was a boy, which appeared improbable; and at the shining tables, where I saw myself reflected, in unruffled depths of old mahogany; and at the lamps, without a flaw in their trimming or cleaning; and at the comfortable green curtains, with their pure brass rods, snugly enclosing the boxes; and at the two large coal fires, brightly burning; and at the rows of decanters, burly as if with the consciousness of pipes of expensive old port wine below; and both England and the law appeared to me to be very difficult indeed to be taken by storm. I went up to my bedroom to change my wet clothes; and the vast extent of that old wainscoted apartment (which was over the archway leading to the Inn, I remember), and the sedate immensity of the four-post bedstead, and the indomitable gravity of the chests of drawers, all seemed to unite in sternly frowning on the fortunes of Traddles, or on any such daring youth. I came down again to my dinner; and even the slow comfort of the meal, and the orderly silence of the place—which was bare of guests, the Long Vacation not yet being over—were eloquent on the audacity of Traddles, and his small hopes of a livelihood for twenty years to come.

I had seen nothing like this since I went away, and it quite dashed my hopes for my friend. The chief waiter had had enough of me. He came near me no more; but devoted himself to an old gentleman in long gaiters, to meet whom a pint of special port seemed to come out of the cellar of its own accord, for he gave no order. The second waiter informed me, in a whisper, that this old gentleman was a retired conveyancer living in the Square, and worth a mint of money, which it was expected he would leave to his laundress's daughter; likewise that it was rumoured that he had a service of plate in a bureau, all tarnished with lying by, though more than one spoon and a fork had never yet been beheld in his chambers by mortal vision. By this time, I quite gave Traddles up for lost; and settled in my own mind that there was no hope for him.

Being very anxious to see the dear old fellow, nevertheless, I despatched my dinner, in a manner not at all calculated to raise me in the opinion of the chief waiter, and hurried out by the back way. Number two in the Court was soon reached; and an inscription on the door-post informing me that Mr. Traddles occupied a set of chambers on the top storey, I ascended the staircase. A crazy old staircase I found it to be, feebly lighted on each landing by a club-headed little oil wick, dying away in a little dungeon of dirty glass.

In the course of my stumbling up-stairs, I fancied I heard a pleasant sound of laughter; and not the laughter of an attorney or barrister, or attorney's clerk or barrister's clerk, but of two or three merry girls. Happening, however, as I stopped to listen, to put my foot in a hole where the Honourable Society of Gray's

Inn had left a plank deficient, I fell down with some noise, and when I recovered my footing all was silent.

Groping my way more carefully, for the rest of the journey, my heart beat high when I found the outer door, which had MR. TRADDLES painted on it, open. I knocked. A considerable scuffling within ensued, but nothing else. I therefore knocked again.

A small sharp-looking lad, half-footboy and half-clerk, who was very much out of breath, but who looked at me as if he defied me to prove it legally, presented himself.

"Is Mr. Traddles within?" I said.

"Yes, sir, but he's engaged."

"I want to see him."

After a moment's survey of me, the sharp-looking lad decided to let me in; and opening the door wider for that purpose, admitted me, first, into a little closet of a hall, and next into a little sitting-room; where I came into the presence of my old friend (also out of breath), seated at a table, and bending over papers.

"Good God!" cried Traddles, looking up. "It's Copperfield!" and rushed into my arms, where I held him tight.

"All well, my dear Traddles?"

"All well, my dear, dear Copperfield, and nothing but good news!"

We cried with pleasure, both of us.

"My dear fellow," said Traddles, rumpling his hair in his excitement, which was a most unnecessary operation, "my dearest Copperfield, my long-lost and most welcome friend, how glad I am to see you! How brown you are! How glad I am! Upon my life and honour, I never was so rejoiced, my beloved Copperfield, never!"

I was equally at a loss to express my emotions. I was quite unable to speak, at first.

"My dear fellow," said Traddles. "And grown so famous! My glorious Copperfield! Good gracious me, *when* did you come, *where* have you come from, *what* have you been doing?"

Never pausing for an answer to anything he said, Traddles, who had clapped me into an easy-chair by the fire, all this time impetuously stirred the fire with one hand, and pulled at my neckerchief with the other, under some wild delusion that it was a great coat. Without putting down the poker, he now hugged me again, and I hugged him; and, both laughing, and both wiping our eyes, we both sat down, and shook hands across the hearth.

"To think," said Traddles, "that you should have been so nearly coming home as you must have been, my dear old boy, and not at the ceremony!"

"What ceremony, my dear Traddles?"

"Good gracious me!" cried Traddles, opening his eyes in his old way. "Didn't you get my last letter?"

"Certainly not, if it referred to any ceremony."

"Why, my dear Copperfield," said Traddles, sticking his hair upright with both hands, and then putting his hands on my knees, "I am married!"

"Married!" I cried joyfully.

"Lord bless me, yes!" said Traddles—"by the Rev. Horace—to Sophy—down in Devonshire. Why, my dear boy, she's behind the window curtain! Look here!"

To my amazement, the dearest girl in the world came at that same instant, laughing and blushing, from her place of concealment. And a more cheerful, amiable, honest, happy, bright-looking bride, I believe (as I could not help saying on the spot) the world never saw. I kissed her as an old acquaintance should, and wished them joy with all my might of heart.

"Dear me," said Traddles, "what a delightful re-union this is! You are so extremely brown, my dear Copperfield! God bless my soul, how happy I am!"

"And so am I," said I.

"And I am sure I am!" said the blushing and laughing Sophy.

"We are all as happy as possible!" said Traddles. "Even the girls are happy. Dear me, I declare I forgot them!"

"Forgot?" said I.

"The girls," said Traddles. "Sophy's sisters. They are staying with us. They have come to have a peep at London. The fact is, when—was it you that tumbled up-stairs, Copperfield?"

"It was," said I, laughing.

"Well, then, when you tumbled up-stairs," said Traddles, "I was romping with the girls. In point of fact, we were playing at Puss in the Corner, But as that wouldn't do in Westminster Hall, and as it wouldn't look quite professional if they were seen by a client, they decamped. And they are now—listening, I have no doubt," said Traddles, glancing at the door of another room.

"I am sorry," said I, laughing afresh, "to have occasioned such a dispersion."

"Upon my word," rejoined Traddles, greatly delighted, "if you had seen them running away, and running back again, after you had knocked, to pick up the combs they had dropped out of their hair, and going on in the maddest manner, you wouldn't have said so. My love, will you fetch the girls?"

Sophy tripped away, and we heard her received in the adjoining room with a peal of laughter.

"Really musical, isn't it, my dear Copperfield?" said Traddles. "It's very agreeable to hear. It quite lights up these old rooms. To an unfortunate bachelor of a fellow who has lived alone all his life, you know, it's positively delicious. It's charming. Poor things, they have had a great loss in Sophy—who, I do assure you, Copperfield, is, and ever was, the dearest girl!—and it gratifies me beyond expression to find them in such good spirits. The society of girls is a very delightful thing, Copperfield. It's not professional, but it's very delightful."

Observing that he slightly faltered, and comprehending that in the goodness of his heart he was fearful of giving me some pain by what he had said, I expressed my concurrence with a heartiness that evidently relieved and pleased him greatly.

"But then," said Traddles, "our domestic arrangements are, to say the truth, quite unprofessional altogether, my dear Copperfield. Even Sophy's being here, is unprofessional. And we have no other place of abode. We have put to sea in a cock-boat, but we are quite prepared to rough it. And Sophy's an extraordinary manager! You'll be surprised how those girls are stowed away. I am sure I hardly know how it's done!"

"Are many of the young ladies with you?" I inquired.

"The eldest, the Beauty is here," said Traddles, in a low confidential voice, "Caroline. And Sarah's here—the one I mentioned to you as having something the matter with her spine, you know. Immensely better! And the two youngest that Sophy educated are with us. And Louisa's here."

"Indeed!" cried I.

"Yes," said Traddles. "Now the whole set—I mean the chambers—is only three rooms; but Sophy arranges for the girls in the most wonderful way, and they sleep as comfortably as possible. Three in that room," said Traddles, pointing. "Two in that."

I could not help glancing round, in search of the accommodation remaining for Mr. and Mrs. Traddles. Traddles understood me.

"Well!" said Traddles, "we are prepared to rough it, as I said just now, and we *did* improvise a bed last week, upon the floor here. But there's a little room in the roof—a very nice room, when you're up there—which Sophy papered herself, to surprise me; and that's our room at present. It's a capital little gipsy sort of place. There's quite a view from it."

"And you are happily married at last, my dear Traddles!" said I. "How rejoiced I am!"

"Thank you, my dear Copperfield," said Traddles, as we shook hands once more. "Yes, I am as happy as it's possible to be. There's your old friend, you see," said Traddles, nodding triumphantly at the flower-pot and stand; "and there's the table with the marble top! All the other furniture is plain and serviceable, you perceive. And as to plate, Lord bless you, we haven't so much as a tea-spoon."

"All to be earned?" said I, cheerfully.

"Exactly so," replied Traddles, "all to be earned. Of course we have something in the shape of tea-spoons, because we stir our tea. But they're Britannia metal."

"The silver will be the brighter when it comes," said I.

"The very thing we say!" cried Traddles, "You see, my dear Copperfield," falling again into the low confidential tone, "after I had delivered my argument in DOE *dem.* JIPES *versus* WIGZELL, which did me great service with the profession, I went down into Devonshire, and had some serious conversation in private with the Reverend Horace. I dwelt upon the fact that Sophy —who I do assure you, Copperfield, is the dearest girl!——"

"I am certain she is!" said I.

"She is, indeed!" rejoined Traddles. "But I am afraid I am wandering from the subject. Did I mention the Reverend Horace?"

"You said that you dwelt upon the fact——"

"True! Upon the fact that Sophy and I had been engaged for a long period, and that Sophy, with the permission of her parents, was more than content to take me—in short," said Traddles, with his old frank smile, "on our present Britannia-metal footing. Very well. I then proposed to the Reverend Horace—who is a most excellent clergyman, Copperfield, and ought to be a Bishop; or at least ought to have enough to live upon, without pinching himself—that if I could turn the corner, say of two hundred and fifty pounds, in one year; and could see my way pretty clearly to that, or something better, next year; and could plainly furnish a little place like this, besides; then, and in that case, Sophy and I should be united. I took the liberty of representing that we had been patient for a good many years; and that the circumstance of Sophy's being extraordinarily useful at home, ought not to operate with her affectionate parents, against her establishment in life—don't you see?"

"Certainly it ought not," said I.

"I am glad you think so, Copperfield," rejoined Traddles, "because, without any imputation on the Reverend Horace, I do think parents, and brothers, and so forth, are sometimes rather selfish in such cases. Well! I also pointed out, that my most earnest desire was, to be useful to the family; and that if I got on in the world, and anything should happen to him—I refer to the Reverend Horace—"

"I understand," said I.

"—Or to Mrs. Crewler—it would be the utmost gratification of my wishes, to be a parent to the girls. He replied in a most admirable manner, exceedingly flattering to my feelings, and undertook to obtain the consent of Mrs. Crewler to this arrangement. They had a dreadful time of it with her. It mounted from her legs into her chest, and then into her head—"

"What mounted?" I asked.

"Her grief," replied Traddles, with a serious look. "Her feelings generally. As I mentioned in a former occasion, she is a very superior woman, but has lost the use of her limbs. Whatever occurs to harass her, usually settles in her legs; but on this occasion it mounted to the chest, and then to the head, and, in short, pervaded the whole system in a most alarming manner. However, they brought her through it by unremitting and affectionate attention; and we were married yesterday six weeks. You have no idea what a Monster I felt, Copperfield, when I saw the whole family crying and fainting away in every direction! Mrs. Crewler couldn't see me before we left—couldn't forgive me, then, for depriving her of her child—but she is a good creature, and has done so since. I had a delightful letter from her, only this morning."

"And in short, my dear friend," said I, "you feel as blest as you deserve to feel!"

"Oh! That's your partiality!" laughed Traddles. "But, indeed, I am in a most enviable state. I work hard, and read Law insatiably. I get up at five every morning, and don't mind it at all. I hide the girls in the day-time, and make merry with them in the evening. And I assure you I am quite sorry that they are going home on Tuesday, which is the day before the first day of Michaelmas Term. But here," said Traddles, breaking off in his confidence, and speaking aloud, "*are* the girls! Mr. Copperfield, Miss Crewler—Miss Sarah—Miss Louisa—Margaret and Lucy!"

They were a perfect nest of roses; they looked so wholesome and fresh. They were all pretty, and Miss Caroline was very handsome; but there was a loving, cheerful, fireside quality in Sophy's bright looks, which was better than that, and which assured me that my friend had chosen well. We all sat round the fire; while the sharp boy, who I now divined had lost his breath in putting the papers out, cleared them away again, and produced the tea-things. After that, he retired for the night, shutting the outer door upon us with a bang. Mrs. Traddles, with perfect pleasure and composure beaming from her household eyes, having made the tea, then quietly made the toast as she sat in a corner by the fire.

She had seen Agnes, she told me, while she was toasting. "Tom" had taken her down into Kent for a wedding trip, and there she had seen my aunt, too; and both my aunt and Agnes were well, and they had all talked of nothing but me. "Tom" had never had me out of his thoughts, she really believed, all the time I had been away. "Tom" was the authority for everything. "Tom" was evidently the idol of her life; never to be shaken on his pedestal by any commotion; always to be believed in, and done homage to with the whole faith of her heart, come what might.

The deference which both she and Traddles showed towards the Beauty, pleased me very much. I don't know that I thought it very reasonable; but I thought it very delightful, and essentially a part of their character. If Traddles ever for an instant missed the tea-spoons that were still to be won, I have no doubt it was when he handed the Beauty her tea. If his sweet-tempered wife could have got up any self-assertion against any one, I am satisfied it could only have been because she was the Beauty's sister. A few slight indications of a rather petted and capricious manner, which I observed in the Beauty, were manifestly considered, by Traddles and his wife, as her birthright and natural endowment. If she had been born a Queen Bee, and they labouring Bees, they could not have been more satisfied of that.

But their self-forgetfulness charmed me. Their pride in these girls, and their submission of themselves to all their whims, was the pleasantest little testimony to their own worth I could have desired to see. If Traddles were addressed as "a darling," once in the course of that evening; and besought to bring something here, or carry something there, or take something up, or put something down, or find something, or fetch something, he was so addressed, by one or other of his sisters-in-law, at least twelve times in an hour. Neither could they do anything without Sophy. Somebody's hair fell down, and nobody but Sophy could put it up. Somebody forgot how a particular tune went, and nobody but Sophy could hum that tune right. Somebody wanted to recall the name of a place in Devonshire, and only Sophy knew it. Something was wanted to be written home, and Sophy alone could be trusted to write before breakfast in the morning. Somebody broke down in a piece of knitting, and no one but Sophy was able to put the defaulter in the right direction. They were entire mistresses of the place, and Sophy and Traddles waited on them. How many children Sophy could have taken care of in her time, I can't imagine; but she seemed to be famous for knowing every sort of song that ever was addressed to a child in the English tongue; and she sang dozens to order with the clearest little voice in the world, one after another (every sister issuing directions for a different tune, and the Beauty generally striking in last), so that I was quite fascinated. The best of all was, that, in the midst of their exactions, all the sisters had a great tenderness and respect both for Sophy and Traddles. I am sure, when I took my leave, and Traddles was coming out to walk with me to the coffee-house, I thought I had never seen an obstinate head of hair, or any other head of hair, rolling about in such a shower of kisses.

Altogether, it was a scene I could not help dwelling on with pleasure, for a long time after I got back and had wished Traddles good-night. If I had beheld a thousand roses blowing in a top set of chambers, in that withered Gray's Inn, they could not have brightened it half so much. The idea of those Devonshire girls, among the dry law-stationers and the attorney's offices; and of the tea and toast, and children's songs, in that grim atmosphere of pounce and parchment, red-tape, dusty wafers, ink-jars, brief and draft paper, law reports, writs, declarations, and bills of costs, seemed almost as pleasantly fanciful as if I had dreamed that the Sultan's famous family had been admitted on the roll of attorneys, and had brought the talking bird, the singing tree, and the golden water into Gray's Inn Hall. Somehow, I found that I had taken leave of Traddles for the night, and come back to the coffee-house, with a great change in my despondency about him. I began to think he would get on, in spite of all the many orders of chief waiters in England.

Drawing a chair before one of the coffee-room fires to think about him at my leisure, I gradually fell from the consideration of his happiness to tracing prospects in the live-coals, and to thinking, as they broke and changed, of the principal vicissitudes and separations that had marked my life. I had not seen a coal fire, since I had left England three years ago: though many a wood fire had I watched, as it crumbled into hoary ashes, and mingled with the feathery heap upon the hearth, which not inaptly figured to me, in my despondency, my own dead hopes.

I could think of the past now, gravely, but not bitterly; and could contemplate the future in a brave spirit. Home, in its best sense, was for me no more. She in whom I might have inspired a dearer love, I had taught to be my sister. She would marry, and would have new claimants on her tenderness: and in doing it, would never know the love for her that had grown up in my heart. It was right that I should pay the forfeit of my headlong passion. What I reaped, I had sown.

I was thinking. And had I truly disciplined my heart to this, and could I resolutely bear it, and calmly hold the place in her home which she had calmly held in mine,—when I found my eyes resting on a countenance that might have arisen out of the fire, in its association with my early remembrances.

Little Mr. Chillip the Doctor, to whose good offices I was indebted in the very first chapter of this history, sat reading a newspaper in the shadow of an opposite corner. He was tolerably stricken in years by this time; but being a mild, meek, calm little man, had worn so easily, that I thought he looked at that moment just as he might have looked when he sat in our parlour, waiting for me to be born.

Mr. Chillip had left Blunderstone six or seven years ago, and I had never seen him since. He sat placidly perusing the newspaper, with his little head on one side, and a glass of warm sherry negus at his elbow. He was so extremely conciliatory in his manner that he seemed to apologise to the very newspaper for taking the liberty of reading it.

I walked up to where he was sitting, and said, "How do you do, Mr. Chillip?"

He was greatly fluttered by this unexpected address from a stranger, and replied, in his slow way, "I thank you, sir, you are very good. Thank you, sir. I hope *you* are well."

"You don't remember me?" said I.

"Well, sir," returned Mr. Chillip, smiling very meekly, and shaking his head as he surveyed me, "I have a kind of an impression that something in your countenance is familiar to me, sir; but I couldn't lay my hand upon your name, really."

"And yet you knew it, long before I knew it myself," I returned.

"Did I indeed, sir?" said Mr. Chillip. "Is it possible that I had the honour, sir, of officiating when——?"

"Yes," said I.

"Dear me!" cried Mr. Chillip. "But no doubt you are a good deal changed since then, sir?"

" Probably," said I.

" Well, sir," observed Mr. Chillip, " I hope you'll excuse me, if I am compelled to ask the favour of your name? "

On my telling him my name, he was really moved. He quite shook hands with me—which was a violent proceeding for him, his usual course being to slide a tepid little fish-slice, an inch or two in advance of his hip, and evinced the greatest discomposure when anybody grappled with it. Even now, he put his hand in his coat-pocket as soon as he could disengage it, and seemed relieved when he had got it safe back.

" Dear me, sir! " said Mr. Chillip, surveying me with his head on one side. " And it's Mr. Copperfield, is it? Well, sir, I think I should have known you, if I had taken the liberty of looking more closely at you. There's a strong resemblance between you and your poor father, sir."

" I never had the happiness of seeing my father," I observed.

" Very true, sir," said Mr. Chillip, in a soothing tone. " And very much to be deplored it was, on all accounts! We are not ignorant, sir," said Mr. Chillip, slowly shaking his little head again, " down in our part of the country, of your fame. There must be great excitement here, sir," said Mr. Chillip, tapping himself on the forehead with his forefinger. " You must find it a trying occupation, sir! "

" What is your part of the country now? " I asked, seating myself near him.

" I am established within a few miles of Bury St. Edmund's, sir," said Mr. Chillip. " Mrs. Chillip coming into a little property in that neighbourhood, under her father's will, I bought a practice down there, in which you will be glad to hear I am doing well. My daughter is growing quite a tall lass now, sir," said Mr. Chillip, giving his little head another shake. " Her mother let down two tucks in her frocks only last week. Such is time, you see, sir! "

As the little man put his now empty glass to his lips, when he made this reflection, I proposed to him to have it refilled, and I would keep him company with another. " Well, sir," he returned, in his slow way, " it's more than I am accustomed to; but I can't deny myself the pleasure of your conversation. It seems but yesterday that I had the honour of attending you in the measles. You came through them charmingly, sir! "

I acknowledged this compliment, and ordered the negus, which was soon produced. " Quite an uncommon dissipation! " said Mr. Chillip, stirring it, " but I can't resist so extraordinary an occasion. You have no family, sir? "

I shook my head.

"I was aware that you sustained a bereavement, sir, some time ago," said Mr. Chillip. "I heard it from your father-in-law's sister. Very decided character there, sir?"

"Why, yes," said I, "decided enough. Where did you see her, Mr. Chillip?"

"Are you not aware, sir," returned Mr. Chillip, with his placidest smile, "that your father-in-law is again a neighbour of mine?"

"No," said I.

"He is indeed, sir!" said Mr. Chillip. "Married a young lady of that part, with a very good little property, poor thing.—And this action of the brain now, sir? Don't you find it fatigue you?" said Mr. Chillip, looking at me like an admiring Robin.

I waived that question, and returned to the Murdstones. "I was aware of his being married again. Do you attend the family?" I asked.

"Not regularly. I have been called in," he replied. "Strong phrenological development of the organ of firmness, in Mr. Murdstone and his sister, sir."

I replied with such an expressive look, that Mr. Chillip was emboldened by that, and the negus together, to give his head several short shakes, and thoughtfully exclaim. "Ah, dear me! We remember old times, Mr. Copperfield."

"And the brother and sister are pursuing their old course, are they?" said I.

"Well, sir," replied Mr. Chillip, "a medical man, being so much in families, ought to have neither eyes nor ears for anything but his profession. Still, I must say, they are very severe, sir: both as to this life and the next."

"The next will be regulated without much reference to them, I dare say," I returned: "what are they doing as to this?"

Mr. Chillip shook his head, stirred his negus, and sipped it.

"She was a charming woman, sir!" he observed in a plaintive manner.

"The present Mrs. Murdstone?"

"A charming woman indeed, sir," said Mr. Chillip: "as amiable, I am sure, as it was possible to be! Mrs. Chillip's opinion is, that her spirit has been entirely broken since her marriage, and that she is all but melancholy mad. And the ladies," observed Mr. Chillip, timorously, "are great observers, sir."

"I suppose she was to be subdued and broken to their detestable mould, Heaven help her!" said I. "And she has been."

"Well, sir, there were violent quarrels at first, I assure you," said Mr. Chillip; " but she is quite a shadow now. Would it be considered forward if I was to say to you, sir, in confidence, that since the sister came to help, the brother and sister between them have nearly reduced her to a state of imbecility? "

I told him I could easily believe it.

" I have no hesitation in saying," said Mr. Chillip, fortifying himself with another sip of negus, " between you and me, sir, that her mother died of it—or that tyranny, gloom, and worry have made Mrs. Murdstone nearly imbecile. She was a lively young woman, sir, before marriage, and their gloom and austerity destroyed her. They go about with her, now, more like her keepers than her husband and sister-in-law. That was Mrs. Chillip's remark to me, only last week. And I assure you, sir, the ladies are great observers. Mrs. Chillip herself is a *great* observer! "

" Does he gloomily profess to be (I am ashamed to use the word in such association) religious still? " I inquired.

" You anticipate, sir," said Mr. Chillip, his eyelids getting quite red with the unwonted stimulus in which he was indulging, " one of Mrs. Chillip's most impressive remarks. Mrs. Chillip," he proceeded, in the calmest and slowest manner, " quite electrified me, by pointing out that Mr. Murdstone sets up an image of himself, and calls it the Divine Nature. You might have knocked me down on the flat of my back, sir, with the feather of a pen, I assure you, when Mrs. Chillip said so. The ladies are great observers, sir! "

" Intuitively," said I, to his extreme delight.

" I am very happy to receive such support in my opinion, sir," he rejoined. " It is not often that I venture to give a non-medical opinion, I assure you. Mr. Murdstone delivers public addresses sometimes, and it is said,—in short, sir, it is said by Mrs. Chillip,—that the darker tyrant he has lately been, the more ferocious is his doctrine.

" I believe Mrs. Chillip to be perfectly right " said I.

" Mrs. Chillip does go so far as to say," pursued the meekest of little men, much encouraged, " that what such people miscall their religion, is a vent for their bad humours and arrogance. And do you know I must say, sir," he continued, mildly laying his head on one side, " that I *don't* find authority for Mr. and Miss Murdstone in the New Testament? "

" I never found it either! " said I.

" In the meantime, sir," said Mr. Chillip, " they are much disliked; and as they are very free in consigning everybody who dislikes them to perdition, we really have a good deal of perdition going on in our neighbourhood! However, as Mrs. Chillip says, sir, they undergo a continual punishment; for they are turned inward, to feed upon their own hearts, and their own hearts are very bad feeding. Now, sir, about that brain of yours, if you'll excuse my returning to it. Don't you expose it to a good deal of excitement, sir?"

I found it not difficult, in the excitement of Mr. Chillip's own brain, under his potations of negus, to divert his attention from this topic to his own affairs, on which, for the next half hour, he was quite loquacious; giving me to understand, among other pieces of information, that he was then at the Gray's Inn Coffee-house to lay his professional evidence before a Commission of Lunacy, touching the state of mind of a patient who had become deranged from excessive drinking.

"And I assure you, sir," he said, "I am extremely nervous on such occasions. I could not support being what is called Bullied, sir. It would quite unman me. Do you know it was some time before I recovered the conduct of that alarming lady, on the night of your birth, Mr. Copperfield?"

I told him that I was going down to my aunt, the Dragon of that night, early, in the morning; and that she was one of the most tender-hearted and excellent of women, as he would know full well if he knew her better. The mere notion of the possibility of his ever seeing her again, appeared to terrify him. He replied with a small pale smile, "Is she so, indeed, sir? Really?" and almost immediately called for a candle, and went to bed, as if he were not quite safe anwhere else. He did not actually stagger under the negus; but I should think his placid little pulse must have made two or three more beats in a minute, than it had done since the great night of my aunt's disappointment, when she struck at him with her bonnet.

Thoroughly tired, I went to bed too, at midnight; passed the next day on the Dover coach; burst safe and sound into my aunt's old parlour while she was at tea (she wore spectacles now); and was received by her, and Mr. Dick, and dear old Peggotty, who acted as housekeeper, with open arms and tears of joy. My aunt was mightily amused, when we began to talk composedly, by my account of my meeting with Mr. Chillip, and of his holding her in such dread remembrance; and both she and Peggotty had a great deal to say about my poor mother's second husband, and "that murdering woman of a sister,"—on whom I think no pain or penalty would have induced my aunt to bestow any Christian or Proper Name, or any other designation.

60

AGNES

MY AUNT AND I, WHEN WE WERE LEFT ALONE, TALKED far into the night. How the emigrants never wrote home, otherwise than cheerfully and hopefully; how Mr. Micawber had actually remitted divers small sums of money, on account of those " pecuniary liabilities," in reference to which he had been so business-like as between man and man; how Janet, returning into my aunt's service when she came back to Dover, had finally carried out her renunciation of mankind by entering into wedlock with a thriving tavern-keeper; and how my aunt had finally set *her* seal on the same great principle, by aiding and abetting the bride, and crowning the marriage-ceremony with her presence; were among our topics—already more or less familiar to me through the letters I had had. Mr. Dick, as usual, was not forgotten. My aunt informed me how he incessantly occupied himself in copying everything he could lay his hands on, and kept King Charles the First at a respectful distance by that semblance of employment; how it was one of the main joys and rewards of her life that he was free and happy, instead of pining in monotonous restraint; and how (as a novel general conclusion) nobody but she could ever fully know what he was.

" And when, Trot," said my aunt, patting the back of my hand, as we sat in our old way before the fire, " when are you going over to Canterbury? "

" I shall get a horse, and ride over to-morrow morning, aunt, unless you will go with me? "

" No! " said my aunt, in her short abrupt way. " I mean to stay where I am."

Then, I should ride, I said. I could not have come through Canterbury to-day without stopping, if I had been coming to any one but her.

She was pleased, but answered, " Tut, Trot; *my* old bones would have kept till to-morrow! " and softly patted my hand again, as I sat looking thoughtfully at the fire.

Thoughtfully, for I could not be here once more, and so near

Agnes, without the revival of those regrets with which I had so long been occupied. Softened regrets they might be, teaching me what I had failed to learn when my younger life was all before me, but not the less regrets. " Oh, Trot," I seemed to hear my aunt say once more; and I understood her better now—" Blind, blind, blind! "

We both kept silence for some minutes. When I raised my eyes, I found that she was steadily observant of me. Perhaps she had followed the current of my mind; for it seemed to me an easy one to track now, wilful as it had been once.

" You will find her father a white-haired old man," said my aunt, " though a better man in all other respects—a reclaimed man. Neither will you find him measuring all human interests, and joys, and sorrows, with his one poor little inch-rule now. Trust me, child, such things must shrink very much, before they can be measured off in *that* way."

" Indeed they must," said I.

" You will find her," pursued my aunt, " as good, as beautiful, as earnest, as disinterested, as she has always been. If I knew higher praise, Trot, I would bestow it on her."

There was no higher praise for her; no higher reproach for me. Oh, how had I strayed so far away!

" If she trains the young girls whom she has about her, to be like herself," said my aunt, earnest even to the filling of her eyes with tears, " Heaven knows, her life will be well employed! Useful and happy, as she said that day! How could she be otherwise than useful and happy! "

" Has Agnes any—" I was thinking aloud, rather than speaking.

" Well? Hey? Any what? " said my aunt, sharply.

" Any lover," said I.

" A score," cried my aunt, with a kind of indignant pride. " She might have married twenty times, my dear, since you have been gone! "

" No doubt," said I. " No doubt. But has she any lover who is worthy of her? Agnes could care for no other."

My aunt sat musing for a little while, with her chin upon her hand. Slowly raising her eyes to mine, she said:

" I suspect she has an attachment, Trot."

" A prosperous one? " said I.

" Trot," returned my aunt gravely, " I can't say. I have no right to tell you even so much. She has never confided it to me, but I suspect it."

She looked so attentively and anxiously at me (I even saw her tremble), that I felt now, more than ever, that she had followed my late thoughts. I summoned all the resolutions I had made, in all those many days and nights, and all those many conflicts of my heart.

"If it should be so," I began, "and I hope it is—"

"I don't know that it is," said my aunt curtly. "You must not be ruled by my suspicions. You must keep them secret. They are very slight, perhaps. I have no right to speak."

"If it should be so," I repeated, "Agnes will tell me at her own good time. A sister to whom I have confided so much, aunt, will not be reluctant to confide in me."

My aunt withdrew her eyes from mine, as slowly as she had turned them upon me; and covered them thoughtfully with her hand. By and by she put her other hand on my shoulder; and so we both sat, looking into the past, without saying another word, until we parted for the night.

I rode away, early in the morning, for the scene of my old school days. I cannot say that I was yet quite happy, in the hope that I was gaining a victory over myself; even in the prospect of so soon looking on her face again.

The well-remembered ground was soon traversed, and I came into the quiet streets, where every stone was a boy's book to me. I went on foot to the old house, and went away with a heart too full to enter. I returned; and looking, as I passed, through the low window of the turret-room where first Uriah Heep, and afterwards Mr. Micawber, had been wont to sit, saw that it was a little parlour now, and that there was no office. Otherwise the staid old house was, as to its cleanliness and order, still just as it had been when I first saw it. I requested the new maid who admitted me to tell Miss Wickfield that a gentleman who waited on her from a friend abroad, was there; and I was shown up the grave old staircase (cautioned of the steps I knew so well), into the unchanged drawing-room. The books that Agnes and I had read together, were on their shelves; and the desk where I had laboured at my lessons, many a night, stood yet at the same old corner of the table. All the little changes that had crept in when the Heeps were there, were changed again. Everything was as it used to be, in the happy time.

I stood in a window, and looked across the ancient street at the opposite houses, recalling how I had watched them on wet afternoons, when I first came there; and how I had used to speculate about the people who appeared at any of the windows, and had followed them with my eyes up and down stairs, while women went clicking along the pavement in pattens, and the dull rain fell in slanting lines, and poured out of the waterspout yonder, and flowed into the road. The feeling with which I used to watch the tramps, as they came into the town on those wet evenings, at dusk, and limped past, with their bundles drooping over their shoulders at the ends of sticks, came freshly back to me; fraught, as then, with the smell of damp earth, and wet leaves and briar, and the sensation of the very airs that blew upon me in my own toilsome journey.

The opening of the little door in the panelle wall made me start and turn. Her beautiful serene eyes met mine as she came towards me. She stopped and laid her hand upon her bosom, and I caught her in my arms.

"Agnes! my dear girl! I have come too suddenly upon you."

"No, no! I am so rejoiced to see you, Trotwood!"

"Dear Agnes, the happiness it is to me, to see you once again!"

I folded her to my heart, and for a little while we were both silent. Presently we sat down, side by side; and her angel-face was turned upon me with the welcome I had dreamed of, waking and sleeping, for whole years.

She was so true, she was so beautiful, she was so good,—I owed her so much gratitude, she was so dear to me, that I could find no utterance for what I felt. I tried to bless her, tried to thank her, tried to tell her (as I had often done in letters) what an influence she had upon me; but all my efforts were in vain. My love and joy were dumb.

With her own sweet tranquillity she calmed my agitation; led me back to the time of our parting; spoke to me of Emily, whom she had visited, in secret, many times; spoke to me tenderly of Dora's grave. With the unerring instinct of her noble heart, she touched the chords of my memory so softly and harmoniously, that not one jarred within me; I could listen to the sorrowful, distant music, and desire to shrink from nothing it awoke. How could I, when, blended with it all, was her dear self, the better angel of my life?

"And you, Agnes," I said, by-and-by. "Tell me of yourself. You have hardly ever told me of your own life, in all this lapse of time!"

"What should I tell?" she answered, with her radiant smile. "Papa is well. You see us here, quiet in our own home; our anxieties set at rest, our home restored to us: and knowing that, dear Trotwood, you know all."

"All, Agnes?" said I.

She looked at me, with some fluttering wonder in her face.

"Is there nothing else, sister?" I said.

Her colour, which had just now faded, returned, and faded again. She smiled; with a quiet sadness, I thought; and shook her head.

I had sought to lead her to what my aunt had hinted at; for, sharply painful to me as it must be to receive that confidence, I was to discipline my heart, and do my duty to her. I saw, however, that she was uneasy, and I let it pass.

"You have much to do, dear Agnes?"

"With my school?" said she, looking up again, in all her bright composure.

"Yes. It is laborious, is it not?"

"The labour is so pleasant," she returned, "that it is scarcely grateful in me to call it by that name."

"Nothing good is difficult to you," said I.

Her colour came and went once more; and once more, as she bent her head, I saw the same sad smile.

"You will wait and see papa," said Agnes, cheerfully, "and pass the day with us? Perhaps you will sleep in your own room? We always call it yours."

I could not do that, having promised to ride back to my aunt's at night; but I would pass the day there, joyfully.

"I must be a prisoner for a little while," said Agnes, "but here are the old books, Trotwood, and the old music."

"Even the old flowers are here," said I, looking round; "or the old kinds."

"I have found a pleasure," returned Agnes, smiling, "while you have been absent, in keeping everything as it used to be when we were children. For we were very happy then, I think."

"Heaven knows we were!" said I.

"And every little thing that has reminded me of my brother," said Agnes, with her cordial eyes turned cheerfully upon me, "has been a welcome companion. Even this," showing me the basket-trifle, full of keys, still hanging at her side, "seems to jingle a kind of old tune!"

She smiled again, and went out at the door by which she had come.

It was for me to guard this sisterly affection with religious care. It was all that I had left myself, and it was a treasure. If I once shook the foundations of the sacred confidence and usage, in virtue of which it was given to me, it was lost, and could never be recovered. I set this steadily before myself. The better I loved her, the more it behoved me never to forget it.

I walked through the streets; and, once more seeing my old

adversary the butcher—now a constable, with his staff hanging up in the shop—went down to look at the place where I had fought him; and there meditated on Miss Shepherd and the eldest Miss Larkins, and all the idle loves and likings, and dislikings, of that time. Nothing seemed to have survived that time but Agnes; and she, ever a star above me, was brighter and higher.

When I returned, Mr. Wickfield had come home, from a garden he had, a couple of miles or so out of town, where he now employed himself almost every day. I found him as my aunt had described him. We sat down to dinner, with some half-dozen little girls; and he seemed but the shadow of his handsome picture on the wall.

The tranquillity and peace belonging, of old, to that quiet ground in my memory, pervaded it again. When dinner was done, Mr. Wickfield taking no wine, and I desiring none, we went up-stairs; where Agnes and her little charges sang and played, and worked. After tea the children left us; and we three sat together, talking of the bygone days.

" My part in them," said Mr. Wickfield, shaking his white head, " has much matter for regret—for deep regret, and deep contrition, Trotwood, you well know. But I would not cancel it, if it were in my power."

I could readily believe that, looking at the face beside him.

" I should cancel with it," he pursued, " such patience and devotion, such fidelity, such a child's love, as I must not forget, no! even to forget myself."

" I understand you, sir," I softly said. " I hold it—I have always held it—in veneration."

" But no one knows, not even you," he returned, " how much she has done, how much she has undergone, how hard she has striven. Dear Agnes! "

She had put her hand entreatingly on his arm, to stop him; and was very, very pale.

" Well, well! " he said with a sigh, dismissing, as I then saw, some trial she had borne, or was yet to bear, in connection with what my aunt had told me. " Well! I have never told you, Trotwood, of her mother. Has any one? "

" Never, sir."

" It's not much—though it was much to suffer. She married me in opposition to her father's wish, and he renounced her. She prayed him to forgive her, before my Agnes came into this world. He was a very hard man, and her mother had long been dead. He repulsed her. He broke her heart."

Agnes leaned upon his shoulder, and stole her arm about his neck.

" She had an affectionate and gentle heart," he said; " and it was broken. I knew its tender nature very well. No one could, if I did not. She loved me dearly, but was never happy. She was always labouring, in secret, under this distress; and being delicate and downcast at the time of his last repulse—for it was not the first, by many—pined away and died. She left me Agnes, two weeks old; and the grey hair that you recollect me with, when you first came."

He kissed Agnes on her cheek.

" My love for my dear child was a diseased love, but my mind was all unhealthy then. I say no more of that. I am not speaking of myself, Trotwood, but of her mother, and of her. If I gave you any clue to what I am, or to what I have been, you will unravel it, I know. What Agnes is, I need not say. I have always read something of her poor mother's story, in her character; and so I tell it you to-night, when we three are again together, after such great changes. I have told it all."

His bowed head, and her angel-face and filial duty, derived a more pathetic meaning from it than they had had before. If I had wanted anything by which to mark this night of our re-union, I should have found it in this.

Agnes rose up from her father's side, before long; and going softly to her piano, played some of the old airs to which we had often listened in that place.

" Have you any intention of going away again? " Agnes asked me, as I was standing by.

" What does my sister say to that? "

" I hope not."

" Then I have no such intention, Agnes."

" I think you ought not, Trotwood, since you ask me," she said, mildly. " Your growing reputation and success enlarge your power of doing good; and if *I* could spare my brother," with her eyes upon me, " perhaps the time could not."

" What I am, you have made me, Agnes. You should know best."

" *I* made you, Trotwood? "

" Yes! Agnes, my dear girl! " I said, bending over her. " I tried to tell you, when we met today, something that has been in my thoughts since Dora died. You remember, when you came down to me in our little room—pointing upward, Agnes? "

" Oh, Trotwood! " she returned, her eyes filled with tears. " So loving, so confiding, and so young! Can I ever forget? "

"As you were then, my sister, I have often thought since, you have ever been to me. Ever pointing upward, Agnes; ever leading me to something better; ever directing me to higher things!"

She only shook her head; through her tears I saw the same sad quiet smile.

"And I am so grateful to you for it, Agnes, so bound to you, that there is no name for the affection of my heart. I want you to know, yet don't know how to tell you, that all my life long I shall look up to you, and be guided by you, as I have been through the darkness that is past. Whatever betides, whatever new ties you may form, whatever changes may come between us, I shall always look to you, and love you, as I do now, and have always done. You will always be my solace and resource as you have always been. Until I die, my dearest sister, I shall see you always before me, pointing upward!"

She put her hand in mine, and told me she was proud of me, and of what I said; although I praised her very far beyond her worth. Then she went on softly playing, but without removing her eyes from me.

"Do you know, what I have heard to-night, Agnes," said I, "strangely seems to be a part of the feeling with which I regarded you when I saw you first—with which I sat beside you in my rough school days?"

"You knew I had no mother," she replied with a smile, "and felt kindly towards me."

"More than that, Agnes, I knew, almost as if I had known this story, that there was something inexplicably gentle and softened, surrounding you; something that might have been sorrowful in some one else (as I can now understand it was), but was not so in you."

She softly played on, looking at me still.

"Will you laugh at my cherishing such fancies, Agnes?"

"No!"

"Or at my saying that I really believe I felt, even then, that you could be faithfully affectionate against all discouragement, and never cease to be so, until you ceased to live?—Will you laugh at such a dream?"

"Oh, no! Oh, no!"

For an instant, a distressful shadow crossed her face; but even in the start it gave me, it was gone; and she was playing on, and looking at me with her own calm smile.

As I rode back in the lonely night, the wind going by me like a restless memory. I thought of this, and feared she was not happy. *I* was not happy; but, thus far, I had faithfully set the seal upon the Past, and, thinking of her, pointing upward, thought of her as pointing to that sky above me, where, in the mystery to come, I might yet love her with a love unknown on earth, and tell her what the strife had been within me when I loved her here.

61

I AM SHOWN TWO INTERESTING PENITENTS

FOR A TIME—AT ALL EVENTS UNTIL MY BOOK SHOULD be completed, which would be the work of several months—I took up my abode in my aunt's house at Dover; and there, sitting in the window from which I had looked out at the moon upon the sea, when that roof first gave me shelter, I quietly pursued my task.

In pursuance of my intention of referring to my own fictions only when their course should incidentally connect itself with the progress of my story, I do not enter on the aspirations, the delights, anxieties, and triumphs of my art. That I truly devoted myself to it with my strongest earnestness, and bestowed upon it every energy of my soul, I have already said. If the books I have written be of any worth, they will supply the rest. I shall otherwise have written to poor purpose, and the rest will be of interest to no one.

Occasionally I went to London; to lose myself in the swarm of life there, or to consult with Traddles on some business point. He had managed for me, in my absence, with the soundest judgment; and my worldly affairs were prospering. As my notoriety began to bring upon me an enormous quantity of letters from people of whom I had no knowledge—chiefly about nothing, and extremely difficult to answer—I agreed with Traddles to have my name painted up on his door. There the devoted postman on that beat delivered bushels of letters for me; and there, at intervals, I laboured through them, like a Home Secretary of State without the salary.

Among this correspondence, there dropped in, every now and

then, an obliging proposal from one of the numerous outsiders always lurking about the Commons, to practise under cover of my name (if I would take the necessary steps remaining to make a proctor of myself), and pay me a percentage on the profits. But I declined these offers; being already aware that there were plenty of such covert practitioners in existence, and considering the Commons quite bad enough, without my doing anything to make it worse.

The girls had gone home, when my name burst into bloom on Traddles's door; and the sharp boy looked, all day, as if he had never heard of Sophy, shut up in a back room, glancing down from her work into a sooty little strip of garden with a pump in it. But there I always found her, the same bright housewife; often humming her Devonshire ballads when no strange foot was coming up the stairs, and blunting the sharp boy in his official closet with melody.

I wondered, at first, why I so often found Sophy writing in a copy-book; and why she always shut it up when I appeared, and hurried it into the table-drawer. But the secret soon came out. One day, Traddles (who had just come home through the drizzling sleet from Court) took a paper out of his desk, and asked me what I thought of that handwriting?

"Oh, *don't*, Tom!" cried Sophy, who was warming his slippers before the fire.

"My dear," returned Tom, in a delighted state, "why not? What do you say to that writing, Copperfield?"

"It's extraordinarily legal and formal," said I. "I don't think I ever saw such a stiff hand."

"Not like a lady's hand, is it?" said Traddles.

"A lady's!" I repeated. "Bricks and mortar are more like a lady's hand!"

Traddles broke into a rapturous laugh, and informed me that it was Sophy's writing; that Sophy had vowed and declared he would need a copying-clerk soon, and she would be that clerk; that she had acquired this hand from a pattern; and that she could throw off—I forget how many folios an hour. Sophy was very much confused by my being told all this, and said that when "Tom" was made a judge he wouldn't be so ready to proclaim it. Which "Tom" denied; averring that he should always be equally proud of it, under all circumstances.

"What a thoroughly good and charming wife she is, my dear Traddles!" said I, when she had gone away, laughing.

"My dear Copperfield," returned Traddles, "she is, without any exception, the dearest girl! The way she manages this place;

her punctuality, domestic knowledge, economy, and order; her cheerfulness, Copperfield!"

"Indeed, you have reason to commend her!" I returned. "You are a happy fellow. I believe you make yourselves, and each other, two of the happiest people in the world."

"I am sure we *are* two of the happiest people," returned Traddles. "I admit that, at all events. Bless my soul, when I see her getting up by candle-light on these dark mornings, busying herself in the day's arrangements, going out to market before the clerks come into the Inn, caring for no weather, devising the most capital little dinners out of the plainest materials, making puddings and pies, keeping everything in its right place, always so neat and ornamental herself, sitting up at night with me if it's ever so late, sweet-tempered and encouraging always, and all for me, I positively sometimes can't believe it, Copperfield!"

He was tender of the very slippers she had been warming, as he put them on, and stretched his feet enjoyingly upon the fender.

"I positively sometimes can't believe it," said Traddles. "Then, our pleasures! Dear me, they are inexpensive, but they are quite wonderful! When we are at home here of an evening, and shut the outer door, and draw those curtains—which she made—where could we be more snug? When it's fine, and we go out for a walk in the evening, the streets abound in enjoyment for us. We look into the glittering windows of the jewellers' shops; and I show Sophy which of the diamond-eyed serpents, coiled up on white satin rising grounds, I would give her if I could afford it; and Sophy shows me which of the gold watches that are capped and jewelled and engine-turned, and possessed of the horizontal lever-escape-movement, and all sorts of things, she would buy for me if *she* could afford it; and we pick out the spoons and forks, fish-slices, butter-knives, and sugar-tongs, we should both prefer if we could both afford it; and really we go away as if we had got them! Then, when we stroll into the squares and great streets, and see a house to let, sometimes we look up at it, and say, how would *that* do, if I was made a judge? And we parcel it out—such a room for us, such rooms for the girls, and so forth; until we settle to our satisfaction that it would do, or it wouldn't do, as the case may be. Sometimes, we go at half-price to the pit of the theatre—the very smell of which is cheap, in my opinion, at the money—and there we thoroughly enjoy the play: which Sophy believes every word of, and so do I. In walking home, perhaps we buy a little bit of something at a cook's-shop, or a little lobster at the fishmonger's, and bring it here, and make a splendid supper, chatting about what we have seen. Now, you know, Copperfield, if I was Lord Chancellor, we couldn't do this!"

"You would do something, whatever you were, my dear Traddles," thought I, "that would be pleasant and amiable. And by the way," I said aloud, "I suppose you never draw any skeletons now?"

"Really," replied Traddles, laughing, and reddening, "I can't wholly deny that I do, my dear Copperfield. For being in one of the back rows of the King's Bench the other day, with a pen in my hand, the fancy came into my head to try how I had preserved that accomplishment. And I am afraid there's a skeleton—in a wig—on the ledge of the desk."

After we had both laughed heartily, Traddles wound up by looking with a smile at the fire, and saying, in his forgiving way, "Old Creakle!"

"I have a letter from that old—Rascal here," said I. For I never was less disposed to forgive him the way he used to batter Traddles, than when I saw Traddles so ready to forgive him himself.

"From Creakle the schoolmaster?" exclaimed Traddles. "No!"

"Among the persons who are attracted to me in my rising fame and fortune," said I, looking over my letters, "and who discover that they were always much attached to me, is the self-same Creakle. He is not a schoolmaster now, Traddles. He is retired. He is a Middlesex Magistrate'"

I thought Traddles might be surprised to hear it, but he was not so at all.

"How do you suppose he comes to be a Middlesex Magistrate?" said I.

"Oh, dear me!" replied Traddles, "it would be very difficult to answer that question. Perhaps he voted for somebody, or lent money to somebody, or bought something of somebody, or otherwise obliged somebody, or jobbed for somebody, who knew somebody who got the lieutenant of the county to nominate him for the commission."

"On the commission he is, at any rate," said I. "And he writes to me here, that he will be glad to show me, in operation, the only true system of prison discipline; the only unchallenge-able way of making sincere and lasting converts and penitents —which, you know, is by solitary confinement. What do you say?"

"To the system?" inquired Traddles, looking grave.

"No. To my accepting the offer, and your going with me?"

"I don't object," said Traddles.

"Then I'll write to say so. You remember (to say nothing of our treatment) this same Creakle turning his son out of doors, I suppose, and the life he used to lead his wife and daughter?"

"Perfectly," said Traddles.

"Yet, if you'll read his letter, you'll find he is the tenderest of men to prisoners convicted of the whole calendar of felonies," said I; "though I can't find that his tenderness extends to any other class of created beings."

Traddles shrugged his shoulders, and was not at all surprised. I had not expected him to be, and was not surprised myself; or my observation of similar practical satires would have been but scanty. We arranged the time of our visit, and I wrote accordingly to Mr. Creakle that evening.

On the appointed day—I think it was the next day, but no matter—Traddles and I repaired to the prison where Mr. Creakle was powerful. It was an immense and solid building, erected at a vast expense. I could not help thinking, as we approached the gate, what an uproar would have been made in the country, if any deluded man had proposed to spend one half the money it had cost, on the erection of an industrial school for the young, or a house of refuge for the deserving old.

In an office that might have been on the ground-floor of the Tower of Babel, it was so massively constructed, we were presented to our old schoolmaster; who was one of a group, composed of two or three of the busier sort of magistrates, and some visitors they had brought. He received me, like a man who had formed my mind in bygone years, and had always loved me tenderly. On my introducing Traddles, Mr. Creakle expressed, in like manner, but in an inferior degree, that he had always been Traddles's guide, philosopher, and friend. Our venerable instructor was a great deal older, and not improved in appearance. His face was as fiery as ever; his eyes were as small, and rather deeper set. The scanty, wet-looking grey hair, by which I remembered him, was almost gone; and the thick veins in his bald head were none the more agreeable to look at.

After some conversation among these gentlemen, from which I might have supposed that there was nothing in the world to be legitimately taken into account but the supreme comfort of prisoners, at any expense, and nothing on the wide earth to be done outside prison-doors, we began our inspection. It being then just dinner-time, we went first into the great kitchen, where every prisoner's dinner was in course of being set out separately (to be handed to him in his cell), with the regularity and precision of clock-work. I said aside, to Traddles, that I wondered whether it occurred to anybody, that there was a striking contrast between these plentiful repasts of choice quality, and the dinners, not to say of paupers, but of soldiers, sailors, labourers, the great bulk of the honest, working community; of whom not one man in five hundred ever dined half so well. But I learned that the " system " required high living; and, in short, to dispose of the system, once for all, I found that on that head and on all others, " the system" put an end to all doubts, and disposed of all anomalies. Nobody appeared to have the least idea that there was any other system, but *the* system, to be considered.

As we were going through some of the magnificent passages, I inquired of Mr. Creakle and his friends what were supposed to be the main advantages of this all-governing and universally over-riding system? I found them to be the perfect isolation of prisoners—so that no one man in confinement there, knew anything about another; and the reduction of prisoners to a wholesome state of mind, leading to sincere contrition and repentance.

Now, it struck me, when we began to visit individuals in their cells, and to traverse the passages in which those cells were, and to have the manner of the going to chapel and so forth, explained to us, that there was a strong probablilty of the prisoners knowing a good deal about each other, and of their carrying on a pretty complete system of intercourse. This, at the time I write, has been proved, I believe, to be the case; but as it would have been flat blasphemy against the system to have hinted such a doubt then, I looked out for the penitence as diligently as I could.

And here again, I had great misgivings. I found as prevalent a fashion in the form of the penitence, as I had left outside in the forms of the coats and waistcoats in the windows of the tailors' shops. I found a vast amount of profession, varying very little in character: varying very little (which I thought exceedingly suspicious) even in words. I found a great many foxes, disparaging whole vineyards of inaccessible grapes; but I found very few foxes whom I would have trusted within reach of a bunch. Above all, I found that the most professing men were the greatest objects of interest: and that their conceit, their vanity, their want of excitement, and their love of deception (which many of them possessed to an almost incredible extent, as their histories showed), all prompted to these professions, and were all gratified by them.

However, I heard so repeatedly, in the course of our goings to and fro, of a certain Number Twenty Seven, who was the favourite, and who really appeared to be a Model Prisoner, that I resolved to suspend my judgment until I should see Twenty Seven. Twenty Eight, I understood, was also a bright particular star; but it was his misfortune to have his glory a little dimmed by the extraordinary lustre of Twenty Seven. I heard so much of Twenty Seven, of his pious admonitions to everybody around him, and of the beautiful letters he constantly wrote to his mother (whom he seemed to consider in a very bad way), that I became quite impatient to see him.

I had to restrain my impatience for some time, on account of Twenty Seven being reserved for a concluding effect. But at last we came to the door of his cell; and Mr. Creakle, looking through a little hole in it, reported to us, in a state of the greatest admiration, that he was reading a Hymn Book.

There was such a rush of heads immediately, to see Number Twenty Seven reading his Hymn Book, that the little hole was blocked up, six or seven heads deep. To remedy this inconvenience, and give us an opportunity of conversing with Twenty Seven in all his purity, Mr. Creakle directed the door of the cell to be unlocked, and Twenty Seven to be invited out into the passage. This was done; and whom should Traddles and I then behold, to our amazement, in this converted Number Twenty Seven, but Uriah Heep!

He knew us directly; and said, as he came out—with the old writhe,—

"How do you do, Mr. Copperfield? How do you do, Mr. Traddles?"

This recognition caused a general admiration in the party. I rather thought that every one was struck by his not being proud, and taking notice of us.

"Well, Twenty Seven," said Mr. Creakle, mournfully admiring him. "How do you find yourself to-day?"

"I am very umble, sir!" replied Uriah Heep.

"You are always so, Twenty Seven," said Mr. Creakle.

Here, another gentleman asked, with extreme anxiety: "Are you quite comfortable?"

"Yes, I thank you, sir!" said Uriah Heep, looking in that direction. "Far more comfortable here, than ever I was outside. I see my follies now, sir. That's what makes me comfortable."

Several gentlemen were much affected; and a third questioner, forcing himself to the front, inquired with extreme feeling: "How do you find the beef?"

"Thank you, sir," replied Uriah, glancing in the new direction of this voice, "it was tougher yesterday than I could wish;

but it's my duty to bear. I have committed follies, gentlemen," said Uriah, looking round with a meek smile, "and I ought to bear the consequences without repining."

A murmur, partly of gratification at Twenty Seven's celestial state of mind, and partly of indignation against the Contractor who had given him any cause of complaint (a note of which was immediately made by Mr. Creakle), having subsided, Twenty Seven stood in the midst of us, as if he felt himself the principal object of merit in a highly meritorious museum. That we, the neophytes, might have an excess of light shining upon us all at once, orders were given to let out Twenty Eight.

I had been so much astonished already, that I only felt a kind of resigned wonder when Mr. Littimer walked forth, reading a good book!

"Twenty Eight," said a gentleman in spectacles, who had not yet spoken, "you complained last week, my good fellow, of the cocoa. How has it been since?"

"I thank you, sir," said Mr. Littimer, "it has been better made. If I might take the liberty of saying so, sir, I don't think the milk which is boiled with it is quite genuine; but I am aware, sir, that there is great adulteration of milk in London, and that the article in a pure state is difficult to be obtained."

It appeared to me that the gentleman in spectacles backed his Twenty Eight against Mr. Creakle's Twenty Seven, for each of them took his own man in hand.

"What is your state of mind, Twenty Eight?" said the questioner in spectacles.

"I thank you, sir," returned Mr. Littimer; "I see my follies now, sir. I am a good deal troubled when I think of the sins of my former companions, sir; but I trust they may find forgiveness."

"You are quite happy yourself?" said the questioner, nodding encouragement.

"I am much obliged to you, sir," returned Mr. Littimer. "Perfectly so."

"Is there anything at all on your mind now?" said the questioner. "If so, mention it, Twenty Eight."

"Sir," said Mr. Littimer, without looking up, "if my eyes have not deceived me, there is a gentleman present who was acquainted with me in my former life. It may be profitable to that gentleman to know, sir, that I attribute my past follies entirely to having lived a thoughtless life in the service of young men; and to having allowed myself to be led by them into weaknesses, which I had not the strength to resist. I hope that gentleman will take warning, sir, and will not be offended at my freedom. It is for his good. I am conscious of my own past follies. I hope he may repent of all the wickedness and sin to which he has been a party."

I observed that several gentlemen were shading their eyes, each with one hand, as if they had just come into church.

"This does you credit, Twenty Eight," returned the questioner. "I should have expected it of you. Is there anything else?"

"Sir," returned Mr. Littimer, slightly lifting up his eyebrows, but not his eyes, "there was a young woman who fell into dissolute courses, that I endeavoured to save, sir, but could not rescue. I beg that gentleman, if he has it in his power, to inform that young woman from me that I forgive her her bad conduct towards myself; and that I call her to repentance—if he will be so good."

"I have no doubt, Twenty Eight," returned the questioner, "that the gentleman you refer to feels very strongly—as we all must—what you have so properly said. We will not detain you.'

"I thank you, sir," said Mr. Littimer. "Gentlemen, I wish you a good day, and hoping you and your families will also see your wickedness, and amend!"

With this, Number Twenty Eight retired, after a glance between him and Uriah; as if they were not altogether unknown to each other, through some medium of communication; and a murmur went round the group, as his door shut upon him, that he was a most respectable man, and a beautiful case.

"Now, Twenty Seven," said Mr. Creakle, entering on a clear stage with *his* man, "is there anything that any one can do for you? If so, mention it."

"I would umbly ask, sir," returned Uriah, with a jerk of his malevolent head, "for leave to write again to mother."

"It shall certainly be granted," said Mr. Creakle.

"Thank you, sir! I am anxious about mother. I am afraid she ain't safe."

Somebody incautiously asked, what from? But there was a scandalised whisper of "Hush!"

"Immortally safe, sir," returned Uriah, writhing in the direction of the voice. "I should wish mother to be got into my state. I never should have been got into my present state if I hadn't come here. I wish mother had come here. It would be better for everybody, if they got took up, and was brought here."

This sentiment gave unbounded satisfaction—greater satisfaction, I think, than anything that had passed yet.

"Before I come here," said Uriah, stealing a look at us, as if he would have blighted the outer world to which we belonged, if he could, "I was given to follies; but now I am sensible of my follies. There's a deal of sin outside. There's a deal of sin in mother. There's nothing but sin everywhere—except here."

"You are quite changed?" said Mr. Creakle.

"Oh dear, yes, sir!" cried this hopeful penitent.

"You wouldn't relapse, if you were going out?" asked somebody else.

"Oh de-ar no, sir!"

"Well!" said Mr. Creakle, "this is very gratifying. You have addressed Mr. Copperfield, Twenty Seven. Do you wish to say anything further to him?"

"You knew me a long time before I came here and was changed, Mr. Copperfield," said Uriah, looking at me; and a more villainous look I never saw, even on his visage. "You knew me when, in spite of my follies, I was umble among them that was proud, and meek among them that was violent—you was violent to me yourself, Mr. Copperfield. Once, you struck me a blow in the face, you know."

General commiseration. Several indignant glances directed at me.

"But I forgive you, Mr. Copperfield," said Uriah, making his forgiving nature the subject of a most impious and awful parallel, which I shall not record. "I forgive everybody. It would ill become me to bear malice. I freely forgive you, and I hope you'll curb your passions in future. I hope Mr. W. will repent, and Miss W., and all of that sinful lot. You've been visited with affliction, and I hope it may do you good; but you'd better have come here. Mr. W. had better have come here, and Miss W. too. The best wish I could give you, Mr. Copperfield, and give all of you gentlemen, is, that you could be took up and brought here. When I think of my past follies, and my present state, I am sure it would be best for you. I pity all who ain't brought here!"

He sneaked back into his cell, amidst a little chorus of approbation; and both Traddles and I experienced a great relief when he was locked in.

It was a characteristic feature in this repentance, that I was fain to ask what these two men had done, to be there at all. That appeared to be the last thing about which they had anything to say. I addressed myself to one of the two warders, who, I suspected, from certain latent indications in their faces, knew pretty well what all this stir was worth.

"Do you know," said I, as we walked along the passage, "what felony was Number Twenty Seven's last 'folly'?"

The answer was that it was a Bank case.

"A fraud on the Bank of England?" I asked.

"Yes, sir. Fraud, forgery, and conspiracy. He and some others. He set the others on. It was a deep plot for a large sum. Sentence, transportation for life. Twenty Seven was the knowingest bird of the lot, and had very nearly kept himself safe; but not quite. The Bank was just able to put salt upon his tail—and only just."

"Do you know Twenty Eight's offence?"

"Twenty Eight," returned my informant, speaking throughout in a low tone, and looking over his shoulder as we walked along the passage, to guard himself from being overheard, in such an unlawful reference to these Immaculates, by Creakle and the rest; "Twenty Eight (also transportation) got a place, and robbed a young master of a matter of two hundred and fifty pounds in money and valuables, the night before they were going abroad. I particularly recollect his case, from his being took by a dwarf."

"A what?"

"A little woman. I have forgot her name."

"Not Mowcher?"

"That's it! He had eluded pursuit, and was going to America in a flaxen wig and whiskers, and such a complete disguise as never you see in all your born days; when the little woman, being in Southampton, met him walking along the street—picked him out with her sharp eye in a moment—ran betwixt his legs to upset him—and held on to him like grim Death."

"Excellent Miss Mowcher!" cried I.

"You'd have said so, if you had seen her, standing on a chair in the witness-box at the trial, as I did," said my friend. "He cut her face right open, and pounded her in the most brutal manner, when she took him; but she never loosed her hold till he was locked up. She held so tight to him, in fact, that the officers were obliged to take 'em both together. She gave her evidence in the gamest way, and was highly complimented by the Bench, and cheered right home to her lodgings. She said in Court that she'd have took him single-handed (on account of what she knew concerning him), if he had been Samson. And it's my belief she would!"

It was mine too, and I highly respected Miss Mowcher for it.

We had now seen all there was to see. It would have been in

vain to represent to such a man as the worshipful Mr. Creakle, that Twenty Seven and Twenty Eight were perfectly consistent and unchanged; that exactly what they were then, they had always been; that the hypocritical knaves were just the subjects to make that sort of profession in such a place; that they knew its market-value at least as well as we did, in the immediate service it would do them when they were expatriated; in a word, that it was a rotten, hollow, painfully suggestive piece of business altogether. We left them to their system and themselves, and went home wondering.

"Perhaps it's a good thing, Traddles," said I, "to have an unsound Hobby ridden hard; for it's the sooner ridden to death."

"I hope so," replied Traddles.

62

A LIGHT SHINES ON MY WAY

THE YEAR CAME ROUND TO CHRISTMAS-TIME, AND I HAD been at home above two months. I had seen Agnes frequently. However loud the general voice might be in giving me encouragement, and however fervent the emotions and endeavours to which it roused me, I heard her lightest word of praise as I heard nothing else.

At least once a week, and sometimes oftener, I rode over there, and passed the evening. I usually rode back at night; for the old unhappy sense was always hovering about me now —most sorrowfully when I left her—and I was glad to be up and out, rather than wandering over the past in weary wakefulness or miserable dreams. I wore away the longest part of many wild sad nights, in those rides; reviving, as I went, the thoughts that had occupied me in my long absence.

Or, if I were to say rather that I listened to the echoes of those thoughts, I should better express the truth. They spoke to me from afar off. I had put them at a distance, and accepted my inevitable place. When I read to Agnes what I wrote; when

I saw her listening face; moved her to smiles or tears; and heard her cordial voice so earnest on the shadowy events of that imaginative world in which I lived; I thought what a fate mine might have been—but only thought so, as I had thought after I was married to Dora, what I could have wished my wife to be.

My duty to Agnes, who loved me with a love which, if I disquieted, I wronged most selfishly and poorly, and could never restore; my matured assurance that I, who had worked out my own destiny, and won what I had impetuously set my heart on, had no right to murmur and must bear; comprised what I felt and what I had learned. But I loved her; and now it even became some consolation to me, vaguely to conceive a distant day when I might blamelessly avow it; when all this should be over; when I could say " Agnes, so it was when I came home; and now I am old, and I never have loved since! "

She did not once show me any change in herself. What she always had been to me, she still was; wholly unaltered.

Between my aunt and me there had been something, in this connection, since the night of my return, which I cannot call a restraint, or an avoidance of the subject, so much as an implied understanding, that we thought of it together, but did not shape our thoughts into words. When, according to our old custom, we sat before the fire at night, we often fell into this train; as naturally, and as consciously to each other, as if we had unreservedly said so. But we preserved an unbroken silence. I believed that she had read, or partly read, my thoughts that night; and that she fully comprehended why I gave mine no more distinct expression.

This Christmas-time being come, and Agnes having reposed no new confidence in me, a doubt that had several times arisen in my mind—whether she could have that perception of the true state of my breast, which restrained her with the apprehension of giving me pain—began to oppress me heavily. If that were so, my sacrifice was nothing; my plainest obligation to her unfulfilled; and every poor action I had shrunk from, I was hourly doing. I resolved to set this right beyond all doubt;—if such a barrier were between us, to break it down at once with a determined hand.

It was—what lasting reason have I to remember it!—cold, a harsh, winter day. There had been snow some hours before; and it lay, not deep, but hard-frozen on the ground. Out at sea, beyond my window, the wind blew ruggedly from the north. I had been thinking of it, sweeping over those mountain wastes of snow in Switzerland, then inaccessible to any human foot;

and had been speculating which was the lonelier, those solitary regions, or a deserted ocean.

"Riding to-day, Trot?" said my aunt, putting her head in at the door.

"Yes," said I, "I am going over to Canterbury. It's a good day for a ride."

"I hope your horse may think so, too," said my aunt; "but at present he is holding down his head and his ears, standing before the door there, as if he thought his stable preferable."

My aunt, I may observe, allowed my horse on the forbidden ground, but had not at all relented toward the donkeys.

"He will be fresh enough, presently!" said I.

"The ride will do his master good, at all events," observed my aunt, glancing at the papers on my table. "Ah, child, you pass a good many hours here! I never thought, when I used to read books, what work it was to write them."

"It's work enough to read them, sometimes," I returned. "As to the writing, it has its own charms, aunt."

"Ah! I see!" said my aunt. "Ambition, love of approbation, sympathy, and much more, I suppose? Well: go along with you!"

"Do you know anything more," said I, standing composedly before her—she had patted me on the shoulder, and sat down in my chair—"of that attachment of Agnes?"

She looked up in my face a little while, before replying:

"I think I do, Trot."

"Are you confirmed in your impression?" I inquired.

"I think I am, Trot."

She looked so steadfastly at me: with a kind of doubt, or pity, or suspense in her affection: that I summoned the stronger determination to show her a perfectly cheerful face.

"And what is more Trot—" said my aunt.

"Yes!"

"I think Agnes is going to be married."

"God bless her!" said I, cheerfully.

"God bless her!" said my aunt, "and her husband too!"

I echoed it, parted from my aunt, went lightly down-stairs, mounted, and rode away. There was greater reason than before to do what I had resolved to do.

How well I recollect the wintry ride! The frozen particles of ice, brushed from the blades of grass by the wind, and borne across my face; the hard clatter of the horse's hoofs, beating a tune upon the ground; the stiff-tilled soil; the snowdrift, lightly eddying in the chalk-pit as the breeze ruffled it; the smoking team with the wagon of old hay, stopping to breathe on the hill-top, and shaking their bells musically; the whitened slopes and sweeps of Down-land lying against the dark sky, as if they were drawn on a huge slate!

I found Agnes alone. The little girls had gone to their own homes now, and she was alone by the fire, reading. She put down her book on seeing me come in; and having welcomed me as usual, took her work-basket and sat in one of the old-fashioned windows.

I sat beside her on the window-seat, and we talked of what I was doing, and when it would be done, and of the progress I had made since my last visit. Agnes was very cheerful; and laughingly predicted that I should soon become too famous to be talked to, on such subjects.

" So I make the most of the present time, you see," said Agnes, " and talk to you while I may."

As I looked at her beautiful face, observant of her work, she raised her mild clear eyes, and saw that I was looking at her.

" You are thoughtful to-day, Trotwood! "

" Agnes, shall I tell you what about? I came to tell you."

She put aside her work, as she was used to do when we were seriously discussing anything; and gave me her whole attention.

" My dear Agnes, do you doubt my being true to you? "

" No! " she answered, with a look of astonishment.

" Do you doubt my being what I always have been to you? "

" No! " she answered, as before.

" Do you remember that I tried to tell you, when I came home, what a debt of gratitude I owed you, dearest Agnes, and how fervently I felt towards you? "

" I remember it," she said, gently, " very well."

" You have a secret," said I. " Let me share it, Agnes."

She cast down her eyes, and trembled.

" I could hardly fail to know, even if I had not heard—but from other lips than yours, Agnes, which seems strange—that there is some one upon whom you have bestowed the treasure of your love. Do not shut me out of what concerns your happiness so nearly! If you can trust me as you say you can, and as I know you may, let me be your friend, your brother, in this matter, of all others! "

With an appealing, almost a reproachful, glance, she rose from the window; and hurrying across the room as if without knowing where, put her hands before her face, and burst into such tears as smote me to the heart.

And yet they awakened something in me, bringing promise

to my heart. Without my knowing why, these tears allied themselves with the quietly sad smile which was so fixed in my remembrance, and shook me more with hope than fear or sorrow.

"Agnes! Sister! Dearest! What have I done?"

"Let me go away, Trotwood. I am not well. I am not myself. I will speak to you by-and-bye—another time. I will write to you. Don't speak to me now. Don't! don't!"

I sought to recollect what she had said, when I had spoken to her on that former night, of her affection needing no return. It seemed a very world that I must search through in a moment.

"Agnes, I cannot bear to see you so, and think that I have been the cause. My dearest girl, dearer to me than anything in life, if you are unhappy, let me share your unhappiness. If you are in need of help or counsel, let me try to give it to you. If you have indeed a burden on your heart, let me try to lighten it. For whom do I live now, Agnes, if it is not for you?"

"Oh, spare me! I am not myself! Another time!" was all I could distinguish.

Was it a selfish error that was leading me away? Or, having once a clue to hope, was there something opening to me that I had not dared to think of?

"I must say more. I cannot let you leave me so! For Heaven's sake, Agnes, let us not mistake each other after all these years, and all that has come and gone with them! I must speak plainly. If you have any lingering thought that I could envy the happiness you will confer; that I could not resign you to a dearer protector, of your own choosing; that I could not, from my removed place, be a contented witness of your joy; dismiss it, for I don't deserve it! I have not suffered quite in vain. You have not taught me quite in vain. There is no alloy of self in what I feel for you."

She was quiet now. In a little time, she turned her pale face towards me, and said in a low voice, broken here and there, but very clear:

"I owe it to your pure friendship for me, Trotwood—which, indeed, I do not doubt—to tell you, you are mistaken. I can do no more. If I have sometimes, in the course of years, wanted help and counsel, they have come to me. If I have sometimes been unhappy, the feeling has passed away. If I have ever had a burden on my heart, it has been lightened for me. If I have any secret, it is—no new one; and is—not what you suppose. I cannot reveal it, or divide it. It has long been mine, and must remain mine."

"Agnes! Stay! A moment!"

She was going away, but I detained her. I clasped my arm

about her waist. "In the course of years!" "It is not a new one!" New thoughts and hopes were whirling through my mind, and all the colours of my life were changing.

"Dearest Agnes! Whom I so respect and honour—whom I so devotedly love! When I came here to-day, I thought that nothing could have wrested this confession from me. I thought I could have kept it in my bosom all our lives, till we were old. But, Agnes, if I have indeed any new-born hope that I may ever call you something more than Sister, widely different from Sister!——"

Her tears fell fast; but they were not like those she had lately shed, and I saw my hope brighten in them.

"Agnes! Ever my guide and best support! If you had been more mindful of yourself, and less of me, when we grew up here together, I think my heedless fancy never would have wandered from you. But you were so much better than I, so necessary to me in every boyish hope and disappointment, that to have you to confide in, and rely upon in everything, became a second nature, supplanting for the time the first and greater one of loving you as I do!"

Still weeping, but not sadly—joyfully! And clasped in my arms as she had never been, as I had thought she never was to be!

"When I loved Dora—fondly, Agnes, as you know——"

"Yes!" she cried, earnestly. "I am glad to know it!"

"When I loved her—even then, my love would have been incomplete, without your sympathy. I had it, and it was perfected. And when I lost her, Agnes, what should I have been without you, still!"

Closer in my arms, nearer to my heart, her trembling hand upon my shoulder, her sweet eyes shining through her tears, on mine!

"I went away, dear Agnes, loving you. I stayed away, loving you. I returned home, loving you!"

And now, I tried to tell her of the struggle I had had, and the conclusion I had come to. I tried to lay my mind before her, truly and entirely. I tried to show her how I had hoped I had come into the better knowledge of myself and of her; how I had resigned myself to what that better knowledge brought: and how I had come there, even that day, in my fidelity to this. If she did so love me (I said) that she could take me for her husband, she could do so, on no deserving of mine, except upon the truth of my love for her, and the trouble in which it had ripened to be what it was; and hence it was that I revealed it. And O, Agnes, even out of thy true eyes, in that same time, the spirit of my child-wife looked upon me, saying it was well; and winning me, through thee, to tenderest recollections of the Blossom that had withered in its bloom!

"I am so blest, Trotwood—my heart is so overcharged—but there is one thing I must say."

"Dearest, what?"

She laid her gentle hands upon my shoulders, and looked calmly in my face.

"Do you know, yet, what it is?"

"I am afraid to speculate on what it is. Tell me, my dear."

"I have loved you all my life!"

Oh, we were happy, we were happy! Our tears were not for the trials (hers so much the greater) through which we had come to be thus, but for the rapture of being thus, never to be divided more!

We walked, that winter evening, in the fields together; and the blessed calm within us seemed to be partaken by the frosty air. The early stars began to shine while we were lingering on, and looking up to them, we thanked our God for having guided us to this tranquillity.

We stood together in the same old-fashioned window at night, when the moon was shining; Agnes with her quiet eyes raised up to it; I following her glance. Long miles of road then opened out before my mind; and, toiling on, I saw a ragged wayworn boy forsaken and neglected, who should come to call even the heart now beating against mine, his own.

It was nearly dinner-time next day when we appeared before my aunt. She was up in my study, Peggotty said: which it was her pride to keep in readiness and order for me. We found her, in her spectacles, sitting by the fire.

"Goodness me!" said my aunt, peering through the dusk, "who's this you're bringing home?"

"Agnes," said I.

As we had arranged to say nothing at first, my aunt was not a little discomfited. She darted a hopeful glance at me, when I said "Agnes;" but seeing that I looked as usual, she took off her spectacles in despair, and rubbed her nose with them.

She greeted Agnes heartily, nevertheless; and we were soon in the lighted parlour down-stairs, at dinner. My aunt put on her spectacles, twice or thrice, to take another look at me, but as often took them off again, disappointed, and rubbed her nose with them—much to the discomfiture of Mr. Dick, who knew this to be a bad symptom.

" By-the-bye, aunt," said I, after dinner; " I have been speaking to Agnes about what you told me."

" Then, Trot," said my aunt, turning scarlet, " you did wrong, and broke your promise."

" You are not angry, aunt, I trust? I am sure you won't be, when you learn that Agnes is not unhappy in any attachment."

" Stuff and nonsense! " said my aunt.

As my aunt appeared to be annoyed, I thought the best way was to cut her annoyance short. I took Agnes in my arm to the back of her chair, and we both leaned over her. My aunt with one clap of her hands, and one look through her spectacles, immediately went into hysterics, for the first and only time in all my knowledge of her.

The hysterics called up Peggotty. The moment my aunt was restored, she flew at Peggotty, and calling her a silly old creature, hugged her with all her might. After that, she hugged Mr. Dick (who was highly honoured, but a good deal surprised); and after that, told them why. Then we were all happy together.

I could not discover whether my aunt, in her last short conversation with me, had fallen on a pious fraud, or had really mistaken the state of my mind. It was quite enough, she said, that she had told me Agnes was going to be married; and that I now knew better than any one how true it was.

We were married within a fortnight. Traddles and Sophy, and Doctor and Mrs. Strong, were the only guests at our quiet wedding. We left them full of joy; and drove away together. Clasped in my embrace, I held the source of every worthy aspiration I had ever had; the centre of myself, the circle of my life, my own, my wife; my love of whom was founded on a rock!

" Dearest husband! " said Agnes. " Now that I may call you by that name, I have one thing more to tell you."

" Let me hear it, love."

" It grows out of the night when Dora died. She sent you for me."

" She did."

" She told me that she left me something. Can you think what it was? "

I believed I could. I drew the wife who had so long loved me, closer to my side.

" She told me that she made a last request to me, and left me a last charge."

" And it was——"

" That only I would occupy this vacant place."

And Agnes laid her head upon my breast, and wept; and I wept with her, though we were so happy.

63

A VISITOR

WHAT I HAVE PURPOSED TO RECORD IS NEARLY FINISHED; but there is yet an incident conspicuous in my memory, on which it often rests with delight, and without which one thread in the web I have spun would have a ravelled end.

I had advanced in fame and fortune, my domestic joy was perfect, I had been married ten happy years. Agnes and I were sitting by the fire, in our house in London, one night in spring, and three of our children were playing in the room, when I was told that a stranger wished to see me.

He had been asked if he came on business, and had answered, No; he had come for the pleasure of seeing me, and had come a long way. He was an old man, my servant said, and looked like a farmer.

As this sounded mysterious to the children, and moreover was like the beginning of a favourite story Agnes used to tell them, introductory to the arrival of a wicked old Fairy in a cloak who hated everybody, it produced some commotion. One of our boys laid his head in his mother's lap to be out of harm's way, and little Agnes (our eldest child) left her doll in a chair to represent her, and thrust out her little heap of golden curls from between the window-curtains, to see what happened next.

" Let him come in here! " said I.

There soon appeared, pausing in the dark doorway as he entered, a hale, grey-haired old man. Little Agnes, attracted by his looks, had run to bring him in, and I had not yet clearly seen his face, when my wife, starting up, cried out to me, in a pleased and agitated voice, that it was Mr. Peggotty!

It *was* Mr. Peggotty. An old man now, but in a ruddy, hearty, strong old age. When our first emotion was over, and he sat before the fire with the children on his knees, and the blaze shining on his face, he looked, to me, as vigorous and robust, withal as handsome, an old man, as ever I had seen.

"Mas'r Davy," said he. And the old name in the old tone fell so naturally on my ear! "Mas'r Davy, 'tis a joyful hour as I see you, once more, 'long with your own trew wife!"

"A joyful hour indeed, old friend!" cried I.

"And these heer pretty ones," said Mr. Peggotty. "To look at these heer flowers! Why, Mas'r Davy, you was but the heighth of the littlest of these, when I first see you! When Em'ly warn't no bigger, and our poor lad were *but* a lad!"

"Time has changed me more than it has changed you since then," said I. "But let these dear rogues go to bed; and as no house in England but this must hold you tell me where to send for your luggage (is the old black bag among it, that went so far, I wonder), and then, over a glass of Yarmouth grog, we will have the tidings of ten years!"

"Are you alone?" asked Agnes.

"Yes, ma'am," he said, kissing her hand, "quite alone."

We sat him between us, not knowing how to give him welcome enough; and as I began to listen to his old familiar voice, I could have fancied he was still pursuing his long journey in search of his darling niece.

"It's a mort of water," said Mr. Peggotty, "fur to come across, and on'y stay a matter of fower weeks. But water ('specially when 'tis salt!) comes nat'ral to me; and friends is dear, and I am heer.—Which is verse," said Mr. Peggotty, surprised to find it out, "though I hadn't such intentions."

"Are you going back those many thousand miles, so soon?" asked Agnes.

"Yes, ma'am," he returned. "I give the promise to Em'ly, afore I come away. You see, I doen't grow younger as the years comes round, and if I hadn't sailed as 'twas, most like I shouldn't never have done 't. And it's allus been on my mind, as I *must* come and see Mas'r Davy and your own sweet blooming self, in your wedded happiness, afore I got to be too old."

He looked at us, as if he could never feast his eyes on us sufficiently. Agnes laughingly put back some scattered locks of his grey hair, that he might see us better.

"And now tell us," said I, "everything relating to your fortunes."

"Our fortuns, Mas'r Davy," he rejoined, "is soon told. We haven't fared nohows, but fared to thrive. We've allus thrived.

We've worked as we ought to 't, and maybe we lived a leetle hard at first or so, but we have allus thrived. What with sheep-farming, and what with stock-farming, and what with one thing and what with t'other, we are as well to do, as well could be. Theer's been kiender a blessing fell upon us," said Mr. Peggotty, reverentially inclining his head, "and we've done nowt but prosper. That is, in the long run. If not yesterday, why then to-day. If not to-day, why then to-morrow."

"And Emily?" said Agnes and I, both together.

"Em'ly," said he, "arter you left her, ma'am—and I never heerd her saying of her prayers at night, t'other side the canvas screen, when we was settled in the Bush, but what I heerd your name—and after she and me lost sight of Mas'r Davy, that theer shining sundown—was that low, at first, that, if she had know'd then what Mas'r Davy kep from us so kind and thowtful, 'tis my opinion she'd have drooped away. But theer was some poor folks aboard as had illness among 'em, and she took care of *them*; and theer was the children in our company, and she took care of *them*; and so she got to be busy, and to be doing good, and that helped her."

"When did she first hear of it?" I asked.

"I kep it from her arter I heerd on 't," said Mr. Peggotty, "going on nigh a year. We was living then in a solitary place, but among the beautifullest trees, and with the roses a-covering our Bein' to the roof. Theer come along one day, when I was out a-working on the land, a traveller from our own Norfolk or Suffolk in England (I doen't rightly mind which), and of course we took him in, and give him to eat and drink, and made him welcome. We all do that, all the colony over. He'd got an old newspaper with him, and some other account in print of the storm. That's how she know'd it. When I came home at night, I found she know'd it."

He dropped his voice as he said these words, and the gravity I so well remembered overspread his face.

"Did it change her much?" we asked.

"Aye, for a good long time," he said, shaking his head; "if not to this present hour. But I think the solitoode done her good. And she had a deal to mind in the way of poultry and the like, and minded of it, and come through. I wonder," he said thoughtfully, "if you could see my Em'ly now, Mas'r Davy, whether you'd know her!"

"Is she so altered?" I inquired.

"I doen't know. I see her ev'ry day, and doen't know; but, odd-times, I have thowt so. A slight figure," said Mr. Peggotty, looking at the fire, "kiender worn; soft, sorrowful, blue eyes; a delicate face; a pritty head, leaning a little down; a quiet voice and way—timid a'most. That's Em'ly!"

We silently observed him as he sat, still looking at the fire.

"Some thinks," he said, "as her affection was ill-bestowed; some, as her marriage was broke off by death. No one knows how 'tis. She might have married well a mort of times, 'but, uncle,' she says to me, 'that's gone for ever.' Cheerful along with me; retired when others is by; fond of going any distance fur to teach a child, or fur to tend a sick person, or fur to do some kindness tow'rds a young girl's wedding (and she's done a many, but has never seen one); fondly loving of her uncle; patient; liked by young and old; sowt out by all that has any trouble. That's Em'ly!"

He drew his hand across his face, and with a half-suppressed sigh looked up from the fire.

"Is Martha with you yet?" I asked.

"Martha," he replied, "got married, Mas'r Davy, in the second year. A young man, a farm-labourer, as come by us on his way to market with his mas'r's drays—a journey of over five hundred mile, theer and back—made offers fur to take her fur his wife (wives is very scarce theer), and then to set up fur their two selves in the Bush. She spoke to me fur to tell him her trew story. I did. They was married, and they live fower hundred mile away from any voices but their own and the singing birds."

"Mrs. Gummidge?" I suggested.

It was a pleasant key to touch, for Mr. Peggotty suddenly burst into a roar of laughter, and rubbed his hands up and down his legs, as he had been accustomed to do when he enjoyed himself in the long-shipwrecked boat.

"Would you believe it!" he said. "Why, someun even made offers fur to marry *her*! If a ship's cook that was turning settler, Mas'r Davy, didn't make offers fur to marry Missis Gummidge, I'm Gormed—and I can't say no fairer than that!"

I never saw Agnes laugh so. This sudden ecstasy on the part of Mr. Peggotty was so delightful to her, that she could not leave off laughing; and the more she laughed the more she made me laugh, and the greater Mr. Peggotty's ecstasy became, and the more he rubbed his legs.

"And what did Mrs. Gummidge say?" I asked, when I was grave enough.

"If you'll believe me," returned Mr. Peggotty, "Missis Gummidge, 'stead of saying 'thank you, I'm much obleeged to you, I ain't a-going fur to change my condition at my time of life,' up'd with a bucket as was standing by, and laid it over that theer ship's cook's head 'till he sung out fur help, and I went in and reskied of him."

Mr. Peggotty burst into a great roar of laughter, and Agnes and I both kept him company.

"But I must say this for the good creetur," he resumed, wiping his face when we were quite exhausted; "she has been all she said she'd be to us, and more. She's the willingest, the trewest, the honestest-helping woman, Mas'r Davy, as ever draw'd the breath of life. I have never know'd her to be lone and lorn, for a single minute, not even when the colony was all afore us, and we was new to it. And thinking of the old 'un is a thing she never done, I do assure you, since she left England!"

"Now, last, not least, Mr. Micawber," said I. "He has paid off every obligation he incurred here—even to Traddles's bill, you remember, my dear Agnes—and therefore we may take it for granted that he is doing well. But what is the latest news of him?"

Mr. Peggotty, with a smile, put his hand in his breast-pocket, and produced a flat-folded paper parcel, from which he took out, with much care, a little odd-looking newspaper.

"You are to understan', Mas'r Davy," said he, "as we have left the Bush now, being so well to do; and have gone right away round to Port Middlebay Harbour, wheer theer's what *we* call a town."

"Mr. Micawber was in the Bush near you?" said I.

"Bless you, yes," said Mr. Peggotty, "and turned to with a will. I never wish to meet a better gen'l'man for turning to with a will. I've seen that theer bald head of his a-perspiring in the sun, Mas'r Davy, till I al'most thowt it would have melted away. And now he's a Magistrate."

"A Magistrate, eh?" said I.

Mr. Peggotty pointed to a certain paragraph in the newspaper, where I read aloud as follows, from the "Port Middlebay Times":

"→ The public dinner to our distinguished fellow-colonist and townsman, WILKINS MICAWBER, ESQUIRE, Port Middlebay District Magistrate, came off yesterday in the large room of the Hotel, which was crowded to suffocation. It is estimated that not fewer than forty-seven persons must have been accommodated with dinner at one time, exclusive of the company in the passage and on the stairs. The beauty, fashion, and exclusiveness of Port

Middlebay, flocked to do honour to one so deservedly esteemed, so highly talented, and so widely popular. Doctor Mell (of Colonial Salem-House Grammar School, Port Middlebay) presided, and on his right sat the distinguished guest. After the removal of the cloth, and the singing of Non Nobis (beautifully executed, and in which we were at no loss to distinguish the bell-like notes of that gifted amateur, WILKINS MICAWBER, ESQUIRE, JUNIOR), the usual loyal and patriotic toasts were severally given and rapturously received. Dr. Mell, in a speech replete with feeling, then proposed 'Our distinguished Guest, the ornament of our town. May he never leave us but to better himself, and may his success among us be such as to render his bettering himself impossible!' The cheering with which the toast was received defies description. Again and again it rose and fell, like the waves of ocean. At length all was hushed, and WILKINS MICAWBER, ESQUIRE, presented himself to return thanks. Far be it from us, in the present comparatively imperfect state of the resources of our establishment, to endeavour to follow our distinguished townsman through the smoothly-flowing periods of his polished and highly-ornate address! Suffice it to observe, that it was a masterpiece of eloquence; and that those passages in which he more particularly traced his own successful career to its source, and warned the younger portion of his auditory from the shoals of ever incurring pecuniary liabilities which they were unable to liquidate, brought a tear into the manliest eye present. The remaining toasts were DOCTOR MELL; MRS. MICAWBER (who gracefully bowed her acknowledgements from the side-door, where a galaxy of beauty was elevated on chairs, at once to witness and adorn the gratifying scene), MRS. RIDGER BEGS (late Miss Micawber); MRS. MELL; WILKINS MICAWBER, ESQUIRE, JUNIOR (who convulsed the assembly by humorously remarking that he found himself unable to return thanks in a speech, but would do so, with their permission, in a song); MRS. MICAWBER'S FAMILY (well known, it is needless to remark, in the mother-country), &c. &c. &c. At the conclusion of the proceedings the tables were cleared as if by art-magic for dancing. Among the votaries of TERPSICHORE, who disported themselves until Sol gave warning for departure, Wilkins Micawber, Esquire, Junior, and the lovely and accomplished Miss Helena, fourth daughter of Doctor Mell, were particularly remarkable."

I was looking back to the name of Doctor Mell, pleased to have discovered, in these happier circumstances, Mr. Mell, formerly poor pinched usher to my Middlesex magistrate, when Mr. Peggotty pointing to another part of the paper, my eyes rested on my own name, and I read thus:

"TO DAVID COPPERFIELD, ESQUIRE,
THE EMINENT AUTHOR.

"MY DEAR SIR,

"Years have elapsed, since I had an opportunity of ocularly perusing the lineaments, now familiar to the imaginations of a considerable portion of the civilized world.

"But, my dear sir, though estranged (by the force of circumstances over which I have had no control) from the personal society of the friend and companion of my youth, I have not been unmindful of his soaring flight. Nor have I been debarred,

Though seas between us braid ha' roared,

(BURNS) from participating in the intellectual feasts he has spread before us.

"I cannot, therefore, allow of the departure from this place of an individual whom we mutually respect and esteem, without, my dear sir, taking this public opportunity of thanking you, on my own behalf, and, I may undertake to add on that of the whole of the Inhabitants of Port Middlebay, for the gratification of which you are the ministering agent.

"Go on, my dear sir! You are not unknown here, you are not unappreciated. Though 'remote,' we are neither 'unfriended,' 'melancholy,' nor (I may add) 'slow.' Go on, my dear sir, in your Eagle course! The inhabitants of Port Middlebay may at least aspire to watch it, with delight, with entertainment, with instruction!

"Among the eyes elevated towards you from this portion of the globe, will ever be found, while it has light and life,

"The
"Eye
"Appertaining to
"WILKINS MICAWBER,
"Magistrate."

I found, on glancing at the remaining contents of the newspaper, that Mr. Micawber was a diligent and esteemed correspondent of that Journal. There was another letter from him in the same paper, touching a bridge; there was an advertisement of a collection of similar letters by him, to be shortly republished, in a neat volume, "with considerable additions;"

and, unless I am very much mistaken, the Leading Article was his also.

We talked much of Mr. Micawber, on many other evenings while Mr. Peggotty remained with us. He lived with us during the whole term of his stay,—which, I think, was something less than a month,—and his sister and my aunt came to London to see him. Agnes and I parted from him aboard-ship, when he sailed; and we shall never part from him more, on earth.

But before he left, he went with me to Yarmouth, to see a little tablet I had put up in the churchyard to the memory of Ham. While I was copying the plain inscription for him at his request, I saw him stoop, and gather a tuft of grass from the grave, and a little earth.

" For Em'ly," he said, as he put it in his breast. " I promised, Mas'r Davy."

64

A LAST RETROSPECT

AND NOW MY WRITTEN STORY ENDS. I LOOK BACK, once more—for the last time—before I close these leaves.

I see myself, with Agnes at my side, journeying along the road of life. I see our children and our friends around us; and I hear the roar of many voices, not indifferent to me as I travel on.

What faces are the most distinct to me in the fleeting crowd? Lo, these; all turning to me as I ask my thoughts the question!

Here is my aunt in stronger spectacles, an old woman of fourscore years and more, but upright yet, and a steady walker of six miles at a stretch in winter weather.

Always with her, here comes Peggotty, my good old nurse, likewise in spectacles, accustomed to do needlework at night very close to the lamp, but never sitting down to it without a bit of wax candle, a yard measure in a little house, and a work-box with a picture of St. Paul's upon the lid.

The cheeks and arms of Peggotty, so hard and red in my

childish days, when I wondered why the birds didn't peck her in preference to apples, are shrivelled now; and her eyes, that used to darken their whole neighbourhood in her face, are fainter (though they glitter still); but her rough forefinger, which I once associated with a pocket nutmeg-grater, is just the same, and when I see my least child catching at it as it totters from my aunt to her, I think of our little parlour at home, when I could scarcely walk. My aunt's old disappointment is set right, now. She is godmother to a real living Betsey Trotwood; and Dora (the next in order) says she spoils her.

There is something bulky in Peggotty's pocket. It is nothing smaller than the Crocodile Book, which is in rather a dilapidated condition by this time, with divers of the leaves torn and stitched across, but which Peggotty exhibits to the children as a precious relic. I find it very curious to see my own infant face, looking up at me from the Crocodile stories; and to be reminded by it of my old acquaintance Brooks of Sheffield.

Among my boys, this summer holiday time, I see an old man making giant kites, and gazing at them in the air, with a delight for which there are no words. He greets me rapturously, and whispers, with many nods and winks, "Trotwood, you will be glad to hear that I shall finish the Memorial when I have nothing else to do, and that your aunt's the most extraordinary woman in the world, sir!"

Who is this bent lady, supporting herself by a stick, and showing me a countenance in which there are some traces of old pride and beauty, feebly contending with a querulous, imbecile, fretful wandering of the mind? She is in a garden; and near her stands a sharp, dark, withered woman, with a white scar on her lip. Let me hear what they say.

"Rosa, I have forgotten this gentleman's name."

Rosa bends over her, and calls to her, "Mr. Copperfield."

"I am glad to see you, sir. I am sorry to observe you are in mourning. I hope Time will be good to you."

Her impatient attendant scolds her, tells her I am not in mourning, bids her look again, tries to rouse her.

"You have seen my son, sir," says the elderly lady, "Are you reconciled?"

Looking fixedly at me, she puts her hand to her forehead, and moans. Suddenly, she cries in a terrible voice, "Rosa, come to me. He is dead!" Rosa kneeling at her feet, by turns caresses her, and quarrels with her; now fiercely telling her, "I loved him better than you ever did!"—now soothing her to sleep on her breast like a sick child. Thus I leave them; thus I always find them; thus they wear their time away, from year to year.

What ship comes sailing home from India, and what English lady is this, married to a growling old Scotch Croesus with great flaps of ears? Can this be Julia Mills?

Indeed it is Julia Mills, peevish and fine, with a black man to carry cards and letters to her on a golden salver, and a copper-coloured woman in linen, with a bright handkerchief round her head, to serve her Tiffin in her dressing-room. But Julia keeps no diary in these days; never sings Affection's Dirge; eternally quarrels with the old Scotch Croesus, who is a sort of yellow bear with a tanned hide. Julia is steeped in money to the throat, and talks and thinks of nothing else. I liked her better in the Desert of Sahara.

Or perhaps this *is* the Desert of Sahara! For, though Julia has a stately house, and mighty company, and sumptuous dinners every day, I see no green growth near her; nothing that can ever come to fruit or flower. What Julia calls "society," I see; among it Mr. Jack Maldon, from his Patent Place, sneering at the hand that gave it him, and speaking to me of the Doctor as "so charmingly antique." But when society is the name for such hollow gentlemen and ladies, Julia, and when its breeding is professed indifference to everything that can advance or can retard mankind, I think we must have lost ourselves in that same Desert of Sahara, and had better find the way out.

And lo, the Doctor, always our good friend, labouring at his Dictionary (somewhere about the letter D), and happy in his home and wife. Also the Old Soldier, on a considerably reduced footing, and by no means so influential as in days of yore!

Working at his chambers in the Temple, with a busy aspect, and his hair (where he is not bald) made more rebellious than ever by the constant friction of his lawyer's wig, I come, in a later time, upon my dear old Traddles. His table is covered with thick piles of papers; and I say, as I look around me:

"If Sophy were your clerk, now, Traddles, she would have enough to do!"

"You may say that, my dear Copperfield! But those were capital days, too, in Holborn Court! Were they not?"

"When she told you you would be a Judge? But it was not the town talk *then*!"

"At all events," says Traddles, "if I ever am one—"

"Why, you know you will be."

"Well, my dear Copperfield, *when* I am one, I shall tell the story, as I said I would."

We walk away, arm in arm. I am going to have a family dinner with Traddles. It is Sophy's birthday; and, on our road, Traddles discourses to me of the good fortune he has enjoyed.

" I really have been able, my dear Copperfield, to do all that I had most at heart. There's the Reverend Horace promoted to that living at four hundred and fifty pounds a year; there are our two boys receiving the very best education, and distinguishing themselves as steady scholars and good fellows; there are three of the girls married very comfortably; there are three more living with us; there are three more keeping house for the Reverend Horace since Mrs. Crewler's decease; and all of them happy."

" Except—" I suggest.

" Except the Beauty," says Traddles. " Yes. It was very unfortunate that she should marry such a vagabond. But there was a certain dash and glare about him that caught her. However, now we have got her safe at our house, and got rid of him, we must cheer her up again."

Traddles's house is one of the very houses—or it easily may have been—which he and Sophy used to parcel out, in their evening walks. It is a large house; but Traddles keeps his papers in his dressing-room and his boots with his papers; and he and Sophy squeeze themselves into upper rooms, reserving the best bedrooms for the Beauty and the girls. There is no room to spare in the house; for more of "the girls" are here, and always are here, by some accident or other, than I know how to count. Here, when we go in, is a crowd of them, running down to the door, and handing Traddles about to be kissed, until he is out of breath. Here, established in perpetuity, is the poor Beauty, a widow with a little girl; here, at dinner on Sophy's birthday, are the three married girls with their three husbands, and one of the husband's brothers, and another husband's cousin, and another husband's sister, who appears to me to be engaged to the cousin. Traddles, exactly the same simple, unaffected fellow as he ever was, sits at the foot of the large table like a Patriarch; and Sophy beams upon him, from the head, across a cheerful space that is certainly not glittering with Britannia metal.

And now, as I close my task, subduing my desire to linger yet, these faces fade away. But one face, shining on me like a Heavenly light by which I see all other objects, is above them and beyond them all. And that remains.

I turn my head, and see it, in its beautiful serenity, beside me.

My lamp burns low, and I have written far into the night;

but the dear presence, without which I were nothing, bears me company.

Oh Agnes, oh my soul, so may thy face be by me when I close my life indeed; so may I, when realities are melting from me like the shadows which I now dismiss, still find thee near me, pointing upward!

THE END

BIBLIOGRAPHY

MAIN WORKS BY DICKENS:

1833 A Dinner at Poplar Walk (In *Old Monthly Magazine*).
1836 Sketches by Boz (2 vols.).
The Posthumous Papers of the Pickwick Club.
The Strange Gentleman (Play).
The Village Coquette (Comic Opera).
1837 Pickwick Papers.
1838 Oliver Twist.
Memoirs of George Grimaldi.
Sketches of Young Gentlemen.
1839 Life and Adventures of Nicholas Nickleby.
1840 Sketches of Young Couples.
1841 Master Humphrey's Clock (A weekly periodical which included The Old Curiosity Shop and Barnaby Rudge).
1842 American Notes (2 vols.), The Lamplighter (Play).
1843 A Christmas Carol in Prose.
1844 Martin Chuzzlewit, The Chimes.
1845 The Cricket on the Hearth.
1846 Pictures from Italy, The Battle of Life.
1848 Dealings with the Firm of Dombey & Son, The Haunted Man, The Ghost's Bargain.
1850 David Copperfield.
1852 Bleak House, Stories for Christmas.
1854 Hard Times for These Times.
1857 Little Dorrit.
1858 A House to Let, The Haunted House.
1859 A Tale of Two Cities.
1860 The Uncommercial Traveller.
1861 Great Expectations.
1865 Our Mutual Friend.
1867 No Thoroughfare (Play with Wilkie Collins).
1870 The Mystery of Edwin Drood (unfinished).
1871 A Child's Dream of a Star.
1877 Is She His Wife? (Play).
1880 Mud Frog Papers.

COLLECTED WORKS:

Works	1847–68	(17 vols.)
Library edition	1858–59	(22 vols.)
Gadshill edition	1897–1908	(36 vols.)
Nonesuch edition	1938	(23 vols.)

The following contain information on his life and works:

Childhood & Youth of Dickens by Robert Langton (1883).
Life of Charles Dickens by R. S. Mackenzie (Philadelphia, 1870).
A Short Life of Charles Dickens by C. H. Jones (New York, 1880).
Charles Dickens as I Knew Him by George Dolby (1885).
Charles Dickens: A Critical Study by George Gissing (1898).
Charles Dickens by G. K. Chesterton (1906).
Dickens in America by W. Glyde Wilkins (1911).
Life of Charles Dickens by John Foster (1913).
Memories of Charles Dickens by P. H. Fitzgerald (1913).
Dickens: A Portrait in Pencil by Ralph Strauss (1928).
Charles Dickens by Osbert Sitwell (1932).
Charles Dickens by Stephen Leacock (1933).
The Sentimental Journey by Hugh Kingsmill (1934).
Life of Charles Dickens by T. Wright (1935).
The Letters of Charles Dickens Ed. by Walter Dexter (3 vols.) (1939).
Charles Dickens by Una Pope Hennessy (1945).
Dickens: His Character, Comedy and Career by H. Pearson (1949).
Charles Dickens by Jack Lindsay (1950).
Charles Dickens by Julian Symons (1951).
Charles Dickens: His Tragedy and Triumph (2 vols.) by Edgar Johnson (1953).
Letters from Charles Dickens to Angela Burdett Coutts edited by Edgar Johnson (1953).
Charles Dickens by K. J. Fielding ("Writers and their Works" Series) (1953).
The Heart of Charles Dickens Ed. by Edgar Johnson (1953).
Dickens and Ellen Ternan by Ada Nisbet (1953).
Charles Dickens by Michael Harrison (1953).
Dickens and His Readers by George H. Ford (1956).
Georgina Hogarth and the Dickens Circle by A. Adrian (1957).
Charles Dickens by K. J. Fielding (1958).
Charles Dickens: The World of His Novels by J. Killis Miller (1959).
The Maturity of Dickens by Monroe Engel (1959).
The Speeches of Charles Dickens Ed. by K. J. Fielding (1959).
Dickens Incognito by Felix Aylmer (1959).
The Imagination of Charles Dickens by A. O. J. Cockshut (1961).
The Love-Lives of Charles Dickens by C. G. L. Du Cann (1961).
Charles Dickens: A Pictorial Biography by J. B. Priestley (1961).
The Dickens Critics Ed. by George H. Ford and Lauriat Lane, Jr. (1962).
Dickens and the Twentieth Century Ed. by John Gross and Gabriel Pearson (1962).
Dickens and Crime by Philip Collins (1962).
Dickens and Education by Philip Collins (1963).
The Making of Charles Dickens by Christopher Hibbert (1967).
Love and Property in the Novels of Charles Dickens by Ross H. Dabney (1968).
The World of Charles Dickens by Agnes Wilson (1970).
Charles Dickens (2 vols.) by Edgar Johnson (1970).
Novels of the Eighteen Forties by Kathleen Tillotson (1970).

Dickens and his World by J. B. Priestley (1970).
Language of Dickens by G. L. Brook (1970).